Murder Most Royal

Murder Most Royal

JEAN PLAIDY

HARPER
WEEKEND

HarperCollins books may be purchased
for educational, business,
or sales promotional use through our
Special Markets Department.

HarperCollins Publishers Ltd
2 Bloor Street East, 20th Floor
Toronto, Ontario, Canada
M4W 1A8

www.harpercollins.ca

Library and Archives Canada
Cataloguing in Publication information
is available upon request

ISBN 978-1-44340-465-5

Printed in the United States
RRD 9 8 7 6 5 4 3 2 1

Defiled is my name, full sore
Through cruel spite and false report,
That I may say for evermore,
Farewell to joy, adieu comfort.

For wrongfully ye judge of me;
Unto my fame a mortal wound,
Say what ye list, it may not be,
Ye seek for that shall not be found.

Written by ANNE BOLEYN in the Tower of London

Murder Most Royal

The King's Pleasure

In the sewing-room at Hever, Simonette bent over her work and, as she sat there, her back to the mullioned window through which streamed the hot afternoon sunshine—for it was the month of August and the sewing-room was in the front of the castle, overlooking the moat—a little girl of some seven years peeped round the door, smiled and advanced towards her. This was a very lovely little girl, tall for her age, beautifully proportioned and slender; her hair was dark, long and silky smooth, her skin warm and olive, her most arresting feature her large, long-lashed eyes. She was a precocious little girl, the most brilliant little girl it had ever been Simonette's good fortune to teach; she spoke Simonette's language almost as well as Simonette herself; she sang prettily and played most excellently those magical instruments which her father would have her taught.

Perhaps, Simonette had often thought, on first consideration it might appear that there was something altogether too perfect about this child. But no, no! There was never one less perfect than little Anne. See her stamp her foot when she wanted something really badly and was determined at all costs to get it; see her playing shuttlecock with the little Wyatt girl! She would play to win; she would have her will. Quick to anger, she was ever ready to speak her mind, reckless of punishment; she was strong-willed as a boy, adventurous as a boy, as ready to explore those dark dungeons that lay below the castle as her brother George or young Tom Wyatt. No, no one could say she was perfect; she was just herself, and of all the Boleyn children Simonette loved her best.

From whom, Simonette wondered, do these little Boleyns acquire their charm? From Sir Thomas, their father, who with the inheritance from his merchant ancestors had bought Blickling in Norfolk and Hever in Kent, as well as an aristocratic wife to go with them? But no! One could not say it came from Sir Thomas; for he was a mean man, a grasping man, a man who was determined to make a place for himself no matter at what cost to others. There was no warmth in his heart, and these young Boleyns were what Simonette would call warm little people. Reckless they might be; ambitious one could well believe they would be; but every one of them—Mary, George and Anne—were loving people; one could touch their hearts easily; they gave love, and so received it. And that, thought Simonette, is perhaps the secret of charm. Perhaps then from their lady mother? Well . . . perhaps a little. Though her ladyship had been a very pretty woman her charm was a fragile thing compared with that of her three children. Mary, the eldest, was very pretty, but one as French as Simonette must tremble more for Mary than for George and Anne. Mary at eleven was a woman already; vivacious and shallow as a pleasant little brook that babbled incessantly because it liked people to pause and say: "How pretty!" Unwise and lightsome, that was Mary. One trembled to think of the little baggage already installed in a foreign court where the morals—if one could believe all one heard—left much to be desired by a prim French governess. And handsome George, who had always a clever retort on his lips, and wrote amusing poetry about himself and his sisters—and doubtless rude poetry about Simonette—he had his share of the Boleyn charm. Brilliant were the two youngest; they recognized each other's brilliance and loved each other well. How often had Simonette seen them, both here at Hever and at Blickling, heads close together, whispering, sharing a secret! And their cousins, the Wyatt children, were often with them, for the Wyatts were neighbours here in Kent as they were in Norfolk. Thomas, George and Anne; they were the three friends. Margaret and Mary Wyatt with Mary Boleyn were outside that friendship; not that they cared greatly, Mary Boleyn at any rate, for she could always amuse herself planning what she would do when she was old enough to go to court.

Anne came forward now and stood before her governess, her demure pose—hands behind her back—belying the sparkle in her lovely eyes. The pose was graceful as well as demure, for grace was as natural to Anne as breathing. She was unconsciously graceful, and this habit of standing thus had grown out of a desire to hide her hands, for on the little finger of her left one there grew the beginning of a sixth nail. It was not unsightly; it would scarcely be noticed if the glance were cursory; but she was a dainty child, and this difference in her—it could hardly be called a deformity—was most distasteful to her. Being herself, she had infused into this habit a charm which was apparent when she stood with others of her age; one thought then how awkwardly they stood, their hands hanging at their sides.

"Simonette," she said in Simonette's native French, "I have wonderful news! It is a letter from my father. I am to go to France."

The sewing-room seemed suddenly unbearably quiet to Simonette; outside she heard the breeze stir the willows that dripped into the moat; the tapestry slipped from her fingers. Anne picked it up and put it on the governess's lap. Sensitive and imaginative, she knew that she had broken the news too rashly; she was at once contrite, and flung her arms round Simonette's brown neck.

"Simonette! Simonette! To leave you will be the one thing to spoil this news for me."

There were real tears in her eyes, but they were for the hurt she had given Simonette, not for the inevitable parting; for she could not hide the excitement shining through her tears. Hever was dull without George and Thomas, who were both away continuing their education. Simonette was a darling; Mother was a darling; but it is possible for people to be darlings and at the same time be very, very dull; and Anne could not endure dullness.

"Simonette!" she said. "Perhaps it will be for a very short time." She added, as though this should prove some consolation to the stricken Simonette, "I am to go with the King's sister!"

Seven is so young! Even a precocious seven. This little one at the court of France! Sir Thomas was indeed an ambitious man. What did he care for these tender young things who, because they were of an unusual brilliance, needed special care! This is the end, thought Simonette. Ah, well! And who am I to undertake the education of Sir Thomas Boleyn's daughter for more than the very early years of her life!

"My father has written, Simonette. . . . He said I must prepare at once. . . ."

How her eyes sparkled! She who had always loved the stories of kings and queens was now to take part in one herself; a very small part, it was true, for surely the youngest attendant of the princess must be a very small part; Simonette did not doubt that she would play it with zest. No longer would she come to Simonette with her eager questions, no longer listen to the story of the King's romance with the Spanish princess. Simonette had told that story often enough. "She came over to England, the poor little princess, and she married Prince Arthur and he died, and she married his brother, Prince Henry . . . King Henry." "Simonette, have you ever seen the King?" "I saw him at the time of his marriage. Ah, there was a time!

Big and handsome, and fair of skin, rosy like a girl, red of hair and red of beard; the handsomest prince you could find if you searched the whole world." "And the Spanish princess, Simonette?" Simonette would wrinkle her brows; as a good Frenchwoman she did not love the Spaniards. "She was well enough. She sat in a litter of cloth of gold, borne by two white horses. Her hair fell almost to her feet." Simonette added grudgingly: "It was beautiful hair. But he was a boy prince; she was six years older." Simonette's mouth would come close to Anne's ear: "There are those who say it is not well that a man should marry the wife of his brother." "But this is not a man, Simonette. This is a king!"

Two years ago George and Thomas would sit in the window seats and talk like men about the war with France. Simonette did not speak of it; greatly she had feared that she, for the sins of her country, might be turned from the castle. And the following year there had been more war, this time with the treacherous Scots; of this Anne loved to talk, for at the battle of Flodden Field it was her grandfather the Duke of Norfolk and her two uncles, Thomas and Edmund, who had saved England for the King. The two wars were now satisfactorily concluded, but wars have reverberating consequences; they shake even the lives of those who believe themselves remote. The echoes extended from Paris and Greenwich to the quiet of a Kentish castle.

"I am to go in the train of the King's sister who is to marry the King of France, Simonette. They say he is very, very old and . . ." Anne shivered. "I should not care to marry a very old man."

"Nonsense!" said Simonette, rising and throwing aside her tapestry. "If he is an old man, he is also a king. Think of that!"

Anne thought of it, her eyes glistening, her hands clasped behind her back. What a mistake it is, thought Simonette, if one is a governess, to love too well those who come within one's care.

"Come now," she said. "We must write a letter to your father. We must express our pleasure in this great honour."

Anne was running towards the door in her eagerness to speed up events, to bring about more quickly the exciting journey. Then she thought sadly once more of Simonette . . . dear, good, kind, but so dull Simonette. So she halted and went back and slipped one hand into that of her governess.

In their apartments at Dover Castle the maids of honour giggled and whispered together. The youngest of them, whom they patronized shamefully—more because of her youth than because she lacked their noble lineage—listened eagerly to everything that was said.

How gorgeous they were, these young ladies, and how different in their own apartments from the sedate creatures they became when they attended state functions! Anne had thought them too lovely to be real, when she had stood with them at the formal solemnization of the royal marriage at Greenwich, where the Duke of Longueville had acted as proxy for the King of France. Then her feet had grown weary with so much standing, and her eyes had ached with the dazzle, and in spite of all the excitement she had thought longingly of Simonette's strong arms picking her up and carrying her to bed. Here in the apartment the ladies threw aside their brilliant clothes and walked about without any, discussing each other and the lords and esquires with a frankness astonishing—but at the same time very interesting—to a little girl of seven.

The King was at Dover, for he had accompanied his favourite sister to the coast; and here in the castle they had tarried a whole month, for outside the waves rose high against the cliffs, and the wind shrieked about the castle walls, rattling its windows and doors and bellowing down the great chimneys as if it mocked the plans of kings. Challengingly the wind and the waves tossed up the broken parts of ships along that coast, to show what happened to those who would ignore the sea's angry mood. There was nothing to be done but wait; and in the castle the time was whiled away with masques, balls and banquets, for the King must be amused.

Anne had had several glimpses of him—a mountain of a man with fair, glowing skin and bright hair; when he spoke, his voice, which matched his frame, bellowed forth, and his laughter shook him; his jewel-trimmed clothes were part of his dazzling personality; men went in fear of him, for his anger came sudden as his laughter; and his little mouth, ready enough to smile at a jest which pleased him, could as readily become the most cruel in the world.

Here in the apartment the ladies talked constantly of the King, of his Queen, and—to them all just now the most fascinating of the royal family group—of Mary Tudor, whom they were accompanying across the Channel to Louis of France.

"Would it not be strange," said Lady Anne Grey, "if my lady ran off with Suffolk!"

"Strange indeed!" answered her sister Elizabeth. "I would not care to be in her shoes, nor in my Lord Suffolk's, if she were to do that. Imagine the King's anger!"

Little Anne shivered, imagining it. She might be young, but she was old enough to sense the uneasy atmosphere that filled the castle. The waiting had been too long, and Mary Tudor—the loveliest creature, thought Anne, she had ever set eyes on—was wild as the storm that raged outside, and about as dependable as the English climate. Eighteen she was, and greatly loved by the King; she possessed the same auburn-coloured hair, fair skin, blue eyes; the same zest for living. The resemblance between them was remarkable, and the King, it was said, was moved to great tenderness by her. Wilful and passionate, there were two ingredients in her nature which mixed together to make an inflammable brew; one was her ambition, which made her eager to share the throne of France; the other was her passionate love for handsome Charles Brandon; and as her moods were as inconstant as April weather, there was danger in the air. To be queen to a senile king, or duchess to a handsome duke? Mary could not make up her mind which she wanted, and with her maids she discussed her feelings with passion, fretful uncertainty and Tudor frankness.

"It is well," she had said to little Anne, for the child's grace and precocity amused her, "that I do not have to make up my mind myself, for I trow I should not know which way to turn." And she would deck herself with a gift of jewels from the King of France and demand that Anne should admire her radiant beauty. "Shall I not make a beautiful Queen of France, little Boleyn?" Then she would wipe her eyes. "You cannot know . . . how could you, how handsome he is, my Charles! You are but a child; you know nothing of the love of men. Oh, that I had him here beside me! I swear I would force him to take me here and now, and then perhaps the old King of France would not be so eager for me, eh, Anne?" She wept and laughed alternately; a difficult mistress.

How different the castle of Dover from that of Hever! How one realized, listening to this talk, of which one understood but half, that one was a child in worldly matters. What matter if one did speak French as well as the Ladies Anne and Elizabeth Grey! What was a knowledge of French when one was in almost complete ignorance of the ways of the world? One must learn by listening.

"The King, my dear, was mightily affected by the lady in scarlet. Did you not see?"

"And who was she?"

Lady Elizabeth put her fingers to her lips and laughed cunningly.

"What of the Queen?" asked little Anne Boleyn; which set the ladies laughing.

"The Queen, my child, is an old woman. She is twenty-nine years old."

"Twenty-nine!" cried Anne, and tried to picture herself at that great age, but she found this impossible. "She is indeed an old woman."

"And looks older than she is."

"The King—he too is old," said Anne.

"You are very young, Anne Boleyn, and you know nothing . . . nothing at all. The King is twenty-three years old, and that is a very good age for a man to be."

"It seems a very great age," said little Anne, and set them mocking her. She hated to be mocked, and reproved herself for not holding her tongue; she must be silent and listen; that was the way to learn. The ladies twittered together, whispering secrets which Anne must not hear. "Hush! She is but a child! She knows nothing. . . ." But after awhile they grew tired of whispering.

"They say he has long since grown tired of her. . . ."

"No son yet . . . no child of the marriage!"

"I have heard it whispered that she, having been the wife of his brother . . ."

"Hush! Do you want your head off your shoulders?"

It was interesting, every minute of it. The little girl was silent, missing nothing.

As she lay in her bed, sleeping quietly, a figure bent over

her, shaking her roughly. She opened startled eyes to find Lady Elizabeth Grey bending over her.

"Wake up, Anne Boleyn! Wake up!"

Anne fought away sleep which was reluctant to leave her.

"The weather has changed," said Lady Elizabeth, her teeth chattering with cold and excitement. "The weather has changed; we are leaving for France at once."

It had been comforting to know her father was with her. Her grandfather was there also—her mother's father, that was, the Duke of Norfolk—and with them sailed too her uncle Surrey.

It was just getting light when they set off, being not quite four o'clock in the morning. The sea was calmer than Anne had seen it since her arrival at Dover. Mary was gay, fresh from the fond farewell kiss of her brother.

"I will have the little Boleyn to sit near me," she had said. "Her quaintness amuses me."

The boat rocked, and Anne shivered and thought, my father is sailing with us . . . and my uncle and my grandfather. But she was glad she was with Mary Tudor and not with any of these men, for she knew them little, and what time would such important people have to bestow on a seven-year-old girl, the least important in the entire retinue!

"How would you feel, Anne," asked Mary, "if you were setting out to a husband you had never seen in the flesh?"

"I think I should be very frightened," said Anne, "but I should like to be a queen."

"Marry and you would! You are a bright little girl, are you not? You would like to be a queen! Do you think the old man will dote on me?"

"I think he will not be able to help himself."

Mary kissed her.

"They say the French ladies are very beautiful. We shall see. Oh, Charles, Charles, if you were only King of France! But what am I, little Anne? Nothing but a clause in a treaty, a pawn in the game which His Grace, my brother, and the French King, my husband, play together. . . . How the boat rocks!"

"The wind is rising again," said Anne.

"My faith! You are right, and I like it not."

Anne was frightened. Never had she known the like of this. The ship rocked and rolled as though it was out of control; the waves broke over it and crashed down on it. Anne lay below, wrapped in a cloak, fearing death and longing for it.

But when the sickness passed a little, and the sea still roared and it seemed that this inadequate craft would be overturned and all its crew and passengers sucked down to the bottom of the ocean, Anne began to cry because she now no longer wished to die. It is sad to die when one is but seven and the world is proving to be a colourful pageant in which one is destined to play a part, however insignificant. She thought longingly of the quiet of Hever, of the great avenues at Blickling, murmuring: "I shall never see them again. My poor mother

will be filled with sorrow . . . George too; my father perhaps
. . . if he survives, and Mary will hear of this and cry for me.
Poor Simonette will weep for me and be even more unhappy
than she was when she said goodbye." Then Anne was afraid
for her wickedness. "I lied to Simonette about the piece of
tapestry. It did not hurt anyone that I should lie? But it was a
lie, and I did not confess it. It was wrong to pull up the trap
door in the ballroom and show Margaret the dungeons, for
Margaret was frightened; it was wrong to take her there and
pretend to leave her. . . . Oh, dear, if I need not die now, I
will be so good. I fear I have been very wicked and shall burn
in hell."

Death was certain; she heard voices whispering that they
had lost the rest of the convoy. Oh, to be so young, to be so
full of sin, and to die!

But later, when the sickness had passed completely, her spirits revived, for she was by nature adventurous. It was something to have lived through this; even when the boat was run
aground in Boulogne harbour, and Anne and the ladies were
taken off into small waiting boats, her exhilaration persisted.
The wind caught at her long black hair and flung it round her
face, as though it were angry that the sea had not taken her and
kept her forever; the salt spray dashed against her cheeks. She
was exhausted and weary.

But a few days later, dressed in crimson velvet, she rode in
the procession, on a white palfrey, towards Abbeville.

"How crimson becomes the little Boleyn!" whispered the

ladies one to another; and were faintly jealous even though she was but a child.

✳

When Anne came to the French court, it had not yet become the most scintillating and the gayest court in Europe; which reputation it was to acquire under Francois. Louis, the reigning king, was noted for his meanness; he would rather be called mean, he had said, than burden his people with taxes. He indulged in few excesses; he drank in moderation; he ate in moderation; he had a quiet and unimaginative mind; there was nothing brilliant about Louis; he was the essence of mediocrity. His motto was France first and France above all. His court still retained a good deal of that austerity, so alien to the temperament of its people, which had been forced on it during the life of his late queen; and his daughters, the little crippled Claude and young Renee, were like their mother. It was small wonder that the court was all eagerness to fall under the spell of gorgeous Francois, the heir apparent. Francois traced his descent to the Duke of Orleans as did Louis, and though Francois was in the direct line of succession, he would only attain the throne if Louis had no son to follow him; and with his mother and sister, Francois impatiently and with exasperation awaited the death of the King who, in their opinion, had lived too long. Imagine their consternation at this marriage with a young girl! Their impatience turned to anger, their exasperation to fear.

Louise of Savoy, the mother of Francois, was a dark, swarthy woman, energetic in her ambition for her son—her Caesar, as she called him—passionate in her devotion to his interests. They were a strange family, this mother and her son and daughter; their devotion to each other had something of a frenzy in it; they stood together, a trinity of passionate devotion. Louise consulted the stars, seeking good omens for her son; Marguerite, Duchess of Alençon, one of the most intellectual women of her day, trembled at the threat to her brother's accession to the throne; Francois himself, the youngest of the trio, twenty years old, swarthy of skin with his hooked nose and sensuous mouth, already a rake, taking, as it was said, his sex as he took his meals, was as devoted a member of the trinity as the other two. At fifteen years of age he had begun his amorous adventures; he was lavishly generous, of ready wit, a poet of some ability, an intellectual, and never a hypocrite. With him one love affair followed another, and he liked to see those around him indulging in similar pleasures. "Toujours l'amour!" cried Francois. "Hands off love!" Only fools were not happy, and what happiness was there to compare with the delight of satisfied love? Only the foolish did not use this gift which the kindliest gods had bestowed on mankind. Only blockheads prided themselves on their virtue. Another name for virginity was stupidity!

Louise looked on with admiration at her Caesar; Marguerite of Alençon said of her stupid husband: "Oh, why is he not like my brother!" And the court of France, tired of the niggardly

Louis and the influence of the Queen whom they had called "the vestal," awaited eagerly that day when Francois should ascend the throne.

And now the old King had married a young wife who looked as if she could bear many children; Louise of Savoy raged against the Kings of France and England. Marguerite grew pale, fearing that her beloved brother would be cheated of his inheritance. Francois said: "Oh, but how she is charming, this little Mary Tudor!" and he looked with distaste on his affianced bride, the little limping Claude.

Anne Boleyn was very sorry for Claude. How sad it was to be ill-favoured, to look on while he who was to be your husband flitted from one beautiful lady to another like a gorgeous dragonfly in a garden of flowers! How important it was to be beautiful! She went on learning, by listening, her eyes wide to miss nothing.

Mary, the new French Queen, was wild as a young colt, and much more beautiful. Indiscreetly she talked to her attendants, mostly French now, for almost her entire retinue of English ladies had been sent home. The King had dismissed them; they made a fence about her, he said, and if she wanted advice, to whom should she go but to her husband? She had kept little Anne Boleyn, though. The King had turned his sallow face, on which death was already beginning to set its cold fingers, towards the little girl and shrugged his shoulders. A little girl of such tender years could not worry him. So Anne had stayed.

"He is old," Mary murmured, "and he is all impatience for

me. Oh, it can be amusing . . . he can scarcely wait. . . ." And she went off into peals of laughter, reconstructing with actions her own coy reluctance and the King's impatience.

"Look at the little Boleyn! What long ears she has! Wait till you are grown up, my child . . . then you will not have to learn by listening when you think you are not observed. I trow those beautiful black eyes will gain for you an opportunity to experience the strange ways of men for yourself."

And Anne asked herself: "Will it happen so? Shall I be affianced and married?" And she was a little afraid, and then glad to be only seven, for when you are seven marriage is a long way off.

"Monsieur mon beau-fils, he is very handsome, is he not?" demanded Mary. And she laughed, with secrets in her eyes.

Yes, indeed, thought Anne, Francois was handsome. He was elegant and charming, and he quoted poetry to the ladies as he walked in the gardens of the palace. Once he met Anne herself in the gardens, and he stopped her and she was afraid; and he, besides being elegant and charming, was very clever, so that he understood her fear which, she was wise enough to see, amused him vastly. He picked her up and held her close to him, so that she could see the dark, coarse hair on his face and the bags already visible beneath his dark, flashing eyes; and she trembled for fear he should do to her that which it was whispered he would do to any who pleased him for a passing moment.

He laughed his deep and tender laugh, and as he laughed

the young Queen came along the path, and Francois put Anne down that he might bow to the Queen.

"Monsieur mon beau-fils . . ." she said, laughing.

"Madame . . . la reine . . ."

Their eyes flashed sparks of merriment one to the other; and little Anne Boleyn, having no part in this sport that amused them so deeply, could slip away.

I am indeed fortunate to learn so much, thought Anne. She had grown a long way from that child who had played at Hever and stitched at a piece of tapestry with Simonette. She knew much; she learned to interpret the smiles of people, to understand what they meant, not so much from the words they used as from their inflection. She knew that Mary was trying to force Francois into a love affair with her, and that Francois, realizing the folly of this, was yet unable to resist it. Mary was a particularly enticing flower full of golden pollen, but around her was a great spider's web, and he hovered, longing for her, yet fearing to be caught. Louise and her daughter watched Mary for the dreaded signs of pregnancy, which for them would mean the death of hope for Caesar.

"Ah, little Boleyn," said Mary, "if I could but have a child! If I could come to you and say 'I am enceinte,' I would dance for joy; I would snap my fingers at that grim old Louise, I would laugh in the face of that clever Marguerite. But what is the good! That old man, what can he do for me! He tries though . . . he tries very hard . . . and so do I!"

She laughed at the thought of their efforts. There was always laughter round Mary Tudor. All around the court those words were whispered—"Enceinte! Is the Queen enceinte? If only . . . the Queen is enceinte!"

Louise questioned the ladies around the Queen; she even questioned little Anne. The angry, frustrated woman buried her head in her hands and raged; she visited her astrologer; she studied her charts. "The stars have said my son will sit on the throne of France. That old man . . . he is too old, and too cold . . ."

"He behaves like a young and hot one," said Marguerite.

"He is a dying fire. . . ."

"A dying fire has its last flicker of warmth, my mother!"

Mary loved to tease them, feigning sickness. "I declare I cannot get up this morning. I do not know what it can be, except that I may have eaten too heartily last evening. . . ." Her wicked eyes sparkling; her sensuous lips pouting.

"The Queen is sick this morning . . . she looked blooming last night. Can it be . . . ?"

Mary threw off her clothes and pranced before her mirror.

"Anne, tell me, am I not fattening? Here . . . and here. Anne, I shall slap you unless you say I am!" And she would laugh hysterically and then cry a little. "Anne Boleyn, did you never see my Lord of Suffolk? How my body yearns for that man!" Ambition was strong in Mary. "I would be mother to a king of France, Anne. Ah, if only my beautiful beau-fils were King of France! Do you doubt, little Boleyn, that he would have had me with child ere this? What do I want from life? I do not know, Anne. . . . Now, if I had never known Charles . . ." And she grew soft, thinking of Charles Brandon, and the King would come and see her softness, and it would amuse her maliciously to pretend the softness was for him. The poor old King was completely infatuated by the giddy creature; he would give her presents, beautiful jewels one at a time, so that she could express her gratitude for each one. The court tittered, laughing at the old man. "That one will have his money's worth!" It was a situation to set a French court, coming faster and faster under the influence of Francois, rocking with laughter.

Wildly, Mary coquetted with the willing Francois. If she cannot get a child from the King, whispered the court, why not from Francois? She would not lose from such a bargain; only poor Francois would do that. What satisfaction could there be in seeing yourself robbed of a throne by your own offspring? Very little, for the child could not be acknowledged as his. Oh, it was very amusing, and the French were fond of those who amused them. And that it should be Mary Tudor from that gloomy island across the Channel, made it more amusing still. Ah, these English, they were unaccountable. Imagine it! An English princess to give them the best farce in history! Francois was cautious; Francois was reckless. His ardour cooled; his passion flared. There was none, he was sure, whom he could enjoy as heartily as the saucy, hot-blooded little Tudor. There were those who felt it their duty to warn him. "Do you not see the web stretched out to catch you?" Francois saw, and reluctantly gave up the chase.

On the first day of January, as Anne was coming from the Queen's apartment, she met Louise—a distraught Louise, her black hair disordered, her eyes wild.

Anne hesitated, and was roughly thrust aside.

"Our of my way, child! Have you not heard the news? The King is dead."

Now the excitement of the court was tuned to a lower key, though it had increased rather than abated. Louise and her daughter were overjoyed at the death of the King, but their happiness in the event was overshadowed by their fear. What of the Queen's condition? They could scarcely wait to know; they trembled; they were suspicious. What did this one know? What had that one overheard? Intrigue . . . and, at the heart of it, mischievous Mary Tudor.

The period of mourning set in, and the Queen's young body was seen to broaden with the passing of the days. Louise endured agonies; Francois lost his gaiety. Only the Queen, demure and seductive, enjoyed herself. In her apartments Louise pored over charts; more and more men, learned in the study of the stars, came to her. Is the Queen enceinte? She begged, she implored to be told this was not so, for how could she bear it if it were! During those days of suspense she brooded on the past; her brief married life, her widowhood; the birth of her clever Marguerite, and then that day at Cognac nearly twenty-one years ago when she had come straight from the agony of childbirth to find her Caesar in her arms. She thought of her husband, the profligate philanderer who had died when Francois was not quite two years old, and whom she had mourned wholeheartedly and then had given over her life to her children, superintending the education of both of them herself, delighting in their capacity for learning, their intellectual powers which surely set them apart from all others; they were both of them so worthy of greatness—a brilliant pair, her world, or at least Caesar was; and where that king of men was concerned, was not Marguerite in complete accord with her mother? He should be King of France, for he was meant to be King of France since there was never one who deserved the honour more than he, the most handsome, the most courteous, the most virile, the most learned Francois. And now this fear! This cheating of her beautiful son by a baggage from England! A Tudor! Who were the Tudors? They did not care to look far back into their history, one supposed!

"My Caesar shall be King!" determined Louise. And, unable to bear the suspense any longer, she went along to the Queen's apartments and, making many artful inquiries as to her health, she perceived that Her Majesty was not quite as large about the middle as she had been yesterday. So she—for, after all, she was Louise of Savoy, a power in France even in the days of her old enemy and rival, Anne of Brittany—shook the naughty Queen until the padding fell from the creature's clothes. And . . . oh, joy! Oh, blessed astrologers who had assured her that her son would have the throne! There was the wicked girl as straight and slender as a virgin.

So Mary left the court of France, and in Paris, secretly and in great haste, she married her Charles Brandon; and the court of France tittered indulgently until it began to laugh immoderately, for it was whispered that Brandon, not daring to tell his King of his unsanctioned marriage with the Queen of France and the sister of the King of England, had written his apologia to Wolsey, begging the great Cardinal to break the news gently to the King.

Francois triumphantly mounted the throne and married Claude, while Louise basked in the exquisite pleasure of ambition fulfilled; she was now Madame of the French court.

Little Anne stayed on to serve with Claude. The Duchesse d'Alençon had taken quite a fancy to the child, for her beauty and grace and for her intelligence; she was not yet eight years old, but she had much worldly wisdom; she knew that crippled Claude was submissive, ignored by her husband, and that it was the King's sister who was virtually Queen of France. Anne would see brother and sister wandering in the palace grounds, their arms about each other, talking of affairs of state; for Marguerite was outstanding in a court where intellect was given the respect it deserved, and she could advise and help her brother; or Marguerite would read her latest writing to the King, and the King would show a poem he had written; he called her his pet, his darling, ma mignonne. She wanted nothing but to be his slave; she had declared she would be willing to follow her brother as his washerwoman, and for him she would cast to the wind her ashes and her bones.

The shadow of Anne of Brittany was banished from the court, and the King amused himself, and the court grew truly

Gallic, and gayer than any in Europe. It was elegant; it was distinctive; its gallantry was of the highest order; its wit flowed readily. It was the most scintillating of courts, the most intellectual of courts, and Marguerite of Alençon, the passionately devoted slave and sister to the King, was queen of it.

It was in this court that Anne Boleyn cast off her childishness and came to premature womanhood, and with the passing of the years and the nourishing of that friendship which she enjoyed with the strange and fascinating Marguerite, she herself became one of the brightest of its brilliant lights.

Between the towns of Guisnes and Ardres was laid a brilliant pageant. A warm June sun showed the palace of Guisnes in all its glittering glory. A fairy-tale castle this, though a temporary one; and one on which many men had worked since February, to the great expense of the English people. It was meant to symbolize the power and riches of Henry of England. At its gates and windows had been set up sham men-at-arms, their faces made formidable enough to terrify those who looked too close; they represented the armed might of the little island across the Channel, not perhaps particularly significant in the eyes of Europe until the crafty statesman, that wily Wolsey, had got his hands on the helm of its ship of state. The hangings of cloth of gold, the gold images, the chairs decorated with pommels of gold, all the furnishings and hangings ornamented wherever possible with the crimson Tudor rose—these represented the wealth of England. The great fountain in the courtyard, from which flowed wine— claret, white wine, red wine—and over which presided the great stone Bacchus round whose head was written in Tudor gold, "Faietes bonne chere qui vouldra"—this was to signify Tudor hospitality.

The people of England, who would never see this lavish display and who had contributed quite a large amount of money towards it, might murmur; those lords who had been commanded by their King to set out on this most opulent and most expensive expedition in history might think uneasily of return to their estates, impoverished by the need to pay for their participation in it; but the King thought of none of these things. He was going to meet his rival, Francis; he was going to prove to Francis that he was the better king, which was a matter of opinion; he was going to show himself to be a better man, which some might think doubtful; he was going to show he was a richer king, which, thanks to his cautious father, was a fact; and that he was a power in Europe, of which there could no longer be a doubt. He could smile expansively at this glittering palace which he had erected as fitting to be the temporary resting place of his august self; he could smile complacently because in spite of its size it could not accommodate his entire retinue, so that all around the palace were the brightly coloured tents of his less noble followers. He could congratulate himself that Francis's lodging at Ardres was less magnificent than his; and these matters filled the King of England with a satisfaction which was immense.

In the pavilion which was the French King's lodging, Queen Claude prepared herself for her meeting with Queen Katharine. Her ladies, too, prepared themselves; and among these was one whose beauty set her aside from all others. She was now in her fourteenth year, a lovely, slender girl who wore her dark hair in silken ringlets, and on whose head was an aureole made of plaited gauze, the colour of gold. The blue of her garments was wonderfully becoming to her dark beauty; her vest was of blue velvet spattered with silver stars; her surcoat of watered silk was lined with miniver and the sleeves of the surcoat were of her own designing; they were wide and long, and hung below her hands, hiding them, for she was more sensitive about her hands than she had been at Blickling and Hever. Over this costume she wore a blue velvet cape trimmed with points, and from the end of each of these points hung little golden bells; her shoes were covered in the same blue velvet as her vest, and diamond stars twinkled on her insteps. She was one of the very fashionable ladies in the smart court of France, and even now the ladies of the court were striving to copy those long hanging sleeves, so that what had been a ruse to hide a deformity was becoming a fashion. She was the gayest of the young ladies. Who would not be gay, sought after as she was? She was quick of speech, ready of wit; in the dance she excelled all others; her voice was a delight; she played the virginals competently; she composed a little. She was worldly wise, and yet there was about her a certain youthful innocence.

Francois himself had cast covetous eyes upon her, but Anne was no fool. She laughed scornfully at those women who were content to hold the King's attention for a day. Marguerite was her friend, and Marguerite had imbued her with a new, advanced way of thinking, the kernel of which was equality of the sexes. "We are equal with men," Marguerite had said, "when we allow ourselves to be." And Anne determined to allow herself to be. So cleverly and with astonishing diplomacy she held off Francois, and he, amused and without a trace of malice, gracefully accepted defeat.

Now Anne was in her element; there was nothing she enjoyed more than a round of gaiety, and here was gaiety such as even she had never encountered before. She was proud of her English birth, and eagerly she drank in the news of English splendour. "My lord Cardinal seemed as a king," she heard, and there followed an account of his retinue, the gorgeousness of his apparel, the display of his wealth. "And he is but the servant of his master! The splendour of the King of England it would be difficult to describe." Anne saw him now and then— the great red King; he had changed a good deal since she had last seen him, at Dover. He was more corpulent, coarser; perhaps without his dazzling garments he would not be such a handsome man. His face was ruddier, his cheeks more pouchy; his voice, though, bellowed as before. What a contrast he presented with the dark and subtle Francois! And Anne was not the only one who guessed that these two had little love for each other in spite of the gushing outward displays of affection.

During the days that followed the meeting of the Kings, Anne danced and ate and flirted with the rest. Today the French court were guests of the English; pageants, sports, jousting, a masked ball and a banquet. Tomorrow the French court would entertain the English. Everything must be lavish; the French court must outshine the English, and then again the English must be grander still. Never mind the cost to nations groaning under taxations; never mind if the two Kings, beneath the show of jovial good fellowship, are sworn enemies! Never mind! This is the most brilliant and lavish display in history; and if it is also the most vulgar, the most recklessly stupid, what of that! The Kings must amuse themselves.

Mary Boleyn had come to attend Queen Katharine at Guisnes. She was eighteen then—a pretty, plumpish, voluptuous creature. It was years since she had seen her young sister, and it was therefore interesting to meet her in the pavilion at Ardres. Mary had returned to England from the Continent with her reputation in shreds; and her face, her manner, her eager little body suggested that rumour had not been without some foundation. She looked what she was—a lightly loving little animal, full of desire, sensuous, ready for adventure, helpless to avert it, saying with her eyes, "This is good; why fret about tomorrow?"

Anne read these things in her sister's face, and was disturbed by them, for it hurt Anne's dignity to have to acknowledge this wanton as her sister. The Boleyns were no noble family; they were not a particularly wealthy family. Anne was half French in outlook; impulsive, by nature she was also practical. The sisters were as unlike as two sisters could be. Anne set a high price upon herself; Mary, no price at all. The French court opened one's eyes to worldly matters when one was very young; the French shrugged philosophical shoulders; l'amour was charming—indeed what was there more charming? But the French court taught one elegance and dignity too. And here was Mary, Anne's sister, with her dress cut too low and her bosom pressed upwards provocatively; and in her open mouth and her soft doe's eyes there was the plea of the female animal, begging to be taken. Mary was pretty; Anne was beautiful. Anne was clever, and Mary was a fool.

How she fluttered about the ladies' apartments, examining her sister's belongings, her little blue velvet brodiquins, her clothes! Those wonderful sleeves! Trust Anne to turn a disadvantage into an asset! I will have those sleeves on my new gown, thought Mary; they give an added grace to the figure—but is that because grace comes naturally to her? Mary could not but admire her. Simple Anne Boleyn looked elegant as a duchess, proud as a queen.

"I should not have known you!" cried Mary.

"Nor I you."

Anne was avid for news of England.

"Tell me of the court of England."

Mary grimaced. "The Queen . . . oh, the Queen is very dull. You are indeed fortunate not to be with Queen Katharine. We must sit and stitch, and there is mass eight times a day. We kneel so much, I declare my knees are worn out with it!"

"Is the King so devoted to virtue?"

"Not as the Queen, the saints be praised! He is devoted to other matters. But for the King, I would rather be home at Hever than be at court; but where the King is there is always good sport. He is heartily sick of her, and deeply enamoured of Elizabeth Blount; there was a son born to them some little while since. The King is delighted . . . and furious."

"Delighted with the son and furious with the Queen because it is not hers?" inquired Anne.

"That is surely the case. One daughter has the Queen to show for all those years of marriage; and when he gets a son, it is from Elizabeth Blount. The Queen is disappointed; she turns more and more to her devotions. Pity us . . . who are not so devoted and must pray with her and listen to the most mournful music that was ever made. The King is such a beautiful prince, and she such a plain princess."

Anne thought of Claude then—submissive and uncomplaining—not a young woman enjoying being alive, but just a machine for turning out children. I would not be Claude, she thought, even for the throne of France. I would not be Katharine, ugly and unwanted Katharine of the many miscarriages. No! I would be as myself . . . or Marguerite.

"What news of our family?" asked Anne.

"Little but what you must surely know. Life is not unpleasant for us. I heard a sorry story, though, of our uncle, Edmund Howard, who is very, very poor and is having a family very rapidly; all he has is his house at Lambeth, and in that he breeds children to go hungry with him and his lady."

"His reward for helping to save England at Flodden!" said Anne.

"There is talk that he would wish to go on a voyage of discovery, and so doing earn a little money for his family."

"Is it not depressing to hear such news of members of our family!"

Mary looked askance at her sister; the haughtiness had given place to compassion; anger filled the dark eyes because of the ingratitude of a king and a country towards a hero of Flodden Field.

"You hold your head like a queen," said Mary. "Grand ideas have been put into your head since you have been living at the French court."

"I would rather carry it like a queen than a harlot!" flashed Anne.

"Marry and you would! But who said you should carry it like a harlot?"

"No one says it. It is I who say I would prefer not to."

"The Queen," said Mary, "is against this pageantry. She does not love the French. She remonstrated with the King; I wonder she dared, knowing his temper."

Mary prattled lightly; she took to examining the apartment still further, testing the material of her sister's gown; she asked questions about the French court, but did not listen to the answers. It was late when she left her sister. She would be reprimanded perhaps; it would not be the first time Mary had been reprimanded for staying out late.

But for a sister! thought Mary, amused by her recollections.

In a corridor of the gorgeous palace at Guisnes, Mary came suddenly upon a most brilliantly clad personage, and hurrying as she was, she had almost run full tilt into him before she could pull herself up. She saw the coat of russet velvet trimmed with triangles of pearls; the buttons of the coat were diamonds. Mary's eyes opened wide in dismay as confusedly she dropped onto her knee.

He paused to look at her. His small bright eyes peered out from the puffy red flesh around them.

"How now! How now!" he said, and then, "Get up!" His voice was coarse and deep, and it was that perhaps and his brusque manner of speech which had earned him the adjective "bluff."

The little eyes travelled hastily all over Mary Boleyn, then rested on the provocative bosom, exposed rather more than fashion demanded, on the parted lips and the soft, sweet eyes.

"I have seen you at Greenwich . . . Boleyn's girl! Is that so?"

"Yes . . . if it please Your Grace."

"It pleases me," he said. The girl was trembling. He liked his subjects to tremble, and if her lips were a little dumb, her eyes paid him the homage he liked best to receive from pretty subjects in quiet corridors where, for once in a while, he found himself unattended.

"You're a pretty wench," he said.

"Your Majesty is gracious . . ."

"Ah!" he said, laughing and rumbling beneath the russet velvet. "And ready to be more gracious still when it's a pretty wench like yourself."

There was no delicacy about Henry; if anything he was less elegant, more coarse, during this stay in France. Was he going to ape these prancing French gallants! He thought not. He liked a girl, and a girl liked him; no finesse necessary. He put a fat hand, sparkling with rings, on her shoulder. Any reluctance Mary might have felt—but, being Mary, she would of course have felt little—melted at his touch. Her admiration for him was in her eyes; her face had the strained set look of a desire that is rising and will overwhelm all else. To her he was the perfect man, because, being the King, he possessed the strongest ingredient of sexual domination—power. He was the most powerful man in England, perhaps the most powerful in France as well. He was the most handsome prince in Christendom, or perhaps his clothes were more handsome than those worn by any others, and Mary's lust for him, as his for her, was too potent and too obvious to be veiled.

Henry said, "Why, girl . . ." And his voice slurred and faded out as he kissed her, and his hands touched the soft bosom which so clearly asked to be touched. Mary's lips clung to his flesh, and her hands clung to his russet velvet. Henry kissed her neck and her breasts, and his hands felt her thighs beneath the velvet of her gown. This attraction, instantaneous and mutual, was honey-sweet to them both. A king such as he was could take when and where he would in the ordinary course of events; but this coarse, crude man was a complex man, a man who did not fully know himself; a deeply sentimental man. He had great power, but because of this power of his which he loved to wield, he wanted constant reassurance. When a man's head can be taken off his shoulders for a whim, and when a woman's life can hang on one's word, one has to accept the uncertainty that goes with this power; one is surrounded by sycophants and those who feign love because they dare show nothing else. And in the life of a king such as Henry there could only be rare moments when he might feel himself a man first, a king second; he treasured such moments. There was that in Mary Boleyn which told him she desired him—Henry the man, divested of his diamond-spattered clothes; and that man she wanted urgently. He had seen her often enough sitting with his pious Queen, her eyes downcast, stitching away at some woman's work. He had liked her mildly; she was a pretty piece enough; he had let his eyes dwell lightly on her and thought of her, naked in bed, as he thought of them all; nothing more than that. He liked her family; Thomas was a good servant; George, a bright boy; and Mary . . . well, Mary was just what he needed at this moment.

Yesterday the King of France had thrown him in a wrestling match, being more skilled than he in a game which demanded quickness of action rather than bullock strength such as his. He had smarted from the indignity. And again, while he had breakfasted, the King of France had walked unheralded into his apartment and sat awhile informally; they had laughed and joked together, and Francis had called him Brother, and something else besides. Even now while the sex call sounded insistently in his ears, it rankled sorely, for Francis had called him "My prisoner!" It was meant to be a term of friendship, a little joke between two good friends. And so taken aback had Henry been that he had no answer ready; the more he thought of it, the more ominous it sounded; it was no remark for one king to make to another, when they both knew that under their displays of friendship they were enemies. He needed homage after that; he always got it when he wanted it; but this which Mary Boleyn offered him was different; homage to himself, not to his crown. Francis disconcerted him and he wanted to assure himself that he was as good a man as the French King. Francis shocked him; Francis had no shame; he glorified love, worshipped it shamelessly. Henry's affairs were never entirely blatant; he regarded them as sins to be confessed and forgiven; he was a pious man. He shied away from the thought of confession; one did not think of it before the act. And here was little Mary Boleyn ready to tell him that he was the perfect man as well as the perfect king. She was as pretty a girl as he would find in the two courts. French women! Prancing, tittering, elegant ladies! Not for him! Give him a good English bedfellow! And here was one ready enough. She was weak at the knees for him; her little hands fluttering for him, pretending to hold him off, while what they meant really was "Please . . . now . . . no waiting."

He bit her ear, and whispered into it: "You like me then, sweetheart?"

She was pale with desire now. She was what he wanted. In an excess of pleasure, the King slapped her buttocks jovially and drew her towards his privy chamber.

This was the way, the way to wash the taste of this scented French gallantry out of his mouth! There was a couch in this chamber. Here! Now! No matter the hour, no matter the place.

She opened her eyes, stared at the couch in feigned surprise, tried to simulate fear; which made him slap his thigh with mirth. They all wanted to be forced . . . every one of them. Well, let them; it was a feminine trait that didn't displease him. She murmured: "If it please Your Grace, I am late and . . ."

"It does please Our Grace. It pleases us mightily. Come hither to me, little Mary. I would know if the rest of you tastes as sweet as your lips."

She was laughing and eager, no longer feigning feminine modesty when she could not be anything but natural. The King was amused and delighted; not since he had set foot on this hated soil had he been so delighted.

He laughed and was refreshed and eased of his humiliation.

He'd take this girl the English way—no French fripperies for him! He would say what he meant, and she could too.

He said: "Why, Mary, you're sweet all over. And where did you hide yourself, Mary? I'm not sure you have not earned a punishment, Mary, for keeping this from your King so long; we might say it was treason, that we might!"

He laughed, mightily pleased, as he always was, with his own pleasantries; and she was overawed and passive, then responsive and pretending to be afraid she had been over-presumptuous to have so enjoyed the King. This was what he wanted, and he was grateful enough to those of his subjects who pleased him. In an exuberance of good spirits he slapped her buttocks—no velvet to cover them now—and she laughed, and her saucy eyes promised much for other times to come.

"You please me, Mary," he said, and in a rush of crude tenderness added: "You shall not suffer for this day."

When he left her and when she was scrambling into her clothes, she still trembled from the violence of the experience.

In the Queen's apartment she was scolded for her lateness; demurely, with eyes cast down, she accepted the reprimand.

∗

Coming from Mary Boleyn, the King met the Cardinal.

Ah, thought the Cardinal, noting the flushed face of his royal master, and guessing something of what had happened, who now?

The King laid his hand on the Cardinal's shoulder, and they walked together along the corridor, talking of the entertainment they would give the French tonight, for matters of state could not be discussed in the palace of Guisnes; these affairs must wait for Greenwich or York House; impossible to talk of important matters, surrounded by enemies.

This exuberance, thought the Cardinal, means one thing—success in sport. And as sport the Cardinal would include the gratification of the royal senses. Good! said the Cardinal to himself; this has put that disastrous matter of the wrestling from his thoughts.

The Cardinal was on the whole a contented man—as contented, that is, as a man of ambition can ever be. He was proud of his sumptuous houses, his rich possessions; it was a good deal to be, next to the King, the richest man in England. But that which he loved more than riches, he also had; and to those who have known obscurity, power is a more intoxicating draught than riches. Men might secretly call him "Butcher's cur," but they trembled before his might, for he was greater than the King. He led the King, and if he managed this only because the King did not know he was led, that was of little account. Very pleasant it was to reflect that his genius for statecraft, his diplomacy, had put the kingdom into the exalted position it held today. This King was a good king, because the goodness of a king depends upon his choice of ministers. There could be no doubt that Henry was a good king, for he had chosen Thomas Wolsey.

It pleased the statesman therefore to see the King happy with a woman, doubtless about to launch himself on yet another absorbing love affair, for then the fat, bejewelled hands, occupied in caressing a woman's body, could be kept from seeking a place on the helm of the ship of state. The King must be amused; the King must be humoured; when he would organize this most ridiculous pageant, this greatest farce in history, there was none that dare deny him his pleasures. Buckingham, the fool, had tried; and Buckingham should tread carefully, for, being so closely related to the King, his head was scarcely safe on his shoulders, be he the most docile of subjects. Francis was not to be trusted. He would make treaties one week, and discard them the next. But how could one snatch the helm from those podgy hands, once the King had decided they must have a place on it? How indeed! Diplomacy forever! thought the Cardinal. Keep the King amused. It was good to see the King finding pleasure in a woman, for well the Cardinal knew that Elizabeth Blount, who had served her purpose most excellently, was beginning to tire His Majesty.

They parted affectionately at the King's apartments, both smiling, well pleased with life and with each other.

The Queen was retiring. She had dismissed her women when the King came in. Her still-beautiful auburn hair hung about her shoulders; her face was pale, thin and much lined, and there were deep shadows under her eyes.

The King looked at her distastefully. With Mary Boleyn still in his thoughts, he recalled the cold submissiveness to duty of this Spanish woman through the years of their marriage. She had been a good wife, people would say; but she would have been as good a wife to his brother Arthur had he lived. Being a good wife was just another of the virtues that irritated him. And what had his marriage with her been but years of hope that never brought him his desires? The Queen is with child; prepare to sing a Te Deum. Prepare to let the bells of London ring. And then . . . miscarriage after miscarriage; five of them in four years. A stillborn daughter, a son who lived but two months, a stillborn son, one who died at birth and another prematurely born. And then . . . a daughter!

He had begun to be afraid. Rumours spread quickly through a country, and it is not always possible to prevent their reaching the kingly ear. Why cannot the King have a son? murmured his people. The King grew fearful. I am a very religious man, he thought. The fault cannot be mine. Six times I hear mass each day, and in times of pestilence or war or bad harvest, eight times a day. I confess my sins with regularity; the fault cannot be mine.

But he was superstitious. He had married his brother's widow. It had been sworn that the marriage had never been consummated. Had it though? The fault could not be his. How could God deny the dearest wish of such a religious man as Henry VIII of England! The King looked round for a scapegoat, and because her body was shapeless with much fruitless child-bearing, and because he never had liked her pious Spanish ways for more than a week or two, because he was beginning to dislike her heartily, he blamed the Queen. Resentfully he thought of those nights when he had lain with her. When he prayed for male issue he reminded his God of this. There were women in his court who had beckoned him with their charms, who had aroused his ready desire; and for duty's sake he had lain with the Queen, and only during her pregnancies had he gone where he would. What virtue . . . to go unrewarded! God was just; therefore there was some reason why he had been denied a son. There it was . . . in that woman on whom he had squandered his manhood without reward.

He knew, when Elizabeth Blount bore his son, that the fault could not lie with him. He had been in an ecstasy of delight when that boy had been born. His virility vindicated, the guilt of Katharine assured, his dislike had become tinged with hatred on that day.

But on this evening his dislike for the Queen was mellowed by the pleasure he had had in Mary Boleyn; he smiled that remote smile which long experience had taught the Queen was born of satisfied lust. His gorgeous clothing was just a little disarranged; the veins stood out more than usual on the great forehead.

He had thrown himself into a chair, and was sitting, his knees wide apart, the glazed smile on his face, making plans which included Mary Boleyn.

The Queen would say a special prayer for him tonight.

Meanwhile she asked herself that question which had been in the Cardinal's mind—"Who now?"

"Venus etait blonde, l'on m'a dit.
L'on voit bien qu'elle est brunette."

So sang Francois to the lady who excited him most in his wife's retinue of ladies. Unfortunately for Francois, she was the cleverest as well as the most desirable.

"Ah!" said Francois. "You are the wise one, Mademoiselle Bouillain. You have learned that the fruit which hangs just out of reach is the most desired."

"Your Majesty well knows my mind," explained Anne. "What should I be? A king's mistress. The days of glory for such are very short; we have evidence of that all around us."

"Might it not depend on the mistress, Mademoiselle Bouillain?"

She shrugged her shoulders in the way which was so much more charming than the gesture of the French ladies, because it was only half French.

"I do not care to take the risk," she said.

Then he laughed and sang to her, and asked that she should sing to him. This she did gladly, for her voice was good and she was susceptible to admiration and eager to draw it to herself at every opportunity. Contact with the Duchesse d'Alençon had made her value herself highly, and though she was as fond of amorous adventures as any, she knew exactly at what moment to retire. She was enjoying every moment of her life at the court of France. There was so much to amuse her that life could never be dull. Lighthearted flirtations, listening to the scandal of the court, reading with Marguerite, and getting a glimmer of the new religion that had begun to spring up in Europe, since a German monk named Martin Luther had nailed a set of theses on a church door at Wittenberg. Yes, life was colourful and amusing, stimulating mind and body. Though the news that came from England was not so good; disaster had set in after the return from the palace of Guisnes. Poverty had swept over the country; the harvest was bad, and people were dying of the plague in the streets of London. The King was less popular than he had been before his love of vulgar show and pageantry had led him to that folly which men in England now called "The Field of the Cloth of Gold."

There was not very exhilarating news from her family. Uncle Edmund Howard had yet another child, and that a daughter. Catherine, they called her. Anne's ready sympathy went out to poor little Catherine Howard, born into the poverty of that rambling old house at Lambeth. Then Mary had married—hardly brilliantly—a certain William Carey. Anne would have liked to hear of a better match for her sister; but both she and George, right from Hever days, had known Mary was a fool.

And now war clouds were looming up afresh, and this time there was fear of a conflict between France and England. At the same time there was talk of a marriage for Anne which was being arranged in England to settle some dispute one branch of her family was having with another.

So Anne left France most reluctantly, and sailed for England. At home they said she was most Frenchified; she was imperious, witty, lovely to look at, and her clothes caused comment from all who beheld them.

She was just sixteen years old.

Anne's grandfather, the old Duke of Norfolk, was not at home when Anne, in the company of her mother, visited Norfolk's house at Lambeth. The Duchess was a somewhat lazy, empty-headed woman who enjoyed listening to the ambitious adventures of the younger members of her family, and she had learned that her granddaughter Anne had returned from France a charming creature. Nothing therefore would satisfy the Duchess but that this visit should be paid, and during it she found an especial delight in sitting in the grounds of her lovely home on the river's edge, dozing and indulging in light conversation with the girl whom she herself would now be ready to admit was the most interesting member of the family. And, thought the vain old lady, the chit has a look of me about her; moreover, I declare at her age I looked very like her. What honours, she wondered, were in store for Anne Boleyn, for the marriage with the Butlers was not being brought at any great speed to a satisfactory conclusion; and how sad if this bright child must bury herself in the wilds of that dreary, troublesome, uncivilized Ireland! But—and the Duchess sighed deeply—what were women but petty counters to be bartered by men in the settlement of their problems? Thomas Boleyn was too ambitious. Marry! An the girl were mine, to court she should go, and a plague on the Butlers.

She watched Anne feeding the peacocks; a figure of grace in scarlet and grey, she was not one whit less gorgeous than those arrogant, elegant birds. She's Howard, mused the Duchess with pride. All Howard! Not a trace of Boleyn there.

"Come and sit beside me, my dear," she said. "I would talk to you."

Anne came and sat on the wooden seat which overlooked the river; she gazed along its bank at the stately gabled houses whose beautiful gardens sloped down to the water, placing their owners within comfortable distance of the quickest and least dangerous means of transport. Her gaze went quickly towards those domes and spires that seemed to pierce the blue and smokeless sky. She could see the heavy arches of London Bridge and the ramparts of the Tower of London—that great, impressive fortress whose towers, strong and formidable, stood like sentinels guarding the city.

Agnes, Duchess of Norfolk, saw the girl's eager expression, and guessed her thoughts. She tapped her arm.

"Tell me of the court of France, my child. I'll warrant you found much to amuse you there."

As Anne talked, the Duchess lay back, listening, now and

46

then stifling a yawn, for she had eaten a big dinner and, interested as she was, she was overcome by drowsiness.

"Why, bless us!" she said. "When you went away, your father was of little import; now you return to find him a gentleman of much consequence—Treasurer of the Household now, if you please!"

"It does please," laughed Anne.

"They tell me," said Agnes, "that the office is worth a thousand pounds a year! And what else? Steward of Tonbridge. . . ." She began enumerating the titles on her fingers. "Master of the Hunt. Constable of the Castle. Chamberlain of Tonbridge. Receiver and Bailiff of Bradsted, and the Keeper of the Manor of Penshurst. And now it is whispered that he is to be appointed Keeper of the Parks at Thundersley, to say nothing of Essex and Westwood. Never was so much honour done a man in so short a time!"

"My father," said Anne, "is a man of much ability."

"And good fortune," said Agnes slyly, eyeing the girl mischievously, thinking: Can it be that she does not know why these honours are heaped on her father, and she fresh from the wicked court of France? "And your father is lucky in his children," commented Agnes mischievously.

The girl turned puzzled eyes on her grandmother. The old lady chuckled, thinking: She makes a pretty pose of ignorance, I'll swear!

Anne said, her expression changing: "I would it were as well with every member of our family." And her eyes went towards a house less than half a mile away along the river's bank.

"Ah!" sighed the Duchess. "There is a man who served his country well, and yet . . ." She shrugged her shoulders. "His children are too young to be of any use to him."

"I hear there is a new baby," said Anne. "Do they not visit you?"

"My dear, Lord Edmund is afraid to leave his house for fear he should be arrested. He has many debts, poor man, and he's as proud as Lucifer. Ah, yes . . . a new baby. Why, little Catherine is but a baby yet."

"Grandmother, I should like to see the baby."

The Duchess yawned. It had ever been her habit to push unpleasant thoughts aside, and the branch of her family which they were now discussing distressed her. What she enjoyed hearing was of the success of Sir Thomas and the adventures of his flighty daughter. She could nod over them, simper over them, remember her own youth and relive it as she drowsed in her pleasant seat overlooking the river. Still, she would like the Edmund Howards to see this lovely girl in her pretty clothes. The Duchess had a mischievous turn of mind. The little Howards had a distinguished soldier for a father, and they might starve; the Boleyn children had a father who might be a clever enough diplomatist, but, having descended from merchants, was no proud Howard; still, he had a most attractive daughter. There were never two men less alike than Lord Edmund Howard and Sir Thomas Boleyn. And to His Majesty, thought the Duchess, smiling into a lace handkerchief, a sword grown rusty is of less use than a lovely, willing girl.

"Run to the house and get cloaks," she said. "We will step

along to see them. A walk will do me good and mayhap throw off this flatulence which, I declare, attacks me after every meal these days."

"You eat too heartily, Grandmother."

"Off with you, impudent child!"

Anne ran off. It does me good to look at her, thought her grandmother. And what when the King claps eyes on her, eh, Thomas Boleyn? Though it occurs to me that she might not be to his taste. I declare were I a man I'd want to spank the haughtiness out of her before I took her to bed. And the King would not be one to brook such ways. Ah, if you go to court, Anne Boleyn, you will have to lose your French dignity—if you hope to do as well as your saucy sister. Though you'll not go to court; you'll go to Ireland. The Ormond title and the Ormond wealth must be kept in the family to satisfy grasping Thomas, and he was ever a man to throw his family to the wolves.

The Duchess rose, and Anne, who had come running up, put a cloak about her shoulders; they walked slowly through the gardens and along the river's edge.

The Lambeth house of the Edmund Howards was a roomy place, cold and drafty. Lady Edmund was a delicate creature on whom too frequent child-bearing and her husband's poverty were having a dire effect. She and her husband received their visitors in the great panelled hall, and wine was brought for them to drink. Lord Edmund's dignity was great, and it touched Anne deeply to see his efforts to hide his poverty.

"My dear Jocosa," said the Duchess to her daughter-in-law, "I have brought my granddaughter along to see you. She has recently returned from France, as you know. Tell your aunt and uncle all about it, child."

"Uncle Edmund would doubtless find my adventuring tame telling," said Anne.

"Ah!" said Lord Edmund. "I remember you well, niece. Dover Castle, eh? And the crossing! Marry, I thought I should never see your face again when your ship was missed by the rest of us. I remember saying to Surrey: 'Why, our niece is there, and she but a baby!'"

Anne sipped her wine, chatting awhile with Lord Edmund of the court of France, of old Louis, of gay Francois, and of Mary Tudor who had longed to be Queen of France and Duchess of Suffolk, and had achieved both ambitions.

The old Duchess tapped her stick imperiously, not caring to be left to Jocosa and her domesticity. "Anne was interested in the children," she said. "I trow she will be disappointed if she is not allowed to catch a glimpse of them."

"You must come to the nursery," said Jocosa. "Though I doubt that the older ones will be there at this hour. The babies love visitors."

In the nursery at the top of the house, there was more evidence of the poverty of this branch of the Howard family. Little Catherine was shabbily dressed; Mary, the baby, was wrapped in a piece of darned flannel. There was an old nurse who, Anne guessed, doubtless worked without her wages for very love of the family. Her face shone with pride in the children, with affection for her mistress; but she was inclined to be resentful towards Anne and her grandmother. Had I known, thought Anne, I could have put on a simpler gown.

"Here is the new baby, Madam," said the nurse, and put the flannel bundle into Anne's arms. Its little face was puckered and red; a very ugly little baby, but it was amusing and affecting to see the nurse hovering over it as though it were very, very precious.

A little hand was stroking the silk of Anne's surcoat. Anne looked down and saw a large-eyed, very pretty little girl who could not have been very much more than a year old.

"This is the next youngest," said Jocosa.

"Little Catherine!" said the Duchess, and stooping picked her up. "Now, Catherine Howard, what have you to say to Anne Boleyn?"

Catherine could say nothing; she could only stare at the lovely lady in the gorgeous, bright clothes. The jewels at her throat and on her fingers dazzled Catherine. She wriggled in the Duchess's arms in an effort to get closer to Anne, who, always susceptible to admiration, even from babies, handed the flannel bundle back to the nurse.

"Would you like me to hold you, Cousin Catherine?" she asked, and Catherine smiled delightedly.

"She does not speak," said the Duchess.

"I fear she is not as advanced as the others," said Catherine's mother.

"Indeed not!" said the Duchess severely. "I remember well

this girl here as a baby. I never knew one so bright—except perhaps her brother George. Now, Mary . . . she was more like Catherine here."

At the mention of Mary's name Jocosa stiffened, but the old Duchess went on, her eyes sparkling: "Mary was a taking little creature, though she might be backward with her talk. She knew though how to ask for what she wanted, without words . . . and I'll warrant she still does!"

Anne and Catherine smiled at each other.

"There!" said the Duchess. "She is wishing she had a child of her own. Confess it, Anne!"

"One such as this, yes!" laughed Anne.

Catherine tried to pluck out the beautiful eyes.

"She admires you vastly!" said Jocosa.

Anne went to a chair and sat down, holding Catherine on her lap, while her grandmother drew Jocosa into a corner and chatted with her of the proposed match for Anne, of the advancement of Sir Thomas and George Boleyn, of Mary and the King.

Catherine's little hands explored the lovely dress, the glittering jewels; and the child laughed happily as she did so.

"They make a pretty picture," said the Duchess. "I think I am proud of my granddaughters, Anne Boleyn and Catherine Howard. They are such pretty creatures, both of them."

Catherine's fingers had curled about a jewelled tablet which hung by a silken cord from Anne's waist; it was a valuable trinket.

"Would you like to have it for your own, little Catherine?"

whispered Anne, and detached it. They can doubtless sell it, she thought. It is not much, but it is something. I can see it would be useless to offer help openly to Uncle Edmund.

When they said farewell, Catherine shed tears.

"Why, look what the child has!" cried the Duchess. "It is yours, is it not, Anne? Catherine Howard, Catherine Howard, are you a little thief then?"

"It is a gift," said Anne hastily. "She liked it, and I have another."

It was pleasant to be back at Hever after such a long absence. How quiet were the Kentish woods, how solitary the green meadows! She had hoped to see the Wyatts, but they were not in residence at Allington Castle just now; and it was a quiet life she led, reading, sewing, playing and singing with her mother. She was content to enjoy these lazy days, for she had little desire to marry the young man whom it had been ordained she should. She accepted the marriage as a matter of course, as she had known from childhood that when she reached a certain age a match would be made for her. This was it; but how pleasant to pass these days at quiet Hever, wandering through the grounds which she would always love because of those childhood memories they held for her.

Mary paid a visit to Hever; splendidly dressed—Anne considered her overdressed—she was very gay and lively. Her laughter rang through the castle, shattering its peace. Mary admired her sister, and was too good-natured not to admit it wholeheartedly. "You should do well at court, sister Anne," she told her. "You would create much excitement, I trow. And those clothes! I have never seen the like; and who but you could wear them with effect!"

They lay under the old apple trees in the orchard together; Mary, lazy and plump, carefully placing a kerchief over her bosom to prevent the sun from spoiling its whiteness.

"I think now and then," said Mary, "of my visit to you. . . . Do you remember Ardres?"

"Yes," said Anne, "I remember perfectly."

"And how you disapproved of me then? Did you not? Confess it."

"Did I show it then?"

"Indeed you did, Madam! You looked down your haughty nose at me and disapproved right heartily. You cannot say you disapprove now, I trow."

"I think you have changed very little," said Anne.

Mary giggled. "You may have disapproved that night, Anne, but there was one who did not!"

"The tastes of all are naturally not alike."

"There was one who approved most heartily—and he of no small import either!"

"I perceive," said Anne, laughing, "that you yearn to tell me of your love affairs."

"And you are not interested?"

"Not very. I am sure you have had many, and that they are all monotonously similar."

"Indeed! And what if I were to tell His Majesty of that!"

"Do you then pour your girlish confidences into the royal ear?"

"I do now and then, Anne, when I think they may amuse His Grace."

"What is this?" said Anne, raising herself to look more closely at her sister.

"I was about to tell you. Did I not say that though you might disapprove of me, there was one who does not? Listen, sister. The night I left you to return to the Guisnes Palace I met him; he spoke to me, and we found we liked each other."

Anne's face flushed, then paled; she was understanding many things—the chatter of her grandmother, the glances of her Aunt Jocosa, the nurse's rather self-righteous indignation. One of the heroes of Flodden may starve, but the family of Boleyn shall flourish, for the King likes well one of its daughters.

"How long?" asked Anne shortly.

"From then to now. He is eager for me still. There never was such a man! Anne, I could tell you . . ."

"I beg that you will not."

Mary shrugged her shoulders and rolled over on the grass like an amorous cat.

"And William, your husband?" said Anne.

"Poor William! I am very fond of him."

"I understand. The marriage was arranged, and he was given

a place at court so that you might be always there awaiting the King's pleasure, and to place a very flimsy cover of propriety over your immorality."

Mary was almost choked with laughter.

"Your expressions amuse me, Anne. I declare, I shall tell the King; he will be vastly amused. And you fresh from the court of France!"

"I am beginning to wish I were still there. And our father . . ."

"Is mightily pleased with the arrangements. A fool he would be otherwise, and none could say our father is a fool."

"So all these honours that have been heaped upon him . . ."

" . . . are due to the fact that your wicked sister has pleased the King!"

"It makes me sick."

"You have a poor stomach, sister. But you are indeed young, for all your air of worldly wisdom and for all your elegance and grace. Why, bless you, Anne, life is not all the wearing of fine clothes."

"No? Indeed it would seem that for you it is more a matter of putting them off."

"You have a witty tongue, Anne. I cannot compete with it. You would do well at court, would you but put aside your prudery. Prudery the King cannot endure; he has enough of that from his Queen."

"She knows of you and . . ."

"It is impossible to keep secrets at court, Anne."

"Poor lady!"

"But were it not I, 'twould be another, the King being as he is."

"The King being a lecher!" said Anne fiercely.

"That is treason!" cried Mary in mock horror. "Ah! It is easy for you to talk. As for me, I could never say no to such a man."

"You could never say no to any man!"

"Despise me if you will. The King does not, and our father is mightily pleased with his daughter Mary."

Now the secret was out; now she understood the sly glances of servants, her father's looks of approbation as his eyes rested on his elder daughter. There was no one to whom Anne could speak of her perturbation until George came home.

He was eighteen years old, a delight to the eye, very like Anne in appearance, full of exuberant animal spirits; a poet and coming diplomat, and he already had the air of both. His eyes burned with his enthusiasm for life; and Anne was happy when he took her hands, for she had been afraid that the years of separation might divide them and that she would lose forever the beloved brother of her childhood. But in a few short hours those fears were set aside; he was the same George, she the same Anne. Their friendship, she knew, could not lose from the years, only gain from them. Their minds were of similar calibre; alert, intellectual, they were quick to be amused, quick to anger, reckless of themselves. They had therefore a perfect understanding of each other, and, being troubled, it was natural that she should go to him.

She said as they walked together through the Kentish lanes, for she had felt the need to leave the castle so that she might have no fear of being overheard: "I have learned of Mary and the King."

"That does not surprise me," said George. "It is common knowledge."

"It shocked me deeply, George."

He smiled at her. "It should not."

"But our sister! It is degrading."

"She would degrade herself sooner or later, so why should it not be in that quarter from which the greatest advantages may accrue."

"Our father delights in this situation, George, and our mother is complaisant."

"My sweet sister, you are but sixteen. Ah, you look wonderfully worldly wise, but you are not yet grown up. You are very like the little girl who sat in the window seats at Blickling, and dreamed of knightly deeds. Life is not romantic, Anne, and men are not frequently honourable knights. Life is a battle or a game which each of us fights or plays with all the skill at his command. Do not condemn Mary because her way would not be yours."

"The King will tire of her."

"Assuredly."

"And cast her off!"

"It is Mary's nature to be happy, Anne. Do not fear. She will find other lovers when she is ejected from the royal bed. She has poor Will Carey, and she has been in favour for the best part of three years and her family have not suffered for it yet. Know, my sweet sister, that to be mistress of the King is an honour; it is only the mistress of a poor man who degrades herself."

His handsome face was momentarily set in melancholy lines, but almost immediately he was laughing merrily.

"George," she said, "I cannot like it."

"What! Not like to see your father become a power in the land! Not like to see your brother make his way at court!"

"I would rather they had done these things by their own considerable abilities."

"Bless you!" said George. "There are more favours won this way than by the sweat of the brow. Dismiss the matter from your mind. The Boleyns' fortunes are in the ascendant. Who knows whither the King's favour may lead—and all due to our own plump little Mary! Who would have believed it possible!"

"I like it not," she repeated.

Then he took her hands and kissed them lightly, wishing to soothe her troubled mind.

"Fear not, little sister."

Now he had her smiling with him—laughing at the incongruity of this situation. Mary—the one who was not as bright as the rest—was leading the Boleyns to fame and fortune.

It seemed almost unbearably quiet after Mary and George had gone. Anne could not speak of Mary's relationship with the

King to her mother, and it irked her frank nature perpetually to have to steer the conversation away from a delicate topic. She was glad when her father returned to the court, for his obvious delight in his good fortune angered Anne. Her father thought her a sullen girl, for she was not one, feeling displeased, to care about hiding her displeasure. Mary was his favourite daughter; Mary was a sensible girl; and Anne could not help feeling that he would be relieved when the arrangements for the Butler marriage were completed. She spent the days with her mother, or wandered often alone in the lanes and gardens.

Sir Thomas returned to Hever in a frenzy of excitement. The King would be passing through Kent, and it was probable that he would spend a night at Hever. Sir Thomas very quickly roused the household to his pitch of excitement. He went to the kitchen and gave orders himself; he had flowers set in the ballroom and replaced by fresh ones twice a day; he grumbled incessantly about the inconvenience of an old castle like Hever, and wished fervently that he had a modern house in which to entertain the King.

"The house is surely of little importance," said Anne caustically, "as long as Mary remains attractive to the King!"

"Be silent, girl!" thundered Sir Thomas. "Do you realize that this is the greatest of honours?"

"Surely not the greatest!" murmured Anne, and was silenced by a pleading look from her mother, who greatly feared discord; and, loving her mother while deploring her attitude in the case of Mary and the King, Anne desisted.

The King's having given no date for his visit, Sir Thomas fumed and fretted for several days, scarcely leaving the castle for fear he should not be on the spot to welcome his royal master.

One afternoon Anne took a basket to the rose garden that she might cut some of the best blooms for her mother. It was a hot afternoon, and she was informally dressed in her favourite scarlet; as the day was so warm she had taken off the caul from her head and shaken out her long, silky ringlets. She had sat on a seat in the rose garden for an hour or more, half dozing, when she decided it was time she gathered the flowers and returned to the house; and as she stood by a tree of red roses she was aware of a footfall close by, and turning saw what she immediately thought of as "a Personage" coming through the gap in the conifers which was the entrance to this garden. She felt the blood rush to her face, for she knew him at once. The jewels in his clothes were caught and held by the sun, so that it seemed as if he were on fire; his face was ruddy, his beard seemed golden, and his presence seemed to fill the garden. She could not but think of Mary's meeting with him in the palace of Guisnes, and her resentment towards him flared up within her, even as she realized it would be sheer folly to show him that resentment. She sought therefore to compose her features and, with admirable calm—for she had decided now that her safest plan was to feign ignorance of his identity—she went on snipping the roses.

Henry was close. She turned as though in surprise to find

herself not alone, gave him the conventional bow of acknowledgement which she would have given to one of her father's ordinary acquaintances, and said boldly: "Good day, sir."

The King was taken aback. Then inwardly he chuckled, thinking: She has no notion who I am! He studied her with the utmost appreciation. Her informal dress was more becoming, he thought, than those elaborate creations worn by some ladies at a court function. Her beautiful hair was like a black silk cloak about her shoulders. He took in each detail of her appearance and thought that he had never seen one whose beauty delighted him more.

She turned her head and snipped off a rose.

"My father is expecting the King to ride this way. I presume you to be one of his gentlemen!"

Masquerade had ever greatly appealed to Henry. There was nothing he enjoyed as much as to appear disguised at some ball or banquet, and after much badinage with his subjects and at exactly the appropriate moment, to make the dramatic announcement—"I am your King!" And how could this game be more delightfully played out than in a rose garden on a summer's afternoon with, surely, the loveliest maiden in his kingdom!

He took a step closer to her.

"Had I known," he said, "that I should come face to face with such beauty, depend upon it, I should have whipped up my horse."

"Would you not have had to await the King's pleasure?"

"Aye!" He slapped his gorgeous thigh. "That I should!"

She, who knew so well how to play the coquette, now did so with a will, for in this role she could appease that resentment in herself which threatened to make her very angry as she contemplated this lover of her sister, Mary. Let him come close, and she—in assumed ignorance of his rank—would freeze him with a look. She snipped off a rose and gave it to him.

"You may have it if you care to."

He said: "I do care. I shall keep it forever."

"Bah!" she answered him contemptuously. "Mere court gallantry!"

"You like not our court gallants?"

Her mocking eyes swept his padded, jewelled figure.

"They are somewhat clumsy when compared with those of the French court."

"You are lately come from France?"

"I am. A match has been arranged for me with my cousin."

"Would to God I were the cousin! Tell me . . ." He came yet closer, noting the smooth skin, the silky lashes, the proud tilt of the head and its graceful carriage on the tiny neck. "Was that less clumsy?"

"Nay!" she said, showing white teeth. "Not so! It was completely without subtlety; I saw it coming."

Henry found that, somewhat disconcerting as this was, he was enjoying it. The girl had a merry wit, and he liked it; she was stimulating as a glass of champagne. And I swear I never clapped eyes on a lovelier wench! he told himself. The airs she gives herself! It would seem I were the subject—she the Queen!

She said: "The garden is pretty, is it not? To me this is one of the most pleasant spots at Hever."

They walked around it; she showed him the flowers, picked a branch of lavender and held it to her nose; then she rolled it in her hands and smelled its pleasant fragrance there.

Henry said: "You tell me you have recently come from the court of France. How did you like it there?"

"It was indeed pleasant."

"And you are sorry to return?"

"I think that may be, for so long have I been there that it seems as home to me."

"I like not to hear that."

She shrugged her shoulders. "They say I am as French as I am English."

"The French," he said, the red of his face suddenly tinged with purple that matched his coat, "are a perfidious set of rascals."

"Sir!" she said reproachfully and, drawing her skirts about her, she walked from him and sat on the wooden seat near the pond. She looked at him coldly as he hurried towards her.

"How now!" he said, thinking he had had enough of the game.

He sat down beside her, pressing his thigh against hers, which caused her immediate withdrawal from him. "Perfidious!" she said slowly. "Rascals! And when I have said I am half French!"

"Ah!" he said. "I should not use such words to you. You have the face of an angel!"

She was off the seat, as though distrusting his proximity. She threw herself onto the grass near the pond and looked into still waters at her own reflection, a graceful feminine Narcissus, her hair touching the water.

"No!" she said imperiously, as he would have risen: "You stay there, and mayhap I will tarry awhile and talk to you."

He did not understand himself. The joke should have been done with ere this. It was time to explain, to have her on her knees craving forgiveness for her forwardness. He would raise her and say: "We cannot forgive such disrespectful treatment of your sovereign. We demand a kiss in payment for your sins!" But he was unsure; there was that in her which he had never before discovered in a woman. She looked haughty enough to refuse a kiss to a king. No, no! he thought. Play this little game awhile.

She said: "The French are an interesting people. I was fortunate there. My friend was Madame la Duchesse d'Alençon, and I count myself indeed happy to have such a friend."

"I have heard tales of her," he said.

"Her fame travels. Tell me, have you read Boccaccio?"

The King leaned forward. Had he read Boccaccio! Indeed he had, and vastly had the fellow's writing pleased him.

"And you?" he asked.

She nodded, and they smiled at each other in the understanding of a pleasure shared.

"We would read it together, the Duchess and I. Tell me, which of the stories did you prefer?"

Finding himself plunged deep into a discussion of the literature of his day, Henry forgot he was a king, and an amorous king at that. There was in this man, in addition to the coarse, crude, insatiable sensualist, a scholar of some attainment. Usually the sensualist was the stronger, ever ready to stifle the other, but there was about this girl sitting by the pond a purity that commanded his respect, and he found he could sit back in his seat and delight in her as he would in a beautiful picture or piece of statuary, while he could marvel at her unwomanly intellect. Literature, music and art could have held a strong position in his life, had he not in his youth been such a healthy animal. Had he but let his enthusiasm for them grow in proportion to that which he bestowed on tennis, on jousting, on the hunting of game and of women, his mind would assuredly have developed as nobly as his body. An elastic mind would have served him better than his strong muscles; but the jungle animal in him had been strong, and urgent desires tempered by a narrow religious outlook had done much to suppress the finer man, and from the mating of the animal and the zealot was born that monster of cruelty, his conscience. But that was to come; the monster was as yet in its infancy, and pleasant it was to talk of things of the mind with an enchanting companion. She was full of wit, and Marguerite of Alençon talked through her young lips. She had been allowed to peep into the *Heptameron*—that odd book which, under the influence of Boccaccio, Marguerite was writing.

From literature she passed to the pastimes of the French

court. She told of the masques, less splendid perhaps than those he indulged in with such pleasure, but more subtle and amusing. Wit was to the French court what bright colours and sparkling jewels were to the English. She told of a play which she had helped Marguerite to write, quoting lines from it which set him laughing with appreciative merriment. He was moved to tell her of his own compositions, reciting some verses of his. She listened, her head on one side, critical.

She shook her head: "The last line is not so good. Now this would have been better . . ." And so would it! Momentarily he was angered, for those at court had declared there never were such verses written as those penned by his hand. From long practice he could pretend, even to himself, that his anger came from a different cause than that from which it really sprang. Now it grew—he assured himself—not from her slighting remarks on his poetry, but from the righteous indignation he must feel when he considered that this girl, though scarcely out of her childhood, had been exposed to the wickedness of the French court. Where he himself was concerned he had no sense of the ridiculous; he could, in all seriousness, put aside the knowledge that even at this moment he was planning her seduction, and burn with indignation that others—rakes and libertines with fancy French manners—might have had similar intentions. Such a girl, he told himself, smarting under the slights which she, reared in that foreign court, had been able to deliver so aptly, should never have been sent to France.

He said with dignity: "It grieves me to think of the dangers to which you have been exposed at that licentious court presided over by a monarch who . . ." His voice failed him, for he pictured a dark, clever face, a sly smile and lips which had referred to him as "My prisoner."

She laughed lightly. "The King of France is truly of an amorous nature, but never would I be a king's mistress!"

It seemed to him that this clever girl then answered a question which he had yet to ask. He felt worsted, and angry to be so.

He said severely: "There are some who would not think it an indignity to be a king's mistress, but an honour."

"Doubtless there are those who sell themselves cheaply."

"Cheaply!" he all but roared. "Come! It is not kingly to be niggardly with those that please."

"I do not mean in worldly goods. To sell one's dignity and honour for momentary power and perhaps riches—that is to sell cheaply those things which are beyond price. Now I must go into the house." She stood up, throwing back her hair. He stood too, feeling deflated and unkingly.

Silently he walked with her from the rose garden. Now was the time to disclose his identity, for it could not much longer be kept secret.

"You have not asked my name," he said.

"Nor you mine."

"You are the daughter of Sir Thomas Boleyn, I have gathered."

"Indeed, that was clever of you!" she mocked. "I am Anne Boleyn."

"You still do not ask my name. Have you no curiosity to know it?"

"I shall doubtless learn in good time."

"My name is Henry."

"It is a good English name."

"And have you noticed nothing yet?"

She turned innocent eyes upon him. "What is there that I should have noticed?"

"It is the same as the King's." He saw the mockery in her eyes now. He blurted out: "By God! You knew all the time!"

"Having once seen the King's Grace, how could one of his subjects ever forget him?"

He was uncertain now whether to be amused or angry; in vain did he try to remember all she had said to him and he to her. "Methinks you are a saucy wench!" he said.

"I hope my sauciness has pleased my mighty King."

He looked at her sternly, for though her words were respectful, her manner was not.

"Too much sauce," he said, "is apt to spoil a dish."

"And too little, to destroy it!" she said, casting down her eyes. "I had thought that Your Majesty, being a famous epicure, would have preferred a well-flavoured one."

He gave a snort of laughter and put out a hand which he would have laid on her shoulders, but without giving him a glance she moved daintily away, so that he could not know whether by accident or design.

He said: "We shall look to see you at court with your sister."

He was unprepared for the effect of those words; her cheeks were scarlet as her dress, and her eyes lost all their merriment. Her father was coming across the lawn towards them; she bowed low and turning from him ran across the grass and into the castle.

"You have a beautiful daughter there, Thomas!" exclaimed the King. And Thomas, obsequious, smiling, humbly conducted Henry into Hever Castle.

The sight of the table in the great dining-hall brought a glister of pride into Sir Thomas's eyes. On it were laid out in most lavish array great joints of beef, mutton and venison, hare and seasoned peacocks; there were vegetables and fruit, and great pies and pastries. Sir Thomas's harrying of his cooks and scullions had been well worthwhile, and he felt that the great kitchens of Hever had done him justice. The King eyed this display with an approval which might have been more marked, had not his thoughts been inclined to dwell more upon Sir Thomas's daughter than on his table.

They took their seats, the King in the place of honour at the right hand of his host, the small company he had brought with him ranged about the table. There was one face for which the King looked in vain; Sir Thomas, ever eager to anticipate the smallest wish of his sovereign, saw the King's searching look and understood it; he called a serving maid to him and whispered sharply to her to go at once to his daughter and bid her to the table without a second's delay. The maid returned with the disconcerting message that Sir Thomas's daughter suffered from a headache and would not come to the table that day. The King, watching this little by-play with the greatest interest, heard every word.

"Go back at once," said Sir Thomas, "and tell the lady I command her presence here at once!"

"Stay!" interceded Henry, his voice startling Sir Thomas by its unusual softness. "Allow me to deal with the matter, good Thomas. Come hither, girl."

The poor little serving maid dropped a frightened curtsey and feared she would not be able to understand the King's commands, so overawed was she by his notice.

"Tell the lady from us," said Henry, "that we are indeed sorry for the headache. Tell her it doubtless comes from lingering too daringly in the rays of the sun. Tell her we excuse her and wish her good speed in her recovery."

He did not see Anne again, for she kept to her room. Next morning he left Hever. He looked up at its windows, wondering which might be hers, telling himself that no girl, however haughty, however self-possessed, would be able to prevent herself from taking one glimpse at her King. But there was no sign of a face at any window. Disconsolate, bemused, the King rode away from Hever.

✦

The great Cardinal, he who was Lord Chancellor of the realm, rode through the crowds. Before him and behind went his gentlemen attendants, for the great man never rode abroad but that he must impress the people with his greatness. He sat his mule with a dignity which would have become a king. What though his body were weak, his digestion poor, that he was very far from robust and suffered many ailments! His mind was the keenest, the most able, the most profound in the kingdom; and thus, first through the King's father, and more effectively through his gracious son, had Thomas Wolsey come to his high office. His success, he knew well, lay with his understanding of the King—that fine robustious animal—and when he was but almoner to his gracious lord he had used that knowledge and so distinguished himself. There had been those counsellors who might urge the King to leave his pleasure and devote more time to affairs of state. Not so Thomas Wolsey! Let the King leave tiresome matters to his most dutiful servant. Let the King pursue his pleasures. Leave the wearisome matters to his most obedient—and what was all-important—to his most able Wolsey! How well the King loved those who did his will! This King, this immense man—in whom all emotions matched his huge body—hated fiercely and could love well. And he had loved Wolsey, in whose hands he could so safely place those matters that were important to his kingdom but so monotonously dull to his royal mind. And never was a man more content than Wolsey that this should be so. He, arrogant, imperious as his master, had had the indignity to be born the son of a poor man of Ipswich, and by his own fine brain had replaced indignity with honour. The Ipswich merchant's son was the best loved friend of the English King, and how doubly dear were those luxuries and those extravagances with which he, who had once suffered from obscurity, now surrounded himself! If he were over-lavish, he forgave himself; he had to wash the taste of Ipswich from his mouth.

As he rode on his ceremonious way, the people watched him. To his nose he held what might appear to be an orange, and what was really a guard against disease; for all the natural matter had been taken from the orange and in its place was stuffed part of a sponge containing vinegar and such concoctions as would preserve a great man from the pestilence which floated in the London air. Perhaps the people murmured against him; there were those who gave him sullen looks. Is this a man of God? they asked each other. This Wolsey—no higher born than you or I—who surrounds himself with elegance and luxury at the expense of the hard-pressed people! This gourmet, who must get special dispensation from the Pope that he need not follow the Lenten observances! They say he never forgives a slight. They say his hands are as red as his robes. What of brave Buckingham! A marvel it is that the headless ghost of the Duke does not haunt his murderer!

If Wolsey could have spoken to them of Buckingham, he could have told them that a man, who will at any cost hold the King's favour, must often steep his hands in blood. Buckingham had been a fool. Buckingham had insulted Wolsey, and Wolsey had brought a charge against him of treasonable sorcery. Buckingham went to the block, not for his treasonable sorcery; he died because he had committed the unforgivable sin of being too nearly related to the King. He stood too close to the throne, and the Tudors had not been in possession of it long enough to be able to regard such an offence lightly. Thus it was one kept the favour of kings; by learning their unuttered desires and anticipating their wishes; thus one remained the power behind the throne, one's eyes alert, one's ears trained to catch the faintest inflection of the royal voice, fearful lest the mighty puppet might become the master.

In the presence-chamber Wolsey awaited audience of the King. He came, fresh from his Kentish journey, flushed with health, his eyes beaming with pleasure as they rested on his best-loved statesman.

"I would speak with Your Majesty on one or two matters," said the Chancellor-Cardinal when he had congratulated the King on his healthy appearance.

"Matters of state! Matters of state, eh? Let us look into these matters, good Thomas."

Wolsey spread papers on the table, and the royal signature was appended to them. The King listened, though his manner was a little absent.

"You are a good man, Thomas," he said, "and we love you well."

"Your Majesty's regard is my most treasured possession."

The King laughed heartily, but his voice was a trifle acid when he spoke. "Then the King is pleased, for to be the most treasured of all your possessions, my rich friend, is indeed to be of great price!"

Wolsey felt the faintest twinge of uneasiness, until he saw in his sovereign's face a look he knew well. There was a glaze over the bright little eyes, the cruel mouth had softened, and when the King spoke, his voice was gentle.

"Wolsey, I have been discoursing with a young lady who has the wit of an angel, and is worthy to wear a crown."

Wolsey, alert, suppressed his smile with the desire to rub his hands together in his glee.

"It is sufficient if Your Majesty finds her worthy of your love," he whispered.

The King pulled at his beard.

"Nay, Thomas, I fear she would never condescend that way."

"Sire, great princes, if they choose to play the lover, have that in their power to mollify a heart of steel."

The King shook his great head in melancholy fashion, seeing her bending over the pond, seeing her proud young head on the small neck, hearing her sweet voice: "I would never be a king's mistress!"

"Your Majesty has been saddened by this lady," said Wolsey solicitously.

"I fear so, Wolsey."

"This must not be!" Wolsey's heart was merry. There was nothing he desired so much at this time as to see his master immersed in a passionate love affair. It was necessary at this moment to keep the fat, jewelled finger out of the French pie.

"Nay, my master, my dear lord, your chancellor forbids such

sadness." He put his head closer to the flushed face. "Could we not bring the lady to court, and find a place for her among the Queen's ladies?"

The King placed an affectionate arm about Wolsey's shoulders.

"If Your Majesty will but whisper the name of the lady . . ."

"It is Boleyn's daughter . . . Anne."

Now Wolsey had great difficulty in restraining his mirth. Boleyn's daughter! Anne! Off with the elder daughter! On with the younger!

"My lord King, she shall come to the court. I shall give a banquet at Hampton Court—a masque it shall be! I shall ask my Gracious Liege to honour me with his mighty presence. The lady shall be there!"

The King smiled, well pleased. A prince, had said this wise man, has that power to mollify a heart of steel. Good Wolsey! Dear Thomas! Dear friend and most able statesman!

"Methinks, Thomas," said the King with tears in his eyes, "that I love thee well."

Wolsey fell on his knees and kissed the ruby on the forefinger of the fat hand. And I do love this man, thought the King; for he was one to whom it was not necessary to state crude facts. The lady would be brought to court, and it would appear that she came not through the King's wish. That was what he wanted, and not a word had he said of it; yet Wolsey had known. And well knew the King that Wolsey would arrange this matter with expedience and tact.

Life at the English court offered amusement in plenty, and the coming of one as vivacious and striking as Anne Boleyn could not pass unnoticed. The ladies received her with some interest and much envy, the gentlemen with marked appreciation. There were two ways of life at court; on the one hand there was the gay merrymaking of the King's faction, on the other the piety of the Queen. As queen's attendant, Anne's actions were restricted; but at the jousts and balls, where the Queen's side must mingle with the King's, she attracted a good deal of attention for none excelled her at the dance, and whether it was harpsichord, virginals or flute she played there were always those to crowd about her; when she sang, men grew sentimental, for there was that in her rich young voice to move men to tears.

The King was acutely aware of her while feigning not to notice her. He would have her believe that he had been not entirely pleased by her disrespectful manners at Hever, and that he still remembered the levity of her conversation with pained displeasure.

Anne laughed to herself, thinking: Well he likes a masquerade, when he arranges it; well he likes a joke against others! Is he angry at my appointment to attend the Queen? How I hope he does not banish me to Hever!

Life had become so interesting. As lady-in-waiting to the Queen, she was allowed a woman attendant and a spaniel of her own; she was pleased with the woman and delighted with the spaniel. The three of them shared a breakfast of beef and bread, which they washed down with a gallon of ale between them. Other meals were taken with the rest of the ladies in the great chamber, and at all these meals ale and wine were served in plenty; meat was usually the fare—beef, mutton, poultry, rabbits, peacocks, hares, pigeons—except on fast days when, in place of the meats, there would be a goodly supply of salmon or flounders, salted eels, whiting, or plaice and gurnet. But it was not the abundance of food that delighted Anne; it was the gaiety of the company. And if she had feared to be dismissed from the court in those first days, no sooner had she set eyes on Henry, Lord Percy, eldest son of the Earl of Northumberland, than she was terrified of that happening.

These two young people met about the court, though not as often as they could have wished, for whilst Anne, as maid of honour to Queen Katharine, was attached to the court, Percy was a protege of the Cardinal. It pleased Wolsey to have in his retinue of attendants various high-born young men, and so great was his place in the kingdom that this honour was sought by the noblest families in the realm. Young Percy must therefore attend the Cardinal daily, accompany him to court, and consider himself greatly honoured by the patronage of this low-born man.

Lord Percy was a handsome young man of delicate features and of courteous manners; and as soon as he saw the Queen's newest lady-in-waiting he was captivated by her personal charms. And Anne, seeing this handsome boy, was filled with such a tenderness towards him, which she had experienced for none hitherto, that whenever she knew the Cardinal to be in audience with the King she would look for the young nobleman. Whenever he came to the palace he was alert for a glimpse of her. They were both young; he was very shy; and so, oddly enough, was she, where he was concerned.

One day she was sitting at a window overlooking a courtyard when into this courtyard there came the lord Cardinal and his attendants; and among these latter was Henry, Lord Percy. His eyes flew to the window, saw Anne, and emboldened by the distance which separated them, flashed her a message which she construed as "Wait there, and while the Cardinal is closeted with the King I will return. I have so long yearned to hold speech with you!"

She waited, her heart beating fast as she pretended to stitch a piece of tapestry; waiting, waiting, feeling a sick fear within her lest the King might not wish to see the Cardinal, and the young man might thus be unable to escape.

He came running across the courtyard, and she knew by his haste and his enraptured expression that his fear had been as hers.

"I feared to find you gone!" he said breathlessly.

"I feared you would not come," she answered.

"I look for you always."

"I for you."

They smiled, beautiful both of them in the joyful discovery of loving and being loved.

Anne was thinking that were he to ask her, she, who had laughed at Mary for marrying Will Carey, would gladly marry him though he might be nothing more than the Cardinal's Fool.

"I know not your name," said Percy, "but your face is the fairest I ever saw."

"It is Anne Boleyn."

"You are daughter to Sir Thomas?"

She nodded, blushing, thinking Mary would be in his mind, and a fear came to her that her sister's disgrace might discredit herself in his eyes. But he was too far gone in love to find her anything but perfect.

"I am recently come to court," she said.

"That I know! You could not have been here a day but that I should have found you."

She said: "What would your master say an he found you lingering beneath this window?"

"I know not, nor care I!"

"Were you caught, might there not be those who would prevent you from coming again? Already you may have been missed."

He was alarmed. To be prevented from enjoying the further bliss of such meetings was intolerable.

"I go now," he said. "Tomorrow . . . you will be here at this hour?"

"You will find me here."

"Tomorrow," he said, and they smiled at each other.

Next day she saw him, and the next. There were many

meetings, and for each of those two young lovers the day was good when they met, and bad when they did not. She learned of his exalted rank, and she could say with honesty that this mattered to her not at all, except of course that her ambitious father could raise no objection to a match with the house of Northumberland.

One day her lover came to her and pleasure was written large on his face.

"The Cardinal is to give a ball at his house at Hampton. All the ladies of the court will be invited!"

"You will be there?"

"You too!" he replied.

"We shall be masked."

"I shall find you."

"And then . . . ?" she said.

His eyes held the answer to that question.

Anne had dreamed of such happiness, though of late her observation of those about her had led her to conclude that it was rarely known. But to her it had come; she would treasure it, preserve it, keep it forever. She could scarcely wait for that day when Thomas Wolsey would entertain the court at his great house at Hampton on the Thames.

The King was uneasy. The Cardinal had thought to help him when he had had Anne appointed a maid of honour to the

Queen; but had he? Never, for the sake of a woman, had the King been so perplexed. He must see her every day, for how could he deny his eyes a sight of the most charming creature they had ever rested on! Yet he dared not speak with her. And why? For this reason; no sooner had the girl set foot in the Queen's apartments than that old enemy, his conscience, must rear its ugly head to leer at him.

"Henry," said the conscience, "this girl's sister, Mary Boleyn, has shared your bed full many a night, and well you know the edict of the Pope. Well you know that association with one sister gives you an affinity with the other. Therein lies sin!"

"That I know well," answered Henry the King. "But as there was no marriage. . . ."

Such reasoning could not satisfy the conscience; it was the same—marriage ceremony or no marriage ceremony—and well he knew it.

"But there was never one like this girl; never was I so drawn to a woman; never before have I felt myself weak as I would be with her. Were she my mistress, I verily believe I should be willing to dispense with all others, and would not that be a good thing, for in the eyes of the Holy Church, is it not better for a man to have one mistress than many? Then, would not the Queen be happier? One mistress is forgivable; her distress comes from there being so many."

He was a man of many superstitions, of deep religious convictions. The God of his belief was a king like himself, though a more powerful being since, in place of the axe, he was able to wield a more terrifying weapon whose blade was supernatural phenomena. Vindictive was the King's god, susceptible to flattery, violent in love, more violent in hate—a jealous god, a god who spied, who recorded slights and insults, and whose mind worked in the same simple way as that of Henry of England. Before this god Henry trembled as men trembled before Henry. Hence the conscience, the uneasiness, his jealous watchfulness of Anne Boleyn, and his reluctance to make his preference known.

In vain he tried to soothe his senses. All women are much alike in darkness. Mary is very like her sister. Mary is sweet and willing; and there are others as willing.

He tried to placate his conscience. "I shall not look at the girl; I will remember there is an affinity between us."

So those days, which were a blissful heaven to Anne and another Henry, were purgatory to Henry the King, racked alternately by conscience and desire.

She was clad in scarlet, and her vest was cloth of gold. She wore what had become known at court as the Boleyn sleeves, but they did not divulge her identity, for many wore the Boleyn sleeves since she had shown the charm of this particular fashion. Her hair was hidden by her gold cap, and only the beautiful eyes showing through her mask might proclaim her as Anne Boleyn.

He found her effortlessly, because she had described to him in detail the costume she would wear.

"I should have known you though you had not told me. I should always know you."

"Then, sir," she answered pertly, "I would I had put you to the test!"

"I heard the music on the barges as they came along the river," he said, "and I do not think I have ever been so happy in my life."

He was a slender figure in a coat of purple velvet embroidered in gold thread and pearls. Anne thought there was no one more handsome in this great ballroom, though the King, in his scarlet coat on which emeralds flashed, and in his bonnet dazzling rich with rubies and diamonds, was a truly magnificent sight.

The lovers clasped hands, and from a recess watched the gay company.

"There goes the King!"

"Who thinks," said Anne, laughing, "to disguise himself with a mask!"

"None dare disillusion him, or 'twould spoil the fun. It seems as though he searches for someone."

"His latest sweetheart, doubtless!" said Anne scornfully.

Percy laid his hand on her lips.

"You speak too freely, Anne."

"That was ever a fault of mine. But do you doubt that is the case?"

"I doubt it not—and you have no faults! Let us steal away from these crowds. I know a room where we can be alone. There is much I would say to you."

"Take me there then. Though I should be most severely reprimanded if the Queen should hear that one of her ladies hides herself in lonely apartments in the house."

"You can trust me. I would die rather than allow any hurt to come to you."

"That I know well. I like not these crowds, and would hear what it is that you have to say to me."

They went up a staircase and along a corridor. There were three small steps leading into a little antechamber; its one window showed the river glistening in moonlight.

Anne went to that window and looked across the gardens to the water.

"There was surely never such a perfect night!" she exclaimed.

He put his arms about her, and they looked at each other, marvelling at what they saw.

"Anne! Make it the most perfect night there ever was, by promising to marry me."

"If it takes that to make this night perfect," she answered softly, "then now it is so."

He took her hands and kissed them, too young and mild of nature to trust entirely the violence of his emotion.

"You are the most beautiful of all the court ladies, Anne."

"You think that because you love me."

"I think it because it is so."

"Then I am happy to be so for you."

"Did you ever dream of such happiness, Anne?"

"Yes, often . . . but scarce dared hope it would be mine."

"Think of those people below us, Anne. How one pities them! For what can they know of happiness like this!"

She laughed suddenly, thinking of the King, pacing the floor, trying to disguise the fact that he was the King, looking about him for his newest sweetheart. Her thoughts went swiftly to Mary.

"My sister . . ." she began.

"What of your sister! Of what moment could she be to us!"

"None!" she cried, and taking his hand, kissed it. "None, do we but refuse to let her."

"Then we refuse, Anne."

"How I love you!" she told him. "And to think I might have let them marry me to my cousin of Ormond!"

"They would marry me to Shrewsbury's daughter!"

A faint fear stirred her then. She remembered that he was the heir of the Earl of Northumberland; it was meet that he should marry into the Shrewsbury family, not humble Anne Boleyn.

"Oh, Henry," she said, "what if they should try to marry you to the Lady Mary?"

"They shall marry me to none but Anne Boleyn!"

It was not difficult, up here in the little moonlight chamber, to defy the world; but they dare not tarry too long. All the company must be present when the masks were removed, or absent themselves on pain of the King's displeasure.

In the ballroom the festive air was tinged with melancholy. The Cardinal was perturbed, for the King clearly showed his annoyance. A masked ball was not such a good idea as it had at first seemed, for the King had been unable to find her whom he sought.

The masks were removed; the ball over, and the royal party lodged in the two hundred and forty gorgeous bedrooms which it was the Cardinal's delight to keep ready for his guests.

The news might seem a rumour just at first, but before many days had passed the fact was established that Henry, Lord Percy, eldest son and heir to the noble Earl of Northumberland, was so far gone in love with sparkling Anne Boleyn that he had determined to marry her.

And so the news came to the ear of the King.

The King was purple with fury. He sent for him to whom he always turned in time of trouble. The Cardinal came hastily, knowing that to rely on the favour of a king is to build one's hopes on a quiet but not extinct volcano. Over the Cardinal flowed the molten lava of Henry's anger.

"By Christ!" cried the King. "Here is a merry state of affairs! I would take the fool and burn him at the stake, were he not such a young fool. How dare he think to contract himself without our consent!"

"Your Majesty, I fear I am in ignorance . . ."

"Young Percy!" roared His Majesty. "Fool! Dolt that he is!

He has, an it please you, decided he will marry Anne Boleyn!"

Inwardly the Cardinal could smile. This was a mere outbreak of royal jealousy. I will deal with this, thought the Cardinal, and deplored that his wit, his diplomacy must be squandered to mend a lover's troubles.

"Impertinent young fool!" soothed the Cardinal. "As he is one of my young men, Your Majesty must allow me to deal with him. I will castigate him. I will make him aware of his youthful . . . nay, criminal folly, since he has offended Your Majesty. He is indeed a dolt to think Northumberland can mate with the daughter of a knight!"

Through the King's anger beamed his gratitude to Wolsey. Dear Thomas, who made the way easy! That was the reason, he told his conscience—Northumberland cannot mate with a mere knight's daughter!

"'Twere an affront to us!" growled mollified Henry. "We gave our consent to the match with Shrewsbury's girl."

"And a fitting match indeed!" murmured the Cardinal.

"A deal more fitting than that he should marry Boleyn's girl. My dear Wolsey, I should hold myself responsible to Shrewsbury and his poor child if anything went amiss. . . ."

"Your Grace was ever full of conscience. You must not blame your royal self for the follies of your subjects."

"I do, Thomas . . . I do! After all, 'twas I who brought the wench to court."

Wolsey murmured: "Your Majesty . . . ? Why, I thought 'twas I who talked to Boleyn of his younger daughter. . . ."

"No matter!" said the King, his eyes beaming with affection. "I thought I mentioned the girl to you. No matter!"

"I spoke to Boleyn, Your Grace, I remember well."

The King's hand patted the red-clad shoulder.

"I know this matter can be trusted to you."

"Your Majesty knows well that I shall settle it most expeditiously."

"They shall both be banished from the court. I will not be flouted by these young people!"

Wolsey bowed.

"The Shrewsbury marriage can be hastened," said the King.

Greatly daring, Wolsey asked: "And the girl, Your Majesty? There was talk of a marriage . . . the Ormond estates were the issue. . . . Perhaps Your Majesty does not remember."

The brows contracted; the little eyes seemed swallowed up in puffy flesh. The King's voice cracked out impatiently: "That matter is not settled. I like not these Irish. Suffice it that we banish the girl."

"Your Majesty may trust me to deal with the matter in accordance with your royal wishes."

"And, Thomas . . . let the rebuke come from you. I would not have these young people know that I have their welfare so much at heart; methinks they already have too high a conceit of themselves."

After Wolsey retired, the King continued to pace up and down. Let her return to Hever. She should be punished for daring to fall in love with that paltry boy. How was she in love?

Tender? It was difficult to imagine that. Eager? Ah! Eager with a wretched boy! Haughty enough she had been with her lord the King! To test that eagerness he would have given the brightest jewel in his crown, but she would refuse her favours like a queen. And in a brief acquaintance, she had twice offended him; let her see that even she could not do that with impunity!

So she should be exiled to Hever, whither he would ride one day. She should be humble; he would be stern . . . just at first.

He threw himself into a chair, legs apart, hands on knees, thinking of a reconciliation in the rose garden at Hever.

His anger had passed away.

✦

Immediately on his return to his house at Westminster, Wolsey sent for Lord Percy.

The young man came promptly, and there in the presence of several of his higher servants Wolsey began to upbraid him, marvelling, he said, at his folly in thinking he might enter into an engagement with a foolish girl at the court. Did the young fool not realize that on his father's death he would inherit and enjoy one of the noblest earldoms in the kingdom? How then could he marry without the consent of his father? Did Percy think, he thundered, that either his father or the King would consent to his matching himself with such a one? Moreover, continued the Cardinal, working himself up to a fine frenzy of indignation such as struck terror into the heart of the boy, he would have Percy know that the King had at great trouble prepared a suitable match for Anne Boleyn. Would he flout the King's pleasure!

Lord Percy was no more timid than most, but he knew the ways of the court well enough to quail before the meaning he read into Wolsey's words. Men had been committed to the Tower for refusing to obey the King's command, and Wolsey clearly had the King behind him in this matter. Committed to the Tower! Though the dread Cardinal did not speak the words, Percy knew they were there ready to be pronounced at any moment. Men went to the Tower and were heard of no more. Dread happenings there were in the underground chambers of the Tower of London. Men were incarcerated, and never heard of again. And Percy had offended the King!

"Sir," he said, trembling, "I knew not the King's pleasure, and am sorry for it. I consider I am of good years, and thought myself able to provide me a convenient wife as my fancy should please me, not doubting that my lord and father would have been well content. Though she be but a simple maid and her father a knight, yet she is descended of noble parentage, for her mother is of high Norfolk blood and her father descended from the Earl of Ormond. I most humbly beseech Your Grace's favour therein, and also to entreat the King's Majesty on my behalf for his princely favour in this matter which I cannot forsake."

The Cardinal turned to his servants, appealing to them to observe the wilful folly of this boy. Sadly he reproached Percy for knowing the King's pleasure and not readily submitting to it.

"I have gone too far in this matter," said Percy.

"Dost think," cried Wolsey, "that the King and I know not what we have to do in weighty matters such as this!"

He left the boy, remarking as he went that he should not seek out the girl, or he would have to face the wrath of the King.

The Earl arrived, coming in haste from the north since the command was the King's, and hastened to Wolsey's house. A cold man with an eye to his own advantage, the Earl listened gravely, touched his neck uneasily as though he felt the sharp blade of an axe there—for heads had been severed for less than this—hardened his face, and said that he would set the matter to rights.

He went to his son and railed at him, cursing his pride, his licentiousness, but chiefly the fact that he had incurred the King's displeasure. So he would bring his father to the block and forfeit the family estate, would he! He was a waster, useless, idle. . . . He would return to his home immediately and proceed with the marriage to the Lady Mary Talbot, to which he was committed.

Percy, threatened by his father, dreading the wrath of the King, greatly fearing the mighty Cardinal, and not being possessed of the same reckless courage as his partner in romance, was overpowered by this storm he and Anne had aroused. He could not stand out against them. Wretchedly, brokenheartedly he gave in, and left the court with his father.

He was, however, able to leave a message for Anne with a kinsman of hers, in which he begged that she would remember her promise from which none but God could loose her.

And the Cardinal, passing through the palace courtyard with his retinue, saw a dark-eyed girl with a pale, tragic face at one of the windows.

Ah! thought the Cardinal, turning his mind from matters of state. The cause of all the trouble!

The black eyes blazed into sudden hatred as they rested on him, for there had been those who had overheard Wolsey's slighting remarks about herself and hastened to inform her. Wolsey she blamed, and Wolsey only, for the ruin of her life.

Insolently she stared at him, her lips moving as though she cursed him.

The Cardinal smiled. Does she think to frighten me? A foolish girl! And I the first man in the kingdom! I would reprove her, but for the indignity of noting one so lacking in significance!

The next time he passed through the courtyard, he did not see Anne Boleyn. She had been banished to Hever.

At home in Hever Castle, a fierce anger took possession of her. She had waited for a further message from her lover. There was no message. He will come, she had told herself. They would ride away together, mayhap disguised as country folk, and they would care nothing for the anger of the Cardinal.

She would awake in the night, thinking she heard a tap on her window; walking in the grounds, she would feel her heart hammering at the sound of crackling bracken. She longed for him, thinking constantly of that night in the little chamber at Hampton Court, which they had said should be a perfect night and which by promising each other marriage they had made so; she thought of how sorry they had been for those who were dancing below, knowing nothing of the enchantment they were experiencing.

She would be ready when he came for her. Where would they go? Anywhere! For what did place matter! Life should be a glorious adventure. Taking her own courage for granted, why should she doubt his?

He did not come, and she brooded. She grew bitter, wondering why he did not come. She thought angrily of the wicked Cardinal whose spite had ruined her chances of happiness. Fiercely she hated him. "This foolish girl . . ." he had said. "This Anne Boleyn, who is but the daughter of a knight, to wed with one of the noblest families in the kingdom!"

She would show the lord Cardinal whether she was a foolish girl or not! Oh, the hypocrite! The man of God! He who kept house as a king and was vindictive as a devil and hated by the people!

When she and Percy went off together, the Cardinal should see whether she was a foolish girl!

And still her lover did not come.

"I cannot bear this long separation!" cried the passionate

girl. "Perhaps he thinks to wait awhile until his father is dead, for they say he is a sick man. But I do not wish to wait!"

She was melancholy, for the summer was passing and it was sad to see the leaves fluttering down.

The King rode out to Hever. In her room she heard the bustle his presence in the castle must inevitably cause. She locked her door and refused to go down. If Wolsey had ruined her happiness, the King—doubtless at the wicked man's instigation—had humiliated her by banishing her from the court. Unhappy as she was, she cared for nothing—neither her father's anger nor the King's.

Her mother came and stood outside the door to plead with her.

"The King has asked for you, Anne. You must come . . . quickly."

"I will not! I will not!" cried Anne. "I was banished, was I not? Had he wished to see me, he should not have sent me from the court."

"I dare not go back and say you refuse to come."

"I care not!" sobbed Anne, throwing herself on her bed and laughing and weeping simultaneously, for she was beside herself with a grief that she found herself unable to control.

Her father came to her door, but his threats were as vain as her mother's pleas.

"Would you bring disgrace on us!" stormed Sir Thomas. "Have you not done enough!"

"Disgrace!" she cried furiously. "Yes, if it is a disgrace to love and wish to marry, I have disgraced you. It is an honour to be mistress of the King. Mary has brought you honour! An I would not come for my mother, assuredly I will not come for you!"

"The King commands your presence!"

"You may do what you will," she said stubbornly. "He may do what he will. I care for nothing . . . now." And she burst into fresh weeping.

Sir Thomas—diplomatic over a family crisis as on a foreign mission—explained that his daughter was sadly indisposed; and the King, marvelling at his feelings for this wilful girl, replied, "Disturb her not then."

The King left Hever, and Anne returned to that life which had no meaning—waiting, longing, hoping, fearing.

One cold day, when the first touch of winter was in the air and a fresh wind was bringing down the last of the leaves from the trees in the park, Sir Thomas brought home the news.

He looked at Anne expressionlessly and said: "Lord Percy has married the Lady Mary Talbot. This is an end of your affair."

She went to her room and stayed there all that day. She did not eat; she did not sleep; she spoke to none; and on the second day she fell into a fit of weeping, upbraiding the Cardinal, and with him her lover. "They could have done what they would with me," she told herself bitterly. "I would never have given in!"

Drearily the days passed. She grew pale and listless, so that her mother feared for her life and communicated her fears to her husband.

Sir Thomas hinted that if she would return to court, such action would not be frowned on.

"That assuredly I will not do!" she said, and so ill was she that none dared reason with her.

She called to mind then the happiness of her life in France, and it seemed to her that her only hope of tearing her misery from her heart lay in getting away from England. She thought of one whom she would ever admire—the witty, sparkling Duchess of Alençon; was there some hope, with that sprightly lady, of renewing her interest in life?

Love she had experienced, and found it bitter; she wanted no more such experience.

"With Marguerite I could forget," she said; and, fearing for her health, Sir Thomas decided to humour her wishes; so once more Anne left Hever for the court of France.

The King's Secret Matter

The house at Lambeth was wrapped in deepest gloom. In the great bed which Jocosa had shared with Lord Edmund Howard since the night of her marriage, she now lay dying. She was very tired, poor lady, for her married life had been a wearying business. It seemed that no sooner had one small Howard left her womb than another was growing there; and poverty, in such circumstances, had been humiliating.

Death softened bitter feelings. What did it matter now, that her distinguished husband had been so neglected! Why, she wondered vaguely, were people afraid of death? It was so easy to die, so difficult to live.

"Hush! Hush!" said a voice. "You must not disturb your mother now. Do you not see she is sleeping peacefully?"

Then came to Jocosa's ears the sound of a little girl's sobbing. Jocosa tried to move the coverlet to attract attention. That was little Catherine crying, because, young as she was, she was old enough to understand the meaning of hushed voices, the air of gloom, old enough to smell the odour of death.

Jocosa knew suddenly why people were afraid of death. The fear was for those they left behind.

"My children . . ." she murmured, and tried to start up from her bed.

"Hush, my lady," said a voice. "You must rest, my dear."

"My children," she breathed, but her lips were parched, too stiff for the words to come through.

She thought of Catherine, the prettiest of her daughters, yet somehow the most helpless. Gentle, loving little Catherine, so eager to please that she let others override her. Some extra sense told the mother that her daughter Catherine would sorely miss a mother's care.

With a mighty effort she spoke. "Catherine. . . . Daughter . . ."

"She said my name!" cried Catherine. "She is asking for me."

"C . . . Catherine . . ."

"I am here," said Catherine.

Jocosa lifted the baby fingers to her parched lips. Perhaps, she thought, she will acquire a stepmother. Stepmothers are not always kind; they have their own children whom they would advance beyond those of the woman they have replaced, and a living wife has power a dead one lacks. Perhaps her aunt Norfolk would take this little Catherine; perhaps her grandmother Norfolk. No, not the Norfolks, a hard race! Catherine, who was soft and young and tender, should not go to them.

Jocosa thought of her own childhood at Hollingbourne, in the lovely old house of her father, Sir Richard Culpepper. Now her brother John was installed there; he had a son of his own who would be playing in her nursery. She remembered happy days spent there, and in her death-drugged thoughts it was Catherine who seemed to be there, not herself. It was soothing to the dying mother to see her daughter Catherine in her own nursery, but the pleasure passed and she was again conscious of the big, bare room at Lambeth.

"Edmund . . ." she said.

Catherine turned her tearful eyes to the nurse.

"She speaks my father's name."

"Yes, my lady?" asked the nurse, bending over the bed.

"Edmund . . ."

"Go to your father and tell him your mother would speak to him."

He stood by the bedside—poor, kind, bitter Edmund, whose life with her had been blighted by that pest, poverty. Now he was sorry for the sharp words he had spoken to her, for poverty had ever haunted him, waylaid him, leered at him, goaded him, warping his natural kindness, wrecking that peace he longed to share with his family.

"Jocosa . . ." There was such tenderness in his voice when he said her name that she thought momentarily that this was their wedding night, and he her lover; but she heard then the rattle in her throat and was conscious of her body's burning heat, and thus remembered that this was not the prologue but the epilogue to her life with Edmund, and that Catherine—gentlest of her children—was in some danger, which she sensed but did not comprehend.

"Edmund . . . Catherine . . ."

He lifted the child in his arms and held her nearer the bed.

"Jocosa, here is Catherine."

"My lord . . . let her go . . . let Catherine go . . ."

His head bent closer, and with a great effort the words came out.

"My brother John . . . at Hollingbourne . . . in Kent. Let Catherine . . . go to my brother John."

Lord Edmund said: "Rest peacefully, Jocosa. It shall be as you wish."

She sank back, smiling, for it was to be, since none dared disregard a promise made to a dying woman.

The effort had tired her; she knew not where she lay, but she believed it must be at Hollingbourne in Kent, so peaceful was she. The weary beating of her heart was slowing down. "Catherine is safe," it said. "Catherine is . . . safe."

At Hollingbourne, whither Catherine had been brought at her father's command, life was different from that lived in the house at Lambeth. The first thing that struck Catherine was the plenteous supply of good plain country fare. There was a simplicity at Hollingbourne which had been entirely lacking at Lambeth; and Sir John, in his country retreat, was lord of the neighbourhood, whereas Lord Edmund, living his impecunious life among those of equally noble birth, had seemed of little importance. Catherine looked upon her big uncle John as something like a god.

The nurseries were composed of several airy rooms at the top of the house, and from these it was possible to look over the pleasant Kentish country undisturbed by the sombre grandeur of the great city on whose outskirts the Lambeth house had sat. Catherine had often looked at the forts of the great Tower of London, and there was that in them to frighten the little girl. Servants were not over-careful; and though there were some who had nothing but adulation to give to Lord Edmund and his wife, poverty proved to be a leveller, and there were others who had but little respect for one who feared to be arrested at any moment for debt, even though he be a noble lord; and these servants were careless of what was said before the little Howards. There was a certain Doll Tappit who had for lover one who was a warder at the Tower, and fine stories he could tell her of the blood-curdling shrieks which came from the torture chambers, of the noble gentlemen who had displeased the King and who were left to starve in the rat-infested dungeons. Therefore Catherine was glad to see green and pleasant hills against the skyline, and leafy woods in place of the great stone towers.

There was comfort at Hollingbourne, such as there had never been at Lambeth.

She was taken to the nurseries, and there put into the charge of an old nurse who had known her mother; and there she was introduced to her cousin Thomas and his tutor.

Shyly she studied Thomas. He, with his charming face in which his bold and lively eyes flashed and danced with merriment, was her senior by a year or so, and she was much in awe of him; but, finding the cousin who was to share his nursery to be but a girl—and such a little girl—he was inclined to be contemptuous.

She was lonely that first day. It was true she was given food; and the nurse went through her scanty wardrobe, clicking her tongue over this worn garment and that one, which should have been handed to a servant long ago.

"Tut-tut!" exclaimed the nurse. "And how have you been brought up, I should wonder!" Blaming little Catherine Howard for her father's poverty; wondering what the world was coming to, when such beggars must be received in the noble house of Culpepper.

Catherine was by nature easygoing, gay and optimistic; never saying, "This is bad"; always, "This might be worse." She had lost her mother whom she had loved beyond all else in the world, and she was heartbroken; but she could not but enjoy the milk that was given her to drink; she could not but be glad that she was removed from Lambeth. Her sisters and brothers she missed, but being one of the younger ones, in games always the unimportant and unpleasant roles were given to her; and if there were not enough parts to go round, it was

Catherine who was left out. The afternoon of her first day at Hollingbourne was spent with the nurse who, tutting and clicking her tongue, cut up garments discarded by her lady, to make clothes for Catherine Howard. She stood still and was fitted; was pushed and made to turn about; and she thought the clothes that would soon be hers were splendid indeed.

Through the window she saw Thomas ride by on his chestnut mare, and she ran to the window and knelt on the window seat to watch him; and he, looking up, for he suspected she might be there, waved to her graciously, which filled Catherine with delight, for she had decided, as soon as he had looked down his haughty nose at her, that he was the most handsome person she had ever seen.

She had a bedroom to herself—a little panelled room with latticed windows which adjoined the main nursery. At Lambeth she had shared her room with several members of her family.

Even on that first day she loved Hollingbourne, but at that time it was chiefly because her mother had talked to her of it so affectionately.

But on the first night, when she lay in the little room all by herself, with the moon shining through the window and throwing ghostly shadows, she began to sense the solitude all about her and her quick love for Hollingbourne was replaced by fear. There was no sound from barges going down the river to Greenwich or up it to Richmond and Hampton Court; there was only silence broken now and then by the weird hooting of an owl. The strange room seemed menacing in this half-light, and suddenly she longed for the room at Lambeth with the noisy brothers and sisters; she thought of her mother, for Catherine Howard had had that sweet companionship which so many in her station might never know, since there was no court life to take Jocosa from her family, and her preoccupations were not with the cut of a pair of sleeves but with her children; that, poverty had given Catherine, but cruel life had let it be appreciated only to snatch it away. So in her quiet room at Hollingbourne, Catherine shed bitter tears into her pillow, longing for her mother's soft caress and the sound of her gentle voice.

"You have no mother now," they had said, "so you must be a brave girl."

But I'm not brave, thought Catherine, and immediately remembered how her eldest brother had jeered at her because she, who was so afraid of ghosts, would listen to and even encourage Doll Tappit to tell tales of them.

Doll Tappit's lover, Walter the warder, had once seen a ghost. Doll Tappit told the story to the nurse as she sat feeding the baby; Catherine had sat, round-eyed, listening.

"Now you know well how 'tis Walter's task to walk the Tower twice a night. Now Walter, as you know, is nigh on six foot tall, near as tall as His Majesty the King, and not a man to be easily affrighted. It was a moonlit night. Walter said the clouds kept hurrying across the moon as though there was terrible sights they wanted to hide from her. There is terrible sights, Nurse, in the Tower of London! Walter, he's heard some terrible groaning there, he's heard chains clanking, he's heard scream and shrieking. But afore this night he never see anything. . . . And there he was on the green, right there by the scaffold, when . . . clear as I see you now, Nurse . . . the Duke stood before him; his head was lying in a pool of blood on the ground beside him, and the blood ran down all over His Grace's fine clothes!"

"What then?" asked Nurse, inclined to be skeptical. "What would my lord Duke of Buckingham have to say to Walter the warder?"

"He said nothing. He was just there . . . just for a minute he was there. Then he was gone."

"They say," said Nurse, "that the pantler there is very hospitable with a glass of metheglin . . ."

"Walter never takes it!"

"I'll warrant he did that night."

"And when the ghost had gone, Walter stooped down where it was . . ."

"Where what was?"

"The head . . . all dripping blood. And though the head was gone, the blood was still there. Walter touched it; he showed me the stain on his coat."

Nurse might snort her contempt, but Catherine shivered; and there were occasions when she would dream of the headless Duke, coming towards her, and his head making stains on the nursery floor.

And here at Hollingbourne there were no brothers and sisters to help her disbelief in ghosts. Ghosts came when people were alone, for all the stories Catherine had ever heard of ghosts were of people who were alone when they saw them. Ghosts had an aversion to crowds of human beings, so that, all through her life, being surrounded by brothers and sisters, Catherine had felt safe; but not since she had come to Hollingbourne.

As these thoughts set Catherine shivering, outside her window she heard a faint noise, a gentle rustling of the creeper; it was as though hands pulled at it. She listened fearfully, and then it came again.

She was sitting up in bed, staring at the window. Again there came that rustle; and with it she could hear the deep gasps of one who struggles for breath.

She shut her eyes; she covered her head with the clothes; then, peeping out and seeing a face at her window, she screamed. A voice said: "Hush!" very sternly, and Catherine thought she would die from relief, for the voice was the voice of her handsome young cousin, Thomas Culpepper.

He scrambled through the window.

"Why, 'tis Catherine Howard! I trust I did not startle you, Cousin?"

"I . . . thought you . . . to be a . . . ghost!"

That made him rock with merriment.

"I had forgotten this was your room, Cousin," he lied, for well he had known it and had climbed in this way in order to impress her with his daring. "I have been out on wild adventures." He grimaced at a jagged tear in his breeches.

"Wild adventures . . . !"

"I do bold things by night, Cousin."

Her big eyes were round with wonder, admiring him, and Thomas Culpepper, basking in such admiration that he could find nowhere but in this simple girl cousin, felt mightily pleased that Catherine Howard had come to Hollingbourne.

"Tell me of them," she said.

He put his fingers to his lips.

"It is better not to speak so loudly, Cousin. In this house they believe me to be but a boy. When I am out, I am a man."

"Is it witchcraft?" asked Catherine eagerly, for often had she heard Doll Tappit speak of witchcraft.

He was silent on that point, silent and mysterious; but before he would talk to her, he would have her get off her bed to see the height of the wall which he had climbed with naught to help him but the creeper.

She got out, and naked tiptoed to the window. She was greatly impressed.

"It was a wonderful thing to do, Cousin Thomas," she said.

He smiled, well pleased, thinking her prettier in her very white skin than in the ugly clothes she had worn on her arrival.

"I do many wonderful things," he told her. "You will be cold, naked thus," he said. "Get back into your bed."

"Yes," she said, shivering, half with cold and half with excitement. "I am cold."

She leaped gracefully into bed, and pulled the clothes up to her chin. He sat on the bed, admiring the mud on his shoes and the unkempt appearance of his clothes.

"Do tell me," she said, her knees at her chin, her eyes sparkling.

"I fear it is not for little girls' ears."

"I am not such a little girl. It is only because you are big that it seems so."

"Ah!" he mused, well pleased to consider it in that way. "That may well be so; perhaps you are not so small. I have been having adventures, Cousin; I have been out trapping hares and shooting game!"

Her mouth was a round O of wonder.

"Did you catch many?"

"Hundreds, Cousin! More than a little girl like you could count."

"I could count hundreds!" she protested.

"It would have taken you days to count these. Do you know that, had I been caught, I could have been hanged at Tyburn?"

"Yes," said Catherine, who could have told him more gruesome stories of Tyburn than he could tell her, for he had never known Doll Tappit.

"But," said Thomas, "I expect Sir John, my father, would not have allowed that to happen. And then again 'twas scarcely poaching, as it happened on my father's land which will be one day mine, so now, Cousin Catherine, you see what adventures I have!"

"You are very brave," said Catherine.

"Perhaps a little. I have been helping a man whose acquaintance I made. He is a very interesting man, Cousin; a poacher. So I for fun, and he for profit, poach on my father's land."

"Were he caught, he would hang by the neck."

"I should intercede for him with my father."

"I would that I were brave as you are!"

"Bah! You are just a girl . . . and frightened that you might see a ghost."

"I am not now. It is only when I am alone."

"Will you be afraid when I have gone?"

"Very much afraid," she said.

He surveyed her in kingly fashion. She was such a little girl, and she paid such pleasant tribute to his masculine superiority. Yes, assuredly he was glad his cousin had come to Hollingbourne.

"I shall be here to protect you," he said.

"Oh, will you? Cousin Thomas, I know not how to thank you."

"You surely do not think I could be afraid of a ghost!"

"I know it to be impossible."

"Then you are safe, Catherine."

"But if, when I am alone . . ."

"Listen!" He put his head close to hers conspiratorially. "There"—he pointed over his shoulder—"is my room. Only one wall dividing me from you, little Cousin. I am ever alert for danger, and very lightly do I sleep. Now listen very attentively, Catherine. Should a ghost come, all you must do is tap on this wall, and depend upon it you will have me here before you can bat an eyelid. I shall sleep with my sword close at hand."

"Oh, Thomas! You have a sword too?"

"It is my father's, but as good as mine because one day it will be so."

"Oh, Thomas!" Sweet was her adulation to the little braggart.

"None dare harm you when I am by," he assured her. "Dead or living will have to deal with me."

"You would make yourself my knight then, Thomas," she said softly.

"You could not have a braver . . ."

"Oh, I know it. I do not think I shall cry very much now."

"Why should you cry?"

"For my mother, who is dead."

"No, Catherine, you need not cry; for in place of your mother you have your brave cousin, Thomas Culpepper."

"Shall I then tap on the wall if . . . ?"

He wrinkled his brows. "For tonight, yes. Tomorrow we shall find a stick for you . . . a good, stout stick I think; that will make a good banging on the wall, and you could, in an emergency, hit the ghost should it be necessary before I arrive."

"Oh, no, I could not! I should die of fear. Besides, might a ghost not do terrible things to one who made so bold as to hit it?"

"That may be so. The safest plan, my cousin, is to wait for me."

"I do not know how to thank you."

"Thank me by putting your trust in me."

He stood back from the bed, bowing deeply.

"Good night, Cousin."

"Good night, dear, brave Thomas."

He went, and she hugged her pillow in an ecstasy of delight. Never had one of her own age been so kind to her; never had she felt of such consequence.

As for ghosts, what of them! What harm could they do to Catherine Howard, with Thomas Culpepper only the other side of her bedroom wall, ready to fly to her rescue!

There was delight in the hours spent at Hollingbourne. Far away in a hazy and unhappy past were the Lambeth days; and the sweetest thing she had known was the ripening of her friendship with her cousin Thomas. Catherine, whose nature was an excessively affectionate one, asked nothing more than that she should be allowed to love him. Her affection he most graciously accepted, and returned it in some smaller measure. It was a happy friendship, and he grew more fond of her than his dignity would allow him to make known; she, so sweet already, though so young, so clingingly feminine, touched something in his manhood. He found great pleasure in protecting her, and thus love grew between them. He taught her to ride, to climb trees, to share his adventures, though he never took her out at night; nor did he himself adventure much this way after her coming, wishing to be at hand lest in the lonely hours of evening she might need his help.

Her education was neglected. Sir John did not believe over-much in the education of girls; and who was she but a dependant, though the child of his sister! She was a girl, and doubtless a match would be made for her; and bearing such a name as Howard, that match could be made without the unnecessary adornment of a good education. Consider the case of his kinsman, Thomas Boleyn. He had been, so Sir John had heard, at great pains to educate his two younger children who, in the family, had acquired the reputation of possessing some brilliance. Even the girl had been educated, and what had education done for her? There was some talk of a disaster at court; the girl had aspired to marry herself to a very highly born nobleman—doubtless due to her education. And had her education helped her? Not at all! Banishment and disgrace had been her lot. Let girls remain docile; let them cultivate charming manners; let them learn how to dress themselves prettily and submit to their husbands. That was all a girl needed from life. And did she want to construe Latin verse to do these things; did she want to give voice to her frivolous thoughts in six different languages! No, the education of young Catherine Howard was well taken care of.

Thomas tried to teach his cousin a little, but he quickly gave up the idea. She had no aptitude for it; rather she preferred to listen to the tales of his imaginary adventures, to sing and dance and play musical instruments. She was a frivolous little creature, and having been born into poverty, well pleased to have stepped out of it, happy to have for her friend surely the most handsome and the dearest cousin in the world. What more could she want?

And so the days passed pleasantly—riding with Thomas, listening to Thomas's stories, admiring him, playing games in which he took the glorious part of knight and rescuer, she the role of helpless lady and rescued; now and then taking a lesson at the virginals, which was not like a lesson at all because she had been born with a love of music; she had singing lessons too which she loved, for her voice was pretty and promised to be good. But life could not go on in this even tenor forever. A young man such as Thomas Culpepper could not be left to the care of a private tutor indefinitely.

He came to the music room one day while Catherine sat over the virginals with her teacher, and threw himself into a window seat and watched her as she played. Her auburn hair fell about her flushed face; she was very young, but there was always in Catherine Howard, even when a baby, a certain womanliness. Now she was aware of Thomas there, she was playing with especial pains to please him. That, thought Thomas, was so typical of her; she would always care deeply about pleasing those she loved. He was going to miss her very much; he found that watching her brought a foolish lump into his throat, and he contemplated running from the room for fear his sentimental tears should betray him. It was really but a short time ago that she had come to Hollingbourne, and yet she had made a marked difference to his life. Strange it was that that should be so; she was meek and self-effacing, and yet her very wish to please made her important to him; and he, who had longed for this childish stage of his education to be completed, was now sorry that it was over.

The teacher had stood up; the lesson was ended.

Catherine turned a flushed face to her cousin.

"Thomas, do you think I have improved?"

"Indeed yes," he said, realizing that he had hardly heard what she had played. "Catherine," he said quickly, "let us ride together. There is something I would say to you."

They galloped round the paddock, he leading, she trying to catch up but never succeeding—which made her so enchanting. She was the perfect female, forever stressing her subservience to the male, soft and helpless, meek, her eyes ever ready to fill with tears at a rebuke.

He pulled up his horse, but did not dismount; he dared not, because he felt so ridiculously near tears himself. He must therefore be ready to whip up his horse if this inclination became a real danger.

"Catherine," he said, his voice hardly steady, "I have bad news. . . ."

He glanced at her face, at the hazel eyes wide now with fear, at the little round mouth which quivered.

"Oh, sweet little Cousin," he said, "it is not so bad. I shall come back; I shall come back very soon."

"You are going away then, Thomas?"

The world was suddenly dark; tears came to her eyes and brimmed over. He looked away, and sought refuge in hardening his voice.

"Come, Catherine, do not be so foolish. You surely did not imagine that my father's son could spend all his days tucked away here in the country!"

"No . . . no."

"Well then! Dry your eyes. No handkerchief? How like you, Catherine!" He threw her his. "You may keep that," he said, "and think of me when I am gone."

She took the handkerchief as though already it were a sacred thing.

He went on, his voice shaking: "And you must give me one of yours, Catherine, that I may keep it."

She wiped her eyes.

He said tenderly: "It is only for a little while, Catherine."

Now she was smiling.

"I should have known," she said. "Of course you will go away."

"When I return we shall have very many pleasant days together, Catherine."

"Yes, Thomas." Being Catherine, she could think of the reunion rather than the parting, even now.

He slipped off his horse, and she immediately did likewise; he held out his hands, and she put hers into them.

"Catherine, do you ever think of when we are grown up . . . really grown up, not just pretending to be?"

"I do not know, Thomas. I think perhaps I may have."

"When we are grown up, Catherine, we shall marry . . . both of us. Catherine. I may marry you when I am of age."

"Thomas! Would you?"

"I might," he said.

She was pretty, with the smile breaking through her tears.

"Yes," he said, "I think mayhap I will. And now, Catherine, you will not mind so much that I must go away, for you must know, we are both young in actual fact. Were we not, I would marry you now and take you with me."

They were still holding hands, smiling at each other; he, flushed with pleasure at his beneficence in offering her such a glorious prospect as marriage with him; she, overwhelmed by the honour he did her.

He said: "When people are affianced, Catherine, they kiss. I am going to kiss you now."

He kissed her on either cheek and then her soft baby mouth. Catherine wished he would go on kissing her, but he did not, not over-much liking the operation and considering it a necessary but rather humiliating formality; besides, he feared that there might be those to witness this and do what he dreaded most that people would do, laugh at him.

"That," he said, "is settled. Let us ride."

Catherine had been so long at Hollingbourne that she came to regard it as her home. Thomas came home occasionally, and there was nothing he liked better than to talk of the wild adventures he had had; and never had he known a better audience than his young cousin. She was so credulous, so ready to admire. They both looked forward to these reunions, and although they spoke not of their marriage which they had long ago in the paddock decided should one day take place, they neither of them forgot nor wished to repudiate the promises. Thomas was not the type of boy to think over-much of girls except when they could be fitted into an adventure where, by their very helplessness and physical inferiority, they could help to glorify the resourcefulness and strength of the male. Thomas was a normal, healthy boy whose thoughts had turned but fleetingly to sex; Catherine, though younger, was conscious of sex, and had been since she was a baby; she enjoyed Thomas's company most when he held her hand or lifted her over a brook or rescued her from some imaginary evil fate. When the game was a pretense of stealing jewels, and she must pretend to be a man, the adventure lost its complete joy for her. She remembered still the quick, shamefaced kisses he had given her in the paddock, and she would have loved to have made plans for their marriage, to kiss now and then. She dared not tell Thomas this, and little did he guess that she was all but a woman while he was yet a child.

So passed the pleasant days until that sad afternoon when a serving maid came to her, as she sat in the wide window seat of the main nursery, to tell her that her uncle and aunt would have speech with her, and she was to go at once to her uncle's chamber.

As soon as Catherine reached that room she knew that something was amiss, for both her uncle and her aunt looked very grave.

"My dear niece," said Sir John, who frequently spoke for both, "come hither to me. I have news for you."

Catherine went to him and stood before him, her knees trembling, while she prayed: "Please, God, let Thomas be safe and well."

"Now that your grandfather Lord Thomas the Duke is no more, said Sir John in the solemn voice he used when speaking of the dead, your grandmother feels that she would like much to have you with her. You know your father has married again. . . ." His face stiffened. He was a righteous man; there was nothing soft in his nature; it seemed to him perfectly reasonable that, his sister's husband having married a new wife, his own responsibility for his sister's child should automatically cease.

"Go . . . from here . . . ?" stammered Catherine.

"To your grandmother in Norfolk."

"Oh . . . but I . . . do not wish . . . Here, I have been . . . so happy. . . ."

Her aunt put an arm about her shoulders and kissed her cheek.

"You must understand, Catherine, your staying here is not in our hands. Your father has married again . . . he wishes that you should go to your grandmother."

Catherine looked from one to the other, her eyes bright with tears which overflowed, for she could never control her emotion.

Her aunt and uncle waited for her to dry her eyes and listen to them.

Then Sir John said: "You must prepare yourself for a long journey, so that you will be ready when your grandmother sends for you. Now you may go."

Catherine stumbled from the room, thinking, When he comes next time, I shall not be here! And how shall I ever see him . . . he in Kent and I in Norfolk?

In the nursery the news was received with great interest.

"Well may you cry!" she was told. "Why, when you are at your grandmother's house you will feel very haughty towards us poor folk. I have heard from one who served the Duchess that she keeps great state both at Horsham and Lambeth. The next we shall hear of you is that you are going to court!"

"I do not care to go to court!" cried Catherine.

"Ah!" she was told. "All you care for is your cousin Thomas!"

Then Catherine thought, is it so far from here to Norfolk? Not so far but that he could come to me. He will come; and then in a few years we shall be married. The time will pass quickly. . . .

She remembered her grandmother—plumpish, inclined to poke her with a stick, lazy Grandmother who sat about and laughed to herself and made remarks which set her wheezing and chuckling, such as, "You have pretty eyes, Catherine Howard. Keep them; they will serve you well!" Grandmother, with sly eyes and chins that wobbled, and an inside that gurgled since she took such delight in the table.

Catherine waited for the arrival of those who would take her to her grandmother, and with the passage of the days her fears diminished; she lived in a pleasant dream in which Thomas came to Horsham and spent his holidays there instead of at Hollingbourne; and Catherine, being the granddaughter of such a fine lady as the Dowager Duchess of Norfolk, wore beautiful clothes and jewels in her hair. Thomas said: "You are more beautiful in Norfolk than you were in Kent!" And he kissed her, and Catherine kissed him; there was much kissing and embracing at Horsham. "Let us elope," said Thomas. Thus pleasantly passed the last days at Hollingbourne, and when the time came for her departure to Norfolk, she did not greatly mind, for she had planned such a happy future for herself and Thomas.

The house at Horsham was indeed grand. It was built round the great hall; it had its ballroom, its many bedrooms, numerous small chambers and unpredictable corridors; from its mullioned windows there were views of gracious parklands; there was comfort in its padded window seats; there was luxury in its elegant furniture. One could lose oneself with ease in this house, and so many servants and attendants waited on her grandmother that in the first weeks she spent there, Catherine was constantly meeting strangers.

On her arrival she was taken to her grandmother, whom she found in her bed, not yet having risen though the afternoon was advancing.

"Ah!" said the Dowager Duchess. "So here you are, little Catherine Howard! Let me look at you. Have you fulfilled the promise of your babyhood that you would be a very pretty girl?"

Catherine must climb onto the bed and kiss one of the plump hands, and be inspected.

"Marry!" said the Duchess. "You are a big girl for your years! Well, well, there is time yet before we must find a husband for you." Catherine would have told her of her contract with Thomas Culpepper, but the Duchess was not listening. "How neat you look! That is my Lady Culpepper, I'll swear. Catherine Howard and such neatness appear to me as though they do not belong one to the other. Give me a kiss, child, and you must go away. Jenny!" she called, and a maid appeared suddenly from a closet. "Call Mistress Isabel to me. I would talk with her of my granddaughter." She turned to Catherine. "Now, Granddaughter, tell me, what did you learn at Hollingbourne?"

"I learned to play the virginals and to sing."

"Ah! That is well. We must look to your education. I will not have you forget that, though your father is a poor man, you are a Howard. Ah! Here is Mistress Isabel."

A tall, pale young woman came into the room. She had small eyes and a thin mouth; her eyes darted at once to Catherine Howard, sitting on the bed.

"This is my little granddaughter, Isabel. You knew of her coming."

"Your Grace mentioned it to me."

"Well, the child has arrived. Take her, Isabel . . . and see that she lacks nothing."

Isabel curtseyed, and the Duchess gave Catherine a little push to indicate that she was to get off the bed and follow Isabel. Together they left the Duchess's apartment.

Isabel led the way upstairs and along corridors, occasionally turning, as though to make sure that Catherine followed. Catherine began to feel afraid, for this old house was full of shadows, and in unexpected places were doors and sudden passages; all her old fear of ghosts came back to her, and her longing for Thomas brought tears to her eyes. What if they should put her in a bedroom by herself, remote from other rooms! If Hollingbourne might have contained a ghost, this house assuredly would! Isabel, looking over her shoulder at her, alone stopped her from bursting into tears, for there was something about Isabel which frightened Catherine more than she cared to admit to herself.

Isabel had thrown open a door, and they were in a large room which contained many beds; this dormitory was richly furnished, as was every room in this house, but it was an untidy room; across its chairs and beds were flung various garments; shoes and hose littered the floor. There was perfume in the air.

"This room," said Isabel, "is where Her Grace's ladies sleep; she has told me that temporarily you are to share it with us."

Relief flooded Catherine's heart; there was now nothing to fear; her pale face became animated, flushed with pleasure.

"That pleases you?" asked Isabel.

Catherine said it did, adding: "I like not solitude."

Another girl had come into the room, big bosomed, wide hipped and saucy of eye.

"Isabel . . ."

Isabel held up a warning hand.

"Her Grace's granddaughter has arrived."

"Oh . . . the little girl?"

The girl came forward, saw Catherine, and bowed.

"Her Grace has said," began Isabel, "that she is to share our room."

The girl sat down upon a bed, drew her skirts up to her knees, and lifted her eyes to the ornate ceiling.

"It delights her, does it not . . . Catherine?"

"Yes," said Catherine.

The girl, whose name it seemed was Nan, threw a troubled glance at Isabel, which Catherine intercepted but did not understand.

Nan said: "You are very pretty, Catherine."

Catherine smiled.

"But very young," said Isabel.

"Marry!" said Nan, crossing shapely legs and looking down at them in an excess of admiration. "We must all be young at some time, must we not?"

Catherine smiled again, liking Nan's friendly ways better than the quiet ones of Isabel.

"And you will soon grow up," said Nan.

"I hope to," said Catherine.

"Indeed you do!" Nan giggled, and rose from the bed. From a cabinet she took a box of sweetmeats, ate one herself and gave one to Isabel and one to Catherine.

Isabel examined Catherine's clothes, lifting her skirts and feeling the material between thumb and finger.

"She has lately come from her uncle Sir John Culpepper of Hollingbourne in Kent."

"Did they keep grand style in Kent?" asked Nan, munching.

"Not such as in this house."

"Then you are right glad to be here where you will find life amusing?"

"Life was very good at Hollingbourne."

"Isabel," laughed Nan, "the child looks full of knowledge. . . . I believe you had a lover there, Catherine Howard!"

Catherine blushed scarlet.

"She did! She did! I swear she did!"

Isabel dropped Catherine's skirt, and exchanged a glance with Nan. Questions trembled on their lips, but these questions went unasked, for at that moment the door opened and a young man put his head round the door.

"Nan!" he said.

Nan waved her hand to dismiss him, but he ignored the signal, and came into the room.

Catherine considered this a peculiar state of affairs, for at Hollingbourne gentlemen did not enter the private apartments of ladies thus unceremoniously.

"A new arrival!" said the young man.

"Get you gone!" said Isabel. "She is not for you. She is Catherine Howard, Her Grace's own granddaughter."

The young man was handsomely dressed. He bowed low to Catherine, and would have taken her hand to kiss it, had not Isabel snatched her up and put her from him. Nan pouted on the bed, and the young man said: "How is my fair Nan this day?" But Nan turned her face to the wall and would not speak to him; then the young man sat on the bed and put his arms round Nan, so that his left hand was on her right breast, and his right hand on her left breast; and he kissed her neck hard, so that there was a red mark there. Then she arose and slapped him lightly on the face, laughing the while, and she leaped across the bed, he after her and so gave chase, till Isabel shooed him from the room.

Catherine witnessed this scene with much astonishment, thinking Isabel to be very angry indeed, expecting her to castigate the laughing Nan; but she did nothing but smile, when, after the young man had left, Nan threw herself onto the bed laughing.

Nan sat up suddenly and, now that the youth was no longer there to claim her interest, once more bestowed it on Catherine Howard.

"You had a lover at Hollingbourne, Catherine Howard! Did you not see how her cheeks were on fire, Isabel, and still are, I'll warrant! I believe you to be a sly wench, Catherine Howard."

Isabel put her hands on Catherine's shoulders.

"Tell us about him, Catherine."

Catherine said: "It was my cousin, Thomas Culpepper."

"He who is son of Sir John?"

Catherine nodded. "We shall marry when that is possible."

"Tell us of Thomas Culpepper, Catherine. Is he tall? Is he handsome?"

"He is both tall and handsome."

"Tell me, did he kiss you well and heartily?"

"But once," said Catherine. "And that in the paddock when he talked of marriage."

"And he kissed you," said Nan. "What else?"

"Hush!" said Isabel. "What if she should tell Her Grace of the way you have talked!"

"Her Grace is too lazy to care what her ladies may say or do."

"You will be dismissed the house one day," said Isabel. "Caution!"

"So your cousin kissed you, Catherine, and promised he would marry you. Dost not know that when a man talks of marriage it is the time to be wary."

Catherine did not understand; she was aware of a certain fear, and yet a vivid interest in this unusual conversation.

"Enough of this," said Isabel, and Nan went to her bed and lay down, reaching for the sweetmeats.

"Your bed," said Isabel, "shall be this one. Are you a good sleeper?"

"Yes," said Catherine; for indeed the only occasions when she could not sleep were those when she was afraid of ghosts, and if she were to sleep in a room so full of beds, each of which would contain a young lady, she need have no fear of gruesome company, and she could say with truth that she would sleep well.

Isabel looked at her clothes, asked many questions about Lambeth and Hollingbourne; and while Catherine was answering her, several ladies came in, and some gave her sweetmeats, some kissed her. Catherine thought them all pretty young ladies; their clothes were bright, and they wore gay ribands in their hair; and many times during that afternoon and evening a young man would put his head round the door and be waved away with the words: "The Duchess's granddaughter, Catherine Howard, is come to share our apartment." The young men bowed and were as kind to Catherine as the ladies were; and often one of the ladies would go outside and speak with them, and Catherine would hear muffled laughter. It was very gay and pleasant, and even Isabel, who at first had appeared to be a little stern, seemed to change and laugh with the rest.

Catherine had food and drink with the ladies and their kindness persisted through the evening. At length she went to bed, Isabel escorting her and drawing the curtains around her bed. She was very soon asleep for the excitement of the day had tired her.

She awoke startled and wondered where she was. She remembered and was immediately aware of whispering voices. She lay listening for some time, thinking the ladies must just be retiring, but the voices went on and Catherine, in astonishment, recognized some of them as belonging to men. She stood up and peeped through the curtains. There was no light in the room but sufficient moonlight to show her the most unexpected sight.

The room seemed to be full of young men and women; some sitting on the beds, some reclining on them, but all of them in affectionate poses. They were eating and drinking, and stroking and kissing each other. They smacked their lips over the dainties, and now and then one of the girls would make an exclamation of surprise and feigned indignation, or another would laugh softly; they spoke in whispers. The clouds, hurrying across the face of the moon which looked in at the windows, made the scene alternately light and darker; and the wind which was driving the clouds whined now and then, mingling its voice with those of the girls and young men.

Catherine watched, wide-eyed and sleepless for some time. She saw the youth who had aroused Nan's displeasure now kissing her bare shoulders, taking down the straps of her dress and burying his face in her bosom. Catherine watched and wondered until her eyes grew weary and her lids pressed down on them. She lay down and slept.

She awakened to find it was daylight and Isabel was drawing her bed curtains. The room was now occupied by girls only, who ran about naked and chattering, looking for their clothes which seemed to be scattered about the floor.

Isabel was looking down at Catherine slyly.

"I trust you slept well?" she asked.

Catherine said she had.

"But not through the entire night?"

Catherine could not meet Isabel's piercing eyes, for she was afraid that the girl should know she had looked on that scene, since something told her it was not meant that she should.

Isabel sat down heavily on the bed, and caught Catherine's shoulder.

"You were awake part of last night," she said. "Dost think I did not see thee, spying through the curtains, listening, taking all in?"

"I did not mean to spy," said Catherine. "I was awakened, and the moon showed me things."

"What things, Catherine Howard?"

"Young gentlemen, sitting about the room with the ladies."

"What else?"

Isabel looked wicked now. Catherine began to shiver, thinking perhaps it would have been better had she spent the night in a lonely chamber. For it was daylight now, and it was only at night that Catherine had great fear of ghosts.

"What else?" repeated Isabel. "What else, Catherine Howard?"

"I saw that they did eat. . . ."

The grip on Catherine's shoulder increased.

"What else?"

"Well . . . I know, not what else, but that they did kiss and seem affectionate."

"What shall you do, Catherine Howard?"

"What shall I do? But I know not what you mean, Mistress Isabel. What would you desire me to do?"

"Shall you then tell aught of what you have seen . . . to Her Grace, your grandmother?"

Catherine's teeth chattered, for what they did must surely be wrong since it was done at her grandmother's displeasure.

Isabel released Catherine's shoulder and called to the others. There was silence while she spoke.

"Catherine Howard," she said spitefully, "while feigning sleep last night, was wide awake, watching what was done in this chamber. She will go to Her Grace the Duchess and tell her of our little entertainment."

There was a crowd of girls round the bed, who looked down on Catherine, while fear and anger were displayed in every face.

"There was naught I did that was wrong," said one girl, almost in tears.

"Be silent!" commanded Isabel. "Should what happens here of nights get to Her Grace's ears, you will all be sent home in dire disgrace."

Nan knelt down by the bed, her pretty face pleading. "Thou dost not look like a teller of tales."

"Indeed I am not!" cried Catherine. "I but awakened, and being awake what could I do but see. . . ."

"She will, I am sure, hold her counsel. Wilt thou not, little Catherine?" whispered Nan.

"If she does not," said Isabel, "it will be the worse for her. What if we should tell Her Grace of what you did, Catherine Howard, in the paddock with your cousin, Thomas Culpepper!"

"What . . . I . . . did!" gasped Catherine. "But I did nothing wrong. Thomas would not. He is noble . . . he would do no wrong."

"He kissed her and he promised her marriage," said Isabel.

All the ladies put their mouths into round O's, and looked terribly shocked.

"She calls that naught! The little wanton!"

Catherine thought: Did we sin then? Was that why Thomas was ashamed and never kissed me again?

Isabel jerked off the clothes, so that she lay naked before them; she stooped and slapped Catherine's thigh.

"Thou darest not talk!" said Nan, laughing. "Why 'twould go harder with thee than with us. A Howard! Her Grace's own granddaughter! Doubtless he would be hanged, drawn and quartered for what he did to you!"

"Oh, no!" cried Catherine, sitting up. "We did no wrong."

The girls were all laughing and chattering like magpies.

Isabel put her face close to Catherine's: "You have heard! Say nothing of what you have seen or may see in this chamber, and your lover will be safe."

Nan said: "'Tis simple, darling. Say naught of our sins, and we say naught of thine!"

Catherine was weeping with relief.

"I swear I shall say nothing."

"Then that is well," said Isabel.

Nan brought a sweetmeat to her, and popped it into her mouth.

"There! Is not that good? They were given to me last night by a very charming gentleman. Mayhap one day some fine gentleman will bring sweetmeats to you, Catherine Howard!"

Nan put her arms about the little girl, and gave her two

hearty kisses, and Catherine, munching, wondered why she had been so frightened. There was nothing to fear; all that was necessary was to say nothing.

∗

The days passed as speedily as they had at Hollingbourne, and a good deal more excitingly. There were no lessons at Horsham. There was nothing to do during the long, lazy days but enjoy them. Catherine would carry notes from ladies to gentlemen; she was popular with them all, but especially with the young gentlemen. Once one said to her: "I have awaited this, and 'tis double sweet to me when brought by pretty Catherine!" They gave her sweetmeats too and other dainties. She played a little, played the flute and the virginals; she sang; they liked well to hear her sing, for her voice was indeed pretty. Occasionally the old Duchess would send for her to have a talk with her, and would murmur: "What a little tomboy you are, Catherine Howard! I declare you are an untidy chit; I would you had the grace of your cousin Anne Boleyn. . . . Though much good her grace did her!"

Catherine loved to hear of her cousin, for she remembered seeing her now and then at Lambeth before she went to Hollingbourne. When she heard her name she thought of beauty and colour, and sparkling jewels and sweet smiles; she hoped that one day she would meet her cousin again. The Duchess often talked of her, and Catherine knew by the softening of her voice that she liked her well, even though, when she spoke of her disgrace and banishment from court, her eyes would glint slyly as though she enjoyed contemplating her granddaughter's downfall.

"A Boleyn not good enough for a Percy, eh! Marry, and there's something in that! But Anne is part Howard, and a Howard is a match for a Percy at any hour of the day or night! And I would be the first to tell Northumberland so, were I to come face to face with him. As for the young man, a plague on him! They tell me his Lady Mary hates him and he hates her; so much good that marriage did to either of them! Aye! I'll warrant he does not find it so easy to forget my granddaughter. Ah, Catherine Howard, there was a girl. I vow I never saw such beauty . . . such grace. And what did it do for her? There she goes . . . to France! And what has become of the Ormond marriage? She will be growing on into her teens now . . . I hope she will come back soon. Catherine Howard, Catherine Howard, your hair is in need of attention. And your dress, my child! I tell you, you will never have the grace of Anne Boleyn."

It was not possible to tell the Duchess that one could not hope to have the grace of one's cousin who had been educated most carefully and had learned the ways of life at the French court; who had been plenteously supplied with the clothes she might need in order that Sir Thomas Boleyn's daughter might do her father credit in whatever circles she moved. One could not explain that the brilliant Anne had a natural gift for choosing the most becoming clothes, and knew how to wear them. The Duchess should have known these things.

But she rocked in her chair and dozed, and was hardly aware of Catherine's standing there before her. "Marry! And the dangers that girl was exposed to! The French court! There were adventures for her, I'll warrant, but she keeps her secrets well. Ah! How fortunate it is, Catherine, that I have taken you under my wing!"

And while the Duchess snored in her bedroom, her ladies held many midnight feasts in their apartments. Catherine was one of them now, they assured themselves. Catherine could be trusted. It was no matter whether she slept or not; she was little but a baby and there were those times when she would fall asleep suddenly. She was popular; they would throw sweetmeats onto her bed. Sometimes she was kissed and fondled.

"Is she not a pretty little girl!"

"She is indeed, and you will keep your eyes off her, young sir, or I shall be most dismayed."

Laughter, slapping, teasing. . . . It was fun, they said; and with them Catherine said: "It is fun!"

Sometimes they lay on the tops of the beds with their arms about each other; sometimes they lay under the clothes, with the curtains drawn.

Catherine was accustomed to this strange behaviour by now, and hardly noticed it. They were all very kind to her, even Isabel. She was happier with them than she was when attending her grandmother, sitting at her feet or rubbing her back where it itched. Sometimes she must massage the old lady's legs, for she had strange pains in them and massage helped to soothe the pain. The old lady would wheeze and rattle, and say something must be done about Catherine's education, since her granddaughter, a Howard, could not be allowed to run wild all the day through. The Duchess would talk of members of her family; her stepsons and her numerous stepdaughters who had married wealthy knights because the Howard fortunes needed bolstering up. "So Howards married with Wyatts and Bryans and Boleyns," mused the Duchess. "And mark you, Catherine Howard, the children of these marriages are goodly and wise. Tom Wyatt is a lovely boy. . . ." The Duchess smiled kindly, having a special liking for lovely boys. "And so is George Boleyn . . . and Mary and Anne are pleasant creatures. . . ."

"Ah!" said the Duchess one day. "I hear your cousin Anne is back in England and at court."

"I should like well to see her," said Catherine.

"Rub harder, child! There! Clumsy chit! You scratched me. Ah! Back at court, and a beauty more lovely than when she went away. . . ." The Duchess wheezed, and was so overcome with laughter that Catherine feared she would choke. "They say the King is deeply affected by her," said the Duchess happily. "They say too that she is leading him a merry dance!"

When the Duchess had said that the King was deeply affected by Anne Boleyn, she had spoken the truth. Anne had left the court of France and returned to that of England, and no sooner had she made her spectacular appearance than once more she caught the King's eye. The few years that had elapsed had made a great change in Anne; she was not one whit less beautiful than she had been when Henry had seen her in the garden at Hever; indeed she was more so; she had developed a poise which before would have sat oddly on one so young. If she had been bright then, now she was brilliant; her beauty had matured and gained in maturity; the black eyes still sparkled and flashed; her tongue was more ready with its wit, she herself more accomplished. She had been engaged in helping Marguerite to fete Francois, so recently released from captivity, a Francois who had left his youth behind in a Madrid prison in which he had nearly died and would have done so but for his sister's loving haste across France and into Spain to nurse him. But Francois had made his peace treaty with his old enemy, Charles V, although he did repudiate it immediately, and it was the loving delight of his sister and his mother to compensate him for the months of hardship. Anne Boleyn had been a useful addition to the court; she could sing and dance, write lyrics, poetry, music; could always be relied upon to entertain and amuse. But her father, on the Continent with an embassy, had occasion to return to England, and doubtless feeling that a girl of nineteen must not fritter away her years indefinitely, had brought her back to the court of her native land. So Anne had returned to find the entire family settled at the palace. George, now Viscount Rochford, was married, and his wife, who had been Jane Parker and granddaughter to Lord Morley and Monteagle, was still one of the Queen's ladies. Meeting George's wife had been one of the less pleasant surprises on Anne's return, since she saw that George was not very happy in this marriage with a wife who was frivolous and stupid and was not accepted into the brilliant set of poets and intellectuals—most of them cousins of the Boleyns—in which George naturally took a prominent place. This was depressing. Anne, still smarting from the Percy affair—though none might guess it—would have wished for her brother that married happiness which she herself had missed. Mary, strangely enough, seemed happy with William Carey; they had one boy—who, it was whispered, was the King's—and none would guess that their union was not everything that might be desired. Anne wondered then if she and George asked too much of life.

There was no sign of melancholy about Anne. She could not but feel a certain glee—though she reproached herself for this—when she heard that Percy and his Mary were the most wretched couple in the country. She blamed Percy for his weakness; it was whispered that the Lady Mary was a shrew, who never forgave him, being contracted to her, for daring to fall in love with Anne Boleyn and make a scandal of the affair. Very well, thought Anne, let Percy suffer as she had! How many times during the last years had she in her thoughts reproached him for his infidelity! Perhaps he realized now that the easy way is not always the best way. She held her head higher, calling her lost lover weak, wishing fervently that he had been more like Thomas Wyatt who had pursued her ever since her return to court, wondering if she were not a little in love—or ready to fall in love—with her cousin Thomas, surely the most handsome, the most reckless, the most passionate man about the court. There was no doubt as to his feelings for her; it was both in his eyes and in his verses; and he was reckless enough not to care who knew it.

There was one other who watched her as she went about the court; Anne knew this, though others might not, for though he was by no means a subtle man, he had managed so far to keep this passion, which he felt for one of his wife's ladies-in-waiting, very secret.

Anne did not care to think too much of this man. She did not care to feel those little eyes upon her. His manner was correct enough, yet now there were those who were beginning to notice something. She had seen people whispering together, smiling slyly. Now the King is done with the elder sister, is it to be the younger? What is it about these Boleyns? Thomas is advanced as rapidly as my lord Cardinal ever was; George has posts that should have gone to a grey-haired man; Mary . . . of course we understand how it was with Mary; and now, is it to be the same story with Anne?

No! Anne told herself fiercely. Never!

If Thomas Wyatt had not a wife already, she thought, how pleasant it would be to listen to his excellent verses, which were chiefly about herself. She could picture the great hall at Allington Castle decked out for the Christmas festivities, herself and Thomas taking chief parts in some entertainment they had written for the amusement of their friends. But that could not be.

Her position at court had become complicated. She was thinking of a conversation she had had with the King, when he, who doubtless had seen her walking in the palace grounds, had come down to her unattended and had said, his eyes burning in his heated face, that he would have speech with her.

He had asked her to walk with him to a little summer-house he knew of where they could be secret. She had felt limp with terror, had steeled herself, had realized full well that in the coming interview she would have need of all her wits; she must flatter him and refuse him; she must soothe him, pacify him, and pray that he might turn his desirous eyes upon someone more willing.

She had entered the summer-house, feeling the colour in her cheeks, but her fear made her hold her head the higher; her very determination helped to calm her. He had stood looking at her as he leaned against the doors, a mighty man, his padded clothes, glittering and colourful, adding to his great stature. He would have her accept a costly gift of jewels; he told her that he had favoured her from the moment he had seen her in her father's garden, that never had he set eyes on one who pleased him more; in truth he loved her. He spoke with confidence, for at that time he had believed it was but necessary to explain his feelings towards her to effect her most willing surrender. Thus it had been on other occasions; why should this be different?

She had knelt before him, and he would have raised her, saying lightly and gallantly: No, she must not kneel; it was he who should kneel to her, for by God, he was never more sure of his feelings towards any in his life before.

She had replied: "I think, most noble and worthy King, that Your Majesty speaks these words in mirth to prove me, without intent of degrading your noble self. Therefore, to ease you of the labour of asking me any such question hereafter, I beseech Your Highness most earnestly to desist and take this my answer, which I speak from the depth of my soul, in good part. Most noble King! I will rather lose my life than my virtue, which will be the greatest and best part of the dowry I shall bring my husband."

It was bold; it was clever; it was characteristic of Anne. She had known full well that something of this nature would happen, and she had therefore prepared herself with what she would say when it did. She was no Percy to be browbeaten, she was a subject and Henry was King, well she knew that; but this matter of love was not a matter for a king and subject—it was for a man and woman; and Anne was not one to forget her rights as a woman, tactful and cautious as the subject in her might feel it necessary to be.

The King was taken aback, but not seriously; she was so beautiful, kneeling before him, that he was ready to forgive her for putting off her surrender. She wanted to hold him off; very well, he was ever a hunter who liked a run before the kill. He bade her cease to kneel, and said, his eyes devouring her since already in his mind he was possessing her, that he would continue to hope.

But her head shot up at that, the colour flaming in her cheeks.

"I understand not, most mighty King, how you should retain such hope," she said. "Your wife I cannot be, both in respect of mine own unworthiness and also because you have a Queen already." And then there came the most disturbing sentence of all: "Your mistress I will not be!"

Henry left her; he paced his room. He had desired her deeply when she had been a girl of sixteen, but his conscience had got between him and desire; he had made no protest when she had wrenched open the cage door and flown away. Now here she was back again, more desirable, a lovely woman where there had been a delightful girl. This time, he had thought, she shall not escape. He believed he had but to say so and it would be so. He had stifled the warnings of his conscience and now he had to face the refusal of the woman. It could not be; in a long and amorous life it had never been so. He was the King; she the humblest of his Queen's ladies. No, no! This was coquetry; she wished to keep him waiting, that he might burn the fiercer. If he could believe that was all, how happy he would be!

For his desire for Anne Boleyn astonished him. Desire he knew well; how speedily it came, how quickly it could be gratified. One's passion flamed for one particular person; there was a sweet interlude when passion was slaked and still asked to be slaked; then . . . the end. It was the inevitable pattern. And here was one who said with a ring of determination in her voice: "Your mistress I will not be!" He was angry with her;

had she forgotten he was the King? She had spoken to him as though he were a gentleman of the court . . . any gentleman. Thus had she spoken to him in her father's garden at Hever. The King grew purple with fury against her; then he softened, for it was useless to rail against that which enslaved him; it was her pride, it was her dignity which would make the surrender more sweet.

The King saw himself in his mirror. A fine figure of a man . . . if the size of him was considered. The suit he was wearing had cost three thousand pounds, and that not counting all the jewels that adorned it. But she was not the one to say yes to a suit of clothes; it would be the man inside it. He would smile at himself; he could slap his thigh; he was sure enough of eventual success with her.

He too had changed since those days when he allowed his conscience to come between him and this Anne Boleyn. The change was subtle, but definite enough. The conscience was still the dominating feature in his life. There it was, more than life size. The change was this: The conscience no longer ruled him; he ruled the conscience. He soothed it and placated it, and put his own construction on events before he let the conscience get at them. There was Mary Boleyn; he had done with Mary; he had decided that when Anne returned. He would cease to think of Mary. Oh, yes, yes, he knew there were those who might say there was an affinity between him and Anne, but in the course of many years of amorous adventures had this never happened before? Was there no man at court who had loved two sisters, perhaps unwittingly? Mayhap he himself had! For—and on this point Henry could be very stern—court morals being as they were, who could be sure who was closely related to whom? Suppose these sisters had had a different father! There! Was not the affinity reduced by one half? One could never know the secret of families. What if even the one mother did not give birth to the two daughters! One could never be sure; there had been strange stories of changeling children. This matter was not really worth wasting another moment's thought on. What if he were to eschew Anne on account of this edict, and make a match for her, only to discover then that she was not Mary's sister after all! Would it not be more sinful to take another man's wife? And this desire of his for this unusual girl could but be slaked one way, well he knew. Better to take her on chance that she might be Mary Boleyn's sister. He would forget such folly!

There was another matter too, about which his conscience perturbed him deeply and had done so for some time, in effect ever since he had heard that Katharine could bear no more children. Very deeply was he perturbed on this matter; so deeply that he had spoken of it to his most trusted friends. For all the years he had been married to Katharine there was but one daughter of the union. What could this mean? Why was it that Katharine's sons died one after the other? Why was it that only one of their offspring—and this a girl—had been allowed to live? There was some deep meaning in this, and Henry thought he had found it. There was assuredly some blight upon his union with Katharine, and what had he done,

in the eyes of a righteous god, to deserve this? He knew not
. . . except it be by marrying his brother's wife. Was it not
written in the book of Leviticus that should a man marry his
brother's wife their union should be childless? He had broken
off all marital relations with Katharine when the doctors had
told him she would never have any more children. Ah! Well he
remembered that day; pacing up and down his room in a cold
fury. No son for Henry Tudor! A daughter! And why? Why?
Then his mind had worked fast and furiously on this matter
of a divorce. Exciting possibility it had seemed. Divorces—
forbidden by Holy Church on principle—could be obtained
for political reasons from the Pope, who was ever ready to
please those in high places. I must have an heir! Henry told his
conscience. What would happen, should I die and not leave
an heir? There is mine and Katharine's daughter, Mary; but a
woman on the throne of England! No! I must have a male heir!
Women are not made to rule great countries; posterity will
reproach me, an I leave not an heir.

There in his mirror looked back the great man. He saw the
huge head, the powerful, glittering shoulders; and this man
could not produce a son for England! A short while ago he
had had his son by Elizabeth Blount brought to him, and had
created him Duke of Richmond, a title which he himself had
carried in his youth; that he had done in order to discomfort
Katharine. I could have a son, he implied. See! Here is my son.
It is you who have failed! And all the tears she shed in secret, and
all her prayers, availed her little. She had nothing to give him but

a daughter, for—and when he thought of this, the purple veins stood out on Henry's forehead—she had lied; she had sworn that her marriage with Arthur had never been consummated; she had tricked him, deceived him; this pale, passionless Spanish woman had tricked him into marriage, had placed in jeopardy the Tudor dynasty. Henry was filled with self-righteous anger, for he wanted a divorce and he wanted it for the noblest of reasons . . . not for himself, but for the house of Tudor; not to establish his manhood and virility in the eyes of his people, not to banish an aging, unattractive wife . . . not for these things, but because he, who had previously not hesitated to plunge his people into useless war, feared civil war for them; because he lived in sin with one who had never been his wife, having already lived with his brother. This, his conscience—now so beautifully controlled— told Henry. And all these noble thoughts were tinged rose colour by a beautiful girl who was obstinately haughty, whose cruel lips said, "I will never be your mistress!" But it was not necessary for his conscience to dwell upon that matter as yet, for a king does not raise a humble lady-in-waiting to be his queen, however desirable she may be. No, no! No thought of that had entered his head . . . not seriously, of course. The girl was there, and it pleased him to think of her in his arms, for such reflections were but natural and manly; and how she was to be got into that position was of small consequence, being a purely personal matter, whereas this great question of divorce was surely an affair of state.

So was his mind active in these matters, and so did he view

the reluctance of her whom he desired above all others with a kindly tolerance, like a good hunter contented to stalk awhile, and though the stalking might be arduous, that would be of little account when the great achievement would be his.

Thus was there some truth in the remarks of the Duchess of Norfolk when she had said to her granddaughter Catherine Howard that Anne Boleyn was leading the King a merry dance.

✦

In their apartments at the palace Jane Boleyn was quarrelling with her husband. He sat there in the window seat, handsome enough to plague her, indifferent enough to infuriate her. He was writing on a scrap of paper, and he was smiling as he composed the lyrics that doubtless his clever sister would set to music, that they might be sung before the King.

"Be silent, Jane," he said lightly, and it was his very lightness that maddened her, for well she knew that he did not care sufficiently for her even to lose his temper. He was tapping with his foot, smiling, well pleased with his work.

"What matters it," she demanded bitterly, "whether I speak or am silent? You do not heed which I do."

"As ever," said George, "you speak without thought. Were that so, why should I beg you for silence?"

She shrugged her shoulders impatiently.

"Words! Words! You would always have them at your disposal. I hate you. I wish I had never married you!"

"Sentiments, my dear Jane, which it may interest you to know are reciprocated by your most unwilling husband."

She went over to him, and sat on the window seat.

"George . . ." she began tearfully.

He sighed. "Since your feelings towards me are so violent, my dear, would it not be wiser if you removed yourself from this seat, or better still from this room? Should you prefer it, of course, I will be the one to go. But you know full well that you followed me hither."

As he spoke his voice became weary; the pen in his hand moved as though it were bidding him stop this stupid bickering and get on with what was of real moment to him. His foot began to tap.

Angrily she took the quill from him and threw it to the floor.

He sat very still, looking at it, not at her. If she could have roused him to anger, she would have been less angry with him; it was his indifference—it always had been—that galled her.

"I hate you!" she said again.

"Repetition detracts from, rather than adds to, vehemence," he said in his most lightsome tone. "Venom is best expressed briefly; overstatement was ever suspect, dear Jane."

"Dear Jane!" she panted. "When have I ever been dear to you?"

"There you ask a question which gallantry might bid me answer one way, truth another."

He was cruel, and he meant to be cruel; he knew how to

hurt her most; he had discovered her to be jealous, possessive and vindictive, and having no love for her he cared nothing for the jealousy, while the possessiveness irked him, and her vindictiveness left him cold; he was careless of himself and reckless as to what harm might come to him.

Her parents had thought it advantageous to link their daughter's fortunes with those of the Boleyns, which were rising rapidly under the warming rays of royal favour; so she had married, and once married had fallen victim to the Boleyn charm, to that ease of manner, to that dignity, to that cleverness. But what hope had Jane of gaining George's love? What did she know of the things for which he cared so deeply? He thought her stupid, colourless, illiterate. Why, she wondered, could he not be content to make merry, to laugh at the frivolous matters which pleased her; why could he not enjoy a happy married life with her, have children? But he did not want her, and foolishly she thought that by quarrelling, by forcing him to notice her, she might attract him; instead of which she alienated him, wearied him, bored him. They were strange people, thought Jane, these two younger Boleyns; amazingly alike, both possessing in a large degree the power of attracting not only those who were of the same genre as themselves, but those who were completely opposite. Jane believed them both to be cold people; she hated Anne; indeed she had never been so wretched in her life until the return of her sister-in-law; she hated her, not because Anne had been unpleasant to her, for indeed Jane must admit that Anne had in the first instance made efforts to be most sisterly; but she hated Anne because of the influence she had over her brother, because he could give her who was merely his young sister much affection and admiration, while for Jane, his wife who adored him, he had nothing but contempt.

So now she tried to goad him, longed for him to take her by the shoulders and shake her, that he might lay hands on her if only in anger. Perhaps he knew this, for he was diabolically clever and understood most uncomfortably the workings of minds less clever than his own. Therefore he sat, arms folded; looking at the pen stuck in the polished floor, bored by Jane, weary of the many scenes she created, and heartlessly careless of her feelings.

"George. . . ."

He raised weary eyebrows in acknowledgement.

"I . . . I am so unhappy!"

He said, with the faintest hint of softness in his voice: "I am sorry for that."

She moved closer; he remained impassive.

"George, what are you writing?"

"Just an airy trifle," he said.

"Are you very annoyed that I interrupted?"

"I am not annoyed," he replied.

"That pleases me, George. I do not mean to interrupt. Shall I get your pen?"

He laughed and, getting up, fetched it himself with a smile at her. Any sign of quiet reason on her part always pleased him;

she struggled with her tears, trying to keep the momentary approval she had won.

"I am sorry, George."

"It is of no matter," he said. "I'll warrant also that I should be the one to be sorry."

"No, George, it is I who am unreasonable. Tell me, is that for the King's masque?"

"It is," he said, and turned to her, wanting to explain what he, with Wyatt, Surrey and Anne, was doing. But he knew that to be useless; she would pretend to be interested; she would try very hard to concentrate, then she would say something that was maddeningly stupid, and he would realize that she had not been considering what he was saying, and was merely trying to lure him to an amorous interlude. He had little amorous inclination towards her; he found her singularly unattractive and never more so than when she tried to attract him.

She came closer still, leaning her head forward to look at the paper. She began to read.

"It is very clever, George."

"Nonsense!" said George. "It is very bad and needs a deal of polishing."

"Will it be sung?"

"Yes, Anne will write the music."

Anne! The very mention of that name destroyed her good resolutions.

"Anne, of course!" she said with a sneer.

She saw his eyes flash; she wanted to control herself, but she had heard the tender inflection of his voice when he said his sister's name.

"Why not Anne?" he asked.

"Why not Anne?" she mimicked. "I'll warrant the greatest musician in the kingdom would never write music such as Anne's . . . in your eyes!"

He did not answer that.

"The King's own music," she said, "you would doubtless consider inferior to Anne's!"

That made him laugh.

"Jane, you little fool, one would indeed be a poor musician if one was not more talented in that direction than His Majesty!"

"Such things as you say, George Boleyn, were enough to take a man's head off his shoulders."

"Reported in the right quarter, doubtless. What do you propose, sweet wife? To report in the appropriate quarter?"

"I swear I will one day!"

He laughed again. "That would not surprise me, Jane. You are a little fool, and I think out of your vindictive jealousy might conceivably send your husband to the scaffold."

"And he would richly deserve it!"

"Doubtless! Doubtless! Do not all men who go to the scaffold deserve their fate? They have spoken their minds, expressed an opinion, or have been too nearly related to the King . . . all treasonable matters, my dear Jane."

For this recklessness she loved him. How she would have

liked to be as he was, to have snapped her fingers at life and enjoyed it as he did!

"You are a fool, George. It is well for you that you have a wife such as I!"

"Well indeed, Jane!"

"Mayhap," she cried, "you would rather I looked like your sister Anne, dressed like your sister Anne, wrote as she wrote. . . . Then I might find approval in your sight!"

"You never could look like Anne."

She flashed back: "It is not given to all of us to be perfect!"

"Anne is far from that."

"What! Sacrilege! In your eyes she is perfect, if ever any woman was in man's eyes."

"My dear Jane, Anne is charming, rather because of her imperfections than because of her good qualities."

"I'll warrant you rage against Fate that you could not marry your sister!"

"I never was engaged in such a foolish discussion in all my life." She began to cry.

"Jane," he said, and put a hand on her shoulder. She threw herself against him, forcing the tears into her eyes, for they alone seemed to have the power to move him. And as they sat thus, there was the sound of footsteps in the corridor, and these footsteps were followed by a knock on the door.

George sat up, putting Jane from him.

"Enter!" he called.

They trooped in, laughing and noisy.

Handsome Thomas Wyatt was a little ahead of the others, singing a ballad. Jane disliked Thomas Wyatt; indeed she loathed them all. They were all of the same calibre, the most important set at court these days, favourites of the King every one of them, and all connected by the skein of kinship. Brilliant of course they were; the songsters of the court. One-eyed Francis Bryan, Thomas Wyatt, George Boleyn, all of them recently returned from France and Italy, and eager now to transform the somewhat heavy atmosphere of the English court into a more brilliant copy of other courts they had known. These gay young men were anxious to oust the duller element, the old set. No soldiers nor grim counsellors to the King these; they were the poets of their generation; they wished to entertain the King, to make him laugh, to give him pleasure. There was nothing the King asked more; and as this gay crowd circulated round none other than the lady who interested him so deeply, they were greatly favoured by His Majesty.

Jane's scowl deepened, for with these young men was Anne herself.

Anne threw a careless smile at Jane, and went to her brother.

"Let us see what thou hast done," she said, and snatched the paper from him and began reading aloud; and then suddenly she stopped reading and set a tune to the words, singing them, while the others stood round her. Her feet tapped, as her brother's had done, and Wyatt, who was bold as well as handsome, sat down between her and George on the window seat, and his eyes stayed on Anne's face as though they could not tear themselves away.

Jane moved away from them, but that was of no account

for they had all forgotten Jane's presence. She was outside the magic circle; she was not one of them. Angrily she watched them, but chiefly she watched Anne. Anne, with the hanging sleeves to hide the sixth nail; Anne, with a special ornament at her throat to hide what she considered to be an unbecoming mole on her neck. And now all the ladies at the court were wearing such ornaments. Jane put her hand to her throat and touched her own. Why, why was life made easy for Anne? Why did everyone applaud what she did? Why did George love her better than he loved his wife? Why was clever, brilliant and handsome Thomas Wyatt in love with her?

Jane went on asking herself these questions as she had done over and over again; bitter jealousy ate deeper and deeper into her heart.

Wyatt saw her sitting by the pond in the enclosed garden, a piece of embroidery in her hands. He went to her swiftly. He was deeply and passionately in love.

She lifted her face to smile at him, liking well his handsome face, his quick wit.

"Why, Thomas. . . ."

"Why, Anne. . . ."

He threw himself down beside her.

"Anne, do you not find it good to escape from the weary ceremony of the court now and then?"

"Indeed I do."

Her eyes were wistful, catching his mood. They were both thinking of Hever and Allington in quiet Kent.

"I would I were there," he said, for such was the accord between them that they sometimes read the other's thoughts.

"The gardens at Hever will be beautiful now."

"And at Allington, Anne."

"Yes," she said, "at Allington also."

He moved closer.

"Anne, what if we were to leave the court . . . together? What if we were to go to Allington and stay there . . . ?"

"You to talk thus," she said, "and you married to a wife!"

"Ah!" His voice was melancholy. "Anne, dost remember childhood days at Hever?"

"Well," she answered. "You locked me in the dungeons once, and I declare I all but died of fright. A cruel boy you were, Thomas."

"I! Cruel . . . and to you! Never! I swear I was ever tender. Anne, why did we not know then that happiness for you and me lay in the one place?"

"I suppose, Thomas, that when we are young we are so unwise. It is experience that teaches us the great lessons of life. How sad that, in gaining experience, we so often lose what we would most cherish!"

He would have taken her hand, but she held him off.

"Methinks we should return," she said.

"Now . . . when we are beginning to understand each other!"

"You, having married a wife . . ." she began.

"And therein being most unhappy," he interrupted; but she would have none of his interruptions.

"You are in no position to speak in this wise, Thomas."

"Anne, must we then say a long farewell to happiness?"

"If happiness would lie in marriage between us two, then we must."

"You would condemn me to a life of melancholy."

"You condemned yourself to that, not I!"

"I was very young."

"You were, I mind well, a most precocious boy."

He smiled back sadly over his youth. A boy of great precocity, they had sent him to Cambridge when he was twelve, and at seventeen had married him to Elizabeth Brooke, who was considered a good match for him, being daughter of Lord Cobham.

"Why," he said, "do our parents, thinking to do well for us, marry us to their choice which may well not be our own? Why is the right sort of marriage so often the unhappy one?"

Anne said: "You are spineless, all of you!" And her eyes flashed as her thoughts went to Percy. Percy she had loved and lost, for Percy was but a leaf wafted by the winds. The wicked Cardinal whom she hated now as she had ever done, had said, "It shall not be!" And meekly Percy had acquiesced. Now he would complain that life had denied him happiness, forgetting he had not made any great effort to attain it. And Wyatt, whom she could so easily love, complained in much the same manner. They obeyed their parents; they married, not where they listed, but entered into any match that was found for them; then they bitterly complained!

"I would never be forced!" she said. "I would choose my way, and, God help me, whatever I might encounter I would not complain."

"Ah! Why did I not know then that my happiness was with Anne Boleyn!"

She softened. "But how should you know it . . . and you but seventeen, and I even less?"

"And," he said, "most willing to engage yourself to Percy!"

"That!" She flushed, remembering afresh the insults of the Cardinal. "That. . . . Ah! That failed just as your marriage has failed, Thomas, though differently. Perchance I am glad it failed, for I never could abide a chicken-livered man!"

Now he was suddenly gay, throwing aside his melancholy; he would read to her some verses he had written, for they were of her and for her, and it was meet that she should hear them first.

So she closed her eyes and listened and thrilled to his poetry, and was sad thinking of how she might have loved him. And there in the pond garden it occurred to her that life had shown her little kindness in her love for men. Percy she had lost after a brief glimpse into a happy future they were to have shared; Wyatt she had lost before ever she could hope to have him.

What did the future hold for her? she wondered. Was she going on in this melancholy way, loving but living alone? It was unsatisfactory.

Thomas finished reading and put the poem into his pocket, his face flushed with appreciation for his work. He has his poetry, she mused, and what have I? Yes, the rest of us write a little; it is to us a pleasant recreation, it means not to us what it does to Wyatt. He has that, and it is much. But what have I?

Wyatt leaned forward; he said earnestly: "I shall remember this day forever, for in it you all but said you loved me!"

"There are times," she said, "when I fear that love is not for me."

"Ah, Anne! You are gloomy today. Whom should love be for, if not for those who are most worthy to receive it! Be of good cheer, Anne! Life is not all sadness. Who knows but that one day you and I may be together!"

She shook her head. "I have a melancholy feeling, Thomas."

"Bah! You and melancholy mate not well together." He leaped to his feet and held out his hands to her; she put hers in his, and he helped her to rise. He refused to release her hands; his lips were close to hers. She felt herself drawn towards him, but it seemed to her that her sister was between them. . . . Mary, lightsome, wanton, laughing, leering. She drew away coldly. He released her hands at once, and they fell to her side; but his had touched a jewelled tablet she wore and which hung from her pocket on a golden chain. He took it and held it up, laughing. "A memento, Anne, of this afternoon when you all but said you loved me!"

"Give it back!" she demanded.

"Not I! I shall keep it forever, and when I feel most melancholy

I shall take it out and look at it, and remember that on the afternoon I stole it you all but said you loved me."

"This is foolishness," she said. "I do not wish to lose that tablet."

"Alas then, Anne! For lost it you have. It is a pleasing trinket—it fills me with hope. When I feel most sad I shall look at it, for then I shall tell myself I have something to live for."

"Thomas, I beg of you. . . ."

She would have snatched it, but he had stepped backwards and now was laughing.

"Never will I give it up, Anne. You would have to steal it back."

She moved towards him. He ran, she after him; and running across the enclosed pond garden, trying to retrieve that which he had stolen, was poignantly reminiscent of happy childhood days at Allington and Hever.

The Cardinal rode through the crowds, passing ceremoniously over London Bridge and out of the capital on his way to France, whither he had been bidden to go by the King. Great numbers of his attendants went before him and followed after him; there were gentlemen in black velvet with gold chains about their necks, and with them their servants in their tawny livery. The Cardinal himself rode on a mule whose trappings were of crimson velvet, and his stirrups were of copper and gold. Before him were borne his two crosses of silver, two pillars of silver, the Great Seal of England, his Cardinal's hat.

The people regarded him sullenly, for it was now whispered, even beyond the court, of that which had come to be known as the King's Secret Matter; and the people blamed the Cardinal, whispering that he had put these ideas into the King's head. Whither went he now, but to France? Mayhap he would find a new wife to replace the King's lawful one, their own beloved Queen Katharine. They found new loyalty towards their quiet Queen, for they pictured her as a poor, wronged woman, and the London crowd was a sentimental crowd ever ready to support the wronged.

In the crowd was whispered the little ditty which malicious Skelton had written, and which the public had taken up, liking its simple implication, liking its cutting allusions to a Cardinal who kept state like a king.

> *"Why come ye not to court?*
> *To which court?*
> *To the King's court*
> *Or to Hampton Court!"*

He was well hated, as only the successful man can be hated by the unsuccessful. That he had risen from humble circumstances made the hatred stronger. "We are as good as this man!" "With his luck, there might I have gone!" So whispered the people, and the Cardinal knew of their whisperings and was grieved; for indeed many things grieved this man as he passed through London on his way to Sir Richard Wiltshire's house in Dartford wherein he would spend the first night of his journey to the coast.

The Cardinal was brooding on the secret matter of the King's. It was for him to smooth the way for his master, to get him what he desired at the earliest possible moment; and he who had piloted his state ship past many dangerous rocks was now dismayed. Well he could agree with His Majesty that the marriages of kings and queens depend for their success on the male issue, and what had his king and queen to show for years of marriage but one daughter! The Cardinal's true religion was statecraft; thus most frequently he chose to forget that as Cardinal he owed allegiance to the Church. When he had first been aware of the King's passion for Mistress Anne Boleyn, many fetes had he given at his great houses, that the King and this lady might meet. Adultery was a sin in the eyes of the Holy Church; not so in the liberal mind of Thomas Wolsey. The adultery of the King was as necessary as the jousts and tourneys he himself arranged for His Majesty's diversion. And though he was ever ready to give the King opportunities for meeting this lady, he gave but slight thought to the amorous adventures of His Majesty. This affair seemed to him but one of many; to absorb, to offer satiety; that was inevitable. And then . . . the next. So when this idea of divorce had been passed to him by the King, glorious possibilities of advancing England's interests through an advantageous marriage began to take hold of the Cardinal's mind.

Should England decide to ally herself with France against the Emperor Charles, what better foundation for such an alliance could there be than marriage! Already he had put out feelers for Francis's widowed sister, Marguerite of Alençon, but her brother, uncertain of Henry who still had an undivorced wife—and she none other than the aunt of the Emperor Charles himself—had dallied over negotiations, and married his sister to the King of Navarre. There was, however, Renee of France, sister to the late Queen Claude, and Wolsey's heart glowed at the prospect of such a marriage. Had not Claude borne Francis many children? Why, therefore, should Renee not bear Henry many sons? And to make the bargain complete, why not contract the King's daughter Mary to Francis's son, the Duke of Orleans? Of these matters had Wolsey spoken to the King, and craftily the King appeared to consider them, and whilst considering them he was thinking of none but Anne Boleyn, so did he yearn towards her; and so had her reluctance inflamed his passion that already he was toying with the idea of throwing away Wolsey's plans for a marriage which would be good for England; he was planning to defy his subjects' disapproval, to throw tradition to the wind, to satisfy his desires only and marry Anne Boleyn. He knew his Chancellor; wily, crafty, diplomatic; let Wolsey consider this divorce to be a state affair, and all his genius for statecraft would go into bringing it about; let him think it was but to satisfy his master's overwhelming desire for a humble gentlewoman of his court—who persistently and obstinately refused to become his mistress—and could Wolsey's genius then be counted on to work as well? The King thought not; so he listened to Wolsey's plans with feigned interest and approval, but unknown to the Cardinal, he dispatched his own secretary as messenger to the Pope, for he wished to appease his conscience regarding a certain matter which worried him a little. This was his love affair with Mary Boleyn, which he feared must create an affinity between himself and Anne, though he had determined it should be of small consequence should his secretary fail to obtain the Pope's consent to remove the impediment.

Riding on to Dartford, the Cardinal was busily thinking. There was within him a deep apprehension, for he was aware that this matter of the divorce was to be a delicate one and one less suited to his genius, which loved best to involve itself in the intricacies of diplomacy and was perhaps less qualified to deal with petty domesticities. Of Anne Boleyn he thought little. To him the King's affair with this foolish girl was a matter quite separate from the divorce, and unworthy of much thought. It appeared to him that Anne was a light o' love, a younger version of her sister, Mary, a comely creature much prone to giving herself airs. He smiled on her, for, while not attaching over-much importance to the King's favourites whose influence had ever been transient, it was well not to anger them. Vaguely he remembered some affair with Percy; the Cardinal smiled faintly at that. Could it be then that the King had remained faithful so long?

He fixed his eyes on his Cardinal's hat being borne before him, and that symbol of his power, the Great Seal of England; and his mind was busy and much disturbed, recent events having complicated the matter of divorce. He thought of the three men of consequence in Europe—Henry, Charles and Francis. Francis—even enfeebled as he was just now—had the enviable role of looker-on, sly and secret, waiting to see advantage and leap on it; Henry and Charles must take more active parts in the drama, for Henry's wife was Charles's aunt, and it was unlikely that Charles would stand calmly by to see Henry humiliate Spain through such a near relation. Between these two the Pope, a vacillating man, was most sorely perplexed; he dared not offend Henry; he dared not offend Charles. He had granted a divorce to Henry's sister Margaret on the flimsiest of grounds, but that had proved simple; there was no mighty potentate to be offended by such a divorce. Henry, ranting, fuming, urgently wanting what, it seemed to him, others conspired to keep from him, was a dangerous man; and to whom should he look to gratify his whims but Wolsey? And on whom would he vent his wrath, were his desires frustrated?

This sorry situation had been vastly aggravated by a recent event in Europe; the most unexpected, horrible and sacrilegious event the Cardinal could conceive, and the most disastrous to the divorce. This was the sack of Rome by the Duke of Bourbon's forces in the name of the Empire.

Over the last few years Wolsey had juggled dexterously in Europe; and now, riding on to Dartford, he must wonder whether out of his cunning had not grown this most difficult situation. For long Wolsey had known of the discord which existed between Francis and one of the most powerful nobles of France, the mighty Duke of Bourbon. This nobleman, to safeguard his life, had fled his country, and being a very proud and high-spirited gentleman was little inclined to rest in exile all his life; indeed for years before his flight he had been in treasonable communication with the Emperor Charles, France's hereditary enemy, and when he left his country he went to Charles with plans for making war on the French King.

Now it had occurred to Wolsey that if the Duke could be supplied secretly with money he could raise an army from his numerous supporters and thus be, as it were, a general under the King of England while none need know that the King of England had a hand in this war. Therefore would England be in secret alliance with Spain against France. Henry had felt the conception of such an idea to be sheer genius, for the weakening of France and the reconquering of that country had ever been a dream of his. A secret ambassador had been sent to Emperor Charles, and the King and Wolsey with their council laughed complacently at their own astuteness. Francis, however, discovered this and sent a secret messenger to make terms with England, with the result that Bourbon's small army—desperate and exhausted—awaited in vain the promised help from England. Wolsey had calculated without the daring of the Duke and the laxity of the French forces, without Francis's poor generalship which alternately hesitated and then was over-bold. At Pavia the French King's forces were beaten, and the King taken prisoner; and among his documents was found the secret treaty under the Great Seal of England. Thus was Francis a prisoner in the hands of the Emperor, and thus was English double-dealing exposed. Francis was to languish and come near to death in a Madrid prison; and Charles would not be overeager to link himself with England again. So that the master stroke which was to have put England in the enviable position of being on the winning side—whichever it was to be—had failed.

That had happened two years ago; yet it was still unpleasant to contemplate, as was Wolsey's failure, in spite of bribery, to be elected Pope. And now had come the greatest blow; Bourbon had turned his attentions to the city of Rome itself. True, this had cost the hasty Duke his life, but his men went on with his devilish scheme, and the city was ransacked, laid waste by fire and pillage, its priests desecrated, its virgins raped; and the sacred city was the scene of one of the most terrible massacres in history. But most shocking of all was the fact that the Pope, who was to grant Henry's divorce, was a prisoner at Castle Angell—prisoner of the Emperor Charles, the nephew of that lady who was to be most deeply wronged by the divorce.

Small wonder that the Cardinal's head ached, but even as it ached it buzzed with plans, for it had ever been this man's genius to turn every position in which he found himself to his own advantage; and now an idea had come to him that should make him more famous, make his master love him more. A short while ago it had seemed to him that a vast cloud was beginning to veil the sun of his glory, as yet so vapourish that the sun was but slightly obscured and blazed hotly through. He trusted in the sun's fierce rays to disperse that cloud; and so it should be. The Pope was a prisoner; why not set up a Deputy-Pope while he was thus imprisoned? And who more fitted for the office than Cardinal Wolsey? And would not such a deputy feel kindly disposed towards his master's plea for a divorce?

On rode the Cardinal, renewed and refreshed, until he came to Canterbury; and there he was the leader of a mighty procession that went into the Abbey; and, gorgeously attired, wearing his Cardinal's hat, he prayed for the captive Pope and wept for him, while his mind was busy with the plans for reigning in Clement's stead, granting the divorce, and marrying his master to a French princess.

And so passed the Cardinal on to France where he was received royally by the Regent, Louise of Savoy—who reigned during the absence of her son Francois—and by the King's gifted sister, Marguerite of Navarre. He assured them of his master's friendship with their country; he arranged the marriage of the King's daughter to the Duke of Orleans; and he hinted at the King's divorce and his marriage with Renee. He was entertained lavishly, well assured of French friendship.

But among the people of France the Cardinal was no more popular than he was in England; and although he came with offers of friendship, and though he brought English gold with him, the humble people of France did not trust him and made his journey through their land an uncomfortable one. He was robbed in many places where he rested, and one morning when he arose from his bed, he went to his window and there saw that on the leaning stone some mischievous person had engraved a Cardinal's hat, and over it a gallows.

.✳.

The whole court whispered of nothing else but the King's Secret Matter. Anne heard it; Katharine heard it. The Queen was afraid. Great pains she took with her toilet, hoping thereby to please the King, that there might yet be a hope of defying the doctors and producing an heir. Katharine was melancholy; she prayed more fervently; she fretted.

Anne heard it and was sorry for the Queen, for though she was as different from Anne as one woman could be from another, a gloomy woman, rarely heard to laugh, yet had Anne a deep respect for such piety as her mistress's while feeling herself unable to emulate it.

But Anne was busy with thoughts of her own affairs. Wyatt was plaguing her, making wild and impossible suggestions; and she feared she thought too much and too often of Wyatt. There came to her little scraps of paper with his handwriting, and in the poems inscribed on these he expressed his passion for her, the unhappiness of his marriage, the hope he might have, would she but give it, of the future. There had been those who had said that Anne was half French; in character this was so. She was frivolous, sentimental, excessively fond of admiration; but mingling with these attributes was something essentially practical. Had Wyatt been unmarried, ready would she have been to listen to him; and now, admitting this to herself—at the same time giving him no hope that his plans would ever reach fruition—she found it impossible to refuse his attentions entirely. She looked for him; she was ever ready to dally with him. With her cousin Surrey and her brother to ensure the proprieties, she was often to be found with Wyatt. They were the gayest and most brilliant quartet at the court; their cousinship was a bond between them. Life was pleasant for Anne with such friends as these, and she was enjoying it as a butterfly flutters in the sunshine even when the first cool of evening is setting in.

Preparing herself for the banquet which was to be given at the palace of Greenwich in honour of the departing French ambassadors, Anne thought of Wyatt. This banquet was to be the most gorgeous of its kind as a gesture of friendship towards the new allies. At Hampton these gentlemen had been entertained most lavishly by the lord Cardinal, who had recently returned from France, and so magnificent a feast had the Cardinal prepared for them that the King, jealous that one of his subjects could provide such a feast fit only for a king's palace, would have Wolsey's hospitality paled to insignificance by his own.

George, Anne, Surrey, Bryan and Wyatt had organized

a most lavish carnival for the entertainment of these French gentlemen. They were delighted with their work, sure of the King's pleasure. Such events were ever a delight to Anne; she revelled in them, for she knew that, with her own special gifts she excelled every other woman present, and this was intoxicating to Anne, dispersing that melancholy which she had experienced periodically since she had lost Percy and which was returning more frequently, perhaps on account of Wyatt.

Anne's dress was of scarlet and cloth of gold; there were diamonds at her throat and on her vest. She discarded her headdress, deciding it made her look too much like the others; she would wear her beautiful hair flowing and informal.

She was, as she had grown accustomed to be, the shining light of the court. Men's eyes turned to watch her; there was Henry Norris, the groom of the stole, Thomas Wyatt, smouldering and passionate, the King, his eyes glittering. To Norris she was indifferent; of Thomas Wyatt she was deeply aware; the King she feared a little; but admiration, no matter whence it came, was sweet. George smiled at her with approval; Jane watched her with envy, but there was little to disturb in that, as all the women were envious; though perhaps with Jane the envy was tinged with hatred. But what did Anne care for her brother's foolish wife! Poor George! she thought. Better to be alone than linked with such a one. It could be good to be alone, to feel so many eyes upon her, watching, admiring, desiring; to feel that power over these watching men which their need of her must give her.

About her, at the banquet, the laughter was louder, the fun more riotous. The King would join the group which surrounded her, because he liked to be with gay young people; and all the time his eyes burned to contemplate her who was the centre of this laughing group.

The Queen sat, pale and almost ugly. She was a sad and frightened woman who could not help thinking continually of the suggested divorce; and this feast in itself was a humiliation to her, since she, a Spaniard, could find little joy in friendship with the French!

The King's distaste for his Queen was apparent; and those courtiers who were young and loved gaiety scarcely paid her the homage due to her; they preferred to gather round Anne Boleyn, because to be there was to be near the King, joining in his fun and laughter.

Now, from his place at the head of the table, the King was watching Wyatt. Wine had made the poet over-bold and he would not move from Anne's side though he was fully aware of Henry's watching eyes. There was hardly anyone at the table who was ignorant of the King's passion, and there was an atmosphere of tension in the hall, while everyone waited for the King to act.

Then the King spoke. There was a song he wished the company to hear. It was of his own composing. All assumed great eagerness to hear the song.

The musicians were called. With them came one of the finest singers in the court. There was a moment's complete silence, for no one dared move while the King's song was about to be sung. The King sat forward and his eyes never left Anne's face until the song was finished and the applause broke out.

> "The eagle's force subdues each bird that flies:
> What metal can resist the flaming fire?
> Doth not the sun dazzle the clearest eyes
> And melt the ice, and make the frost retire?
> The hardest stones are pierced through with tools,
> The wisest are with princes made but fools."

There could be no doubt of the meaning of these arrogant words; there could be no doubt for whom they were written. Anne was freshly aware of the splendour of this palace of Greenwich, of the power it represented. The words kept ringing in her ears. He was telling her that he was weary of waiting; princes, such as he was, did not wait over-long.

This evening had lost its joy for her now; she was afraid. Wyatt had heard those words and realized their implication; George had heard them, and his eyes smiled into hers reassuringly. She wanted to run to her brother, she wanted to say: "Let us go home; let us go back to being children. I am afraid of the glitter of this court. His eyes watch me now. Brother, help me! Take me home!" George knew her thoughts. She saw the reckless tilt of his head, and imitated it, feeling better, returning his smile. George was reassuring. "Never fear, Anne!" he seemed to convey. "We are the Boleyns!"

The company was applauding. Great poetry, was the verdict. Anne looked to him who, some said, was the literary genius of the court, Sir Thomas More; his *Utopia* she had just read with much pleasure. Sir Thomas was gazing at his large and rather ugly hands; he did not, she noticed, join in the effusive praise of the others. Was it the poetry or the sentiments, of which Sir Thomas did not approve?

The King's song was the prelude of the evening's entertainment, and Anne with her friends would have a big part in this. She thrust aside her fears; she played that night with a fervour she had rarely expressed before in any of these masquerades and plays which the quartet contrived. Into her fear of the King there crept an element which she could not have defined. What was it? The desire to make him admire her more? The company were over-courteous to her; even her old enemy, Wolsey, whom she had never ceased to hate, had a very friendly smile! The King's favourites were to be favoured by all, and when you had known yourself to be slighted on account of your humble birth . . . when such a man as Wolsey had humiliated you . . . yes, there was pleasure mingling with the fear of this night.

She was like a brilliant flame in her scarlet and gold. All eyes were upon her. For months to come they would talk of this night, on which Anne had been the moon to all these pale stars.

The evening was to end with a dance, and in this each gentleman would choose his partner. The King should take the Queen's hand and lead the dance, whilst the others fell in behind them. The Queen sat heavy in her chair, brooding and disconsolate. The King did not give her a look. There was a moment of breathless silence while he strode over to Anne Boleyn, and thus, choosing her, made public his preference.

His hand held hers firmly; his was warm and strong; she felt he would crush her fingers.

They danced. His eyes burned bright as the jewels on his clothes. Different this from the passion of Wyatt; fiercer, prouder, not sad but angry passion.

He would have speech with her away from these people, he said. She replied that she feared the Queen's disapproval should she leave the ballroom.

He said: "Do you not fear mine if you stay!"

"Sir," she said, "the Queen is my mistress."

"And a hard one, eh?"

"A very kind one, Sir, and one whose displeasure I should not care to incur."

He said angrily: "Mistress, you try our patience sorely. Did you like our song?"

"It rhymed well," she said, for now she sat with him she could see that his anger was not to be feared; he would not hurt her, since mingling with his passion there was a tenderness, and this tenderness, which she observed, while it subdued her fear, filled her with a strange and exalted feeling.

"What mean you?" he cried, and he leaned closer, and though he would know himself to be observed he could not keep away.

"Your Majesty's rhyme I liked well; the sentiments expressed, not so well."

"Enough of this folly!" he said. "You know I love you well."

"I beg your Majesty . . ."

"You may beg anything you wish an you say you love me."

She repeated the old argument. "Your Majesty, there can be no question of love between us . . . I would never be your mistress."

"Anne," he said earnestly, pleadingly, "should you but give yourself to me body and soul there should be no other in my heart I swear. I would cast off all others that are in competition with you, for there is none that ever have delighted me as you do."

She stood up, trembling; she could see he would refuse to go on taking no for an answer, and she was afraid.

She said: "The Queen watches us, Your Majesty. I fear her anger."

He arose, and they joined the dancers.

"Think not," he said, "that this matter can rest here."

"I crave Your Majesty's indulgences. I see no way that it can end that will satisfy us both."

"Tell me," he said, "do you like me?"

"I hope I am a loving subject to Your Majesty. . . ."

"I doubt not that you could be a very loving one, Anne, if you gave your mind to it; and I pray you will give your mind to it. For long have I loved you, and for long have I had little satisfaction in others for my thoughts of you."

"I am unworthy of Your Majesty's regard."

She thought: Words! These tiresome words! I am frightened. Oh, Percy, why did you leave me! Thomas, if you loved me when you were a child, why did you let them marry you to a wife!

The King towered over her, massive and glittering in his power. He breathed heavily; his face was scarlet; desire in his eyes, desire in his mouth.

She thought: Tomorrow I shall return secretly to Hever.

The Queen was sulky. She dismissed her maids and went into that chamber wherein was the huge royal bed which she still shared with Henry, but the sharing of which was a mere formality. She lay at one extreme edge; he at the other.

She said: "It is useless to pretend you sleep."

He said: "I had no intention of pretending, Madam."

"It would seem to be your greatest pleasure to humiliate me."

"How so?" he said.

"It is invariably someone; tonight it was the girl Boleyn. It was your kingly duty to have chosen me."

"Chosen you, Madam!" he snorted. "That would I never have done; not now, nor years ago, an the choice were mine!"

She began to weep and to murmur prayers; she prayed for self-control for herself and for him. She prayed that he might soften towards her, and that she might defy the doctors who had prophesied that he would never get a male heir from her.

He lay listening to her but paying little attention, being much accustomed to her prayers, thinking of a girl's slender body in scarlet and gold, a girl with flowing hair and a clever, pointed face, and the loveliest dark eyes in the court. Anne, he thought, you witch! I vow you hold off to provoke me. . . . Pleasant thoughts. She was holding off to plague him. But enough, girl. How many years since I saw you in your father's garden, and wanted you then! What do you want, girl? Ask for it; you shall have it, but love me, love me, for indeed I love you truly.

The Queen had stopped praying.

"They give themselves such airs, these women you elevate with your desires."

"Come," he said, gratified, for did not she give herself airs, and was it then because of his preference for her? "It is natural, is it not, that those noticed by the King should give themselves airs?"

"There are so many," she said faintly.

Ah! he thought, there would be but one, Anne, and you that one!

The Queen repeated: "I would fain Your Majesty controlled himself."

Oh, her incessant chatter wearied him. He wished to be left alone with his dream of her whose presence enchanted him.

He said cruelly: "Madam, you yourself are little inducement to a man to forsake his mistresses."

She quivered; he felt that, though the width of the vast bed separated them.

"I am no longer young," she said. "Am I to blame because our children died?" He was silent; she was trembling violently now. "I have heard the whispering that goes on in the court. I have heard of this they call the King's Secret Matter."

Now she had dragged his mind from the sensuous dream which soothed his body. So the whispering had reached her ears, had it! Well, assuredly it must reach them some time; but he would rather the matter had been put before her in a more dignified manner.

She said appealingly: "Henry, you do not deny it?"

He heaved his great body up in the bed. "Katharine," he said, "you know well that for myself I would not replace you; but a king's life does not belong to him but to his kingdom. And Katharine, serious doubts have arisen in my mind, not lately but for some time past; and well would I have suppressed them had my conscience let me. I would have you know, Katharine, that when our daughter's marriage with the Duke of Orleans was proposed, the French ambassador raised the question of her legitimacy."

"Legitimacy!" cried Katharine, raising herself. "What meant he? My lord, I hope you reproved him most sternly!"

"Ah! That I did! And sorely grieved was I." The King felt happier now; he was no longer the erring husband being reproved by his too faithful wife; he was the king, who put his country first, before all personal claims; and in this matter, he could tell himself, the man must take second place to the king. He could, lying in this bed with a woman whose pious ways, whose shapeless body had long since ceased to move him except with repugnance, assure himself that the need to remain married to her was removed.

He had married Katharine because there had been England's need to form a deep friendship with Spain, because England had then been weak, and across a narrow strip of channel lay mighty France, a perennial enemy. In those days of early marriage it had been a hope of Henry's to conquer France once more; with Calais still in English hands, this had not seemed an impossibility; he had hoped that with the Emperor's help this might be effected, but since the undignified affair at Pavia, Charles was hardly likely to link himself with English allies; thus was the need for friendship with Spain removed; Wolsey's schemes had been called to a halt; the new allies were the French. Therefore, what could be better for England than to dissolve the Spanish marriage! And in its place . . . But no matter, dissolve the Spanish marriage since it could no longer help England.

These were minor matters compared with the great issue which disturbed his conscience. God bless the Bishop of Tarbes, that ambassador who had the tact at this moment to question the legitimacy of the Princess Mary.

"'Twere a matter to make a war with France," said Katharine hotly. "My daughter a bastard! Your daughter . . ."

"These matters are not for women's wits," said the King. "Wars are not made on such flimsy pretexts."

"Flimsy!" she cried, her voice sharp with fear. Katharine was no fool; to the suppers given in her apartments there came the most learned of men, the more serious courtiers, men such as Sir Thomas More; she was more fastidious than the English ladies, and she had never tried to learn the English ways. She did not enjoy the blood sports so beloved by her husband. At first he had protested when she had told him that Spanish ladies did not follow the hawk and hound. But that was years ago; he thought it well now that she did not attend sporting displays, since he had no wish for her company. But there was that in her which must make him respect her, her calm dignity, her religious faith; and even now, when this great catastrophe threatened her, she had not shown publicly—apart from her melancholy, which was natural to her—that she knew what was afoot. But she was tenacious; she would fight, he knew, if not for herself, for her daughter. Her piety would tell her that she fought for Henry as well as for herself, that divorce was wrong in the eyes of the Church, and she would fight with all her quiet persistence against it.

"Katharine," said the King, "dost thou remember thy Bible?" He began to quote a passage from Leviticus wherein it was said that for a man to take his brother's wife was an unclean thing, for thus had he uncovered his brother's nakedness, they should therefore be childless. He repeated the last sentence.

"Thou knowest I was never truly thy brother's wife."

"It is a matter which perplexes me greatly."

"You would say you believe me not?"

"I know not what to say. Your hopes of an heir have been blighted; it looks like Providence. Is it natural that our sons should die one after the other? Is it natural that our efforts should be frustrated?"

"Not all," she said plaintively.

"A daughter!" he retorted contemptuously.

"She is a worthy girl. . . ."

"Bah! A girl! What good are women on the throne of England! She is no answer to our prayers, Katharine. Sons have been denied to us. The fault does not lie in me. . . ."

Tears were in the Queen's eyes. She would hate this man if most of her natural instincts had not been suppressed by piety; she knew not now whether she hated or loved; she only knew she must do what was right according to her religion. She must not hate the King; she must not hate her husband; for therein was mortal sin. So all through the years when he had slighted her, humiliated her, shown utter carelessness of the hurt his lack of faith might cause her, she had assured herself that she loved him. Small wonder that he found her colourless; small wonder that now he compared this woman of forty-one with a laughing, wilful girl of nineteen years! He was thirty-five; surely a good age for a man—his prime. But he must be watchful of the years, being a king who had so far failed to give his kingdom an heir.

A short while ago he had brought his illegitimate son to court, and heaped honours upon him to the deep humiliation of the Queen, whose fears were then chiefly for her daughter.

This huge man cared nothing for her, little for her daughter; he only cared that he should get what he wanted, and that the world should think that in procuring his own needs he did it not for his own, but for duty's sake.

When he said that the fault was not with him, he meant she had lied when she declared herself a virgin; he meant that she had lived with his brother as his wife. She began to weep as she prayed for strength to fight this powerful man and his evil intentions to displace her daughter from the throne with a bastard he might beget through one whom he would call his wife.

"Search your soul!" he said now, his voice trembling with righteousness. "Search your soul, Katharine, for the truth. Does the blame for this disaster to our kingdom lie with you or with me? I have a clear conscience. Ah, Katharine, can you say you have the same?"

"That I can," she said, "and will!"

He could have struck her, but he calmed himself and said in melancholy fashion: "Nothing would have made me take this step, but that my conscience troubled me."

She lay down and was silent; he lay down too; and in a very short while he had forgotten Katharine and was thinking of her who, he had determined, should be his.

★

Anne arrived at Hever with the words of the King's song still in her thoughts. She found it difficult to analyze her feelings, for to be the object of so much attention from one as powerful as the King was to reflect that power; and to Anne, bold and eager for life, power, though perhaps not the most cherished gift life could bestow, was not to be despised.

She wondered what he would say when the news of her departure reached him. Would he be angry? Would he decide that it was beneath his dignity to pursue such an unappreciative female? Would he banish her from court? She fervently hoped not that, for she needed gaiety as she never had before. She could suppress her melancholy in feverish plans for the joust, and moreover her friends were at court—George and Thomas, Surrey and Francis Bryan; with them she could laugh and frivol; and indeed talk most seriously too, for they were all—perhaps with the exception of Surrey—interested in the new religion of which she had learned a good deal from Marguerite, now the Queen of Navarre. They leaned towards that religion, all of them, perhaps because they were young and eager to try anything that was different from the old way, liking it by virtue of its very novelty.

She had not been at Hever more than a day, when the King arrived. If she had any doubt of his intense feeling for her, she need have no doubt any longer. He was inclined to be angry, but at the sight of her his anger melted; he was humble, which was somehow touching in one in whom humility was such a rare virtue; he was eager and passionate, anxious that she should have no doubt of the nature of his feelings for her.

They walked in that garden which had been the scene of

their first encounter; and that was at his wish, for he was a sentimental man when it pleased him to be so.

"I have seriously thought of this matter of love between us," he told her. "I would have you know that I understand your feelings. I must know—so stricken am I in my love for you— what your feelings to me are, and what they would be if I no longer had a wife."

She was startled. Dazzling possibilities had presented themselves. Herself a queen! The intoxicating glory of power! The joy of snapping her fingers at the Cardinal! Queen of England . . . !

"My lord . . ." she stammered. "I fear I am stupid. I understand not . . ."

He put a hand on her arm, and she felt his fingers burning there; they crept up to her forearm, and she faced him, saw the intensity of his desire for her, and thrilled to it because, though he might not be a man she loved, he was King of England, and she felt his power, and she felt his need of her, and while he was in such urgent need it was she who held the power, for the King of England would be soft in her hands.

She cast down her eyes, fearful lest he should read her thoughts. He said she was fairer than any lady he had ever seen, and that he yearned to possess her, body and soul.

"Body and soul!" he repeated, his voice soft and humble, his eyes on her small neck, her slender body; and his voice slurred suddenly with desire as, in his mind, he took her, just as he had when he had lain beside the Queen and conjured up pictures of her so vividly that it had seemed she was there with him.

She was thinking of Percy and of Wyatt, and it seemed to her that these two mingled together and were one, representing love; and before her beckoned this strong, powerful, bejewelled man who represented ambition.

He was kissing her hand with swift, devouring kisses; there was a ring on her forefinger which she wore always; he kissed this ring, and asked that he might have it as a token, but she clenched her hands and shook her head. There was a large diamond on his finger that he would give to her, he said; and these two rings would be symbols of the love between them.

"For now I shall soon be free," he said, "to take a wife."

She lifted her eyes incredulously to his face. "Your Majesty cannot mean he would take me!"

He said passionately: "I will take none other!"

Then it was true; he was offering her marriage. He would lift her up to that lofty eminence on which now sat Queen Katharine, the daughter of a king and queen. She, humble Anne Boleyn, was to be placed there . . . and higher, for Katharine might be Queen, but she had never had the King's regard. It was too brilliant to be contemplated. It dazzled. It gave her a headache. She could not think clearly, and it seemed as though she saw Wyatt smiling at her, now mocking, now melancholy. It was too big a problem for a girl who was but nineteen and who, longing to be loved, had been grievously disappointed in her lovers.

"Come, Anne!" he said. "I swear you like me."

"It is too much for me to contemplate. . . . I need . . ."

"You need me to make up your mind for you!" he said, and there and then he had her in his arms, his lips hard and hot against her own. She felt his impatience, and sought to keep her wits. Already she knew something of this man; a man of deep needs ever impatient of their immediate gratification; now he was saying to her: "I've promised marriage. Why wait longer? Here! Now! Show your gratitude to your King and your trust in him, and believe that he will keep his promise!"

The Secret Matter . . . would it be granted? And if so . . . what would her old enemy, Wolsey, have to say of such a marriage? There would be powerful people at court who would exert all their might to prevent it. No, she might be falling in love with the thought of herself as queen, but she was not in love with the King.

She said, with that haughty dignity which while it exasperated him never failed to subdue him: "Sire, the honour you do me is so great that I would fain . . ."

With a rough edge to his voice he interrupted: "Enough of such talk, sweetheart! Let us not talk as king and subject, but as man and woman." One hand was at her throat. She felt his body hot against her own. With both hands she held him off.

"As yet," she said coldly, "I am unsure."

The veins stood out on his forehead.

"Unsure!" he roared. "Your King has said he loves you . . . aye, and will marry you, and you are unsure!"

"Your Majesty suggested we should talk as man and woman, not as king and subject."

She had freed herself and was running towards the hedge of fir trees which enclosed this garden; he ran after her, and she allowed herself to be caught at the hedge. He held both her hands tightly in his.

"Anne!" he said. "Anne! Dost seek to plague me?"

She answered earnestly: "I never felt less like plaguing anyone, and why should I plague Your Majesty who has done me this great honour! You have offered me your love, which is to me the greatest honour, you being my King and I but a humble girl; but it was Your Majesty's command that I should cease to think of you as King . . ."

He interrupted: "You twist my words, Anne. You clever little minx, you do!" And, forcing her against the hedge, he put his hands on her shoulders and kissed her lips; then those hands sought to pull apart her dress.

She wriggled free.

He said sternly: "I would have you regard me now as your king. I would have you be my obedient, loving little subject."

She was breathless with fear. She said, greatly daring: "You could never win my love that way! I beg of you, release me."

He did so, and she stood apart from him, her eyes flashing, her heart beating madly; for she greatly feared that he would force on her that which till now she had so cleverly avoided. But suddenly she saw her advantage, for there he stood before her, not an angry king but a humble man who, besides desiring her, loved her; and thus she knew that it was not for him to say what should be, but for herself to decide. Such knowledge was sweet; it calmed her sorely troubled mind, and calm she was indeed mistress of the situation. Here he was, this great bull of a man, for the first time in his life in love, and therefore inexperienced in this great emotion which swept over him, governing his actions, forcing him to take orders instead of giving them; forcing him to supplicate instead of demanding.

"Sweetheart . . ." he began hoarsely; but she lifted a hand.

"Your rough treatment has grieved me."

"But my love for you . . ."

She looked at the red marks his hands had made on her shoulder, where he had torn the neck of her gown.

"It frightens me," she said, looking not the least frightened, but mistress of herself and of him. "It makes me uncertain. . . ."

"Have no uncertainty of me, darling! When I first met you I went back and said to Wolsey: 'I have been discoursing with one who is worthy to wear a crown!'"

"And what said my lord Cardinal? He laughed in your face I dare swear!"

"Dost think he would dare!"

"There are many things my lord Cardinal might dare that others would not. He is an arrogant, ill-bred creature!"

"You wrong him, sweetheart . . . nor do we wish to speak of him. I beg of you, consider this matter in all seriousness, for I swear there is none that can make me happy but yourself."

"But Your Majesty could not make me your queen! I have said your mistress I would never be."

Now he was eager, for his mind, which had weighed this

point since she began to torment him, was now firmly made up.

"I swear," he said, "I would never take another queen but that she was Anne Boleyn. Give me the ring, sweetheart, and take you this so that I may have peace in my mind."

These were sweet words to her, but still she wavered. Love first; power second. Ah, she thought, could I but love this man!

"Your Grace must understand my need to think this matter over well."

"Think it over, Anne? I ask you to be my queen!"

"We do not discuss kings and queens," she reproved him, and the reproof enchanted him. "This is a matter between a man and a woman. Would you then wish me to be your queen and not to be wholly sure that I loved you more than a subject loves a king?"

This was disarming. Where was there a woman who could hesitate over such a matter! Where was one like her! In wit, in beauty, he had known she had no equal; but in virtue too she stood alone. She was priceless, for nothing he could give would buy her. He must win her love.

He was enchanted. This was delightful—for how could he doubt that she would love him! There was none who excelled as he did at the jousts; always he won—or almost always. His songs were admired more than Wyatt's or Surrey's even; and had he not earned the title of Defender of the Faith by his book against Luther! Could More have written such a book? No! He was a king among men in all senses of the words. Take away the throne tomorrow and he would still be king. In love . . . ah! He had but to look at a woman and she was ripe for him. So it had always been . . . except with Anne Boleyn. But she stood apart from others; she was different; that was why she should be his queen.

"I would have time to think on this matter," she said, and her words rang with sincerity, for this man's kisses had aroused in her a desire for those of another man, and she was torn between love and ambition. If Wyatt had not had a wife, if it was a dignified love he could have given her, she would not have hesitated; but it was the King who offered dignity, and he offered power and state; nor was Wyatt such a humble lover as this man, for all his power, could be; and, lacking humility herself, she liked it in others.

"I stay here till I have your answer," said the King. "I swear I will not leave Hever till I wear your ring on my finger and you mine on yours."

"Give me till tomorrow morning," she said.

"Thus shall it be, sweetheart. Deal kindly with me in your thoughts."

"How could I do aught else, when from you I and mine have had naught but kindness!"

He was pleased at that. What had he not done for these Boleyns! Aye, and would do more still. He would make old Thomas's daughter a queen. Then he wondered, did she mean to refer to Mary? Quick of speech was his love; sharp of wits; was she perhaps a little jealous of her sister, Mary?

He said soberly: "There shall be none in competition with you, sweetheart."

And she answered disconcertingly: "There would need to be none, for I could not believe in the love of a man who amused himself with mistresses." Then she was all smiles and sweetness. "Sire, forgive my forwardness. Since you tell me you are a man who loves me, I forget you are the King."

He was enraptured; she would come to him not for what the coming would mean to her in honour; she would come to him as the man.

That evening was a pleasant one. After the meal in the great dining hall she played to him and sang a little.

He kissed her hands fervently on retiring.

"Tomorrow," he said, "I must have that ring."

"Tomorrow," she answered, "you shall know whether or not you shall have it."

He said, his eyes on her lips: "Dost think of me under this roof knowing you so near and refusing me?"

"Perhaps it will not always be so," she said.

"I will dream you are already Queen of England. I will dream that you are in my arms."

She was afraid of such talk; she bade him a hasty good night, repeating her promise that he should hear her decision in the morning. She went to her chamber and locked her door.

Anne passed a night that was tortured with doubts. To be Queen of England! The thought haunted her, dominated her. Love, she had lost—the love she had dreamed of. Ambition beckoned. Surely she was meant to be a queen, she on whom the Fates had bestowed great gifts. She saw her ladies about her, robing her in the garments of state; she saw herself stately and gracious, imperious. Ah! she thought, There are so many people I can help. And her thoughts went to a house in Lambeth and a little girl tugging at her skirts. That would be indeed gratifying, to lift her poor friends and members of her family out of poverty; to know that they spoke of her lovingly and with respect. . . . We owe this to the Queen—the Queen, but a humble girl whose most unusual gifts, whose wit and beauty so enslaved the King that he would make her his Queen. And then . . . there were some who had laughed at her, her enemies who had said: "Ah! There goes Anne Boleyn; there she goes, the way of her sister!" How pleasant to snap the fingers at them, to make them bow to her!

Her eyes glittered with excitement. The soft girl who had loved Percy, who was inclined to love Wyatt, had disappeared, and in her place was a calculating woman. Ambition was wrestling desperately with love; and ambition was winning.

I do not dislike the King, she thought—for how could one dislike a man who had the good taste to admire one so wholeheartedly.

And the Queen? Ah! Something else to join the fight against ambition. The poor Queen, who was gentle enough, though melancholy, she a queen to be wronged. Oh, but the glitter of queenship! And Anne Boleyn was more fit to occupy a throne than Katharine of Aragon, for queenship is innate; it is not to be bestowed on those who have nothing but their relationship to other kings and queens.

Thomas, Thomas! Why are you not a king, to arrange a divorce, to take a new queen!

Would you be faithful, Thomas? Are any men? And if not, is love the great possession to be prized above all else? Thomas and his wife! George and Jane! The King and the Queen! Look around the court; where has love lasted? Is it not overrated? And ambition . . . Wolsey! How high he had come! From a butcher's shop, some said, to Westminster Hall. From a tutor's cold attic to Hampton Court! Ambition beckoned. Cardinals may be knocked down from their proud perches, but it would need a queen to knock them down; and who could displace a queen of the King's choice!

A queen! A queen! Queen Anne!

While Henry, restless, dreamed of her taking off those elegant clothes, of caressing the shapely limbs, she, wakeful, pictured herself riding in a litter of cloth of gold, while on either side crowds of people bared their heads to the Queen of England.

The next day Henry, after extracting a promise from her that she would return to court at once, rode away from Hever wearing her ring on his finger.

✦

The Cardinal wept; the Cardinal implored; all his rare gifts were used in order to dissuade the King. But Henry was more determined on this than he had ever been on any matter. As wax in the hands of the crafty Wolsey he had been malleable indeed; but Wolsey had to learn that he had been so because, being clever enough to recognize the powers of Wolsey, he had been pleased to let him have his way. Now he desired the divorce, he desired marriage with Anne Boleyn as he had never desired anything except the throne, and he would fight for these with all the tenacity of the obstinate man he was; and being able to assure himself that he was in the right he could do so with unbounded energy. The divorce was right, for dynastic reasons; Anne was right for him, for she was young and healthy and would bear him many sons. An English queen for the English throne! That was all he asked.

In vain did Wolsey point out what the reaction in France must surely be. Had he not almost affianced Henry to Renee? And the people of England? Had His Grace, the King, considered their feelings in the matter? There was murmuring against the divorce throughout the capital. Henry did what he ever did when crossed; he lost his temper, and in his mind were sown the first seeds of suspicion towards his old friend and counsellor. Wolsey had no illusions; well he knew his royal master. He must now work with all his zest and genius for the divorce; he must use all his energies to put on the throne one whom he knew to be his enemy, whom he had discovered to be more than a feckless woman seeking admiration and gaiety, whom he knew to be interested in the new religion, to be involved in a powerful party comprising her uncle of Norfolk, her father, her brother, Wyatt and the rest; this he must do, or displease the King. He could see no reward for himself in this. To please the King he must put Anne Boleyn on the throne, and to put Anne Boleyn on the throne was to advance one who would assuredly have the King under her influence, and who was undoubtedly—if not eager to destroy him—eager to remove him from that high place to which years of work had brought him.

But he was Wolsey the diplomat, so he wrote to the Pope extolling the virtues of Anne Boleyn.

Anne herself had returned to court a changed person. Now she must accept the adulation of all; there were those who, disliking her hitherto, now eagerly sought her favour; she was made to feel that she was the most important person at court, for even the King treated her with deference.

She was nineteen—a girl, in spite of an aura of sophistication. Power was sweet, and if she was a little imperious it was because of remembered slights when she had been considered not good enough for Percy—she who was to be Queen of England. If she was a little hard, it was because life had been unkind to her, first with Percy, then with Wyatt. If she were inclined to be over-fond of admiration and seek it where it was unwise to do so, was not her great beauty responsible? She was accomplished and talented, and it was but human that she should wish to use these gifts. Very noble it might seem for Queen Katharine to dress herself in sober attire; she was aging and shapeless, and never, even in her youth, had she been beautiful. Anne's body was perfectly proportioned, her face animated and charming; it was as natural for her to adorn herself as it was for Wyatt to write verses, or for the King in his youth to tire out many horses in one day at the hunt. People care about doing things which they do well, and had Katharine possessed the face and figure of Anne, doubtless she would have spent more time at her mirror and a little less with her chaplain. And if Anne offended some a little at this point, she was but nineteen, which is not very old; and she was gay by nature and eager to live an exciting, exhilarating and stimulating life.

Her pity for the Queen was diminished when that lady, professing friendship for her, would have her play cards every evening to keep her from the King, and that playing she might show that slight deformity on her left hand. Ah! These pious ones! thought Anne. Are they as good as they would seem? How often do they use their piety to hurt a sinner like myself!

She was over-generous perhaps, eager to share her good fortune with others, and one of the keenest joys she derived from her newly won power was the delight of being able to help the needy. Nor did she forget her uncle Edmund Howard but besought the King that something might be done for him. The King, becoming more devoted with each day and caring not who should know it, promised to give the Comptrollership of Calais to her uncle. This was pleasant news to her; and she enjoyed many similar pleasures.

But she, seeming over-gay, not for one moment relaxed in the cautious game she must continue to play with the King; for the divorce was long in coming, and the King's desire was hard to check; forever must she be on her guard with him, since it was a difficult game with a dangerous opponent.

Nor did she forget it, for with her quickness of mind very speedily did she come to know her royal lover; and there were times in this gay and outwardly butterfly existence when fears beset her.

Wyatt, reckless and bold, hovered about her, and though she knew it was unwise to allow his constant attendance, she was very loath to dismiss him from her companionship. Well she had kept her secret, and Wyatt did not yet know of the talk of marriage which had taken place between her and the King. Wyatt himself was similar to Anne in character, so that the relationship between them often seemed closer than that of first cousin. He was reckoned the handsomest man at court; he was certainly the most charming. Impulsive as Anne herself, he would slip unthinking into a dangerous situation.

There was such an occasion when he was playing bowls with the King. The Duke of Suffolk and Sir Francis Bryan completed the quartet. There was a dispute over the game, which any but Wyatt would have let pass; not so Wyatt; he played to win, as did the King, and he would not allow even Henry to take what was not his. Henry was sure he had beaten Wyatt in casting the bowl. Wyatt immediately replied: "Sire, by your leave, it is not so."

The King turned his gaze upon this young man whom he could not help but like for his charm, his gaiety and his wit; his little eyes travelled over Wyatt's slim body, and he remembered that he had seen him but that morning hovering about Anne. Wyatt was handsome, there was no denying that. Wyatt wrote excellent verses. The King also wrote verses. He was a little piqued by Wyatt's fluency. And Anne? He had heard it whispered, before it was known that such whispers would madden him, that Wyatt was in love with Anne.

He was suddenly angry with Wyatt. He had dared to raise a dispute over a game. He had dared write better verses than Henry. He had dared to cast his eyes on Anne Boleyn, and was young enough, handsome enough, plausible enough to turn any girl's head.

Significantly, and speaking in the parables he so loved to use, Henry made a great show of pointing with his little finger on which was the ring Anne had given him. Wyatt saw the ring, recognized it and was nonplussed; and that again added fuel to Henry's anger. How dared Wyatt know so well a ring which had been Anne's! How often, wondered Henry, had he lifted her hand to his lips!

"Wyatt!" said the King; and smiling complacently and significantly: "I tell thee it is mine!"

Wyatt, debonair, careless of consequences, looked for a moment at the ring and with a nonchalant air brought from his pocket the chain on which hung the tablet he had taken from Anne. He said with equal significance to that used by the King: "And if it may please Your Majesty to give me leave to measure the cast with this, I have good hopes yet it will be mine!"

Gracefully he stooped to measure, while Henry, bursting with jealous fury, stood by.

"Ah!" cried Wyatt boldly. "Your Majesty will see that I am right. The game is mine!"

Henry, his face purple with fury, shouted at Wyatt: "It may be so, but then I am deceived!" He left the players staring after him.

"Wyatt," said Bryan, "you were ever a reckless fool! Why did you make such a pother about a paltry game?"

But Wyatt's eyes had lost their look of triumph; he shrugged his shoulders. He knew that he had lost, and guessed the ring Anne had given the King to be a symbol.

Henry stormed into the room where Anne was sitting with some of the ladies. The ladies rose at his entrance, curtseyed timidly, and were quick to obey the signal he gave for their departure.

"Your Majesty is angry," said Anne, alarmed.

"Mistress Anne Boleyn," said the King, "I would know what there is betwixt thee and Wyatt."

"I understand not," she said haughtily. "What should there be?"

"That to make him boast of his success with you."

"Then he boasts emptily."

He said: "I would have proof of that."

She shrugged her shoulders. "You mean that you doubt my words."

She was as quick to anger as he was, and she had great power over him because, though he was deeply in love with her, she was but in love with the power he could give her, and she was as yet uncertain that this honour was what she asked of life. That was the secret of her power over him. She wavered, swaying away from him, and he, bewitched and inflamed with the strong sexual passion which coloured his whole existence, was completely at her mercy.

He said: "Anne, I know well that you would speak the truth. But tell me now with good speed, sweetheart, that there is naught between you and Wyatt."

"You would blame me," she said haughtily, "since he writes his verse to me?"

"Nay, sweetheart. I would blame you for nothing. Tell me now that I have naught to fear from this man, and restore my happiness."

"You have naught to fear from him."

"He had a jewelled tablet of yours."

"I remember it. He took it one day; he would not return it, and I, valuing it but little, did not press the matter."

He sat heavily beside her on the window seat, and put an arm about her.

"You have greatly pleased me, sweetheart. You must excuse my jealousy."

"I do excuse it," she said.

"Then all is well." He kissed her hand hungrily, his eyes asking for much that his lips dared not. He had angered her; he could not risk doing so again, for he sensed the uncertainty in her. Thus he marvelled at his infatuation for this girl; as did the court. He had never loved like this; nay, he had never loved before. He was thirty-six, an old thirty-six in some ways, for he lived heartily; this was the last flare-up of youth, and the glow lighted everything about him in fantastic colours. He was the middle-aged man in love with youth; he felt inexpressibly tender towards her; he was obsessed by her; he chafed against the delay of the divorce.

After this affair of the bowls, Anne knew she was committed. Wyatt's glance was sardonic now; Wyatt was resigned. She had chosen the power and the glory; his rival had tempted her with the bait of marriage.

> "And wilt thou leave me thus
> That hath loved thee so long
> In wealth and woe among:
> And is thy heart so strong
> As for to leave me thus?"

Her heart must be strong; she must cultivate ambition; she must tread warily, since in that court of glittering men and women she now began to find her enemies, and if their malice was cloaked in soft words, they were nonetheless against her. The Cardinal, watchful and wary; the Duke of Suffolk and his wife—that Mary with whom she had gone to France—who now saw her throwing a shadow over the prospects of their descendants' claim to the throne; Chapuys, the Spaniard who was more of a spy for his master, the Emperor Charles, than his ambassador; Katharine, the Queen whom she would displace; Mary, the princess who would be branded as illegitimate. All these there were in high places to fight against her. There was a more dangerous enemy still—the people of London. Discontent was rampant in the city; the harvest had been a poor one, and the sober merchants felt that an alliance with France was folly, since it merely changed old friends for new ones who had previously shown they were not to be trusted. There was famine throughout the country, and though the King might lend to the city corn from his own granaries, still the people murmured. The cloth merchants fretted, for the trouble with Spain meant losing the great Flanders market. The County of Kent petitioned the King, in view of their poverty, to repay a loan made to him two years before. The Archbishop of Canterbury did what he could to soothe these people, but they remained restive.

For these troubles did the people of England blame Wolsey. During the prosperous years the King received the homage of his subjects; he had been taken to their hearts during the period of his coronation when he, a magnificent figure of an Englishman, fair and tall and skilled in sport, had ridden among them—such a contrast to his ugly, mean old father. During the dark years, however, they blamed Wolsey; for Wolsey had committed the sin of being of the people and rising above them. The whispers went round: "Which court? Hampton Court or the King's court?" This was the twilight hour of Wolsey's brilliant day. And the starving and wretched gazed at a bright and beautiful girl, reclining in her barge or riding out with friends from court; more gaily dressed than the other ladies, she sparkled with rich jewels, presents from the King—a sight to raise the wrath of a starving people. "We'll have none of Nan Bullen!" they murmured together. "The King's whore shall not be our queen. Queen Katharine forever!"

From the choked gutters there arose evil smells; decaying matter lay about for weeks; rats, tame as cats, walked the cobbles; overhanging gables, almost touching across narrow streets, shut out the sun and air, held in the vileness. And in those filthy streets men and women were taken suddenly sick; many died in the streets, the sweat pouring from their bodies; and all men knew that the dreaded sweating sickness had returned to England. Thus did the most sorely afflicted people of London wonder at this evil which had fallen upon them; thus did they murmur against her who by her witch's fascination had turned the King from his pious ways. The sick and suffering of London whispered her name; the rebellious people of Kent talked of her; in the weaving counties her name was spoken with distaste. Everywhere there was murmuring against the devil's instrument, Wolsey, and her who had led the King into evil ways and brought down the justice of heaven upon their country. Even at Horsham, where the news of the sweating sickness had not yet reached, they talked of Anne Boleyn. The old Duchess chuckled in great enjoyment of the matter.

"Come here, Catherine Howard. Rub my back. I declare I

must be full of lice or suffering from the itch! Rub harder, child. Ah! Fine doings at the court, I hear. The King is bewitched, it seems, by your cousin Anne Boleyn, and I am not greatly surprised to hear it. I said, when she came visiting me at Lambeth: 'Ah! There is a girl the King would like!' Though I will say I added that he might feel inclined to spank the haughtiness out of her before carrying her off to bed. Don't scratch, child! Gently . . . gently. Now I wonder if . . ." The Duchess giggled. "You must not look so interested, child, and I should not talk to you of such matters. Why, of course . . . As if he would not . . . From what I know of His Majesty . . . Though there are those that say . . . It is never wise to give in . . . and yet what can a poor girl do . . . and look how Mary kept him dancing attendance all those years! There is something about the Boleyns, and of course it comes from the Howards . . . though I swear I see little of it in you, child. Why, look at your gown! Is that a rent? You should make Isabel look after you better. And what do you do of nights when you should be sleeping? I declare I heard such a noise from your apartment that I was of good mind to come and lay about the lot of you. . . ."

It was merely the Duchess's talk; she would never stir from her bed. But Catherine decided she must tell the others.

"And your cousin, I hear, is to do something for your father, Catherine Howard. Oh, what it is to have friends at court! Why, you are dreaming there . . . rub harder! Or leave that . . . you may do my legs now."

Catherine was dreaming of the beautiful cousin who had

come to the house at Lambeth. She knew what it meant to be a king's favourite, for Catherine had a mixed knowledge; she knew of the attraction between men and women, and the methods in which such attraction was shown; of books she knew little, as the Duchess, always meaning to have her taught, was somehow ever forgetful of this necessity. The cousin had given her a jewelled tablet, and she had it still; she treasured it.

"One day," said the Duchess, "I shall go to Lambeth that I may be near my granddaughter who is almost a queen."

"She is not really your granddaughter," said Catherine. "You were her grandfather's second wife."

The Duchess cuffed the girl's ears for that. "What! And you would deny my relationship to the queen-to-be! She who is all but queen has never shown me such disrespect. Now do my legs, child, and no more impertinence!"

Catherine thought: Nor are you my real grandmother either! And she was glad, for it seemed sacrilege that this somewhat frowsy old woman—Duchess of Norfolk though she might be—should be too closely connected with glorious Anne.

When Catherine was in the room which she still shared with the ladies-in-waiting, she took out the jewelled tablet and looked at it. It was impossible in the dormitory to have secrets, and several of them wanted to know what she had.

"It is nothing," said Catherine.

"Ah!" said Nan. "I know! It is a gift from your lover."

"It is not!" declared Catherine. "And I have no lover."

"You should say so with shame! A fine big girl like you!" said a tall, lewd-looking girl, even bolder than the rest.

"I'll swear it is from her lover," said Nan. "Why, look! It has an initial on it—A. Now who is A? Think hard, all of you."

Catherine could not bear their guessings, and she blurted out: "I will tell you then. I have had it since I was a very little baby. It was given to me by my cousin Anne Boleyn."

"Anne Boleyn!" screamed Nan. "Why, of course, our Catherine is first cousin to the King's mistress!" Nan leaped off the bed and made a mock bow to Catherine. The others followed her example, and Catherine thrust away the tablet, wishing she had not shown it.

Now they were all talking of the King and her cousin Anne, and what they said made Catherine's cheeks flush scarlet. She could not bear that they should talk of her cousin in this way, as though she were one of them.

The incorrigible Nan and the lewd-faced girl were shouting at each other.

"We will stage a little play . . . for tonight. . . . You may take the part of the King. I shall be Anne Boleyn!"

They were rocking with laughter. "I shall do this. You shall do that. . . . I'll warrant we'll bring Her Grace up with our laughter. . . ."

"We must be careful. . . ."

"If she discovered . . ."

"Bah! What would she do?"

"She would send us home in disgrace."

"She is too lazy. . . ."

"What else? What else?"

"Little Catherine Howard shall be lady of the bedchamber!"

"Ha! That is good. She being first cousin to the lady. . . . Well, Catherine Howard, we have brought you up in the right way, have we not? We have trained you to wait on your lady cousin, even in the most delicate circumstances, with understanding and . . ."

"Tact!" screamed Nan. "And discretion!"

"She'll probably get a place at court!"

"And Catherine Howard, unless you take us with you, we shall tell all we know about you and . . ."

"I have done nothing!" said Catherine hastily. "There is nothing you could say against me."

"Ah! Have you forgotten Thomas Culpepper so soon then?"

"I tell you there was nothing. . . ."

"Catherine Howard! Have you forgotten the paddock and what he did there. . . ."

"It was nothing . . . nothing!"

Nan said firmly: "Those who excuse themselves, accuse themselves. Did you know that, Catherine?"

"I swear . . ." cried Catherine. And then, in an excess of boldness: "If you do not stop saying these things about Thomas, I will go and tell my grandmother what happens in this room at night."

Isabel, who had been silent amidst the noise of the others, caught her by her wrist.

"You would not dare. . . ."

"Don't forget," cried Nan, "we should have something to say of you!"

"There is nothing you could say. I have done nothing but look on. . . ."

"And enjoyed looking on! Now, Catherine Howard, I saw a young gentleman kiss you last evening."

"It was not my wish, and that I told him."

"Oh, well," said Nan, "it was not my wish that such and such happened to me, and I told him; but it happened all the same."

Catherine moved to the door. Isabel was beside her.

"Catherine, take no heed of these foolish girls."

There were tears in Catherine's eyes.

"I will not hear them say such things of my cousin."

"Heed them not, the foolish ones! They mean it not."

"I will not endure it."

"And you think to stop it by telling your grandmother?"

"Yes," said Catherine, "for if she knew what happened here, she would dismiss them all."

"I should not tell, Catherine. You have been here many nights yourself; she might not hold you guiltless. Catherine, listen to me. They shall say nothing of your cousin again; I will stop them. But first you must promise me that you will not let a word of what happens here get to your grandmother's ears through you."

"It is wrong of them to taunt me."

"Indeed it is wrong," said Isabel, "and it must not be. Trust me to deal with them. They are foolish girls. Now promise you will not tell your grandmother."

"I will not tell unless they taunt me to it."

"Then rest assured they shall not."

Catherine ran from the room, and Isabel turned to the girls who had listened open-eyed to this dialogue.

"You fools!" said Isabel. "You ask for trouble. It is well enough to be reckless when there is amusement to be had, but just to taunt a baby. . . . What do you achieve but the fear of discovery?"

"She would not dare to tell," said Nan.

"Would she not! She has been turning over in her baby mind whether she ought not to tell ever since she came here. Doubtless the saintly Thomas warned her it was wrong to tell tales."

"She dared not tell," insisted another girl.

"Why not, you fool? She is innocent. What has she done but be a looker-on? We should be ruined, all of us, were this known to Her Grace."

"Her Grace cares nothing but for eating, sleeping, drinking, scratching and gossip!"

"There are others who would care. And while she is innocent, there is danger of her telling. Now if she were involved . . ."

"We shall have to find a lover for her," said Nan.

"A fine big girl such as she is!" said the lewd-faced girl who had promised to take the part of Henry.

The girls screamed together lightheartedly. Only Isabel, aloof from their foolish chatter, considered this.

✦

The King sat alone and disconsolate in his private apartments. He was filled with apprehension. Through the southeastern corner of England raged that dread disease, the sweating sickness. In the streets of London men took it whilst walking; many died within a few hours. People looked suspiciously one at the other. Why does this come upon us to add to our miseries! Poverty we have; famine; and now the sweat! Eyes were turned to the palaces, threatening eyes; voices murmured: "Our King has turned his lawful wife from his bed, that he might put there a witch. Our King has quarrelled with the holy Pope. . . ."

Wolsey had warned him, as had others of his council: "It would be well to send Mistress Anne Boleyn back to her father's castle until the sickness passes, for the people are murmuring against her. It might be well if Your Majesty appeared in public with the Queen."

Angry as the King had been, he realized there was wisdom in their words.

"Sweetheart," he said, "the people are murmuring against us. This matter of divorce, which they cannot understand, is at the heart of it. You must go to Hever for awhile."

She, with the recklessness of youth, would have snapped her

fingers at the people. "Ridiculous," she said, "to associate this sickness with the divorce! I do not want to leave the court. It is humiliating to be sent away in this discourteous manner."

Was ever a man so plagued, and he a king! To his face she had laughed at his fears, despising his weakness in bowing to his ministers and his conscience. She would have defied the devil, he knew. He had forced himself to be firm, begging her to see that it was because he longed for her so desperately that he wished this matter of the divorce concluded with the minimum of trouble. Ever since she had gone he had been writing letters to her, passionate letters in which he bared his soul, in which he clearly told her more than it was wise to tell her. "Oh," he wrote. "Oh, that you were in my arms!" He was not subtle with the pen; he wrote from the heart. He loved her; he wanted her with him. He told her these things, and so did he, the King of England, place himself at the mercy of a girl of nineteen.

He believed, with his people, that the sweat was a visitation from heaven. It had come on other occasions; there had been one epidemic just before his accession to the throne. Ominous this! Was God saying he was not pleased that the Tudors should be the heirs of England? Again it had come in 1517, at about the time when Martin Luther was denouncing Rome. Was it God's intention to support the German, and did He thus show disapproval of those who followed Rome? He had heard his father's speaking of its breaking out after Bosworth . . . and now, here it was again when Henry was thinking of divorce.

Assuredly it was alarming to contemplate these things!

So he prayed a good deal; he heard mass many times a day. He prayed aloud and in his thoughts. "Thou knowest it was not for my carnal desires that I would make Anne my wife. There is none I would have for wife but Katharine, were I sure that she was my wife, that I was not sinning in continuing to let her share my bed. Thou knowest that!" he pleaded. "Thou hast taken William Carey, O Lord. Ah! He was a complaisant husband to Mary, and mayhap this is his punishment. For myself, I have sinned in this matter and in others, as Thou knowest, but always I have confessed. I have repented. . . . And if I took William's wife, I gave him a place at court beyond his deserts, for, as Thou knowest, he was a man of small ability."

All his prayers and all his thoughts were tinged with his desire for Anne. "There is a woman who will give sons to me and to England! That is why I would elevate her to the throne." It was reassuring to be able to say, "England needs my sons!" rather than, "I want Anne."

Henry was working on his treatise, in which he was pointing out the illegality of his marriage, and which he would dispatch to the Pope. He was proud of it; for its profound and wise arguments; its clarity; its plausibility; its literary worth. He had shown what he had done to Sir Thomas More; had eagerly awaited the man's compliments; but More had merely said that he could not judge it since he knew so little of such matters. Ah! thought Henry. Professional jealousy, eh! And he had scowled at More, feeling suddenly a ridiculous envy of the man, for there was in More an agreeable humour, deep learning, wit, charm and a serenity of mind which showed in his countenance. Henry had been entertained at More's riverside house; had walked in the pleasant garden and watched More's children feed his peacocks; had seen this man in the heart of his family, deeply loved and reverenced by them; he had watched his friendship with men like the learned Erasmus, the impecunious Hans Holbein who, poor as he might be, knew well how to wield a brush. And being there, he the King—though he could not complain that they gave him not his rightful homage—had been outside that magic family circle, though Erasmus and Holbein had obviously been welcomed into it.

A wild jealousy had filled his heart for this man More who was known for his boldness in stating his opinions, for his readiness to crack a joke, for his love of literature and art, and for his practical virtue. Henry could have hated this man, had the man allowed him to, but ever susceptible to charm in men as well as women, he had fallen a victim to the charm of Sir Thomas More; and so he found, struggling in his breast, a love for this man, and even when More refused to praise his treatise, and even though he knew More was amongst those who did not approve of the divorce, he must continue to respect the man and seek his friendship. How many of his people, like More, did not approve of the divorce! Henry grew hot with righteous indignation and the desire to make them see this matter in the true light.

He had written a moralizing letter to his sister Margaret of

Scotland, accusing her of immorality in divorcing her husband on the plea that her marriage had not been legal, thus making her daughter illegitimate. He burned with indignation at his niece's plight while he—at that very time—was planning to place his daughter Mary in a similar position. He did this in all seriousness, for his thoughts were governed by his muddled moral principles. He saw himself as noble, the perfect king; when the people murmured against Anne, it was because they did not understand! He was ready to sacrifice himself to his country. He did not see himself as he was, but as he wished himself to be; and, surrounded by those who continually sought his favour, he could not know that others did not see him as he wished to be seen.

One night during this most unsatisfactory state of affairs occasioned by Anne's absence, an express messenger brought disquieting news.

"From Hever!" roared the King. "What from Hever?"

And he hoped for a letter, for she had not answered his in spite of his entreaties, a letter in which she was more humble, in which she expressed a more submissive mood of sweet reasonableness. It was not however a letter, but the alarming news that Anne and her father had taken the sickness, though mildly. The King was filled with panic. The most precious body in his kingdom was in danger. Carey had died. Not Anne! he prayed. Not Anne!

He grew practical; grieving that his first physician was not at hand, he immediately dispatched his second, Doctor Butts, to Hever. Desperately anxious, he awaited news.

He paced his room, forgetting his superstitious fears, forgetting to remind God that it was just because she was healthy and could give England sons that he proposed marrying her; he thought only of the empty life without her.

He sat down, and poured out his heart to her in his direct and simple manner.

"The most displeasing news that could occur came to me suddenly at night. On three accounts I must lament it. One, to hear of the illness of my mistress whom I esteem more than all the world, and whose health I desire as I do mine own; I would willingly bear half of what you suffer to cure you. The second, from the fear that I shall have to endure thy wearisome absence much longer, which has hitherto given me all the vexation that was possible. The third, because my physician (in whom I have most confidence) is absent at the very time when he could have given me the greatest pleasure. But I hope, by him and his means, to obtain one of my chief joys on earth; that is the cure of my mistress. Yet from the want of him I send you my second (Doctor Butts) and hope he will soon make you well. I shall then love him more than ever. I beseech you to be guided by his advice in your illness. By your doing this, I hope soon to see you again. Which will be to me a greater comfort than all the precious jewels in the world.

"Written by the hand of that secretary who is, and forever will be, your loyal and most assured servant. H.R."

And having written and dispatched this, he must pace his apartment in such anxiety as he had never known, and marvel that there could be such a thing as love, all joy and sorrow, to assail even the hearts of princes.

∗

The Queen was jubilant. Was this God's way of answering her prayers? She rejoiced with her daughter, because Anne Boleyn lay ill of the sweating sickness at Hever.

"Oh," cried the Queen to her young daughter, "this is the vengeance of the Lord. This is a judgment on the girl's wickedness."

Twelve-year-old Mary listened wide-eyed, thinking her mother a saint.

"My father . . ." said the girl, "loves he this woman?"

Her mother stroked her hair. Loving her dearly, she had until now superintended her education, kept her with her, imbued her with her own ideas of life.

"He thinks to do so, daughter. He is a lusty man, and thus it is with men. It is no true fault of his; she is to blame."

"I have seen her about the court," said Mary, her eyes narrowed, picturing Anne as she had seen her. That was how witches looked, thought Mary; they had flowing hair and huge dark eyes, and willowy bodies which they loved to swath in scarlet; witches looked like Anne Boleyn!

"She should be burned at the stake, Mother!" said Mary.

"Hush!" said her mother. "It is not meet to talk thus. Pray for her, Mary. Pity her, for mayhap at this moment she burns in hell."

Mary's eyes were glistening; she hoped so. She had a vivid picture of flames the colour of the witch's gown licking her white limbs; in her imagination she could hear the most melodious voice at court, imploring in vain to be freed from hideous torment.

Mary understood much. This woman would marry her father; through her it would be said that Mary's mother was no wife, and that she, Mary, was a bastard. Mary knew the meaning of that; she would no longer be the Princess Mary; she would no longer receive the homage of her father's subjects; she would never be Queen of England.

Mary prayed each night that her father would tire of Anne, that he would banish her from the court, that he would grow to hate her, commit her to the Tower where she would be put in a dark dungeon to be starved and eaten by rats, that she might be put in chains, that her body might be grievously racked for every tear she had caused to fall from the eyes of Mary's saintly mother.

Mary had something of her father in her as well as of her mother; her mother's fanaticism perhaps, but her father's cruelty and determination.

Once her mother had said: "Mary, what if your father should make her his queen?"

Mary had answered proudly: "There could be but one Queen of England, Mother."

Katharine's heart had rejoiced, for deeply, tenderly, she loved her daughter. While they were together there could not be complete despair. But all their wishes, all their prayers, were without effect.

When the news came to Henry that Anne had recovered, he embraced the messenger, called for wine to refresh him, fell on his knees and thanked God.

"Ha!" said he to Wolsey. "This is a sign! I am right to marry the lady; she will give me many lusty sons."

Poor Katharine! She could but weep silently; and then her bitterness was lost in fear, for her daughter had taken the sickness.

Anne convalesced at Hever. At court she was spoken of continually. Du Bellay, the witty French ambassador, joked in his light way. He wagered the sickness of the lady had spoiled her beauty in some measure; he was certain that during her absence some other one would find a way to the King's susceptible heart. Chapuys, the Spanish ambassador, laughed with him, and gleefully wrote to his master of the "concubine's" sickness. Blithely he prophesied an end of this—in Spain's eyes—monstrous matter of the divorce.

But Henry did not wait for her convalescence to end. How could he wait much longer! He had waited enough already. Privately he would ride from Greenwich or from Eltham to Hever Castle, and Anne, from the castle grounds, hearing his bugle call on a nearby hill, would go out to meet him. They would walk the gallery together, or sit in the oak-panelled chamber while he told her how the matter of the divorce progressed; he would talk of his love, would demand in fierce anger—or meek supplication—why now she could not make him the happiest of men.

And when the pestilence had passed over and she returned to court, Du Bellay reported to his government: "I believe the King to be so infatuated with her that God alone can abate his madness."

.✦.

Thomas Wolsey, knowing sickness of heart, feigned sickness of body. He knew his master; sentimental as a girl, and soft as wax in the fiery hands of Anne Boleyn.

Wolsey saw his decline, now, as clearly as he had so often seen the sun set; for him, though, there would be no rising again after the coming of night.

He did not complain; he was too wise for that. Well he knew that he had made his mistake, and where. He had humiliated her who had now the King's ear. And she was no soft, weak woman; she was strong and fierce, a good friend and a bad enemy. Oh! he thought, There is a night crow that possesses the royal ear and misrepresents all my actions.

He must not complain. He remembered the days of his own youth. He could look back to the humble life when he was tutor to the sons of Lord Marquess Dorset. Then there had been a certain knight, one Sir Amyas Pawlet, who had dared to humiliate young Wolsey; and had young Wolsey forgotten? He had not! Sir Amyas Pawlet grew to wish he had considered awhile before heaping indignities upon a humble tutor. So it was with Mistress Anne Boleyn and Thomas Wolsey. He could go to her; he could say: "I would explain to you. It was not I who wished to hurt you. It was not I who would have prevented your marriage with Percy. It was my lord King. I was but his servant in this matter." It might well be that she, who was noted for her generous impulses, would forgive him; it might be that she would not continue to plan against him. It might be . . . but she was not his only enemy. Her uncle Norfolk was with her in this matter; the Duke of Suffolk, also; and that Percy of Northumberland who had loved her and still brooded on his loss. These powerful men had had enough of Wolsey's rule.

He was very weary; defeated by this divorce, feigning sickness that he might appeal to the sentiment of the King, that he might make him sorry for his old friend; hiding himself away until Campeggio whom the Pope was sending from Rome was due to arrive. This was Wolsey in decline.

Foolishly he had acted over this matter of Eleanor Carey. He was in disgrace with the King over that matter, and he had received such a rebuke as he had never had before, and one which told him clearly that the King was no longer his to command. The night crow and her band of vultures watched him, waiting for his death. Yet stupidly and proudly he had acted over the Eleanor Carey affair; she was the sister-in-law of Anne, and with characteristic generosity, when the woman had asked Anne to make her Abbess of Wilton—which place had fallen vacant—Anne had promised she should have her wish. And he, Wolsey, had arrogantly refused Eleanor Carey and given the place to another. Thus was Mistress Anne's anger once more raised against him; how bitterly had she complained of his action to the King! Wolsey had explained that Eleanor was unfit for the post, having had two illegitimate children by a priest. Knowing that, Henry, whose attitude towards others was rigorously moral, must see the point of this refusal. Gently and with many apologies for the humiliation she had suffered in the matter, the King explained this to Anne. "I would not," wrote Henry to his sweetheart, "for all the gold in the world clog your conscience and mine to make her a ruler of a house. . . ."

Anne, who was by nature honest, had no great respect for her lover's conscience; she was impatient, and showed it; she insisted that Wolsey's arrogance should not be allowed to pass. And Henry, fearing to lose her, ready to give her anything she wished, wrote sternly to Wolsey; and that letter showed Wolsey more clearly than anything that had gone before that he was slipping dangerously, and he knew no way of gaining a more steady foothold on the road of royal favour.

Now at last he understood that she who had the King's ear was indeed a rival to be feared. And he was caught between Rome and Henry; he had no plans; he could see only disaster coming out of this affair. So he feigned sickness to give himself time to prepare a plan, and sick at heart, he felt defeat closing in on him.

The legate had arrived from Rome, and old gouty Campeggio was ready to try the case of the King and Queen. Crowds collected in the streets; when Queen Katharine rode out, she was loudly cheered, and so likewise was her daughter, Mary. Katharine, pale and wan from worry, Mary, pale from her illness, were martyrs in the eyes of the people of London; and the King begged Anne not to go abroad for fear the mob might do her some injury.

Anne was wretched, longing now to turn from this thorny road of ambition; not a moment's real peace had she known since she had started to tread it. The King was continually trying to force her surrender, and she was weary with the fight she must put up against him. And when Henry told her she must once more go back to Hever, as the trial was about to begin, she was filled with anger.

Henry said humbly: "Sweetheart, your absence will be hard to bear, but my one thought is to win our case. With you here . . ."

Her lips curled scornfully, for did she not know that he would plead his lack of interest in a woman other than his wife? Did she not know that he would tell the Cardinals of his most scrupulous conscience?

She was wilful and cared not; she was foolish, she knew, for did she not want the divorce? She was hysterical with fear sometimes, wishing fervently that she was to marry someone who was more agreeable to her, seeing pitfalls yawning at the feet of a queen.

"An I go back," she said unreasonably, "I shall not return. I will not be sent back and forth like a shuttlecock!"

He pleaded with her. "Darling, be reasonable! Dost not wish this business done with? Only when the divorce is complete can I make you my queen."

She went back to Hever, having grown suddenly sick of the palace, since from her window she saw the angry knots of people and heard their sullen murmurs. "Nan Bullen! The King's whore. . . . We want no Nan Bullen!"

Oh, it was shameful, shameful! "Oh, Percy!" she cried. "Why did you let them do this to us?" And she hated the Cardinal afresh, having convinced herself that it was he who, in his subtle, clever way, had turned the people against her. At Hever her father treated her with great respect—more respect than he had shown to Mary; Anne was not to be the King's mistress, but his wife, his queen. Lord Rochford could not believe in all that good fortune; he would advise her, but scornfully she rejected his advice.

Two months passed, during which letters came from the King reproaching her for not writing to him, assuring her that she was his entirely beloved; and at length telling her it would now be safe for her to return to court.

The King entreated her; she repeated her refusals to all the King's entreaties.

Her father came to her. "Your folly is beyond my understanding!" said Lord Rochford. "The King asks that you will return to court! And you will not!"

"I have said I will not be rushed back and forth in this uncourtly way."

"You talk like a fool, girl! Dost not realize what issues are at stake?"

"I am tired of it all. When I consented to marry the King, I thought 'twould be but a simple matter."

"When you consented . . . !" Lord Rochford could scarcely believe his ears. She spoke as though she were conferring a favour on His Majesty. Lord Rochford was perturbed. What if the King should grow weary at this arrogance of his foolish daughter!

"I command you to go!" he roared; which made her laugh at him. Oh, how much simpler to manage had been his daughter Mary! He would have sent Anne to her room, would have said she was to be locked in there, but how could one behave so to the future Queen of England!

Lord Rochford knew a little of this daughter. Wilful and unpredictable, stubborn, reckless of punishment, she had been from babyhood; he knew she wavered even yet. Ere long she would be telling the King she no longer wished to marry him.

"I command you go!" he cried.

"You may command all you care to!" And at random she added, "I shall not go until a very fine lodging is found for me."

Lord Rochford told the King, and Henry, with that pertinacity of purpose which he ever displayed when he wanted something urgently, called in Wolsey; and Wolsey, seeking to reinstate himself, suggested Suffolk House in place of Durham House, which the King had previously placed at her disposal.

"For, my lord King, my own York House is next to Suffolk House, and would it not be a matter of great convenience to you, if, while the lady is at Suffolk House, Your Highness lived at York House?"

"Thomas, it is a plan worthy of you!" The fat hand rested on the red-clad shoulder. The small eyes smiled into those of his Cardinal; the King was remembering that he had ever loved this man.

Anne came to Suffolk House. Its grandeur overawed even her, for it was the setting for a queen. There would be her ladies-in-waiting, her train-bearer, her chaplain; she would hold levees, and dispense patronage to church and state.

"It is as if I were a queen!" she told Henry, who was there to greet her.

"You are a queen," he answered passionately.

Now she understood. The fight was over. He who had waited so long had decided to wait no longer.

They would eat together informally at Suffolk House, he told her. Dear old Wolsey had lent him York House, next door, that he might be close and could visit her unceremoniously. Did she not think she had judged the poor old fellow too harshly?

There was about the King an air of excitement this day. She understood it, and he knew she understood it.

"Mayhap we judge him too hardly," she agreed.

"Darling, I would have you know that you must lack nothing. Everything that you would have as my queen—which I trust soon to make you—shall be yours." He put burning hands on her shoulders. "You have but to ask for what you desire, sweetheart."

"That I know," she said.

Alone in her room, she looked at herself in her mirror. Her heart was beating fast. "And what have you to fear, Anne Boleyn?" she whispered to her reflection. "Is it because after tonight there can be no turn back, that you tremble? Why should you fear? You are beautiful. There may be ladies at court with more perfect features, but there is none so intoxicatingly lovely, so ravishingly attractive as Anne Boleyn! What have you to fear from this? Nothing! What have you to gain? You have made up your mind that you will be Queen of England. There is nothing to fear."

Her eyes burned in her pale face; her beautiful lips were firm. She put on a gown of black velvet, and her flesh glowed as lustrous as the pearls that decorated it.

She went out to him, and he received her with breathless wonder. She was animated now, warmed by his admiration, his passionate devotion.

He led her to a table where they were waited upon discreetly; and this tête-à-tête meal, which he had planned with much thought, was to him complete happiness. Gone was her wilfulness now; she was softer; he was sure of her surrender; he had waited so long, he had lived through this so often in his dreams; but nothing he had imagined, he was sure, could be as wonderful as the reality.

He tried to explain his feelings for her, tried to tell her of how she had changed him, how he longed for her, how she was different from any other woman, how thoughts of her coloured his life; how, until she came, he had never known love. Nor had he, and Henry in love was an attractive person; humility was an ill-fitting garment that sat oddly on those great shoulders, but not less charming because it did not fit. He was tender instead of coarse, modest instead of arrogant; and she warmed towards him. She drank more freely than was her custom: she had confidence in herself and the future.

Henry said, when they rose from the table: "Tonight I think I am to be the happiest man on earth!" Apprehensively he waited for her answer, but she gave no answer, and when he would have spoken again he found his voice was lost to him; he had no voice, he had no pride; he had nothing but his great need of her.

She lay naked in her bed, and seeing her thus he was speechless, nerveless, fearful of his own emotion; until his passion rushed forth and he kissed her white body in something approaching a frenzy.

She thought: I have nothing to fear. If he was eager before, he will be doubly eager now. And, as she lay crushed by his great weight, feeling his joy, his ecstasy, she laughed inwardly and gladly, because now she knew there was to be no more wavering and she, being herself, would pursue this thing to the end.

His words were incoherent, but they were of love, of great love and desire and passion and pleasure.

"There was never one such as thee, my Anne! Never, never I swear . . . Anne, Queen Anne . . . my queen. . . ."

He lay beside her, this great man, his face serene and completely happy, so she knew how he must have looked when a very small boy; his face was purged of all that coarseness against which her fastidiousness had turned in disgust; and she felt she must begin to love him, that she almost did love him, so that on impulse she leaned over to him and kissed him. He seized her then, laughing, and told her again that she was beautiful, that she excelled his thoughts of her.

"And many times have I taken you, my queen, in my thoughts. Dost remember the garden at Hever? Dost remember thy haughtiness? Why, Anne! Why I did not take thee there and then I do not know. Never have I wanted any as I wanted thee, Anne, my queen, my little white queen!"

She could laugh, thinking: Soon he will be free, and I shall be truly queen . . . and after this he will never be able to do without me.

"Aye, and I wonder I was so soft with you, my entirely beloved, save that I loved you, save that I could not hurt you. Now you love me truly not as your King, you said, but as a man. . . . You love me as I love you, and you find pleasure in this, as I do. . . ."

And so he would work himself to a fresh frenzy of passion; so he would stroke and caress her, lips on her body, his hands at her hair and her throat and her breasts.

"There was never love like this!" said Henry of England to Anne Boleyn.

Happiest of Women

At Horsham there was preparation for the Christmas festivities; excitement was high in the ladies' dormitory. There should be a special Yuletide feast, they said, a good deal more exciting than that one which would be held in the great hall to be enjoyed by all; the ladies were busy getting together gifts for their lovers, speculating as to what they would receive.

"Poor little Catherine Howard!" they said, laughing. "She has no lover!"

"What of the gallant Thomas? Alas, Catherine! He soon forgot thee."

Catherine thought guiltily that, though she would never forget him, she had thought of him less during the last months; she wondered if he ever thought of her; if he did, he evidently did not think it necessary to let her know.

"It is unwise," said Isabel, "to think of those who think not of us."

In the Duchess's rooms, where Catherine often sat with her grandmother, the old lady fretted about the monotony of life in the country.

"I would we were at Lambeth. Fine doings I hear there are at court."

"Yes," answered Catherine, rubbing her grandmother's back. "My cousin is a most important lady now."

"That I swear she is! Ah! I wonder what Lord Henry Algernon Percy . . . I beg his pardon, the Earl of Northumberland . . . has to say now! He was too high and mighty to marry her, was he? 'Very well,' says Anne, 'I'll take the King instead.' Ha! Ha! And I declare nothing delights me more than to hear the haughty young man is being made wretched by his wife; for so does anyone deserve who thinks himself too fine for my granddaughter."

"The granddaughter of your husband," Catherine reminded her once more; and, was cuffed for her words.

"How I should like to see her at Suffolk House! I hear that she holds daily levees, as though she is already Queen. She dispenses charity, which is the Queen's task. There are those who storm against her, for, Catherine, my child, there will always be the jealous ones. Ah! How I should love to see my granddaughter reigning, at Greenwich! I hear the Queen was most discomfited, and that last Christmas Anne held her revels apart from those of Katharine—which either shocked or delighted all. Imagine her revels! Imagine poor Katharine's! Herself, my granddaughter, the centre of attraction, with George and

Wyatt and Surrey and Bryan with her; and who could stand up against them, eh? And the King so far gone in love, dear man, that everything she asks must be hers. Ah! How I should love to be there to see it! And Wolsey, that old schemer, trembling in his shoes, I dare swear. And so he should . . . trying to keep our sovereign lord from marrying her who should be his queen—for if ever woman was born to be a queen, that woman was my granddaughter Anne!"

"I should love to see her too," said Catherine wistfully. "Grandmother, when will you go to court?"

"Very soon. I make my plans now. Why, I have only to let her know my desires, and she would send for me. She was ever my favourite granddaughter, and it has always seemed to me that I was a favourite of hers. Bless her! God bless Queen Anne Boleyn!"

"God bless her!" said Catherine.

Her grandmother regarded the girl through narrowed eyes.

"I declare I never saw one so lacking in dignity. I would hear you play to me awhile, Catherine. Music is the only thing for which you seem to have the least aptitude. Go over and play me a tune."

Catherine eagerly went to the virginals; she hated the ministrations to her grandmother, and regretted that they must be an accompaniment to her racy conversation, which she always enjoyed.

The Duchess, her foot tapping, was only half listening, for her thoughts were far away, at Greenwich, at Eltham, at

Windsor, at Suffolk House, at York House. She saw her beautiful granddaughter, queening it in all these places; she saw the King, humble in his love; the colour, the music, the gorgeous clothes, the masques; the terror of that man Wolsey whom she had ever hated; and Anne, the loveliest woman in the kingdom, queen of the court.

To be there! To be favoured of her who was most favoured of the King! "My granddaughter, the Queen." To see her now and then, lovely, vital; to think of her, loved passionately by the King; mayhap to be on the best of terms oneself with His Majesty, for he would be kind to those beloved of his beloved; and Anne had always had a regard for her scandal-loving, lazy old grandmother—even if she were only the wife of her grandfather!

"I shall go to Lambeth!" said the Duchess. And little Catherine there should have a place at court, she thought. . . . Attendant to her cousin the Queen? Why not? As soon as this wearisome divorce was done with, she would go to Lambeth. And surely it would not be long now; it had been dragging on for more than two years; and now that the King's eyes were being opened to that Wolsey's wickedness, surely it could not be long.

Yes, little Catherine should have a place at court. But how very unfitted she was for that high honour! Anne, my child, you were at the French court at her age, a little lady delighting all who beheld you, I swear, with your grace and your charm and your delicious clothes and the way you wore them. Ah, Catherine Howard! You will never be an Anne Boleyn; one could not hope for that. Look at the child! Sitting humped over the virginals.

And yet she was not unattractive; she already had the air of a woman; her little body had that budding look which meant that Catherine might well flower early. But she had about her a neglected look, and it was that which made the Duchess angry. What right had Catherine Howard to look neglected! She lived in the great establishment of the Duchess; she was in the charge of the Duchess's ladies. Something should be done about the child, thought the Duchess, and knowing herself to blame—had she not often taken herself to task about the girl's education, promised herself that it should be attended to and then forgotten all about it?—she felt suddenly angry with Catherine, and rising from her chair, went over and slapped the girl at the side of her head.

Catherine stopped playing and looked up in surprise; she was not greatly disturbed by the blow, as the Duchess often cuffed her and there was no great strength in her flabby muscles.

"Disgraceful!" stormed the old lady.

Catherine did not understand. Playing musical instruments was one of the few things she did really well; she did not know that the Duchess, her thoughts far away at Suffolk House where another granddaughter was a queen in all but name, had not heard what she played; she thought that her playing was at fault, for how should she realize that the Duchess was comparing her with Anne and wondering how this child could possibly go to court uneducated as she was.

"Catherine Howard," said the Duchess, trying to convince herself that she was in no way to blame for the years of neglect, "you are a disgrace to this house! What do you think Queen Anne would say if I asked for a place at court for you—which she of course would find, since I asked it—and then I presented you to her . . . her cousin? Look at your hair! You are bursting forth from your clothes, and your manners are a disgrace! I declare I will give you such a beating as you never had, you untidy, ignorant little chit! And worse, it seems to me that were you less lazy, you might be quite a pretty girl. Now we shall begin your education in earnest; we are done with this dreaming away of the days. You will work, Catherine Howard, and if you do not, you shall answer to me. Did you hear that?"

"I did hear, Grandmother."

The Duchess rang a bell, and a serving maid appeared.

"Go bring to me at once young Henry Manox."

The maid complied, and in a very short time a young man with hair growing low upon his brow but a certain handsome swagger in his walk and an elegance about his person, combined with a pair of very bold black eyes to make him an attractive creature, appeared and bowed low before the Duchess.

"Manox, here is my granddaughter. I fear she needs much tuition. Now I would you sat down at the virginals and played awhile."

He flashed a smile at Catherine which seemed to suggest that they were going to be friends. Catherine, ever ready to respond to friendship, returned the smile, and he sat down and played most excellently, so that Catherine, loving music as she did, was delighted and clapped her hands when he ended.

"There, child!" said the Duchess. "That is how I would have you play. Manox, you shall teach my granddaughter. You may give her a lesson now."

Manox stood up and bowed. He came to Catherine, bowed again, took her hand and led her to the virginals.

The Duchess watched them; she liked to watch young people; there was something, she decided, so delightful about them; their movements were graceful. Particularly she liked young men, having always had a fondness for them from the cradle. She remembered her own youth; there had been a delightful music master. Nothing wrong about that of course; she had been aware of her dignity at a very early age. Still it had been pleasant to be taught by one who had charm; and he had grown quite fond of her, although always she had kept him at a distance.

There they sat, those two children—for after all he was little more than a child compared with her old age—and they seemed more attractive than they had separately. If Catherine were not so young, thought the Duchess, I should have to watch Manox; I believe he has quite a naughty reputation and is fond of adventuring with the young ladies.

Watching her granddaughter take a lesson, the Duchess thought: From now on I shall superintend the child's education myself. After all, to be cousin to the queen means a good deal. When her opportunity comes, she must be ready to take it.

Then, feeling virtuous, grandmotherly devotion rising within her, she told herself that even though Catherine was such a child, she would not allow her to be alone with one of Manox's reputation; the lessons should always take place in this room and she herself would be there.

For the thousandth time the Duchess assured herself that it was fortunate indeed that little Catherine Howard should have come under her care; after all, the cousin of a queen needs to be very tenderly nurtured, for who can say what honours may await her?

Anne was being dressed for the banquet. Her ladies fluttered about her, flattering her. Was she happy? she asked herself, as her thoughts went back over the past year which had seen her rise to the height of glory, and which yet had been full of misgivings and apprehensions, even fears.

She had changed; none knew this better than herself; she had grown hard, calculating; she was not the same girl who had loved Percy so deeply and defiantly; she was less ready with sympathy, finding hatreds springing up in her, and with them a new, surprising quality which had not been there before— vindictiveness.

She laughed when she saw Percy. He was changed from that rather delicate, beautiful young man whom she had loved; he was still delicate, suffering from some undefined disease; and such unhappiness was apparent in his face that should have made her weep for him. But she did not weep; instead she was filled with bitter laughter, thinking: You fool! You brought this on yourself. You spoiled your life—and mine with it—and now you must suffer for your folly, and I shall benefit from it!

But did she benefit? She was beginning to understand her royal lover well; she could command him; her beauty and her wit, being unsurpassed in his court, must make him their slave. But how long does a man, who is more polygamous than most, remain faithful? That was a question that would perplex her now and then. Already there was a change in his attitude towards her. Oh, he was deeply in love, eager to please, anxious that every little wish she expressed should be granted. But who was it now who must curse the delay, Anne or Henry? Henry desired the divorce; he wanted very much to remove Katharine from the throne and put Anne on it, but he was less eager than Anne. Anne was his mistress; he could wait to make her his wife. It was Anne who must rail against delay, who must fret, who must deplore her lost virtue, who must ask herself, Will the Pope ever agree to the divorce?

Sometimes her thoughts would make her frantic. She had yielded in spite of her protestations that she would never yield. She had yielded on the King's promise to make her queen; her sister Mary had exacted no promise. Where was the difference between Anne and Mary, since Mary had yielded for lust, and Anne for a crown! Anne had a picture of herself returning home to Hever defeated, or perhaps married to one as ineffectual as the late William Carey.

Henry had given Thomas Wyatt the post of High Marshal of Calais, which would take him out of England a good deal. Anne liked to dwell on that facet of Henry's character; he loved some of his friends, and Wyatt was one of them. He did not commit Wyatt to the Tower—which would have been easy enough—but sent him away. . . . Oh, yes, Henry could feel sentimental where one he had really loved was concerned, and Henry did love Thomas. Who could help loving Thomas? asked Anne, and wept a little.

Anne tried now to think clearly and honestly of that last year. Had it been a good year? It had—of course it had! How could she say that she had not enjoyed it—she had enjoyed it vastly! Proud, haughty, as she was, how pleasant it must be to have such deference shown to her. Aware of her beauty, how could she help but wish to adorn it! Such as Queen Katharine might call that vanity; is pride in a most unusual possession, then, vanity? Must she not enjoy the revels when she herself was acclaimed the shining light, the star, the most beautiful, the most accomplished of women, greatly loved by the King?

She had her enemies, the Cardinal the chief among them. Her uncle Norfolk was outwardly her friend, but she could never like and trust him, and she believed him now to be annoyed because the King had not chosen to favour his daughter the Lady Mary Howard, who was of so much nobler birth than Anne Boleyn. Suffolk! There was another enemy, and Suffolk was a dangerous, cruel man. Her thoughts went back to windy days and nights in Dover Castle, when Mary Tudor talked of the magnificence of a certain Charles Brandon. And this was he, this florid, cruel-eyed, relentless and ambitious man! An astute man, he had married the King's sister and placed himself very near the throne, and because a strange fate had placed Anne even nearer, he had become her enemy. These thoughts were frightening.

How happy she had been, dancing with the King at Greenwich last Christmas, laughing in the faces of those who would criticize her for holding her revels at Greenwich in defiance of the Queen; hating the Queen, who so obstinately refused to go into a nunnery and to admit she had consummated her marriage with Arthur! She had danced wildly, had made brilliantly witty remarks about the Queen and the Princess, had flaunted her supremacy over them—and afterwards hated herself for this, though admitting the hatred to none but the bright-eyed reflection which looked back at her so reproachfully from the mirror.

The Princess hated her and took no pains to hide the fact; and had not hesitated to whisper to those who had been ready to carry such talk to the ears of Anne, of what she would do to Anne Boleyn, were she queen.

"I would commit her to the Tower, where I would torture her; we should see if she would be so beautiful after the tormentors had done with her! I should turn the rack myself. We should see if she could make such witty remarks to the rats who came to the Pit to gnaw her bones and bite her to death. But I would not leave her to die that way; I would burn her alive. She is all but a witch, and I hear that she has those about her who are of the new faith. Aye! I would pile the faggots at her feet and watch her burn, and before she had burned, I would remove her that she might burn and burn again, tasting on earth that which she will assuredly meet in hell."

The eyes of the Princess, already burning with fanatical fervour, rested on Anne with loathing, and Anne laughed in the face of the foolish girl and feigned indifference to her, but those eyes haunted her when she was awake and when she slept. But even as she professed scorn and hatred for the girl, Anne well understood what her coming must have meant to Mary, who had enjoyed the privileges of being her father's daughter, Princess Mary and heiress of England. Now the King sought to make her but a bastard, of less importance than the Duke of Richmond, who was at least a boy.

As she lay in the King's arms, Anne would talk of the Princess.

"I will not be treated thus by her! I swear it. There is not room for both of us at court."

Henry soothed her while he put up a fight for Mary. His sentimental streak was evident when he thought of his daughter; he was not without affection for her and, while longing for a son, he had become—before the prospect of displacing Katharine had come to him, and Anne declared she would never be his mistress—reconciled to her.

Anne said: "I shall go back to Hever. I will not stay to be insulted thus."

"I shall not allow you to go to Hever, sweetheart. Your place is here with me."

"Nevertheless," said Anne coldly, "to Hever I shall go!"

The fear that she would leave him was a constant threat to Henry, and he could not bear that she should be out of his sight; she could command him by threatening to leave him.

When Mary fell into disgrace with her father, there were those who, sorry for the young girl, accused Anne of acute vindictiveness. It was the same with Wolsey. It was true that she did not forget the slights she had received from him, and that she pursued him relentlessly, determined that he should fall from that high place on which he had lodged himself. Perhaps it was forgotten by those who accused her that Anne was fighting a desperate battle. Behind all the riches and power, all the admiration and kingly affection which was showered upon her, Anne was aware of that low murmur of the people, of the malicious schemes of her enemies who even now were seeking to ruin her. Prominent among these enemies were Wolsey and Princess Mary. What therefore could Anne do but fight these people, and if she at this time held the most effective weapons, she merely used them as both Wolsey and Mary would have done, had they the luck to hold them.

But her triumphs were bitter to her. She loved admiration; she loved approval, and she wanted no enemies. Wolsey and she, though they flattered each other and feigned friendship, knew that both could not hold the high positions they aspired to; one must go. Anne fought as tenaciously as Wolsey had ever fought, and because Wolsey's star was setting and Anne's was rising, she was winning. There were many little pointers to indicate this strife between them, and perhaps one of the most significant—Anne was thinking—was the confiscation of a book of hers which had found its way into the possession of her equerry, young George Zouch. Anne, it was beginning to be known—and this knowledge could not please the Cardinal—was interested in the new religion which was becoming a matter of some importance on the Continent, and one of the reformers had presented her with Tindal's translation of the holy scriptures.

Anne had read it, discussed it with her brother and some of her friends, found it of great interest and passed it on to one of the favourite ladies of her retinue, for Mistress Gaynsford was an intelligent girl, and Anne thought the book might be of interest to her. However, Mistress Gaynsford was loved by George Zouch who, one day when he had come upon her quietly reading, to tease her snatched the book and refused to return it; instead he took it with him, to the King's chapel, where, during the service, he opened the book and becoming absorbed in its contents attracted the attention of the dean who, demanding to see it and finding it to be a prohibited one, lost no time in conveying it to Cardinal Wolsey. Mistress Gaynsford was terrified at the course of events, and went trembling to Anne, who, ever ready to complain against the Cardinal, told the King that he had confiscated her book and demanded its immediate return. The book was brought back to Anne at once.

"What book is this that causes so much pother?" Henry wanted to know.

"You must read it," Anne answered and added: "I insist!"

Henry promised and did; the Cardinal was disconcerted to learn that His Majesty was as interested as young George Zouch had been. This was a deeply significant defeat for Wolsey.

This year, reflected Anne as the coif was fixed upon her hair and her reflection looked back at her, had been a sorry one for the Cardinal. The trial had gone wrong. Shall we ever get this divorce, wondered Anne. The Pope was adamant; the people murmured: "Nan Bullen shall not be our queen!"

Henry would say little of what had happened at Blackfriars Hall, but Anne knew something of that fiasco; of Katharine's coming into the court and kneeling at the feet of the King, asking for justice. Anne could picture it—the solemn state, the May sunshine filtering through the windows, the King impatient with the whole proceedings, grey-faced Wolsey praying that the King might turn from the folly of his desire to marry Anne Boleyn, gouty old Campeggio procrastinating, having no intention of giving a verdict. The King had made a long speech about his scrupulous conscience and how—Anne's lips curled with scorn—he did not ask for the divorce out of his carnal desires, how the Queen pleased him as much as any woman, but his conscience . . . his conscience . . . his most scrupulous conscience. . . .

And the trial had dragged on through the summer months, until Henry, urged on by herself, demanded a decision. Then had Campeggio been forced to make a statement, then had he been forced to show his intention—which was, of course, not to grant the divorce at all. He must, he had said—to Henry's extreme wrath—consult with his master, the Pope. Then had Suffolk decided to declare open war on the Cardinal, for he had stood up and shouted: "It was never merry in England whilst we had cardinals among us!" And the King strode forth from the court in an access of rage, cursing the Pope, cursing the delay, cursing Campeggio and with him Wolsey, whom he was almost ready to regard as Campeggio's confederate. Anne's thoughts went to two men who, though obscure before, had this year leaped into prominence—the two Thomases, Cromwell and Cranmer. Anne thought warmly of them both, for from these two did she and Henry hope for much. Cranmer had distinguished himself because of his novel views, particularly on this subject of the divorce. He was tactful and discreet, clever and intellectual. As don, tutor, priest and Cambridge man, he was interested in Lutherism. He had suggested that Henry should appeal to the English ecclesiastical courts instead of to Rome on this matter of the divorce; he voiced this opinion constantly, until it had been brought to Henry's notice.

Henry, eager to escape from the meshes of Rome, was ready to welcome anyone who could wield a knife to cut him free. He liked what he heard of Cranmer. "By God!" he cried. "That man hath the right sow by the ear!"

Cranmer was sent for. Henry was crafty, clever enough when he gave his mind to a matter; and never had he given as much thought to anything as he had to this matter of the divorce. Wolsey, he knew, was attached to Rome, for Rome had its sticky threads about the Cardinal as a spider has about the fly in its web. The King was crying out for new men to take the place of Wolsey. There could never be another Wolsey; of that he was sure; but might there not be many who together could carry the great burdens which Wolsey had carried alone? When Cranmer had talked with Henry a few times, Henry saw great possibilities in the man. He was obedient, he was docile, he was a loyal; he was going to be of inestimable value to a Henry who had lost his Wolsey to the Roman web.

Anne's thoughts went to that other Thomas—Cromwell. Cromwell was of the people, just as Wolsey had been, but with a difference. Cromwell bore the marks of his origins and could not escape from them; Wolsey, the intellectual, had escaped, though there were those who said that he showed the marks of his upbringing in his great love of splendour, in his vulgar displays of wealth. (But, thought Anne, laughing to herself, had not the King even greater delight in flamboyant display!) Cromwell, however—thickset, impervious to insult, with his fish-like eyes and his ugly hands—could not hide his origins and made but little attempt to do so. He was serving Wolsey well, deploring the lack of fight he was showing. Cromwell was not over-nice; Henry knew this and, while seeing in him enormous possibilities, had never taken to him. "I love not that man!" said Henry to Anne. "By God! He has a touch of the sewer about him. He sickens me! He is a knave!"

There was a peculiar side to Henry's nature which grew out of an almost childish love and admiration for certain people, which made him seek to defend them even while he planned their destruction. He had had that affection for Wolsey, Wolsey the wit, in his gorgeous homes, in his fine clothes; he had liked Wolsey as a man. This man Cromwell he could never like, useful as he was; more useful as he promised to be. Cromwell was blind to humiliation; he worked hard and took insults; he was clever; he helped Wolsey, advised him to favour Anne's friends, placated Norfolk, and so secured a seat in parliament. Would there always be those to spring up and replace others when the King needed them? What if she herself lost the King's favour! It was simpler to replace a mistress than a Wolsey. . . .

Pretty Anne Saville, Anne's favourite attendant, whispered that she was preoccupied tonight. Anne answered that indeed she was, and had been thinking back over the past year.

Anne Saville patted Anne's beautiful hair lovingly.

"It has been a great and glorious year for your ladyship."

"Has it?" said Anne, her face so serious that the other Anne looked at her in sudden alarm.

"Assuredly," said the girl. "Many honours have come your ladyship's way, and the King grows more in love with you with the passing of each day."

Anne took her namesake's hand and pressed it for awhile, for she was very fond of this girl.

"And you grow more beautiful with each day," said Anne

Saville earnestly. "There is no lady in the court who would not give ten years of her life to change places with you."

In the mirror the coif glittered like a golden crown. Anne trembled a little; in the great hall she would be gayer than any, but up here away from the throng she often trembled, contemplating the night before her, and afraid to think further than that.

Anne was ready; she would go down. She would take one last look at herself—the Lady Anne Rochford now, for recently her father had been made Earl of Wiltshire, George became Lord Rochford, and she herself was no longer plain Anne Boleyn. The Boleyns had come far, she thought, and was reminded of George, laughing-eyed and only sad when one caught him in repose.

When she thought of George she would feel recklessness stealing over her, and the determination to live dangerously rather than live without adventure.

Thoughts of George were pleasant. She realized with a pang that of all her friends who now, with the King at their head, swore they would die for her, there was only one she could really trust. There was her father, her uncle Norfolk, the man who would be her husband . . . but on those occasions when Fear came and stood menacingly before her, it was of her brother she must think. "There is really none but George!"

"Thank God for George!" she said to herself, and dismissed gloomy thoughts.

In the great hall the King was waiting to greet her. He was magnificent in his favourite russet, padded and sparkling, larger than any man there, ruddy from the day's hunting, flushed already and flushing more as his eyes rested on Anne.

He said: "It seems long since I kissed you!"

"'Tis several hours, I'll swear!" she answered.

"There is none like you, Anne."

He would show his great love for her tonight, for of late she had complained bitterly of the lack of courtesy shown her by the Queen and Princess.

He had said: "By God! I'll put an end to their obstinacy. They shall bow the knee to you, sweetheart, or learn our displeasure!" The Princess should be separated from her mother, and they should both be banished from court; he had said last night that he was weary of them both; weary of the pious obstinacy of the Queen, who stuck to her lies and refused to make matters easy by going into a nunnery; weary of the rebellious daughter who refused to behave herself and think herself fortunate—she, who was no more than a bastard, though a royal one—in receiving her father's affection. "I tell thee, Anne," he had said, his lips on her hair, "I am weary of these women."

She had answered: "Need I say I am too?" And she had thought, they would see me burn in hell; nor do I blame them for that, for what good have I done them! But what I cannot endure is their attitude of righteousness. They burn with desire for revenge, and they pray that justice shall be dealt me; they pray to God to put me in torment. Hearty sinful vengeance I can forgive; but when it is hidden under a cloak of piety and called justice . . . never! Never! And so will I fight against these

250

two, and will not do a thing to make their lot easier. I am a sinner; and so are they; nor do sins become whiter when cloaked in piety.

But this she did not tell her lover, for was he not inclined to use that very cloak of piety to cover his sins? When he confessed what he had done this night, last night, would he not say: "It is for England; I must have a son!" Little eyes, greedy with lust; hot straying hands; the urgent desire to possess her again and again. And this, not that she might give the King pleasure, but that she should give England a son!

Was it surprising that sometimes in the early hours of the morning, when he lay beside her breathing heavily in sleep, his hand laid lightly on her body smiling as he slept the smile of remembrance, murmuring her name in his sleep—was it surprising that then she would think of her brother's handsome face, and murmur to herself: "Oh, George, take me home! Take me to Blickling, not to Hever, for at Hever I should see the rose garden and think of him. But take me to Blickling where we were together when we were very young . . . and where I never dreamed of being Queen of England."

But she could not go back now. She must go, on and on. I want to go on! I want to go on! What is love? It is ethereal, so that you cannot hold it; it is transient, so that you cannot keep it. But a queen is always a queen. Her sons are kings. I want to be a queen; of course I want to be a queen! It is only in moments of deepest depression that I am afraid.

Nor was she afraid this night as he, regardless of all these watching ladies and gentlemen, pressed his great body close to hers and showed that he was impatient for the night.

Tonight he wished to show her how greatly he loved her; that he wished all these people to pay homage to his beautiful girl who had pleased him, who continued to please him, and whom, because of an evil Fate in the shape of a weak Pope, an obstinate Queen, and a pair of scheming Cardinals, he could not yet make his queen.

He would have her take precedence over the two most noble ladies present, the Duchess of Norfolk and his own sister of Suffolk.

These ladies resented this, Anne knew, and suddenly a mood of recklessness came over her. What did she care! What mattered it, indeed. She had the King's love and none of her enemies dared oppose her openly.

The King's sister? She was aging now; different indeed from the giddy girl who had led poor Louis such a dance, who had alternated between her desire to bear a king of France and marry Brandon; there was nothing left to her but ambition; and ambition for what? Her daughter Frances Brandon? Mary of Suffolk wanted her daughter on the throne. And now here was Anne Boleyn, young and full of life, only waiting for the divorce to bear the King many sons and so set a greater distance between Frances Brandon and the throne of England.

And the Duchess of Norfolk? She was jealous, as was her husband, on account of the King's having chosen Anne instead of their daughter the Lady Mary Howard. She was angry because of Anne's friendship with the old Dowager Duchess of Norfolk.

What do I care? What have I to fear!

Nothing! For the King was looking at her with deep longing; nor could he bear that she should not be with him. She only had to threaten to leave him, and she could have both of these arrogant ladies banished from court.

So she was bold and defiant, and flaunted her supremacy in the faces of all those who resented her. Lady Anne Rochford, beloved of the King, leader of the revels, now taking precedence over the highest in the land as though she were already Queen.

She had seen the Countess Chateau-briant and the Duchess d'Estampes treated as princesses by poor little Claude at the court of Francis. So should she be treated by these haughty Duchesses of Norfolk and Suffolk; yes, and by Katharine of Aragon and her daughter Mary!

But of course there was a great difference between the French ladies and the Lady Anne Rochford. They were merely the mistresses of the King of France; the Lady Anne Rochford was to be Queen of England!

In her chair the Dowager Duchess of Norfolk dozed; her foot tapped automatically, but she was not watching the pair at the virginals. She was thinking of the court and the King's passion for that gorgeous lady, her dear granddaughter. Ah! And scheming Thomas now has his earldom and all that goes with it; and well pleased he is, I'll swear, for money means more to Thomas than aught else. And she is the Lady Anne Rochford, if you please, and George on very pleasant terms with the King . . . though not with his own sly little wife! Poor George! A pity there can't be a divorce. Why not a princess wife for your brother, eh, Queen Anne? Eh? Of course you are Queen! But she'll look after George . . . those two would stick together no matter what befell. Ah, how I wish she would send for me! I trow she would if she knew how eager I am to be gone. . . . What if I sent a messenger. . . . Ah! The court, the masques . . . though indeed I am a little old for such pleasures. Charming, if she came to visit me at Lambeth. . . . We would sit in the gardens, and I would make her talk to me of the King. . . . My granddaughter, the Queen of England! My granddaughter . . . Queen Anne . . .

She was asleep, and Henry Manox, sensing this, threw a sly glance over his shoulder at her.

"There!" said Catherine. "Was that better?"

He said, moving nearer to Catherine: "That was perfect!"

She flushed with pleasure, and he noticed the delicate skin and the long, fair lashes, and the charming strand of auburn hair that fell across her brow. Her youth was very appealing; he had never made love to one so young before; and yet, in spite of her youth, already she showed signs of an early ripening.

"Never," he whispered, "have I enjoyed teaching anyone as I have enjoyed our lessons!"

The Duchess snored softly.

Catherine laughed, and he joined in the laugh; he leaned forward suddenly and kissed the tip of her nose. Catherine felt a pleasurable thrill; it was exciting because it had to be done while the Duchess slept; and he was handsome, she thought, with his dark, bold eyes; and it was flattering to be admired by one so much older than herself; it was gratifying to be treated as though one were charming, after the reproaches her grandmother had showered upon her.

"I am glad I am a good pupil."

"You are a very good pupil!" he said. "Right glad I am that it is my happy lot to teach you."

"Her Grace, my grandmother, thinks me very stupid."

"Then it is Her Grace, your grandmother, who is stupid!"

Catherine hunched her shoulders, laughing.

"I take it, sir, that you do not then think me stupid."

"Indeed not; but young, very young, and there is much you have to learn yet."

The Duchess awoke with a start, and Catherine began to play.

"That was better," said the Duchess, "was it not, Manox?"

"Indeed, Your Grace, it was!"

"And you think your pupil is improving?"

"Vastly, Madam!"

"So thought I. Now you may go, Catherine. Manox, you may stay awhile and talk with me."

Catherine went, and he stayed and talked awhile; they talked of music, for they had nothing in common but music. But the Duchess did not mind of what her young men talked as long as they talked and entertained her. It was their youth she liked, it was their flattery. And as Manox talked to her, she drifted back to the days of her own youth, and then forward again to the court as it was today, ruled by her loveliest of granddaughters.

"Methinks I shall go to Lambeth," she announced, and dismissed Manox.

Catherine went to the apartment, where she found Isabel.

"How went the lesson?" asked Isabel.

"Very well."

"How you love your music!" said Isabel. "You look as if you had just left a lover, not a lesson."

Their talk was continually of lovers; Catherine did not notice this, as it seemed natural enough to her. To have lovers was not only natural but the most exciting possibility; it was all part of the glorious business of growing up, and now Catherine longed to be grown up.

She still thought of Thomas Culpepper, but she could only with difficulty remember what he looked like. She still dreamed that he rode out to Horsham and told her they were to elope together, but his face, which for so long had been blurred in her mind, now began to take on the shape of Henry Manox. She looked forward to her lessons; the most exciting moment of her days was when she went down to the Duchess's room and found him there; she was always terrified that he would not be there, that her grandmother had decided to find her a new teacher; she looked forward with gleeful anticipation to those spasmodic snores of the Duchess which set both her and Manox giggling, and made his eyes become more bold.

As he sat very close to her, his long musician's fingers would come to rest on her knee, tapping tightly that she might keep in time. The Duchess nodded; her head shook; then she would awake startled and look round her defiantly, as though to deny the obvious fact that she had dozed.

There was one day, some weeks after the first lesson, which was a perfect day, with spring in the sunshine filtering through the window, in the songs of the birds in the trees outside it, in Catherine's heart and in Manox's eyes.

He whispered: "Catherine! I think of you constantly."

"Have I improved so much then?"

"Not of your music, but of you, Catherine . . . of you."

"I wonder why you should think constantly of me."

"Because you are very sweet."

"Am I?" said Catherine.

"And not such a child as you would seem!"

"No," said Catherine. "Sometimes I think I am very grown up."

He laid his delicate hands on the faint outline of her breasts.

"Yes, Catherine, I think so too. It is very sweet to be grown up, Catherine. When you are a woman you will wonder how you could ever have borne your childhood."

"Yes," said Catherine, "I believe that. I have had some unhappy times in my childhood; my mother died, and then I went to Hollingbourne, and just when I was beginning to love my life there, that was over."

"Do not look so sad, sweet Catherine! Tell me, you are not sad, are you?"

"Not now," she said.

He kissed her cheek.

He said: "I would like to kiss your lips."

He did this, and she was astonished by the kiss, which was different from those Thomas had given her. Catherine was stirred; she kissed him.

"I have never been so happy!" he said.

They were both too absorbed in each other to listen for the Duchess's snores and heavy breathing; she awoke suddenly, and hearing no music, looked towards them.

"Chatter, chatter, chatter!" she said. "I declare! Is this a music lesson!"

Catherine began to play, stumbling badly.

The Duchess yawned; her foot began to tap; in five minutes she was asleep again.

"Do you think she saw us kiss?" whispered Catherine.

"Indeed I do not!" said Manox, and he meant that, for he well knew that if she had he would have been immediately turned out, possibly dismissed from the house; and Mistress Catherine would have received a sound beating.

Catherine shivered ecstatically.

"I am terrified that she might, and will stop the lessons."

"You would care greatly about that?"

Catherine turned candid eyes upon him. "I should care very much!" she said. She was vulnerable because her mind was that of a child, though her body was becoming that of a woman; and the one being so advanced, the other somewhat backward, it was her body which was in command of Catherine. She liked the proximity of this man; she liked his kisses. She told him so in many ways; and he, being without scruples, found the situation too novel and too exciting not to be exploited.

He was rash in his excitement, taking her in his arms before the sleeping Duchess and kissing her lips. Catherine lifted her face eagerly, as a flower will turn towards the sun.

The Duchess was sleeping, when there was a faint tap on the door and Isabel entered. The lesson had extended beyond its appointed time, and she, eager to see the teacher and pupil together, had an excuse ready for intruding. Isabel stood on the threshold, taking in the scene—the sleeping Duchess, the young man, his face very pale, his eyes very bright; Catherine, hair in some disorder, her eyes wide, her lips parted, and with a red mark on her chin. Where he has kissed her, the knave! thought Isabel.

The Duchess awoke with a start.

"Come in! Come in!" she called, seeing Isabel at the door.

Isabel approached and spoke to the Duchess. Catherine rose, and so did Manox.

"You may go, Catherine," said the Duchess. "Manox! Stay awhile. I would speak to you."

Catherine went, eager to be alone, to remember everything

he had said, how he had looked; to wonder how she was going to live through the hours until the next lesson on the morrow.

When Isabel was dismissed, she waited for Manox to come out.

He bowed low, smiling when he saw her, thinking that he had made an impression on her, for his surface charm and his reputation had made him irresistible to quite a number of ladies. He smiled at Isabel's pale face and compared it with Catherine's round childish one. He was more excited by Catherine than he had been since his first affair; for this adventuring with the little girl was a new experience, and though it was bound to be slow, and needed tact and patience, he found it more intriguing than any normal affair could be.

Isabel said: "I have never seen you at our entertainments."

He smiled and said that he had heard of the young ladies' revels, and it was a matter of great regret that he had never attended one.

She said: "You must come . . . I will tell you when. You know it is a secret!"

"Never fear that I should drop a hint to Her Grace."

"It is innocent entertainment," said Isabel anxiously.

"I could not doubt it!"

"We frolic a little; we feast; there is nothing wrong. It is just amusing."

"That I have heard."

"I will let you know then."

"You are the kindest of ladies."

He bowed courteously, and went on his way, thinking of Catherine.

✦

Through the gardens at Hampton Court Anne walked with Henry. He was excited, his head teeming with plans, for the Cardinal's palace was now his. He had demanded of a humiliated Wolsey wherefore a subject should have such a palace; and with a return of that wit which had been the very planks on which he had built his mighty career, the Cardinal, knowing himself lost and hoping by gifts to reinstate himself a little in the heart of the King, replied that a subject might build such a palace only to show what a noble gift a subject might make to his king.

Henry had been delighted by that reply; he had all but embraced his old friend, and his eyes had glistened to think of Hampton Court. Henry had inherited his father's acquisitive nature, and the thought of riches must ever make him lick his lips with pleasure.

"Darling," he said to Anne, "we must to Hampton Court, for there are many alterations I would make. I will make a palace of Hampton Court, and you shall help in this."

The royal barge had carried them up the river; there was no ceremony on this occasion. Perhaps the King was not eager for it; perhaps he felt a little shame in accepting this magnificent gift from his old friend. All the way up the river he laughed with Anne at the incongruity of a subject's daring to possess such a place.

"He was another king . . . or would be!" said Anne. "You were most lenient with him."

"'Twas ever a fault of mine, sweetheart, to be over-lenient with those I love."

She raised her beautifully arched eyebrows, and surveyed him mockingly.

"I fancy it is so with myself."

He slapped his thigh—a habit of his—and laughed at her; she delighted him now as ever. He grew sentimental, contemplating her. He had loved her long, nor did his passion for her abate. To be in love was a pleasant thing; he glowed with self-sacrifice, thinking: She shall have the grandest apartments that can be built! I myself will plan them.

He told her of his ideas for the alterations.

"Work shall be started for my queen's apartments before aught else. The hangings shall be of tissue of gold, sweetheart. I myself will design the walls." He thought of great lovers' knots with the initials H and A entwined. He told her of this; sentimental and soft, his voice was slurred with affection. "Entwined, darling! As our lives shall be and have been ever since we met. For I would have the world know that naught shall come between us two."

Unceremoniously they left the barge. The gardens were beautiful—but a cardinal's gardens, said Henry, not a king's!

"Dost know I have a special fondness for gardens?" he asked. "And dost know why?"

She thought it strange and oddly perturbing that he could remind her of his faithfulness to her here in this domain which he had taken—for the gift was enforced—from one to whom he owed greater loyalty. But how like Henry! Here in the shadow of Wolsey's cherished Hampton Court, he must tell himself that he was a loyal friend, because he had been disloyal to its owner.

"Red and white roses," said the King, and he touched her cheek. "We will have this like your father's garden at Hever, eh? We will have a pond, and you shall sit on its edge and talk to me, and watch your own reflection. I'll warrant you will be somewhat kinder to me than you were at Hever, eh?"

"It would not surprise me," she laughed.

He talked with enthusiasm of his plans. He visualized beds of roses—red and white to symbolize the union of the houses of York and Lancaster, to remind all who beheld them that the Tudors represented peace; he would enclose those beds with wooden railings painted in his livery colours of white and green; he would set up posts and pillars which should be decorated with heraldic designs. There would be about the place a constant reminder to all, including himself, that he was a faithful man; that when he loved, he loved deeply and long. H and A! Those initials should be displayed in every possible spot.

"Come along in, sweetheart," he said. "I would choose your apartments. They shall be the most lavish that were ever seen."

They went up the staircase, across a large room. It was Anne who turned to the right and descended a few steps into the panelled rooms which had been Wolsey's own. Henry had not wished to go into those rooms, but when he saw their splendid furnishings, their rich hangings, the magnificent plate, the window seats padded with red window carpets, the twisted gold work on the ceilings, he was loath to leave them. He had seen this splendour many times before; but then it had been Wolsey's, now it was his.

Anne pointed to the damask carpets which lay about the floors, and reminded the King of how, it was whispered, Wolsey had come by these.

Henry was less ready to defend his old favourite than usual. He recounted the story of the Venetian bribe, and his mouth was a thin line, though previously he had laughed at it, condoned it.

They went through the lavishly furnished bedrooms, admired the counterpanes of satin and damask, the cushions of velvet and satin and cloth of gold.

"Good sweetheart," said Henry, "I think your apartment shall be here, for I declare it to be the finest part of Hampton Court. The rooms shall be enlarged; I will have new ceilings; everything here shall be of the best. It shall be accomplished as soon as possible."

"It will take many years," said Anne, and added: "So therefore it is just possible that the divorce may be done with by then, if it ever is!"

He put an arm about her shoulders.

"How now, darling! We have waited long, and are impatient, but methinks we shall not wait much longer. Cranmer is a man of ideas . . . and that knave, Cromwell, too! My plans for your apartments may take a year or two completely to carry out, but never fear, long ere their accomplishment you shall be Queen of England!"

They sat awhile on the window seat, for the day was warm. He talked enthusiastically of the changes he would make. She listened but listlessly; Hampton Court held memories of a certain moonlit night, when she and Percy had looked from one of those windows and talked of the happiness they would make for each other.

She wondered if she would ever occupy these rooms which he planned for her. Wolsey had once made plans in this house.

"Our initials entwined, sweetheart," said the King. "Come! You shiver. Let us on."

In his house at Westminster, Wolsey awaited the arrival of Norfolk and Suffolk. His day was over, and Wolsey knew it; this was the end of his brightness; he would live the rest of his life in the darkness of obscurity, if he were lucky; but was it not a proven fact that when great men fell from favour their heads were not long in coming to the block? Those who lived gloriously must often die violently. Wolsey was sick, of mind and body; there was a pain in his solar plexus, a pain in his throat; and this was what men called heartbreak. And the most heartbreaking moment of his career was when he had arrived at Grafton with Campeggio, to find that there was no place for him at the court. For his fellow cardinal there were lodgings prepared in accordance with his state, but for Thomas Wolsey, once beloved of the King, there was no bed on which to rest his weary body. Then did he know to what depths of disfavour he had sunk. But for young Henry Norris, he knew not what he would have done; already had he suffered enough humiliation to break the heart of a proud man.

Norris, groom of the stole, a young handsome person with compassion in his pleasant eyes, had offered his own apartment to the travel-stained old man; such moments were pleasant in a wretched day. And yet, next day when he and Campeggio had had audience with the King, had not His Majesty softened to him, his little eyes troubled, his little mouth pursed with remembrance? Henry would never hate his old friend when he stood face to face with him; there were too many memories they shared; between them they had given birth to too many successful schemes for all to be forgotten. It is the careless, watching, speculating eyes which hurt a fallen man. He knew those callous courtiers laid wagers on the King's conduct towards his old favourite. Wolsey had seen the disappointment in their faces when Henry let his old affection triumph; and Lady Anne's dark eyes had glittered angrily, for she believed that the resuscitation of Wolsey's dying influence meant the strangulation of her own. Her beautiful face had hardened, though she had smiled graciously enough on the Cardinal; and Wolsey, returning her smile, had felt fear grip his heart once more, for what hope had he with such an enemy!

It had come to his ears, by way of those who had waited on her and the King when they dined, that she had been deeply offended by Henry's show of affection for the Cardinal; and she, bold and confident in her power over the King, did not hesitate to reprove him. "Is it not a marvellous thing," so he had heard she said, "to consider what debt and danger the Cardinal hath brought you in with your subjects?" The King was puzzled. "How so, sweetheart?" Then she referred to that loan which the Cardinal had raised from his subjects for the King's use. And she laughed and added: "If my lord Norfolk, my lord Suffolk, my lord my father, or any other noble person within your realm had done much less than he, they should have lost their heads ere this." To which the King answered: "I perceive ye are not the Cardinal's friend." "I have no cause!" she retorted. "Nor more any other that love Your Grace, if ye consider well his doings!"

No more had been heard at the table, but Wolsey knew full well how gratifying it would be for the King to imagine her hatred for the Cardinal had grown out of her love for the King. She was an adversary to beware of. He had no chance of seeing the King again, for the Lady Anne had gone off riding with him next morning, and had so contrived it that His Majesty did not return until the cardinals had left. What poison did this woman pour into his master's ears by day and night? But being Wolsey he must know it was himself whom he must blame; he it was who had taken that false step. He was too astute not to realize that had he been in Lady Anne's place he would have acted as she did now. Imagination had helped to lift him, therefore it was easy to see himself in her position. He could even pity her, for her road was a more dangerous one than his, and those who depend for prosperity upon a prince's favour—and such a prince—must consider each step before they take it, if they wish to survive. He had failed with the divorce, and looking back, that seemed inevitable, for as Cardinal he owed allegiance to Rome, and the King was straining to break those chains which bound him to the Holy See. He, who was shrewd, diplomatic, had failed. She was haughty, imperious, impulsive; what fate awaited her? Where she was concerned he had been foolish; he had lacked imagination. A man does not blame himself when enemies are made by his greatness; it is only when they are made by his folly that he does this. Perhaps humiliation was easier to bear, knowing he had brought it on himself.

His usher, Cavendish, came in to tell him that the Dukes of Norfolk and Suffolk had arrived. The Cardinal received them ceremoniously—the cold-eyed Norfolk, the cruel-eyed Suffolk, both rejoicing in his downfall.

"It is the King's pleasure," said Suffolk, "that you should hand over the Great Seal into our hands, and that you depart simply unto Esher."

Esher! To a house near splendid Hampton Court which was

his through the Bishopric of Winchester. He summoned all his dignity.

"And what commission have you, my lords, to give me such commandment?"

They said they came from the King, that they had received the commission from his royal mouth.

"Then that is not sufficient," said Wolsey, "for the Great Seal of England was delivered me by the King's own person, to enjoy during my life. I have the King's letters to show it."

The Dukes were angered by this reply, but seeing the King's letters, all they could do was return to Henry.

Wolsey knew he but put off the evil day. The Great Seal, the symbol of his greatness, remained in his hands for but one more day; on the morrow the Dukes returned from Windsor with letters from the King, and there was nothing more that Wolsey could do but deliver up the seal.

The ex-chancellor was filled with deep foreboding and set his servants to make inventories of all the rich possessions in his house; these goods he would give to the King, for if his master could not be touched by affection it might well be that he could by rich gifts; many times had Wolsey noted that the little eyes glinted with envy when they rested on these things. When a man is in danger of drowning, thought Wolsey, he throws off all his fine apparel that he may swim more easily. What are possessions, compared with life itself!

He took his barge at his privy stairs, having ordered horses to be awaiting him at Putney; and the river, he saw, was crowded with craft, for news had travelled quickly and there were those who find the spectacle of a fallen man pleasurable indeed. He saw their grins; he heard their jeers; he sensed the speculation, the disappointment that he was not going straightway to the Tower.

Riding through Putney town, he saw Norris coming towards him, and his heart was lightened, since he had come to look upon Norris as a friend. And so it proved, for the King's peace of mind had been profoundly disturbed by the story which Norfolk and Suffolk had told him of the giving up of the seal. The King could not forget that he had once loved Wolsey; he was haunted by a pale, sick face under a cardinal's hat; and he remembered how this man had been his friend and counsellor; and though he knew that he had done with Wolsey, he wanted to reassure his conscience that it was not he who had destroyed his old friend, but others. Therefore, to appease that conscience, he sent Norris to Putney with a gold ring which Wolsey would recognize by the rich stone it contained, as they had previously used this ring for a token. He was to be of good cheer, Norris told him, for he stood as high as ever in the King's favour.

Wolsey's spirits soared; his body gained strength; the old fighting spirit came back to him. He was not defeated. He embraced Norris, feeling great affection for this young man, and took a little chain of gold from his neck to give to him; on this chain there hung a tiny cross. "I desire you to take this small reward from my hand," he said, and Norris was deeply moved.

Then did the Cardinal look about his retinue; and saw one

who had been close to him, and in whom he delighted, for the man's wit and humour were of the subtlest, and many times had he brought mirth into the Cardinal's heaviest hours.

"Take my fool, Norris," he said. "Take him to my lord the King, for well I know His Majesty will like well the gift. Fool!" he called. "Here, Fool!"

The man came, his eyes wide with fear and with love for his master; and seeing this, the Cardinal leaned forward and said almost tenderly: "Thou shalt have a place at court, Fool."

But the fool knelt down in the mire and wept bitterly. Wolsey was much moved that his servant should show such love, since to be Fool to the King, instead of to a man who is sinking in disgrace, was surely a great step forward.

"Thou art indeed a fool!" said Wolsey. "Dost not know what I am offering thee?"

All foolery was gone from those droll features; only tears were in the humorous eyes now.

"I will not leave you, master."

"Didst not hear I have given thee to His Majesty?"

"I will not serve His Majesty. My lord, I have but one master."

With tears in his eyes the Cardinal called six yeomen to remove the man; and struggling, full of rage and sorrow, went the fool. Then on rode Wolsey, and when he reached his destination to find himself in that barren house in which there were not even beds nor dishes, plates nor cups, his heart was warmed that in this world there were those to love a man who is fallen from his greatness.

Lady Anne Rochford sat in her apartment, turning the leaves of a book. She had found this book in her chamber, and even as she picked it up she knew that someone had put it there that she might find it. As she looked at this book, the colour rose from her neck to her forehead, and she was filled with anger. She sat for a long time, staring at the open page, wondering who had put it there, how many of her attendants had seen it.

The book was a book of prophecies; there were many in the country, she knew, who would regard such prophecies as miraculous; it was alarming therefore to find herself appearing very prominently in them.

She called Anne Saville to her, adopting a haughty mien, which was never difficult with her.

"Nan!" she called. "Come here! Come here at once!"

Anne Saville came and, seeing the book in her mistress's hand, grew immediately pale.

"You have seen this book?" asked Anne.

"I should have removed it ere your ladyship set eyes on it."

Anne laughed.

"You should have done no such thing, for this book makes me laugh so much that it cannot fail to give me pleasure."

She turned the pages, smiling, her fingers steady.

"Look, Nan! This figure represents me . . . and here is the King. And here is Katharine. This must be so, since our initials are on them. Nan, tell me, I do not look like that! Look, Nan, do not turn away. Here I am with my head cut off!"

Anne Saville was seized with violent trembling.

"If I thought that true, I would not have him were he an emperor!" she said.

Anne snapped her fingers scornfully, "I am resolved to have him, Nan."

Anne Saville could not take her eyes from the headless figure on the page.

"The book is a foolish book, a bauble. I am resolved that my issue shall be royal, Nan. . . ." She added: "Whatever may become of me!"

"Then your ladyship is very brave."

"Nan! Nan! What a little fool you are! To believe a foolish book!"

If Anne Saville was very quiet all that day as though her thoughts troubled her, Lady Anne Rochford was especially gay, though she did not regard the book as lightly as she would have those about her suppose. She did not wish to give her enemies the satisfaction of knowing that she was disturbed. For one thing was certain in her mind—she was surrounded by her enemies who would undermine her security in every possible way; and this little matter of the book was but one of those ways. An enemy had put the book where she might see it, hoping thereby to sow fear in her mind. What a hideous idea! To cut off her head!

She was nervous; her dreams were disturbed by that picture in the book. She watched those about her suspiciously, seeking her enemies. The Queen, the Princess, the Duke and Duchess of Suffolk, the Cardinal . . . all of the most important in the land. Who else? Who had brought the book into her chamber?

Those about her would be watching everything she did; listening to everything she said. She felt very frightened. Once she awoke trembling in a cold sweat; she had dreamed that Wolsey was standing before her, holding an axe, and the blade was turned towards her. The King lay beside her, and terrified, she awoke him.

"I had an evil dream. . . ."

"Dreams are nothing, sweetheart."

She would not let him dismiss her dream so. She would insist that he put his arms about her, assure her of his undying love for her.

"For without your love, I should die," she told him. He kissed her tenderly and soothed her.

"As I should, without yours."

"Nothing could hurt you," she said.

"Nothing could hurt you, sweetheart, since I am here to take care of you."

"There are many who are jealous of your love for me, who seek to destroy me." She blurted out the story of her finding the book.

"The knave who printed it shall hang, darling. We'll have his head on London Bridge. Thus shall people see what happens to those who would frighten my sweetheart."

"This you say, but will you do it, when you suffer those who hate me to enjoy your favour?"

"Never should any who hated you receive my favour!"

"I know of one."

"Oh, darling, he is an old, sick man. He wishes you no ill. . . ."

"No!" she cried fiercely. "Has he not fought against us consistently! Has he not spoken against us to the Pope! I know of those who will confirm this."

She was trembling in his arms, for she felt his reluctance to discuss the Cardinal.

"I fear for us both," she said. "How can I help but fear for you too, when I love you! I have heard much of his wickedness. There is his Venetian physician, who has been to me. . . ."

"What!" cried the King.

"But no more! You think so highly of him that you will see him my enemy, and leave him to go unpunished. He is in York, you say. Let him rest there! He is banished from Westminster; that is enough. So in York he may pursue his wickedness and set the people against me, since he is of more importance to you than I am."

"Anne, Anne, thou talkest wildly. Who could be of more importance to me than thou?"

"Your late chancellor, my lord Cardinal Wolsey!" she retorted. She was seized with a wild frenzy, and drew his face close to hers and kissed him, and spoke to him incoherently of her love and devotion, which touched him deeply; and out of his tenderness for her grew passion such as he had rarely experienced before, and he longed to give her all that she asked, to prove his love for her and to keep her loving him thus.

He said: "Sweetheart, you talk with wildness!"

"Yes," she said, "I talk with wildness; it is only your beloved Cardinal who talks with good sense. I can see that I must not stay here. I will go away. I have lost those assets which were dearer to me than aught else—my virtue, my honour. I shall leave you. This is the last night I shall lie in your arms, for I see that I am ruined, that you cannot love me."

Henry could always be moved to terror when she talked of leaving him; before he had given her Suffolk House, she had so often gone back and forth to Hever. The thought of losing her was more than he could endure; he was ready to offer her Wolsey if that was the price she asked.

He said: "Dost think I should allow thee to leave me, Anne?"

She laughed softly. "You might force me to stay; you could force me to share your bed!" Again she laughed. "You are big and strong, and I am but weak. You are a king and I am a poor woman who from love of you has given you her honour and her virtue. . . . Yes, doubtless you could force me to stay, but though you should do this, you would but keep my body; my love, though it has destroyed me, would be lost to you."

"You shall not talk thus! I have never known happiness such as I have enjoyed with you. Your virtue . . . your honour! My God, you talk foolishly, darling! Shall you not be my queen?"

"You have said so these many years. I grow weary of waiting.

You surround yourself with those who hinder you rather than help. I have proof that the Cardinal is one of these."

"What proof?" he demanded.

"Did I not tell you of the physician? He knows that Wolsey wrote to the Pope, asking him to excommunicate you, an you did not dismiss me and take back Katharine."

"By God! And I will not believe it."

She put her arms about his neck, and with one hand stroked his hair.

"Darling, see the physician, discover for yourself. . . ."

"That will I do!" he assured her.

Then she slept more peacefully, but in the morning her fears were as strong as ever. When the physician confirmed Wolsey's perfidy, when her cousin Francis Bryan brought her papers which proved that Wolsey had been in communication with the Pope, had asked for the divorce to be delayed; when she took these in triumph to the King and saw the veins stand out on his forehead with anger against the Cardinal, still she found peace of mind elusive. She remembered the softness of the King towards this man; she remembered how, when he had lain ill at Esher, he had sent Butts, his physician—the man he had sent to her at Hever—to attend his old friend. She remembered how he had summoned Butts, recently returned from Esher, and had asked after Wolsey's health; and when Butts had said he feared the old man would die unless he received some token of the King's regard, then had the King sent him a ruby ring, and—greater humiliation—he had turned to her and bidden her send a token too. Such was the King's regard for this man; such was his reluctance to destroy him.

But she would not let her enemy live; and in this she had behind her many noblemen, at whose head were the powerful Dukes of Norfolk and Suffolk, men such as would let the grass grow under their feet in the matter. George had talked with her of Wolsey. "There will be no peace for us, Anne, while that man lives. For, if ever you had an enemy, that man is he!" She trusted George completely. He had said: "You can do this, Anne. You have but to command the King. Hesitate not, for well you know that had Wolsey the power to destroy you, he would not hesitate."

"That I do know," she answered, and was suddenly sad. "George," she went on, "would it not be wonderful if we could go home and live quietly, hated by none!"

"I would not wish to live quietly, sister," said George. "Nor would you. Come! Could you turn back now, would you?" She searched her mind and knew that he was right. "You were meant to be Queen of England, Anne. You have all the attributes."

"I feel that, but I could wish there were not so much hating to be done!"

But she went on hating furiously; this was a battle between herself and Wolsey, and it was one she was determined to win. Norfolk watched; Suffolk watched; they were waiting for their opportunity.

There was a new charge against the Cardinal. He had been guilty of asserting and maintaining papal jurisdiction in England.

Henry must accept the evidence; he must appease Anne; he must satisfy his ministers. Wolsey was to be arrested at Cawood Castle in York, whither he had retired these last months.

"The Earl of Northumberland should be sent to arrest him," said Anne, her eyes gleaming, This was to be. She went to her apartment, dismissed her ladies, and flung herself upon her bed overcome by paroxysms of laughter and tears. She felt herself to be, not the woman who aspired to the throne of England, but a girl in love who through this man had lost her lover.

Now he would see! Now he should know! "That foolish girl!" he had said. "Her father but a knight, and yours one of the noblest houses in the land . . ."

Her father was an earl now; and she all but Queen of England.

Oh, you wise Cardinal! How I should love to see your face when Percy comes for you! You will know then that you were not so wise in seeking to destroy Anne Boleyn.

✦

As the Cardinal sat at dinner in the dining-hall at Cawood Castle, his gentleman usher came to him and said: "My lord, His Grace, the Earl of Northumberland is in the castle!"

Wolsey was astounded.

"This cannot be. Were I to have the honour of a visit from such a nobleman, he would surely have warned me. Show him in to me that I may greet him."

The Earl was brought into the dining-hall. He had changed a good deal since Wolsey had last seen him, and Wolsey scarcely recognized him as the delicate, handsome boy whom he had had occasion to reprimand at the King's command because he had dared to fall in love with the King's favourite.

Wolsey reproached Northumberland: "My lord Earl, you should have let me know, that I might have done you the honour due to you!"

Northumberland was quiet; he had come to receive no honour, he said. His eyes burned oddly in his pallid face. Wolsey remembered stories he had heard of his unhappy marriage with Shrewsbury's daughter. A man should not allow a marriage to affect him so strongly; there were other things in life. A man in Northumberland's position had much; was he not reigning lord of one of the noblest houses in the land! Bah! thought Wolsey enviously, An I were earl . . .

He had an affection for this young man, remembering him well when he had served under him. A docile boy, a charming boy. He had been grieved when he had to send him away.

"It is well to meet again," said Wolsey. "For old times' sake."

"For old times' sake!" said Northumberland, and he spoke as a man speaks in his sleep.

"I mind thee well," said Wolsey. "Thou wert a bright, impetuous boy."

"I mind thee well," said Northumberland.

With malice in his heart, he surveyed the broken old man. So were the mighty fallen from their high places! This man had done that for which he would never forgive him, for he had taken from him Anne Boleyn whom in six long years of wretched marriage he had never forgotten; nor had he any intention of forgiving Wolsey. Anne should have been his, and he Anne's. They had loved; they had made vows; and this man, who dared now to remind him of the old times, had been the cause of all his misery. And now that he was old and broken, now that his ambition had destroyed him, Wolsey would be kind and full of tender reminiscence. But Percy also remembered!

"I have often thought of you," he said, and that was true. When he had quarrelled with Mary, his wife, whom he hated and who hated him, he thought of the Cardinal's face and the stern words that he had used. "Thou foolish boy . . ." Would he never forget the bitter humiliation? No, he never would; and because he would never cease to reproach himself for his own misery, knowing full well that had he shown sufficient courage he might have made a fight for his happiness, he hated this man with a violent hatred. He stood before him, trembling with rage, for well he knew that she had contrived this, and that she would expect him to show now that courage he had failed to show seven years ago.

Northumberland laid his hand on Wolsey's arm. "My lord, I arrest you of High Treason!"

The Earl was smiling courteously, but with malice; the Cardinal began to tremble.

Revenge was a satisfying emotion, thought the Earl. He who had made others to suffer, must now himself suffer.

"We shall travel towards London at the earliest possible moment," he said.

This they did; and, trembling with his desire for vengeance, the Earl caused the Cardinal's legs to be bound to the stirrups of his mule; thus did he proclaim to the world: "This man, who was once great, is now naught but a common malefactor!"

About Cawood the people saw the Cardinal go; they wept; they called curses on his enemies. He left Cawood with their cries ringing in his ears. "God save Your Grace! The foul evil take them that have taken you from us! We pray God that a very vengeance may light upon them!"

The Cardinal smiled sadly. Of late weeks, here in York, he had led that life which it would have become him as a churchman to have led before. Alms had he given to the people at his gates; his table had been overflowing with food and wine, and at Cawood Castle had he entertained the beggars and the needy to whom he had given scarcely a thought at Hampton Court and York House; for Wolsey, who had once sought to placate his sense of inferiority, to establish his social standing, now sought a place in heaven by his good deeds. He smiled at himself as he rode down to Leicester; his body was sick, and he doubted whether it would—indeed he prayed that it would not—last the journey to London. But he smiled, for he saw himself a man who has climbed high and has fallen low. Pride was my enemy, he said, as bitter an enemy as ever was the Lady Anne.

The rejoicing of the Boleyn faction at the death of Wolsey was shameless. None would have believed a year before that the greatest man in England could be brought so low. Wolsey, it was said, had died of a flux, but all knew he had died of a broken heart, for melancholy was as sure a disease as any other; and having lost all that he cared to live for, why should the Cardinal live? He to be taken to the Tower! He, who had loved his master, to be tried for High Treason!

Here was triumph for Anne. People sought her more than ever, flattered her, feted her. To be favoured by Anne was to be favoured by the King. She enjoyed her triumph and gave special revels to commemorate the defeat of her enemy. She was led into the bad taste of having a play enacted which treated the great Cardinal as a figure of fun.

George was as recklessly glad about Wolsey's fall as she was. "While that man lived, I trembled for you," he said. He laughed shortly. "I hear that near his end he told Kingston that had he served God as diligently as he had served the King, he would not have been given over in his grey hairs. I would say that had he served his God as diligently as he served himself, he would have gone to the scaffold long ere this!" People hearing this remark took it up and laughed over it.

The King did not attend these revels of the Boleyns. Having given the order for the arrest of Wolsey, he wished to shut the matter from his mind. He was torn between remorse and gladness. Wolsey had left much wealth, and into whose hands should this fall but the King's!

Henry prayed: "O Lord, thou knowest I loved that man. I would I had seen him. I would I had not let his enemies keep him from me. Did I not send him tokens of my regard? Did I not say I would not lose the fellow for twenty thousand pounds?"

But he could not stop his thoughts straying to the Cardinal's possessions. There was more yet that he must get his hands upon. Hampton Court was his; York House was his, for he had never given it back after Anne went to Suffolk House, liking it too well.

But he wept for the old days of friendship; he wept for Wolsey; and he was able to deplore his death whilst considering how much more there was in gold to come to him.

Soon after this there were two matters which caused Anne some misgiving. The first came in the form of a letter which the Countess of Northumberland had written to her father, the Earl of Shrewsbury. Shrewsbury had thought it wise to show this letter to the Duke of Norfolk, who had brought it to his niece with all speed.

Anne read the letter. There was no doubt of its meaning. Mary of Northumberland was leaving her husband; she told her father that in one of their more violent quarrels her husband had told her that he was not really married to her, being previously contracted to Anne Boleyn.

Anne's heart beat fast. Here was yet another plot to discredit her in the eyes of the King. She had been his mistress for nearly two years, and it seemed to her that she was no nearer becoming queen than she had been on that first night in Suffolk House. She was becoming anxious, wondering how long she could expect to keep the King her obedient slave. For a long time she had watched for some lessening of his affection; she had found none; she studied herself carefully for some deterioration of her beauty; if she were older, a little drawn, there were many more gorgeous clothes and priceless jewels to set against that. But she was worried, and though she told herself that she longed for a peaceful life and would have been happy had she married Percy or Wyatt she knew that the spark of ambition inside her had been fanned into a great consuming fire; and when she had said to Anne Saville that she would marry the King, no matter what happened to herself, she meant that. She was quite sure that, once she was queen, she would give the King sons, that not only could she delight him as his mistress, but as mother of the future Tudor King of England. Having tasted power, how could she ever relinquish it! And this was at the root of her fear. The delay of the divorce, the awareness of powerful enemies all about her—this was what had made her nervous, imperious, hysterical, haughty, frightened.

Therefore she trembled when she read this letter.

"Give it to me," she commanded.

"What will you do with it?" asked her uncle. She was unsure. He said: "You should show it to the King."

She studied him curiously. Cold, hard, completely without

sentiment, he despised these families which had sprung up, allied to his own house simply because the Norfolk fortunes were in decline at Henry VII's accession on account of the mistake his family had made in backing Richard III. She weighed his words. He was no friend of hers; yet was he an enemy? It would be more advantageous to see his niece on the throne of England than another's niece.

She went to the King.

He was sitting in a window seat, playing a harp and singing a song he had written.

"Ah! Sweetheart, I was thinking of you. Sit with me, and I will sing to you my song. . . . Why, what ails you? You are pale and trembling."

She said: "I am afraid. There are those who would poison your mind against me."

"Bah!" he said, feeling in a merry mood, for Wolsey had left riches such as even Henry had not dreamed of, and he had convinced himself that the Cardinal's death was none of his doing. He had died of a flux, and a flux will attack a man, be he chancellor or beggar. "What now, Anne? Have I not told you that naught could ever poison my mind against you!"

"You would not remember, but when I was very young and first came to court, Percy of Northumberland wished to marry me."

The King's eyes narrowed. Well he remembered. He had got Wolsey to banish the boy from court, and he had banished Anne too. For years he had let her escape him. She was a bud of a girl then, scarce awake at all, but very lovely. They had missed years together.

Anne went on: "It was no contract. He was sent from the court, being pre-contracted to my Lord Shrewsbury's daughter. Now they have quarrelled, and he says he will leave her, and she says he tells her he was never really married to her, being pre-contracted to me."

The King let out an exclamation, and put aside his harp.

"This were not true?" he said.

"Indeed not!"

"Then we must put a stop to such idle talk. Leave this to me, sweetheart. I'll have him brought up before the Archbishop of Canterbury. I'll have him recant this, or 'twill be the worse for him!"

The King paced the floor, his face anxious.

"Dost know, sweetheart," he said, "I fear I have dolts about me. Were Wolsey here . . ."

She did not speak, for she knew it was unnecessary to rail against the Cardinal now; he was done with. She had new enemies with whom to cope. She knew that Henry was casting a slur on the new ministry of Norfolk and More; that he was reminding her that though Wolsey had died, he had had nothing to do with his death. She wished then that she did not know this man so well; she wished that she could have been as lightheartedly gay as people thought her, living for the day, thinking not of the morrow. She had set her skirts daintily about her, aware of her grace and charm, knowing that they drew men irresistibly to her, wondering what would happen to her when she was old, as her grandmother Norfolk. Then I suppose, she thought, I will doze in a chair and recall my adventurous youth, and poke my grand-daughters with an ebony stick. I would like my grandmother to come and see me; she is a foolish old woman assuredly, but at least she would be a friend.

"Sweetheart," said the King, "I shall go now and settle this matter, for there will be no peace of mind until Northumberland admits this to be a lie."

He kissed her lips; she returned his kiss, knowing well how to enchant him, being often sparing with her caresses so that when he received them he must be more grateful than if they had been lavished on him. He was the hunter; although he talked continually of longing for peace of mind, she knew that that would never satisfy him. He must never be satisfied, but always be looking for satisfaction. For two years she had kept him thus in difficult circumstances. She must go on keeping him thus, for her future depended on her ability to do so.

Fain would he have stayed, but she bid him go. "For," she said, "although I know this matter to be a lie, until my lord of Northumberland admits it I am under a cloud. I could not marry you unless we had his full confession that there is no grain of truth in this claim."

She surveyed him through narrowed eyes; she saw return to him that dread fear of losing her. He was easy to read, simple in his desires, ready enough to accept her own valuation of her-self. What folly it would have been to have wept, to have told him that Northumberland lied, to have caused him to believe that her being Queen of England was to her advantage, not to his. While he believed she was ready to return to Hever, while he believed that she wished to be his wife chiefly because she had given way to his desires and sacrificed her honour and virtue, he would fight for her. She had to make him believe that the joy she could give him was worth more than any honours he could heap on her.

And he did believe this. He went storming out of the room; he had Northumberland brought before the Archbishops; he had him swear there had never been a contract with Anne Boleyn. It was made perfectly clear that Northumberland was married to Shrewsbury's daughter, and Anne Boleyn free to marry the King.

Anne knew that her handling of that little matter had been successful.

It was different with the trouble over Suffolk.

Suffolk, jealous, ambitious, seeking to prevent her marriage to the King, was ready to go to any lengths to discredit Anne, provided he could keep his head on his shoulders.

He started a rumour that Anne had had an affair with Thomas Wyatt even while the King was showing his preference for her. There was real danger in this sort of rumour, as there was no one at court who had not witnessed Thomas's loving attitude towards Anne; they had been seen by all, spending much time together, and it was possible that she had shown how she preferred the poet.

Anne, recklessly deciding that one rumour was as good as another, repeated something completely damaging to Suffolk. He had, she had heard, and she did not hesitate to say it in quarters where it would be quickly carried to Suffolk's ears, more than a fatherly affection for his daughter, Frances Brandon, and his love for her was nothing less than incestuous. Suffolk was furious at the accusation; he confronted Anne; they quarrelled; and the result of this quarrel was that Anne insisted he should absent himself from the court for a while.

This was open warfare with one who—with perhaps the exception of Norfolk—was the most powerful noble in the land, and the King's brother-in-law to boot. Suffolk retired in smoldering anger; he would not, Anne knew, let such an accusation go unpaid for, and she had always been afraid of Suffolk.

She shut herself in her room, feeling depressed; she wept a little and told Anne Saville that whoever asked for her was not to be admitted, even should it be the King himself.

She lay on her bed, staring at the ornate ceiling, seeing Suffolk's angry eyes wherever she looked; she pictured his talking over with his friends the arrogance of her who, momentarily, had the King's ear. Momentarily! It was a hideous word. The influence of all failed sooner or later. Oh, my God, were I but queen! she thought. Were I but queen, how happy I should feel! It is this perpetual waiting, this delay. The Pope will never give in; he is afraid of the Emperor Charles! And how can I be Queen of England while Katharine lives!

There was a tap on the door, and Anne Saville's head appeared.

"I told you I would see no one!" cried Anne impatiently. "I told you—no one! No one at all! Not the King himself. . . ."

"It is not the King," said Anne Saville, "but my Lord Rochford. I told him you might see him. . . ."

"Bring him to me," said Anne.

George came in, his handsome face set in a smile, but she knew him well enough to be able to see the worried look behind the smile.

"I had the devil's own job to get them to tell you I was here, Anne."

"I had said I would see no one."

He sat on the bed and looked at her.

"I have been hearing about Suffolk, Anne," he said, and she shivered. "It is a sorry business."

"I fear so."

"He is the King's brother-in-law."

"Well, what if that is so? I am to be the King's wife!"

"You make too many enemies, Anne."

"I do not make them! I fear they make themselves."

"The higher you rise, sister, the more there will be, ready to pull you down."

"You cannot tell me more than I know about that, George."

He leaned towards her.

"When I saw Suffolk, when I heard the talk . . . I was afraid. I would you had been more reasonable, Anne."

"Did you hear what he said of me? He said Wyatt and I were, or had been, lovers!"

"I understand your need to punish him, but not your method."

"I have said he shall be banished from the court, and so he is. I have but to say one shall be banished, and it is done."

"The King loves you deeply, Anne, but it is best to be wise. A queen will have more need of friends than Anne Rochford, and Anne Rochford could never have too many."

"Ah, my wise brother! I have been foolish . . . that I well know."

"He will not let the matter rest here, Anne; he will seek to work you some wrong."

"There will always be those who seek to do me wrong, George, no matter what I do!"

"It is so senseless to make enemies."

"Sometimes I am very weary of the court, George."

"So you tell yourself, Anne. Were you banished to Hever, you would die of boredom."

"That I declare I would, George!"

"If you were asked what was your dearest wish, and spoke truthfully, you would say, 'I would I were settled firmly on the throne of England.' Would you not?"

"You know me better than I know myself, George. It is a glorious adventure. I am flying high, and it is a wonderful, exhilarating, joyous flight; but when I look down I am sometimes giddy; then I am afraid." She held out a hand and he took it. "Sometimes I say to myself: 'There is no one I trust but George.'"

He kissed her hand. "George you can always trust," he said. "Others too, I'll warrant; but always George." Suddenly his reserve broke down, and he was talking as freely as she did. "Anne, Anne, sometimes I too am afraid. Whither are we going, you and I? From simple folk we have become great folk; and yet . . . and yet . . . Dost remember how we scorned poor Mary? And yet . . . Anne, whither are we going, you and I? Are you happy? Am I? I am married to the most vindictive of women; you contemplate marrying the most dangerous of men. Anne, Anne, we have to tread warily, both of us."

"You frighten me, George."

"I did not come to frighten you, Anne."

"You came to reprove me for my conduct towards Suffolk. And I have always hated the man."

"When you hate, Anne, it is better to hide your hatred. It is only love that should be shown."

"There is nothing to be done about Suffolk now, George. In future I shall remember your words. I shall remember you coming to my room with a worried frown looking out from behind your smiles."

The door opened and Lady Rochford came in. Her eyes darted to the bed.

"I thought to find you here."

"Where is Anne Saville?" said Anne coldly, for she hated to have this tête-à-tête disturbed; there was much yet that she wished to say to her brother.

"Do you want to reprove her for letting me in?" asked Jane

maliciously. "Marry! I thought when my husband came into a lady's chamber, there should I follow him!"

"How are you, Jane?" said Anne.

"Very well, I thank you. You do not look so, sister. This affair of Suffolk must have upset you. I hear he is raging. You accused him of incest, so I heard."

Anne flushed hotly. There was that in her sister-in-law to anger her even when she felt most kindly towards the world; now, the woman was maddening.

Jane went on: "The King's sister will be most put about. She retains her fiery temper. . . . And what Frances will say I cannot think!"

"One would not expect you to think about any matter!" said Anne cuttingly. "And I do not wish you to enter my apartment without announcement."

"Indeed, Anne, I am sorry. I thought there would be no need to stand on ceremony with your brother's wife."

"Let us go, Jane," said George wearily; and she was aware that he had not looked at her since that one first glance of distaste when she entered the room.

"Oh, very well. I am sure I know when I am not wanted; but do not let me disturb your pleasant conversation—I am sure it was most pleasant . . . and loving."

"Farewell, Anne," said George. He stood by the bed, smiling at her, his eyes flashing a message: "Be of good cheer. All will be well. The King adores you. Hast forgotten he would make you queen? What of Suffolk! What of any, while the King loves you!"

She said: "You have done me so much good, George. You always do."

He stooped and kissed her forehead. Jane watched jealously. When had he last kissed her—kissed her voluntarily, that was—a year ago, or more? I hate Anne, she thought, reclining there as though she were a queen already; her gowns beautifully furred—paid for by the King doubtless! Herself bejewelled as though for a state function, here in her private apartments. I hope she is never queen! Katharine is Queen. Why should a man put away his wife because he is tired of her? Why should Anne Boleyn take the place of the true queen, just because she is young and sparkling and vivacious and witty and beautifully dressed, and makes people believe she is more handsome than anyone at court? Everyone speaks of her; everywhere one goes one hears her name!

And he loves her . . . as he never loved me! And am I not his wife?

"Come, Jane!" he said, and his voice was different now that he spoke to her and not to his sister.

He led her out, and they walked silently through the corridors to their apartments in the palace.

She faced him and would not let him walk past her.

"You are as foolish about her as is the King!"

He sighed that weary sigh which always made her all but want to kill him, but not quite, because she loved him, and to kill him would be to kill her hopes of happiness.

"You will talk such nonsense, Jane!"

"Nonsense!" she cried shrilly, and then burst into weeping, covering her face with her hands; and waited for him to take her hands, plead with her to control herself. She wept noisily, but nothing happened; and taking down her hands, she saw that he had left her.

Then did she tremble with cold rage against him and against his sister.

"I would they were dead, both of them! They deserve to die; she for what she has done to the Queen; he for what he has done to me! One day . . ." She stopped, and ran to her mirror, saw her face blotched with tears and grief, thought of the cool, lovely face of the girl on the bed, and the long black hair which looked more beautiful in its disorder than it did when neatly tied. "One day," she went on muttering to herself, "I believe I shall kill one of them . . . both of them, mayhap."

They were foolish thoughts, which George might say were worthy of her, but nevertheless she found in them an outlet for her violent feelings, and they brought her an odd comfort.

A barge passed along the river. People on the banks turned to stare after it. In it sat the most beautiful lady of the King's court. People saw how the fading sunlight caught her bejewelled person. Her hair was caught up in a gold coif that sat elegantly on her shapely head.

"Nan Bullen!" The words were like a rumble of thunder among the crowd.

"They say the poor Queen, the true Queen, is dying of a broken heart. . . ."

"As is her daughter, Mary."

"They say Nan Bullen has bribed the Queen's cook to administer poison unto Her Most Gracious Majesty. . . ."

"They say she has threatened to poison the Princess Mary."

"What of the King?"

"The King is the King. It is no fault of his. He is bewitched by this whore."

"She is very lovely!"

"Bah! That is her witchery."

"'Tis right. A witch may come in any guise. . . ."

Women in tattered rags drew their garments about them and thought angrily of the satins and velvets and cloth of gold worn by the Lady Anne Rochford . . . who was really plain Nan Bullen.

"Her grandfather was but a merchant in London town. Why should we have a merchant's daughter for our queen?"

"There cannot be a second queen while the first queen lives."

"I lost two sons of the sweat. . . ."

They trampled through the muck of the gutter, rats scuttled from under their feet, made bold by their numbers and the lack of surprise and animosity their presence caused. In the fever-ridden stench of the cobbled streets, the people blamed Anne Boleyn.

Over London Bridge the heads of traitors stared out with glassy eyes; offal floated up the river; beggars with sore-encrusted limbs asked for alms; one-legged beggars, one-eyed beggars and beggars all but eaten away with some pox.

"'Tis a poor country we live in, since the King would send the rightful Queen from his bed!"

"I mind the poor lady at her coronation; beautiful she was then, with her lovely long hair flowing, and her in a litter of cloth of gold. Nothing too good for her then, poor lady."

"Should a man, even if he be a king, cast off his wife because she is no longer young?"

It was the cry of fearful women, for all knew that it was the King who set examples. It was the cry of aging women against the younger members of their sex who would bewitch their husbands and steal them from them.

The murmurs grew to a roar. "We'll have no Nan Bullen!"

There was one woman with deep cadaverous eyes and her front teeth missing. She raised her hands and jeered at the women who gathered about her.

"Ye'll have no Nan Bullen, eh? And what'll ye do about it, eh? You'll be the first to shout 'God save Your Majesty' when the King makes his whore our queen!"

"Not I!" cried one bold spirit, and the others took it up.

The fire of leadership was in the woman. She brandished a stick.

"We'll take Nan Bullen! We'll go to her and we'll take her, and when we've done with her we'll see if she is such a beauty, eh? Who'll come? Who'll come?"

Excitement was in the air. There were many who were ever

ready to follow a procession, ever ready to espouse a cause; and what more worthy than this, for weary housewives who had little to eat and but rags to cover them, little to hope for and much to fear?

They had seen the Lady Anne Rochford in her barge, proud and imperious, so beautiful that she was more like a picture to them than a woman; her clothes looked too fine to be real . . . And she was not far off . . . her barge had stopped along the river.

Dusk was in the sky; it touched them with adventure, dangerous adventure. They were needy; they were hungry; and she was rich, and doubtless on her way to some noble friends' house to supper. This was a noble cause; it was Queen Katharine's cause; it was the cause of Princess Mary.

"Down with Nan Bullen!" they shouted.

She would have jewels about her, they remembered. Cupidity and righteousness filled their minds. "Shall we let the whore sit on the throne of England? They say she carries a fortune in jewels about her body!"

Once, it was said, in the days of the King's youth when he feasted with his friends, the mob watched him; and so dazzled were they by his person, that they were unable to keep away from him; they seized their mighty King; they seized Bluff King Hal, and stripped him of his jewels. What did he do? He was a noble king, a lover of sport. What did he do? He did naught but smile and treat the matter as a joke. He was a bluff king! A great king! But momentarily he was in the hands of a witch.

There were men who had picked up a fortune that night. Why should not a fortune be picked up from Nan Bullen? And she was no bluff, good king, but a scheming woman, a witch, a poisoner, a usurper of the throne of England! It was a righteous cause; it was a noble cause; it might also prove a profitable cause!

Someone had lighted a torch; another sprang up, and another. In the flickering glow from the flares the faces of the women looked like those of animals. Cupidity was in each face . . . cruelty, jealousy, envy. . . .

"Ah! What will we do to Nan Bullen when we find her? I will tear her limbs apart . . . I will tear the jewels off her. Nan Bullen shall not be our queen. Queen Katharine forever!"

They fell into some order, and marched. There were more flares; they made a bright glow in the sky.

They muttered, and each dreamed of the bright jewel she would snatch from the fair body. A fortune . . . a fortune to be made in a night, and in the righteous cause of Katharine the Queen.

"What means this?" asked newcomers.

"Nan Bullen!" chanted the crowd. "We'll have no Nan Bullen! Queen Katharine forever!"

The crowd was swollen now; it bulged and sprawled, but it went forward, a grimly earnest, glowing procession.

Anne, at the riverside house where she had gone to take supper, saw the glow in the sky, heard the low chanting of voices.

"What is it they say?" she asked of those about her. "What is it? I think they come this way."

Anne and her friends went out into the riverside garden, and listened. The voices seemed thousands strong.

"Nan Bullen . . . Nan Bullen. . . . We'll not have the King's whore. . . ."

She felt sick with fear. She had heard that cry before, never at such close quarters, never so ominous.

"They have seen you come here," whispered her hostess, and trembled, wondering what an ugly mob would do to the friends of Anne Boleyn.

"What do they want?"

"They say your name. Listen. . . ."

They stood, straining their ears.

"We'll have none of Nan Bullen. Queen Katharine forever!"

The guests were pale; they looked at each other, shuddering. Outwardly calm, inwardly full of misery, Anne said: "Methinks I had better leave you, good people. Mayhap when they find me not here they will go away."

And with the dignity of a queen, unhurried, and taking Anne Saville with her, she walked down the riverside steps to her barge. Scarcely daring to breathe until it slipped away from the bank, she looked back and saw the torches clearly, saw the dark mass of people, and thought for a moment of what would have happened to her if she had fallen into their hands.

Silently moved the barge; down the river it went towards Greenwich. Anne Saville was white and trembling, sobbing, but Lady Anne Rochford appeared calm.

She could not forget the howls of rage, and she felt heavy

with sadness. She had dreamed of herself a queen, riding through the streets of London, acclaimed on all sides. "Queen Anne. Good Queen Anne!" She wanted to be respected and admired.

"Nan Bullen, the whore! We'll not have a whore on the throne. . . . Queen Katharine forever!"

"I will win their respect," she told herself. "I must . . . I must! One day . . . one day they shall love me."

Swiftly went the barge. She was exhausted when she reached the palace; her face was white and set, more haughty, more imperious, more queenly than when she had left to join the riverside party.

There was a special feast in the dormitory at Horsham. The girls had been giggling together all day.

"I hear," said one to Catherine Howard, "that this is a special occasion for you. There is a treat in store for you!"

Catherine, wide-eyed, listened. What? she wondered. Isabel was smiling secretly; they were all in the secret but Catherine.

She had her lesson that day, and found Manox less adventurous than usual. The Duchess dozed, tapped her foot, admonished Catherine—for it was true she stumbled over her playing. Manox sat upright beside her—the teacher rather than the admiring and passionate friend. Catherine knew then how much she looked forward to the lessons.

She whispered to him: "I have offended you?"

"Offended me! Indeed not; you could never do aught but please me."

"Methought you seemed aloof."

"I am but your instructor in the virginals," he whispered. "It has come to me that were the Duchess to discover we are friends, she would be offended; she might even stop the lessons. Would that make you very unhappy, Catherine?"

"Indeed it would!" she said guilelessly. "More than most things I love music."

"And you do not dislike your teacher?"

"You know well that I do not."

"Let us play. The Duchess is restive; she will hear our talking at any moment now."

She played. The Duchess's foot tapped in a sprightly way; then it slowed down and stopped.

"I think of you continually," said Manox. "But with fear."

"Fear?"

"Fear that something might happen to stop these lessons."

"Oh, nothing must happen!"

"And yet how easily it could! Her Grace has but to decide that she would prefer you to have another teacher."

"I would beg her to let you stay."

His eyes showed his alarm.

"You should not do that, Catherine!"

"But I should! I could not bear to have another teacher."

"I have been turning over in my mind what I would say

to you today. We must go cautiously, Catherine. Why, if Her Grace knew of our . . . our friendship. . . ."

"Oh, we will be careful," said Catherine.

"It is sad," he said, "for only here do we meet, under the Duchess's eyes."

He would talk no more. When she would have spoken, he said: "Hush! Her Grace will awaken. In future, Catherine, I shall appear to be distant to you, but mistake me not, though I may seem merely your cold, hard master, my regard for you will be as deep as ever."

Catherine felt unhappy; she thrived on caresses and demonstrations of affection, and so few came her way. When the Duchess dismissed her, she returned to the young ladies' apartments feeling deflated and sad at heart. She lay on her bed and drew the curtains round it; she thought of Manox's dark eyes and how on several occasions he had leaned close to her and kissed her swiftly.

In the dormitory she could hear the girls laughing together, preparing for tonight. She heard her own name mentioned amidst laughter.

"A surprise . . ."

"Why not . . ."

"Safer too . . ."

She did not care for their surprises; she cared only that Manox would kiss her no more. Then it occurred to her that he had merely liked her as a young and attractive man might like a little girl. It was not the same emotion as the older people felt for each other; that emotion of which Catherine thought a good deal, and longed to experience. She must live through the weary years of childhood before that could happen; the thought made her melancholy.

Through her curtains she listened to running footsteps. She heard a young man's voice; he had brought sweetmeats and dainties for the party tonight, he said. There were exclamations of surprise and delight.

"But how lovely!"

"I declare I can scarce keep my hands off them."

"Tonight is a special occasion, didst know? Catherine's coming of age. . . ."

What did they mean? They could laugh all they liked; she was not interested in their surprises.

Evening came. Isabel insisted on drawing back the curtains of Catherine's bed.

"I am weary tonight," said Catherine. "I wish to sleep."

"Bah!" laughed Isabel. "I thought you would wish to join in the fun! Great pains have I taken to see that you should enjoy this night."

"You are very kind, but really I would rather retire."

"You know not what you say. Come, take a little wine."

The guests began to arrive; they crept in, suppressing their laughter. The great room was filled with the erotic excitement which was always part of these entertainments. There were slapping and kisses and tickling and laughter; bed curtains pulled back and forth, entreaties for caution, entreaties for less noise.

"You'll be the death of me, I declare!"

"Hush! Her Grace . . ."

"Her Grace is snoring most elegantly. I heard her."

"People are often awakened by their snores!"

"The Duchess is. I've seen it happen."

"So has Catherine, has she not, when she is having her lesson on the virginals with Henry Manox!"

That remark seemed to be the signal for great laughter, as though it were the most amusing thing possible.

Catherine said seriously: "That is so. Her snores do awaken her."

The door opened. There was a moment's silence. Catherine's heart began to hammer with an odd mixture of fear and delight. Henry Manox came into the room.

"Welcome!" said Isabel. Then: "Catherine, here is your surprise!"

Catherine raised herself, and turned first red, then white. Manox went swiftly to her and sat on her bed.

"I had no notion . . ." began Catherine breathlessly.

"We decided it should be a secret. . . . You are not displeased to see me?"

"I . . . of course not!"

"Dare I hope that you are pleased?"

"Yes, I am pleased."

His black eyes flashed. He said: "'Twas dangerous, little Catherine, to kiss you there before the Duchess. I did it because of my need to kiss you."

She answered: "It is dangerous here."

"Bah!" he said. "I would not fear the danger here . . . among so many. And I would have you know, Catherine, that no amount of danger would deter me."

Isabel came over.

"Well, my children? You see how I think of your happiness!"

"This was your surprise, Isabel?" said Catherine.

"Indeed so. Are you not grateful, and is it not a pleasant one?"

"It is," said Catherine.

One of the young gentlemen came over with a dish of sweetmeats, another with wine.

Catherine and Manox sat on the edge of Catherine's bed, holding hands, and Catherine thought she had never been so excited nor so happy, for she knew that she had stepped right out of an irksome childhood into womanhood, where life was perpetually exciting and amusing.

Manox said: "We can be prim now before Her Grace, and what care I! I shall be cold and aloof, and all the time you will know that I long to kiss you." Thereupon he kissed her and she kissed him. The wine was potent; the sweetmeats pleasant. Manox put an arm about Catherine's waist.

Darkness came to the room, as on these occasions lights were never used for fear they should be detected in their revels.

Manox said: "Catherine, I would be alone with you completely. . . . Let us draw these curtains." And so saying he drew the curtains, and they were shut in, away from the others.

October mists hung over Calais. Anne was reminded of long ago feasting at Ardres and Guisnes, for then, as now, Francis and Henry had met and expressed their friendship; then Queen Katharine had been his queen; now the chief lady from England was the Marchioness of Pembroke, Anne herself. Anne felt more at ease than she had for four years. Never had she felt this same certainty that her ambition would be realized. The King was ardent as ever, impatient with the long delay; Thomas Cromwell had wily schemes to present to His Majesty; there was something ruthless about the man; he was the sort one would employ to do any deed, however dangerous, however murky—and, provided the reward was great enough, one felt the deed would be done.

So, at the highest peak of glory she had so far reached, she could enjoy the pomp and ceremony of this visit to France, which was being conducted as a visit of a king and his queen. The King was ready to commit to the Tower any who did not pay her full honour. When, a month ago, she had been created Marchioness of Pembroke she had acquired with this high honour the establishment of a queen. She must have her train-bearer, her ladies of the bedchamber, her maids of honour, her gentlemen-in-waiting, her officers, and at least thirty domestics for her own use. What Henry wished the world to know was that the only thing that kept the Marchioness from being queen in name was the marriage ceremony. "By God!" said

Henry to Anne. "That shall take place before you are much older, sweetheart!"

They had stayed four days at Boulogne, and there Anne had met with some slight rebuff, being unable to attend the festivities which the French arranged for Henry, as the French ladies had not come with Francis. It was understandable that Francis's wife should not come, for on the death of Claude he had married Charles's sister Eleanor, and Henry was known to have said, when the visit was being discussed, that he would rather see a devil than a lady in Spanish dress. The Queen of France therefore could not come. There remained Francis's sister, the Queen of Navarre, but she had pleaded illness. Consequently there were no ladies of the French court to greet Henry and his Marchioness. Doubtless it was a slight, but such slights would be quickly remedied once Anne wore a crown.

Now they were back at Calais and very soon, with her ladies, Anne would go down to the great hall for the masked ball; she must however wait until supper was concluded, since the banquet was attended only by men. Contentedly she browsed, thinking of the past months, thinking of that state ceremony at Windsor, when the King had made her Marchioness of Pembroke—the first woman ever to be created a peer of the realm. What a triumph that had been! And how she, with her love of admiration and pomp, of which she was the centre, had enjoyed every minute of it! Ladies of noble birth, who previously had thought themselves so far above her, had been forced to attend her in all humility; Lady Mary Howard to carry her state robes; the Countesses of Rutland and Sussex to conduct her to the King; the lords of Norfolk and Suffolk with the French ambassador to attend the King in the state apartments. And all this ceremony that they might do honour to Anne Boleyn. She pictured herself afresh, in her surcoat of crimson velvet that was lined with ermine, her lovely hair flowing; herself kneeling before the King while he very lovingly and tenderly placed the coronet on the brow of his much-loved Marchioness.

And then to France, with Wyatt in their train, and her uncle Norfolk and, best of all, George. With George and Wyatt there, she had felt secure and happy. Wyatt loved her as he ever did, though now he dared not show his love. He poured it out in his poetry.

> *"Forget not! O, forget not this!—*
> *How long ago hath been, and is,*
> *The mind that never meant amiss—*
> *Forget not yet!*
>
> *Forget not then thine own approved,*
> *The which so long hath thee so loved,*
> *Whose steadfast faith yet never moved:*
> *Forget not this!"*

She quoted those words as her ladies helped to dress her. Wyatt would never forget; he asked her not to. She smiled happily. No, she would not forget Wyatt; but she was happy tonight for she was assured of the King's steadfastness in his intention to marry her. He had declared this, but actions speak so much louder than words; would he have created her Marchioness of Pembroke, would he have brought her to France if he were not even more determined to make her his queen than he had been two years ago? She felt strong and full of power, able to bind him to her, able to keep him. How could she help but be happy, knowing herself so loved! George was her friend; Wyatt had said he would never forget. Poor Wyatt! And the King had met the disapproval of his people, even faced the possibility of a tottering throne, rather than relinquish her.

Courage made her eyes shine the brighter, made her cheeks to glow. Tonight she was dressed in masquing costume; her gown was of cloth of gold with crimson tinsel satin slashed across it in unusual fashion, puffed with cloth of silver and ornamented with gold laces. All the ladies were dressed in this fashion, and they would enter the hall masked, so that none should know who was who. And then, after the dancing, Henry himself would remove the masks, and the ladies would be exhibited with national pride, for they had been chosen for their beauty.

The Countess of Derby came in to tell her it was time they went down, and four ladies in crimson satin, who were to lead them into the hall, were summoned, and they descended the stairs.

There was an expectant hush as they entered the hall which

at great cost Henry had furnished specially for this occasion. The hangings were of tissue of silver and gold; and the seams of these hangings had been decorated with silver, pearls and stones.

Each masked lady was to select her partner, and Anne chose the King of France.

Francis had changed a good deal since Anne had last seen him; his face was lined and debauched; she had heard alarming stories of him when she had been in France, and she remembered one of these was of the daughter of a mayor at whose house Francis had stayed during one of his campaigns. He had fancied the girl, and she, dreading his advances and knowing too well his reputation, had ruined her looks with acid.

Francis said he could think of no more delight to follow supper than the English King's idea of a ball in which the ladies were masked.

"One is breathless with suspense, awaiting that moment when the masks are removed." He tried to peer lasciviously beneath hers, but laughingly she replied that she was surprised he should be breathless. "It is the inexperienced, not the connoisseur, is it not, who is more likely to be reduced to such a state?"

"Even connoisseurs are deeply moved by masterpieces, Madam!"

"This is what our lord King would doubtless call French flattery."

"'Tis French truth nevertheless."

Henry watched her, jealous and alert, knowing well the French King's reputation, distrusting him, disliking to see him in conversation with Anne.

Francis said: "It is indeed exciting to contemplate that we have the Lady Anne here with us tonight. I declare I long to see the face that so enchants my brother of England."

"Your curiosity will be satisfied ere long," she said.

"I knew the lady once," he said, feigning not to know it was with none other that he now danced.

"That must have been very long ago."

"A few years. But such a lady, Madam, one would never forget, you understand."

She said: "Speak French, if you wish it. I know the language."

He spoke French; he was happier in it. He told her she spoke it enchantingly. He told her that he would wager she was more fair than the Lady Anne herself, for he had never set eyes on such a lithesome figure, nor heard such a melodious voice; and he trusted she had the fairest face in England and France, for he would be disappointed if she had not!

Anne, feeling Henry's eyes upon her, rejoiced in Henry. He was a king and a great king; she could not have endured Francis for all the kingdoms in the world.

Henry, impatient of watching, would now remove the masks; and did so, going first to Anne.

"Your Majesty has been dancing with the Marchioness of Pembroke," he told Francis, who declared himself astonished and delighted.

Henry moved on, leaving Anne with Francis.

"And what did I say of my old friend little Anne Boleyn?" he said.

Anne laughed. "Your Majesty was fully aware with whom he danced."

"I should have known that one so full of grace, so pleasant to the eye and the ear, could be none other than she who will soon, I trust, be my sister of England. I congratulate myself that she chose to dance with me."

"Ceremony, as Your Majesty will well understand, demanded it."

"You were ever unkind, fair lady! That I well remember."

"Tell me of your sister."

They talked long together; Anne's laughter rang out now and then, for they had many reminiscences to share of the French court, and each could bring back memories to the other.

Henry watched, half proud, half angry. He had ever been jealous of Francis; he wondered whether to join them or leave them together. He did not care to see Anne in such close conversation with the lecher Francis, and yet it must be so for he was the King of France, and honour shown to Anne was honour shown to Henry. Francis's approval at Rome could mean a good deal, for though Charles was the most important man in Europe, might not Henry and Francis together carry more weight than Katharine's nephew?

The dance broke up; the ladies retired. Henry talked with his royal guest. Francis suggested he should marry Anne without the Pope's consent. Henry did not see how this could be, but enjoyed such talk; it was pleasant to think he had French support behind him.

He went to Anne's chamber, and dismissed her ladies.

"You were indeed a queen tonight!" he said.

"I trust I did not disgrace my King."

She was gay tonight, savouring the success of the evening; adorable in her costume of cloth of gold and crimson.

He went to her and put his arms about her.

"The dresses were the same, but you stood out among them all. Had one not known who you were, it would have been easily seen that you were she who should be queen."

"You are very gracious to me."

"And you are glad I love you, eh?"

She was so very happy this night that she wanted to shower happiness all about her; and on whom should it fall but on her royal benefactor!

"I was never happier in my life!" she said.

Later, when she lay in his arms, he confessed to jealousy of the French King.

"You seemed to like him too well, sweetheart."

"Would you have had me ungracious to him? If I seemed to like him, it was because he was your guest."

"Methought you appeared to coquette with him a little."

"I did only what I thought would please you."

"'Twould never please me, Anne, to see your smiles given to another!"

"My smiles! Bah! If I smiled too warmly then 'twas because I compared him with you and was happy in the comparing."

Henry was overjoyed.

"I declare he puts on years as one would put on state robes; he is weighed down with them. I never thought him handsome. . . ."

"Debauchery is apparent in his face," said Anne.

Henry's prudish little mouth lifted into a smile.

"I would not care to own his reputation!"

Then she amused him with an imitation of the French King, recounting what he had said and what she had answered; and the King laughed and was very happy with her.

In the morning Francis sent Anne a jewel as a gift. Henry examined it, was delighted with its worth, and jealous that it had not come from himself.

He gave her more jewellery; he gave of his own and Katharine's and even his sister Mary of Suffolk's. The King was more deeply in love than ever.

When it was time for them to leave Calais there was a high wind and it was unsafe to cross the Channel. Anne was reminded of that stay at Dover; but then she had been a seven-year-old girl of no importance whatever, trying to listen to those about her and learn something of life. Pleasant it was to think back, when one had come so far.

They beguiled the days with dice and cards, at which the King lost heavily and Anne almost always won; nor did it matter if she lost, for the King would pay her debts. One of the players was a handsome young man named Francis Weston for whom Anne conceived a genuine liking, and he for her. They played by day and danced at night; they were hilarious over the cards; there was much fun to be had at "Pope Julius," the favourite game of the court, with its allusions to matrimony, intrigue and the Pope—they all found it so apt in view of the pending divorce. Thus passed the days, with Anne happier than she had been since deciding to occupy the throne, more secure, more content.

The old year was dying, and Christmas came. Still the Pope was adamant; still action hung fire. Four years ago Anne had become the King's mistress, and now, at Christmas of the year 1532, still she waited to be his queen.

She was pale and listless.

"Does aught ail thee, sweetheart?" the King asked her.

"Much ails me," she told him.

The King was alarmed.

"Darling, tell me instantly. I would know what is wrong, and right it."

She said very clearly: "I fear he who should follow Your Majesty as King of England will after all be but a bastard."

Henry was beside himself with the importance of this news. Anne was pregnant! A son was what he wanted more than any-thing—next to Anne herself—on earth. Anne, who should have been the queen long ere this—and had they married she would have given him a son by now, for it had ever been her wish that no children should be born to them until she was queen—Anne was with child. His child! His son! He who should be King of England!

"And by God," said the King, "he shall be!" Now he was all tenderness, all loving care; that body which sheltered his son had become doubly precious. "Fret not, sweetheart. Be done with fretting for evermore. I declare I'll endure this delay no longer. I'll be cut free from that canting Pope, or, by God, much blood will flow!"

Anne could smile; this was the happiest thing that could have happened; this would decide him. She was determined that her son should be born in wedlock; and so was Henry.

Well he remembered how he had looked with something like fury on his son, the Duke of Richmond—that fine boy so like himself, who, had he been born of Katharine instead of Elizabeth Blount, would have spared him much heart-burning. No! There should be no repetition of that!

He called Cromwell to him; he would see Cranmer; he would leave nothing undone, no way out unexplored. Divorce he must have, and quickly, for Anne was pregnant with a son.

Henry's determination was vital; it swept all opposition before it; none who valued his future, or his head, dared go against him, whilst those who worked with him and were blessed with success were sure of favour.

Warham had died in August, and who should replace

him but Cranmer, the man who, when the idea of divorce was first being considered, had the right sow by the ear! The Archbishopric of Canterbury could therefore be placed in good hands. Then Cromwell: Cromwell's daring scheme of separating England from Rome, which had on first hearing seemed too wild to be put into action, now presented itself as the only sure solution. Cromwell, unlike so many, suffered not at all from a superstitious dread of consequences; he was not by any means scrupulous; he could bring in evidence against Rome as fast as his master cared to receive it. What had Henry to lose by the separation? he demanded of his king. And see what he had to gain!

Henry's eyes glistened, contemplating the dissolution of those storehouses of treasure, the monasteries . . . treasures which would naturally be thrown into the King's chests. The state would be free of Rome; it would be strong, beholden to no one. Moreover, free from the Pope, why should Henry care for his verdict on the divorce? Henry, all powerful, might make his own divorce! The Continent, in the grip of the reformation, had weakened the Church. Everywhere in Europe men were challenging the Pope's authority; a new religion was springing up. It was simple; it merely meant that the headship was transferred from the Pope to Henry. Henry had hesitated, turning this truly delightful plan over and over in his mind. He had to consider his conscience, which troubled him incessantly. He was afraid of isolation. How would it affect him politically? Wolsey—the wisest man he had ever known—

would have opposed Cromwell's scheme; he did not like Cromwell, he considered him a knave. Was Cromwell right? Could Cromwell be trusted? Cromwell might be a knave, but was he a wise man?

Henry shilly-shallied. He had always considered his accession to be influenced by the Holy See, and through the Holy See, by God; but he was ever ready to support an idea he liked. He was superstitious to a great degree; he had looked upon the Pope as holy; it was not easy for a superstitious man with a conscience to overthrow a lifetime's tradition. He was afraid of God's wrath, although he did not fear the vacillating Clement. He had been proud of his title "Defender of the Faith." Who was it who had written the most brilliant denouncement of Luther? Henry of England. How could he then overthrow that which he had so ardently defended!

Cromwell had talked slyly and persuasively for if he would keep in favour, this matter of the divorce must be settled, and he saw no way of settling it but this. He explained this was nothing to do with Lutherism; the religion of the country remained the same; it was merely the headship of the church that was involved. Was it not more seemly that a nation's great good king should lead its church?

Henry tried to justify this procedure morally. Once he had made a case for the breakaway, it would be done. Warham had died at the most convenient moment; that was a sign perhaps. Who better to head a country's church than its king! Anne was pregnant. This was a sign. He must have the divorce if he was to legitimize Anne's child. The time was short. There was no longer occasion for conferences, for shilly-shallying. Sir Thomas More, a few months previously, had retired from the office of Chancellor. More had ever been one to discountenance Henry. He liked the man, he could not help it, but he had been rather shaken when More had said, on taking office, that he would "first look unto God and after God to his Prince," for that was a most uncomfortable thing for a minister to say; but More was an uncomfortable man; he was beloved by the people, he was honest, religious in that true sense to which so few do, or even try to, attain. He had calmly walked out and gone home to his family and friends; he begged to be allowed to do this on the plea of ill health, and Henry had to accept that plea; but he had always liked the man, and he knew his lack of ease was more mental than bodily. More could not reconcile himself to the divorce; that was why he had resigned and gone to the peace of his Chelsea home. The King had outwardly taken his resignation in good part; he had visited Chelsea; but at the same time he was disturbed on More's account, since More was known as a good man, and the King would have preferred him to be less arbitrary.

Cromwell was whispering in the King's ear. Cromwell was smart; Cromwell was cunning; any delicate job could be left to Cromwell.

Divorce! Why divorce? When a marriage has not been valid, what need of divorce? He had never been married to Katharine! She was his brother's wife, and therefore the ceremony was illegal.

Henry dared delay no longer. Anne's child must be legitimate. So, on a January day, he summoned one of his chaplains to a quiet attic of White Hall, and when the chaplain arrived, he found there—much to his astonishment, for he had been told he was merely to celebrate mass—the King attended by two grooms of the chamber, one of them being that Norris whose sympathy for Wolsey had lightened the Cardinal's last hours. The chaplain had not been there more than a few minutes when who should arrive but the Marchioness of Pembroke accompanied by Anne Saville!

The King then took the chaplain aside, and told him he would be required to marry him to the Marchioness.

The chaplain began to tremble at this, looking fearfully about him, at which the King stamped impatiently. Greatly did the chaplain fear the King, but more so did he fear Rome. Henry, seeing himself in a quandary, hastily told the man that the Pope had granted the divorce, and he need fear nothing. The ceremony was over before the light of morning, and all the party went secretly away.

Henry was disturbed and not a little alarmed; he had done a bold thing, and not even Cranmer knew he had intended to do it in this way. For, by marrying Anne as he had, he had irrevocably broken with Rome and placed himself at the head of the English Church. The council could do nothing but accept this state of affairs; Henry was their King. But what of the people, that growling mass of the populace who had come through pestilence and poverty, and were less inclined to bend the knee than his courtiers? In the streets they murmured against Anne. Some murmured against the King.

If the King trembled, Anne was triumphant. She was Queen after four years of waiting; Queen of England. Already she carried the King's child within her. She was mentally exhausted by the long struggle, and only now did she realize what a struggle it had been, what nervous energy she had put into maintaining it, how she had feared she would never reach this pinnacle of power. She could now relax and remember that she was to be a mother. Love was not to be denied her then. She carried a child, and the child would inherit the throne of England. She slept peacefully, dreaming the child—a son—was already born, that her attendants laid it in her arms; and her heart was full of love for this unborn child. "September!" she said on waking. "But September is such a long way off."

George Boleyn was preparing for a journey; he would leave the palace before dawn. Jane came gliding to him as he buttoned his coat.

"George . . . where are you going?"

"A secret mission," he said.

"So early?"

"So early."

"Could I not accompany you?"

He did not answer such folly.

"George, is it very secret? Tell me where you go."

He contemplated her; he always felt more kindly towards her when he was going to leave her.

"It is a secret, so if I tell you, you must keep it entirely to yourself."

She clasped her hands, feeling suddenly happy because he smiled in such a friendly way.

"I will, George! I swear I will! I can see it is good news."

"The best!"

"Tell me quickly, George."

"The King and Anne were married this morning. I go to carry the news to the King of France."

"The King . . . married to Anne! But the Pope has not given the divorce, so how can that be possible?"

"With God—and the King—all things are possible."

She was silent, not wishing to spoil this slight friendliness he was showing towards her.

"So you are the Queen's brother now, George, and I am her sister-in-law."

"That is so. I must away. I must leave the palace before the day begins."

She watched him go, smiling pleasantly; then all her bitter jealousy burst forth. It was so unfair. So she was Queen of England, and she would be more arrogant than ever now. Why should a man displace his wife because he tired of her!

A marriage had been arranged for Isabel; she was leaving the Duchess's retinue. Catherine was not really sorry, never having liked Isabel; and then she was too absorbed in Henry Manox to care much what happened to anyone else.

Manox had been to the dormitory on several occasions; he was recognized now as Catherine's lover. There was much petting and caressing and whispering, and Catherine found this a delightful state of affairs. She was grown up at last, revelling in intrigue, receiving little gifts from Manox; she never wrote to him, since she had never been taught how to write properly; but oral messages were exchanged between her and Manox by way of their friends.

During the lessons they were very conventional in their behaviour—which seemed to Catherine a great joke. The old Duchess might fall into a deep sleep, and all Manox and Catherine would do was exchange mischievous glances.

"I declare, Manox," said the Duchess on one occasion, "you are too stern with the child. You do nothing but scold!"

They would laugh at that when she lay in his arms in her bed with the curtains drawn. Catherine, though a child in years, was highly sexed, precocious, a budding woman; over-excitable, generous, reckless, this affair with Manox seemed the high spot of her life. He said he had loved her ever since he had first set eyes on her; Catherine was sure she had loved him ever since her very first lesson. Love was the excuse for everything they did. He brought her sweetmeats and ribands for her hair; they laughed and joked and giggled with the rest.

It was the Duchess who told Catherine that she was engaging another woman in place of Isabel.

"She is from the village, and her name is Dorothy Barwicke. She will take Isabel's place among the ladies. She is a serious young lady, as Isabel was, and I feel I can trust her to keep you young people in some sort of order. I'll whisper something else to you, Catherine. . . . We really are going to Lambeth ere the month is out! I declare I grow weary of the country, and now that my granddaughter is in truth the Queen . . ."

She never tired of talking of Anne, but Catherine who had loved to hear such talk was hardly interested now.

"Imagine poor old Katharine's face when he took Anne to France! If ever a king proclaimed his queen, he did then! And I hear she was a great success. How I should have loved to see her dancing with the French King! Marchioness of Pembroke, if you please! I'll warrant Thomas—I beg his pardon, the Earl of Wiltshire—is counting what this means in gold. Oh, Thomas, Earl of Wiltshire, who would not have beautiful daughters!"

"Grandmother, will you really go to Lambeth?"

"Don't look so startled, child. Assuredly I shall go. Someone must assist at the dear Queen's coronation. I feel sure I shall be invited, in view of my rank and my relationship to Her Majesty the Queen."

"And . . . will you take the whole household?" asked Catherine, her voice trembling. But the Duchess was too absorbed by her thoughts and plans for the coronation to notice that.

"What foolish questions you ask, child! What matter . . ."

"You would take your musicians, would you not, Grandmother? You would take me?"

"Ah! So that is what you are thinking, is it? You fear to be left out of the excitement. Never fear, Catherine Howard, I doubt not the Queen your cousin will find a place at court for you when you are ready."

There was no satisfaction to be gained from the Duchess; in any case she changed her plans every day.

"Isabel! Isabel!" said Catherine. "Do you think the whole household will remove to Lambeth?"

"Ah!" cried Isabel, who in view of her coming marriage was not interested in the Duchess's household. "You are thinking of your lover!" She turned to Dorothy Barwicke, a dark woman with quick, curious eyes and a thin mouth. "You would think Catherine Howard but a child, would you not? But that is not so; she has a lover; he visits her in our bedroom of nights. He is a very bold young man, and they enjoy life; do you not, Catherine?"

Catherine flushed and, looking straight at Dorothy Barwicke, said: "I love Henry and he loves me."

"Of course you do!" said Isabel. "And a very loving little girl she is, are you not, Catherine? She is very virtuous, and would not allow Manox in her bed an she did not love him!"

"And, loving him," said Dorothy Barwicke, "I'll warrant she finds it difficult to refuse his admittance."

The two young women exchanged glances, and laughed.

"You will look after Catherine when I leave, will you not?" said Isabel.

"I do not need looking after."

"Indeed you do not!" said Dorothy. "Any young lady not yet in her teens, who entertains gentlemen in her bed at night, is quite able to look after herself, I'd swear!"

"Not gentlemen," said Isabel ambiguously. "It is only Manox."

Catherine felt they were mocking her, but she always felt too unsure of all the ladies to accuse them of so doing.

"I shall expect you to look after Catherine when I have gone," said Isabel.

"You may safely leave that to me."

Catherine lived in agony of fear while the Duchess set the household bustling with preparations for her journey to Lambeth. She talked perpetually of "my granddaughter, the Queen," and having already heard that she was to attend the coronation—fixed for May—was anxious to get to Lambeth in good time, for there would be her state robes to be put in order, and many other things to be seen to; and she hoped to have a few informal meetings with the Queen before the great event.

Catherine was wont to lie in bed on those nights when there were no visitors to the dormitory and ask herself what she would do were the Duchess to decide not to take Manox. Catherine loved Manox because she needed to love someone; there were two passions in Catherine's life; one was music, and the other was loving. She had loved her mother and lost her; she had loved Thomas Culpepper, and lost him; now she loved

Manox. And on all these people had she lavished unstintingly her capacity for loving, and that was great. Catherine must love; life for her was completely devoid of interest without love. She enjoyed the sensational excitement of physical love in spite of her youth; but her love for Manox was not entirely a physical emotion. She loved to give pleasure as well as to take it, and there was nothing she would not do for those she loved. All that she asked of life was to let her love; and she was afraid of life, for it seemed to her that her love was ill-fated; first her mother, then Thomas Culpepper, now Manox. She was terrified that she would have to go to Lambeth without Manox.

There came a day when she could no longer bear the suspense. She asked her grandmother outright.

"Grandmother, what of my lessons at Lambeth?"

"What of them, child?"

"Shall Henry Manox accompany us, that he may continue to instruct me?"

The Duchess's reply sent a shiver down her spine.

"Dost think I would not find thee a teacher at Lambeth?"

"I doubt not that you would, but when one feels that one can do well with one teacher. . . ."

"Bah! I know best who will make a good teacher. And why do you bother me with lessons and teachers? Dost not realize that this is to be the coronation of your own cousin Anne!"

Catherine could have wept with mortification, and her agony of mind continued.

Manox came often to the dormitory.

"Do you think I could ever leave you?" he asked. "Why, should you go to Lambeth without me I would follow."

"And what would happen to you if you so disobeyed?"

"Whatever the punishment it would be worth it to be near you, if but for an hour!"

But no! Catherine would not hear of that. She remembered the tales Doll Tappit had gleaned of Walter the warder. She remembered then that, though she ran wild through the house and her clothes were so shabby as to be almost those of a beggar, she was Catherine Howard, daughter of a great and noble house, while he was plain Henry Manox, instructor at the virginals. Though he seemed so handsome and clever to her, there would be some—and her grandmother and her dreaded uncle the Duke among them—who would consider they had done great wrong in loving. What if they, both, should be committed to the Tower! It was for Manox she trembled, for Catherine's love was complete. She could endure separation, but not to think of Manox's body cramped in the Little Ease, or rotting, and the food of rats in the Pit. She cried and begged that he would do nothing rash; and he laughed and said did she not think he did something rash every night that he came to her thus, for what did she think would happen to him if her grandmother were to hear of their love?

Then was Catherine seized with fresh fears. Why must the world, which was full of so many delights, hold so much that was cruel! Why did there have to be stern grandmothers and terrifying uncles! Why could not everybody understand what a good thing it was to love and be loved in this most exciting and sensational way which she had recently discovered!

Then Catherine found the world was indeed a happy place, for when she left for Lambeth in her grandmother's retinue, Manox was in it too.

$$\ast$$

Lambeth was beautiful in the spring, and Catherine felt she had never been so completely happy in her life. The fruit trees in the orchards which ran down to the river's brink were in blossom; she spent whole days wandering through the beautiful gardens, watching the barges go down the river.

With Manox at Lambeth, they were often able to meet out of doors; the Duchess was even more lax than she had been at Horsham, so busy was she with preparations for the coronation. Anne visited her grandmother, and they sat together in the garden, the Duchess's eyes sparkling to contemplate her lovely granddaughter. She could not resist telling Anne how gratified she was, how lucky was the King, and how, deep in her heart, she had ever known this must happen.

Catherine was brought to greet her cousin.

"Your Majesty remembers this one?" asked the Duchess "She was doubtless but a baby when you last saw her."

"I remember her well," said Anne. "Come hither, Catherine, that I may see you more closely."

Catherine came, and received a light kiss on her cheek.

Catherine still thought her cousin the most beautiful person she had ever seen, but she was less likely to idealize, because all her devotion was for Manox.

"Curtsey, girl!" thundered the Duchess. "Do you not know that you stand before your Queen?"

Anne laughed. "Oh, come! No ceremony in the family . . . No, Catherine, please. . . ."

Anne thought, Poor little thing! She is pretty enough, but how unkempt she looks!

"Perhaps Your Majesty will find a place for her at court. . . ."

"Assuredly I will," said Anne, "but she is young yet."

"On your knees, girl, and show some gratitude!"

"Grandmother," laughed the Queen, "I would have you remember this is but our family circle. I am weary of ceremony; let me drop it awhile. What do you like doing, Catherine? Are you fond of music?"

Catherine could glow when she talked of music. They remembered how they had once felt affection, which was spontaneous, for one another, and as they talked it came back to them.

After Catherine had been dismissed, Anne said: "She is a sweet child, but a little gauche. I will send her some clothes; they could be altered to fit her."

"Ah! You would dress up Catherine Howard! She is a romp, that child. And what a sheltered life she has led! I have kept her away in the country, perhaps too long."

A new woman joined the Duchess's household while they

were at Lambeth. Her name was Mary Lassells, and she was of lower birth than most of the Duchess's attendants; she had been nurse to Lord William Howard's first child, and on the death of his wife, the Duchess had agreed to take her in. During her first week in the Duchess's establishment, Mary Lassells met a young man who was dark and handsome with bold roving eyes, and to whom she felt immediately drawn. She was sitting on an overturned tree trunk in the Lambeth orchard, when he strolled by.

"Welcome, stranger!" he said. "Or am I wrong in calling you stranger? I declare I should recognize you, had I ever seen you before!"

And so saying he sat down beside her.

"You are right in supposing me to be a stranger. I have been in the Duchess's establishment but a few days. You have been here long?"

"I made the journey up from Norfolk."

His bold eyes surveyed her. She was well enough, but not worth risking trouble with little Catherine, who, with her naivete, her delight, her willingness, was giving him the most amusing and absorbing affair he had enjoyed for a long time.

"I rejoice to see you here," he continued.

"Indeed, sir, you are very kind."

"It is you who are kind, to sit thus beside me. Tell me, how do you like it here?"

She did not greatly like it, she told him; she found the behaviour of some of the ladies shocking. She was rather bitter, acutely feeling herself to be low-born, inexperienced in the ways of etiquette, having been merely a nurse before she entered the Duchess's household. She had been delighted when she was offered the position, and owing to the unconventional ways of the household Mary had been accepted into it without ceremony. But among these ladies she felt awkward—awkward in speech, awkward in manners; she fancied that they watched her, sneered at her behind her back. This was pure imagination on Mary's part, for in actual fact the ladies were much too absorbed in their own affairs to give much attention to her; but she nursed her grievances, aired them to herself with great bitterness, until they grew out of all proportion to the truth. She occupied a bed in the dormitory with the rest, but there had been no feasting nor lovemaking in her presence yet, as at the Lambeth house the dormitory was not so conveniently situated. Still, she could not help but notice the levity of the ladies; young gentlemen had looked in on some of them during the day; she had seen many a kiss and indications of greater familiarity. Mary had thought bitterly: And these are those who would look down on a good woman such as I am!

She told him that she did not like what she had so far seen of the conduct of those who were called ladies.

He raised his eyebrows.

"There is much familiarity between them and the young men."

Manox laughed inwardly, thinking it would be amusing to lead her on. He feigned shocked surprise.

Warming to the subject, she went on: "Gentlemen—or those who would call themselves gentlemen—look in at the dormitory at all hours of the day. I was never more startled in my life. There was one, who would doubtless call herself a lady, changing her dress, and a gentleman looked round the door and she pretended to hide herself by running behind a screen and was much delighted when he peeped over the top. I declare I wondered whether I should not go at once to Her Grace!"

Manox looked sharply at her. The severely practical head-dress, the thin disapproving lips, the pale eyes—all these belonged to a bearer of tales. She was a virgin, he doubted not. A virgin of necessity! he thought cynically; and of such material were made the tale-bearers, the really dangerous women.

He laid a hand over hers. She started, and a flush spread over her face, beginning at her modest collar and running swiftly to her flat and simply arranged hair. She was nearer to being pretty at that moment than she would ever be.

He said gently: "I understand . . . of course I understand. But would you take a word of advice?"

She turned her eyes upon him, smiling, thinking him the handsomest and most charming person she had met since entering the house.

"I am ever ready to take good advice," she said.

"It would be most unwise to carry tales of this matter to Her Grace."

"Why so?"

"You have told me that you were a nurse before you came here. I am but a musician. I instruct ladies at whichever musical instrument it is decreed they shall learn to play." His voice became caressing. "You and I are but humble folk; do you think we should be believed? Nay! It is you who would be turned from the house, were you to tell Her Grace what you have seen!"

This was fuel to the bitterness in her; she had lived in noble houses, and had longed to be one of the nobility; she saw every situation from this angle. I am as good as they are. . . . Why should I have to serve them, just because I was born in a humble house, and they in castles!

"Well I can believe that the blame would be put on me, rather than on those delinquents."

He leaned closer to her. "Depend upon it, it most assuredly would! That is the way of life. Be silent about what you see, fair lady."

"I cannot tell you what it means to me to have met you," she said. "Your sympathy warms me, gives me courage."

"Then I am indeed glad that I walked this way."

Mary Lassells was trembling with excitement. No young man had ever taken notice of her before. The eyes of this one were warm and friendly, one might say bold. Mary began to feel very happy, very glad that she had joined the Duchess's retinue after all.

"Do you often walk this way?" she asked.

He kissed her hand. "We shall meet again ere long."

She was anxious to make it definite. "I shall doubtless walk here tomorrow."

"That is well to know," he said.

They walked through the orchards down to the river's edge. It was a lovely spring day, and she thought there had never been any scene more beautiful than that of the river gliding by the blossoming trees. The sun, she was sure, was warmer today, and the birds seemed to sing more joyously. Manox sang too; he sang pleasantly; music was his passion, the only one to which he could remain faithful through his life. Mary thought: He means he is happy too, to sing thus.

They went into the house. That encounter had changed Mary; everything to her looked different, and people looked at her and thought her less plain than they had imagined. She hummed the song which Manox had sung; she was pleasant and smiling, forgetting the social barriers between her and most of the others. She smiled in a kindly way on the Duchess's little granddaughter. It is well, thought Mary, that I am not of noble birth; a musician would be a tolerable match for me.

In less than a week she was rudely awakened. She had seen Manox on several occasions, and on each he had continued to charm her. On this day she went to the dormitory in the middle of the morning, having been down to the orchards, having sat for a full hour on the overturned tree trunk, waiting in vain. She opened the door of the dormitory; the curtains were drawn back from most of the beds, and on one in a corner—young

Catherine Howard's—sat the little girl, and with her Henry Manox. They sat side by side, their arms about each other; he was caressing the child, and Catherine was flushed and laughing. It was a great shock to Mary; she stood still, staring at them. Then Manox rose and said: "Ah! Here is Mistress Lassells!"

Mary stood, struggling with her emotions, thinking: How foolish of me! He likes children; he doubtless came here on some errand, saw the child, and made much of her. But what business could Henry Manox have in the ladies' dormitory! And had he not known that this was the hour when she would be waiting to see him in the orchards!

Manox was plausible. In his numerous love affairs he had found himself in many a delicate situation; with grace he had ever managed to set matters right, if only temporarily.

He went swiftly to Mary and said to her: "I had a message to bring here; I am really but a servant; and when I came here, the little girl needed comforting."

She accepted his explanation; because she felt Catherine to be but a child, it did not occur to her that they could possibly be lovers. She smiled again, quite happy. Manox thought, My God! She would be a vindictive woman! And he cursed himself for having lightheartedly indulged in this mild flirtation with her. She had been so prim, so seemingly virtuous, that he could not resist the temptation; he had wanted to show her that what she lacked was, not the desire to sin, but the opportunity.

He escaped, and the situation was saved; but this could not always be so, and he would not give up Catherine for Mary Lassells.

There came a night when Manox, unable to stay away longer, recklessly went to Catherine though he knew Mary would discover this. Mary pulled the curtains about her bed, and wept tears of bitter humiliation. If she had hated the world before she had met Manox, now she hated it a thousand times more; and her hatred was directed, not against Manox, but against Catherine Howard. The wanton! The slut! she thought. And she a great lady to be! A Howard! So much for the nobility—a cousin to the Queen! And who is the Queen? Another such as Catherine Howard. Why, in this wicked world does sin go unpunished and virtue unrewarded?

Her eyes were narrow with weeping. She would go to the Duchess at once, were it not that Manox would suffer. Catherine Howard would be beaten, possibly sent away, but they would hush the matter up so that scandal should not be brought to the house of Howard. It would be Manox who would suffer most, for he was low-born like herself, of no importance; it was such as they who suffered for the sins of the nobility.

Who knew that Manox might not come to his senses, that he might not learn to cherish virtue, that he might discard that vile slut, Catherine Howard, who was not yet in her teens and yet had sunk to the very depths of wickedness! Sexual immorality was surely the most violent form of sin; for such did one burn in hell. To steal and to murder were to commit evil crimes, it was true; but what crime could compare with the wickedness of Catherine Howard!

She would not tell though, for Manox's sake; she would hope

that one day he would see his folly, that he would repent . . . that before the blossom gave way to leaves on the trees in the orchard, he would come to her and tell her he had been a fool.

He did not, and there was mockery in his eyes. One day she met him by the river, and telling herself that she must save him from his folly, she went to him, and with burning eyes and lips that trembled demanded: "Man, what meanest thou to play the fool of this fashion! Knowest thou not that an my lady of Norfolk knew of the love between thee and Mistress Howard she will undo thee? She is of a noble house; and if thou shouldst marry her, some of her blood will kill thee."

Manox threw back his head and laughed, knowing full well what had caused her to utter such warning, mocking her, laughing at her. He said that she need have no fear for him, since his intentions were strictly of a dishonourable nature.

Angry and humiliated, Mary went into the house. If Manox would not accept her warning against the folly of pursuing this affair, perhaps Catherine would. She found Catherine stitching at a piece of tapestry in the sewing-room.

"I would have speech with you, Mistress Howard."

Catherine looked up; she knew little of Mary Lassells, and had not greatly liked what she did know, agreeing with most of the others that the woman was prudish and dull.

"Yes?" said Catherine.

"I have come to warn you. You are very young, and I do not think you realize what you do. What you do with Manox is . . . criminal!"

"I understand you not," said Catherine haughtily, and would have moved away, but Mary caught her arm.

"You must listen. Manox is amusing himself with you. He jokes about your willingness."

"You lie!" said Catherine.

"I have just come from him," said Mary with a virtuous air, "having wished—for indeed I feel it would be but Her Grace's pleasure—to beg him to cease his attentions to yourself. I pointed out to him what reckless folly this was, and how, if he married you, one of your house would surely work his ruin. He boasted that his intentions were only dishonourable."

Catherine flushed hotly, hating the pale, prim face of Mary Lassells, suddenly afraid, suddenly seeing this beautiful love of hers in a different light. It was sordid now, not beautiful at all. She had been wrong to indulge in it. Manox despised her; many people would despise her; heaven help her if what she had done should ever get to her grandmother's ears! But chiefly she suffered from Manox's words. His intentions were dishonourable! What a wicked thing for him to have said! Could it be that he was not the adoring, the faithful and gallant, the courteous lover she had believed him to be?

Catherine was hot with rage.

"Fie upon him!" she cried. "Where is he now? I will go to him, and you shall come with me. I will demand of him whether you have spoken the truth."

There was nothing Mary could do but conduct Catherine to him there in the orchards, where the thick trees helped to shield those who wished to meet clandestinely. Mary had one thought—and that to break up this foolish affair of Manox's with Catherine Howard. She visualized Manox's repentance, her own great understanding; a marriage between them would be so suitable.

Manox looked startled to see them both; Catherine flushed and angry, Mary smiling secretly.

"I would have you know," said Catherine in such a fine temper that she could not control it, "that I despise you, that I hate you, that I never wish to see you again!"

"Catherine!" gasped Manox. "What does this mean?"

"I know what you have said to this . . . woman, of me."

He was shaken. There was something tremendously attractive about Catherine Howard; her complete enjoyment of physical contact made for his enjoyment; never had he known one so innocently abandoned and responsive; she was a lovely child; her youth was enchanting, and must add piquancy to the affair; he had never had such an experience. And he was not going to lose her if he could help it. He threw a venomous glance at Mary Lassells, which she saw, and which wounded her deeply.

"Catherine," he said, and would have embraced her there in front of Mary Lassells, but she held off haughtily.

"Do not touch me! I would have you know that I shall never again allow you to do so."

"I must make you understand," said Manox, covering his face with his hands and forcing tears into his eyes. "I love you entirely, Catherine, I have said nothing that could offend. How could I, when my only thought is for your happiness!"

She repeated what Mary had told her. Mary burst out spitefully: "Thou canst not deny it, Manox, to my face!"

"I know not what I say," said Manox, his voice shaking with anguish. "All I know is that my passion for you so transports me beyond the bounds of reason that I wist not what I say!"

Catherine could never bear to see anyone in distress; her heart softened at once.

"I am very displeased," she said, and it was obvious that she was weakening.

Ignoring Mary Lassells, Manox slipped an arm about Catherine; Mary, in bitter defeat, turned and ran into the house.

Catherine walked in friendly fashion through the orchards, listening to his protestations of love, but although she said she forgave him, it not being in her nature to harbour ill feeling for long, as she was always ready to believe the best of people and could not happily see anyone suffer, she was shaken, and badly shaken.

Mary Lassells had made her see this love affair in a different light. She never felt the same towards Manox again; and, being Catherine, in need of love, she must look about her for a more worthy object on which to lavish her affection.

Every citizen who could find a boat to hold him was on the Thames that May morning; along the banks of the river the crowd thronged. Beggars had come into the city to view the procession, and pickpockets hoped to ensure a profitable day's work among the press of people. The taverns were full and overflowing; at all points of vantage people stood, sat or knelt, mounted posts or one another's shoulders to get a good view of the celebrations in honour of Queen Anne's coronation.

From the river bank, Catherine watched with some of the ladies, among them Dorothy Barwicke and Mary Lassells. There was festivity and recklessness in the air today. All the ladies giggled and looked for someone with whom to flirt; they had decked themselves out in their gayest clothes in order to do honour to the new Queen. Most of the young people were ready to admire her; it was chiefly the old ones who continued to murmur against her, and even they were lethargic in their disapproval on this day. When she had been the King's mistress it was one thing; now she was Queen it was another. The King had married her; the Pope had not sanctioned the divorce; Rome considered the marriage illegal; but what matter! England was no longer under the Pope; it owed allegiance to none but its own great King. Weighty matters these, which the people did not fully understand; they worshipped in the same way as before, and the same religious rites were observed, so what matter! And even those who pitied sad Katharine and reviled flaunting, wicked Anne, enjoyed a day's pleasure.

And this honour which the King would do to his newly made Queen was to be such a spectacle, so lavish in its display, as to outdo even Tudor splendour.

The Queen was to come from Greenwich to the Tower, and the coronation would take place at Westminster; there would be days of rejoicing, days of processions, and the citizens of London ever loved such occasions.

Mary Lassells would have liked to voice her opinions of the new Queen, but thought it wise to keep quiet. Here was another example of sin's being lauded and feted; but she knew well enough the folly of talking too freely. The King was determined to have no opposition; already she had heard that the dungeons at the Tower of London were full of those who spoke rashly; well she knew that the instruments of torture were being overworked. It was not for a humble person to run into danger.

Silly Catherine Howard was filled with childish glee, talking incessantly of her dear, beautiful cousin whom she loved devotedly. "I declare I shall die of pride . . ." babbled Catherine Howard. "I declare I can scarce wait for her royal barge. . . ."

Mary Lassells talked with Dorothy Barwicke about the wickedness of Manox and Catherine. Dorothy listened and feigned disgust, not mentioning that she had carried many a message from Manox to Catherine, had helped to make their meetings easy, that she had taken over Isabel's task of advancing Catherine's love affair so that she, Catherine, might be involved in the practices which occurred in the ladies' apartments and thereby be prevented from carrying stories to her grandmother. Not, thought Dorothy, that Isabel need have feared. Catherine was no tale-bearer, but the last person in the world to wish to make trouble for others. With Mary Lassells it was quite another matter; Dorothy knew she must go cautiously with Mary.

Catherine's bright eyes had seen a little group of gentlemen along the riverbank. The gentlemen looked interested in the party of young ladies, recognizing them as of the Duchess's retinue.

"I can tell you who they are," whispered one laughing-eyed girl to Catherine. "They are your uncle the Duke's young gentlemen."

This was so, for the Duke of Norfolk kept in his household certain gentlemen of good birth and low fortune, most of whom could claim some connection—however distant—with himself. He called them his household troop; they were really pensioners; their only duty was to guard his interests wherever they might be, in time of war to follow him in the field, to back him in his quarrels, to be ever ready to defend him should the need arise. For this he paid them well, fed and clothed them, and gave them little to do—except when he should need them—but amuse themselves. The Earl of Northumberland had a similar retinue in his house; they had always had such, and found it difficult to discard this relic of the feudal system. The gentlemen, having nothing to do but amuse themselves, did this with gusto; they were a high-spirited group, reckless and daring, seeking adventure in any form.

It was a little band of these gentlemen who now found an opportunity of speaking to the ladies of the Duchess's household whom they had seen often, for the Duke's residence was close by his stepmother's, and its gardens and orchards also ran down to the river.

"Look!" cried Dorothy Barwicke, and Catherine's attention was taken from the young men to the river. Numerous barges, containing the chief citizens of London with their Lord Mayor, were passing by on their way to greet the Queen. The merchants presented a brilliant sight in their scarlet clothes and the great heavy chains about their necks. A band of musicians was playing in the city state barge.

Catherine began to sing, keeping time with the band; one of the young men on the river bank joined in. Catherine noticed that he was quite the handsomest of the group, and as she sang, she could not take her eyes from him. He pointed to a barge, calling her attention to what appeared to be a dragon which capered about the deck, shaking its great tail and spitting fire into the river, to the intense delight of all who beheld it. Catherine laughed gleefully, and the young man laughed; she believed he was urging his companions to get nearer to her and her friends. Catherine shrieked with excitement, watching the monsters who were helping the dragon to entertain the citizens. Catherine's eyes filled with ready tears as a barge came into view containing a choir of young girls, singing softly. Catherine could hear the words they sang, which were of the beauty and virtue of Queen Anne.

There was a long wait before the return of the procession bringing with it the Queen. There was however plenty with which to beguile themselves, on such a day.

Sweetmeats were handed round; there was wine to drink and little cakes to nibble. It was all very pleasant, especially when Catherine found the handsome young man standing beside her, offering sweets.

"I watched you from the crowd," he said.

"Indeed, sir, you need not tell me that, for I saw that you watched!"

She looked older than her years; she was flushed with pleasure; her experience with Manox had matured her. Francis Derham judged her to be about fifteen—a delightful age, he thought.

"I thought you might care to sample these sweetmeats."

"Indeed I do care." She munched them happily, childishly. "I long for the moment when the Queen comes by!"

"Have you ever seen Her Majesty? I hear she is wondrously beautiful."

"Have I ever seen her! I would have you know, sir, that the Queen is first cousin to me."

"Cousin to you! I know you are of my lady of Norfolk's house. Tell me, are you then her granddaughter?"

"I am."

He was surprised that Her Grace of Norfolk should allow her granddaughter—so young and so attractive—to run wild in this way, but he suppressed his surprise. He said in tones of excitement: "Then verily I believe you to be a kinswoman of mine!"

Catherine was delighted. They talked of their relations; he was right, there was a connection, though distant.

"Ah!" said Catherine. "I feel safe then with you!"

That was a pleasant reflection, for she was realizing that she could feel safe no longer with Manox, that she was beginning to fear his embraces, that she sought excuses not to be with him. His sordid words to Mary Lassells had shocked and frightened her, and though she did not wish to hurt him, she had no desire to see him. Moreover, now that she had met Francis Derham, she felt more estranged from Manox than before, for Francis was an entirely different type—a gentleman, a man of good manners, good breeding—and being with him, even in those first hours, and seeing that he was attracted by her as Manox had been, she could not help but compare the two; and every vestige of admiration she had had for the musician vanished.

Francis thought: Her grandmother is waiting on the Queen, and that accounts for her freedom; but she is young to be abroad alone. He made up his mind to protect her.

He stayed at her side; they wandered along the bank of the river, they saw the Queen in her royal barge from which issued sweet music; and there followed the Queen, the barges of her father, the Duke of Suffolk, and all the nobility.

"She goes to the Tower!" said Derham.

"The Tower!" Catherine shivered, and he laughed at her. "Why do you laugh?" she asked.

"Because you look afraid."

Then she was telling him of her childhood, of Doll Tappit and Walter the warder, of the Little Ease and the Pit; and the screams the warder had heard coming from the torture chambers.

"I would," said Catherine simply, "that my sweet cousin were not going to the Tower."

He laughed at this simplicity. "Do you not know that all our sovereigns go to the Tower on their coronation? The state apartments there are very different from the dungeons and torture chambers, I'll warrant you!"

"Still, I like it not."

"You are a dear little girl." He thought again: She should not be allowed to run free like this! And he was angry towards those who were in charge of her. He liked her company; she was so youthful, so innocent, and yet . . . womanly. She would attract men, he knew, perhaps too strongly for her safety. He said: "You and I should see the celebrations together, should we not? We could meet and go together."

Catherine was ever eager for adventure, and she liked this young man because he inspired her with trust. She wanted someone to think of affectionately, so that she might no longer brood on Manox.

"You are very kind."

"You would need to wear your plainest garments, for we should mingle with the crowds."

"My plainest! They are all plain!"

"I mean you would cease to be Catherine Howard of

Norfolk in a crowd of citizens; you would be plain Catherine Smith or some such. How like you this plan?"

"I like it vastly!" laughed Catherine.

And so they made their plans, and it was with him that Catherine saw the Queen's procession after her sojourn at the Tower; it was with Derham that she watched the royal progress through the city. In Gracechurch Street, hung with crimson and scarlet, they mingled with the crowd; they marvelled at the sight of the Chepe decorated with cloth and velvet. They saw the Lord Mayor receive the Queen at the Tower Gate; they saw the French ambassador, the judges, the knights who had been newly honoured in celebration of the coronation; they saw the abbots and the bishops; they espied the florid Duke of Suffolk, who must bury his animosity this day, bearing the verge of silver which showed him to hold the office of High Constable of England.

Catherine looked at this man, and held Derham's hand more firmly. Her companion looked down at her questioningly.

"What ails Catherine Smith?"

"I but thought of his wife, the King's sister, who I have heard is dying. He shows no sorrow."

"He shows nothing," whispered Derham. "Not his antagonism to the Queen. . . . But let us not speak of such matters."

Catherine shivered, then burst into sudden laughter.

"I think it more pleasant to wear a plain hood and be of the crowd, than to be a queen. I trow I'm as happy as my cousin!"

He pressed her hand; he had begun by feeling friendship,

but friendship was deepening into warmer feelings. Catherine Howard was so sweet, such a loving and entrancing little creature!

Catherine gasped, for now came none but the Queen herself, breathtakingly lovely, borne by two white palfreys in white damask in an open litter covered with cloth of gold. Her beautiful hair was flowing in her favourite style, and on her head was a coif whose circlet was set with precious stones. Her surcoat was of silver tissue, and her mantle of the same material lined with ermine. Even those who had murmured against her must stop their murmurings, for never had they beheld such beauty, and while she was among them they must come under her spell.

Catherine was entirely fascinated by her; she had no eyes for those following; she did not see the crimson-clad ladies nor the chariots that followed, all covered in red cloth of gold, until Derham pointed out her grandmother in the first of these with the Marchioness of Dorset. Catherine smiled, wondering what the old lady would say, could she see her in this crowd. But the old Duchess would be thinking of nothing but the lovely woman in the litter, her granddaughter, Queen of England, and that this was the proudest day of her long life.

Through the city the pageant continued. In Gracechurch Street they fought their way through the crowd clustered round a fountain from which spurted most lavishly good Rhenish wine. The pageant of the white falcon was enchanting, thought Catherine, for the white falcon represented Anne, and it sat uncrowned among the red and white roses; and then, as the Queen came close, there was a burst of sweet music and an angel flew down and placed a golden crown on the falcon's head. In Cornhill the Queen must pause before a throne on which sat the Three Graces, and in front of which was a spring which ran continually with wine; and she rested there while a poet read a poem which declared that the Queen possessed the qualities represented by the three ladies on the throne. The conduits of Chepe Side ran at one end white wine, and at the other claret, during the whole of that afternoon.

All through this pageantry rode Anne, her eyes bright with triumph—this was the moment for which she had waited four long years—on to Westminster Hall to thank the Lord Mayor and those who had organized the pageantry. Weary and very happy, she ate, and changed from the state garments, staying there at Westminster with the King that night.

Next morning—the coronation day itself, the first of June and a glorious Sunday—Catherine and Derham were again together. They caught a glimpse of the Queen in her surcoat and mantle of purple velvet lined with ermine, with rubies glistening in her hair.

"There is my grandmother!" whispered Catherine. And so it was, for on this day it was the old Duchess's delight and joy to hold the train of her granddaughter. Following the Dowager Duchess were the highest ladies in the land, clad splendidly in scarlet velvet, and the bars of ermine which decorated their stomachers denoted by their number the degree of nobility possessed by each; after these ladies came the knights' wives and the Queen's gentlewomen all clad in gay scarlet. Neither Catherine nor Derham went into the Abbey to see Cranmer set the crown on Anne's head. Mingling with the crowd outside, they both thought they had never been so happy in their lives.

"This is a great adventure indeed for me!" said Derham. "And glad I am I saw thee!"

"Glad I am too!"

They looked at each other and laughed. Then he, drawing her into an alley, laid his lips against hers. He was surprised by the warmth with which she returned his kiss. He kissed her again and again.

Passersby saw them and smiled.

"The city is as full of lovers as pickpockets this day!" said one.

"Aye! All eager to follow the royal example doubtless!"

There was laughter, for who could but laugh at such a time, when these streets, in which but a few years before people had died of that plague called the sweating sickness, were now running with good wine!

There was one member of Anne's family who did not attend the coronation. Jane Rochford's jealousy had become uncontrollable, and in her mad rage against her sister-in-law she was even more indiscreet than was habitual with her.

She had said: "This marriage . . . it is no marriage. A man may not take a wife while he has another. Anne is still the

King's mistress, no matter what ceremonies there may be. There is only one Queen, and she is Queen Katharine."

There were many in support of Queen Katharine, many who shook their heads sadly over the melancholy fate which had befallen the woman whom they had respected as Queen for over twenty years; indeed even those who supported Anne through love or fear could have little to say against Queen Katharine. She must be admired for that calm and queenly dignity which had never deserted her throughout her reign; she had suffered deeply; she had been submitted to mental torture by her unfaithful husband, even before he had brutally told her he would divorce her since she was of no more use to him; she had, by her tactful behaviour, managed to endow the King with some of her own dignity, covering his blatant amours, saying and believing, "This is but the way of kings!" She who suffered bitter humiliations at the hands of Henry VII during those years which had elapsed between Arthur's death and her marriage with Henry, bore few grudges; she was meek, and submissive when she considered it her duty to be so; when she considered it her duty to be strong she could be as firm and tenacious as Henry himself. Duty was the keynote of her life. She would suffer the severest torture rather than deviate from what she considered right. She had been taught her religion by her mother, Isabella, who in her turn had been taught by that grim zealot, Torquemada.

In these great people—Katharine, Isabella, Torquemada—there burned fierce fires of fanaticism which purged them of fear. Their religion was the rock to which they clung; life on earth was to them but a dream, compared with the reality to come. Katharine, bound irrevocably to Rome, believing there could be no divorce, was ready to go to the stake rather than give Henry what he demanded; for to her mind earthly torment was a small price to pay for that eternal bliss which was reserved only for those true servants of the Roman Catholic Faith. With all the strength she had possessed she had stood out against her blustering, furious husband, so nobly, so fearlessly, so assured of the right, that even in defeat she appeared to triumph, and there were none who could go into her presence and not treat her as a queen. There was her passionate devotion to her daughter to touch the hearts of all; to this daughter she had given all the affection her husband did not want; she lived for this daughter, and delighted in the belief that one day she would sit on the throne of England; she had superintended her education with the greatest care, had glowed with pleasure at Mary's aptitude for learning, at her youthful charm, at her father's affection for her.

The only earthly joy which had lighted Katharine's sombre life was in her daughter, the Princess Mary. Henry, raging against her, cursing her obstinacy, unable to believe she could not see what was so clear to his scrupulous conscience, cursing her because she would not admit having consummated her marriage with his brother, hating her because she could have solved the whole difficulty by going into a nunnery, had struck at her in the most effective way possible, when he had separated her from her daughter.

In doing this he had acted foolishly, for the sympathy of the great mass of people was ever ready to be given to the victim of injustice, and they were all for Katharine and Mary. Mothers wept for them and, with their own children beside them, though they might be humble fishwives, could well understand the sufferings of a queen.

Henry, whose nature demanded homage and admiration, was hurt and alarmed by the sympathy shown to Katharine. Previous to the time when the divorce was mooted, it was he who had strutted across the stage, he on whom all attention was focused—he, large and magnificent, the goodliest of princes, the most handsome of princes, the most sporting of princes, the most loved and admired prince in the world. Katharine had been beside him, but only as a satellite shining with the reflected brilliance from his blazing personality. And now in the hearts of the susceptible and sentimental people she was enshrined as a saint, while he was looked upon as a bully, a promiscuous husband, a brutal man. He could not bear it; it was so unfair. Had he not told them he had merely obeyed the promptings of his conscience? They judged him as a man, not as a king. Then he grew angry. He had explained patiently; he had bared his soul; he had suffered the humiliation of a trial at Westminster Hall; and they did not understand! He had done with patience. He would have all these sullen people know who was their absolute master! A word, a look, would be enough to send any one of them, however high, however low, to the Tower.

Jane's motives were not of the highest, since it was her jealousy which overcame her prudence. She was a little hysterical. George was so often with the Queen; she had seen emotion in his face at a fancied slight to his sister; he was alert, anxious for her, admonishing her for her impulsiveness, and ridiculously, as people do when they love, loving her the more for it. My faults, thought Jane tearfully, are treated as such; hers are considered virtues.

People were looking furtively at her. When she railed against the Queen, they moved away from her, not wishing to be involved in such recklessness. Jane was too unhappy to care what she said, and gave herself up to the bitter satisfaction of reviling Anne.

Now in her apartment at the palace, she felt about her an ominous calm; those of her associates who had been wont to chat with her or sit with her, were not to be found. Her jealousy burned out, she had time to be frightened, and as she sat and brooded, longing for the return of George that she might tell him of her fears—feeling that he, seeing her in danger, might find her at least worthy of his pity—she heard on the staircase close to her door the sound of footsteps. She leaped up, for there was something in those footsteps of precision and authority; they stopped outside her door; there was a peremptory knocking.

Suppressing a desire to hide, Jane called in a trembling voice: "Come in!"

She knew him. His face was hard; he would have seen much suffering and grown accustomed to it; for he was Sir William Kingston, the Constable of the Tower of London.

Jane's fingers clutched the scarlet hangings. Her face was drained of colour, her lips trembled.

"Lady Jane Rochford, I am to conduct you to the Tower of London on a charge of High Treason."

Treason! That dreaded word. And she was guilty of it, for it was treason to speak against the king, and in speaking against Anne, this was what she had done.

She felt the room swing round her; one of Sir William's attendants caught her. They held her head down until the blood rushed back, and they did this naturally, as though they expected it. The room righted itself, but there was a rushing sound in her ears, and the faces of the men were blurred.

She faltered: "There is some mistake."

"There is no mistake," Sir William told her. "Your ladyship is requested to leave immediately."

"My husband . . ." she began. "My sister the Queen . . ."

"I have a warrant for your ladyship's arrest," she was told. "I must obey orders. And I must ask your ladyship to accompany us at once."

Quietly she went out, across the courtyard to the waiting barge. Silently they went up the river. She looked back at the sprawling palace on the riverbank with its squat towers and its mullioned windows—the favourite palace of the King, for he was born there and he liked its situation, which gave him a perfect view of the rising and falling of the river. When, wondered Jane, would she see Greenwich again?

Past the riverside houses of the rich went the barge until it came to that great fortress which now looked sullen in the grey light, forbidding and ominous. How many had passed through the Traitor's Gate and been swallowed up by that grey stone monster, and so lost to the world outside! It could not happen to me, thought Jane. Not to me! What have I done? Nothing . . . nothing. I did but voice an opinion.

Then she remembered some cynical remark of George's about those who voiced their opinions and those who were too nearly related to the King, deserving to die.

The barge was made fast; up the stone stairs Jane was led. She felt stifled by the oppressive atmosphere of the place. She was taken through a postern, across a narrow stone bridge, and was brought to the entrance of a grey tower. Trembling, Jane entered the Tower of London and was led up narrow spiral staircases, along cold corridors, to the room she would have to occupy. The door was locked on her. She ran to the window and looked out; below her was the dark water of the Thames.

Jane threw herself onto the narrow bed and burst into hysterical tears. This was her own folly! What did she care for Queen Katharine! What did she care for the Princess Mary! She wished to be no martyr. Well did she know that, had she tried to be Anne's friend, she could have been, for Anne did not look for enemies—she only fought those who stood against her. And how could poor little Jane Rochford stand against Queen Anne!

She was a fool. Looking back over her married life, she could see how foolish she had been. Oh, for another chance! She was humble, she was repentant, blaming herself. If she went to Anne, confessed her folly, asked for forgiveness, it would be granted, she knew well. She resolved that if she came out of the Tower she would overcome her jealousy of her brilliant sister-in-law; who knew, by so doing might she not gain a little of George's affection?

She was soothed and calmed, and so remained for some time, until that day which marked the beginning of the celebrations. And then, gazing from her window, she saw the arrival at the Tower of Anne, dressed in cloth of gold and attended by many ladies; and at the sight of her, all Jane's enmity returned, for the contrast between herself and her sister-in-law was too great to be endured stoically. She had arrived by way of the Traitor's Gate, while Anne had come in triumph as the Queen. No! Jane could not endure it. Here in this very place was her sister-in-law, feted and honoured, adored openly by that mighty and most feared man, Henry VIII. It was too much. Jane was overcome by fresh weeping.

"She has many enemies," said Jane aloud. "There is the true Queen and her daughter; there is Suffolk, Chapuys . . . to name but a few, and all of them powerful people. But Anne Boleyn, though there are many who hate you," she sobbed bitterly, "none does so as wholeheartedly as your despised Jane Rochford!"

The King was not happy. All through the hot month of June he had been aware of his dissatisfaction with life. He had thought that when Anne became his queen he would know complete happiness; she had been that for five months, and instead of his happiness growing it had gradually diminished.

The King still desired Anne, but he was no longer in love with her; which meant that he had lost that tenderness for her which had dominated him for six years, which had softened him and mellowed his nature. Never had the King loved any but himself, for even his love for Anne was based on his need of her. She had appeared on his horizon, a gay, laughing girl; to him she represented delightful youth; she was unique in her refusal to surrender; she appeared to be unimpressed by his kingship, and had talked of the need to love the man before the king. In his emotions Henry was as simple as a jungle lion; he stalked his quarry, and at these times stalking was his main preoccupation. The stalking of Anne was finished; she had managed to make it arduous; she had made him believe that the end of the hunt was not her surrender, but her place beside him on the throne; together they had stalked a crown for Anne; now it was hers, and they were both exhausted with the effort.

The relationship of mistress and lover was more exciting to a man of Henry's temperament than that of wife and hus-band; though his conscience would never allow him to admit this. The one was full of excitement, with clandestine meet-ings, with doubts and fears, and all the ingredients of romance;

the other was prosaic, arranged, and—most objectionable of all—inescapable, or almost. Gradually the relationship had been changing ever since January. She could still arouse in him moments of wild passion; she would always do that, she would always be to him the most attractive woman in his life; but he was essentially polygamous, and he possessed a wonderful and elastic conscience to explain all his actions.

Anne was clever; she could have held him; she could have kept him believing he had achieved happiness. But she had always been reckless, and the fight had tired her far more than it had Henry; she had more to gain and more to lose; now she felt she had reached her goal and needed to rest. Moreover she was able now to see this man she had married, from a different angle. She was no longer the humble subject climbing up to the dizzy heights on which he stood secure as King; she was level with him now, not a humble knight's daughter, but a queen looking at a king—and the closer view was less flattering to him. His youthful looks had gone. He was in his forties, and he had lived too well; he had done most things to excess, and this was apparent; stripped of his glittering clothes he was by no means wholesome; he had suffered the inevitable consequences of a promiscuous life. His oblique gaze at facts irritated Anne beyond endurance. She rebelled against his conscience; she looked at him too closely, and he knew she did. He had seen her lips curl at certain remarks of his; he had seen her face harden at some display of coarseness. This would enrage him, for he would remind himself that he was the son of a king, and that it was entirely due to him that she had gained her high eminence.

They quarrelled; they were both too easily roused to anger to avoid it; but so far the quarrels were little more than tiffs, for she could still enchant him, and moreover he did not forget that she carried the Tudor heir. Anne did not forget it either; in fact it absorbed her; she was experiencing the abandonment of the mother—all else was of small importance, set beside the life that moved within her. She was obsessed by it; she wished to be left alone that she might dream of this child, this son, for whom she must wait for three long, dreary months.

This was all very right, thought Henry; the child was all-important, but there was no need for her to change so completely. He rejoiced to see her larger; it was a goodly sight. The boy was well and happy inside her, and God speed his coming! But . . . she should not forget the baby's father, as she appeared to do. She was languid, expressing no delight in the attentions he paid to her, preferring to talk of babies with her ladies than to have him with her. Henry was disappointed. He missed too their passionate lovemaking. He was in the forties; he could not expect to enjoy his manly vigour for many more years. Sometimes he felt quite old; then he would say to himself: "What I have endured these last years for her has done this to me; brought me a few years nearer the grave, I trow!" Then he would be indignant with her, indignant that she, while carrying his child, must deny him those blissful moments which he could enjoy with none as he could with her. He would think back over his faithfulness to her. This was astonishing; it amazed him. Ah, well, a man must be faithful to a mistress if he wishes to keep her, but a wife is a different matter altogether!

The thought took hold of Henry, haunting his mind. He thought of the days before Anne had come to Suffolk House; they had a piquancy, a charm, since the excitement of adventure is in its unexpectedness. "It is more pleasing to pluck an apple from the branch which you have seized, than to take one up from a graven dish." There was truth enough in that, he assured himself, thinking of sudden amorous adventures.

There came a day in July when the rain was teeming down and there was little to do. One played the harp, one sang . . . but the day flagged, for he was uneasy in his mind. Affairs of state weighed heavily upon him. In spite of his separation from Rome, he was eager that the Pope should sanction his marriage; he was disappointed of this, for instead of the sanction there came an announcement that Cranmer's sentence on Henry's former marriage was to be annulled; unless, he was threatened, he left Anne before September and returned to Katharine, both he and she he called his new queen would be excommunicated.

This was disquieting news which set Henry trembling; Anne's defiance of Rome, her lack of superstitious dread, angered him against her, for he did not care that she should show more courage than he; although his conscience explained that his feeling was not fear but eagerness to assure himself that he had acted with the will of God. Some priests, particularly in the north, were preaching against the new marriage. At Greenwich, Friar Peyto had even had the temerity to preach before Henry and Anne, hinting at the awful judgment that awaited them. Cardinal Pole, who had decided it would be well to live on the Continent owing to his close relationship to the King, wrote reproachful letters abusing Anne. Henry did not trust the Spanish ambassador; the man was sly and insolent and over-bold; he had dared to ask Henry if he could be sure of having children, making a reference to the state of the kingly body which was outwardly manifested by a malignant sore on the leg, which refused to heal.

Henry had reason to believe that Chapuys had reported to his master on the state of English defences; and if this were so, might he not advise the Emperor to make an attack?

Would a conquest of England be difficult for such a skilled general as Charles? Henry knew that most of his nobles—with perhaps the exception of Norfolk—would be ready to support Katharine's side; the Scots were ever eager to be troublesome. Why should not Charles, on the pretext of avenging an ill-treated aunt, do that which would be of inestimable advantage to himself—subdue England? There was one gleam of hope in this prospect; Charles was fully occupied in his scattered possessions, and he was too cautious to stretch his already overstrained resources in another cause. Henry raged and fumed and said he would send Chapuys home, but that was senseless, he knew well; better to have the spy whose evil ways were known to him than another sent in his place who might be possessed of even greater cunning. Henry bottled up his indignation temporarily, holding in his anger, but storing it, nourishing it. The only brightness on the political horizon was that Francis had sent congratulations to both himself and Anne; Henry had invited the French King to sponsor his son, which Francis had cordially agreed to do. Henry felt that, once his son was born, the mass of the people—the element he feared most—would be so overjoyed that it would be forgotten that various unorthodox methods had been followed in order to bring about such a joyous event. Astrologers and physicians had assured him that there could be no doubt of the sex of the child, so all Henry needed to do was to wait for September; but never had a month seemed so long in coming, and it was but July, and wet. The King therefore felt himself in need of diversion.

It came in the voluptuous form of one of the ladies attending Anne. This girl was in complete contrast to her mistress, round-faced, possessed of large baby blue eyes, plump and inviting. No haughtiness there; no dignity; Henry was ever attracted by change.

She glanced at him as she flitted about the chamber, and Anne, absorbed in maternity, did not at first notice what was going on. The girl curtseyed to him, glanced sideways at him; he smiled at her, forgetting Chapuys and astute Charles, and all those who preached against him.

He came upon her suddenly in the quiet of a corridor.

She curtseyed, throwing at him that bold glance of admiration which he remembered so well from the days before his thoughts had been given entirely to Anne. He kissed the girl; she caught her breath; he remembered that too; as though they were overwhelmed by him! He felt a king again; pleasant indeed to bestow favours like a king, instead of having to beg for them like a dog.

He left her though, for Anne still largely occupied his thoughts. There was none to be compared with Anne, and he was afraid of her still, afraid of her reactions should she discover any infidelity. He could not forget how she had gone back to Hever; moreover she was to bear him a son. He felt sentimental towards her still; but a kiss was nothing.

The weather cleared, and he felt better. August came. Invitations to the christening of the prince were made ready. Anne, languid on her couch, watched the King obliquely, wondering what gave him that secret look, noting the sly glances of her attendant, noting a certain covert boldness in the girl's manner towards herself. Anne could not believe that he who had been faithful for so many years in the most difficult circumstances had so quickly lapsed, and at such a time, when she was to give him a son. But the secretiveness of him, that irritability towards herself which a man of his type would feel towards someone he had wronged or was about to wrong made her feel sure of what was afoot.

Anne was no patient Griselda, no Katharine of Aragon. She was furious, and the more so because her fury must be tinged with fear. What if history were to repeat itself! What if that which had happened to Queen Katharine was about to happen to Queen Anne! Would she be asked to admit that her marriage was illegal? Would she be invited to go into a nunnery? She must remember that she had no powerful Emperor Charles behind her.

She watched the King; she watched the girl. Henry was overwrought; he drank freely; the days seemed endless to him; he was nervous and irritable sometimes, at others over-exuberant. But this was understandable, for the birth of a son was of the utmost importance since not only would it ensure the Tudor dynasty, but to Henry it would come like a sign from heaven that he had been right to displace Katharine.

Anne lived uncomfortably through the hot days, longing for the birth of her child. She felt upon her the eyes of all; she felt them to be waiting for that all-deciding factor, the birth of a male child. Her friends prayed for a son; her enemies hoped for a daughter or a stillborn child.

One day at the end of August it seemed to her that the girl whom she watched with such suspicion was looking more sly and a trifle arrogant. She saw Henry give her a look of smoldering desire.

"Shall I endure this before my very eyes?" Anne asked herself. "Am I not Queen?"

She waited until Henry was alone in the chamber with her; then she said, her eyes blazing: "If you must amuse yourself, I would prefer you did not do it under my eyes and with one of my own women!"

Henry's eyes bulged with fury. He hated being caught; he had had this matter out with his conscience; it was nothing, this light little affair with a wench who had doubtless lost her virginity long ago; it was hardly worth confessing. It was a light and airy nothing, entered into after the drinking of too much wine, little more than a dream.

"Am I to be defied by one wife," he asked himself, "dictated to by another?"

He had had enough of this; he was the King, he would have her know. It was not for her to keep up her arrogance to him now.

As he struggled for words to express his indignation, one of Anne's attendants entered; that did not deter him. It should be known throughout the court that he was absolute King, and that the Queen enjoyed her power through him.

He shouted: "You close your eyes, as your betters did before you!"

Her cheeks flushed scarlet; she lifted herself in the bed; angry retorts rose to her lips, but something in the face of the King subdued her suddenly, so that her anger left her; she had no room for any other emotion than deadly fear. His face had lost its flushed appearance too; his eyes peered out from his quivering flesh, suddenly cold and very cruel.

Then he continued to speak, slowly and deliberately: "You ought to know that it is in my power in a single instant to lower you further than I raised you up."

He went from the room; she sank back, almost fainting.

The attendant came to her hastily, ministering to her anxiously, knowing the deep humiliation that must have wounded one so proud. Had Anne been alone she would have retorted hotly; she would have flayed him with her tongue; but they were not alone—yet he had not cared for that! In the court her enemies would hear of this; they would talk of the beginning of the end of Anne Boleyn.

Her hands were cold and wet; she overcame a desire to burst into passionate tears. Then the child began to move inside her, reassuring her. Her son. Once he was born, she was safe, for Henry would never displace the mother of his son whatever the provocation.

Henry did not go near her again for several days. He found a fresh and feverish excitement in the knowledge that to be in lust was satisfying and more congenial to his nature than to be in love. The girl was a saucy wench, God knew, but ready enough, over-ready, to obey her king. To love was to beg and plead; to lust was but to demand satisfaction.

He thought of Anne often, sometimes when he was with the girl. His thoughts were so mixed he could not define them. Sometimes he thought, When the confinement's over, she'll be herself again. Then he thought of a lithesome girl leaning over a pond at Hever, a lovely woman entertaining him at Suffolk House. Anne, Anne . . . there is none on earth as delightful as Anne! This is naught, Anne; this is forgotten once you are with me again.

Then at mass or confession his thoughts would be tinged

with fear. Suppose the Almighty should show his displeasure by a daughter or a stillborn child! Marriage with Katharine had been a succession of stillborn children, because his marriage with Katharine had been no marriage. He himself had said that. What if his marriage with Anne should be no marriage either?

But God would show him, for God would always be ready to guide one who followed His laws and praised Him, as did Henry VIII of England.

Throughout the city the news was awaited. People in the barges that floated down the Thames called one to the other.

"Is the prince come yet then?"

There was scarcely a whisper against the new Queen; those who had been her most violent enemies thought of her now, not as the Queen, but as a mother.

"I heard her pains had started, poor lady . . ."

"They say his name will be Henry or Edward . . ."

Mothers remembered occasions when they had suffered as the Queen suffered now, and even those who cared nothing for motherhood were fond of pageantry. They remembered the coronation, when wine had flowed free from fountains. Pageants, feasting, rejoicing would mark the birth of a son to a king who had waited twenty-four years for it; it would be a greater event than a coronation.

"God save the little prince!" cried the people.

The Dowager Duchess of Norfolk scarcely slept at all, so eager was she for the event. She was full of pride and misgivings, assuring herself that Anne was a healthy girl, that the delivery must be effected efficiently, pushing to the back of her mind those fears which came from her knowledge of the King. Poor Katharine had had miscarriage after miscarriage; they said she was diseased, and whence did she come by such diseases? Might it not have been through close contact with His Majesty? One did not speak such thoughts, for it were treason to do so, but how could the most loyal subjects help their coming to mind! But Anne was a healthy girl; this was her first child. She had come safely through the nine months of pregnancy, and everything must be well.

In the orchard, sheltered by the trees whose fruit was beginning to ripen, Catherine Howard and Francis Derham lay in each other's arms with scarcely a thought for the momentous events which would shape the course of history.

Francis said: "Why should they not consent to our marriage? It is true I am poor, but my birth is good."

"They will assuredly consent," murmured Catherine. "They must consent!"

"And why should it not be soon? When the Duchess is recovered from this excitement, she will surely listen to me,

Catherine. Do you think that I might approach her?"

"Yes," said Catherine happily.

"Then we are betrothed!"

"Yes."

"Then call me husband."

"Husband," said Catherine, and he kissed her.

"I would we were away from here, wife, that at we were in our own house. I get so little opportunity for seeing you."

"So little," she sighed.

"And I hear that the Duchess's ladies are unprincipled in some ways, that they are over-bold with men. I like it not that you should be among them."

"I am safe," she said, "loving thee."

They kissed again, Catherine drew him closer, feeling that excessive excitement which physical contact with one who attracted her must always give her.

Derham kissed her fervently, enchanted by her as Manox had been; but he was genuinely in love with her, and his feelings were governed by affection as well as the need to gratify his senses. She was very young, but she was ready for passion. He was a reckless young man, courageous and virile; and Catherine's obvious longing to complete their intimacy was so alluring that he—while tenderly thinking of her age—must seek to arrange it.

He insisted they would marry. He could think of nothing more delightful. They were really married, he told her, because according to the law of the Church it was only necessary for two free people to agree to a contract and it was made. It soothed his fears that she was too young, when he called her wife; when she called him husband, he was transported with joy.

He meant to be tactful and kind. He knew nothing of her experience with Manox. Catherine did not tell him, not because she wished to hide it, but because Manox no longer interested her. She had asked her grandmother if she might have a new music teacher, and the old lady, too full of court matters to care what her granddaughter did, had nodded, and when Catherine had named an ascetic, middle-aged man, her grandmother had nodded again. In any case the Duchess no longer sat as chaperone during the music lessons. Manox had almost passed from Catherine's thoughts, except on those unpleasant occasions when he would try to see her—for he was furious that she had ended the affair so abruptly, blaming Mary Lassells for this and making no secret of his hatred and contempt for the girl. Catherine wished of course that she had never known Manox, but she was too blissful to think of much else but the completion of her love with Francis Derham.

"I have a plan," said Derham.

"Tell me of it."

"What if I were to ask Her Grace to take me into her house?"

"Dost think she would?" Catherine was trembling at the thought.

"I think she might." He smiled complacently, remembering how on one occasion Her Grace had singled him out—as a most personable young man—for her special attention. "I can but try. Then we shall be under the same roof; then I may speak for you. Oh, Catherine, Catherine, how I long for that day!"

Catherine longed for it with equal intensity.

He almost whispered to her that they need not wait; why should they, when they were husband and wife? Catherine was waiting for him to say that; but he did not . . . yet. They lay on the grass, looking up at the ripening fruit.

"I shall never forget the day you first called me husband," he said. "I shall remember it when I die!"

Catherine laughed, for death seemed far away and a most absurd topic for two young people in love.

"I shall never forget it either," she told him, and turned her face to his. They kissed; they trembled; they yearned for each other.

"Soon," he said, "I shall be in the Duchess's house. Then I shall see you often . . . often."

Catherine nodded.

On the gorgeous bed, which had been part of a French Prince's ransom, Anne lay racked with the agony of childbirth. The King paced up and down in an adjoining room. He could hear her groans. How he loved her! For her groaning set his heart beating with fear that she would die. He was that same lover to whom news of her illness had been brought during the pestilence. "I would willingly endure half of what you suffer to cure you." Memories of her came and went in his mind; her laughter, her gaiety; Anne, the centre of attraction at the jousts and masques; sitting beside him watching the jousts in the tiltyard, so beautiful, so apart from all others that he found it difficult to turn his attention from her to the jousting; he thought of her in his arms, his love and his Queen.

He was filled with remorse for that lapse, for the quarrel which had upset her, and—this made him break out into a clammy sweat—might have had some effect on the birth of his son.

He paced up and down, suffering with her. How long? How long? The veins stood out on his forehead. "By God! If anything happens to her, blood will flow—that I swear!"

The girl with whom he had dallied recently looked in at the door, smiling; she had been sent to soothe him. He looked at her without recognizing her.

Up and down he went, straining his ears and then putting his hands over them to shut out the sound of Anne's pain, His fear was suddenly swept away, for distinctly he heard the cry of a child, and in a second he was at the bedside, trembling with eagerness. In the chamber there was a hushed silence. The attendants were afraid to look at him. Anne lay white and exhausted, aware neither of him, nor her room, nor perhaps herself.

"What is it?" he shouted.

They hesitated, one looking at another, hoping that some

other would take on the delicate task of breaking unpleasant news.

His face was purple; his eyes blazing. He roared in his anguish.

"A daughter!" His voice was almost a sob; he was defeated; he was humiliated.

He stood, his hands clenched, words pouring from his mouth, abuse and rage; and his eyes were on Anne, lying still on the bed. This to happen to him! What had he done to deserve it? What had he ever done to deserve it? Had he not always sought to do right? Had he not spent hours of labour, studying theology; had he not written *A Glasse of the Truth*? Had he not delved deep into this matter before he had taken action? Had he not waited for the promptings of his conscience? And for whom had he worked and suffered? Not for himself, but for his people, to save them from the rigours of civil war which during the last century had distressed and ravaged the land. For this he had worked, sparing himself not at all, defying the wrath of his simple people who could not be expected to understand his high motives. And this was his reward . . . a daughter!

He saw tears roll from Anne's closed eyes; her face was white as marble; she looked as though all life had gone from her; those tears alone showed him that she had heard. And then suddenly his disappointment was pushed aside. She too had suffered deeply; she was disappointed as he was. He knelt down and put his arms about her.

He said earnestly: "I would rather beg from door to door than forsake you!"

When he had gone, she lay very still, exhausted by the effort of giving birth to her daughter, her mind unable to give her body the rest it needed. She had failed. She had borne a daughter, not a son! This then was how Katharine of Aragon had felt when Mary was born. The hope was over; the prophecies of the physicians and the soothsayers had proved to be meaningless. "It will be a boy," they had assured her; and then . . . it was a girl!

Her heartbeats, which had been sluggish, quickened. What had he said? "I would rather beg from door to door than forsake you!" Forsake you! Why should he have said that? He would surely only have said it if the thought of forsaking her had been in his mind! He had forsaken Katharine.

Her cheeks were wet; then she must have shed tears. I could never live in a nunnery, she thought, and she remembered how she had once believed that Katharine ought to have gone to such a place. How different the suggestion seemed when applied to oneself! She had never understood Katharine's case until now.

Someone bent over her and whispered: "Your Majesty must try to sleep."

She slept awhile and dreamed she was plain Anne Boleyn at Blickling; she was experiencing great happiness, and when she awoke she thought, Happiness then is a matter of comparison; I never knew such complete happiness, for my body was in agony and now I scarce know I have a body, and that in itself is enough.

Fully conscious, she remembered that she was no longer a girl at Blickling, but a queen who had failed in her duty of bearing a male heir. She remembered that throughout the palace—throughout the kingdom—they would now be talking of her future, speculating as to what effect it would have upon her relationship with the King. Her enemies would be rejoicing, her friends mourning. Chapuys would be writing gleefully to his master. Suffolk would be smiling, well content. Katharine would pray for her; Mary would gloat: She has failed! She has failed! What will the King do now?

The sleep had strengthened her; her weakness of spirit was passing. She had fought to gain her place, she would fight to keep it.

"My baby . . ." she said, and they brought the child and laid it in her arms.

The red, crumpled face looked beautiful to her, because the child was hers; she held it close, examining it, touching its face lightly with her fingers, murmuring, "Little baby . . . my little baby!"

It mattered little to her now that the child was a girl, for, having seen her, she was convinced that there never had been such a beautiful child—so how could she wish to change it! She held her close, loving her and yet feeling fearful for her, for was not the child a possible Queen of England? No, there would be sons to follow. The first child had been a girl; therefore she would never sit on the throne of England, because Anne would have sons, many sons. Still, the mother must tremble for her child, must wish now that she were not the daughter of a king and queen. Suppose this baby had been born in some other home than royal Greenwich, where her sex would not have been a matter of such great importance. How happy she would have been then! There would have been nothing to think of but tending the child.

They would have taken the baby from her, but she would not let her go. She wanted her with her, to hold her close, to protect her.

She thought of Mary Tudor's fanatical eyes. How the birth of this child would add fuel to the fierce fires of Mary's resentment! Another girl to take her place, when she had lost it merely by being a girl! Before, there had been many a skirmish with Mary Tudor; now there must be deciding warfare between her and Queen Anne. For what if there were no more children! What if the fate of Queen Anne was that of Queen Katharine? Then . . . when the King was no more, there would be a throne for this child, a throne which would be coveted most ardently by Mary Tudor; and might not the people of England think Mary had the greater claim? Some considered that Katharine was still Queen, and that this newly born child was the bastard, not Mary Tudor.

"Oh, baby," murmured Anne, "what a troublesome world it is that you have been born into!" Fiercely she kissed the child. "But it shall be as happy for you as I can make it. I would kill Mary Tudor rather than that she should keep from you that which is your right!"

One of the women bent over the bed.

"Your Majesty needs to rest. . . ."

Hands took the baby; reluctantly Anne let her go.

She said: "She shall be called Elizabeth, after my mother and the King's."

The court was tense with excitement. In lowered tones the birth of Elizabeth was discussed, in state apartments, in the kitchens; women weeding in the gardens whispered together. In the streets, the people said: "What now? This is God's answer!" Chapuys was watchful, waiting; he sounded Cromwell. Cromwell was noncommittal, cool. He felt that the King was as yet too fond of the lady to desire any change in their relationship. He was unlike Wolsey; Wolsey shaped the King's policy while he allowed the King to believe it was his own; Cromwell left the shaping to the King, placing himself completely at the royal disposal. Whatever the King needed, Thomas Cromwell would provide. If he wished to disinherit Mary, Cromwell would find the most expeditious way of doing it; if the King wished to discard Anne, Cromwell would work out a way in which this could be done. Cromwell's motto was: "The King is always right."

The King still desired Anne ardently, but though he could be the passionate lover, he wished her to realize that it was not hers to command but to obey. A mistress may command, a wife must be submissive. Yet he missed his mistress; he even felt a need to replace her. He could not look upon Anne—young, beautiful and desirable—as he had looked on Katharine. And yet it seemed to him that wives are always wives; one is shackled to them by the laws of holy church, and to be shackled is a most unpleasant condition. There was an element of spice in sin, which virtue lacked; and even though a man had a perfectly good answer to offer his conscience, the spice was there. Anne could no longer threaten to return home; this was her home, the home of which she was indubitably master. She had given him a daughter—a further proof that she was not all he had believed her to be when he had pursued her so fanatically.

And so, in spite of his still-passionate desire for her, when this was satisfied he would quickly change from lover into that mighty figure, King and master.

This was apparent very soon after Elizabeth's birth. Anne wanted to keep the child with her, to feed her herself, to have her constantly in her care. Apart from her maternal feelings which were strong, she feared ill might befall her daughter through those enemies whom the child would inherit from the mother.

Seeing his daughter's cradle in the chamber which he shared with Anne, the King was startled.

"How now!" he growled. "What means this?"

"I would have her with me," said Anne, used to command, continuing to do so.

"You would have her with you!" he repeated ominously.

"Yes. And I shall feed her myself, for I declare I shall trust no one else with this task."

The King's face was purple with rage.

He stamped to the door and called to a startled maid of honour. She came in, trembling.

"Take the child away!" he roared.

The girl looked from the King to the Queen; the Queen's face was very pale, but she did not speak. She was trembling, remembering what he had said before the child's birth; at that time he had not waited until they were alone. "You ought to know that it is in my power in a single instant to lower you further than I raised you up!" And later, "I would rather beg from door to door than forsake you." He cared not what he said before whom; he was so careless of her feelings that it mattered not to him if, in the court, people speculated as to whether her influence was waning. Therefore she watched the girl remove the baby, and said nothing.

"She would disturb our rest!" said the King.

When they were alone, Anne turned on him fiercely.

"I wished to keep her with me. I wished to feed her myself. What could it matter. . . ."

He looked at her squarely. "Remember," he said slowly, "that I lifted you up to be Queen of England. I ask that you do not behave as a commoner."

His voice matched his eyes for coldness; she had never noticed how very cold they could be, how relentless and cruel was the small mouth.

Still trembling, she turned away from him, holding her head high, realizing that she, who a short while ago would have blazed at him demanding that her wishes be gratified, now dared do nothing but obey.

The King watched; her hair loose about her shoulders, she

reminded him suddenly of the girl in the Hever rose garden. He went to her and laid a heavy hand on her shoulder.

"Come, Anne!" he said, and turning her face to his kissed her. Hope soared in her heart then; she still had power to move him; she had accepted defeat too easily. She smiled.

"You were very determined about that!" she said, trying to infuse a careless note into her voice, for she was afraid to insist on keeping Elizabeth with her, and realized the folly of showing fear to one who was naturally a bully.

"Come, sweetheart!" His voice was thick with the beginnings of passion; she knew him so well; she recognized his moods. "A queen does not suckle her babes. Enough of this!" He laughed. "We have a daughter; we must get ourselves a boy!"

She laughed with him. As he caressed her, her thoughts moved fast. She had believed that, with the birth of her child, her great fight would be over; she would sink back, refreshed by new homage, into a security which could not be shaken. But Fate had been unkind; she had given the King, not that son who would have placed her so securely on the throne, but a daughter. The fight was not over; it was just beginning; for what had gone before must be a skirmish compared with what must follow. She would need all her skill now, since the very weapons which had won for her her first victories were grown blunt; and it was now not only for herself that she must fight.

How she pitied Katharine of Aragon, who had gone through it all before her! Who was still going through it; a veteran whose weapons were endurance and tenacity. Anne would have need of equal endurance, equal tenacity, for she fought in the opposite camp. She was a mother now; she was a tigress who sees her cub in mortal danger. Katharine of Aragon she had thought of as a pitiable woman, Mary as a wilful, outspoken girl; now they were her bitterest enemies, and they stood on their guard, waiting to dishonour her daughter.

She returned Henry's kisses.

He said: "Anne, Anne, there's no one like you, Anne!"

And hot anger rose within her, for she sensed that he was comparing her with the woman whom he had dallied with before her delivery. Once she would have repulsed him, stormed at him, told him what she thought; now she must consider; she must lure him afresh, she must enchant him. It would be more difficult now, but she would do it, because it was imperative that she should.

As he lay beside her, she entwined her fingers in his.

"Henry," she said.

He grunted.

Words trembled on her lips. What if she asked to have the baby in! No, that would be unwise; she could not make conditions now. She must tread carefully; she was only the King's wife now. The Queen of England lacked the power of Anne Rochford and the Marchioness of Pembroke; but the Queen had all the cunning of those ladies, and she would laugh yet in the faces of her enemies who prophesied her destruction.

"Henry, now that we have a child, would it not be well to

declare Mary illegitimate? We know well that she is, but it has never been so stated."

He considered this. He was feeling a little hurt with Mary, who had applauded and supported her mother ever since the divorce had been thought of. Mary was an obstinate girl, an unloving daughter who had dared to flout her father, the King.

"By God!" he said. "I've been too lenient with that girl!"

"Indeed you have! And did I not always tell you so; you must announce her illegitimacy at once, and every man of note in the country must agree to it."

"If they do not," growled Henry, "'twill be the worse for them!"

She kissed his cheek; she had been foolish to worry. She still had the power to manage him.

He said: "We must go cautiously. I fear the people will not like it. They have made a martyr of Katharine, and of Mary too."

She did not attach over-much importance to the will of the people. They had shouted: "We'll have no Nan Bullen!" And here she was, on the throne in spite of them. The people gathered together and grumbled; sometimes they made disturbances; sometimes they marched together with flaming torches in their hands. . . . Still, they should not pay too much attention to the people.

"Mary is a stupid, wayward girl," said Anne. And as the King nodded in agreement, she added: "She should be compelled to act as maid to Elizabeth. She should be made to understand who is the true princess!"

Then she threw herself into his arms, laughing immoderately. He was pleased with her; he was sure that ere long they would have a healthy boy.

✦

Sir Thomas More's daughter, Margaret Roper, was full of fear, for peace had been slowly filched from her home. April was such a pleasant month at Chelsea; in the garden of her father's house, where she had spent her happy childhood and continued to live with her husband, Will Roper, the trees were blossoming; the water of the Thames lapped gently about the privy stairs; and how often had Margaret sat on the wooden seat with her father, listening to his reading to her and her brother and sisters, or watching him as he discoursed most wittily with his good friend Erasmus. Change had crept into the house like a winter fog, and Margaret's heart was filled with a hatred alien to it; the hatred was for one whom she thought of as a brown girl, a girl with a sixth nail on her left hand and a disfiguring mark on her throat, a girl who had bewitched the King, who had cut off England from the Pope, and who had placed Margaret's father in mortal danger.

When Anne Boleyn had gone to court from Hever Castle, the first shadow had been cast over the Chelsea house. Her father would reprove her for her hatred, but Margaret could not subdue it. She was no saint, she reasoned. She had talked of Anne Boleyn most bitterly to her sisters, Elizabeth and Cecily; and now, sitting in the garden watching the river, calm today, bringing with it the mingled smells of tar and seaweed and rotting wood and fish, with the willow trees abudding and drooping sadly over it, she felt fear in the very air. When her adopted sister, Mercy, came running out to sit with her awhile, she had started violently and begun to tremble, fearing Mercy had brought news of some disaster. When her stepsister, Alice, appeared beside her, she felt her knees shake, though Alice had merely come to ask if Margaret would care to help her feed the peacocks.

Margaret recalled this house a few years back; she remembered seeing her father in the heart of his family, reading to them in long summer evenings out of doors, saying prayers in the house; and so often with a joke on his lips. Her father was the centre of his household; they all moved round him; were he removed, what then of the More family? 'Twould be like earth without the sun, thought Margaret. She remembered writing letters to him when he was away from home on an embassy. He had been proud of her, showing her letters to the great scholar Reginald Pole who had complimented him on possessing such a daughter. He had told her this, for he knew well when a compliment might be passed to do the object good, and not to foster pride. He was a saint. And what so often was the end of saints? They became martyrs. Margaret wept softly, controlledly, for she dared not show the others she had wept; it would displease her father. Why must she now recall the memories of her childhood and all those sunny days in which her father moved, the centre of her life, the best-loved one? Fear made her do it; fear of what was coming swiftly towards him. What was waiting for this adored father, tomorrow or the next day, or the next? Gloom had settled in the house; it was in the eyes of her stepmother, usually not eager to entertain it, usually eager to push it away; but it had come too close to be pushed away. Her sisters . . . were they over-gay? Their husbands laughed a little louder than was their wont; and in the garden, or from the windows of the house, their eyes would go to the river as though they were watching, watching for a barge that might come from Westminster or the Tower, and stop at the privy steps of Sir Thomas More's garden.

Her father was the calmest of the household; though often he would look at them all sadly and eagerly, as though he would remember the details of each face that he might recall them after he would be unable to see them. A great calm had settled upon him of late, as though he had grappled with a problem and found the solution. He was a great man, a good man; and yet he was full of fun. One would have expected a saint to be a little melancholy, not fond of partaking of pleasure nor seeing those about him doing so. He was not like that; he loved to laugh, to see his children laugh; he was full of kindly wit. Oh, there was never such a one as Father! sighed Margaret.

He was fifty-six years of age now, and since he had given up the chancellorship he had looked every year of it. As a boy he had been taken into the household of Cardinal Morton who was then Archbishop of Canterbury; from thence he had gone to Oxford, become a lawyer, gone into Parliament, had lectured on the subject of theology, and was soon recognized as a brilliant young man. There was in him the stuff of the martyr; at one time he had come very near to becoming a monk, but he decided to marry. "Did you ever regret that decision, Father?" Margaret once asked, and he laughed and pretended to consider; and she had been filled with happiness to know he did not. That was well, for if ever a man was meant to be a father, that man was Sir Thomas More. There was never such a family as ours, thought Margaret. We were happy . . . happy . . . before Anne Boleyn went to court. Wolsey had admired Sir Thomas, had made use of him; the King had met him, taken a liking to him, sought his help in denouncing the doctrines of Luther. Thus, when Wolsey was discarded, it was on this man that the King's choice fell. "More shall be Chancellor. More shall have the Great Seal of England," said the King. "For rarely liked I a man better!" And so he achieved that high office; but he was never meant to go to court. Had he not remarked that he would serve God first, the Prince second? He would ever say that which would lead to trouble, because honesty was second nature to him. He was a saint; please God he need never show the world that he could be a martyr too! Margaret had been frightened when he became Chancellor, knowing his views on the divorce.

"Anne Boleyn will never be Queen," she had said often enough to her husband, Will. "How can she be, when the Pope will not sanction the divorce?"

"Indeed," had answered Will, "you speak truth, Meg. How can that be! A man who has one wife may not marry another."

She had been afraid for Will then, for he was interested in

the new faith and would read of it secretly, being unsure in his mind; she trembled, for she could not have borne that her beloved father and her dear husband should not be in agreement on these matters. She had discussed Martin Luther and his doctrines with her father, for he was ever ready to talk with her on any serious subject, holding that though she was a woman she had the power to think and reason.

"Father," she had said, "there have been times when I have heard you discourse against the ways of Rome."

"That I have done, Meg. But this is how I see it, daughter. Rome's ways are not always good, but I hold the things we value most in life may best be held to under Rome."

She had not dared to tell him of Will's flirting with the new faith. She did not understand it fully. She supposed that Will, being young, would prefer to try the new, and her father, being not so young, must like the old ways best. She had thought it a great tragedy when she discovered this tendency in Will; but what was that, compared with this which threatened!

The giving up of the Great Seal had been like the first clap of thunder that heralds an unexpected storm on a fine summer's day. After that there was quiet, until that April day a year ago, when three bishops came to the house one morning to bring twenty pounds for his dress, that he might attend the coronation of her who was set up as Queen, and who could never be accepted as Queen in this household. He had refused that invitation. She shivered at the memory. A few days later that refusal brought forth its results; he was charged with bribery and corruption. A ridiculous charge against the most honest man in England; but nothing was too ridiculous to bring against one so prominent who failed to do honour to Anne Boleyn. And recently there had come a further and more alarming charge; a mad nun of Kent, named Elizabeth Barton, had been shocking Anne's supporters and heartening those of Katharine with her lurid prophecies of the evil fates which would await the King and Anne, should they continue in their ungodly ways. The rightful Queen, declared the nun, was Katharine. She had seen visions; she went into trances and then gave voice to prophecies which she declared were put into her mouth by the Holy Ghost. As she had been in touch with Queen Katharine and the Emperor Charles, she was considered dangerous, but on her arrest and examination in the Star Chamber she had confessed she was an imposter. And Sir Thomas More was accused of having instigated this woman to pretend the future had been revealed to her, that she might frighten the King into taking back Katharine and abandoning Anne.

Margaret remembered how they had sat about the table, pretending to eat, pretending it would be well, telling each other that the innocence of the guiltless was their best defence. He had been taken before the council; he had been questioned by the new Archbishop, by His Grace of Norfolk—whom she feared for his cold eyes and his hard, cruel mouth—before Thomas Cromwell, whose thick hands looked as though they would not hesitate to turn on one slow to answer his questions; his fish-like eyes held no warmth, only cunning. But he was clever as well as good, this most loved father; he had out-witted them, for his wit was sharper than theirs; and she had heard that there was none equal to him apart from Cranmer, and on this occasion Cranmer was on the wrong side, so right must prevail. They had dismissed him in exasperation, for they could not trip him; and it was his arguments, she was sure, that had dumbfounded them, not theirs him.

Will had travelled down with him, and told her about this afterwards. Will had said that he knew all must be well, and rejoiced to see him so merry.

Her father had replied that truly he was merry, and would Will know why? He had taken the first step and the first step was the hardest. He had gone so far with those lords that with-out great shame he could never turn back.

This then had been the cause of his merriment. The step was taken down that path which he believed to be the right one; but what a path, where danger lurked at every turn! And what was at the end of it? That had happened a year ago, and now he had come far along that path; and this gloom which hung over them now—did it mean that he was nearing its end?

Mercy was running out to the garden now.

"Meg!" she called. "Meg!" And Margaret dared not turn to look at her, so strong was her fear, so numbing the suspense.

Mercy's pleasant face was hot with running.

"Dinner, Meg! Of what are you thinking . . . dreaming here? We are all waiting for you. Father sent to call you. . . ."

She thought she had never heard more beautiful words than

those, and their beauty was in their sweet normality. "Father sent to call you." She went with Mercy into the house.

They sat round the large table, her stepmother, Alice, Cecily and her husband Giles, Elizabeth and her husband, John and his wife, Mercy and Clement, Margaret and Will. And there at the head of the table he sat, his face more serene than any, as though he were unaware of the dark patches of sorrow that hung about his house. He was laughing, pretending to chide her for daydreaming, giving her a lecture on the evils of unpunctuality which was spattered with fun; and she laughed with the rest, but not daring to meet his eyes for fear he should see the tears there. He knew why she would not look at him, for they were closer than any in the household, and though he loved well his family, it was his daughter Meg who was closest to his heart. So the others laughed, for he was a sorcerer where laughter was concerned, conjuring it up out of nowhere, but not for her; she was too close to the magician, she knew his tricks, she saw the sleight of hand; she knew the merry eyes watched the window, listened for a sign.

It came with a loud knocking on the outer door.

Gillian, their little maid, came running in, her mouth open. There was one outside who must see Sir Thomas.

Sir Thomas arose, but the man was already in the room. He carried the scroll in his hands. He bowed most courteously. His face was sad, as though he did not greatly love his mission, which was a command that Sir Thomas must appear next day before the Commissioners in order to take the Oath of Supremacy.

There was silence round the table; Margaret stared at the dish before her, at the worn wood of the table which she remembered so well, since she had sat at this particular place for as long as she could recall. She wished the birds would not sing so loudly, showing they did not know this was a day of doom; she wished the sun would not shine so hotly on her neck for it made her feel she would be sick. She wanted perfect clarity of mind to remember forever each detail of that well-loved face.

Her stepmother had turned deathly pale; she looked as if she would faint. The whole family might have been petrified; they did not move; they sat and waited.

Margaret looked at her father; his eyes had begun to twinkle. No, no! she thought. Not now! I cannot bear that you should turn this into a joke. Not even for them. Not now!

But he was smiling at her, imploring her. Margaret! You and I, we understand. We have to help one another.

Then she arose from the table and went to the messenger, and looking closely at his face, she said: "Why . . . Dick Halliwell! Mother . . . everybody . . . 'tis only Dick!"

And they fell upon her father, chiding him, telling him he went too far with his jokes. And there he was, laughing among them, believing that it is well not to look at unhappiness until it is close upon you, having often said that once you have passed it, every day lends distance between it and yourself.

Margaret went to her nursery where she stayed with her small daughter, finding solace in the charm of the child and thinking of the child's future when she would have children of her own, so that she might not think of this day and the days that would immediately follow it.

Later, hearing voices beneath her window, she looked out and saw her father walking below with the Duke of Norfolk who, she guessed, had come to have a word with him about the morrow. Margaret, her hand on her heart, as though she feared those below would hear its wild beating, listened to their voices which were wafted up to her.

"'Tis perilous striving with princes," said His Grace. "I could wish you as a friend to incline to the King's pleasure."

Then she heard her father's voice, and it seemed to her that it held little of sorrow. "There will be only this difference between Your Grace and me, that I shall die today and you tomorrow."

That night, she could not sleep. Death seemed already to be hovering over the house. She recalled what she had heard of those committed to the Tower; she thought of that gloomy prison and compared it with this happy home. He would say: "All these years of happiness have I had; I should be grateful to have known them, not sorrowful that because I have loved them well, I now must grieve the more to lose them."

She wept bitter tears, and took her child in her arms, seeking comfort from that small body. But there was no comfort for Margaret Roper. Death hung over the house, waiting to snatch its best-loved member.

He left next day. She watched him go down the privy steps

with Will, his head held high; already he looked a saint. He did not cast a look behind him; he would have them all believe that soon he would be returning to them.

✦

Catherine Howard was in the orchard, looking through the trees at the river. She was plumper than she had been almost a year ago when she had first met Francis Derham at the coronation. Now she deplored the state of her clothes, longed for rich materials, for ribands and flowers to adorn her hair.

She was not yet thirteen years old and looked seventeen—a plump, ripe, seventeen; she was very pretty, very gay, fond of laughter; in love with Francis.

Life was beautiful, she thought, and promised to be more so. Francis was husband to her, she wife to him. One day—and that not far distant—they would be so in earnest.

As she stood gazing at the river, a pair of hands were placed over her eyes; she gave a little cry of pleasure, assured this was Francis. Often he came to her, and they met here in the orchards, for he was still of her uncle's house.

"Guess who!" said the loved and familiar voice.

"Guess!" she cried shrilly. "I do not have to guess—I know!"

She pulled away his hands and swung round to face him; they kissed passionately.

He said: "Such good news I have today, Catherine! I can scarce wait to tell you."

"Good news!"

"The best of news. I hope that you will agree that it is."

"Tell me, tell me! You must tell me."

He stood, surveying her, laughing, harbouring his secret, longing so deeply for the moment of revelation that he must keep it back, savouring afresh the pleasure it would give him to tell her.

"Very well, I will tell you, Catherine. Her Grace is to have a new gentleman usher. What do you think his name is?"

"Francis . . . you!"

He nodded.

"Then you will be here . . . under this very roof! This is wonderful news, Francis."

They embraced.

"It will be so much simpler to meet, Catherine."

She was smiling. Yes, indeed, it would be much easier to meet. There would be many opportunities of which he did not as yet dream.

She was flushed with pleasure, bright-eyed, dreaming of them.

Some young ladies and gentlemen came upon them kissing there. Among them was Francis's great friend Damport.

Francis and Catherine broke free on seeing them, and were greeted with laughter. One of the young men said in mock dismay: "You often kiss Mrs. Catherine Howard, Derham. Is it not very bold of you?"

Derham answered: "Who should hinder me from kissing my wife?"

"I trow this matter will come to pass!" said one of the ladies.

"What is that?" asked Derham.

"Marry! That Mr. Derham shall have Mrs. Catherine Howard."

Derham laughed with pleasure. "By St. John!" he cried. "You may guess twice and guess worse."

They were all laughing merrily, when Catherine broke up their mirth by pointing to a barge that went down the river.

"Look ye all!" she cried. "Is that not Sir Thomas More!"

They all fell silent, thinking of the man. They knew he had come near the block when the nun of Kent had burned for her heresies. What now? they wondered, and a gloom was cast over their merriment. They watched the barge pass along the river on its way to Westminster; and when it was out of sight, they sought to laugh again, but they found they had no mirth in them.

Jane Rochford's brief sojourn in the Tower had frightened her considerably. There, in her prison, as she looked down on the river at the pomp of the coronation, she had realized that only her own folly had brought her to this pass, and that in future she must be wiser. She would always hate Anne, but that was no reason why she should shout the dangerous fact abroad. Her short incarceration had been in the nature of a warning to herself and others, but she came out chastened, determined to curb her hysterical jealousy. She apologized to Anne, who accepted her apology, her dislike for Jane being but mild, and she thinking her too colourless to feel much interest in her. So Jane came back to court as attendant to Anne, and though they were never even outwardly friends, there was a truce between them.

It was about a year after the coronation when Jane, who had a habit of discovering the secrets of those around her, made a great discovery.

There was among Anne's attendants a young girl of some beauty, of modest, rather retiring demeanour, somewhat self-effacing; a member of what had come to be known as the anti-Boleyn faction—that set which had held out for Katharine, and were quiet now, though seeming to be watching and waiting for a turn in events.

Jane had intercepted a glance the King had given this girl, and she had felt a deep exultation. Could it be, wondered Jane, that the King was contemplating taking a mistress . . . that he had already been unfaithful to Anne? The thought made Jane laugh aloud when she was alone. How foolish she had been to murmur against Anne! What a poor sort of revenge, that merely put oneself into the Tower! Revenge should be taken subtly; she had learned that now.

How amusing to carry the news to Anne, to falter, to shed a tear, to murmur: "I am afraid I have some terrible news for you. I am not certain that I should tell. . . . I am grieved that it should fall to my lot to bring you such news. . . ."

She must watch; she must peep; she must go cautiously. She listened at doors; she hid behind curtains. She was really very bold, for well she knew what the wrath of the King could be like. But it was worth it; she discovered what she had hoped to discover.

She then must turn over in her mind how she would use this. She could go to Anne; she could have the story dragged from her seemingly reluctant lips; it would do her good to see the proud eyes flash, the anger burn in those cheeks, to see haughty Anne humiliated. On the other hand, what if she went to George with the news? She would have his complete attention; she would have his approval, as he would say she had done right in coming to him. She could not make up her mind what she wanted most, and she must do so quickly, for there were others in the court who pried and peeped, and would be only too glad to have the pleasure of doing that which she had worked for.

In the end she went to George.

"George, I have something to tell you. I am afraid. I hardly know what to do. Perhaps you can advise me."

He was not very interested, she noticed with a sudden jealous rage; he thought it was her own affair. But wait until he learned it concerned his sister Anne!

"The King is indulging in a love affair with one of Anne's ladies."

George, who had been writing when she came in, hardly looked up from his work. He was perturbed by this news, but not greatly. Knowing the King, he considered such affairs inevitable; they were bound to come sooner or later. The main point was that Anne should realize this and not irritate the King further than he was already irritated by the birth of a daughter. If she remained calm, understanding, she could keep her hold on him; if she were jealous, demanding, she might find herself in a similar position to that of Katharine. He would warn her to treat this matter with the lightness it deserved.

"Well," said Jane, "do you not think it was clever of me to have discovered this before most?"

He looked at her with distaste. She could not hide the triumph in her eyes. He pictured her, spying; he discovered early in their married life that she had a gift for spying. And now she was all excitement, happy—and showing it—because she had knowledge which was certain to hurt Anne.

"I am sure," he said, "that you enjoyed making the discovery and were clever in doing so."

"What mean you?" she demanded.

"Just what I say, Jane."

He stood up, and would have walked past her; she stopped him, putting her hands on his coat.

"I thought to please you, George. I wish I had gone straight to Anne now."

He was glad she had not done that. Anne was nervous; she was irritable; she was inclined to do the first rash thing that came into her head these days.

He forced himself to smile at Jane. He patted her hand.

"I am glad you told me first."

She pouted.

"You seemed angry with me a moment ago. Why, George? Why? Why does everything I do anger you?"

He could feel blowing up, one of those scenes which he dreaded. He said: "Of course I was not angry. You imagine these things."

"You were angry because you think she will be hurt. It does not matter that I risk my life . . ."

"To spy on the King!" he finished. He burst into sudden laughter. "By God, Jane, I should like to have seen His Majesty, had he come upon you peeping through a crack in the door!"

She stamped her foot; her face was white with rage.

"You find this comic!" she said.

"Well, in a measure. The King, taking his guilty pleasure, and you doing that for which you have a perfect genius . . . spying, congratulating yourself . . ."

"Congratulating myself!"

"Oh, come! I swear I never saw you so pleased with anything."

Her lips trembled; tears came into her eyes.

"I know I'm not clever, but why should you laugh at everything I do!"

"Everything?" he said, laughing. "I assure you, Jane, that it is only on rare occasions that I can laugh at what you do."

She turned on him angrily.

"Perhaps you will not find this such a laughing matter when I tell you who the lady is!"

He was startled now, and she had the joy of swing that she had all his attention.

"I forget her name. She is so quiet, one scarcely notices her. She is a friend of Chapuys; she is of those who would very gladly see the Queen displaced from the throne. . . ."

She saw now that he was deeply perturbed; this was not merely a king's light love affair; this was high politics. It was very likely that the girl had been primed to do this by the enemies of Anne.

George began to pace up and down; Jane sat in a window seat, watching him. Quite suddenly he went towards the door, and without a glance at Jane strode from the room. Jane wanted to laugh; but there was no laughter in her; she covered her face with her hands and began to cry.

George went to Anne. She was in her room, reading quietly, making marks with her thumbnail at those passages which she meant Henry to read. She was interesting herself in theology, because the subject interested him. She was trying now to bind him to her in every way she knew; she was uneasy; she thought often of Katharine and what had happened to her; she now wondered why she had not previously been more sympathetic towards Henry's first queen. Bitterly she would laugh at herself; did she not understand the old queen's case because her own was becoming distressingly similar?

"You look alarmed, George," she said, laying aside her book.

"I have alarming news."

"Tell me quickly." She gave a somewhat hysterical laugh. "I think I am prepared for anything."

"The King is philandering."

She threw back her head and laughed.

"I cannot say I am greatly surprised, George."

"This is no ordinary philandering. It is important, when we consider who the girl is."

"Who?"

"Jane does not remember her name."

"Jane!"

They exchanged glances of understanding.

"Jane made it her affair to discover this matter," said George. "This time I think Jane has done us a service. She described the girl as meek and mild as milk."

"Ah!" cried Anne. "I can guess who she is!"

"She is of our enemies," said George. "It may well be that she has been made to do this to work your ruin, Anne."

Anne stood up, her cheeks flaming.

"She shall be banished from the court! I myself will see her. She shall come to me at once . . . I . . ."

He lifted a restraining hand.

"Anne, you terrify me. These sudden rages . . ."

"Sudden! Rages! Have I not good cause . . ."

"You have every cause in the world, Anne, to go carefully. You must do nothing rash; everything you do is watched;

everything you say is listened to. The throne shakes under you! You must say nothing of this to the King; you must feign ignorance for a while. We must go secretly and in great quiet, for this is no ordinary light flirtation."

"There are times," she said, "when I feel I should like nothing better than to walk out of the palace and never set eyes on the King again."

"Be of good cheer. We'll think of something. There is one point you must not forget: Give no sign to the King that you know anything. We will, between us, think of a plan."

"It is so . . . humiliating!" she cried. "By my faith! I have suffered more indignities since I have been the Queen than I ever did before."

"One of the penalties of being Queen, Anne! Promise . . . promise you will go cautiously!"

"Of course, of course! Naturally I shall . . ."

"No," he said, with a little grimace, "not naturally, Anne; most unnaturally! Remember Mary . . ."

"What of Mary?"

"You know well to what I refer. How could you have been so wild, so foolish, as to say that if the King went to France and you were Regent, you would find a reason for putting Mary out of the way!"

"This girl maddens me. She is foolish, obstinate . . . and . . ."

"That we well know, but the greater foolishness was yours, Anne, in making such unwise statements."

"I know . . . I know. And you do well to warn me."

"I warn you now. Remember previous follies, and keep in good temper with the King."

"I had thought he seemed more tender of late," she said, and began to laugh suddenly. "To think it was naught but his guilty conscience!"

"Ah!" said George. "He was ever a man of much conscience. But, Anne, he is simple; you and I know that, and together we can be frank. He has great pride in himself. His verses . . . If he thought we did not consider them the best ever written in his court, he would be ready to have our heads off our shoulders!"

"That he would! He has indeed great pride in himself and all his works. George . . ." She looked over her shoulder. "There is none other to whom I could say this." She paused, biting her lips, her eyes searching his face. "Katharine had a daughter, and then . . . all those miscarriages! George, I wonder, might it not, be that the King cannot breed sons?"

He stared at her.

"I understand not," he said.

"Not one son," she said, "but Richmond. And Richmond . . . have you noticed? There is a delicate air about him; I do not think he will live to a great age. He is the King's only son. Then there is Mary who is normal, but Mary is a girl and they say that girls survive at birth more easily than boys. There is my own Elizabeth; she is also a girl. . . ." She covered her face with her hands. "And all those stillborn boys, and all those boys who lived to breathe for an hour or so before they died. . . . George, was it due to any weakness in Katharine, think you, or was it . . . ?"

He silenced her with a look. He read the terror behind her words.

She said in a whisper: "He is not wholly well. . . . The place on his leg . . ." She closed her eyes and shivered. "One feels unclean. . . ." She shivered again. "George, what if . . . he . . . cannot have sons?"

He clenched his hands, begging her with his eyes to cease such talk. He got up and strode to the door. Jane was in the corridor, coming towards the room. He wondered, had she heard that? Had she heard him rise from his seat and stride to the door? Had she retreated a few paces from the door, and then, just as it opened, commenced to walk leisurely towards it? He could not tell from her face; her eyes glistened; she had been weeping. It seemed to him that she was always weeping. He would have to be careful with her; he was sure she could be dangerous.

"Oh . . . Jane . . . I was just telling Anne . . ."

Anne threw a haughty glance at her sister-in-law, but Jane did not care, as George was smiling at her.

"Come inside," said George.

Jane went in, and the three of them sat together; but Anne would not speak of this matter before Jane. She wondered at her brother's show of friendship for his wife. Could it be that he was reconciling himself to his unhappy marriage, trying to make something out of it at last?

The King hummed a snatch of a song. Anne watched him. He sparkled with jewels; he looked enormous; he was getting corpulent, he was no longer the handsomest prince in Christendom; he was no longer the golden prince. He was a coarse man whose face was too red, whose eyes were bloodshot, and whose leg was a hideously unwholesome ulcer. His eyes were gleaming; he was the lover now, and she remembered the lover well. How often had she seen that look in his eyes! Always before, the look had been for her. Strange indeed to know his desires were fixed on someone else—strange and terrifying.

She said: "The song is charming. Your own?"

He smiled. She was reclining on the bed he had given her before her confinement. It was a beautiful bed, he thought. By God, she should think herself lucky to have such a fine bed! He doubted whether there was such another bed in the world. Its splendour suited her, he thought indulgently. Anne! There was no one like her, of course; not even little . . . Well, he had never thought she was, but she was sweet, and Anne was fractious and could be maddening—and a man needed a change, if but to prove his manhood. He felt tender towards Anne at moments like this, when she said: "The song is charming. Your own?" It was when those great black eyes of hers seemed to look right through him and see more of his mind than he cared for anyone to see, that he was angry with her. She was more clever than a woman ought to be! Learned foreigners delighted to talk to her of the new Lutheran theories, and did great homage to her because she could converse naturally and easily with them. He liked that not. Any glory that came to a queen should come through her king. Her beauty might be admired; the splendid clothes she wore, also; but her cleverness, her sharp retorts that might be construed as gibes . . . No, no; they angered him.

He would have her keep in mind that he had raised her up, that she owed all she now enjoyed to him. By God, there were moments when she would appear to forget this! She could please him still, could make him see that there never had been any like her, nor ever would be. That in itself irritated him; it bound him, and he did not like to be bound. He could think with increasing longing of the days before he had known Anne, before this accursed leg began to trouble him, when he was a golden-haired, golden-bearded giant of a man, excelling all others in any sport that could be named; riding hard, eating, drinking, loving, all in a grander manner than that of other men; with Wolsey—dear old Wolsey—to take over matters of state. She had killed Wolsey as surely as if she had slain him with her own hands, since but for her Wolsey would have been alive to this day.

More was in the Tower. And she had done this. And yet . . . there was none could satisfy him as she could; haughty, aloof, as she well knew how to be, always he must feel the longing to subdue her. Sometimes his feeling for her was difficult to explain; sudden anger and fury she aroused in him, and then as suddenly desire, blinding desire that demanded satisfaction at any price. Nay, there was no one like her, but she had cut him off from the days of his glowing manhood. He had met her and changed from that bright youth; during the years of his faithfulness he had been steadily undergoing a change; now he would never be the same man again.

But enough of introspection! He was trying hard to regain his youth. There was one—and she soon to be in his arms, looking up at him with sweet humility—who would assure him that he was the greatest of men as well as the mightiest of kings; who asked for nothing but the honour of being his mistress. Sweet balm to the scorching wounds the black-eyed witch on the bed had given him. But at the moment the witch was sweetly complimenting him, and he had ever found her irresistible in that mood. The other could wait awhile.

"My own, yes," he said. "You shall hear me sing it, but not now."

"I shall await the hearing with pleasure."

He looked at her sharply. Did she mock? Did she like his songs? Did she compare them with her brother's, with Wyatt's, with Surrey's? Did she think they suffered by comparison?

She was smiling very sweetly. Absently she twirled a lock of her hair. Her eyes were brilliant tonight, and there was a flush in her cheeks. He was taken aback at the contemplation of her beauty, even though he had come to know it too familiarly.

The little one would be awaiting him. Her homage was very sweet. He would sing his song to her, and have no doubts of her approval—but for that reason it was not as sweet as Anne's. She thought him wonderful. She was not clever; a woman should not

412

be clever; her mission in life was to please her lord. And yet . . . he was proud of his Queen. But what matter? It was but manly to love; there was little harm in a dash of light loving here and there; the ladies expected it, and a king should please his subjects.

"Henry . . ." she said. He paused, patting the diamond which was the centre button of his coat. "There is something I would say to you."

"Can it not wait?"

"I think you would rather hear it now."

"Then tell me quickly."

She sat up on the bed and held out her hands to him, laughing.

"But it is news I would not care to hurry over." She was watching his face eagerly.

"What!" said the King. "Anne . . . what meanest thou?"

He took her hands, and she raised herself to a kneeling position.

"Tell me," she said, putting her face close to his, "what news would you rather I gave, what news would please you more than any?"

His heart was beating wildly. Could it be what he had longed to hear? Could it really be true? And why not? It was the most natural . . . it was what all expected, what all were waiting for.

"Anne!" he said.

She nodded.

He put his arms about her; she slid hers about his neck.

"I thought to please you," she said.

"Please me!" He was hilarious as a schoolboy. "There could be naught to give me greater pleasure."

"Then I am happy."

"Anne, Anne, when . . . ?"

"Not for eight long months. Still . . ."

"You are sure?"

She nodded, and he kissed her again.

"This pleases me more than all the jewels in the world," he told her.

"It pleases me as much as it pleases you. There have been times of late . . . when I have felt . . ."

He stopped her words by kissing her.

"Bah! Then thou wert indeed a foolish girl, Anne!"

"Indeed I was. Tell me, were you about to go on an important mission? For I would fain talk of this . . ."

He laughed. "Important mission! By God! I would desert the most important of missions to hear this news!"

He had forgotten her already, thought Anne exultantly. Here was the tender lover returned. It had only needed this.

He did not leave her, not that night, nor the next. He had forgotten the demure little girl; he had merely been passing the time with her. Anne was with child. This time a son; certainly a son. Why not! All was well. He had done right to marry Anne. This was God's answer!

Henry felt sure of his people's joy, once his son was born. It would but need that to have done with the murmuring and grumbling. He forgot the girl with whom he had been pleasing himself; he was the loyal husband now; the father of a daughter, about to be the father of a son. He gave up the idea of going to France, and instead went on a tour through the midlands with Anne—belligerent and mighty. This is the Queen I have chosen. Be good subjects, and love her—or face my wrath!

Subjects en masse were disconcerting. A king might punish a few with severity, but what of that? The Dacres affair was proof that the people were not with Anne. Dacres was devoted wholeheartedly to the Catholic cause, and thus to Katharine; and for this reason, Northumberland—still a great admirer of Anne—had quarrelled with the man and accused him of treason. To Cromwell and Cranmer it seemed a good moment to conduct Lord Dacres to the block, so they brought him to London, where he was tried by his peers. The Lords, with unexpected courage and with a defiance unheard of under Henry's despotic rule, had acquitted Dacres. This would seem to Henry like treason on the part of the peers, but it was much more; it meant that these gentlemen knew they had public support behind them, and that was backed up by hatred of Anne—whether she was with child or not made no difference. It shook Henry; it shattered Anne and her supporters. It seemed that everyone was waiting now for the son she promised to produce; that of course would make all the difference; Henry could never displace the mother of his son. Once Anne gave birth to a boy, who showed some promise of becoming a man, she was safe; until then she was tottering.

Anne was very uneasy; more so than anyone, with perhaps the exception of George, could possibly guess. She would wander in the grounds around Greenwich, and brood on the future. She wished to be alone; sometimes when she was in the midst of a laughing crowd she would steal away. Anne was very frightened.

Each day she hoped and prayed for some sign that she might be pregnant; there was none. She had planned boldly, and it seemed as if her plan had failed. What will become of me? she wondered. She could not keep her secret much longer.

She had believed, when she told the King that she was with child, that soon she must be. Why was it that she was not? Something told her the fault lay with him, and this idea was supported by Katharine's disastrous experiences and her own inability to produce another child. There was Elizabeth, but Elizabeth would not do. She murmured: "Oh, Elizabeth, my daughter, why wast thou not born a boy!"

She watched the clouds drifting across the summer sky; she looked at the green leaves on the trees and murmured: "Before they fall I shall have to tell him. A woman cannot go on forever pretending she is pregnant!"

Perhaps by then . . . Yes, that had been the burden of her thoughts. . . . Perhaps by then that which had been a fabrication of her tortured mind would be a reality. Perhaps by then there would be a real child in her womb, not an imaginary one.

The days passed. Already people were glancing at her oddly. Is the Queen well? How small she is! Can she really be with child? What think you? Is something wrong? Is this her punishment for the way she treated poor Queen Katharine?

She sat under the trees, praying for a child. How many women had sat under these trees, frightened because they were to bear a child! And now here was one who was terrified because she was not to bear one, because she, feeling herself in a desperate situation, had seen in such a lie a possible way out of her difficulties.

Her sister, Mary, came and sat beside her. Mary was plumper, more matronly, but still the same Mary although perhaps overripe now. Still unable to say no, I'll warrant, thought Anne, and was suddenly filled with sharp envy.

"Anne," said Mary, "I am in great trouble."

Anne's lips curled; she wondered what Mary's trouble was, and how it would compare with her own.

"What trouble?" asked Anne, finding sudden relief as her thoughts necessarily shifted from herself to her sister.

"Anne, dost know Stafford?"

"What!" cried Anne. "Stafford the gentleman usher?"

"The very one," said Mary. "Well . . . he and I . . ."

"A gentleman usher!" said Anne.

"All the world seemed to set so little by me, and he so much," said Mary. "I thought I could take no better way out but to take him and forsake all other ways."

"The King will never consent," said Anne.

"Perhaps when he knows I am to have a child . . ."

Anne turned on her sister in horror. Mary had been a widow

417

for five years. Naturally one would not expect her to live a nun's life, but one did expect her to show a little care. Oh, thought Anne, how like Mary! How like her!

Mary hastened to explain. "He was young, and love overcame us. And I loved him as he did me. . . ."

Anne was silent.

"Ah!" went on Mary, "I might have had a man of higher birth, but I could never have had one who could have loved me so well . . . nor a more honest man."

Anne looked cold, and Mary could not bear coldness now; she did not know of her sister's trials; she pictured her happy and secure, rejoicing in her queenly state. It seemed unkind to have from her no word for reassurance.

Mary stood up. "I had rather be with him than I were the greatest queen!" she cried, and began to run across the grass into the palace.

Anne watched her. Mary—a widow—was with child, and afraid because of it. Anne—a queen and a wife—was not, and far, far more afraid than Mary could understand, because of it! Anne threw back her head and laughed immoderately; and when she had done, she touched her checks and there were tears upon them.

When Anne told Henry there was not to be a child, he was furious.

"How could such a mistake occur!" he demanded suspiciously, his little eyes cold and cruel.

"Simply!" she flared back. "And it did, so why argue about it!"

"I have been tricked!" he cried. "It seems that God has decreed I shall never have a son."

And he turned away, for there was a certain speculation in his eyes which he did not wish her to see. He went to the demure little lady-in-waiting.

"Ha!" he said. "It seems a long time since I kissed you, sweetheart!"

She was meek, without reproaches. How different from Anne! he thought, and remembered resentfully how she had commanded him during the days of his courtship, and how when she had become his mistress she continued to berate him.

By God, he thought, I'll have none of that. Who brought her up, eh? Who could send her back whence she came? Women should be meek and submissive, as this one was.

Anne watched angrily, trying to follow her brother's advice and finding herself unable to do so.

"Madge," she said to her cousin, a lovely girl of whom she was very fond, "go to that girl and tell her I would see her this minute."

Madge went, and awaiting the arrival of the girl, Anne paced up and down, trying to compose herself, trying to rehearse what she would say to her.

The girl came, eyes downcast, very frightened, for Anne's eyes were blazing in spite of her efforts to remain calm.

"I would have you know," said Anne, "that I have been hearing evil reports of my ladies. I am sending you back to your home. Be ready to start as soon as you hear from me that you are to do so."

The girl scarcely looked at Anne; she blushed scarlet, and her lips quivered.

Sly creature! thought Anne angrily. And she the King's mistress! What he can see in the girl I do not understand, except that she is a trifle pretty and very meek. Doubtless she tells him he is wonderful! Her lips twisted scornfully, and then suddenly she felt a need to burst into tears. Here was she, the Queen, and must resort to such methods to rid herself of her rivals! Was everyone in this court against her? Her father was anxious now, she knew, wondering how long she would retain her hold on the King; Norfolk no longer troubled to be courteous; they had quarrelled; he had stamped out of the room on the last occasion she had seen him, muttering that of her which she would prefer not to remember; Suffolk watched, sly, secretly smiling; the Princess Mary was openly defiant. And now this girl!

"Get you gone from my presence!" said Anne. "You are banished from court."

The girl's reply was to go straight to the King, who immediately countermanded the Queen's order.

He left the girl and went to Anne.

"What means this?" he demanded.

"I will not have you parade your infidelities right under my nose!"

"Madam!" roared the King. "I would have you know I am master here!"

"Nevertheless," she said, "you cannot expect me to smile on your mistresses and to treat them as though they were the most faithful of my attendants."

He said coarsely: "If that is what I wish, you shall do it . . . as others did before you!"

"You mistake me," she answered.

"I mistake you not. From where do you derive your authority if not from me! Consider from what I lifted you. I have but to lift my finger to send you back whence you came!"

"Why not lift it then?" she blazed. "Your pretty little mistress doubtless would grace the throne better than I. She is so brilliant! Her conversation is so witty! The people would acclaim her. But, Henry, do you not think she might put you a little in the shade. . . . Such wit . . . such brilliance!"

He looked at her with smoldering eyes; there were occasions when he could forget he was a king and put his hands about that little neck, and press and press until there was no breath left in her. But a king does not do murder; others do it for him. It was a quick thought that passed through his mind and was gone before he had time to realize it had been there.

He turned and strode out of the room.

Jane Rochford had overheard that quarrel. She was excited; it gave her a pleasurable thrill to know that Anne was having difficulties with her husband, just as she herself had with George, though with a difference.

Jane crept away and came back later, begging a word with the Queen. Could the ladies be dismissed? Jane whispered. What she had to say was for Anne's ears alone.

She expressed her sympathy.

"Such a sly wench! I declare she deliberately sets out to trap the King. All that modesty and reluctance . . ." Jane glanced sideways at Anne; had her barb struck a vulnerable spot? Oh, how did it feel, where you have shown reluctance to a king and complete indifference to the feelings of his wife, to find your position suddenly reversed; yourself the neglected wife and another careless of your feelings? Jane was so excited she could scarcely talk; she wanted to laugh at this, because it seemed so very amusing.

"But I have not come to commiserate with you, dear sister. I want to help. I have a plan. Were I to let her people know that she is in danger of disgracing herself—oh, I need not mention His Majesty—it might be a friendly warning. . . . I would try. I trow that, were she removed from court, the King would be the most loyal of husbands; and how can a woman get children when her husband has no time for her, but only for other women!"

Jane spoke vehemently, but Anne was too sick at heart to notice it. Everywhere she looked, disaster was threatening. She was young and healthy, but her husband was neither so young nor so healthy; she could not get a child, when the most urgent matter she had ever known was that she should first get with child, and that the child should be a son. The King's health was doubtless to blame, but the King never blamed himself; when he was in fault he blamed someone else. There was evidence of that all about him, and had been for years. Francis had made an alarming move; he had begun to talk once more of a match between his son and Mary. What could that mean, but one thing! Mary was a bastard; how could a bastard marry the son of the King of France?

There was only one answer: The King of France no longer regarded Mary as a bastard. Her hopes had soared when Clement died and Paul III took his place; Paul had seemed more inclined to listen to reason, but what did she know of these matters? Only what it was deemed wise to tell her! Francis, whom she had regarded as a friend to herself, who had shown decided friendship when they had met at Calais, had decided it was unsafe to quarrel with Charles and with Rome. France was entirely Catholic—that was the answer. Francis could not stand out against his people; his sympathy might be with Anne, but a king's sympathy must be governed by diplomacy; Francis was showing a less friendly face to Anne. She saw now that the whole of Europe would be against the marriage; that would have meant nothing, had Henry been with her, had Henry been the devoted lover he had remained during the waiting years. But Henry was turning from her; this sly, meek, pretty girl from the opposite camp was proof of that. She was filled with terror, for she remembered the negotiations which had gone on before news of a possible divorce had reached Katharine. Everyone at court had known before

Katharine; they had whispered of the King's Secret Matter. Was the King now indulging once more in a secret matter? Terrified, she listened to Jane; she was ready to clutch at any straw. That was foolish—she might have known Jane was no diplomatist. Jane's art was in listening at doors, slyly setting one person against another.

Henry discovered what Jane was about.

"What!" he shouted. "This is the work of Rochford's wife. She shall be committed to the Tower by the Traitor's Gate." She wept and stormed, cursing herself for her folly. To think she had come to this by merely trying to help Anne! What would become of her now? she wondered. If ever she got out of the Tower alive, she would be clever, subtle. . . . Once before she had been careless; this time she had been equally foolish, but she had learned her lesson at last. George would bear her no gratitude for what she had done; he would say: "What a clumsy fool you are, Jane!" Or if he did not say it, he would think it.

All this she had done for George really . . . and he cared not, had no feeling for her at all. "Methinks I begin to hate him!" she murmured, and looked through her narrow windows onto the cobbles beneath.

George came to see his sister; he was secretly alarmed.

"Jane has been sent to the Tower!" he said. Anne told him what had happened. "This grows mightily dangerous, Anne."

"You to tell me that! I assure you I know it but too well."

"Anne, you must go very carefully."

"You tell me that persistently," she answered pettishly. "What must I do now? I have gone carefully, and I have been brought to this pass. What is happening to us? Mary in disgrace, our father quite often absenting himself from court, shamefaced, hardly looking at me! And Uncle Norfolk becoming more and more outspoken! You, alarmed that I will not be cautious, and I . . ."

"We have to go carefully, that is all. We have to stop this affair of the King's with this girl; it must not be allowed to go on."

"I care not! And it were not she, it would be another."

"Anne, for God's sake listen to reason! It matters not if it were another one; it only matters that it should be she!"

"You mean . . . there is more in this than a simple love affair?"

"Indeed I do."

Madge Shelton looked in at the door.

"I beg your pardon. I had thought Your Majesty to be alone." She and George exchanged cousinly greetings, and Madge retired.

"Our cousin is a beautiful girl," said George.

Anne looked at him sharply.

He said: "You'll hate what I am about to say, Anne. It is a desperate remedy, but I feel it would be effective. Madge is delightful, so young and charming. The other affair may well be beginning to pall."

"George! I do not understand. . . ."

"We cannot afford to be over-nice, Anne."

"Oh, speak frankly. You mean—throw Madge to the King, that he may forget that other . . ."

"It is not a woman we have to fight, Anne. It is a party!"

"I would not do it," she said. "Why, Madge . . . she is but a young girl, and he . . . You cannot know, George. The life he has lived. . . ."

"I do know. Hast ever thought we are fighting for thy life?"

She tried to throw off her fears with flippancy. She laughed rather too loudly; he noticed uneasily that of late she had been given to immoderate laughter.

"Ever since I had thought to be Queen, there have been those ready to thrust prophecies under my eyes. I mind well one where I was depicted with my head cut off." She put her hands about her throat. "Fret not, George. My husband, after the manner of most, amuses himself. He was all eagerness for me before our marriage; now?" She shrugged her shoulders and began to laugh again.

"Be silent," said George. "What of Elizabeth?"

She stopped laughing.

"What of Elizabeth?"

"It has been decreed that Mary Tudor is a bastard, because the King tired of her mother and decided—as she could no longer hope to give him a son—that he was no longer married to her. Oh, we know of his conscience, we know of his treatise . . . we know too well the story. But, Anne, we are alone and we need not fear each other. . . . Ah! What a good thing it is to have in this world one person of whom you need not cherish the smallest fear! Anne, I begin to think we are not so unlucky, you and I."

"Please stop," she said. "You make me weep."

"This is no time for tears. I said Mary has been decreed a bastard, though her mother is of Spain and related to the most powerful man in Europe. Anne, you are but the daughter of the Earl of Wiltshire—Sir Thomas Boleyn not long since—and he was only raised to his earldom to do honour to you; he could be stripped of that honour easily enough. He is no Emperor, Anne! Dost see what I mean? Mary was made a bastard; what of Elizabeth? Who need fear her most humble relations?"

"Yes," said Anne breathlessly. "Yes!"

"If the King has no sons, Elizabeth will be Queen of England . . . or Mary will! Oh, Anne, you have to fight this, you have to hold your place for your daughter's sake."

"You are right," she said. "I have my daughter."

"Therefore . . ."

She nodded. "You are right, George. I think you are often right. I shall remember what you said about our being lucky. Yes, I think we are; for who else is there, but each other!"

The next day she sent Madge Shelton with a message to the King. From a window she watched the girl approach him, for he was in the palace grounds. Yes, he was appreciative; who could help being so, of Madge! Madge had beauty; Madge had wit. She had made the King laugh; he was suggesting they should take a turn round the rose garden.

Anne soothed her doubts with the reflection that Madge was a saucy wench, able to take care of herself, and had probably had love affairs before. Besides . . . there was Elizabeth!

✳

The Dowager Duchess of Norfolk was uneasy. Rumours came from the court, and one could not ignore them. All was not well with the Queen. She herself had quarrelled with her stepson, the Duke, because he had spoken as she did not care to hear him speak, and it had been of the Queen. I never did like the man, she mused. Cruel, hard opportunist! One could tell which way the wind was blowing, by what he would have to say. Which way was the wind blowing? She liked not these rumours.

She was to be state governess to the Princess Elizabeth, a further sign of Anne's friendship for her. "I do hope the dear child is well and happy. It is a terrible trial to be a queen, and to such a king!" she murmured to herself.

The Duchess was fractious in her own household. Those girls were noisy in their room at night, and she had heard it whispered that they were over-free with the young men.

She sent for Mary Lassells, whom she did not like overmuch. The girl was of humble birth, apt to look sullen; she was really a serving maid, and should not be with the ladies. I must see to that one day, thought the Duchess, and filed the matter away in that mental pigeonhole which was crammed full of forgotten notes.

"Mary Lassells," she said, when the girl came to her, "there is much noise in the ladies' sleeping apartments at night. These ladies are under my care, and as since my granddaughter's coronation I find myself with less and less leisure, I am going to take a few precautions to make sure of correct behaviour on the part of these young people."

The girl was smiling primly, as though to indicate that there was every reason for the Duchess to take precautions. This angered the Duchess; she did not wish to be reminded that she had been lax; she would have preferred the girl to look as though this were a quite unnecessary precaution being taken by an over-careful duenna.

"It will be your duty, Mary Lassells, every night when the ladies have retired, to see that the key of their apartment is placed in the lock outside the door. Then at a fixed hour I shall send someone to lock the door, and the key will be brought to me."

The Duchess sat back in her chair, well pleased.

"I think that will be a very excellent plan, Your Grace," said Mary Lassells unctuously.

"Your opinion was not asked, Mary Lassells," said the Duchess haughtily. "That will do. Now remember please, and I will send someone for the key this very night."

Mary said nothing. It was shocking to consider what went on in that room at night. Catherine Howard behaved quite shamelessly now with Francis Derham; he would bring fruit and wine for her, and they would sit on her bed and laugh and chatter, telling everyone that as they were really married there was no harm in what they were doing. Derham was very much in love with the child—that was obvious—and she with him;

he salved his conscience by pretending they were married. It was very silly, thought Mary Lassells, and certainly time such wickedness was stopped.

They were planning for tonight. Let them plan! What a shock for them, when they were waiting to receive their lovers, to find the door locked, keeping them out! And so would it be every night. No more games, no more of such wicked folly.

Though Manox never came to the room now, she often thought of him. Some said he was sorely troubled because he had lost little Catherine Howard. And she not fourteen! Thirteen at the most. Was ever such crass wickedness allowed to go unpunished! She will go to hell and suffer eternal torment when she dies, I'll swear! And Mary Lassells felt happier at the thought.

They were all laughing, chattering in their silly way, when Mary Lassells went to the door to obey the Duchess's instructions. "Where go you?" asked one girl.

"Merely to act on Her Grace's orders." Mary put the key in the outer lock. Inside the room they heard her exchanging a few words with someone outside the door. Mary came back into the room, and the door was immediately locked on the outside.

There was a chorus of excitement. "What means this?" "Is it a joke?" "What said you, Mary Lassells?" "Why did you take the key?"

Mary Lassells faced them, her prim mouth working. "Her Grace the Duchess is much displeased. She has heard the laughing and chatter that goes on here of nights. She has taken me on one side and told me what she will do. Every night the door of this apartment is to be locked and the key taken to her."

There were cries of rage.

"Mary Lassells! You have been bearing tales!"

"Indeed I have not!"

"What can one expect of a cook's daughter!"

"I am not a cook's daughter."

"Oh, well . . . something such!"

"This is shameful. Her Grace merely asked me to put the key outside. . . . I suppose because she sees I am more virtuous than the rest of you."

Dorothy Barwicke said: "Do you swear, Mary Lassells, that you have said nothing to Her Grace of what happens in this room?"

"I swear!"

"Then why . . . ?"

"She has heard the noise in here. She says too that she has heard whispers of what goes on. . . . Doubtless the servants. . . ."

"They may have heard the gentlemen creeping up the stairs!" said one girl with a giggle. "I declare Thomas made one devil of a row last time."

"The truth remains," said Mary Lassells, "that you are under suspicion. I only hope Her Grace does not think I have been a party to your follies!"

"Impossible!"

"You would find it difficult, Mary, to discover one who would be a partner."

The girls were rocking on their beds, laughing immoderately.

"Poor Mary!" said Catherine. "I am sure Manox likes you very well."

Everyone shrieked with laughter at that. Catherine was hurt; she had not meant to be unkind. She had seen Manox and Mary together before she had broken with him, and she had thought they seemed friendly. She would have liked Manox to find someone he could care for. Mary too. It seemed a satisfactory settlement, to Catherine.

Mary threw her a glance of hatred.

"Well," said Dorothy Barwicke, "this is an end of our little frolics . . . unless . . ."

"Unless what?" cried several voices.

"There are some very rash and gallant gentlemen among our friends; who knows, one might find a way of stealing the keys!"

"Stealing the keys!" The adventures would have an additional spice if keys had first to be stolen.

The young ladies settled into their beds and talked for a long time. Mary Lassells lay in hers, trembling with rage against them all, and particularly against Catherine Howard.

In his prison in the Tower of London, Margaret Roper stood before her father. He was hollow-eyed, but he was smiling bravely, and she saw that he was more serene in his mind than he had been for a long time. Margaret flung herself at him, reproaches on her lips for those who had brought him to this, for her hatred of them she could not express in his presence, knowing it would disturb him.

They could only look at each other, drinking in each detail of the well-loved faces, knowing that only with the greatest good luck could they hope for another interview. He was braver than she was. Perhaps, she thought, it is easier to die than to be left. He could laugh; she could not. When she would have spoken, tears ran from her eyes.

He understood her feelings. Had he not always understood her?

"Let me look at thee, Meg! Thou hast been too long in the sun. There are freckles across thy nose. Look after the children, Meg. Let them be happy. Meg, thou and I may speak frankly together."

She nodded. She knew that all pretense between them was at an end. He would not say to her, as he might have said to any of the others: "This will pass!" They were too close; they could hide nothing. He knew that it was but a matter of time before he must lay his head on the block.

"Take care of the children, Meg. Frighten them not with gloomy tales of death. Tell them of bright chariots and of beauty. Make them see death as a lovely thing. Do this for me, Meg. Grieve not that I must leave this gloomy prison. My spirit is enclosed in a shell. It longs for the hatching. It longs to be born. Oh, let that shell be cracked. What matter by whom, by the King or his mistress!"

"Speak not of her, Father. . . . But for her . . ."

He must lay his hands on her lips, and say a word for the creature.

"Judge her not, Meg. For how do we know what she may be suffering at this moment?"

She burst out: "At the court there is sport and dances. What do they care that you—the noblest of men—shall die! They must amuse themselves; they must destroy those who would stand in the way of their pleasure. Father, do not ask me not to curse them—for I do, I do!"

"Poor Anne Boleyn!" he said sadly. "Alas, Meg, it pitieth me to consider what misery, poor soul, she will shortly come to. These dances of hers will prove such dances that she will spurn our heads off like footballs, but 'twill not be long ere her head will dance the like dance."

He was saint indeed, thought Margaret, for he could defend her who was to cause his death; he could be sorry for her, could weep a little for her. He talked of the King more frankly than she had ever heard him spoken of. He said there was always cruelty in a man who cannot restrain his passions.

"Be not troubled, sweet daughter, even when you see my head on London Bridge. Remember it is I who will look down on thee and feel pity."

He asked of family affairs, of the garden, of the house, of the peacocks. He could laugh; he could even jest. And sick at heart, yet comforted, she left him.

After his trial she saw him brought back to the Tower. He

walked with his head erect; though she noticed his clothes were creased and looked shabby; well she remembered the gold chain ornamented with double roses, the dark green coat with its fur collar and big sleeves which he favoured as his hands were of awkward shape; she looked at his hands, loving him afresh for his one vanity. Anger surged through her that they should have made him walk between the guards, their bills and halberts ready lest he should attempt an escape. Fools, to think he would try to escape! Did they not know he welcomed this, that he had said to Will: "I am joyful because the first step which is the worst and most difficult, is taken!" Had he not said that to stand out against the King was to lose one's body, but to submit to him was to lose one's soul!

She ran to him, breaking through the guards; she flung her arms about his neck. And the guards turned away that they might not see this which brought tears to their eyes.

"Meg!" he whispered. "For Christ's sake don't unman me!"

She remembered nothing more until she was lying on the ground while those about her chafed her hands and whispered words of comfort; she was conscious of nothing but the hateful, sultry July heat, and the fact that she would never see him alive again.

From the Tower he wrote to her, using a piece of coal, to tell her which day he would be executed. He could not forbear to jest even then. "It will be St. Thomas's Eve, a day very meet and convenient for me. And I never liked your manners better than when you kissed me last. For I like when daughterly love

435

and dear charity hath no leisure to look to worldly courtesy."

She was to go to his burial. The King had given written consent—and this was a privilege—providing that at his execution Sir Thomas would promise not to use many words.

So he died; and his head was impaled on London Bridge to show the people he was a traitor. But the people looked at it with anger; they murmured sullenly; for these people knew they looked at the head of one who was more saint than traitor.

Henry was uneasy; he was tired of women. Women should be a pleasant diversion; matters of state should be those affairs to claim the attention of a king.

The French King was trying to renew negotiations for a marriage with Mary. More was in prison awaiting execution; so was Fisher. He had postponed execution of these men, knowing of the popular feeling towards them. He had ever been afraid of popular feeling.

Anne coloured all his thoughts; he was angry with her who had placed him in this position; angry with his desire for her, brief though it might be, without which his life would be incomplete. Anne had brought him to this pass; he could wish she had never entered his life, yet he could not imagine it without her. He hated her; he loved her. She was a disturbance, an irritation; he could never escape from her; he fancied he never would; worse still, he was not entirely sure that he wanted to.

Obviously a most unfortunate state of affairs for a mighty king to find himself in. He had broken with Rome for Anne's sake; the Pope's name had been struck from the prayer books, and it was not mentioned at Divine Service; yet in the streets the people never ceased to talk of the Pope, and with reverence. Wolsey was gone, and with his going, the policy of England was changed. Wolsey it was who had believed that England must preserve the balance of power in Europe; Henry had pursued a new policy, he had cut off England from Europe. England stood alone.

Those matters, which had once been the concern of the Cardinal's, were now the King's. Cromwell was sly and cunning, but a servant, no leader; Cromwell did what he was told. Why should a man with so much on his shoulders be pestered by women! Madge Shelton was a bright wench, but he had had enough of her. Anne was Anne . . . none like her, but a witch— a nagging witch at that. Too clever, trying to dictate to England through him; advising rashness here, there, everywhere. This state of affairs was such as to make a man's blood—which was ever ready to simmer—bubble and boil over.

He was going to be firm. Anne could not get children; he would be better without Anne; she disturbed him, distracted him from state matters. Women were for bedtime, not to sidle between a king and his country.

The people were dissatisfied. There were too many noble lords ready to support the Catholic cause, possibly conspiring with Chapuys. These were not dangerous at the moment, but there were inevitable perils in such a situation. He had his daughter Mary watched; he believed there was a plot afoot to smuggle her out of the country to the Emperor. What if that warrior thought to raise an army against the King, with the replacement of Katharine and Mary as its cause! How many nobles of England, who now did honour to its king, would slip over to the Emperor's banner? Henry asked himself uneasily. His conscience told him that he had embarked on this matter of divorce that he might produce a son and save England from civil war, but he had produced no son, and his actions had put England nearer to civil war than she had been since the conflicts between the houses of York and Lancaster.

He sounded a few of his most trusted counsellors on a new line of action. What if he divorced Anne? It looked as if she could not have a son. Might not this be a sign from Almighty God that the union with Anne had not found favour in the sight of heaven? It was astonishing; a healthy girl to be so barren. One daughter! One pretended pregnancy! His lips curled. How she had fooled him! How she continued to fool him! How, when he was thinking he would be better without her, she would lure him and tempt him, so that instead of occupying his mind with plans to rid himself of her, he found himself making love to her.

His counsellors shook their heads at the suggestion of a second divorce. There were points beyond which even the most docile men could not go, and the most despotic of kings could not carry them with him. Perhaps these men were thinking of

Sir Thomas More and John Fisher, awaiting death stoically in the Tower; perhaps they were thinking that the people were murmuring against the doings of the King.

Divorce Anne he might, his counsellors thought, but only on condition that he took Katharine back.

Katharine! That made the King roar like a wounded animal. Katharine back! Anne angered him, Anne plagued him, but at least she excited him. Let matters rest. Not for anything would be have Katharine back.

These matters all tended to arouse the wrath of the King. The new Pope aggravated him still further, by raising John Fisher—a man who was in prison for treason—to cardinal's rank. When Henry heard the news, he foamed with rage.

"I'll send the head to Rome for the cap!" he cried fiercely. He had had enough. Fisher was executed. Sir Thomas More was to follow. Nor were these the only traitors; those monks of the Charterhouse who had refused to acknowledge him Supreme Head of the Church were to be punished with the utmost severity. This should be a sign to the people that all those who would not do the will of Henry VIII of England should suffer thus. He would have the people heartily aware of this. There should be public executions; there should be hangings; there should be burned-flesh offerings to the supremacy of the King. Murder was in the King's heart; he murdered now with a greater ferocity than when he had murdered men like Empson, Dudley and Buckingham; the murders of these men were calculated, cold-blooded; now he murdered in revenge and anger. The instruments of torture in those gloomy dungeons of pain beneath the grey buildings of the Tower should be worked night and day. The King was intent on the complete subjugation of all who raised a voice against him.

A pall of smoke hung over London. The people huddled together, watching the mutilation, listening to the shrieks and groans of martyrs.

The Continent was aghast at the news of the death of Fisher and More; the Church infuriated by the murder of Fisher, the political world shocked beyond expression by that of More. The Vatican found its voice, and sent forth vituperation against the monster of England. The Emperor, astonished at the stupidity of a king who could rid himself of the ablest man in the country, said: "Had we been master of such a servant, we would rather have lost the fairest city in our dominion than such a counsellor."

Europe mourned wise men, but London mourned its martyrs, and the King was shaken, afraid. But his blood was up; he was shrewd enough to know that any sign of weakness would not help him now; he had gone too far to retrace his steps. When More had said that a man who cannot restrain his passions is essentially cruel, he spoke the truth. The real Henry emerged from behind the fair, flushed, good-tempered, hail-fellow-well-met personality which his people—as good Englishmen—had admired so long. The cold, cruel, implacable, relentless egoist was exposed.

But there was still the conscience, which could make him

tremble. "What I have done," he told it, "has been done for Anne." He did not say, "I am a great hater!" but, "I am a great lover."

They brought the news of Thomas More's execution to him while he played at the tables with Anne; as he sat opposite her, he pictured beside her brilliant beauty the calm ascetic face of the man whose death he had just brought about.

He stood up. He had no stomach for the game now. He knew that he had murdered a great man, a good man; and he was afraid.

Then he saw Anne sitting there opposite him. The answer to his conscience was clear; he knew how to stifle that persistent voice inside him.

He said: "Thou art the cause of this man's death!"

Then he left the table and shut himself in his private chamber in sudden fright which nothing would allay.

Crossing London Bridge, people could not look up without seeing the ghastly sights exhibited there. The heads of brave men dripped blood; to this pass had their bravery brought them, since it was unwise to be brave in the reign of Bluff King Hal.

On the lips of all were the names of More and Fisher. These men were saints enshrined in the hearts of the people; there could be no open worship of such saints. Many of the monks of the Charterhouse preferred death to admitting that Henry was

Supreme Head of the Church. A large number of them went to the Tower; some were tortured on the rack, that they might betray their friends; many found their way into the embrace of the Scavenger's Daughter, that vile instrument recently invented by Thomas Skevington, which contracted the body in a manner exactly opposite to that of the rack, so that blood was forced from the nose and ears; some were hung from the ceilings of dungeons by their wrists, which were encased in gauntlets, until their hands were bleeding and paralyzed; some had their teeth forced out by the brakes; some were tortured with the thumbscrews or the bilboes. People whispered together of the dreadful things that befell these saintly men in the Tower of London. Some were chained in airless dungeons, and left to starve; some were paralyzed by continued confinement in one of those chambers called the Little Ease, the walls of which were so contrived that its inmate could neither walk, nor sit, nor lie full length; some were put into the Pit, a noisome deep cavern in which rats were as ferocious as wild beasts and lived on those human wrecks who, chained and helpless, standing knee deep in filthy water, must face them while being unable to defend themselves. Some of the more obstinate monks were given an execution which was public and shameful; taken to Tyburn, they were half-hanged, cut down, and while they were conscious their abdomens were ripped open and their bowels dragged forth from their mutilated bodies and burned. Even after death their bodies were further desecrated.

This, the King would have the people know, might be

the fate of any who questioned his supremacy. The people of London heard the screams of the Anabaptists as the flames leaped from the faggots at their feet, scorching and frizzling their bodies. In Europe the people talked of the terror which had befallen England; they talked in hushed, shocked whispers. When Henry heard this he laughed savagely, calling to mind the Spaniards' way of dealing with heretics and how, but a few months before, Francis and his family had marched through Paris chanting piously while Lutherans were burned before the doors of Notre Dame.

Henry knew how to suppress rebellion; he knew how to make the people knuckle under. "I will have this thing an it cost me my crown!" he had been known to say, and he meant it. He was strong and ruthless; all men trembled before him. He was no longer the young and lusty boy seeking pleasure while a cardinal ruled; he was master. He would force all to recognize that, however much blood should flow.

He had a plan now which intrigued him; it was to make Thomas Cromwell his vicar-general, and as such let him visit all the churches and monasteries of England. The Supreme Head of the church would know the state of these monasteries; it worried his conscience that stories he had heard from time to time of the profligacy of the monks and nuns might have some truth in them! What if these monasteries were the bawdy houses he had often heard it whispered that they were! What if there were men living licentious lives, sheltered by their monks' robes! Those nuns, wrapped up in the garments of piety—what of them? He remembered the case of Eleanor Carey, that relative of Anne's who had had two illegitimate children by a priest. These things had come to light, and if there was one thing the Supreme Head of the Church of England would not tolerate in his land, it was immorality! He would suppress it, he would stamp it out! Once it had been no concern of his, but now by God's will he was the head of the Church, and by God, he would put an end to all evil practices.

Thomas Cromwell should go to these places; he should bring back evidence of what he found—and Thomas Cromwell could always be relied upon to bring back the evidence that was expected of him—and if that evidence warranted the dissolution of these places, then dissolved they should be! A list of their valuables should Thomas bring back; it was said they had some fine treasures in their chests—jewels, works of art only suited to a king's palace. This was a good plan; later he would talk with Cromwell.

From his palace he saw the smoke over London. This was done in the name of righteousness. The Anabaptists denied the divinity of Christ; they deserved to die.

In the courtyards of the palace men talked together in whispers. Something was afoot. The King was nervous today; there had been a time in the days of his youth when he had gone among his people unafraid, but now it was not so. If he stayed in a house, even for a night, he took a locksmith with him that new bolts might be put on the door of his sleeping apartment; he had the straw of his bed searched every night for hidden daggers.

"Now what?" he said, and leaning from his windows roared down to be told what fresh news was exciting them.

A little group of courtiers looked up at him in some alarm.

"There is some news. Hide it not!" he shouted.

"'Tis naught, Your Majesty, but that the head of Sir Thomas More is no longer on the bridge."

"What!" cried the King, roaring, that none might guess his voice shook. "Who moved it then?"

There was no answer.

"Who moved it then?" he roared again.

"'Tis not known, Your Majesty. . . . 'Tis but known that it is gone."

He shut the window. His knees trembled; the whole of his great body shook. The head of More the martyr had been removed from the bridge, where it should have remained with the heads of other traitors. What means this? What meant it? A miracle, was it? There had been One who had risen from the dead; what if this man, More, were such another!

He could see the shrewd, kind face, did he but close his eyes; he could recall the humour, the mocking kindliness. He remembered the man so well; often had he walked in the Chelsea garden, his arm about the fellow's neck. He remembered when he had written his book denouncing Luther, who had worked with him, whose lucid style, whose perfect Latin knowledge had largely made the book. And because he had had need to show this man he could not disobey his master, he had murdered him. True he had not wielded the axe; true he had not been the one to place the head among the heads of traitors; but he was the murderer nevertheless. His old friend More—the brightest light in his realm! He remembered how the man had walked with him and Katharine on the terraces of the palace, and talked of the stars, pointing them out to the royal pair, for he and Katharine had been interested in astronomy then. Now he was dead, he who had never wanted to sun himself in the brilliance of court life; who would have preferred to live quietly in the heart of his family with his books. He was dead; and his head had disappeared. This might be a miracle, a sign!

Anne came in, saw that he was distressed, and was unusually soft and ready to comfort him.

"You have had some shock."

He looked at her eagerly; she thought he had the air of a frightened boy who is afraid to be left in the dark.

"More's head has gone from London Bridge!"

She was taken aback; she looked at him, wide-eyed; and they were drawn together in their fear.

"Anne," he said groping for her hand, "what means this, thinkest thou?"

She took his hand and pressed it firmly; she forgot the miracle of the missing head, since the fear which had been with her night and day was evaporating. Henry needed her; at moments such as this, it was to her he turned; she had been too easily humiliated, too ready to show her humiliation. She had nothing to fear. She was the wife of a man who, having absolute power, would have his way, but a clever woman might manage him still. She could see her folly stretching right back to her coronation; she thought she saw why she had appeared to lose her power over him. Now here he was, trembling and afraid, superstitious in an age of superstition, lacking that courage which had made her the reckless creature she was.

She smiled at him.

"My lord, someone has removed the head."

"But who would dare?"

"He was a man who had many friends, and one of these might be ready to take his head from where it belonged."

"I see that, Anne." He was feeling better already; he looked at her through softly sentimental eyes. She was very beautiful, and now she was gentle and very reassuring; she was clever too; the others paled quickly. When Anne reassured, there was a good deal that was truth in the reassurance; the others flattered; it was good to be with Anne. "That was where the head belonged," he said fiercely. "He was a traitor, Anne."

"As all who seek to disobey Your Majesty's commands," she said.

"Thou speakest truth. 'Twas a friend of his that took the head. By God, that in itself was a traitorous act, was it not!"

She stroked his hand.

"Indeed it was. There will be those simple people who ever look on traitors as saints. Mayhap it would be well to leave this matter. Why should it worry us? We know the man deserved to die."

"By God, you're right!" he cried. "'Tis a matter of small importance."

He did not wish to leave her; she distracted his thoughts from the memory of that severed head with its kindly mocking eyes.

It was reconciliation. In the court it was said: "She has a power over him, which none other could exercise."

Her enemies cursed her. If she but give him a son, they said, she is Queen of England till her death.

Chapuys wrote home to the Emperor, Charles, telling him that the King of England was over and over again unfaithful, but that the concubine was cunning and knew how to manage the King. It would be unwise to attach too much importance to his brief infatuations for court ladies.

Anne was preparing the most splendid banquet the court had yet seen. She was feverish with delight. She felt as though she had come through a nightmare of terror, and now here was the morning to prove that the shadows had been conjured up out of her imagination, that they had no existence in truth. How could she have been so foolish; how could she have believed that she who had held the King so well in check, could have lost control now! She was supreme; his need of her was passionate and lasting; now that—as her husband—he was conscious of the shackles that held him to her, all she need do was lengthen the tether. Her fault had been in trying to keep it as tight as a mistress might. All a wife needed was a little more subtlety, and it had taken her two years of doubts and nightmares to realize this. Let him wander away from her, let him dally with others—it would but be to compare them with his incomparable Queen.

She was gayer than she had ever been. She designed new costumes; she called to her the most brilliant courtiers to arrange an entertainment that should enchant the King; witty Wyatt, subtle George, gentle Harry Norris, amusing Francis Bryan, Henry Howard, those gay courtiers Francis Weston and William Brereton; others too, all the brightest stars of the court clustered about her, and she the dazzling centre as it used to be. The King was with her constantly; she planned and thrilled to her plans.

One day she found one of the youngest of the musicians sitting alone playing, and she paused to listen, delighting in his delicate touch, thinking, He is more than ordinarily good. She had Madge Shelton bring him to her. He was young and slender, a rather beautiful boy with long tapering fingers and dreamy, dark eyes.

"Her Majesty heard your music," said Madge. "She thought it good."

The boy was overcome with the honour of being noticed by the Queen, who smiled on him most graciously.

"I would have you play awhile," she said. "I feel you could be of use to us in the revels, for it would seem to me that we have not so many musicians of your talent in the court that we can afford to leave out one who plays as you do."

She was charming, because she at once saw that his admiration was not merely that which he would give to his queen. Her long sleeves hung over the hand with its slight malformation; the other, with long, white, jewel-decked fingers, rested lightly on her chair. He could not take his wondering eyes from her, for he had never been so close to her before.

"What is his name?" she asked, when he had been dismissed.

"It is Smeaton, Your Majesty. Mark Smeaton."

"He was poorly clad," she said.

"He is one of the humbler musicians, Your Majesty."

"See that he has money with which to procure himself clothes. He plays too well to be so shabbily attired. Tell him he may play before me; I will have a part for him to take at the entertainment."

She dismissed him from her mind, and gave herself over to fresh plans. There was an air of lightheartedness among her friends; George seemed younger, excessively gay. The Queen herself was as sparkling as she had ever been when she was the King's mistress. She was the centre of the brilliant pageant, the pivot round which the wit and laughter revolved; she was the most lovely performer. The King watched the entertainment, his eyes for her alone. Anne! he thought, inwardly chuckling. By God, she was meant to be a queen. She could amuse him, she could enchant him, she could divert him, she could cast unpleasant thoughts from his mind.

He had forgotten Fisher; More too almost, for the removal of his head from London Bridge had been no miracle but the bold action of his daughter Margaret Roper who had gone stealthily and by night. Anne had learned this, and brought him the news.

"By God!" he had cried. "'Tis a treasonable offence to go against the King's command!" She had soothed him. "Let be! Let be! 'Twas a brave action. Doubtless the girl loved her father well. People are full of sentiment; they would not care that a girl should be punished because she loved her father well. Let us have done with this gruesome affair of a traitor's head. To please me, I would ask Your Majesty not to pursue the matter."

He had frowned and feigned to be considering it, knowing full well that his people would not care for interference with Margaret Roper; then she had wheedled, and kissed him, and he had patted her thighs and said: "Well then, sweetheart, since you ask it, it shall be done. But I like not treason . . . I like it not at all!" She had smiled, well pleased, and so had he. An unpleasant business was done with.

He watched her now—the loveliest woman in the court— and too many of these young profligates had their eyes upon her, ready to be over-bold an they dared. He liked to know that they fancied her, even while it filled him with this smoldering rage. He could laugh. None dared to give her more than covert looks, for it would be treason to cast over-desirous eyes on what belonged to the King; and well they knew this king's method of dealing with traitors! He called to her, would have her sit by him, would let his hands caress her.

It was borne home to the Queen's enemies that their hopes had been premature, and to her friends that they had feared too soon.

Catherine Howard was joyous as a lark; like the lively young grasshopper, she danced all through the summer months without a thought of winter. She was discovering that she was more than ordinarily pretty; she was the prettiest of all the ladies; she had, said some, a faint resemblance to her cousin the Queen. She developed a love of finery, and being kept short of decorative clothes or the money with which to provide herself with even the smallest addition to her wardrobe, she looked to her lover to provide these. Derham was only too delighted. He was enchanted by the lovely child, who was so very youthful at times, at others completely mature. He would provide her with many little luxuries besides—wines and sweetmeats, fruit and flowers. So when Catherine yearned to possess an ornament called the French Fennel, which was being worn by all the court ladies who would follow the latest fashion, Derham told her that he knew a little woman in London with a crooked back who was most skilled in the making of flowers of silk. Catherine begged him to get this done for her. "I will pay you when I have the means," she told him, which set him smiling and begging her that it should be a present. And so it was, but when she had the precious ornament, she was afraid to wear it until she had let it be known that one of the ladies had given it to her, for the Duchess was more watchful than she had been at Horsham.

It was tiresome of the old lady to have taken the precaution of locking the chamber door each night. Derham was an adventurous young man; he was passionately in love. He was not going to let a key separate him from Catherine. A little planning, a little scheming, a little nodding and looking the other way by those who liked to see good sport, and it was not such a difficult matter to steal the key after it had been brought to the Duchess.

There was the additional spice of planning what should be done, should there be a sudden intrusion.

"You would have to hurry into the gallery and hide there!" said Catherine.

"That I could do with the greatest of ease!" said Derham.

He would come to the chamber at any hour of the night; it was a highly exciting adventure they were both enjoying.

The others watched, rather wistfully. Derham was such a handsome young man and so much in love with the child; there were some, such as Dorothy Barwicke and a newcomer, Jane Acworth, who whispered to each other that Catherine Howard was the sort who would always find men to love her. What use to warn her? She was too addicted to physical love to heed any warning. If she realized that the path she was treading might be dangerous, she might try to reform, but she would surely slip back. She was a lusty little animal, irresistible to men because she found them irresistible. Mary Lassells thought the Duchess should be told, in secret so that she could come up and catch them in the act, but the others were against this. They wanted no probings, nor inquiries. They pointed out that they would all be implicated—even Mary Lassells, since she had been months in the house and had not seen fit to warn Her Grace before.

The Duchess was less comfortable in her mind than she had been. Apart from the rumours she heard at court, she sensed the presence of intrigue in her own household. She watched Catherine, flaunting her new French Fennel. Heaven knew there were plenty of men all too eager to take advantage of a young girl. She saw something in Catherine's face, something secret and knowledgeable, and the memory of it would recur in her uneasy thoughts. Her other granddaughter, she believed, was not happy; the Duchess preferred not to think of what might be happening at court; better to turn her attention to her own house. Were the young men too free with the girls? She would have to be arranging a marriage for young Catherine soon; when she next saw the Queen, she would have a word with her about this. In the meantime the greatest care must be exercised.

Sometimes the Duchess did not sleep very well; sometimes she would wake in the night and fancy she heard footsteps on the stairs, or a muffled burst of laughter overhead. She knew now that for some time she had been suspicious of what went on in the girls' apartments; there were some over-bold wenches there, she believed. I must bestir myself; I must look into this. There is my little granddaughter Catherine to be considered. That French Fennel . . . She had said she got it from Lady Brereton. Now did she? Would her ladyship give such a handsome gift? What if one of the young gentlemen was seeking Catherine's favours by offering gifts! It was not a very pleasant reflection.

Forced by a sense of impending danger both at court and at Lambeth, she roused herself one night soon after twelve, and went to the place where the key of the ladies' apartment should be. It was not there. Puffing and panting with the fear of what she would find if she went to the room, she nevertheless could make no excuse for not going. It had ever been her habit to avoid the unpleasant, but here was something for the avoidance of which it would be most difficult to find an adequate excuse.

She put on a robe and went out of her sleeping apartment to the corridor. Slowly she mounted the staircase. She was distressed, for she was sure she could hear muffled voices coming from that room; she paused outside the door. There was no sound inside the room now. She opened the door and stood on the threshold. All the ladies were in their beds, but there was in that room an atmosphere of such tenseness that she could not but be aware of it, and she was sure that, though they had their eyes shut, they but feigned sleep.

She went first to Catherine's bed. She drew off the clothes

and looked at the naked body of her granddaughter. Catherine feigned sleep too long for innocence.

The Duchess thought she heard the faintest creak of boards in the gallery which ran along one side of the room. She had an alarmed feeling that if she had that gallery searched, the search would not be fruitless. It would set tongues wagging though, and she dared not let that happen.

Her panic made her angry; she wished to blame someone for the negligence of which she knew herself to be guilty. Catherine was lying on her back; the Duchess rolled her over roughly and brought her hand across the girl's buttocks. Catherine yelled; the girls sat up in bed, the curtains were drawn back.

"What has happened? What is this?"

Did their exclamations ring true? wondered the old lady.

Catherine was holding her bruised flesh, for the Duchess's rings had cut into her.

"I would know," said the Duchess sharply, "who it was who stole my keys and opened this door."

"Stole Your Grace's keys . . ."

"Opened the door . . ."

Oh, yes! The sly wenches . . . they knew well enough who it was. Thank God, she thought, I came in time!

Mary Lassells was trying to catch her eye, but she would not look at the sly creature. Didn't the fool realize that what she just did not want to hear was the truth . . . providing of course that the truth was disturbing!

"Tomorrow," said the Duchess, "I shall look into this matter. If any of you had aught to do with this matter of my keys, you shall be soundly whipped and sent home in disgrace. I shall make no secret of your sins, I warn you! I thought I heard noises here. Let me warn you that if I hear more noises it will be the worse for you."

She went out and left them.

"There!" she said, as she settled down to sleep. "I have done my duty. I have warned them. After such a threat, none of them would dare to misbehave herself, and if any of them have already done so, they will take good care to keep quiet about it."

In the morning she found her keys; they were not in their rightful place, which led her to hope and believe that they must have been there all the time, and that there had been an oversight, the doors having been left unlocked all that night.

Still, she was resolved to keep an eye on the young women, and particularly on Catherine.

There came a day when, entering what was known as the maids' room, she saw Catherine and Derham together. The maids' room was a long, pleasant, extremely light room in which the ladies sat to embroider, or to work tapestry, or to spin. Such a room was certainly forbidden to gentlemen.

The Duchess had come to the room, taking her usual laboured steps, and had Derham and Catherine not been noisily engaged in a romp, they would assuredly have heard her approach.

Derham had come in to talk to Catherine, and she feigning greater interest in her piece of needlework than in him, had goaded him to snatch it from her; after which, Catherine immediately sought to retrieve it. They were not interested in the piece of needlework, except as an excuse for titillating their senses by apparent haphazard physical contacts. Derham ran round the room, flourishing the piece of needlework, and Catherine gave chase. Cornering him behind the spinning wheel, she snatched it from him, but he caught her round the waist and she slid to the floor, at which he did likewise. They rolled on the floor together, he with his arms about her, Catherine shrieking her delighted protests. And thus the Duchess found them.

She stood in the doorway, shouting at them for some seconds before they heard her angry voice.

Then she stalked over to them. They saw her and were immediately quiet, standing abashed before her.

She was trembling with rage and fury. Her granddaughter to be guilty of such impropriety! The girl's gown was torn at the neck, noted Her Grace, and that doubtless on purpose! She narrowed her eyes.

"Leave us at once, Derham!" she said ominously. "You shall hear further of this."

He threw Catherine a glance and went out.

The Duchess seized her frightened granddaughter by her sleeve and ripped her clothes off her shoulders.

"You slut!" she cried. "What means this behaviour . . . after all my care!"

She lifted her ebony stick, and would have brought it down on Catherine's head had she not dodged out of the way. The

Duchess was growing a little calmer now, realizing it would not do to make too violent a scene.

She cornered Catherine, pushed her onto the couch and, bending over her, said: "How far has this gone?"

"It was nothing," said Catherine, fearful for Derham as well as for herself. "It was just that he . . . stole my piece of needlework, and I . . . sought to retrieve it . . . and then . . . you came in."

"His hands were on your neck!"

"It was to retrieve the needlework which I had snatched from him."

The Duchess preferred to believe it was but a childish romp. She wanted no scandal. What if it came to the hard-faced Duke's ears, of what went on in her house, what tricks and pranks those under her care got up to! He would not hesitate to whisper it abroad, the wicked man, and then would she be considered the rightful state governess for the Princess Elizabeth!

It must go no further than this room; but at the same time she must make Catherine understand that she must have no dangerous friendships with young men under her roof.

She said: "An I thought there was aught wrong in this romping between thee and Derham, I would have thee sent to the Tower; him too! As it is, I will content myself with giving you the biggest beating you have ever had in your life, Catherine Howard!"

She paused, horror stricken; sitting in a corner, quietly trembling with fear, was one of her attendants, and she must have witnessed the whole scene.

The Duchess turned from Catherine and went over to her.

"Jane Acworth! You think to sit there and allow such behaviour! What do you think your task is? To watch young men make free with Catherine Howard?" The girl, trembling, said: "Your Grace, it was naught . . ."

But a stinging blow at the side of her head silenced the girl. The Duchess continued to slap her for some seconds.

"Let me hear no more of this, girl, or you shall feel a whip across your shoulders. Catherine, go to my private chamber; you shall receive your punishment there!"

She went puffing from the room, very ill at ease. But having beaten Catherine, while Catherine writhed and shrieked, she felt she had done her duty.

She summoned one Margaret Morton, when she had done with Catherine.

"I would have speech with Francis Derham. Send him to me without delay!"

He came. She did not know how to punish him. She should banish him of course. But she had always liked him; he was quite the most charming young man of her household. If anything, he was over-bold, but there is something very attractive about over-boldness. He was a distant kinsman too . . . so perhaps it would be enough to warn him.

"I would have you know that you are without prospects. You could not marry my granddaughter. I would have you remember your position in this house, Francis Derham!"

"Your Grace, I must humbly apologize. It was but animal spirits. . . ."

The animal spirits of youth, she thought. There was something delightful about them. Memories came back, softening her. Suppose she allowed him to stay this time! She had warned him; he would not dare to presume again. He was such a handsome, courtly, charming boy!

✦

With the coming of the autumn, Anne's spirits soared, for she discovered that at last she was pregnant. The King was overjoyed. He was sure that if he would but show the people a male heir, everything that had gone to the producing of it might be forgotten.

Anne, eager to be brought to bed of a healthy child, gave up her life of gaiety and spent a good deal of time reading and thinking of the past. She could not look back with much pride on the two years which had seen her Queen. It seemed to her that much of her time had been spent in worthless machinations and sordid subterfuge. The affair of Madge Shelton stood out from those years, filling her with shame. She herself was now with child again; should she be delivered of a son, her dearest wish would be granted; she would then ask nothing more of life.

She was thoughtfully sitting over her tapestry with her ladies, asking questions about the poor of London. She said: "Would it not be better if, instead of stitching this fine tapestry, we made shirts and suchlike garments for the poor?"

It was strange to see her who had been known to occupy

herself at great length with the planning of her own gowns, to see her who had given orders how should be cut and made yards of black satin and gold arras, now stitching contentedly at garments for the poor. She had changed, and the change had a good deal to do with the terrible fear which had beset her and which had been removed, first by the King's returning affection for her, and then by her pregnancy.

Hugh Latimer had been largely instrumental in her change of heart. She had been interested in the great reformer ever since she had heard of him, and when Stokesley, Bishop of London, had had him committed to the Tower, she used all her influence to get him released. The King, reluctant and yet unable in a fresh return of his passion to refuse what she asked, agreed on the release, and thus postponed Latimer's martyrdom for twenty-five years. On his release, Anne had desired to hear him preach and forthwith did so, when, much to her astonishment, instead of receiving the gratitude she might have expected from the man, he delivered for her benefit a stormy lecture advising those who placed too much reliance on treasures upon earth to turn from their folly and repent. Anne saw the man afterwards and characteristically asked him where he thought she had erred. He answered unflinchingly that she should by her morality and piety set an example to those under her command. Greatly impressed by his honesty—a virtue by which she set great store—she appointed him one of her chaplains and began to veer towards a more spiritual way of life. Always generous in the extreme, she delighted in looking into deserving cases about her, and helping those whom she considered would benefit by such help. She had always done this when cases were brought to her notice, but now she looked for them systematically.

Although less superstitious than the King, she was not entirely free from this weakness. As she stitched at garments for the poor, she asked herself if she were not doing this in return for a healthy boy. Was she placating the Powers above, as Henry did? Was she, she wondered, getting a little like him? She had her moments of fear. Was Henry capable of begetting a healthy boy? His body was diseased. What if this were the reason Katharine had failed, and she too, so far! Perhaps she was, in a way, placating Providence, making conditions.

She was worried about the Princess Mary. She was still afraid of the Princess and of Katharine. It had seemed to her that if these two were together they might plot something against her, and through her against Elizabeth. Chapuys she feared. She knew well there were many powerful nobles who deeply resented the break with Rome. They were all only waiting to rise up and destroy her. She must not allow her new favour with the King to blind her to this.

And as she stitched, she prayed for a son.

The King prayed too. He was pleased with the change in Anne. It was well to see her calmer, quieter; it was well to feel this peace stealing over him because at last their union was flavoured with hope. He needed such hope; the people were being difficult once more. They were saying that it had not rained since More had died; they would always find a reason for a bad harvest, and the crops had failed once more. The Flanders trade was not good. In fact it looked as if the country was getting together a collection of grievances and irritations in order to make trouble.

The King needed distraction. It suddenly dawned on him that one of his wife's attendants was—well, not so much an attractive girl as a different kind of girl. Perhaps he meant that she was quite different from Anne; she was so quiet, she moved about like a little mouse; she was very fair; she had a prim little mouth and quick, glancing eyes. She would never be leader of the revels, she would never shine, she would never outwit a man with her sharp tongue! She was as different from Anne as any woman could be. That was why he first noticed her.

If she caught his eyes upon her, she would drop hers quickly; a soft rose-pink blush would steal into her cheeks. She was very demure.

On one occasion he was sitting alone, thinking that it was a long time before his son could be born, and wondering if there was some holy relic the soothsayers could give him as protection against another girl child. He had some holy water, a tear which Christ had shed over Lazarus, and a vial of the sweat of St. Michael; all of which he had purchased at great cost during the sweating sickness. But in spite of these, Anne's first child had been a girl, and he wondered whether he should buy something especially which might ensure the birth of a boy. As he considered this, the demure maid of honour came into the room and, seeing him, curtseyed in a frightened way and would have hurried off had he not detained her with a "Hi, there! What want you?"

"Her Grace, the Queen . . ." said the girl, so low that he could scarcely hear her.

"What of Her grace, the Queen?" He studied her from head to toe. Small where Anne was tall; slow of movement where Anne was quick; meek where Anne sparkled; slow of speech instead of bright; modest instead of coquettish; willing to listen humbly rather than disconcert a man with her wit.

"I had thought to find her . . ."

"Come hither!" said the King. "And are you very disturbed to come upon the King when you looked for the Queen?"

"Yes, Your Majesty . . . I mean no, Your Majesty. . . ."

"Well," said Henry pleasantly, "make up your mind."

She would not come too close. He did not force her, liking suddenly her demureness, since there were so many of them who were too ready.

She could think of nothing to say, which pleased him and made him remember that Anne was over-ready with her retorts.

"Sit there awhile and I will play. You may listen. Bring my lute to me."

She brought it, cautiously. He tried to touch her fingers over the lute, but she was quick; she had leaped back as though he had tried to sting her. He was not angry. His thoughts were chiefly of his son, and therefore with Anne. But he liked the girl; he was, he told himself, always touched by modesty; he liked and respected it in the young people about his court.

He commanded her to sit; she did so, modestly letting her hands fall into her lap; her mild eyes watched him, and then seemed full of admiration.

When he had finished he saw that her eyes were filled with tears, so moved was she by his music, and he realized that he had not felt so gratified for a long time.

He asked her name. She told him it was Jane Seymour.

He dismissed her then. "You may go. We shall meet again. I like you, Jane!"

It was not a quarrel with Anne, just a slight irritation. A petty argument, and she, in her overpowering way, had proved herself right. Jane Seymour would never be one to prove herself right. She's all woman, thought Henry. And that's how a woman should be. Women are women, and men are men. When the one will dabble with that which is solely within the province of the other, it is a sad thing.

He sent for Jane Seymour. She should have the honour of hearing his new song before he allowed anyone else to hear it. She sat listening, her feet scarce reaching the floor; which made her seem helpless. She was very meek.

He made inquiries about her. She was the daughter of Sir John Seymour of Wolf Hall in Wiltshire; he was by no means a powerful nobleman, but it was interesting to discover that there was a tiny root of royalty in his family tree, provided one dug deep enough to find it. Henry stored such knowledge. And as he played his lute, he thought about Jane; a quiet, mild bedfellow, he thought, pleasant enough, and white skinned;

unawakened and virginal. He grew sentimental; virtue had that effect on him. All women, he told himself, should be virtuous.

The court noticed his preoccupation with the maid of honour. Chapuys and the French ambassador laughed together. They were cynical. The King had been noted of late to extol virginity. "He refers to Jane Seymour!" said the French ambassador, to whom the Spanish ambassador replied that he greatly doubted Jane possessed that quality, having been some time at court. He added that the King might be pleased though that she did not, for then he could marry her on condition that she was a virgin, and when he needed a divorce he could then find many witnesses to the contrary.

But the King continued to view Jane through sentimental eyes. She had been primed by her father and her brothers, when dazzling possibilities had occurred to the minds of these very ambitious men who had the example of the Earl of Wiltshire and the young Lord Rochford before their eyes. They advised Jane: "Do this. . . ." "On no account do that. . . ." Jane herself was not without ambition. She had watched many a quarrel between the King and Queen, and she understood the King more than he would have thought from the demure eyes that met his with such seeming sincerity.

When he tried to kiss her, she was overcome with blushes; she ran away and hid herself, and the King, having become the champion of virtue, could not satisfy his conscience if he forced the girl to anything. His mind began to scheme with his conscience once again. What if this marriage with Anne had been wrong? What if God should show his disapproval over the child? The plans were not very well shaped as yet—they were misty shadows of thought, which allowed him to dally with Jane, while respecting her virtue.

He gave her a locket bearing his picture; she wore it on a chain round her throat, intending this to be a sign that were she not of such unbending virtue she would readily consider his advances, having the greatest admiration for his person. He wanted Jane; he could not have her; and this made her seem very desirable to him.

The story of Anne was to Jane a long object lesson: what to do before, what not to do after. But though Jane knew what she must do, she was not very intelligent, and she could not prevent a new haughtiness creeping into her manner, which Anne was quick to notice. She saw the locket which Jane was wearing, and asked mildly enough if she might see it.

Jane flushed guiltily, and put her hand over the locket; whereat Anne's suspicions flared up. She took the locket, breaking its chain as she did so, and on snapping it open beheld the smiling face of the King crowned in a jewelled cap.

A year ago she would have raged against him; now she was silent and undecided. She saw in sly Jane Seymour, with her much-paraded virtue, a more deadly enemy than any other woman who had taken the King's fancy.

She prayed urgently. A son! I must have a son!

At Kimbolton Castle, Katharine lay dying. She had lived wretchedly during her lingering illness, for money due to her was not paid. She was full of sorrow; not only had she been separated from her beloved daughter, but when she had asked that she might see the Princess before she died, even this request was denied her. She was deeply disturbed by the fate of her former confessor, Father Forrest, who though an old man had, through his allegiance to her, been cruelly treated at the hands of the King; he had been imprisoned and tortured in such a manner that she could not bear to contemplate; she longed to write and comfort him, but she feared that if a letter from her was intercepted, it might cause the old man's execution, and though, in his case, death might be the happiest release from his misery, she could not bring it about. Abell, her other confessor, was treated with equal cruelty; it was unbearable that her friends should suffer thus.

Chapuys had got the King's reluctant permission to visit her, and arrived on New Year's Day. She was delighted to see one whom she knew to be her friend. She was very ill, and looked ten years older than her fifty years. He sat by her bed and she, while expressing genuine sorrow for all those who had suffered in her cause, said that she had never thought for one instant that she had been wrong in her struggle against the King.

To the man who had caused the chief miseries of her life she had no reproaches to offer. She was the daughter of a king and queen, and she believed in the divine right of royalty. The King would bastardize a princess, because he was bewitched; he would, she believed, emerge from that witchery and see the folly of his ways. It was her duty in the interests of royalty to uphold herself and her daughter—not for any personal reasons, but because they were Queen and Princess. Katharine was adamant now as ever, and would have suffered any torture rather than admit that her daughter was not the legitimate heir to the throne of England.

She talked with tears of Fisher, with regret of More; she talked of Abell and Forrest, mercifully knowing nothing of the more horrible deaths that awaited these two of her faithful adherents.

Chapuys, the cynic, thought, She is dying by his hand as surely as More and Fisher did. He thought of the years of misery this woman had endured, the mental torture that had been inflicted on her by her husband. Here was yet another victim of the murderer's hand. What though the method was different!

Chapuys had no real comfort to give her. His master would not wish to be embroiled in a war with England for the sake of Katharine of Aragon and her daughter since he had his hands full elsewhere.

To comfort her though, he hinted at some action from outside on her behalf. She brightened. His visit did much to revive her; it was so rarely that the King allowed her to be visited by her friends.

After he left, another incident occurred which helped to

lighten her grief in being denied the comfort of her daughter's presence.

It was evening of a bitterly cold day, when through the castle there echoed the sound of loud knocking. Her maid came to tell her that it was a poor woman who, making a journey across country, had lost her way and begged to be allowed to spend the night at the castle for fear she and her attendant should freeze to death.

Katharine bade them bring in the poor souls and give them food.

She was dozing, when her bedroom door was opened and a woman came in. Katharine looked at the newcomer in astonishment for one moment, and then the tears began to flow from her eyes. She held out her arms, feeling that she was a girl again, riding the rough seas of the Bay of Biscay, thinking fearfully of the fate which awaited her in an unknown country where she was to marry a boy husband; she was young again, watching the land grow less blurred, as she sailed into Plymouth. With her there had been a band of beautiful Spanish girls, and there was one among them who, during the unhappy years which England had given her, had ever been her faithful friend. This girl had married Lord Willoughby; and they had been together until, by the King's command, Katharine had been banished from the court and cut off from all those she loved. And here was Lady Willoughby coming by stealth, as a stranger lost in the snow, that she might be with Katharine during her last hours in England as she had been during her first.

This was wonderful; she was almost happy.

"If I could but have seen my little daughter . . ." she murmured.

But the coming of her friend had put her in high spirits, and she revived so much that she was well enough to sit up in her bed, though she was too far gone in sickness of body, which had grown out of sickness of mind, to make any real recovery. During the first week of January her condition grew worse. She had mass said in her room on the afternoon of the sixth, and then, ill as she was, asked for materials that she might write a last letter to the King. She did not blame him; she accepted her fate meekly; she only asked that he should be a good father to their daughter Mary, and that he should do right by her servants.

Henry was hilarious when he heard the news of Katharine's death; there followed one moment of apprehension when in a blurred fashion he remembered her sad, pale face, heard her strong voice pleading for justice. He did then what he ever did when remorse touched him; he made the persecution of Katharine someone else's burden, not his own; he assured himself that he had acted from the highest and most disinterested of motives.

"Praise be to God!" he cried. "We are delivered from all fear of war. The time has come for me to manage the French better than before, because in wondering whether I may now ally myself to the Emperor, they will do all I want."

He would now show that he had never been married to

Katharine. He dressed himself in yellow, having a white feather set in his cap, for why should a man go into mourning for one not his wife!

"Bring me my daughter!" he cried, and the nurses brought Elizabeth to him. Although little more than two years old, she was already a very bright and intelligent child who enjoyed being exhibited, and surveyed her great dazzling father with the utmost interest.

He called for all the musical instruments to play; the courtiers must dance. He went from one to the other, demanding they do homage to their little princess. "For," he exclaimed again and again, "we are now delivered from the evil threat of war!"

Anne rejoiced when she heard the news. It was a great relief. For the first time, she thought, I can feel myself to be really Queen; there is no shadowy Queen in the background to whom some could still look. I am Queen. There is no other Queen but me!

She was inordinately gay; she imitated the King's action, and dressed in yellow.

She did not know that he had once discussed the question of divorcing her with his most trusted counsellors; she did not know that he had refrained from doing so because they said he might divorce her, but if he did, he would surely have to take back Katharine.

✦

Now that Katharine was dead, and Anne felt more secure, she decided she could be less harsh to the Princess Mary, so she sent one of her ladies to the girl with a message. Would Mary come to court? Could they not be friends?

"Tell her," said Anne, "that if she will be a good daughter to her father, she may come to court and count me her friend. Tell her she may walk beside me, and I shall not need her to hold my train."

Mary, grief stricken by the death of her mother, brokenhearted so that she cared not what became of her, sent back word that if being a good daughter to her father meant denying that for which martyrs' blood had been shed, she could not accept Anne's offer.

"The foolish girl!" said Anne. "What more can I do?"

Then she was angry, and at the root of her anger was the knowledge that she herself had helped to make this motherless girl's unhappy lot harder than it need have been. She could not forget what she had heard of Katharine's miserable death, and in her new and chastened mood she felt remorse as well as anger.

She tried again with Mary, but Mary was hard and stubborn, neither ready to forgive nor forget. Mary was fanatical; she would have all or nothing. She wanted recognition: Her mother to be recognized as the true Queen, Anne to be displaced, Elizabeth to be acknowledged a bastard. And on these terms only, would Mary come to court.

Anne shrugged impatient shoulders, really angry with the

girl because she would not let her make amends. When my son is born, thought Anne, I shall be in such a strong position that she will do as I say. If I say she shall come to court, she shall come to court, and it will not be so easy for her to find favour with the King when she is forced to do that which she might have done more graciously.

The beginning of that year was disastrously eventful for Anne. The first disturbance was when Norfolk came hurrying into her chamber to tell that the King had taken such a toss from his horse that he feared he was killed. This upset Anne—not that the King, during their married life, had given her any reasons to love him—but in her condition she felt herself unable to cope adequately with the situation which must inevitably arise if he died. She had the interests of her daughter and the child as yet unborn to look to, and she was greatly disturbed. This however proved to be a minor accident; the King's fall had done scarcely any harm, and he was too practised a horseman to suffer much shock from such a fall.

After this escape, the King was in excellent spirits. He found Jane Seymour alone in one of the Queen's apartments. People had a way of disappearing from Jane Seymour's side when the King approached. Demure as she was, she had permitted certain liberties. He was somewhat enamoured of the pretty, pale creature, and she was a pleasant diversion for a man who can scarcely wait to hear that his son is born.

"Come hither, Jane!" he said in the soft, slurred voice of a lover, made husky with good ale and wine. And she came to him most cautiously, until he, seizing her, pulled her onto his knee.

"Well, what did you think, Jane, when that fool Norfolk ran around telling the world I was done for, eh?"

Jane's eyes filled with tears.

"There, there!" he said. "'Tis no matter for weeping. Here I am, hale and hearty as ever, except for a sore leg. . . ."

He liked to talk of his leg; he spent a good deal of time thinking about it.

"Every physician in London has had a go at it, Jane! And to no avail. I've tried charms and potions . . . no avail . . . no avail."

Jane was timidly sympathetic; he stroked her thighs caressingly.

He liked Jane; he could sit thus happily with her, feeling a mild pleasure in her, without that raging desire which must put a man in torment till it was slaked; it was just pleasant, stroking and patting and going so far and then drawing back.

The door opened, and Anne was watching them. All the fears which she had successfully pushed away came rushing back. She knew Jane Seymour . . . sly, waiting, watchful of her opportunities. Anne suddenly realized why they waited, why Henry could be content to wait. They were waiting to see whether she bore a son. If she did, then Jane Seymour would be the King's mistress. If not . . .

Anne's self-control broke. She began to storm and rage. She now said to the King all those things which had been in her mind and which, even in her most frank moments, she had never mentioned before. It was as though she dragged him

476

away from that bright and pleasant picture he had made of himself, and held up her picture of him. She was laughing at his conscience, at his childish method of putting himself right. Did he not think she saw through that! Did he not think that the great men about him did not either!

She was maddened with rage and grief and terror, so that she knew not what she said.

Henry's one idea was to calm her, for he must think of the son, whom she was so soon to bear.

"Be at peace, sweetheart," he pleaded, "and all shall go well for thee."

But Anne was not at peace. Jane Seymour ran and hid herself behind the hangings, covering her face with her hands and audibly murmuring: "Oh, what have I done!" while she rejoiced at what she had done.

For what could she have done to suit herself and her supporters more, since, after that sudden shock, prematurely Anne's son was born dead!

Trembling, they brought the news to the King. He clenched his hands; his eyes seemed to sink into the flesh about them, while the veins stood out knotted on his forehead. In uncontrollable rage he strode into Anne's room. He stood over her as she lay limp, exhausted and defeated. Words flowed from that cruel little mouth. She had done this! She had humiliated him!

She had deceived him into thinking she would give him sons! She was a witch, a sorceress. . . .

Enfeebled as she was by hours of agony, yet she answered with spirit: "There was none to blame but yourself. This is due to the distress of mind you caused me through your philanderings with that sly Seymour wench!"

Henry roared back wrathfully: "You shall have no more sons by me!" And then, cunning and pious: "I see well that God does not wish to give me male children."

But he did not really believe this, not seeing how he himself could possibly be at fault in this matter.

"When you are on your feet, I will speak to you," he said coldly.

Then he went from the room, his thoughts with Jane Seymour. It might well be that this marriage was a mistake, he was thinking. By God, I was forced into it by sorcery! She was irresistible, with her long hair and her wicked little pointed face. It was beyond the power of man to say nay to her. Sorcery! This is why God does not permit me to have male children. Might it not be that I should make a new match?

Jane Seymour sat in her apartments at the palace, awaiting the King. These apartments which were splendid and hung with rich arras and cloth of gold, had a short while before belonged to Thomas Cromwell, but he had vacated them that Jane might use them, because adjoining those of the King they could most easily and secretly be reached by His Majesty.

Jane was rather frightened by the great happenings which had come about ever since that day when the King had glanced in her direction. Her brothers, Thomas and Edward, had planned ambitiously, and their plans, they told their sister, were all for her. Edward was clever, subtle and ambitious; Thomas was fascinating, dashing and also ambitious. Look what came to Anne Boleyn! said these two. Why not to Jane Seymour? True, Jane had not the obvious attractions of Anne Boleyn, but men were strange in their fancies, and was it Anne's beauty and wit that had charmed the King as much as her reluctance? If Jane had not beauty and wit, she could be as reluctant as Anne, and in all probability with more effect, for shyness would seem more natural in Jane than it ever could be in Anne.

So Jane must bow to the wishes of her family. Chapuys and the imperialists were with Jane too, eager to support any who would bring disfavour on the partisans of Martin Luther.

So here was Jane, meek and mild, yet not being entirely without ambition, feeling that it would be somewhat pleasant to wear a crown, and that to discountenance the haughty Anne Boleyn would be most gratifying. She was therefore ready enough to step into her mistress's shoes, yet a little frightened, for she could not but be aware that this role which was being forced upon her—even though she was not altogether reluctant to take it—was a very dangerous one. Anne was losing her place; Anne who had wit and beauty; Anne who had kept the

King for five long years after she had become his mistress; and when she remembered this, Jane dared not think more than a month or two ahead. Her brothers had assured her that all she need do was obey their orders. She admired her brothers; they were clever, which Jane had never been; they were men, whereas Jane was just a weak woman. She was afraid of the King; when he put his face near hers and she smelled the wine on his breath, when she looked at the great face with its purple veins, when the little bloodshot eyes twinkled at her, she did not have to feign a desire to run. Jane, without pity, thought of the Queen who would have to be displaced if she were to sit on the throne; it was not that Jane was cruel or hard-hearted, but merely that she was without imagination. Children could move her a little; they were small and helpless like Jane herself, and she understood their doubts, their fear of their elders, their gropings for enlightenment. She had wept a little for the Princess Mary, for surely that child had suffered a very hard fate; if Jane were ever queen, she would do her best to see that even little Elizabeth was treated fairly, for bastard though she was, she was at least a child, and a little child at that.

Jane's thoughts went back to that important day when the King's messenger had come to her with a letter and purse of gold from the King. Her brothers had been expecting some such approach from the King, and had primed her as to what she must do. Jane was ever obedient; her nature demanded that she should be; so she obeyed her brothers. She kissed the letter to show how greatly she esteemed the King's person, how if he were but free to pay honourable courtship to her, she would so willingly have linked her fortune with his. The purse she refused.

"Kneel to His Grace the King," said Jane, "beseeching him to consider that I am a gentlewoman of good and honourable family. I have no greater wealth than mine honour, and for a thousand deaths I would not sully it. If my lord the King desires to make me a present of money, I pray it shall be when God sends me a good offer of marriage."

The King had evidently not been displeased with this response. Jane had made it tremblingly, doubting whether her brothers had not gone too far and might have displeased His Majesty. But no! Her brothers had been right; the King was enchanted by such modesty and virtue. He would have the world know that the virtue of the ladies of his court was their most admired possession in the eyes of their King. The Seymours were honoured; they should have apartments in the palace near the King, for with Jane's family and friends he was more at ease than with Anne and hers. He was never sure of Anne's friends; they were too clever, too subtle. In future, give him good practical jokes; give him hearty humour that all could understand; he had done with mockery and smartness, and people who wrote and talked in a manner that he was not at all sure did not put him in the shade. No, he liked the company of the Seymours; they soothed him, and it was pleasant to contemplate a good and virtuous woman who appealed to him without arousing too insistent a passion.

He knew what the Seymours were after. Well, well, Anne could not have boys. A daughter from Katharine, a daughter from Anne! He wondered what he would get from Jane. With Anne he had scarcely thought of children at first, so greatly had he desired her, but he would not marry Jane on the chance that she might have a child; he would have to make sure that she was capable of doing so, before he committed himself again. This was a delicate situation for the Seymours, which while it was full of the most dazzling possibilities, was rampant with danger. Jane's strength had been in her aloofness, and how could she remain aloof and at the same time prove to the King that she was capable of bearing his child? The Seymours had to act with extreme tact; they had to take a risk, and they took it boldly. Hence the apartments close to those of His Majesty; hence the secret visits of the King, when he found Edward Seymour and his wife discreetly absent, and Jane alone and not so demure, waiting to receive him.

His courtship of her was a sober matter when he compared it with his courtship of Anne Boleyn. There was something restful about Jane; he never forgot for a moment when he was with her that he was the King, and never did he lose sight of the real meaning of this lovemaking. If Jane was unlike Anne, she was also unlike the King; he looked at their reflections, side by side in the mirror; himself large and red, she small and white; he completely master of the situation, she shrinking, a little afraid. She did not shrink from his coarseness as Anne had often done; cleverly she feigned such innocence as not to understand it; if she made a false move, if she said anything to arouse his anger, she would be meekly apologetic. With Jane Seymour he was enjoying a period of domestic peace which he had not enjoyed since he had banished Katharine and taken Anne to live beside him. In the turbulent years he had longed for that peace which would be brought about by what he thought of as Anne's sweet reasonableness; it had been a goal to which he, in his sentimental hours, had reached out with yearning hands, and never did he succeed in attaining it. Now here was Jane, offering it to him; he could lie back, close his eyes, enjoy it, say what he liked, and be sure of approbation.

The girl was a bit insipid though; he realized that, after the first few nights with her. She was too passive; neither eager nor repulsing him; just meek and submissive. All that a queen should be to a king of course, but . . . Ah! he thought, I think of Anne. I gave too much of myself to that witch, for witch she is, with the devil's own power over me, so that even when I lie with another I cannot forget her. There will be no peace for me, while Anne lives, for the power of a witch is far-reaching, and she can cast spells even when her victim is in a good woman's arms.

Jane was not a little troubled by this most secret love affair between herself and the King; she was terrified of the Queen, whose rages could be awful; she had been maid of honour long enough to witness many a scene between their Majesties, and at these scenes the Queen had been known to outwit the King. The Queen was more physically attractive than any woman at court; it was impossible to be near her and not see the effect she could have on those about her. There were men who, conceiving passions for her ladies, would visit them, and on the coming of the Queen would be unable to take their eyes from her; she had but to throw a stray word in their direction, or a quick smile, and they were ready to do anything for her. She had that power. There might be those who said the King was tired of her; and so he was . . . at times. There might be those who would say that her only hope of holding the King was to give him a son; that was true in part, but not wholly. Jane had seen the many and conflicting moods that had come to the King as he watched this woman; anger and hatred had been there, strong enough to let in murder; but something else too, passionate hunger which Jane could not understand but vaguely feared. "What if through Your Majesty's visits I should be with child?" she had asked. He had patted her thigh indulgently. "Then, my Jane, you would please me mightily; you would show yourself worthy to be my queen." "But how may I be your queen when you have already a queen?" His eyes glinted like tiny diamonds. "Let not thy head bother with matters too big for it, Jane!" A warning, that had been; do not meddle in state affairs, child. It is a dangerous thing for a woman to do.

All the same, Jane was uneasy. She would tell herself that the King was bewitched, the Queen had sorcery in her eyes; it was not necessary to be clever to see that. Those huge, black, flashing eyes had more witchery than was natural for a woman to have; and the Queen was careless of what she said, as though she had some hidden power to protect her; she could draw men to her with a speed and an ease that had magic in their roots. She would weave spells round the King who, having realized her wickedness and his folly in submitting to it, would now escape. She had brought evil into the court when she entered it. She had brought misery and great humiliation to the true Queen and her daughter, Mary. Jane could weep to think of the child. And now her spells were less potent, for though she could weave them about men, she could bring no son to the King, since children were of heaven and Anne's powers came from hell. This was how Jane saw it. When the King caressed her, she would close her eyes tightly and say to herself: "I must endure this, for in this way can I save our lord the King from a witch." She prayed that her body might be fruitful, for she saw that thus could she fulfill her mission.

She thought continually of the Princess Mary. She had known her when she had been a maid to Katharine, before the coming of Anne Boleyn; she had ever deplored the King's infatuation for Anne; she had secretly adhered to Katharine all through the dangerous years, and so had she won the approval of Chapuys and many of the nobles who condemned the break with Rome. Thus they had been pleased when the King's fancy had lighted on her, and had sought to help and advise her.

She said to the King when he came to her: "I have been thinking of the Princess Mary."

"What of her?" he asked indifferently.

"I but thought of the hardship of her life, and how sad it is that she should be banished from the court. I wondered if Your Majesty would most graciously allow her to be brought back; I fear she suffers deeply from the humiliation which has been heaped upon her."

The King looked at Jane with narrowed eyes. He said with exasperation: "You are a fool! You ought to solicit the advancement of the children we shall have between us, and not others."

When he left her Jane assured herself that her duty was to rescue the Supreme Head of the English Church from a wanton witch who would never release him in this life. And as Jane did not know how she could rescue him, except by bearing him a child, she knelt down by her bed and prayed that her union with the King might bring forth fruit.

The Queen was gay, recklessly so. Her eyes were enormous in her pale face; she was almost coquettish; she was lavish with the smiles she bestowed on those about her. The King was spending more and more time with the Seymours, and there was no doubt in Anne's mind that Jane was his mistress; moreover she knew this to be no light affair; there was deep meaning behind it. Those two brothers of Jane's were eager and apprehensive; they watched, they waited; indeed all the court was watching and waiting for something to happen. The loss of her boy, they whispered, had finished Anne. Cynical courtiers murmured together: "Is he trying out Jane? If the King is waiting to produce a child before divorcing Anne, he may wait a very long time!"

It would have been a humiliating position for anyone; for Anne it was agonizing. She thought, This happened to Katharine while we tried for the divorce; it happened to Wolsey when he awaited his downfall; this is how More and Fisher must have waited in their homes . . . waited for a doom they felt coming to them, but knew not from which direction it would come. She was not the sort to show her fear; if during the lonely nights she would awake startled, the sweat on her forehead, having dreamed some nightmare in which the doom was upon her; if she lay awake for hours staring into darkness, thinking of the King with Jane Seymour, wondering if he ever thought of her, she never showed this. After such nightmares, such nocturnal wondering, she would be gayer than ever. Her clothes were still the talk of the court; she would throw herself feverishly into the planning of a new gown; she could no longer sit silently stitching for the poor, though she did not forget them. She would gather round her the most brilliant of the young men and women. Just as there had been Katharine's sober friends in the old days who had held aloof from that set over which she and the King ruled together, so now there was yet another set, and this time it was the Seymour party, but the King was of the Seymour party. Round Anne fluttered the poets and the wits, not seeming to care that they scorched their wings. Her revels were still the wittiest; the Seymours' were heavy and clumsy in comparison, but the King could not be lured from them. Handsome Henry Norris, who was supposed to be in love with Madge Shelton, had eyes for none but the Queen; people smiled at this man who was supposed to be engaging himself to Madge but was forever postponing his marriage. "What good does that do poor Norris?" they asked. "Surely he cannot hope to marry the Queen!" Francis Weston and William Brereton, younger and more sophisticated, were equally enamoured of her; Wyatt was faithful as ever. She encouraged their attentions, finding great solace in the love of these men, wounded when she discovered that the King preferred dull Jane Seymour. She was reckless; she accepted the homage of those who loved her; she would dance and laugh immoderately; she was wittier than ever, and the wildness of her looks gave her beauty a new strangeness that for some augmented it. It would seem that she wished to lure all to her side, that only when she was surrounded by those who admired her did she feel safe. She sought to build up a wall of friendship round her. She had with her, in addition to Madge Shelton, those two friends, Margaret Lee and her sister, Mary Wyatt, in whom she placed the greatest trust. Her own sister Mary came to attend her, and it was good to contemplate the serene happiness of Mary who, happy in her love for Stafford whom she had married, was as comfortable to be near as a glowing fire in winter. Anne felt secure with these people. Even Mark Smeaton, whom she had raised to be one of her chief musicians, might show his passionate admiration of her, and go unreproved.

There were always those to watch her slyly. The black eyes of the Spanish ambassador would meet those of the King's vicar-general, and the Spaniard would guess what thoughts went round and round in Cromwell's ugly shaven head. Jane Rochford was now openly unsympathetic towards Anne, not caring if she did invite her husband's disapproval.

As for George, he seemed to have caught his sister's recklessness; he rarely warned Anne now; he was like a man who had been running from danger and, feeling suddenly there is no escape, turns to face it.

It was pleasant to sit with George and Mary, Margaret Lee, Mary and Thomas Wyatt, talking of childhood days before they had been scattered and lost touch with each other.

"Well I remember," said Anne on one occasion, "how we all played together in Norfolk, and then again in Kent, how we all talked of our ambitions and what we would do."

"Ambition," laughed George, "is like the moon; it looks so close, so easy to grasp, but the nearer knowledge takes you to it, the more unattainable you realize it to be. Ambition is a pernicious thing!"

"You said you would be a great poet," said Anne. "Wyatt too."

"And he at least achieved his ambition," said George.

"Much good did it do him!" said Wyatt, looking meaningly at Anne.

"We hoped for too much," she said, "all of us except Margaret and my sister, Mary, and your sister, Mary. They are the happiest ones."

They could look at those three. Margaret who was happily married to Sir Henry Lee, Mary Wyatt who had no husband but a serene countenance, Mary Boleyn who had many lovers, not for gain but for pleasure. The ambition of these three was happiness; they had found it. For the other three it had been power, and in a measure they had realized it too. There they were—Wyatt whose joy was in his verses and yet, being never satisfied with them, they could not give him complete happiness; Anne who would be a queen and had achieved her ambition and now listened for some sign to herald in disaster, as she scanned people's faces and tried to read behind their eyes; George who through the fortunes of his sisters had come to fame. Three of those children who had played together—the ordinary ones who were not clever or brilliant, or made for greatness—had succeeded; it was the clever ones who had asked for much—though in a measure they had found what they desired—to whom failure had come.

Anne said: "We chose the wrong things; they chose the right. . . ." And none answered her, for this was a matter which it was unwise to discuss.

Mary would talk to her comfortingly.

"The King . . . ah! How well I knew him! Almost as well as you do, Anne." Mary would smile at the memory. "He is wayward; none dare stand between him and his desires, but an a woman pleases she need fear naught."

Ah, but Mary had known him as a mistress; Anne knew him as a wife.

The winter of that year passed into spring. Anne danced and sang as though she had not a care in the world; she would wander through the park at Greenwich, would watch the barges on the river, would sit under the trees; sometimes she would romp with the dogs, laughing gaily at their antics, throwing herself about in a frenzy of enjoyment, but her heart was sad and heavy; she would weep sometimes and mingle her tears with her laughter; this was a dangerous mood, for in it she cared nothing for what she said or what she did, and so laid herself open to attack from all her enemies. She would call Smeaton to her and bid him play, play something gay, something to which she could dance, something to make her gay and joyous; play music that told of love and laughter, not of sorrow. And the musician's great dark eyes watched her passionately, and his long tapering fingers played for her, soothing her.

She gave him a fine ring, for his talent, she said, was great, and those with talent should not go unrewarded. She thought, He may sell it and buy himself clothes, poor man; he has little reward for his labours. But she knew he would never sell the ring, since she had worn it on her finger; and she laughed and was pleased that though the King appeared to be indifferent to her, a poor musician was deep in hopeless love for her.

"Come!" she would cry suddenly. "Let us have a masque. Let us do a witty play. Thomas, you and George shall put your heads together; I would be amused. Mark, you shall play for the dancing; you shall play for my singing. Let us dance and be merry . . . I am tired of melancholy."

Cromwell had retired from court life for several days, on the plea of sickness. Cromwell needed solitude; he had to work out his next moves in this game of politics most carefully. He was no inspired genius; everything that had come to him had been the result of unflagging labour, of cautiously putting one foot forward and waiting until it was securely in its rightful place before lifting the other. He was fully aware that now he faced one of the crises of his career. His master commanded, and he obeyed, though the command of course was not given in so many words. Henry was too conscience ridden to mention his more vile thoughts, so it was the duty of a good servant to discover his master's wishes though not a word be spoken between them. Murder is a dangerous business, and Cromwell must consider whilst carrying out the King's wishes, not what was good for the King and the country, but what was good for Cromwell. Cromwell had a very good head on a pair of sturdy shoulders, and he did not intend that those should part company. The farther one climbed, the more steep the road, the easier it was to slip; one false step now, and Cromwell would go slipping down to the dark valley where waited the block and the executioner's axe.

It had seemed to Emperor Charles that, on the death of

Katharine, new friendship with Henry might be sought, and for this reason Chapuys came to Greenwich for a special audience with the King. But how could Henry become the ally of Charles, when Henry had broken so definitely with Rome, and Charles supported Rome? Rome, it seemed, stood between the Emperor and Henry. Cranmer trembled; he got as near blazing forth his anger as Cranmer could get; he preached a reckless sermon. Cromwell did not feel so deeply. Cranmer made up his mind which course he would take, and was loyal to that course; Cromwell was ready to examine any course; he would use any members of any sect if necessary; he would support them one day, burn them at the stake the next. Cromwell could see that there was some advantage to accrue from a new bond of friendship with the Emperor; therefore he was ready to explore this course of action. Cromwell was at this time very busily engaged in ransacking the monasteries, but he could see that if the Emperor and Henry should cease to be enemies, this could easily be held up for a time. He was prepared for anything. Anne was furious; naturally she would be. A possible reconciliation with the Emperor was a direct insult to her; she had not been overcautious in her treatment of Cromwell, never liking nor trusting him. Until now Cromwell had been meek enough, but he did not believe that he need now treat the Queen with overmuch humility. The King had hinted that Jane Seymour was with child, and Cromwell must think of this matter very seriously. What if this were so? What if there was need for Henry to marry the girl quickly in order to legitimize a possible heir to

493

the throne? Cromwell would be expected to bring this about, and if Cromwell failed to do it in the time at his disposal, what then? It was not so long ago when the King had desired a divorce most urgently, and Cromwell's late master had blundered. Cromwell was ready to profit by the Cardinal's mistakes, for he was resolved that he should not be caught as Wolsey had been. Cromwell would be ready. It was easy to see—and this applied particularly if Jane Seymour was really pregnant—that he need fear nothing from the wrath of Queen Anne. This secret matter of the King's was conducted rather differently from that other secret matter. This was a series of hints and innuendoes: the lady was so demure, so shy, that the King must respect her reserve. She must not suffer—nor the King through her—the pain and scandal of divorce. How did one rid oneself of a wife one no longer wants, if not by divorce?

Cromwell knew a great deal about the peculiar burden of the King's—his conscience. Cromwell knew that it was capable of unexpected twists and turns; Cromwell knew that it must always be placated, and how comparatively easy it was to placate it; how one turned a subject to show the side which the conscience might like and approve; how one carefully covered that which was unpleasant. The conscience was obliging; it could be both blind and deaf when the need arose; therefore, he did not propose to lose much sleep over that accommodating creature.

Cromwell decided to favour alliance with Spain. The Emperor was a better ally than Francis; alliance with the

French had never brought gain to England. Henry had been very difficult at the meeting—which had seemed to Cromwell and to most of the counsellors deplorable. It showed cunning Cromwell one thing—the King was still under the influence of Anne. In spite of Jane Seymour, he would listen to Anne; in spite of her failure to give him an heir, he still hankered after her. It was an alarming state of affairs; Cromwell knew his master well enough to realize that if something was not soon done, he would have Henry throwing aside Jane Seymour, buying fresh holy relics, reconciling himself to his black-browed witch, in one more effort to get himself a son. Were the Queen secure again, what would happen to Thomas Cromwell? What had happened to Thomas Wolsey! It was not so long ago that one could forget.

There must be alliance with Spain, for it meant the downfall of Anne; how disconcerting therefore, when the King must abuse the Emperor before Chapuys himself, must recall all he had done to delay the divorce, must announce here and now that not for a hundred alliances would he give way to Rome! He had made himself head of the Church, and head of the Church he would stay. If there was any humility to be shown, then Emperor Charles must show it. He even went so far as to tell Chapuys that he believed Francis had first claim on Burgundy and Milan.

This seemed to Cromwell sheer folly. The King was not acting with that shrewdness a statesman must always display. Henry was smarting under insults which he had received from Clement and Paul and Charles. He was not thinking of the good of England; he could only think: "They want my friendship—these people who have been against me, who have worked against me, who have humiliated me for years!"

Anne had said: "Ah! So you would be friends with your enemies as soon as they whistle for you, would you! Have you forgotten the insults of Clement? And why did he insult us? Would Clement have dared, had he not been supported? And by whom was he supported? By whom but this Charles who now comes and asks for your friendship, and in a manner that is most haughty! Oh, make friends, accept your humble role, remember not the insults to your kingship, to your Queen!"

He had ever been afraid of her tongue; it could find his weakness. Well he knew that she feared alliance with Spain more than anything, for it would mean her personal defeat; they had humiliated him and her, and as he had made her Queen, insults to her were insults to him. They had doubly insulted him!

This he remembered as he paced the floor with Chapuys, as he talked to Cromwell and Audley—that chancellor who had followed More—both of whom were urging him to sink his grievances and snatch a good thing while he could. But no! It was the Emperor who must come humbly to him. The egoist was wounded; he needed the sweet balm of deference from one he feared to be more mighty than himself, to lay upon his wounds.

Cromwell, for the first time in a long obsequious association, lost his temper; his voice cracked as he would explain; Cromwell and the King shouted at each other.

"Danger, Cromwell! Danger!" said a small voice inside the man, and he had to excuse himself and move away that he might regain control of his temper. He was trembling from head to foot at his folly; he was sick with fear and anger. How simple to abandon his quarrel with Rome! What need to continue it now Katharine was dead. Only the gratification of Henry's personal feelings came into this. Anne and her supporters were at the bottom of it; they would keep alive the King's anger. Could it be that Anne's falling into disfavour really was but a temporary thing? Such thoughts were fraught with great terror for Thomas Cromwell. For the first time in his career with the King, he must act alone; thus he feigned sickness that he might shut himself away from the King, that he might make a plan, study its effect, its reverberations, from all sides before daring to put it into practice.

He emerged from his isolation one mild April day, and asked for permission to see the King.

The King scowled at him, never liking him, liking him less remembering the man's behaviour when he had last seen him. He, who had ever been meek and accommodating, daring to shout at him, to tell him he was wrong! Was this secretary—whom he had made his vicar-general—was humble Thomas Cromwell a spy of Chapuys!

"Sir," said Thomas Cromwell, "I am perplexed."

His Majesty grunted, still retaining his expression of distaste.

"I would have Your Majesty's permission to exceed the powers I now enjoy."

Henry regarded his servant with some shrewdness. Why not? he wondered. He knew his Cromwell—cunning as a fox, stealthy as a cat; since he had attained to great power, he had his spies everywhere; if one wanted to know anything, the simplest way was to ask Cromwell; with speed and efficiency he would bring the answer. He was the most feared man at court. A good servant, thought Henry, though a maddening one; and there'll come a day, was the royal mental comment, when he'll anger me so much by his uncouth manners and his sly, cunning ways, that I'll have his head off his shoulders . . . and doubtless be sorry afterwards, for though he creeps and crawls and is most wondrous sly, I declare he knows what he is about.

Cromwell should have his special powers. Cromwell bowed low and retired well pleased.

A few nights later, he asked Mark Smeaton to come up to dinner at his house at Stepney.

When Mark Smeaton received an invitation to dine at the house of the King's secretary, he was delighted. Here was great honour indeed. The Queen had shown him favour, and now here was Master Secretary Thomas Cromwell himself seeking his company!

It must be, thought Mark, my exceptional skill at music—

though he had not known that Master Cromwell was fond of music. He knew very little of Cromwell; he had seen him now and then at the court, his cold eyes darting everywhere, and he had shivered a little for he had heard it said that none was too insignificant to be of interest to that man. He would know a good deal of most people, and usually of matters they would prefer to keep secret; and every little piece of information he gathered, he would store, cherishing it until he might lay it beside another bit of information, and so make up a true picture of what was happening at court.

Mark had never been so happy as he had this last year or so. He had begun life most humbly in his father's cottage; he had watched his father at work on his bench, mending chairs and such things as people brought to him to be mended. He had heard music in his father's saw and plane; he had heard music in his mother's spinning wheel. Mark had been born with two great gifts—beauty and a love of music. He had a small pointed face with great luminous dark eyes, and hair that hung in curls about his face; his hands were delicate, his fingers tapering; his skin was white. He had danced gracefully from the time he was a small boy, though he had never been taught to dance. He was noticed, and taken to the house of a neighbouring knight where he had taught the knight's daughter to play various musical instruments; and when she had married, his benefactor had found him a place at court—a very humble place, it was true—so that Mark thought himself singularly blessed, which indeed he was, to have gained it. He had seen poor beggars wander past his father's door with never a bite to eat, and their feet sore and bleeding; no such fate for clever Mark! An opening at court; what next?

What next, indeed! He had never known how beautiful a thing life could be until one day when the Queen had passed so close to him that he had seen her long silken lashes lying against her smooth skin, and had heard her sing in the most exquisite voice he had ever heard, very softly to herself. Then she had caught sight of him, noticed his beauty of face, would have him play to her. He had wondered how he had been able to play, so deep had been his emotion.

Not only was she his idol, she was his benefactress. He was in his teens, at that age when it is possible to worship from afar some bright object, and to be completely happy in such worship, to be amply rewarded by a smile; and the Queen was generous with her smiles, especially to those who pleased her—and who could please her more readily than those who played excellently the music she loved!

Sometimes she would send for him and have him play to her when she was sad; he had seen her eyes fill with tears, had seen her hastily wipe them. Then he had yearned to throw himself at her feet, to say: "Let Your Majesty command me to die for you, and gladly will I do it!"

But that was foolish, for what good could his death do her? There were rumours in the court, and thinking he knew the cause of her unhappiness, he longed to comfort her. He could do so by his music, and he played to the Queen as he had never played before in his life. So pleased was she that she gave him a ring with a ruby in it, a most valuable ring which never, never would he remove from his finger.

That was some weeks ago, and it seemed to him as he considered this invitation to dine at Stepney, that events were moving so fast that he could not guess to what they pointed.

There were many about the Queen who loved her and made no great effort to hide their love; playing the virginals close by, he had heard their conversation with her. There was Sir Henry Norris whose eyes never left her, and whom she baited continually, pretending to scold him because he was a careless lover— since he was supposed to be in love with her cousin Madge Shelton, yet was ever at the Queen's side. There were Brereton and Weston too, whom she scolded happily enough as though the scolding was not meant to be taken seriously. There was Wyatt with whom she exchanged quips; they laughed together, those two, and yet there was such sadness in their eyes when they looked on each other, that Mark could not but be aware of it. As for Mark himself, he was but humbly born, unfit to be the companion of such noble lords and their queen, but he could not help his emotions nor could he hide them completely, and those lovely black eyes must see his feelings and regard him with more indulgence because of them.

Two days before Mark had received the invitation, Brereton did not come to the presence chamber. He heard the nobles' speculating on what had happened to him. He had been seen in his barge—going whither? None could be sure.

"On some gay adventure, I'll warrant." said the Queen. "We shall have to exact a confession from gay William, when he again presents himself!" And she was piqued, or feigned to be so; Mark was not sure; he could never be sure of the Queen; when she laughed most gaily, he sensed she was most near tears.

She found him sitting in the window seat, his lute idle in his hands.

She said softly: "Mark, you look sad! Tell me why."

He could not tell her that he had been thinking he was but a foolish boy, a boy whose father was a carpenter, a boy who had come far because of his skill in music, and he at the height of his triumph must be melancholy because he loved a queen.

He said that it was of no importance that he was sad, for how could the sadness of her humblest musician affect so great a lady!

She said then that she thought he might be sad because she may have spoken to him as an inferior person, and he would wish her to speak to him as though he were a nobleman.

He bowed low and, overcome with embarrassment, murmured: "No, no, Madam. A look sufficeth me."

That was disturbing, because she was perhaps telling him that she knew of his ridiculous passion. She was clever; she was endowed with wit and subtlety; how was it possible to keep such a mighty secret from her!

The next day he took a barge to Stepney. Cromwell's house stood back from the river, which lapped its garden. Smeaton scrambled out and ascended the privy steps to the garden. A few years ago he would have been overawed by the splendour of the house he saw before him, but now he was accustomed to Greenwich and Windsor and Hampton Court; he noted it was just a comfortable riverside house.

He went through the gates and across the courtyard. He knocked, and a servant opened the door. Would he enter? He was expected. He was led through the great hall to a small chamber and asked to sit. He did so, taking a chair near the window, through which he gazed at the sunshine sparkling on the river, thinking what a pleasant spot this was.

The door must have been opened some time before he realized it, so silently was it done. In the doorway stood Thomas Cromwell. His face was very pale; his eyes were brilliant, as though they burned with some excitement. Surely he could not be excited by the visit of a humble court musician! But he was. This was decidedly flattering. In the court there were many who feared this man; when he entered a room, Mark had noticed, words died on people's lips; they would lightly change a dangerous subject. Why had the great Thomas Cromwell sent for Mark Smeaton?

Mark was aware of a hushed silence throughout the house. For the first time since he had received the invitation, he began to wonder if it was not as a friend that Cromwell had asked him. He felt the palms of his hands were wet with sweat; he was trembling so much that he was sure that if he were asked to play some musical instrument he would be unable to do so.

Cromwell advanced into the room. He said: "It was good of you to come so promptly and so punctually."

"I would have you know, my lord," said Mark humbly, "that I am by no means insensible of the honour . . ."

Cromwell waved his thick and heavy hands, as though to say "Enough of that!" He was a crude man; he had never cultivated court graces, nor did he care that some might criticize his manners. The Queen might dislike him, turning her face from him fastidiously; he cared not a jot. The King might shout at him, call him rogue and knave to his face; still Thomas Cromwell cared not. Words would never hurt him. All he cared was that he might keep his head safely in the place where it was most natural for it to be.

He walked silently and he gave the impression of creeping, for he was a heavy man. Once again Mark was aware of the silence all about him, and he felt a mad desire to leap through the window, run across the gardens to the privy stairs and take a barge down the river . . . no, not back to court where he could never be safe from this man's cold gaze, but back to his father's cottage, where he might listen to the gentle sawing of wood and his mother's spinning wheel.

He would have risen, but Cromwell motioned him to be seated, and came and stood beside him.

"You have pleasant-looking hands, Master Smeaton. Would they not be called musician's hands?" Cromwell's own hands were clammy as fish skin; he lifted one of Mark's and affected to study it closely. "And what a pleasant ring! A most valuable ring; a ruby, is it not? You are a very fortunate young man to come by such a ring."

Smeaton looked at the ring on his finger, and felt that his face had flushed to the stone's colour; there was something so piercing in the cold eyes; he liked not to see them so close. The big, clumsy fingers touched the stone.

"A gift, was it, Master Smeaton?"

Mark nodded.

"I should be pleased to hear from whom."

Mark tried to conceal the truth. He could not bear those cold hands to touch the ring; he could not bear to say to this crude man, "It was a gift from the Queen." He was silent therefore, and Cromwell's fingers pressed into his wrist.

"You do not answer. Tell me, who gave you that most valuable ring?"

"It was . . . from one of my patrons . . . one who liked my playing."

"Might I ask if it was a man . . . or a lady?"

Mark slipped his hands beneath the table.

"A man," he lied.

His arms were gripped so tightly that he let out a shriek for Cromwell's hands were strong, and Mark was fragile as a girl.

"You lie!" said Cromwell, and his voice was quiet and soft as silk.

"I . . . no, I swear . . . I . . ."

"Will you tell me who gave you the ring?"

Mark stood up. "Sir, I came here on an invitation to dine with you. I had no idea that it was to answer your questions."

"You came here to dine," said Cromwell expressionlessly. "Well, when you dine, boy, will depend on how readily you answer my questions."

"I know not by what authority . . ." stammered the poor boy, almost in tears.

"On the authority of the King, you fool! Now will you answer my questions?"

Sweat trickled down Smeaton's nose. He had never before come face to face with violence. When the beggars had passed his father's door, when he had seen men in the pillory or hanging from a gibbet, he had looked the other way. He could not bear to look on any distressing sight. He was an artist; when he saw misery, he turned from it and tried to conjure up music in his head that he might disperse his unhappy thoughts. And now, looking at Cromwell, he realized that he was face to face with something from which it was not possible to turn.

"Who gave you the ring?" said Cromwell.

"I . . . I told you . . ." Smeaton covered his face with his hands, for tears were starting to his eyes, and he could not bear to look longer into the cold and brutal face confronting him.

"Have done!" said Cromwell. "Now . . . ready?"

Mark uncovered his eyes and saw that he was no longer alone with Cromwell. On either side of him stood two big men dressed as servants; in the hands of one was a stick and a rope.

Cromwell nodded to these men. One seized Smeaton in a grip that paralyzed him. The other placed the rope about his head, making a loop in the rope through which was placed the stick.

"Tighten the rope as I say," commanded Cromwell.

The boy's eyes were staring in terror; they pleaded with

Cromwell: Do not hurt me; I cannot bear it! I could not bear physical pain . . . I never could. . . .

The eyes of Cromwell surveyed his victim, amused, cynical. One of the thick fingers pulled at his doublet.

"Indeed it is a fine doublet . . . a very fine doublet for a humble musician to wear. Tell me, whence came this fine doublet?"

"I . . . I . . ."

"Tighten the rope," said Cromwell. It cut into the pale skin of Mark's forehead. He felt as though his head was about to burst.

"The doublet . . . whence did it come?"

"I . . . I do not understand. . . ."

"Tighter . . . tighter! I have not all the day to spend on such as he."

Something was trickling down his face, something warm and thick. He could see it on his nose, just below his eyes.

"Who gave you the doublet? Tighten the rope, you fools!"

Mark screamed. His head was throbbing; black spots, like notes of music, danced before his eyes.

"Please . . . stop! I . . . will tell you . . . about the doublet . . . Her majesty . . ."

"Her Majesty!" said Cromwell, smiling suddenly.

"Loosen the rope. Bring him a little water. Her Majesty?" he prompted.

"Her Majesty thought I was ill-clad, and since I was to be her musician, she gave money for the doublet. . . ."

"The Queen gave you money. . . ." One large cold finger pointed to the ruby. "And the ring . . . ?"

"I . . ."

"The rope, you fools! Tighten it! You were too soft before. . . ."

"No!" screamed Mark. "You said . . . water . . ."

"Then who gave you the ring?"

"The Queen . . ."

"Give him water. The Queen then gave you the ruby ring."

Mark drank; the room was swimming round and round; the ceiling dipped. He could see the river through the window—it looked faint and far away; he heard the sound of singing on a passing barge. Oh, were I but there! thought Mark.

"I would know why the Queen gave you the ruby."

That was easy. "She was pleased with my playing. . . . She is a most generous lady . . ."

"Over-generous with her favours, I'll warrant!"

He felt sick. This was no way to speak of the Queen. He wanted to stand up, push aside that bland, smiling face, run out into the fresh air, run to the Queen.

"You were most friendly with the Queen?"

"She was most gracious . . ."

"Come, no evasions! You know full well my meaning. The Queen gave you money, clothes, and a ruby ring. Well, why not? She is young, and so are you. You are a handsome boy."

"I understand not . . ."

"Subterfuge will not help you. You are here, on the King's command, to answer questions. You are the Queen's lover!"

The shock of those words set his head throbbing anew; he

could still feel the tight pressure of the rope about his head, although in actual fact it was quite loose now; the torture had stopped for a while. He felt very ill; the blood was still trickling down his face from the cut which the rope had made. Oh, why had he accepted an invitation to dine with Thomas Cromwell! Now he knew what people meant when they talked with fear of Cromwell. Now he knew why they would suddenly stop talking when Cromwell appeared.

Cromwell rapped on the table with his knuckles.

"Tighten the rope."

"No!" screamed Mark.

"Now. Speak the truth, or it will be worse for you. You are the Queen's lover. You have committed adultery with the Queen. Answer! Answer yes!"

"No!" sobbed Mark.

He could not bear this. He was screaming with the pain; it seemed to him that his blood was pounding against the top of his head, threatening to burst it. It gushed from his nose. He alternately moaned and screamed.

Cromwell said: "You must tell the truth. You must admit this crime you and she have committed."

"I have committed no crime! She . . . she . . . is a queen. . . . No, no! Please . . . please . . . I cannot bear it . . . I cannot . . ."

One of the men was putting vinegar beneath his nose, and he realized that he had enjoyed a second or two of blessed unconsciousness.

Cromwell gripped his chin and jerked his head up violently,

so that it seemed as if a hundred knives had been plunged into his head.

"This is nothing to what will follow, if you do not answer my questions. Admit that you have committed adultery with the Queen."

"'Twould be but an untruth . . ."

Cromwell banged on the table; the noise was like hammer blows on his aching head.

"You committed adultery with the Queen. . . . Tighten up. . . . Tighter, you fools! Tighter. . . ."

"No!" screamed Mark. And then the smell of vinegar, mingling with that of blood, told him he had lost consciousness again.

He sobbed: "I cannot . . . I cannot . . ."

"Listen," snarled Cromwell, "you committed adultery with the Queen. . . ." The great hand shot up and seized the stick from the hands of his servant. "There! There! You committed adultery with the Queen. You committed adultery with the Queen. . . . Admit it! Admit it!"

Mark screamed. "Anything . . . anything. . . . Please . . . I cannot . . . I cannot . . . endure . . . my head . . ."

"You admit it then?"

"I admit . . ."

"You committed adultery with the Queen. . . ."

He was crying, and his tears mingled with the blood and sweat . . . and that hateful smell of vinegar would not let him sink into peace. He had longed to die for her, and he could not bear a little pain for her. A little pain! Oh, but it was such exquisite torture;

his head was bursting, bleeding; he had never known there could be agony like this.

Cromwell said; "He admits adultery with the Queen. Take him away."

They had to carry him, for when he stood up he could see nothing but a blur of panelled walls, and light from the window, and a medley of cruel faces. He could not stand; so they carried him to a dark chamber in which they left him, locked in. And as he sank to the floor, he lost consciousness once more.

He lay there, half fainting, not aware of the room nor even what had gone before. He knew nothing except that there was a pain that maddened him, and that it was in his head. In his mouth he tasted blood; the smell of vinegar clung to his clothes, devilishly not allowing him to rest in that dark world for which he longed.

He was semi-conscious, thinking he was in his father's cottage, thinking he sat at the feet of the Queen, and that darkness for which he longed was her eyes, as black as night, as beautiful as forgetfulness.

But now someone was beating with a hammer on his head, and it was hurting him abominably. He awakened screaming, and knew suddenly that he was not in his father's cottage, nor at the feet of the Queen; he was in a dark room in Thomas Cromwell's house at Stepney, and he had been tortured . . . and what had he said? What had he said?

He had lied; he had lied about her for whom he would have died! Sobs shook his slender body. He would tell them . . . he would tell them he lied; he would explain. It hurt me so that

I knew not what I said. She is a great, good lady. How could I have said that of her! How could I so demean her . . . and myself! But I could not bear the pain in my head; it was maddening. I could not endure it, Your Most Gracious Majesty! For that reason I lied.

He must pray for strength. He must do anything, but he must explain that he had lied. He could not let them believe . . .

He lay groaning in the dark, misery of body forgotten because he mourned so sincerely what he had done. Even though I assure them it is not so, I said it . . . I failed her.

He was almost glad when they came to him. That cruel man was with them.

Mark stammered: "I lied. . . . It was not so. The pain was too much for me."

"Can you stand?" asked Cromwell in a voice that was almost solicitous.

He could stand. He felt better. There was a terrible throbbing in his head, but the frightening giddiness had passed. He felt strengthened. No matter what they did to him, he would tell no more lies. He was ready to go to the scaffold for the Queen.

"This way," said Cromwell.

The cool air fanned his burning face, setting his wounds to smart. He reeled, but there were those to support him. He was too dazed to wonder where he was going. They led him down the privy stairs to a barge.

He could feel the river breeze; he could smell the river, tar and sea salt mingling with blood and vinegar. He felt steady with purpose; he pictured himself going to the scaffold for her sake; but first though, he must make it clear that he had lied, that only such frightening, maddening torture could have made him lie about her.

The river was shot with darkness, for evening was advancing. The barge was being moored; he was prodded and told to get out. Above him loomed a dark, grey tower; he mounted the steps and went over the stone bridge. They were going to put him in the Tower! He was suddenly sick; the sight of the Tower had done that to him. What now? Why should they take him to the Tower? What had he done? He had accepted money, he had accepted a ring; they were gifts from a queen to one whose music had pleased her. He had committed no crime.

"This way," said Cromwell. A door was unlocked; they passed through it. They were in a dark passage whose walls were slimy; and there was a noisome smell coming up from below the dismal spiral staircase which they were descending.

A man with a lantern appeared. Their shadows were grotesque on the walls.

"Come along," said Cromwell, almost gently.

They were in one of the many passages which ran under the great fortress. The place was damp and slimy; little streams trickled across the earthen floor, and rats scuttled away at their approach.

"You are in the Tower of London, Smeaton."

"That I have realized. For what reason have I been brought here?"

"You will know soon enough. Methought I would like to show you the place."

"I would rather go back. I would have you know that when I said . . . when I said what I did . . . that I lied . . ."

Cromwell held up a thick finger.

"An interesting place, this Tower of London. I thought you would enjoy a tour of inspection before we continue with our cross-examination."

"I . . . I understand not . . ."

"Listen! Ah! We are nearer the torture chambers. How that poor wretch groans! Doubtless 'tis the rack that stretches his body. These rogues! They should answer questions, and all would be well with them."

Mark vomited suddenly. The smell of the place revolted him, his head was throbbing, he was in great pain, and he felt he could not breathe in this confined space.

"You will be better later," said Cromwell. "This place has a decided effect on those who visit it for the first time. . . . Here! Someone comes. . . ."

He drew Mark to one side of the loathsome passage. Uncanny screams, like those of a madman, grew louder, and peering in the dim light, Mark saw that they issued from the bloody head of what appeared to be a man who was coming towards them; he walked between two strong men in the uniform of warders of the Tower, who both supported and restrained him. Mark gasped with horror; he could not take his eyes from that gory thing which should have been a head; blood dripped from it, splashing Mark's clothes as the man reeled past, struggling in his agony to dash his head against the wall and so put an end to his misery.

Cromwell's voice was silky in his ear.

"They have cut off his ears. Poor fool! I trow he thought it smart to repeat what he'd heard against the King's Grace."

Mark could not move; it seemed to him that his legs were rooted to this noisome spot; he put out a hand and touched the slimy wall.

"Come on!" said Cromwell, and pushed him.

They went on; Mark was dazed with what he had seen. I am dreaming this, he thought. This cannot be; there could never be such things as this!

The passages led past cells, and Cromwell would have the man shine his lantern into these, that Mark might see for himself what befell those who saw fit to displease the King. Mark looked; he saw men more dead than alive, their filthy rags heaving with the movement of vermin, their bones protruding through their skin. These men groaned and blinked, shutting their eyes from that feeble light, and their clanking chains seemed to groan with them. He saw what had been men, and were now mere bones in chains. He saw death, and smelled it. He saw the men cramped in the Little Ease, so paralyzed by this form of confinement that when Cromwell called to one of them to come out, the man, though his face lit up with a sudden hope of freedom, could not move.

The lantern was shone into the gloomy pits where rats

swam and squeaked in a ferocious chorus as they fought one another over dying men. He saw men, bleeding and torn from the torture chambers; he heard their groans, saw their bleeding hands and feet, their mutilated fingers from which the nails had been pulled, their poor, shapeless, bleeding mouths from which their teeth had been brutally torn.

"These dungeons have grown lively during the reign of our most Christian king," said Cromwell. "There will always be fools who know not when they are fortunate. . . . Come, Master Smeaton, we are at our destination."

They were in a dimly lighted chamber which seemed to Mark's dazed eyes to be hung with grotesque shapes. He noticed first the table, for at this table sat a man, and set before him were writing materials. He smelled in this foul air the sudden odour of vinegar, and the immediate effect of this—so reminiscent of his pain—was to make him retch. In the centre of this chamber was a heavy stone pillar from which was projected a long iron bar, and slung around this was a rope at the end of which was a hook. Mark stared at this with wonder, until Cromwell directed his gaze to that ponderous instrument of torture nicknamed the Scavenger's Daughter; it was a simple construction, like a wide iron hoop, which by means of screws could be tightened about its victim's body.

"Our Scavenger's Daughter!" said Cromwell. "One would not care for that wench's embrace. Very different, Smeaton, from the arms of her who is thought by many to be the fairest lady of the court!"

Mark stared at his tormentor, as a rabbit stares at a stoat. He was as if petrified, and while he longed to scream, to run to dash himself against the walls in an effort to kill himself—as that other poor wretch had done—he could do nothing but stand and stare at those instruments of torture which Cromwell pointed out to him.

"The gauntlets, Smeaton! A man will hang from these. . . . Try them on? Very well. I was saying . . . they would be fixed on yonder hook which you see there, and a man would hang for days in such torture as you cannot . . . yet imagine. And all because he will not answer a few civil questions. The folly of men, Smeaton, is past all believing!"

Mark shuddered, and the sweat ran down his body.

"The thumbscrews, Smeaton. See, there is blood on them. The Spanish Collar . . . see these spikes! Not pleasant when pressed into the flesh. How would you like to be locked into such a collar and to stay there for days on end? But no, you would not be unwise, Smeaton. Methinks you are a cultured man; you are a musician; you have musician's hands. Would it not be a pity were those beautiful hands fixed in yon gauntlets! They say men have been known to lose the use of their hands after hanging from that beam."

Mark was trembling so that he could no longer stand.

"Sit here," said Cromwell, and sat with him. Regaining his composure to some small extent, Mark looked about him. They were sitting on a wooden frame shaped like a trough, large enough to contain a human body. At each end of this frame were fixed windlasses on which rope was coiled.

Smeaton screamed aloud. "The rack!" he cried.

"Clever of you, Smeaton, to have guessed aright. But fear not. You are a wise young man; you will answer the questions I ask, and you will have no need of the rack nor her grim sister, the Scavenger's Daughter."

Mark's mouth was dry, and his tongue was too big for it.

"I . . . I cannot . . . I lied . . ."

Cromwell lifted a hand. Two strong men appeared and, laying hands on the shivering boy, began stripping off his clothes.

Mark tried to picture the face of the Queen; he could see her clearly. He must keep that picture before him, no matter what they did to him. If he could but remember her face . . . if . . .

He was half fainting as they laid him in the frame and fastened the loops of the ropes to his wrists and ankles.

Cromwell's face was close to his.

"Smeaton, I would not have them do this to you. Dost know what happens to men who are racked? Some lose their reason. There are some who never walk again. This is pain such as you cannot dream of, Smeaton. Just answer my questions." He nodded to his attendants to be ready. "Smeaton, you have committed adultery with the Queen."

"No!"

"You have admitted it. You admitted it at Stepney; you cannot go back on that."

"I was tortured. . . . The pain . . . it was too much. . . ."

"So you admitted the truth. Did I not tell you that what you have known so far was naught? You are on the rack, Smeaton. One sign from me, and those men will begin to work it. Will you answer my questions?"

"I lied . . . I did not . . ."

He could see her face clearly, smiling at him; her eyes were great wells of blessed darkness; to lose oneself in that darkness would be to die, and death was the end of pain.

"Begin," said Cromwell. The windlasses turned outwards. . . . Smeaton felt his body was being torn apart; he screamed, and immediately lost consciousness.

Vinegar. That hateful smell that would not let a man rest.

"Come, Smeaton! You committed adultery with the Queen."

He could still see her face, but it was blurred now.

"You committed adultery with the Queen. . . ."

There was nothing but pain, pain that was a thousand red-hot needles pressing into the sockets of his arms and legs; he could feel his joints cracking; he felt they must be breaking. He began to groan.

"Yes, yes . . . yes . . . anything . . . but . . ."

"Enough!" said Cromwell, and the man at the table wrote.

Mark was sobbing. It seemed to him that they poured the accursed vinegar over his face. They sprinkled it on with the brush he had seen hanging on the wall, adding fresh smarts to his bleeding head; causing him to shrink, which in its turn made him scream afresh, for every movement was acute torture.

Cromwell's voice came from a long way off.

"There were others, beside yourself, Smeaton."

Others? He knew not what the man meant. He knew nothing but pain, pain, excruciating pain that shot all over his flesh; this was all the pain he had ever thought there could be; this was all the pain in the world. And more than pain of the body—pain of the mind. For he would have died for her, and he had betrayed her, he had lied; he had lied about her; he had said shameful things of her because . . . he . . . could not bear the pain.

"Their names?" said Cromwell.

"I know . . . no names."

Not vinegar again! I cannot bear it . . . I cannot bear pain and vinegar . . . not both! He broke into deep sobs.

"You shall rest if you but tell us their names."

How could he know of what the man was speaking? Names? What names? He thought he was a little boy at his mother's spinning wheel. "Little Mark! He is a pretty boy. Here is a sweet-meat, Mark. . . . And he sings prettily too. And he plays the virginals. . . . Mark, how would you like a place at court? The King loves music mightily. . . ."

"Begin again!" ordered Cromwell.

"No!" shrieked Mark.

"The names," murmured Cromwell.

"I . . . I . . . know . . . not . . ."

It was coming again, the agony. There was never agony such as this. Burning pincers . . . the wrenching apart of his muscles . . . the wicked rack was tearing off his limbs. Vinegar. Accursed vinegar.

"Mark Smeaton, you have committed adultery with the Queen. Not you alone! You were not to blame, Mark; the Queen tempted you, and who were you, a humble musician, to say nay to the Queen! But you were not alone in this, Mark; there were others. There were noble gentlemen, Mark. . . . Come now, you have had enough of this rack; men cannot be racked forever—you know that, Mark. It drives men mad. Just say their names, Mark. Come! Was it Wyatt?"

"There was none . . . I know not. I lied. Not I . . . I . . ."

No, not again. He was going mad. He could not endure more. Her face was becoming blurred. He must stop, stop. He was going mad. He would not say what they told him to. He must not say Wyatt's name . . .

They were putting vinegar under his nose. They were going to turn the rack again.

He saw the court, as clearly as though he were there. She was smiling, and someone was standing beside her.

"Norris!" he screamed. "Norris!"

Cromwell's voice was gentle, soothing.

"Norris, Mark. That is good. That is right. Who else, Mark? Just whisper . . ."

"Norris! Brereton! Weston!" screamed Mark.

He was unconscious as they unbound him and carried his tortured body away.

Cromwell watched them, smiling faintly. It had been a good day's work.

✦

The next day was the first of May. May Day was a favourite court festival which the King never failed to keep. At one time he had been the hero of the tiltyard, but now that his leg was troublesome, he must sit back and watch others take the glory of the day. The chief challenger on this day would be Lord Rochford, and the chief of the defenders, Henry Norris. It was not pleasant, when one had been more skillful than they, to realize age was creeping on, turning one into a spectator instead of a brilliant performer who had held the admiration of the entire court.

Cromwell came to see the King before he went to the tilt-yard. Henry frowned on the man, not wishing to see him now, but for once Cromwell would not be waved aside; he had news, disturbing news, news which should not be withheld from His Majesty one second longer than necessary. Cromwell talked; the King listened. He listened in silence, while his eyes seemed to sink into his head and his face grew as purple as his coat.

Down in the tiltyard they were awaiting the arrival of the King. The Queen was already in her place, but obviously the jousts could not start without the King. He went to the yard, and took his place beside her. The tilt began.

He was aware of her beside him; he was trembling with jealous rage. He was thinking. This is the woman to whom I have given everything; the best years of my life, my love, my throne. For her I broke with Rome; for her I risked the displeasure of my people. And how does she reward me? She betrays me with any man that takes her fancy!

He did not know who tilted below; he did not care. Red mist swam before his eyes. He glanced sideways at her; she was more beautiful than she had ever seemed, and more remote than she had been in her father's garden at Hever. She had tricked him; she had laughed at him; and he had loved her passionately and exclusively. He was a king, and he had loved her; she was a nobody, the daughter of a man who owed his advancement to the favour of his king . . . and she had flouted him. Never had she loved him; she had loved a throne and a crown, and she had reluctantly taken him because she could not have them without him. His throat was dry with the pain she had caused him; his heart beat wildly with anger. His eyes were murderous; he wanted her to suffer all the pain she had inflicted on him—not as he had suffered, but a thousand times more so. It galled him that even now she was not one half as jealous of Jane Seymour as he was of Norris down there in the yard.

He looked at Norris—one of his greatest and most intimate friends—handsome, not as young as those others, Weston, Brereton and Smeaton, but with a distinguished air, a charm of manner, a gracious, gentle, knightly air. He loathed Norris, of whom a short while ago he had been very fond. There was her brother, Rochford; he had liked that young man; he had been glad to raise him for his own sake as well as his sister's; gay, amusing, devilishly witty and attractive . . . and now Cromwell had discovered that Rochford had said unforgivable, disloyal, treasonable things of his royal master; he had laughed at the King's verses, laughed at the King's clothes; he had most shamefully—and for this he deserved to die—disparaged the King's manhood, had laughed at him and whispered that the reason why the King's wives could not have children successfully was that the King himself was at fault.

Smeaton . . . that low-born creature who had nothing to recommend him but his pretty face and his music had pleased her more than he himself had. He, King of England, had begged her, had implored her, had bribed her with offers of greatness, and reluctantly she had accepted—not for love of him, but because she could not refuse a glittering crown.

He was mad with rage, mad with jealousy; furious with her that she could still hurt him thus, and that he was so vulnerable even now when he planned to cast her off. He could leap on her now . . . and if he had a knife in his hand he would plunge it into her heart; nothing would satisfy him, nothing . . . nothing but that her blood should flow; he would stab her himself, rejoicing to see her die, rejoicing that no one else should enjoy her.

The May sunshine was hot on his face; the sweat glistening across his nose. He did not see the jousts; he could see nothing but her making such voluptuous love with others as she had never given him. He had been jealous of her before; he had been ready to torture those who had glanced at her, but that had been complacent jealousy; now he could be jealous by reason of his knowledge, he could even fill in the forms of her lovers—Norris! Weston! Brereton! Wyatt? And that Smeaton! How dare she, she whom he had made a queen! Even a humble boy could please her more than he could!

His attention was suddenly caught, for her handkerchief had fluttered from her hand; she was smiling, smiling at Norris; and Norris picked up the handkerchief, bowed, handed it to her on the point of his lance while they exchanged smiles that seemed like lovers' smiles to Henry's jealous eyes.

The joust continued. His tongue was thick, his throat was dry; he was filled with mad rage which he knew he could not continue to control. If he stayed here he would shout at her, he would take her by the beautiful hair which he had loved to twine about his fingers, and he would twist it about that small white neck, and tighten it and tighten it until there was no life left in the body he had loved too well.

She spoke to him. He did not hear what she said. He stood up; he was the King, and everything he did was of importance. How many of those people, who now turned startled eyes on him, had laughed at him for the complaisant husband he had appeared to be, had laughed at his blind devotion to this woman who had tricked him and deceived him with any man she fancied in his court!

It was the signal for the jousting to end. How could it go on, when the King no longer wished to see it? Anne was not so surprised that she would attach too much importance to the strange behaviour of the King; he had been curt with her often enough of late; she guessed he had left Greenwich for White Hall, as he often went to London to see Jane Seymour.

The King was on his way to White Hall. He had given orders that Rochford and Weston should be arrested as they were leaving the tiltyard. Norris he had commanded to ride back with him.

He could not take his eyes from that handsome profile; there was a certain nobility about Norris that angered the King; he was tall and straight, and his gentle character was apparent in the finely cut profile and the mobile mouth. He was a man to be jealous of. The King had heard that Norris was about to engage himself to Madge Shelton who at one time—and that not so long ago—had pleased the King himself. Henry had wished him well of Madge; she was a very attractive woman, lively and clever and good-looking. The King had tired of her quickly; the only woman he did not tire of quickly was Anne Boleyn. And she . . . The anger came surging up again. The wanton! The slut! To think that he, who had always admired virtue in women, should have been cursed with a wife who was known throughout his court for her wanton ways! It was too much. She had known that he admired virtue in those about him; and she had laughed at him, jeered at him . . . with her brother and Weston and Brereton and Norris. . . .

He leaned forward in his saddle and said, his voice quivering with rage: "Norris, I know thee for what thou art, thou traitor!"

Norris almost fell from the saddle, so great was his surprise.

"Your Majesty . . . I know not . . ."

"You know not! I'll warrant you know well enough. Ha! You start, do you! Think you not that I am a fool, a man to stand aside and let his inferiors amuse themselves with his wife. I accuse you of adultery with the Queen!"

"Sir . . . this is a joke . . ."

"This is no joke, Norris, and well you know it!"

"Then it is the biggest mistake that has ever been made."

"You would dare to deny it?" foamed the King.

"I deny it utterly, Your Majesty."

"Your lies and evasions will carry little weight with me, Norris."

"I can only repeat, Sir, that I am guiltless of that of which you accuse me," said Norris with dignity.

All the rich blood had left the King's usually florid face, showing a network of veins against a skin grown pallid.

"'Twill be better if you do not lie to me, Norris. I am in no mood to brook such ways. You will confess to me here and now."

"There is naught I can confess, my lord. I am guiltless of this charge you bring against me."

"Come, come! You know, as all in the court know, how the Queen conducts herself."

"I assure Your Most Gracious Majesty that I know naught against the Queen."

"You have not heard rumours! Come, Norris, I warn you I am not in the mood for dalliance."

"I have heard no rumours, Sir."

"Norris, I offer you pardon, for you know that I have loved you well, if you will confess to your adultery."

"I would rather die a thousand deaths, my lord, than accuse the Queen of that which I believe her, in my conscience, innocent."

The King's fury almost choked him. He said no more until they reached Westminster. Then, calling to him the burly bully Fitzwilliam, whom Cromwell had chosen to be his lieutenant, he bade the man arrest Norris and dispatch him to the Tower.

✦

Anne, sitting down to supper in Greenwich Palace, felt the first breath of uneasiness.

She said to Madge Shelton: "Where is Mark? He does not seem to be in his accustomed place."

"I do not know what has happened to Mark, Your Majesty," answered Madge.

"If I remember aright, I did not notice him last night. I hope he is not sick."

"I do not know, Madam," said Madge, and Anne noticed that her cousin's eyes did not meet hers; it was as though the girl was afraid.

Later she said: "I do not see Norris. Madge, is it not strange that they should both absent themselves? Where is Norris, Madge? You should know."

"He has said nothing to me, Madam."

"What! He is indeed a neglectful lover; I should not allow it, Madge."

Her voice had an edge to it. She well knew, and Madge well knew that though Norris was supposed to be in love with Madge, it was the Queen who received his attention. Madge was charming; she could attract easily, but she could not hold men to her as her cousin did. Weston had been attracted to Madge once, until he had felt the deeper and irresistible attraction of the Queen.

"I know not what is holding him," said Madge.

Anne said: "You know not who is holding him, you mean!" And when she laughed, her laughter was more than usually high-pitched.

It was a strange evening; people whispered together in the corridors of the palace.

"What means this?"

"Did you see the way His Majesty left the tiltyard?"

"They say Norris, Weston and Brereton are missing."

"Where is Mark Smeaton? Surely they would not arrest little Mark!"

The Queen was aware of this strange stillness about her; she called for the musicians, and while they played to her, sat staring at Mark's empty place. Where was Norris? Where was Weston? Why did Brereton continue to absent himself?

She spent a sleepless night, and in the early morning fell into a heavy doze from which she awakened late. All during the morning the palace abounded in rumour. Anne heard the whispering voices, noted the compassionate glances directed at her, and was increasingly uneasy.

She sat down to dinner, determined to hide the terrible apprehension that was stealing over her. When she did not dine with the King, His Majesty would send his waiter to her with the courteous message: "Much good may it do you!" On this day she waited in vain for the King's messenger; and as soon as the meal was over and the surnap was removed, there came one to announce the arrival at Greenwich of certain members of the council, and with them, to her disgust, was her uncle the Duke of Norfolk.

Her uncle looked truculent and self-righteous, pleased with himself, as though that which he had prophesied had come to pass. He behaved, not as a courtier to a queen, but as a judge to a prisoner.

"What means this?" demanded Anne.

"Pray be seated," said Norfolk.

She hesitated, wanting to demand of him why he thought he might give her orders when to sit and when to stand; but something in his eyes restrained her. She sat down, her head held high, her eyes imperious.

"I would know why you think fit to come to me at this hour and disturb me with your presence. I would know . . ."

"You shall know," said Norfolk grimly. "Smeaton is in the Tower. He had confessed to having committed adultery with you."

She grew very pale, and stood up, her eyes flashing.

"How dare you come to me with such vile accusations!"

"Tut, tut, tut!" said Norfolk, and shook his head at her. "Norris is also in the Tower." He lied: "He also admits to adultery with you."

"I will not believe that he could be guilty of such falsehood! I will not believe it of either. Please leave me at once. I declare you shall suffer for your insolence."

"Forget not," said Norfolk, "that we come by the King's command to conduct you to the Tower, there to abide His Highness's pleasure."

"I must see the King," said Anne. "My enemies have done this. These stories you would tell me would be tragic, were they not ridiculous. . . ."

"It is not possible for you to see the King."

"It is not possible for me to see the King. You forget who I am, do you not? I declare you will wish . . ."

"You must await the King's pleasure, and he has said he does not wish to see you."

She was really frightened now. The King had sent these men to arrest her and take her to the Tower; he had said he did not wish to see her. Lies were being told about her. Norris? Smeaton? Oh, no! Not those two! They had been her friends, and she would have sworn to their loyalty. What did this mean. . . . George, where was George? She needed his advice now as never before.

"If it be His Majesty's pleasure," she said calmly, "I am ready to obey."

In the barge she felt very frightened. She was reminded of another journey to the Tower, of a white falcon which had been crowned by an angel, of the King, waiting to receive her there . . . eager that all the honour he could give her should be hers.

She turned to her uncle. "I am innocent of these foul charges. I swear it! I swear it! If you will but take me to the King, I know I can convince him of my innocence."

She knew she could, if she could but see him . . . if she could but take his hands. . . . She had ever been able to do with him what she would . . . but she had been careless of late. She had never loved him; she had not much cared that he had strayed; she had thought that she had but to flatter him and amuse him, and he would be hers. She had never thought that this could happen to her, that she would be removed from him, not allowed to see him, a prisoner in the Tower.

Norfolk folded his arms and looked at her coldly. One would have thought he was her bitterest enemy rather than her kinsman.

"Your paramours have confessed," he said, shrugging his shoulders. "'Twould be better if you did likewise."

"I have naught to confess. Have I not told you! What should I confess? I do not believe that these men have made confessions; you say so to trap me. You are my enemy; you always have been."

"Calm yourself!" said Norfolk. "Such outbursts can avail you nothing."

They made fast the barge; they led her up the steps; the great gate opened to admit her.

"Oh, Lord, help me," she murmured, "as I am guiltless of that whereof I am accused." Sir William Kingston came out to receive her, as he had on that other occasion. "Mr. Kingston," she asked, "do I go into a dungeon?"

"No, Madam," answered the constable, "to your own lodgings where you lay at your coronation."

She burst into passionate weeping, and then she began to laugh hysterically; and her sobs, mingling with her laughter, were pitiful to hear. She was thinking of then and now—and that in but three short years. A queen coming to her coronation; a queen coming to her doom.

"It is too good for me!" she cried, laughing as the sobs shook her. "Jesus have mercy on me!"

Kingston watched her until her hysteria passed. He was a hard man but he could not but be moved to pity. He had seen some terrible sights in these grey, grim buildings, but he thought that this girl, laughing and crying before him, presented one of the most pathetic he had ever witnessed. He had received her on her first coming to the Tower, thought her very beautiful in her coronation robes with her hair flowing about her; he could not but compare her then with this poor weeping girl, and so was moved in spite of himself.

She wiped her eyes, controlled her laughter, and her dignity returned to her. She listened to a clock strike five, and such a familiar, homely sound reminded her of ordinary matters. Her family—what of them?

She turned to the members of the council, who were about to leave her in Kingston's care.

"I entreat you to beseech the King in my behalf that he will be a good lord unto me," she said; and when they had taken their leave, Kingston conducted her to her apartments.

She said: "I am the King's true wedded wife." Anne added: "Mr. Kingston, do you know wherefore I am here?"

"Nay!" he answered.

"When saw you the King?"

"I saw him not since I saw him in the tiltyard," he said.

"Then Mr. Kingston, I pray you tell me where my lord father is."

"I saw him in the court before dinner," said Kingston.

She was silent awhile, but the question she had longed to ask, now refused to be kept back longer. "Oh, where is my sweet brother?"

He could not look at her; hard as he was he could not face the passionate entreaty in her eyes which pleaded with him to tell her that her brother was safe.

Kingston said evasively that he had last seen him at York Place.

She began to pace up and down, and as though talking to herself, she murmured: "I hear say that I shall be accused with three men, and I can say no more than 'Nay!'" She began to weep softly, as if all the wildness had been drained out of her, and there was only sadness left. "Oh, Norris, hast thou accused me? Thou art in the Tower, and thou and I shall die together; and Mark, thou art here too? Oh, my mother, thou wilt die for sorrow."

She sat brooding awhile, and then turning to him asked: "Mr. Kingston, shall I die without justice?"

He tried to comfort her. "The poorest subject the King hath, has that," he assured her.

She looked at him a moment before she fell into prolonged and bitter laughter.

534

Silence hung over the palace; in the courtyards men and women stood about whispering together, glancing furtively over their shoulders, fearful of what would happen next. Wyatt was in the Tower; who next? No man in the Queen's set felt safe. In the streets the people talked together; they knew that the Queen was a prisoner in the Tower; they knew she was to be tried on a charge of adultery. They remembered how the King had sought to rid himself of Katharine; did he seek to rid himself of Anne? Those who had shouted, "Down with Nan Bullen!" now murmured, "Poor lady! What will become of her?"

Jane Rochford, looking from her window, watched the courtiers and the ladies crossing the courtyard. She had expected trouble, but not such trouble. Anne in the Tower, where she herself had spent many an uneasy hour! George in the Tower! It was Jane's turn to laugh now, for might it not be that her whispered slander had put Cromwell on the scent? Had she not seen grave Norris and gay Weston cast their longing glances at the Queen? Yes, and she had not hesitated to laugh at these matters, to point them out to others. "Ah! The Queen was born gay, and my husband tells me that the King . . . no matter, but what is a woman to do when she cannot got children. . . ." Poor George was in the Tower now, though it was whispered that no harm could come to him. It was others, who had been her lovers, who would die.

Jane threw back her head, and for some moments she was weak with hysterical laughter. Poor little Jane! they had said. Silly little Jane! They had not bothered to explain their clever remarks to her; they had cut her out, considering her too stupid to understand. And yet she had had quite a big part to play in bringing about this event. Ah, Anne! she thought, when I was in the Tower you came thither in your cloth of silver and ermine, did you not! Anne the Queen, and Jane the fool whose folly had got her accused of treason. Now, who is the fool, eh, Anne? You, you and your lovers . . . dear sister! Not Jane, for Jane is free, free of you all . . . yes, even free of George, for now she does not cry and fret for him; she can laugh at him and say, "I hate you, George!"

And he will be freed, for what has he done to deserve death! And he was ever a favourite with the King. It is only her lovers who will die the deaths of traitors. . . . But he loved her as well as any.

Her eyes narrowed; her heart began to pound against her side, but her mind was very calm. She could see his face clearer in her mind's eye—calm and cynical, ever courageous. If he could stand before her, his eyes would despise her, would say, "Very well, Jane, do your worst! You were always a vindictive, cruel woman." Vindictive! He had used that word to describe her. "I think you are the most vindictive woman in the world!" He had laughed at her fondness for listening at doors.

Her cheeks flamed; she ran down the staircase and out into the warm May sunshine.

People looked at her in a shamefaced way, as they looked at those whose loved ones were in danger. They should know that George Boleyn meant nothing to her; she could almost scream at the thought of him. "Nothing! Nothing! He means nothing to me, for if I loved him once, he taught me to hate him!" She was a partisan of the true Queen Katharine. Princess Mary was the rightful heir to the throne, not the bastard Elizabeth!

She joined a little group by a fountain.

"Has aught else happened?"

"You have heard about Wyatt. . . ." said one.

"Poor Wyatt!" added another.

"Poor Wyatt!" Jane's eyes flashed in anger. "He was guilty if ever one was!"

The man who had spoken moved away; he had been a fool to say, "Poor Wyatt!" Such talk was folly.

"Ah! I fear they will all die," said Jane. "Oh, do not look to be sorry for me. She was my sister-in-law, but I always knew. My husband is in the Tower, and he will be released because . . . because . . ." And she burst into wild laughter.

"It is the strain," said one. "It is because George is in the Tower."

"It is funny," said Jane. "He will be released . . . and he . . . he is as guilty as any. . . ."

They stared at her. She saw a man on the edge of that group, whom she knew to be Thomas Cromwell's spy.

"What mean you?" he asked lightly, as though what she meant were of but little importance to him.

"He was her lover as well as any!" cried Jane. "He adored her. He could not keep his hands from her . . . he would kiss and fondle her. . . ."

"George . . . ?" said one, looking oddly at her. "But he is her brother. . . ."

Jane's eyes flashed. "What mattered that . . . to such . . .

monsters! He was her lover. Dost think I, his wife, did not know these things? Dost think I never saw? Dost think I could shut my eyes to such obvious evidence? He was forever with her, forever shut away with her. Often I have surprised them . . . together. I have seen their lovers' embrace. I have seen . . ."

Her voice was shrill as the jealousy of years conjured up pictures for her.

She closed her eyes, and went on shouting. "They were lovers I tell you, lovers! I, his wife, meant nothing to him; he loved his sister. They laughed together at the folly of those around them. I tell you I know. I have seen . . . I have seen . . ."

Someone said in a tone of disgust: "You had better go to your apartment, Lady Rochford. I fear recent happenings have been too much for you; you are overwrought."

She was trembling from head to foot. She opened her eyes and saw that Cromwell's spy had left the group.

The King could not stop thinking of Anne Boleyn. Cromwell had talked to him of her; Cromwell applied enthusiasm to this matter as to all others; he had closed his eyes, pressed his ugly lips together, had begged to be excused from telling the King of all the abominations and unmentionable things that his diligent probing had brought to light. The King dwelt on these matters which Cromwell had laid before him, because they were balm to his conscience. He hated Anne, for she had deceived him; if she had given him the happiest moments of his life, she had given him the most wretched also. He had, before Cromwell had forced the confession from Smeaton, thought of displacing Anne by Jane Seymour; and Jane was with child, so action must take place promptly. He knew what this meant; it could mean but one thing; he was embarking on no more divorces. There were two counts which he could bring forward to make his marriage with Anne null and void; the first was that pre-contract of hers with Northumberland; the second was his own affinity with Anne through his association with her sister Mary. Both of these were very delicate matters, since Northumberland had already sworn before the Archbishop of Canterbury that there had been no pre-contract, and this before he himself had married Anne; moreover he was in full knowledge of the matter. Could he now say that he believed her to have been pre-contracted to Northumberland when he had accepted her freedom and married her? Not very easily. And this affair with Mary; it would mean he must make public his association with Anne's sister; and there was of course the ugly fact that he had chosen to forget about this when he had married Anne. It seemed to him that two opportunities of divorcing Anne were rendered useless by these very awkward circumstances; how could a man, who was setting himself up as a champion of chastity, use either? On the other hand how—unless he could prove his marriage to Anne illegal—could he marry Jane in time to make her issue legitimate?

There was one other way, and that was the way he wanted.

He wanted it fiercely. While she lived he would continue to think of her enjoyed by and enjoying others; he could never bear that; she had meant too much to him, and still did. But their marriage had been a mistake; he had been completely happy with her before it, and he had never known a moment's true peace since; and it was all her fault. She could not get a male child, which meant that heaven disapproved of their marriage. He could see no other way out of this but that that charming head should be cut from those elegant shoulders. His eyes glistened at the thought. Love and hatred, he knew, were closely allied. None other shall have her! was his main thought. She shall enjoy no more lovers; she shall laugh at me no more with her paramours! She shall die . . . die . . . die, for she is a black-browed witch, born to destroy men; therefore shall she be destroyed. She was guilty of adultery, and, worse still, incest; he must not forget that.

Ah, it grieved him that one he had once loved dearly should be too unworthy to live; but so it was . . . so it was. It was his painful duty to see justice done.

He said to Cranmer: "This is painful to me, Cranmer. I would such work as this had not fallen to my bitter lot!"

Cranmer was grieved too; he was terrified that this might turn back the King towards Rome. And then what of those who had urged the break? Cranmer imagined he could smell the pungent smell of burning faggots and feel the hot flames creeping up his legs.

He said that he was hurt and grieved as was His Majesty,

for next to the King's Grace he was most bound unto her of all creatures living. He would ask the King's permission to pray for her; he had loved her for the love he had supposed her to bear to God and the gospel. He hastened to add that all who loved God must now hate her above all others, for there could never have been one who so slandered the gospel.

Poor chicken-hearted Cranmer went in fear and trembling for the next few weeks. He could wish his courage was as strong as his beliefs. What if he who had been helped by the Queen, whose duty really lay towards her now, were clapped into the Tower! Those who were high one day, were brought low the next. He thought of a girl he had loved and married in Nuremburg, whither he had gone to study Lutheran doctrines, and whom he had left in Nuremburg because he had been called home to become Archbishop of Canterbury. It had been heartbreaking to leave her behind; she was sweet and clinging; but Henry believed in the celibacy of priests, and what would he have said to a priest who had married a wife? He had left her for Henry; had left a bride for an archbishopric, had sacrificed love for a high place at court. What if he should fall from that high place to a dungeon in the Tower! From the Tower to the stake or the block was a short step indeed.

Henry found it comforting to talk with Cranmer; Cranmer was eager as he himself to do what was right.

"If she has done wrong," said Cranmer, "then Your Grace will punish her through God."

"Through God," said Henry. "Though I trust she may yet

prove her innocence. I would say to you, my lord, that I have no desire in the world to marry again unless constrained to do so by my subjects."

"Amen!" said Cranmer, and tried not to show by his expression that he must think of Jane Seymour and those reports he had heard that she was already with child.

Henry patted the Archbishop's shoulder, called him his good friend; and Cranmer begged that this sad matter should not cause the King to think less of the gospel.

"I but turn to it more, good Cranmer."

Cranmer left happier, and the King was relieved by his visit.

He called to his son, the young Duke of Richmond, and would have him stand before him that he might embrace him.

"For I feel tender towards you this night, my son."

He was thinking of Anne even as he spoke. How often had she discountenanced him! How often had she disturbed him! And she, laughing at him . . . in the arms of his courtiers . . . Norris . . . Weston. . . . Their faces leaped up in his mind, and were beside Anne's, laughing at him.

Fiercely he embraced his son; tears of self-pity came into his eyes and brimmed over onto the boy's head.

"Your Majesty is deeply disturbed," said the young Duke.

Henry's voice broke on a sob. He remembered a rumour that when he had thought of going to France and leaving Anne as Regent, she had talked wildly of getting rid of Mary; some had said she meant to poison her.

He held the boy against his chest.

"You and your sister Mary ought to thank God for escaping that cursed and venomous whore who tried to poison you both!" he declared.

Anne was desolate. The weary days were passing. There were with her two women, day and night, whom she hated and knew to be her enemies. These had been sent as her attendants by command of the King. They were a certain Mrs. Cosyns, a spy and a tale-bearer, and her aunt Lady Boleyn, who was the wife of her uncle Sir Edward. This aunt had always been jealous of her niece, right from the time when she was a precocious child considered in the family to be clever. These two, at Cromwell's instigation, wore her down with their questions as they tried to trap her into admissions; they were sly-faced, ugly women, envious, jealous women who enjoyed their position and were made most gleeful by the distress of the Queen. Every chance remark that fell from her lips was repeated with some distortion to make it incriminating. This was just what Cromwell wanted, and he was therefore pleased with these two women. Those ladies whom she would have liked to have beside her, were not allowed to come to her. She longed to talk with Margaret Lee and Mary Wyatt, with her own sister, Mary, with Madge; but no, she must be followed, no matter where she went, by these two odious females or by Lady Kingston who was as cold as her husband and had little sympathy, having seen too much suffering in her capacity of wife of the Constable of the Tower to have much to spare for one who, before this evil fate had befallen her, had enjoyed in plenty the good things of life.

But news filtered through to Anne. Her brother had been arrested. On what charge? Incest! Oh, but this was grotesque! How could they say such things! It was a joke; George would laugh; they could not hurt George. What had George done to deserve this? "For myself," she cried, "I have been foolish and careless and over-fond of flattery. I have been vain and stupid. . . . But oh, my sweet brother, what have you ever done but help me! I would die a thousand deaths rather than you should suffer so through me."

The sly women nodded, carefully going over what she had said. By eliminating a word here, a sentence there, they could give a very good account of themselves to Thomas Cromwell.

"Wyatt here!" she exclaimed. "Here in the Tower?" And she wept for Wyatt, calling him Dear Thomas, and was overwrought, recalling the happy days of childhood.

"Norris is here. Norris accused me. . . . Oh, I cannot believe it of Norris. . . . Oh, I cannot! He would never betray me."

She could not believe that Norris would betray her! Then, argued Cromwell, if she cannot believe he would betray her, is not that an admission that there is something to betray?

When she was tired, they would pretend to soothe her, laying wily traps.

"What of the unhappy gentlemen in the Tower?" she wanted to know. "Will any make their beds?"

"No, I'll warrant you; they'll have none to make their beds!" She showed great solicitude for the comfort of her paramours, they reported.

"Ballads will be made about me," she said, smiling suddenly. "None can do that better than Wyatt."

She spoke with great admiration and feeling of Thomas Wyatt, they then told Cromwell.

She wept bitterly for her baby. "What will become of her? Who will care for her now? I feel death close to me, because I know of her whom the King would set up in my place, but how can he set up a new queen when he has a queen already living? And what of my baby? She is not yet three. It is so very young, is it not? Could I not see her? Oh, plead for me please! Have you never thought how a mother might long for a last glimpse of her daughter! No, no. Bring her not to me. What would she think to see me thus! I should weep over her and frighten her, since the thought of her frightens me, for she is so very young to be left alone in a cruel world. . . . Say not that I wish to see my baby."

Her eyes were round with fear. They would be so clever at thinking up fresh mental torture for her to bear. Not that though! Not Elizabeth!

"She will be playing in her nursery now. What will become of her? After all, is she not the King's daughter?"

Then she began to laugh shrilly, and her laughter ended in violent weeping. For she thought, They will call her bastard now perhaps . . . and this is a judgment on me for my unkindness to Katharine's daughter, Mary. Oh, Katharine, forgive me. I knew not then what it meant to have a daughter. And what if the King . . .

But she could not think; she dared not. Oh, but she knew him, cold and relentless and calculating, and having need to rid himself of her. Already she was accused with five men, and one of them her own, and so innocently loved, brother. What if he said Elizabeth were not his child? What will he care for her, hating her mother? And if he married Jane Seymour . . . if she is queen, will she be kind to my baby daughter . . . as I was to Mary? Jesus, forgive me. I was wicked. I was wrong . . . and now this is my punishment. It will happen to me as it happened to Katharine, and there will be none to care for my daughter, as there was none to care for Mary.

Such thoughts must set her weeping; then remembering that when she had become Henry's queen she had chosen as her device, "Happiest of Women," she laughed bitterly and long.

"How she weeps! How she laughs!" whispered the women. "How unstable she is . . . hysterical and afraid! Does not her behaviour tend to show her guilt?"

She talked a good deal; she did not sleep; she lay staring into the darkness, thinking back over the past, trying to peer into the future. Despair enveloped her. The King is cruel and cold; he can always find a righteous answer when he wishes to do some particularly cruel deed. I am lost. There is naught can save me now! Hope came to her. But he loved me once; once there was nothing he would not do for me. Even to the last I could amuse him, and I tried hard enough. . . . I could delight him more than any an I gave myself up to it. He does this but to try me. He will come to me soon; all will be well.

But no! I am here in the Tower and they say evil things of me. My friends are here. George, my darling, my sweet brother, the only one I could truly trust in the whole world. And they know that! That is why they have sent you here, George; that is why they imprison you; so that I shall have none to help me now.

She asked for writing materials. She would write; she would try to forget his cruel eyes; she would try to forget him as he was now and remember him as he used to be when he had said the name of Anne Boleyn was the sweetest music to his ears.

The words flowed impulsively from her pen.

"Your Grace's displeasure and my imprisonment are things so strange unto me, that what to write or what to excuse, I am altogether ignorant. . . ."

She wrote hastily, hope coming back to her as her pen moved swiftly along.

"Never a prince had wife more loyal in all duty, and in all true affection, than you have ever found in Anne Boleyn—with which name and place I could willingly have contented myself if God and Your Grace's pleasure had so been pleased. Neither did I at any time so far forget myself in my exaltation, or received queenship, but that

I always looked for such alteration as I now found; for the ground of my preferment being on no surer foundation than Your Grace's fancy, the least alteration was fit and sufficient (I knew) to draw that fancy to some other subject."

She paused. Was she over-bold? She felt death close to her and cared not.

"You have chosen me from low estate to be your queen and companion, far beyond my desert or desire; if then you found me worthy of such honour, good Your Grace, let not any light fancy or bad counsel of my enemies withdraw your princely favour from me, neither let that stain—that unworthy stain—of a disloyal heart towards Your Good Grace, ever cast so foul a blot on me and on the infant Princess, your daughter Elizabeth.

"Try me, good King, but let me have a lawful trial and let not my sworn enemies sit as my accusers and as my judges; yea, let me receive an open trial, for my truth shall fear no open shames; then shall you see either my innocency cleared, your suspicions and conscience satisfied, the ignominy and slander of the world stopped, or my guilt openly declared. So that whatever God and you may determine of Your Grace may be freed from an open censure, and mine offence being so lawfully proved, Your Grace may be at liberty, both before God and man, not

only to execute worthy punishment on me, as an unfaith-
ful wife, but to follow your affection already settled on
that party, for whose sake I am now as I am; whose name
I could, some good while since, have pointed unto; Your
Grace being not ignorant of my suspicion therein."

Her cheeks burned with anger as her pen flew on.

"But if you have already determined of me, and that
not only my death, but an infamous slander, must bring
you the joying of your desired happiness, then, I desire
of God that he will pardon your great sin herein, and,
likewise, my enemies, the instruments thereof, and that
He will not call you to a strait account of your unprincely
and cruel usage of me, at his general judgment seat, where
both you and myself must shortly appear; and in whose
just judgment I doubt not (whatsoever the world may
think of me) mine innocency shall be openly known, and
sufficiently cleared."

She laid down her pen, a bitter smile about her lips. That
would touch him as she knew so well how to touch him, and
as she, among all those around him, alone had the courage to
touch him. She was reckless of herself, and though she may
have been foolish and vain she clung to her magnificent courage. If he ever read those words with their reference to the
judgment of God he would tremble in his shoes, and no matter

how he might present them to his conscience, they would disturb him to the end of his days. He would think of them when he lay with Jane Seymour; and she exulted in that power over him which she would wield from the grave. She was sure that he intended to murder her; in cold blood he planned this, as any commoner might plan to put away a wife of whom he had tired, by beating her to death or stabbing her with a knife or throwing her body into the dark river. She was terrified, experiencing all the alarm of a woman who knows herself to be followed in the dark by a footpad with murder in his heart. Such women, who were warned of an impending fate, might call for help; but there was none who could come to her aid, for her murderer would be the mightiest man in England whose anger none could curb, for whose crimes the archbishops themselves would find a righteous excuse.

She began to cry in very fear, and her thoughts went from her own troubles to those of the men who would be required to shed their blood with her, and she blamed herself, for was it not her love of flattery that had led them to express their feelings too openly? Was it not her desire to show the King that though he might prefer others, there were always men to prefer her, which had brought about this tragedy?

She took up her pen once more.

> *"My last and only request shall be, that myself may only bear the burden of Your Grace's displeasure, and that it may not touch the innocent souls of those poor gentle-*

men, who, as I understand, are likewise in strait imprisonment for my sake.

"If ever I have found favour in your sight—if ever the name of Anne Boleyn have been pleasing in your ears—then let me obtain this request; and so I will leave to trouble Your Grace any further: with mine earnest prayer to the Trinity to have Your Grace in his good keeping, and to direct you in all your actions.

"From my doleful prison in the Tower, the 6th of May. —Anne Boleyn."

She felt better after having written that letter; she would keep the writing materials with her that she might write now and then. She was wretched though, wondering how her letter would reach the King. She pictured its falling into Cromwell's hands, which was likely, for he had his spies all about her, and it could hardly be hoped that the letter would find its way through them to the King. If by good luck it did, he could not be unmoved by her words, she felt sure. He who had once upbraided her for not writing frequently enough, surely would read this last letter.

But she was afraid, sensing her doom, knowing her husband too well, knowing how he was placed, how he must find a way to marry Jane Seymour and appease his conscience; and thinking on these matters, hope, which had come to her through the writing of the letter, was swallowed up once more in deepest despondency.

Smeaton lay in his cell. He was no longer a beautiful boy; his dark curls were tangled and matted with blood and sweat; his delicate features were swollen with pain and grief. It seemed to him that there were but two emotions in the world—that of suffering pain and that of having no pain. One was agony; the other bliss.

He had scarcely been aware of the solemn atmosphere of the courtroom of the men who stood on trial with him; he had answered when he had been questioned, answered mechanically as they wanted him to answer, for he knew that not to do so would be to invite pain to come to him once more.

"Guilty!" he cried. "Guilty! Guilty!" And before his eyes he saw, not the judge and the jurymen, but the dark room with the smell of blood and death about it, mingling with the odour of vinegar; he saw the dim light, heard the sickening creak of rollers, felt again the excruciating pain of bones being torn from their sockets.

He could but walk slowly to the place assigned to him, every movement was agony; he would never stand up straight again; he would never walk with springy step; he would never let his fingers caress a musical instrument and draw magic from it.

A big, bearded man came to him as he lay in his cell and would have speech with him. He held a paper in his hand. He said Mark must sign the paper.

"Dost know the just reward of low-born traitors, Mark?" a voice whispered in his ear.

No! He did not know; he could not think; pain had robbed him of his power to use both his limbs and his mind.

Hung by the neck, but not to die. Disembowelled. Did Mark wish him to go on? Had not Mark seen how the monks of the Charterhouse had died? They had died traitors' deaths, and Mark was a traitor as they had been.

Pain! He screamed at the thought of it; it was as though every nerve in his body cried out in protest. A prolongation of that torture he had suffered in that gloomy dungeon? No, no! Not that!

He was sobbing, and the great Fitzwilliam, leaning over him, whispered: "'Tis not necessary, Mark. 'Tis not necessary at all. Just pen your name to this paper, and it shall not happen to you. You shall have naught to fear."

Paper? "Where is it?" asked Mark, not, "What is it?" He dared not ask that, though he seemed to see the Queen's beautiful black eyes reproaching him. He was not quite sure whether he was in the cell or in her presence chamber; he was trying to explain to her. Ah, Madam, you know not the pains of the torture chamber; it is more than human flesh can stand.

"Sign here, Mark. Come! Let me guide your hand."

"What then? What then?" he cried. "No more . . . no more. . . ."

"No more, Mark. All you need do is sign your name. Subscribe here, Mark, and you shall see what will come of it."

His hand guided by Fitzwilliam, he put his name to the statement prepared for him.

Sir Francis Weston, the beautiful and very rich young man, whose wife and mother offered the King a very large ransom for his freedom, could face death more stoically. So it was with Sir William Brereton. Handsome, debonair, full of the spirit of adventure they had come to court; they had seen others go to the block on the flimsiest of excuses. They lived in an age of terror and had been prepared for the death sentence from the moment they entered the Tower. Guiltless they were, but what of that? Their jury was picked; so were the judges; the result was a foregone conclusion and the trial a farce; and they were knowledgeable enough to know this. They remembered Buckingham who had gone to the block ostensibly on a charge of treason, but actually because of his relationship to the King; now they, in their turn, would go to the block on a charge of treason, when the real reason for their going was the King's desire to rid himself of his present Queen and take another before her child was born. It was brutal, but it was simple. Court law was jungle law, and the king of beasts was a roaring, man-eating lion who spared none—man nor woman—from his lustful egoistical demands.

They remembered that they were gentlemen; they prayed that no matter what befell them, they might go on remembering it. Mark Smeaton had perjured his soul and sullied his honour; they trusted that whatever torment they were called upon to face, they would not sink so low. They took their cue from their older companion, Norris, who, grave and stoical, faced his judges.

"Not guilty!" said Norris.

"Not guilty!" echoed Weston, and Brereton.

It mattered not; they were found guilty, and sentenced to death, all four of them—the block for three of them and the hangman's noose for Mark on account of his low birth.

The King was angry with these three men. How dared they stand up in the courtroom, looking such haughty heroes, and pronounce in ringing tones that they were not guilty! The people were sentimental, and he thanked God that Anne had ever been disliked and resented by them. They would not have a word to say in favour of her now; they would be glad to see the end of her, the witch, the would-be prisoner, the black-browed sorceress, the harlot. He thanked God there would be none ready to defend her. Her father? Oh, Thomas, Earl of Wiltshire, was not very much in evidence these days. He was sick and sorry, and ready to obey his king, fearful lest he should be brought in to face trial with his wicked daughter and son. Norfolk? There was none more pleased than Norfolk to see Anne brought low. They had been quarrelling for years. Suffolk, her old enemy, was rubbing his hands in glee. Northumberland? A pox on Northumberland! Sick and ailing! A fine champion, he! He should be appointed one of her judges and he should see what would happen to him were he to oppose his King. He had been in trouble over Anne Boleyn before; doubtless he would be so again. There was none to fear. My Lord Rochford, that foul, unnatural monster, was safe under lock and key, and what had he with which to defend himself and his sister but a tongue of venom! Anne should see what price she would pay for laughing at the King, first bewitching him and then deceiving him. No one else, girl, he said viciously, shall kiss your pretty lips, unless they like to kiss them cold; nor would they find the head of you so lovely without the body that goes with it!

But a pox on these men, and all would-be martyrs! There they stood, side by side, on trial for their lives, and though Cromwell could be trusted to find evidence against them, though they were traitors, lechers, all of them, people would murmur: "So young to die! So handsome! So noble! Could such bravery belong to guilty men? And even if they are guilty, who has not loved recklessly in his life? Why, the King himself . . ."

Enough! He called Cromwell to him.

"Go to Norris!" he commanded. "I liked that man. Why, he was an intimate friend of mine. Tell him I know the provocation of the Queen. Tell him I know how she could, an she wished it, be well-nigh irresistible. Go to him and tell him I will be merciful. Offer him his life in exchange for a full confession of his guilt."

Cromwell went, and returned.

"Ah, Your Most Clement Majesty, that there should be such ungrateful subjects in your realm!"

"What said he then?" asked Henry, and he was trembling for the answer. He wanted to show Norris's confession to his court; he would have it read to his people.

"His reply is the same as that he made Your Majesty before. He would rather die a thousand deaths than accuse the Queen who is innocent."

Henry lost control.

"Hang him up then!" he screamed. "Hang him up!"

He stamped out of the room and he seemed to see the body-less head of More and there was a mocking smile about the mouth.

"A thousand curses on all martyrs!" muttered Henry.

The room in which Anne and her brother would be tried had been hastily erected within the great hall of the Tower. Courageously she entered it, and faced that row of peers who had been selected by the King to try her, and she saw at once that he had succeeded in confronting her with her most bitter enemies. Chief among them was the Duke of Suffolk, his hateful red face aglow with pleasure; there was also the young Duke of Richmond who was firmly against her, because he had had hopes of the throne, illegitimate though he might be; he was influenced by his father, the King, and the Duke of Norfolk who had become his father-in-law when he had married the Lady Mary Howard, the Duke's daughter.

Anne had schooled herself for the ordeal; she was determined that she would not break down before her enemies; but she almost lost control to see Percy among those whom the King had named Lord-Triers. He looked at her across the room, and it seemed to them both that the years were swept away and they were young and in love and from the happiness of a little room in Hampton Court were taking a terrified peep into a grim future. Percy, weak with his physical defects, turned deathly pale at the sight of her; but she lifted her head higher and smiled jauntily, shaming him with her readiness to face whatever life brought her. Percy was not of her calibre. He crumpled and fell to the floor in a faint. How could he condemn her whom he had never been able to forget? And yet, how could he not condemn her, when it was the King's wish that she should be condemned? Percy could not face this, as years before he had not been able to face the wrath of Wolsey, his father and the King. He was genuinely ill at the prospect and had to be carried out of the courtroom.

Thank God, thought Anne, that her father was not among those who were to try her! She had feared he would be, for it would have been characteristic of Henry to have forced him to this and characteristic of her father that he would have obeyed his King and sent his daughter to her death. She had escaped the shame of seeing her father's shame.

She listened to the list of crimes for which she was being tried. She had, they were saying, wronged the King with four persons and also her brother. She was said to have conspired with them against the King's life. Cromwell's ingenuity had even supplied the dates on which the acts had taken place; she could smile bitterly at these, for the first offence—supposed to have been committed with Norris—was fixed for an occasion when she, having just given birth to Elizabeth, had not left the lying-in chamber.

As she faced her accusers she seemed to see the doubts that

beset them. There could not be any of these men who did not know that she was here because the King wished to replace her with Jane Seymour. Oh, justice! she thought. If I could but be sure of justice!

The decision of the peers was not required to be unanimous; a majority was all that was necessary to destroy her. But Suffolk's hot eyes were surveying those about him as though to tell them he watched for any who would disobey the King's desires.

Outside in the streets, where men and women stood about in groups, the atmosphere was stormy. If Anne could have seen these people her spirits would have been lightened. Many eyes wept for her, though once their owners had abused her. At the height of her power they had called her whore; now they could not believe that one who carried herself with such nobility and courage could be anything but innocent. Mothers remembered that she had a child scarcely three years old. A terrible, tragic fate overhung her, and she had it before her.

Suffolk knew what people were thinking; he knew what some of the Lord-Triers were thinking. This was a reign of terror. Bluff Hal had removed his mask and shown a monster who thought nothing of murder and of inhuman torture to herald it in. A man would be a fool to run his body into torment for the sake of Anne Boleyn. Suffolk won the day and they pronounced her guilty.

"Condemned to be burned or beheaded, at the King's pleasure!" said the Duke of Norfolk, savouring each word as though it held a flavour very sweet to his palate.

She did not change colour; she did not flinch. She could look into the cruel eyes of her enemies and she could say, her voice firm, her head high, her eyes imperious: "God hath taught me how to die, and he will strengthen my faith."

She smiled haughtily at the group of men. "I am willing to believe that you have sufficient reasons for what you have done, but then they must be other than those which have been produced in court."

Even Suffolk must squirm at those words; even Norfolk must turn his head away in shame.

But her voice broke suddenly when she mentioned her brother.

"As for my brother and those others who are unjustly accused, I would willingly suffer many deaths to deliver them."

The Lord Mayor was very shaken, knowing now for certain what he had before suspected, that they had found nothing against her, only that they had resolved to make an occasion to get rid of her.

Back in her room, Anne relived it over and over again; she thanked God for the strength which had been hers; she prayed that she might have sustained courage.

Lady Kingston unbent a little now that she had been condemned to die and Mary Wyatt was allowed to come to her.

"You cannot know what comfort it is to me to see you here, Mary," she said.

"You cannot know what comfort it gives me to come," answered Mary.

"Weep not, Mary. This was inevitable. Do you not see it now? From the first moments in the garden of Hever. . . . But my thoughts run on. You know not of that occasion; nor do I wish to recall it. Ah, Mary, had I been good and sweet and humble as you ever were, this would never have befallen me. I was ambitious, Mary. I wanted a crown upon my head. Yet, looking back, I know not where I could have turned to tread another road. You must not weep, dear Mary, for soon I shall be past all pain. I should not talk of myself. What of George, Mary? Oh, what news of my sweet brother?"

Mary did not answer, but the tears, which she could not restrain, were answer enough.

"He defended himself most nobly, that I do not need to be told," said Anne. Her eyes sparkled suddenly. "I wonder he did not confound them. Mary, dost remember old days at Blickling and Hever! When he had done aught that merited punishment, could he not always most convincingly defend himself? But this time . . . what had he done? He had loved his sister. May not a brother love his sister, but there must be those to say evil of him? Ah, George, this time when you were truly innocent, you could not save yourself. This was not Blickling, George! This was not Hever! This was the wicked court of Henry, my husband, who now seeks to murder me as he will murder you!"

"Be calm," said Mary. "Anne, Anne, you were so brave before those men. You must be brave now."

"I would rather be the victim of a murderer, Mary, than be a murderer. Tell me of George."

"He was right noble in his defence. Even Suffolk could scarce accuse him. There was much speculation in court. It was said: 'None could name this man guilty!'"

"And what said they of . . . me and George?"

"They said what you would have expected them to say! Jane was there . . . a witness against him."

"Jane!" Anne threw back her head and laughed. "I would not be in Jane's shoes for years of life. Liar and perjurer that she is. She . . . out of jealousy, to bear false witness against her husband! But what could she say of him and me? What could she say?"

"She said that on one occasion he did come to your chamber while you were abed. He came to make some request and he kissed you. There seemed little else. It was shameful. They had naught against him. They could not call him guilty, but he . . ."

"Tell me all, Mary. Hold nothing back from me. Know you not what this means to me to have you here with me at last, after my dreary captivity with them that hate me? Be frank with me, Mary. Hold nothing back, for frankness is for friends."

"They handed him a paper, Anne, for on it was a question they dared not ask and he . . ."

"Yes? What did he?"

"He, knowing how it would sorely discountenance them,

should he read aloud what was written, read it aloud, in his reckless and impulsive way."

"Ah! I know him well. For so would I have done in an unguarded moment. He had nothing but contempt for that group of selected peers—selected by the King whose one object is to destroy us—and he showed it by reading aloud that which was meant to be kept secret. It was of the King?"

Mary nodded. "That the King was not able to have children; that there was no virtue or potency in him. He was asked if he had ever said such things. And he read that aloud. No man could be allowed to live after that. But he meant to show his contempt for them all; he meant to show that he knew he had been condemned to die before the trial began. He asked then to plead guilty, solely that he might prevent his property passing into the hands of the King. The King could have his life but he should not have his goods."

"Oh, George!" cried Anne. "And you to scold me for reckless folly! Mary, I cannot but weep, not for myself but for my brother. I led the way; he followed. I should go to the block for my careless ambition, for my foolish vanity. But that I should take him with me! Oh, Mary, I cannot bear that, so I weep and am most miserable. Oh, Mary, sit by me. Talk to me of our childhood. Thomas! What of Thomas? I cannot bear to think on those I have loved and brought to disaster."

"Grieve not for Thomas. He would not have it so. He would not have you shed one tear for him, for well you know he ever loved you dearly. We hope for Thomas. He was not tried with the rest. Perhaps he will just be a prisoner awhile, for it is strange that he should not be tried with the others."

"Pray for him, Mary. Pray that this awful fate may not befall him. Mayhap they have forgotten Thomas. Oh, pray that they have forgotten Thomas."

When Mary left her she lay on her bed. She felt happier. Rather my lot, she thought, than the King's. Rather my lot, than Jane Rochford's. I would rather mine were the hapless head that rolled in the straw, than mine the murderous hand that signs the death warrant.

She was preparing herself for a journey. A summons had been brought to her that she was to make ready to go to the Archbishop at Lambeth. She was to go quietly; this was the King's order. He wanted no hysterical crowds on the river's bank to cheer her barge. He himself had received a copy of the summons, but he would not go; he would send his old proctor, Doctor Sampson, to represent him. Come face to face with Anne Boleyn! Never! There were too many memories between them. What if she tried her witcheries on him once more!

He felt shaken and ill at ease. He was sleeping badly; he would wake startled from bad dreams, calling her name and, with the daze of sleep still on him, think she was there beside him. He had dispatched Jane Seymour to her father's house, since that was the most seemly place for her to be in. He did not wish to have her with him during the critical days, as he had announced that he was deeply grieved at the falseness of his wife and would not take another unless his people wished it. Jane should therefore not attract much attention. Her condition—early in pregnancy though she was—must be considered. So Henry sat alone, awaiting news from Lambeth; whilst Anne, who would have liked to refuse to answer the summons, left the Tower and went quietly up the river.

She was conducted to the crypt of the Archbishop's residence and awaiting her there were Cranmer, looking troubled but determined to do his duty; Cromwell, looking more sly and ugly than ever; Doctor Sampson, to represent the King; and two doctors, Wotton and Barbour, who, most farcically, were supposed to represent her.

She had not been there for more than a few moments when she realized their cunning purpose.

Cranmer's voice was silky. There was no man who could present a case as he could. His voice almost caressed her, expressing sympathy for her most unhappy state.

She was under the sentence of death, he said, by beheading . . . or burning.

Did he mean to stress that last word, or did she imagine this? The way in which he said it made her hot with fear; she felt as though the flames were already scorching her flesh.

The King's conscience, went on Cranmer, troubled him

sorely. She had been pre-contracted to Northumberland! That, she would understand, would make her marriage with the King illegal.

She cried: "Northumberland was brought before you. You yourself accepted . . ."

Cranmer was quiet and calm, so capable of adjusting his opinion, so clever, so intellectual, so impossible to confound.

The King himself had been indiscreet. Yes, His Majesty was ready to admit it. An association with Anne's sister. An affinity created.

Cranmer spread his hands as though to say, Now, you see how it is. You were never really married to the King!

She could hold her head high in the crypt at Lambeth as she had in that other court where they had condemned her. They would need her acknowledgement of this, would they not? Well, they should never get it.

Cranmer was pained and sad. He had loved her well, he said.

She thought, How I hate all hypocrites! Fool I may be but I am no hypocrite. How I hate you, Cranmer! I helped you to your present position. You too, Cromwell. But neither of you would think of helping me! But Cranmer I hate more than Cromwell for Cranmer is a hypocrite, and perhaps I hate this in men because I am married to the most shameless one that ever lived.

Cranmer was talking in his deep, sonorous voice. He had

a gift for making suggestions without expressing actual statements. She was thinking, I have my little daughter to consider. She shall never be called bastard.

Cranmer's voice went droning on. He was hinting at her release. There was a pleasant convent at Antwerp. What of the young men whose fate she deplored and whose innocence she proclaimed? All the country knew how she esteemed her brother, and he her. Was he to go to the block? What of her daughter? The King would be more inclined to favour a child whose mother had impressed him with her good sense.

Anne's mind was working quickly. It was painfully clear. She must make a choice. If her marriage to the King were proved null and void then that was all he need ask for. He could marry Jane Seymour immediately if his marriage with Anne Boleyn had been no marriage at all. The child Jane carried would be born in wedlock. And for this, Anne was offered a convent in Antwerp, the lives of her brother and those innocent men who were to die with him. And if not . . . Once more she was hot with the imaginary fire that licked her limbs. And what would her refusal mean in any case? If the King had decided to disinherit Elizabeth, he would surely do so. He had ever found excuses for what he wished to do.

She had something to gain and nothing to lose, for if she had not been married to the King, how could she have committed adultery? The affairs of Lady Anne Rochford and the Marchioness of Pembroke could not be called treason to the King.

Her hopes were soaring. She thought, Oh, George, my darling, I have saved you! You shall not die. Gladly I will throw away my crown to save you!

Cromwell went back to his master rubbing his ugly hands with pleasure. Once more he had succeeded. The King was free to take a new wife whenever he wished, for he had never been married to Anne Boleyn. She herself had agreed upon it.

It was over. They had tricked her. At the King's command she had stood and watched them as they passed by her window on their way to Tower Hill. She had sacrificed her own and her daughter's rights in vain. Although she was no queen, these men had died. It was not reasonable; it was not logical; it was simply murder.

She herself had yet another day to live through. Mary Wyatt came to tell her how nobly these men had died, following the example of George, how they had made their speeches, which etiquette demanded, on the scaffold, how they had met their deaths bravely.

"What of Smeaton?" she asked. She thought of him still as a soft-eyed boy, and she could not believe that he would not tell the truth on the scaffold. Mary was silent and Anne cried out: "Has he not cleared me of the public shame he hath done me!" She surveyed Mary's silent face in horror. "Alas," she said at length and in great sorrow, "I fear his soul will suffer from the false witness he hath borne."

Her face lightened suddenly.

"Oh, Mary," she cried, "It will not be long now. My brother and the rest are now, I doubt not, before the face of the greater King, and I shall follow tomorrow."

When Mary left her her sadness returned. She wished they had not given her fresh hope in the Lambeth crypt. She had resigned herself to death, and then they had promised her she should live, and life was so sweet. She was twenty-nine and beautiful; and though she had thought herself weary of living, when they had given her that peep into a possible future, how eagerly she had grasped at it!

She thought of her daughter, and trembled. Three is so very young. She would not understand what had happened to her mother. Oh, let them be kind to Elizabeth.

She asked that Lady Kingston might come to her, and when the woman came she locked the door and with tears running down her cheeks, asked that Lady Kingston would sit in her chair of state.

Lady Kingston herself was moved in face of such distress.

"It is my duty to stand in the presence of the Queen, Madam," she said.

"That title is gone," was the answer. "I am a condemned person, and, I have no estate left me in this life, but for the clearing of my conscience, I pray you sit down."

She began to weep, and her talk was incoherent, and humbly she fell upon her knees and begged that Lady Kingston would go to Mary, the daughter of Katharine, and kneel before her and beg that she would forgive Anne Boleyn for the wrong she had done her.

"For, my Lady Kingston," she said, "till this be accomplished, my conscience cannot be quiet."

After that she was more at peace and did not need to thrust the thought of her daughter from her mind.

The news was brought to her that her death should not take place at the appointed hour; there had been a postponement. She had been most gay, and to learn that she was to have a few more hours on earth was a disappointment to her.

"Mr. Kingston," she said, "I hear I shall not die afore noon, and I am very sorry therefore, for I thought to be dead by this time and past my pain."

"The pain will be little," he told her gently, "it is so subtle."

She answered; "I have heard say the executioner is very good, and I have a little neck."

She embraced it with her hands and laughed; and when her laughter had subsided, a great peace came to her. She had another day to live and she had heard that the King wished the hour of her execution to be kept secret, and that it was not to take place on Tower Hill where any idle spectator might see her die, but on the enclosed green; for the King feared the reactions of the people.

The evening passed; she was gay and melancholy in turns;

she joked about her end. "I shall be easily nicknamed—'Queen Anne . . . sans tête.'"

She occupied herself in writing her own dirge.

"Oh death, rock me asleep,
Bring on my quiet rest,
Let pass my very guiltless ghost
Out of my careful breast.
Ring out the doleful knell
Let its sound my death tell;
For I must die,
There is no remedy,
For now I die. . . ."

She dressed herself with such care that it might have been a state banquet to which she was going instead of to the scaffold. Her robe of grey damask was trimmed with fur and low cut; beneath this showed a kirtle of crimson. Her headdress was trimmed with pearls. She had never looked more beautiful; her cheeks were flushed, her eyes brilliant, and all the misery and fear of the last weeks seemed to have been lifted from her face.

Attended by four ladies, among them her beloved Mary Wyatt, with much dignity and grace she walked to the green before the church of St. Peter ad Vincula. Slowly and calmly she ascended the steps to that platform which was strewn with straw; and she could smile because there were so few people to witness her last moments, smile because the hour and place of her execution had had to be kept secret from the people.

Among those who had gathered about the scaffold she saw the Dukes of Suffolk and Richmond, but she could feel no enmity towards these two now. She saw Thomas Cromwell, whose eldest son was now married to Jane Seymour's sister. Ah, thought Anne, when my head has rolled into the sawdust, he will feel an impediment lifted and his relationship to the King almost an accomplished fact.

She called to her one whom she knew to be of the King's privy chamber, and said she would send a message by him to the King.

"Commend me to His Majesty," she said, "and tell him that he hath ever been constant in his career of advancing me; from a private gentlewoman, he made me a marchioness, from a marchioness a queen, and now he hath left no higher degree of honour, he gives my innocency the crown of martyrdom."

The messenger trembled for she was a woman about to die, and how could he dare carry such a message to the King!

Then she would, after the etiquette of the scaffold, make her dying speech.

"Good Christian people," she said, "I am come hither to die, according to law, for by the law I am judged to die, and therefore I will speak nothing against it. . . ."

Her ladies were so overcome with weeping that she, hearing their sobs, was deeply moved.

"I come hither to accuse no man," she continued, "nor to speak anything of that whereof I am accused, as I know full well that aught that I say in my defence doth not appertain to you. . . ."

When she spoke of the King, her words were choked. Cromwell moved nearer to the scaffold. This was the moment he and the King had most feared. But with death so near she cared nothing for revenge. All the bitterness had gone out of her. Cromwell would arrange the words she spoke, not only as they should best please the King, but also that they should mislead the public into thinking she had died justly. The people must be told that at the end she had only praise for the King, that she spoke of him as a merciful prince and a gentle sovereign lord.

Her voice cleared and she went on: "If any person will meddle with my cause I require them to judge the best. Thus I take my leave of the world and of you, and I heartily desire you all to pray for me."

It was time for her now to lay her head upon the block and there was not one of her attendants whose hands were steady enough to remove her headdress; they could only turn from her in blind misery. She smiled and did this herself; then she spoke to each of them gently, bidding them not to grieve and thanking them for their services to her. Mary she took aside and to her gave a little book of devotions as a parting gift and whispered into her ear a message of good cheer that she might give it to her brother in the Tower.

Then she was ready. She laid her head upon the block. Her lips were murmuring her own verses.

> *"Farewell my pleasures past;*
> *Welcome my present pain,*
> *I feel my torments so increase*
> *That life cannot remain.*
> *Sound now the passing bell,*
> *Rung is my doleful knell,*
> *For its sound my death doth tell.*
> *Death doth draw nigh,*
> *Sound the knell dolefully,*
> *For now I die."*

She was waiting now, waiting for that swift stroke, that quick and subtle pain.

"Oh, Lord God have pity on my soul. Oh, Lord God . . ."

Her lips were still moving as her head lay on the straw.

The Dowager Duchess of Norfolk was weeping bitterly as she went about the Lambeth house. Catherine Howard flung herself onto her bed and wept. Over the city of London hung silence. The Queen was dead.

At Richmond the King waited for the booming of the gun

which would announce the end of Anne Boleyn. He waited in anxiety; he was terrified of what she might say to those watching crowds. He knew that the people who had never accepted her as their Queen were now ready to make of her a martyr.

His horse was restive, longing to be off; but not more so than he. Would he never hear the signal! What were they at, those fools? What if some had planned a rescue! He was hot at the thought. There had been men who loved her dearly and none knew better than he did, how easy it was to do that. She had changed his life when she came into it; what would she do when she went out of it?

He pictured her last moments; he knew she would show great courage; he knew she would show dignity; he knew she would be beautiful enough to stir up pity in the hearts of all who beheld her. It was well that but few were sure of hour and place.

Around him were hounds and huntsmen. This night the hunt would end at Wolf Hall whether the stag led them there or not. But the waiting was long, and try as he might he could not forget Anne Boleyn.

He spoke to his conscience, "Thank God I can now leave Mary without constant fear that she will meet a horrible end. Thank God I discovered the evil ways of this harlot."

He had done right, he assured himself. Katharine had suffered through her; Mary had suffered. Thank God he had found out in time! Thank God he had turned his affections on a more worthy object!

What would the people say when they heard the gun booming from the Tower? What would they say of a man who went to a new bride before the body of his wife was cold?

Along the river came the dismal booming of the gun. He heard it; his mouth twisted into a line of mingling joy and apprehension.

"The deed is done!" he cried. "Uncouple the hounds and away!"

So he rode on, on to Wolf Hall, on to marriage with Jane Seymour.

No Other Will Than His

The Dowager Duchess of Norfolk was in bed and very sad. A new queen reigned in the place of her granddaughter; a pale-faced creature with scarcely any eyebrows so that she looked forever surprised, a meek, insipid, vapid woman and to put her on the throne had the King sent beautiful Anne to the block. The Duchess's dreams were haunted by her granddaughter, and she would awaken out of them sweating and trembling. She had just had such a dream, and thought she had stood among those spectators who had watched Anne submit her lovely head to the executioner's sword.

She began to weep into her bedclothes, seeing again Anne at court, Anne at Lambeth; she remembered promised favours which would never now be hers. She could rail against the King in the privacy her bedchamber offered her. Fat! Coarse! Adulterer! And forty-five! While Anne at twenty-nine had lost her lovely head that that slut Seymour might sit beside him on the throne!

"Much good will she do him!" murmured the Duchess. "Give the King a son quickly, Mistress Seymour, or your head will not stay on your shoulders more than a year or two, I warrant you! And I'll be there to see the deed done; I swear it!" She began to chuckle throatily, remembering that she had heard but a week or so after his marriage to Jane had been announced, the King, on meeting two very beautiful young women, had shown himself to be—and even mentioned this fact—sorry that he had not seen them before he married Jane. It had not been so with Anne. She had absorbed his attention, and it was only when she could not produce a son that her enemies had dared to plot against her. "Bound to Serve and Obey." That was the device chosen by Jane. "You'll serve, my dear!" muttered the Duchess. "But whether you produce a son or not remains to be seen, and if you do not, why then you must very meekly obey, by laying your head on the block. You'll have your enemies just as my sweet Anne did!" The Duchess dried her eyes and set her lips firmly together as she thought of one of the greatest of those enemies, both to Anne and herself, and one with whom she must continually be on her guard—her own stepson and Anne's uncle, the Duke of Norfolk.

Some of the Duchess's ladies came in to help her dress. Stupid girls they were. She scolded them, for she thought their hands over-rough as they forced her bulk into clothes too small for it.

"Katharine Tylney! I declare you scratch me with those nails of yours. I declare you did it apurpose! Take that!"

Katharine Tylney scowled at the blow. The old Duchess's temper had been very bad since the execution of the Queen, and the least thing sent it flaring up. Katharine Tylney shrugged her shoulders at Mistress Wilkes and Mistress Baskerville, the two who were also assisting with the Duchess's toilet. When they were beyond the range of the Duchess's ears they would curse the old woman, laughing at her obscenity and her ill temper, laughing because she who was so fat and old and ugly was vain as a young girl, and would have just the right amount of embroidered kirtle showing beneath her skirt, and would deck herself in costly jewels even in the morning.

The Duchess wheezed and scolded while her thoughts ran on poor Anne and sly Jane and that absurd fancy of the King's, which had made him change the one for the other; she brooded on the cunning of that low-born brute Cromwell, and the cruelty of Norfolk and Suffolk, until she herself felt as though she were standing almost as near the edge of that active volcano as Anne herself had stood.

She dismissed the women and went slowly into her presence chamber to receive the first of her morning callers. She was fond of ceremony and herself kept an establishment here at Lambeth—as she had at Norfolk—like a queen's. As she entered the chamber, she saw a letter lying on a table, and going to it, read her own name. She frowned at it, picked it up, looked at the writing, did not recognize this, unfolded it and began to read; and as she read a dull anger set her limbs shaking. She reread it.

"This is not true!" she said aloud, and she spoke to reassure herself, for had she not for some time suspected the possibility of such a calamity! "It is not true!" she repeated fiercely. "I'll have the skin beaten off the writer of this letter. My granddaughter to behave in this way! Like some low creature in a tavern!"

Puffing with that breathlessness which the least exertion aroused in her, she once more read the letter with its sly suggestion that she should go quietly and unannounced to the ladies' sleeping apartments and see for herself how Catherine Howard and Francis Derham, who called themselves wife and husband, behaved as such.

"Under my roof!" cried the Duchess. "Under my roof!" She trembled violently, thinking of this most sordid scandal's reaching the ears of her stepson.

She paced up and down not knowing what it would be best for her to do. She recalled a certain night when the key of the ladies' apartment had not been in its rightful place, and she had gone up to find the ladies alone, but seeming guilty; she remembered hearing suspicious creaking noises in the gallery. There had been another occasion when going to the maids' room she had found Catherine and Derham romping on the floor.

She sent for Jane Acworth, for Jane had been present and had had her ears boxed in the maids' room for looking on with indifference while Catherine and Derham behaved so improperly.

Jane's eyes glinted with fear when she saw the wrath of the Duchess.

"You know this writing?"

Jane said she did not, and a slap on her cheek told her that she had better think again; but Jane Acworth, seeing Catherine's and Derham's names on that paper, was not going to commit herself. The writing, she said, was doubtless disguised, and she knew it not.

"Get you gone then!" said the Duchess; and left alone once more began her pacing up and down. What would this mean? Her granddaughter Catherine Howard had been seduced by a young man, who, though of good family, being a connection of the Howards, was but a member of an obscure branch of theirs. Catherine, for all her illiteracy, for all that she had been allowed to run wild during her childhood, was yet the daughter of Lord Edmund Howard; and she had been so reckless and foolish, that she had doubtless ruined her chances of making a good marriage.

"The little slut!" whispered the Duchess. "To have that young man in her bed! This will cost him his life! And her . . . and her . . ." The Duchess's fingers twitched. "Let her wait till I lay hands on her. I'll make her wish she had never been so free with Mr. Derham. I'll make her wish she had never been born. After all my care of her . . . ! I always told myself there was a harlot in Catherine Howard!"

Jane Acworth sought Catherine Howard and found her on the point of going to the orchard to meet Derham.

"A terrible thing has happened," said Jane. "I would not care to be in your shoes!"

"What mean you, Jane?"

"Someone has written to Her Grace, telling her what you and Derham are about."

Catherine turned pale.

"No!"

"Indeed yes! Her Grace is in a fury. She showed me the letter and asked if I knew the handwriting. I swore I did not, nor could I be sure, but to my mind . . ."

"Mary Lassells!" whispered Catherine.

"I could not swear, but methought. Let us not waste time. What do you think is going to happen to you and Derham and to us all?"

"I dare not think."

"We shall all be brought into this. I doubt not but that this is the end of our pleasant days and nights. The Duchess cannot ignore this, much as she may wish to do. I would not be you, Catherine Howard; and most assuredly I would not be Derham."

"What dost think they will do to him?"

"I could not say. I could only guess. They will say what he has done to you is criminal. Mayhap he will go to the Tower. Oh, no, it will not be the block for him, because then it would be known that he had seduced Catherine Howard. He would be taken to the dungeons and allowed to rot in his chains, or perhaps be tortured to death. The Howards are powerful, and

I would not be in the shoes of one who had seduced a member of their house!"

"Please say no more. I must go!"

"Yes. Go and warn Derham. He must not stay here to be arrested and committed to the Tower."

Fear made Catherine fleet; tears gushed from her eyes and her childish mouth was trembling; she could not shut from her mind terrible pictures of Francis in the Tower, groaning in his chains, dying a lingering death for her sake.

He was waiting in the orchard.

"Catherine!" he cried on seeing her. "What ails thee, Catherine?"

"You must fly," she told him incoherently. "You must wait for nothing. Someone has written to Her Grace, and you will be sent to the Tower."

He turned pale. "Catherine! Catherine! Where heard you this?"

"Jane Acworth has seen the letter. Her Grace sent for her that she might tell her who wrote it. It was there . . . all about us . . . and my grandmother is furious."

Bold and reckless, very much in love with Catherine, he wished to thrust such unpleasantness aside. He could not fly, and leave Catherine?

"Dost think I would ever leave thee?"

"I could not bear that they should take thee to the Tower."

"Bah!" he said. "What have we done? Are we not married— husband and wife?"

"They would not allow that to be."

"And could they help it? We are! That is good enough for me."

He put his arms about her and kissed her, and Catherine kissed him in such desire that was nonetheless urgent because danger threatened, but all the more insistent. She took his hand and ran with him into that part of the orchard where the trees grew thickest.

"I would put as far between us and my grandmother as possible," she told him.

He said: "Catherine, thou hast let them frighten thee."

She answered; "It is not without cause." She took his face into her hand and kissed his lips. "I fear I shall not see thee for a long time, Francis."

"What!" he cried, throwing himself onto the grass and pulling her down beside him. "Dost think aught could keep me from thee?"

"There is that in me that would send thee from me," she sighed, "and that is my love for thee."

She clung to him, burying her face in his jerkin. She was picturing his young, healthy body in chains; he was seeing her taken from him to be given to some nobleman whom they would consider worthy to be her husband. Fear gave a new savour to their passion, and they did not care in those few moments of recklessness whether they were discovered or not. Catherine had ever been the slave of the moment; Derham was single-minded as a drone in his hymeneal flight; death was no deterrent to desire.

The moment passed, and Catherine opened her eyes to stare at the roof of branches, and her hand touched the cold grass which was her bed.

"Francis . . . I am so frightened."

He stroked her auburn hair that was turning red because the sun was glinting through the leaves of the fruit tree onto it.

"Do not be, Catherine."

"But they know, Francis. They know!"

Now he seemed to feel cold steel at his throat. What would the Norfolks do to one who had seduced a daughter of their house? Assuredly they would decide he was not worthy to live. One night at dusk, as he came into this very orchard, arms mayhap would seize him. There would be a blow on the head, followed by a second blow to make sure life was extinct, and then the soft sound of displaced water and the ripples would be visible on the surface of the river at the spot where his body had fallen into it. Or would it be a charge of treason? It was simple enough for the Norfolks to find a poor man guilty of treason. The Tower . . . the dreaded Tower! Confinement to one who was ever active! Living a life in one small cell when one's spirit was adventurous; one's limbs which were never happy unless active, in heavy chains.

"You must fly from here," said Catherine.

"Thou wouldst have me leave thee?"

"I shall die of sorrow, but I would not have them hurt thee. I would not have thee remember this love between us with aught but the utmost delight."

"I could never think on it but with delight."

She sat up, listening. "Methought I heard . . ."

"Catherine! Catherine Howard!" It was the voice of Mistress Baskerville calling her.

"You must go at once!" cried Catherine in panic. "You must leave Lambeth. You must leave London."

"And leave you! You know not what you ask!"

"Do I not! An you lose me, do I not lose you? But I would rather not keep you with me if it means that they will take you. Francis, terrible things happen to men in the Tower of London, and I fear for you."

"Catherine!" called Mistress Baskerville. "Come here, Catherine!"

Her eyes entreated him to go, but he would not release her.

"I cannot leave you!" he insisted.

"I will come with you."

"We should then be discovered at once."

"An you took me," she said sagely, "they would indeed find us. They would search for us and bring me back, and oh, Francis, what would they do to you?"

Mistress Baskerville was all but upon them.

"I will go to her," said Catherine.

"And I will wait here until you come back to me."

"Nay, nay! Go now, Francis. Do not wait. Something tells me each moment is precious."

They embraced; they kissed long and broken-heartedly.

"I shall wait here awhile and hope that you will come back

to me, Catherine," he said. "I cannot go until we are certain this thing has come to pass."

Catherine left him and ran to Mistress Baskerville.

"What is it?" asked Catherine.

"Her Grace wants you to go to her at once . . . you and Derham. She is well-nigh mad with rage. She has had a whip brought to her. Some of us have been questioned. I heard Jane Acworth crying in her room. I believe she has been whipped . . . and it is all about you and Derham."

Catherine said: "What do you think they will do to Derham?"

"I know not. It is a matter of which one can only guess. They are saying he deserves to die."

Catherine's teeth began to chatter. "Please help me," she pleaded. "Wait here one moment. Will you give me one last moment with him?"

The girl looked over her shoulder. "What if we are watched?"

"Please!" cried Catherine. "One moment. . . . Stay here. . . . Call my name. Pretend that you are still looking for me. I swear I will be with you after one short minute."

She ran through the trees to Derham. "It is all true!" she cried. "They will kill thee, Francis. Please go. . . . Go now!"

He was thoroughly alarmed now, knowing that she did not speak idly. He kissed her again, played with the idea of taking her with him, knew the folly of that, guessing what hardships she would have to face. He must leave her; that was common sense; for if he disappeared they might not try very hard to find him, preferring to let the matter drop, since with him gone, it would be easier to hush up the affair. Besides, he might be able to keep in touch with Catherine yet.

"I will go," said Francis, "but first promise me this shall not be the end."

"Dost think I could bear it an it were?" she demanded tearfully.

"I shall write letters, and thou wilt answer them?"

She nodded. She could not wield a pen very happily, but that there would be those to help her in this matter she doubted not.

"Then I leave thee," he said.

"Do not return to the house for aught, Francis. It would not be safe. Where shall you go?"

"That I cannot say. Mayhap I shall go to Ireland and turn pirate and win a fortune so that I may then come back and claim Catherine Howard as my wife. Never forget, Catherine, that thou art that."

The tears were streaming down Catherine's cheeks. She said with great emotion, "Thou wilt never live to say to me 'Thou hast swerved!'"

One last kiss; one last embrace.

"Not farewell, Catherine. Never that. Au revoir, sweet Catherine. Forget not the promise thou hast made to me."

She watched him disappear through the trees before she ran back to Mistress Baskerville. Fearfully they went into the house and to the Duchess's rooms.

When the old woman saw Catherine, her eyes blazed with rage. She seized her by the hair and flung her against the wall, shouting at her, after first shutting the door, "You little harlot! At your age to allow such liberties! What dost think you have done! Do not look at me so boldly, wench!"

The whip came down on Catherine's shoulders while she cowered against the wall, covering her face with her hands. Across her back, across her thighs, across her legs, the whip descended. There was not much strength behind the Duchess's blows, but the whip cut into Catherine's flesh, and she was crying, not from the infliction of those strokes, but for Derham, since she could know no pain that would equal the loss of him.

The Duchess flung away the whip and pushed Catherine onto a couch. She jerked the girl's head up, and looked into her grief-swollen face.

"It was true then!" cried the Duchess in a fury. "Every word of it was true! He was in your bed most nights! And when you were disturbed he hid in the gallery!" She slapped Catherine's face, first one side, then the other. "What sort of marriage do you expect after this? Tell me that! Who will want Catherine Howard who is known for a slut and a harlot!" She slapped Catherine's face. "We shall marry you to a potman or a pantler!"

Catherine was hysterical with the pain of the blows and the mental anxiety she suffered concerning Derham's fate.

"You would not care!" stormed the Duchess. "One man as good as another to you, eh? You low creature!"

The slapping began again. Catherine had wept so much that she had no more tears.

"And what do you think we shall do with your fine lover, eh? We will teach him to philander. We shall show him what happens to those who creep stealthily into the beds of their betters . . . or those who should be their betters. . . ."

Down came the heavy ringed hands again. Catherine's bodice was in tatters, her flesh red and bruised; and the whip had drawn blood from her shoulders.

The Duchess began to whisper of the terrible things that would be done to Francis Derham, were he caught. Did she think she had been severely punished? Well, that would be naught compared with what would be done to Francis Derham. When they had done with him, he would find himself unable to creep into young ladies' beds of night, for lascivious wenches like Catherine Howard would find little use for him, when they had done with him . . . when they had done with him . . . !

Saliva dripped from Her Grace's lips; her venom eased her fear. What if the Duke heard of this? Oh, yes, his own morals did not bear too close scrutiny and there were scandals enough in the Norfolk family and to spare. What of the washerwoman Bess Holland who was making a Duchess of Norfolk most peevish and very jealous! And the late Queen herself had had Howard blood in her veins and stood accused of incest. But oddly enough it was those who had little cause to judge others who most frequently and most loudly did. The King himself who was over-fond of wine and women was the first to condemn such excesses in others; and did not courtiers ever take their cue from a king! If the Duke heard of this he would laugh his sardonic laugh and doubtless say evil things of his old enemy his stepmother. She was afraid, for this would be traced to her neglect. The girl had been in her charge and she had allowed irreparable harm to be done. What of Catherine's sisters? Such a scandal would impair their chances in the matrimonial field. Then, there must be no scandal, not only for Catherine's sake, but for that of her sisters—and also for the sake of the Dowager Duchess of Norfolk. She quietened her voice and her blows slackened.

"Why," she said slyly, "there are those who might think this thing had gone farther than it has. Why, there are those who will be ready to say there was complete intimacy between you and Francis Derham." She looked earnestly into Catherine's face, but Catherine scarcely heard what she said; much less did she gather the import of her words. "Derham shall suffer nevertheless!" went on the Duchess fiercely; and she went to the door and called to her Mary Lassells and Katharine Tylney. "Take my granddaughter to the apartment," she told them, "and put her to bed. She will need to rest awhile."

They took Catherine away. She winced as they removed her clothes. Katharine Tylney brought water to bathe her skin where the Duchess's ring had broken it.

While Catherine cried softly, Mary Lassells surveyed with satisfaction the plump little body which had been so severely beaten. Her just deserts! thought Mary Lassells. It was a right and proper thing to have done, to have written to the Duchess. Now this immorality would be stopped. No more petting and stroking of those soft white limbs. Mary Lassells did not know how she had so long borne to contemplate such wickedness.

In her room the Duchess was still shaking with agitation. She must have advice, she decided, and she asked her son Lord William Howard, to come to see her. When he arrived she showed him the letter and told him the story. He grumbled about mad wenches who could not be merry among themselves without falling out.

"Derham," said Her Grace, "has disappeared."

Lord William shrugged. Did his mother not attach too much importance to a trifling occurrence, he would know. Young men and women were lusty creatures and they would always frolic. It need not necessarily mean that although Derham had visited the girl's sleeping apartment, there was anything to worry about.

"Forget it! Forget it!" said Lord William. "Give the girl a beating and a talking to. As for Derham, let him go. And pray keep all this from my lord Duke."

It was sound advice. There was no harm done, said the Duchess to herself, and dozed almost serenely in her chair. But out of her dozes she would awake startled, worried by dreams of her two most attractive granddaughters, one dead, and the other so vitally alive.

Then the Duchess made a resolution, and this she determined to keep, for she felt that it did not only involve the future of Catherine Howard, but of her own. Catherine should be kept under surveillance; she should be coached in deportment so that she should cease to be a wild young hoyden and become a lady. And some of those women, whose sly ways the Duchess did not like over-much, should go.

On this occasion the Duchess carried out her resolutions. Most of the young ladies who had shared the main sleeping apartment with Catherine were sent to their homes. Jane Acworth was among those who remained, for a marriage was being arranged for her with Mr. Bulmer of York, and, thought the Duchess, she will soon be going in any case.

The Duchess decided to see more of Catherine, to school her herself, although, she admitted ruefully, it was hardly likely that Jane Seymour would find a place at court for Anne's cousin. Never mind! The main thing was that Catherine's unfortunate past must be speedily forgotten, and Catherine prepared to make the right sort of marriage.

It seemed to the Princess Mary that the happiest event that had taken place since the King had cast off her mother, was the death of Anne Boleyn. Mary was twenty years old, a very serious girl, with bitterness already in her face, and fanaticism peering out through her eyes. She was disappointed and frustrated, perpetually on the defensive and wholeheartedly devoted to Roman Catholicism. She was proud and the branding of illegitimacy did not make her less so. She had friends and supporters, but whereas, while Anne Boleyn lived, these did not wish to have their friendship known, they now were less secretive. The King had put it on record that not in any carnal concupiscence had he taken a wife, but only at the entreaty of his nobility, and he had chosen one whose age and form was deemed to be meet and apt for the procreation of children. His choice had been supported by the imperialists, for he had chosen Jane Seymour who was one who still clung to the old Catholicism; moreover Jane was known to be kindly disposed towards Mary.

It was, as ever, necessary to tread very cautiously, for the King had changed since the death of Anne; he was less jovial; he had aged considerably and looked more than his forty-five years; he did not laugh so frequently, and there was a glitter in his eyes, which could send cold shivers down the spine of a man though he might have no knowledge of having displeased the King. His matrimonial adventures had been conspicuously unsuccessful, and though Jane had been reported to be pregnant before the death of Anne—well, Katharine of Aragon had been pregnant a good many times without much result; and Anne had had no success either. Young Richmond, on whom the King doted, as his only son, had ever since the death of Anne been spitting blood. "She has cast a spell on him," said Mary. "She would murder him as she tried to murder me, for Richmond has death in his face if ever one had." And what if

Richmond died and Jane Seymour was without issue! Elizabeth was a bastard now, no less then Mary.

"It is time," said her friends to Mary, "that you began to woo the King."

"And defame my mother!" cried Mary.

"She who was responsible for your mother's position is now herself cast off and done with. You should try to gain His Majesty's friendship."

"I do not believe he will listen to me."

"There is a way of approaching him."

"Which way is that?"

"Through Cromwell. It is not only the best, but the only possible way for you."

The result was that Cromwell came to visit Mary at Hunsdon whither she had been banished. Cromwell came eagerly enough, seeing good reasons for having Mary taken back into favour. He knew that the King would never receive his daughter unless she agreed that her mother's marriage had been unlawful and incestuous; and if Mary could be brought to such admission, she would cease to have the sympathy of the people. There were many nobles in the land who deplored the break with Rome; who were silently awaiting an opportunity to repair the link. If they were ever able to do this, what would happen to those who had worked for the break! And was not the greatest of them Thomas Cromwell! Cromwell could therefore see much good in the King's reconciliation with his daughter.

Henry's eyes were speculative regarding the prospect laid out before him by Cromwell. How he loathed that man! But what good work he was doing with the smaller abbeys, and what better work he would do with the larger ones! If there was to be a reconciliation with Mary, Cromwell was right in thinking this was the time to make it. Many people considered Mary had been badly treated; the common people were particularly ready to be incensed on her behalf. He had separated her from her mother, had not allowed her to see Katharine on her deathbed. He could not help feeling a stirring of his conscience over Mary. But if he effected a reconciliation at this moment, he himself would emerge from the dangerous matter, not as a monster but as a misguided man who had been under the influence of a witch and a sorceress. Anne, the harlot and would-be prisoner, could be shown to have been entirely responsible for the King's treatment of his daughter. "Why," people would say, "as soon as the whore was sent to her well-deserved death, the King becomes reconciled to his daughter!" A well-deserved death! Henry liked that phrase. He had suffered many disturbed nights of late; he would awaken and think she lay beside him; he would find sleep impossible for hours at a time; and once he dreamed of her looking into a pool at Hever: and when he looked too, he saw her head with its black hair, and blood was streaming from it. A well-deserved death! thought Henry complacently, and he sent Norfolk to see his daughter at Hunsdon.

"Tell the girl," he said, "that she is wilful and disobedient, but that we are ever ready to take pity on those who repent."

Mary saw that she was expected to deny all that she had previously upheld, and was frightened by the storm that she had aroused.

"My mother was the King's true wife," she insisted. "I can say naught but that!"

She was reminded ominously that many had lost their heads for saying what she had said. She was not easily frightened and she tried to assure herself that she would go to the block as readily as More and Fisher had done.

Mary could see now that she had been wrong in blaming Anne for her treatment. Norfolk was brusque with her, insulting even; she had never been so humiliated when Anne was living. It was Anne who had begged that they might bury their quarrel, that Mary should come to court, and had told her that she should walk beside her and need not carry her train. Lady Kingston had come to her with an account of Anne's plea for forgiveness and Mary had shrugged her shoulders at that. Forgiveness! What good would that do Anne Boleyn! When Mary died she would look down on Anne, burning in hell, for burn in hell she assuredly would. She had carried out the old religious rites until her death, but she had listened to and even applauded the lies of Martin Luther and so earned eternal damnation. Mary was not cruel at heart; she knew only two ways, the right and the wrong, and the right way was through the Roman Catholic Church. No true Catholic burned in hell; but this was a fate which those who were not true Catholics could not possibly escape. But she saw that though Anne would assuredly burn in hell for her responsibility in the severance of England from Rome, she could not in all truth be entirely blamed for the King's treatment of his elder daughter. Mary decided that although she could not forgive Anne, she would at least be as kind as she could to Anne's daughter.

Henry was furious at the reports brought back to him. He swore that he could not trust Mary. He was an angry man. It was but a matter of days since he had married Jane Seymour and yet he was not happy. He could not forget Anne Boleyn; he was dissatisfied with Jane; and he was enraged against Mary. A man's daughter to work against him! He would not have it! He called the council together. A man cannot trust those nearest to him! was his cry. There should be an inquiry. If he found his daughter guilty of conspiracy she should suffer the penalty of traitors.

"I'll have no more disobedience!" foamed Henry. "There is one road traitors should tread, and by God, I'll see that they tread it!"

There was tension in court circles. It was well known that, while Anne lived, Mary and her mother had had secret communications from Chapuys; and that the ambassador had had plans for—with the Emperor's aid—setting Katharine or Mary on the throne.

The King, as was his custom, chose Cromwell to do the unpleasant work; he was to go secretly into the houses of suspected persons and search for evidence against the Princess.

The Queen came to the King.

"What ails thee?" growled the newly married husband. "Dost not see I am occupied with matters of state!"

"Most gracious lord," said Jane, not realizing his dangerous mood, "I would have speech with you. The Princess Mary has ever been in my thoughts, and now that I know she repents and longs to be restored in your affections . . ."

Jane got no further.

"Be off!" roared the King. "And meddle not in my affairs!"

Jane wept, but Henry strode angrily from her, and in his mind's eye, he seemed to see a pair of black eyes laughing at him, and although he was furious he was also wistful. He growled: "There is none I can trust. My nearest and those who should be my dearest are ready to betray me!"

Mary's life was in danger. Chapuys wrote to her advising her to submit to the King's demands, since it was unsafe for her not to do so. She must acknowledge her father Supreme Head of the Church; she must agree that her mother had never been truly married to the King. It was useless to think that as his daughter she was safe, since there was no safety for those who opposed Henry. Let her think, Chapuys advised her, of the King's last concubine to whom he had been exclusively devoted over several years; he had not hesitated to send her to the block; nor would he hesitate in his present mood to send his own daughter.

But the shrewd man Henry had become knew that the unpopularity he had incurred, first by his marriage with Anne and then by his murder of her, would be further increased if he shed the blood of his daughter. The enmity of the people, ever a dark bogey in his life since he felt his dynasty to be unsafe, seemed as close as it had when he broke from the Church of Rome. He told Cromwell to write to her telling her that if she did not leave all her sinister councils she would lose her chance of gaining the King's favour.

Mary was defeated, since even Chapuys was against her holding out; she gave in, acknowledged the King Supreme Head of the Church, admitted the Pope to be a pretender, and agreed that her mother's marriage was incestuous and unlawful. She signed the papers she was required to sign and she retired to the privacy of her rooms where she wept bitterly, calling on her saintly mother to forgive her for what she had done. She thought of More and Fisher. "Ah! That I had been brave as they!" she sobbed.

Henry was well pleased; instead of a recalcitrant daughter, he had a dutiful one. Uneasy about the death of Anne, he wished to assure himself and the world that he had done right to rid himself of her. He was a family man; he loved his children. Anne had threatened to poison his daughter, his beloved Mary. Did his people not now see that Anne had met a just fate? Was not Mary once more his beloved daughter? It mattered not that she had been born out of wedlock. She was his daughter and she should come to court. With the death of the harlot who had tried to poison his daughter, everything was well between her and her father.

Jane was jubilant.

"You are the most gracious and clement of fathers," she told Henry.

"You speak truth, sweetheart!" he said and warmed to Jane, liking afresh her white skin and pale eyelashes. He loved her truly, and if she gave him sons, he would love her all the more. He was a happy family man.

Mary sat at the royal table, next in importance to her stepmother, and she and Jane were the best of friends. Henry smiled at them benignly. There was peace in his home, for his obstinate daughter was obstinate no longer. He tried to look at her with love, but though he had an affection for her, it was scarcely strong enough to be called love.

When Jane asked that Elizabeth should also come to court, he said he thought this thing might be.

"An you wish it, sweetheart," he said, making it a favour to Jane. But he liked to see the child. She was attractive and spirited, and there was already a touch of her mother in her.

"The King is very affectionate towards the young Elizabeth," it was said.

When his son, the Duke of Richmond, died, Henry was filled with sorrow. Anne, he declared, had set a spell upon him, for it was but two months since Anne had gone to the block, and from the day she died, Richmond had begun to spit blood.

Such an event must set the King brooding once more on the succession. He was disturbed because young Thomas Howard, half-brother to the Duke of Norfolk, had dared to betroth himself, without Henry's permission, to Lady Margaret Douglas, daughter of Henry's sister Margaret of Scotland. This was a black crime indeed. Henry knew the Howards—ambitious to a man. He was sure that Thomas Howard aspired to the throne through his proposed marriage with Henry's niece and he was reminded afresh of what a slight hold the Tudors had upon the throne.

"Fling young Howard into the Tower!" cried Henry, and this was done.

He was displeased with the Duke also, and Norfolk was terrified, expecting that at any moment he might join his half-brother.

If the Howards were disturbed so was Henry; he hated trouble at home more than trouble abroad. The Henry of this period was a different person from that younger man whose thoughts had been mainly occupied in games and the hunting of women and forest creatures. He had come into the world endowed with a magnificent physique and a shrewd brain; but as the former was magnificent and the latter merely shrewd, he had developed the one at the expense of the other. Excelling as he did in sport, he had passed over intellectual matters; loving his great body, he had decked it in dazzling jewels and fine velvets and cloth of gold; for the glory of his body he had subdued his mind. But at forty-five he was well past his active youth;

the ulcer in his leg was bad enough to make him roar with pain at times; he was inclined to breathlessness, being a heavy man who had indulged too freely in all fleshly lusts. His body being not now the dominating feature in his life, he began to exercise his mind. He was chiefly concerned in the preservation and the glorification of himself, and as this must necessarily mean the preservation and the glorification of England, matters of state were of the utmost interest to him. Under him, the navy had grown to a formidable size; certain monies were set aside each year for the building of new ships and that those already built might be kept in good fighting order; he wished to shut England off from the Continent, making her secure; while he did not wish England to become involved in war, he wished to inflame Charles and Francis to make war on one another, for he feared these two men; but he feared them less when they warred together than when they were at peace. His main idea was to have all potential enemies fighting while England grew out of adolescence into that mighty power which it was his great hope she would one day be. If this was to happen, he must first of all have peace at home, for he knew well that there was nothing to weaken a growing country like civil war. In severing the Church of England from that of Rome, he had done a bold thing, and England was still shaking from the shock. There were many of his people who deplored the break, who would ask nothing better than to be reunited with Rome. Cleverly and shrewdly, Henry had planned a new religious program. Not for one moment did he wish to deprive his people of those rites and ceremonies which were as much a part of their lives as they were of the Roman Catholic Faith. But their acceptance of the King as Supreme Head of the Church must be a matter of life and death.

Peace at home and peace abroad therefore, was all he asked, so that England might grow in the best possible conditions to maturity. Wolsey had moulded him into a political shape very like his own. Wolsey had believed that it was England's task to keep the balance of power in Europe, but Wolsey had been less qualified to pursue this than Henry. Wolsey had been guilty of accepting bribes; he could never resist adding to his treasures; Henry was not so short-sighted as to jeopardize England's position for a gift or two from foreign powers. He was every bit as acquisitive as Wolsey, but the preservation of himself through England was his greatest need. He had England's treasures at his disposal, and at this moment he was finding the dissolution of the abbeys most fruitful. Wolsey never forgot his allegiance to Rome; Henry knew no such loyalty. With Wolsey it was Wolsey first, England second; with Henry, England and Henry meant the same thing. Cromwell believed that England should ally herself with Charles because Charles represented the strongest Power in Europe, but Henry would associate himself with neither Charles nor Francis, clinging to his policy of preserving the balance of power. Neither Wolsey nor Cromwell could be as strong as Henry, for there was ever present with these two the one great fear which must be their first consideration, and this was fear of Henry. Henry therefore was freer to act; he could take advantage of sudden action; he could do what he would, without having to think what excuse he should make if his action failed. It was a great advantage in the subtle game he played.

Looking back, Henry could see whither his laziness had led him. He had made wars which had given nothing to England, and he had drained her of her strength and riches, so that the wealth so cautiously and cleverly amassed by his thrifty father had slowly dwindled away. There was the example of the Field of the Cloth of Gold, on which he could now look back through the eyes of a wiser and far more experienced man, and be shocked by his lack of statecraft at that time. Kings who squandered the treasure and the blood of their subjects also squandered their affections. He could see now that it was due to his father's wealth that England had become a power in Europe, and that with the disappearance of that wealth went England's power. By the middle of the twenties England was of scarcely any importance in Europe, and at home Ireland was being troublesome. When Henry had talked of divorcing his queen, and was living openly with Anne Boleyn, his subjects had murmured against him, and that most feared of all calamities to a wise king—civil war—had threatened. At that time he had scarcely been a king at all, but when he had broken from Rome he had felt his strength, and that was the beginning of Henry VIII as a real ruler.

He would now continue to rule, and brute strength would be his method; never again should any other person than the king govern the country. He was watchful; men were watchful of him. They dreaded his anger, but Henry was wise enough to realize the wisdom of that remark of his Spanish ambassador's: "Whom many fear, must fear many." And Henry feared many, even if many feared him.

His great weakness had its roots in his conscience. He was what men called a religious man, which in his case meant he was a superstitious man. There was never a man less Christian; there was never one who made a greater show of piety. He was cruel; he was brutal; he was pitiless. This was his creed. He was an egoist, a megalomaniac; he saw himself not only as the centre of England but of the world. In his own opinion, everything he did was right; he only needed time to see it in its right perspective, and he would prove it to be right. He took his strength from this belief in himself; and as his belief was strong, so was Henry.

One of the greatest weaknesses of his life was his feeling for Anne Boleyn. Even now, after she had died on his command, when his hands were stained with her innocent blood, when he had gloated over his thoughts of her once-loved, now-mutilated body, when he knew that could he have her back he would do the same again, he could not forget her. He had hated her so violently, only because he had loved her; he had killed her out of passionate jealousy, and she haunted him. Sometimes he knew that he could never hope to forget her. All his life he would seek a way of forgetting. He was now trying the obvious way, through women.

Jane! He was fond enough of Jane. What egoist is not fond of those who continually show him he is all that he would have people believe he is! Yes, he liked Jane well enough, but she maddened him; she irritated him because he always knew exactly what she would say; she submitted to his embraces mildly, and he felt that she did so because she considered it her duty; she annoyed him because she offered him that domestic peace which had ever been his goal, and now having reached it, he found it damnably insipid; she angered him because she was not Anne.

Moreover, now she had disappointed him. She had had her first miscarriage, and that very reason why he had been forced to get rid of Anne so speedily, to resort to all kinds of subterfuge to pacify his subjects, and to tell his people that it was his nobles who had begged him to marry Jane before Anne's mutilated body was cold, had proved to be no worthwhile reason at all. He could have waited a few months; he could have allowed Cromwell and Norfolk to have persuaded him; he could have been led self-sacrificingly into marriage with Jane instead of scuffling into it in the undignified way he had done. It was irritating.

It was also uncanny. Why did all his wives miscarry? He thought of the old Duke of Norfolk's brood, first with one wife, then with another. Why should the King be so cursed? First with Katharine, then with Anne. Katharine he had discarded; Anne he had beheaded; still, he was truly married to Jane, for neither of these two had been living when he married

Jane; therefore he could have done no wrong. If he had displeased God in marrying Anne while Katharine was alive, he could understand that; but he had been a true widower when he had married Jane. No, he was worrying unduly; he would have children yet by Jane, for if he did not . . . why, why had he got rid of Anne?

In his chamber at Windsor, he was brooding on these matters when he was aware of a disturbance in the courtyard below his window; even as he looked out a messenger was at his door with the news that certain men had ridden with all speed to the King as they had alarming news for him.

When they were brought in they fell on their knees before him.

"Sir, we tremble to bring such news to Your Majesty. We come hot speed to tell you that trouble has started, so we hear, in Lincoln."

"Trouble!" cried Henry. "What mean you by trouble?"

"My lord, it was when the men went into Lincoln to deal with the abbeys there. There was a rising, and two were killed. Beaten and roughly handled, please Your Majesty, unto death."

Henry's face was purple; his eyes blazed.

"What means this! Rebellion! Who dares rebel against the King!"

Henry was astounded. Had he steered the country away from civil war, only to find it breaking out at last when he had been congratulating himself on his strength? The people, particularly those in the north, had been bewildered by the break with Rome; but by the pillaging of the abbeys, they had been roused to action. Already bands of beggars were springing up all over the country; they who had been sure of food and shelter from the monks were now desolate, and there was but one sure way for a destitute man to keep himself fed in Tudor England, and that was to rob his fellow men. Over the countryside there roamed hordes of desperate starving men, and to their numbers were added the displaced monks and nuns. There was more boldness in the north than in the south because those far removed from his presence could fear Henry less. So they, smarting from the break with Rome, sympathizing with the monks, resenting the loss of the monasteries, decided that something should be done. They were joined by peasants who, owing to the enclosure acts, and the prevailing policy of turning arable into pasture land, had been rendered homeless. Lords Darcy and Hussey, two of the most powerful noblemen of the north, had always supported the old Catholic faith; the rebels therefore could feel they had these men behind them.

Henry was enraged and apprehensive. He felt this to be a major test. Should he emerge from it triumphant, he would have achieved a great victory; he would prove himself a great king. Two ways lay before him. He could return to Rome and assure peace in his realm; he could fight the rebels and remain not only head of the Church but truly head of the English people. He chose the second course. He would risk his crown to put down the rebels.

It meant reconciliation with Norfolk, for whenever there was a war to be fought, Norfolk must be treated with respect. He would send Suffolk to Lincoln. He stormed against those of his counsellors who advised him against opposing the rebels. Fiercely he reminded them that they were bound to serve him with their lives, lands and goods.

Jane was afraid. She was very superstitious and it seemed to her that this rising was a direct reproach from heaven because of Cromwell's sacrilegious pillaging of the monasteries.

She came to the King and knelt before him, and had her head not been bent she would have seen her danger from his blazing eyes.

"My lord husband," she said, "I have heard the most disquieting news. I fear it may be a judgment on us for ridding ourselves of the abbeys. Could not Your Most Gracious Majesty consider the restoring of them?"

For a few seconds he was speechless with rage; he saw Jane through the red haze in his eyes, and when he spoke his voice was a rumble of thunder.

"Get up!"

She lifted terrified eyes to his face and stood. He came closer to her, breathing heavily, his jowls quivering, his lower lip stuck out menacingly.

"Have I not told you never to meddle in my affairs!" he said very slowly and deliberately.

Tears came into Jane's eyes; she was thinking of all those people who were wandering homeless about the country;

she thought of little babies crying for milk. She had pictured herself saving the people from a terrible calamity; moreover, her friends who longed for the return of the old ways would rejoice in the restoration of the monasteries, and would be very pleased with Queen Jane. Therefore she felt it to be her duty to turn the King back to Rome, or at least away from that wickedness which had sprung up in the world since Martin Luther had made himself heard.

The King gripped her shoulder, and put his face to hers.

"Dost remember what happened to your predecessor?" he asked meaningfully.

She stared at him in horror. Anne had gone to the block because she was guilty of high treason. What could he mean?

His eyes were hot and cruel.

"Forget it not!" he said, and threw her from him.

The men of the north had followed the example of the men from Lincolnshire. This was no mob rising; into the ranks of the Pilgrimage of Grace went sober men of the provinces. The most inspiring of its leaders was a certain Robert Aske, and this man, whose integrity and honesty of purpose were well known, had a talent for organization; he was a born commander, and under him, the northern rebels were made into a formidable force.

Henry realized too well how very formidable. The winter was

beginning; he had no standing army. He acted with foresight and cunning. He invited Aske to discuss the trouble with him.

It did not occur to Aske that one as genial as Henry appeared to him could possibly not be as honest as Aske himself. On the leader, Henry unloosed all his bluffness, all his honest, down-to-earth friendliness. Did Aske wish to spread bloodshed over England? Aske certainly did not. He wanted only hardship removed from the suffering people. Henry patted the man affectionately. Why then, Aske and the King had the same interests at heart. Should they quarrel! Never! All they must do was to find a way agreeable to them both of doing what was right for England.

Aske went back to Yorkshire to tell of the King's oral promises, and the insurgents were disbanded; there was a truce between the north and the King.

There were in the movement less level-headed men than such leaders as Aske and Constable, and in spite of Aske's belief in the King's promises he could not prevent a second rising. This gave Henry an excuse for what followed. He had decided on his action before he had seen Aske; his promises to the leader had meant that he wished to gain time, to gather his strength about him, to wait until the end of winter. He had never swerved from the policy he intended to adopt and which he would continue to follow to the end of his reign. It was brute strength and his own absolute and unquestioned rule.

He decided to make a bloody example and show his people what happened to those who opposed the King. Up to the north went Norfolk and the bloodletting began. Darcy was beheaded; Sir Thomas Percy was brought to Tyburn and hanged; honest men who had looked upon the Pilgrimage of Grace as a sacred movement were hanged, cut down alive, disembowelled, and their entrails burned while they still lived; then they were beheaded. Aske learned too late that he had accepted the promises of one to whom a promise was naught but a tool to be picked up and used for a moment when it might be useful and then to be laid aside and forgotten. In spite of his pardon, he was executed and hanged in chains on one of the towers of York that all might see what befell traitors. Constable was taken to Hull and hanged from the highest gate in the town, a grim warning to all who beheld him.

The King licked his lips over the accounts of cruelties done in his name. "Thus shall all traitors die!" he growled, and warned Cromwell against leniency, knowing well that he could leave bloody work in those ugly hands.

The Continent, hearing of his internal troubles, was on tiptoe waiting and watching. Henry's open enemy Pope Paul could state publicly his satisfaction; Henry's secret enemies, Charles and Francis, though discreetly silent, were nonetheless delighted.

The Pope, deeply resenting this king who had dared set an example which he feared others might follow, began to plan. What if the revolt against Henry were nourished outside England? Reginald Pole was on the Continent; he had left England for two reasons; he did not approve of the divorce and break with Rome; and he being the grandson of that Duke of Clarence who was brother to Edward IV, was too near the throne to make residence in England safe for him. He had written a book against Henry, and Henry feigning interest suggested Pole return to England that they might discuss the differences of opinion. Pole was no careless fly to walk into the spider's web. He declined his sovereign's offer and went to Rome instead where the Pope made him a cardinal and discussed with him a plan for fanning the flames which were at this time bursting out in the north of England. If Pole succeeded in displacing Henry, why should he not marry the Princess Mary, restore England to the papacy and rule as her king?

Henry acted with cunning and boldness. He demanded from Francis Pole's extradition, that he might be sent to England and stand his trial as a traitor. Francis, who did not wish to defy the Pope nor to annoy Henry, ordered Pole to leave his domains. Pole went to Flanders, but Charles was as reluctant as Francis to displease the King of England. Pole had to disguise himself.

The attitude of the two great monarchs showed clearly that they were very respectful towards the island lying off the coast of Europe, for never had a papal legate been so humiliated before.

Henry could purr with pleasure. He was treated with respect and he had crushed a revolt which threatened his throne. The crown was safe for the Tudors, and England was saved from civil war. He knew how to rule his country. He had been strong and he had emerged triumphant from the most dangerous situation of his reign.

There was great news yet. The Queen was paler than usual; she had been sick; she had fancies for special foods.

Henry was joyful. He once more had hopes of getting a son.

While Henry was strutting with pleasure, Jane was beset with fear. There were many things to frighten Jane. Before her lay the ordeal of childbirth. What if it should prove unsuccessful? As she lay in those Hampton Court apartments which the King had lovingly planned for Anne Boleyn, she brooded on these matters. From her window she could see the initials entwined in stonework—J and H, and where the J was there had once been an A, and the A had had to be taken away very suddenly indeed.

The King was in high humour, certain that this time he would get a son. He went noisily about the place, eating and drinking with great heartiness; and hunting whenever his leg was not too painful to deter him. If Jane gave him a son, he told himself, he would at last have found happiness. He would know that he had been right in everything he had done, right to rid himself of Katharine who had never really been his wife, right to execute Anne who was a sorceress, right to marry Jane.

He jollied the poor pale creature, admonishing her to take good care of herself, threatening her that if she did not, he would want to know the reason why; and his loving care was not for her frail body but for the heir it held.

The hot summer passed. Jane heard of the executions and shuddered, and whenever she looked from her windows she saw those initials. The J seemed to turn into an A as she looked, and then into something else, blurred and indistinguishable.

Plague came to London, rising up from the fetid gutters and from the dirty wash left on the riverbanks with the fall of the tide. People died like flies in London. Death came close to Jane Seymour during those months.

She was wan and sickly and she felt very ill, though she dared not mention this for fear of angering the King; she was afraid for herself and the child she carried. She had qualms about the execution of Anne, and her dreams became haunted with visions. She could not forget an occasion when Anne had come upon her and the King together. Then Anne must have felt this sickness, this heaviness, this fear, for she herself was carrying the King's child at that time.

Jane could not forget the words the King had used to her more than once. "Remember what happened to your predecessor!" There was no need to ask Jane to remember what she would never be able to forget.

She became more observant of religious rites, and as her religion was of the old kind, both Cranmer and Cromwell were disturbed. But they dared not approach the King with complaints for they knew well what his answer would be. "Let the Queen eat fish on Fridays. Let her do what she will an she give me a son!"

All over the country, people waited to hear of the birth of a son. What would happen to Jane, it was asked, if she produced a stillborn child? What if she produced a girl?

Many were cynical over Henry's matrimonial affairs, inclined to snigger behind their hands. Already there were Mary and Elizabeth—both proclaimed illegitimate. What if there was yet another girl? Perhaps it was better to be humble folk when it was considered what had happened to Katharine of Aragon and Anne Boleyn.

The Dowager Duchess of Norfolk waited eagerly for the news. Her mouth was grim. Would Jane Seymour do what her granddaughter had failed to do? That pale, sickly creature succeed, where glowing, vital Anne had failed! She thought not!

Catherine Howard fervently hoped the King would get a son. She had wept bitterly at the death of her cousin, but unlike her grandmother she bore no resentment. Let poor Queen Jane be happy even if Queen Anne had not. Where was the good sense in harbouring resentment? She scarcely listened to her grandmother's grim prophecies.

Catherine had changed a good deal since that violent beating her grandmother had given her. Now she really looked like a daughter of the house of Howard. She was quieter; she had been badly frightened by the discovery. She had received lectures from Lord William who insisted on looking on the episode as a foolish, girlish prank; she had received a very serious warning from her grandmother who, when they were alone, did not hide from her that she knew the worst. Catherine must put all that behind her, must forget it had happened, must never refer to it again, must deny what she had done if she were ever questioned by anyone. She had been criminally foolish; let her remember that. Catherine did remember; she was restrained.

She was growing very pretty and her gentle manners gave a new charm to her person. The Duchess was ready to forget unsavoury incidents; she hoped Catherine was too. She did not know that Catherine was still receiving letters from Derham, that through the agency of Jane Acworth, whose pen was ever ready, the correspondence was being kept up.

Derham wrote: "Do not think that I forget thee. Do not forget that we are husband and wife, for I never shall. Do not forget you have said, 'You shall never live to say I have swerved.' For I do not, and I treasure the memory. One day I shall return for you. . . ."

It appealed strongly to Catherine's adventure-loving nature to receive love letters and to have her replies smuggled out of the house. She found it pleasant to be free from those women who had known about her love affair with Derham and who were forever making sly allusions to it. There were no amorous adventures these days, for the Duchess's surveillance was strict. Catherine did not want them; she realized her folly and she was very much ashamed of the freedom she had allowed Manox. She still loved Francis, she insisted; she still loved receiving his letters; and one day he would return for her.

October came, and one morning, very early, Catherine was awakened by the ringing of bells and the sound of guns. Jane Seymour had borne the King a son.

Jane was too ill to feel her triumph. She was hardly aware of what was going on in her chamber. Shapes rose up and faded. There was a huge red-faced man, whose laughter was very loud, drawing her away from the peaceful sleep she sought. She heard whispering voices, loud voices, laughter.

The King would peer at his son anxiously. A poor puny little thing he was, and Henry was terrified that he would, as others of his breed before him, be snatched from his father before he reached maturity. Even Richmond had not survived, though he had been a bonny boy; this little Edward was small and white and weak.

Still, the King had a son and he was delighted. Courtiers moved about the sick room. They must kiss Jane's hand; they must congratulate her. She was too tired? Nonsense! She must rejoice. Had she not done that which her predecessors had failed to do, given the King a son!

Fruit and meat were sent to her, gifts from the King. She must show her pleasure in His Majesty's attentions. She ate without knowing what she ate.

The ceremony of the christening began in her chamber. They lifted her from her bed to the state pallet which was decorated with crowns and the arms of England in gold thread. She lay, propped on cushions of crimson damask, wrapped in a mantle of crimson velvet furred with ermine; but Jane's face looked transparent against the rich redness of her robes. She was exhausted before they lifted her from the bed; her head throbbed and her hands were hot with fever. She longed to sleep, but she reminded herself over and over again that she must do her duty by attending the christening of her son. What would the King say, if he found the mother of his prince sleeping when she should be smiling with pleasure!

It was midnight as the ceremonial procession with Jane in its midst went through the drafty corridors of Hampton Court to the chapel. Jane slipped into unconsciousness, recovered and smiled about her. She saw the Princess Mary present the newly born prince at the font; she saw her own brother carrying the small Elizabeth, whose eyes were small with sleepiness and in whose fat little hands was Edward's chrisom; she saw Cranmer and Norfolk, who were the prince's sponsors; she saw the nurse and the midwife; and so vague was this scene to her that she thought it was but a dream, and that her son was not yet born and her pains about to begin.

Through the mist before her eyes she saw Sir Francis Bryan at the font, and she was reminded that he had been one of those who had not very long ago delighted in the wit of Anne Boleyn. Her eyes came to rest on the figure of a grey old man who carried a taper and bore a towel about his neck; she recognized him as Anne's father. The Earl looked shamefaced, and had the unhappy air of a man who knows himself to be worthy of the contempt of his fellowmen. Was he thinking of his brilliant boy and his lovely girl who had been done to death for the sake of this little prince to whom he did honour because he dared do nothing else?

Unable to follow the ceremony because of the fits of dizziness which kept overwhelming her, Jane longed for the quiet of her chamber. She wanted the comfort of her bed; she wanted darkness and quiet and rest.

"God, in His Almighty and infinite grace, grant good life and long, to the right high, right excellent, and noble Prince Edward, Duke of Cornwall and Earl of Chester, most dear and entirely beloved son of our most dread and gracious Lord Henry VIII."

The words were like a rushing tide that swept over Jane and threatened to drown her; she gasped for breath. She was only hazily aware of the ceremonial journey back to her chamber.

A few days after the christening, Jane was dead.

"Ah!" said the people in the streets. "His Majesty is desolate. Poor dear man! At last he had found a queen he could love; at last he has his heart's desire, a son to follow him; and now this dreadful catastrophe must overtake him."

Certain rebels raised their heads, feeling the King to be too sunk in grief to notice them. The lion but feigned to sleep. When he lifted his head and roared, rebels learned what happened to those who dared raise a voice against the King. The torture chambers were filled with such. Ears were cut off;

tongues were cut out; and the mutilated victims were whipped as they were driven naked through the streets.

Before Jane was buried, Henry was discussing with Cromwell whom he should next take for a wife.

.✦.

Henry was looking for a wife. Politically he was at an advantage; he would be able to continue with his policy of keeping his two enemies guessing. He would send ambassadors to the French court; he would throw out hints to the Emperor; for both would greatly fear an alliance of the other with England.

Henry was becoming uneasy concerning Continental affairs. The war between Charles and Francis had come to an end; and with these two not at each other's throats, but in fact friends, and Pole persisting in his schemes to bring about civil war in England with the assistance of invasion from the Continent, he had cause for anxiety. To be able to offer himself in the marriage market was a great asset at such a time and Henry decided to exploit it to the full.

Although Henry was anxious to make a politically advantageous marriage, he could not help being excited by the prospect of a new wife. He visualized her. It was good to be a free man once more. He was but forty-seven and very ready to receive a wife. There was still in his mind the image of Anne Boleyn. He knew exactly what sort of wife he wanted; she must be beautiful, clever, vivacious; one who was high-spirited as Anne, meek as Jane. He reassured himself that although it was imperative that he should make the right marriage, he would not involve himself unless the person of his bride was pleasing.

He asked Chatillon, the French ambassador who had taken the place of Du Bellay at the English court, that a selection of the most beautiful and accomplished ladies of the French court be sent to Calais; Henry would go there and inspect them.

"Pardi!" mused Henry. "How can I depend on any but myself! I must see them myself and see them sing!"

To this request, Francis retorted in such a way as to make Henry squirm, and he did not go to Calais to make a personal inspection of prospective wives.

There were among others the beautiful Christina of Milan who was a niece of Emperor Charles. She had married the Duke of Milan, who had died, leaving her a virgin widow of sixteen. Henry was interested in reports of her, and after the snub from Francis not averse to looking around the camp of the Emperor. He sent Holbein to make a picture of Christina and when the painter brought it back, Henry was attracted, but not sufficiently so to make him wish to clinch the bargain immediately. He was still keeping up negotiations with the French. It was reported that Christina had said that if she had had two heads one should be at the English King's service, but having only one she was reluctant to come to England. She had heard that her great-aunt Katharine of Aragon had been poisoned; that Anne Boleyn had been put innocently to death; and that Jane Seymour had been lost for lack of keeping in childbirth. She was of course at Charles's command, and these reports might well have sprung out of the reluctance of the Emperor for the match.

Henry's uneasiness did not abate. He was terrified that the growing friendship between Charles and Francis might be a prelude to an attack on England. He knew that Pope Paul was trying to stir up the Scots to invade England from the north; Pole was moving slyly, from the Continent.

Henry's first act was to descend with ferocity on the Pole family in England. He began by committing Pole's young brother Geoffrey to the Tower and there the boy was tortured so violently that he said all Henry wished him to say. The result was that his brother Lord Montague and his cousin the Marquis of Exeter were seized. Even Pole's mother, the aging Countess of Salisbury, who had been governess to the Princess Mary and one of the greatest friends of Katharine of Aragon, was not spared.

These people were the hope of those Catholics who longed for reunion with Rome, and Henry was watching his people closely to see what effect their arrest was having. He had had enough of troubles within his own domains, and with trouble threatening from outside he must tread very cautiously. At this time, he selected as his victim a scholar named Lambert whom he accused of leaning too far towards Lutheranism. The young man was said to have denied the body of God to be in the sacrament in corporal substance but only to be there spiritually. Lambert was tried and burned alive. This was merely Henry's answer to the Catholics; he was telling them that he favoured neither extreme sect. Montague and Exeter went to the block as traitors, not as Catholics. Catholic or Lutheran, it mattered not. No favouritism. No swaying from one sect to another. He only asked allegiance to the King.

Francis thought this would be a good moment to undermine English commerce which, while he and Charles had been wasting their people's energy in war, Henry had been able to extend. Henry shrewdly saw what was about to happen and again acted quickly. He promised the Flemish merchants that for seven years Flemish goods should pay no more duty than those of the English. The merchants—a thrifty people—were overjoyed, seeing years of prosperous trading stretching before them. If their Emperor would make war on England he could hardly hope for much support from a nation benefiting from good trade with that country on whom Charles wished them to make war.

This was a good move, but Henry's fears flared up afresh when the Emperor, visiting his domains, decided to travel through France to Germany, instead of going by sea or through Italy and Austria as was his custom. This seemed to Henry a gesture of great friendship. What plans would the two old enemies formulate when they met in France? Would England be involved in those plans?

Cromwell, to whose great interest it was to turn England from the Catholics and so make more secure his own position, seized this chance of urging on Henry the selection of a wife from one of the German Protestant houses. Cromwell outlined his plan. For years the old Duke of Cleves had wanted an alliance with England. His son had a claim to the Duchy of Guelders, which Duchy was in relation to the Emperor Charles very much what Scotland was to Henry, ever ready to be a cause of trouble. A marriage between England and the house of Cleves would therefore seriously threaten the Emperor's hold on his Dutch dominions.

Unfortunately, Anne, sister of the young Duke, had already been promised to the Duke of Lorraine, but it was not difficult to waive this. Holbein was dispatched; he made a pretty picture of Anne, and Henry was pleasurably excited and the plans for the marriage went forward.

Henry was impatient. Anne! Her very name enchanted him. He pictured her, gentle and submissive and very, very loving. She would have full awareness of her duty; she was no daughter of a humble knight; she had been bred that she might make a good marriage; she would know what was expected of her. He could scarcely wait for her arrival. At last he would find matrimonial happiness, and at the same time confound Charles and Francis.

"Anne!" he mused, and eagerly counted the days until her arrival.

Jane Acworth was preparing to leave.

"How I shall miss you!" sighed Catherine.

Jane smiled at her slyly. "It is not I whom you will miss but your secretary!"

"Poor Derham!" said Catherine. "I fear he will be most unhappy. For I declare it is indeed a mighty task for me to put pen to paper."

Jane shrugged her shoulders; her thoughts were all for the new home she was to go to and Mr. Bulmer whom she was to marry.

"You will think of me often, Jane?" asked Catherine.

Jane laughed. "I shall think of your receiving your letters. He writes a pretty letter and I dare swear seems to love you truly."

"Ah! That he does. Dear Francis! How faithful he had always been to me."

"You will marry him one day?"

"We are married, Jane. You know it well. How else . . ."

"How else should you have lived the life you did together! Well, I have heard it whispered that you were very lavish with your favours where a certain Manox was concerned."

"Oh, speak not of him! That is past and done with. My love for Francis goes on forever. I was foolish over Manox, but I regret nothing I have done with Francis, nor ever shall."

"How lonely you will be without me!"

"Indeed, you speak truthfully."

"And how different this life from that other! Why, scarce anything happens now, but sending letters to Derham and receiving his. What excitement we used to have!"

"You had better not speak of that to Mr. Bulmer!" warned Catherine; and they laughed.

It was well to laugh, and she was in truth very saddened by Jane's departure; the receiving and dispatching of letters had provided a good deal of excitement in a dull existence.

With Jane's going the days seemed long and monotonous. A letter came from Francis; she read it, tucked it into her bodice and was aware of it all day; but she could not read it very easily and it was not the same without Jane, for she, as well as being happy with a pen, was also a good reader. She must reply to Derham, but as the task lacked appeal, she put it off.

The Duchess talked to her of court matters.

"If the King would but take him a wife! I declare it is two years since Queen Jane died, and still no wife! I tell you, Catherine, that if this much-talked-of marriage with the Duchess of Cleves materializes, I shall look to a place at court for you."

"How I wish I could go to court!" cried Catherine.

"You will have to mind your manners. Though I will say they have improved since . . . since. . . ." The Duchess's brows were dark with memory. "You would not do so badly now at court, I trow. We must see. We must see."

Catherine pictured herself at court.

"I should need many new clothes."

"Dost think Lord William would allow you to go to court in rags! Why even His Grace the Duke would not have that! Ha! I hear he is most angry at this proposed marriage. Master

Cromwell has indeed put my noble stepson's nose out of joint. Well, all this is not good for the Howards, and it is a mistake for a house to war within its walls. And so . . . it may not be so easy to find you a place at court. And I know that the King does not like the strife between my stepson and his wife. It is not meet that a Duke of noble house should feel so strongly for a washer in his wife's nurseries that he will flaunt the slut in the face of his lady Duchess. The King was ever a moral man, as you must always remember. Ah! Pat my back, child, lest I choke. Where was I? Oh, yes, the Howards are not in favour while Master Cromwell is, and this Cleves marriage is Cromwell made. Therefore, Catherine, it may not be easy to find you a place at court, for though I dislike my lord Duke with all my heart, he is my stepson, and if he is out of favour at court, depend upon it, we shall be too."

On another occasion the Duchess sent for Catherine. Her old eyes, bright as a bird's, peered out through her wrinkles.

"Get my cloak, child. I would walk in the gardens and have you accompany me."

Catherine obeyed, and they stepped out of the house and strolled slowly through the orchards where Catherine had lain so many times with Derham. She had ever felt sad when she was in the orchards being unable to forget Derham, but now she scarcely thought of him, for she knew by the Duchess's demeanour that she had news for her, and she was hoping it was news of a place at court.

"You are an attractive child," wheezed the Duchess. "I

declare you have a look of your poor tragic cousin. Oh . . . it is not obvious. Her hair was black and so were her eyes, and her face was pointed and unforgettable. You are auburn-haired and hazel-eyed and plump-faced. Oh, no, it is not in your face. In your sudden laughter? In your quick movements? She had an air of loving life, and so have you. There was a little bit of Howard in Anne that looked out from her eyes; there is a good deal of Howard in you; and there is the resemblance."

Catherine wished her grandmother would not talk so frequently of her cousin, for such talk always made her sad.

"You had news for me?" she reminded her.

"Ah, news!" The Duchess purred. "Well, mayhap it is not yet news. It is a thought. And I will whisper this in your ear, child. I doubt not that the stony-hearted Duke would give his approval, for it is a good match."

"A match!" cried Catherine.

"You do not remember your dear mother, Catherine?"

"Vaguely I do!" Catherine's large eyes glistened with tears so that they looked like pieces of topaz.

"Your dear mother had a brother, and it is to his son, your cousin, whom we feel you might be betrothed. He is a dear boy, already at court. He is a most handsome creature. Thomas Culpepper, son of Sir John, your mother's brother. . . ."

"Thomas Culpepper!" whispered Catherine, her thoughts whirling back to a room at Hollingbourne, to a rustle of creeper, to a stalwart protector, to a kiss in the paddock. She repeated: "Thomas Culpepper!" She realized that something very unusual was about to happen. A childhood dream was about to come true. "And he . . . ?" she asked eagerly.

"My dear Catherine, curb your excitement. This is a suggestion merely. The Duke will have to be consulted. The King's consent will be necessary. It is an idea. I was not to tell you yet . . . but seeing you so attractive and marriageable, I could not resist it."

"My cousin . . ." murmured Catherine. "Grandmother . . . when I was at Hollingbourne . . . we played together. We loved each other then."

The Duchess put her finger to her lips.

"Hush, child! Be discreet. This matter must not be made open knowledge yet. Be calm."

Catherine found that very difficult. She wanted to be alone to think this out. She tried to picture what Thomas would be like now. She had only a hazy picture of a little boy, telling her in a somewhat shamefaced way that he would marry her.

Derham's letter scraped her skin. The thought of Thomas excited her so much that she had lost her burning desire to see Francis. She was wishing that all her life had been spent as she had passed the last months.

The Duchess was holding her wrists and the Duchess's hands were hot.

"Catherine, I would speak to you very seriously. You will have need of great caution. The distressing things which have happened to you . . ."

Catherine wanted to weep. Oh, how right her grandmother

was! If only she had listened even to Mary Lassells! If only she had not allowed herself to drift into that sensuous stream which at the time had been so sweet and cooling to her warm nature and which now was so repulsive to look back on. How she had regretted her affair with Manox when she had found Francis! Now she was beginning to regret her love for Francis as her grandmother talked of Thomas.

"You have been very wicked," said her grandmother. "You deserve to die for what you have done. But I will do my best for you. Your wickedness must never get to the Duke's ears."

Catherine cried out in misery rather than in anger: "The Duke! What of him and Bess Holland!"

The Duchess was on her dignity. She might say what she would of her erring kinsman, not so Catherine.

"What if his wife's washerwoman be his mistress! He is a man; you are a woman. There is all the difference in the world."

Catherine was subdued; she began to cry.

"Dry your eyes, you foolish girl, and forget not for one instant that all your wickedness is done with, and it must be as though it never was."

"Yes, grandmother," said Catherine, and Derham's letter pricked her skin.

Derham continued to write though he received no answers. Catherine had inherited some of her grandmother's capacity for shifting her eyes from the unpleasant. She thought continually of her cousin Thomas and wondered if he remembered her, if he had heard of the proposed match and if so what he thought of it.

One day, wandering in the orchard, she heard the rustle of leaves behind her, and turning came face to face with Derham. He was smiling; he would have put his arms about her but she held him off.

"Catherine, I have longed to see thee."

She was silent and frightened. He came closer and took her by the shoulders. "I had no answer to my letters," he said.

She said hastily: "Jane has married and gone to York. You know I was never able to manage a pen."

"Ah!" His face cleared. "That was all then? Thank God! I feared . . ." He kissed her on the mouth; Catherine trembled; she was unresponsive.

His face darkened. "Catherine! What ails thee?"

"Nothing ails me, Francis. It is . . ." But her heart melted to see him standing so forlorn before her, and she could not tell him that she no longer loved him. Let the break come gradually. "Your return is very sudden. Francis . . ."

"You have changed, Catherine. You are so solemn, so sedate."

"I was a hoyden before. My grandmother said so."

"Catherine, what did they do to thee?"

"They beat me with a whip. There never was such a beating. I was sick with the pain of it, and for weeks I could feel it. I was locked up, and ever since I have scarce been able to go out alone. They will be looking for me ere long, I doubt not."

"Poor Catherine! And this you suffered for my sake! But never forget, Catherine, you are my wife."

"Francis!" she said, and swallowed. "That cannot be. They will never consent, and what dost think they would do an you married me in actual fact?"

"We should go away to Ireland."

"They would never let me go. We should die horrible deaths."

"They would never catch us, Catherine."

He was young and eager, fresh from a life of piracy off the coast of Ireland. He had money; he wished to take her away. She could not bear to tell him that they were talking of betrothing her to her cousin Thomas Culpepper.

She said: "What dost think would happen to you if you showed yourself?"

"I know not. To hold you in my arms would suffice for anything they could do to me afterwards."

Such talk frightened her. She escaped, promising to see him again.

She was disturbed. Now that she had seen Derham after his long absence, she knew for truth that which she had begun to suspect. She no longer loved him. She cried herself to sleep, feeling dishonoured and guilty, feeling miserable because she would have to go to her cousin defiled and unclean. Why had she not stayed at Hollingbourne! Why had her mother died! What cruel fate had sent her to the Duchess where there were so many women eager to lead her into temptation! She was not yet eighteen and she had been wicked . . . and all so stupidly and so pointlessly.

She determined to break with Francis; there should be no more clandestine meetings. She would marry Thomas and be such a good wife to him, that when set against years and years of the perfect happiness she would bring him, the sinful years would seem like a tiny mistake on a beautifully written page.

Francis was hurt and angry. He had come back full of hope; he loved her and she was his wife, he reminded her. He had money from his spell of piracy; he was in any case related to the Howards.

She told him she had heard she was to go to court.

"I like that not!" he said.

"But I like it," she told him.

"Dost know the wickedness of court life?" he demanded.

She shrugged her shoulders. She hated hurting people and being forced to hurt Francis who loved her so truly was a terrible sorrow to her; she found herself disliking him because she had to hurt him.

"You . . . to talk of wickedness . . . when you and I . . ."

He would have no misunderstanding about that.

"What we did, Catherine, is naught. Thou art my wife. Never forget it. Many people are married at an early age. We have done no wrong."

"You know we are not husband and wife!" she retorted. "It was a fiction to say we are; it was but to make it easy. We have sinned, and I cannot bear it, I wish we had never met."

Poor Derham was heartbroken. He had thought of no one else all the time he had been away. He begged her to remember how she had felt towards him before he went away. Then he heard the rumour of her proposed betrothal to Culpepper.

"This then," he said angrily, "is the reason for your change of heart. You are going to marry this Culpepper?"

She demanded what right he had to ask such a question, adding: "For you know I will not have you, and if you have heard such report, you heard more than I do know!"

They quarrelled then. She had deceived him, he said. How could she, in view of their contract, think of marrying another man? She must fly with him at once.

"Nay, nay!" cried Catherine, weeping bitterly. "Francis, please be reasonable. How could I fly with you? Dost not see it would mean death to you? I have hurt you and you have hurt me. The only hope for a good life for us both is never to see each other again."

Someone was calling her. She turned to him imploringly. "Go quickly. I dare not think what would happen to you were you found here."

"They could not hurt me, an they put me on the rack, as you have hurt me."

Such words pierced like knives into the soft heart of Catherine Howard. She could not be happy, knowing she had hurt him so deeply. Was there to be no peace for her, no happiness, because she had acted foolishly when she was but a child?

The serving maid who had called her told her her grandmother would speak to her at once. The Duchess was excited.

"I think, my dear, that you are to go to court. As soon as

the new queen arrives you will be one of her maids of honour. There! What do you think of that? We must see that you are well equipped. Fear not! You shall not disgrace us! And let me whisper a secret. While you are at court, you may get a chance to see Thomas Culpepper. Are you not excited?"

Catherine made a great effort to forget Francis Derham and think of the exciting life which was opening out before her. Court . . . and Thomas Culpepper.

Henry was on his way to Rochester to greet his new wife. He was greatly excited. Such a wise marriage this was! Ha! Charles! he thought. What do you think of this, eh? And you, Francis, who think yourself so clever? I doubt not, dear Emperor, that Guelders is going to be a thorn in your fleshy side for many a long day!

Anne! He could not help his memories. But this Anne would be different from that other. He thought of that exquisite miniature of Holbein's; the box it had arrived in was in the form of a white rose, so beautifully executed, that in itself it was a fine work of art; the carved ivory top of the box had to be unscrewed to show the miniature at the bottom of it. He had been joyful ever since the receipt of it. Oh, he would enjoy himself with this Anne, thinking, all the time he caressed her, not only of the delights of her body, but of sardonic Francis and that Charles who believed himself to be astute.

He had a splendid gift of sables for his bride. He was going to creep in on her unceremoniously. He would dismiss her attendants, for this would be the call of a lover rather than the visit of a king. He chuckled. It was so agreeable to be making the right sort of marriage. Cromwell was a clever fellow; his agents had reported that the beauty of Anne of Cleves exceeded that of Christina of Milan as the sun doth the moon!

Henry was fast approaching fifty, but he felt twenty, so eager he was, as eager as a bridegroom with his first wife. Anne was about twenty-four; it seemed delightfully young when one was fifty. She could not speak very much English; he could not speak much German. That would add piquancy to his courtship. Such a practised lover as himself did not need words to get what he wanted from a woman. He laughed in anticipation. Not since his marriage to Anne Boleyn, said those about him, had the King been in such high humour.

When he reached Rochester, accompanied by two of his attendants he went into Anne's chamber. At the door he paused in horror. The woman who curtseyed before him was not at all like the bride of his imaginings. It was the same face he had seen in the miniature, and it was not the same. Her forehead was wide and high, her eyes dark, her lashes thick, her eyebrows black and definitely marked; her black hair was parted in the centre and smoothed down at the sides of her face. Her dress was most unbecoming with its stiff, high collar resembling a man's coat. It was voluminous after the Flemish fashion and English fashions had been following the French ever since Anne Boleyn had introduced them at court. Henry started in dismay, for the face in the miniature had been delicately coloured so that the skin had the appearance of rose petals; in reality Anne's skin was brownish and most disfiguringly pockmarked. She seemed quite ugly to Henry, and as it did not occur to him that his person might have produced a similar shock to her, he was speechless with anger.

His one idea was to remove himself from her presence as quickly as possible; his little scheme, to "nourish love" as he had described it to Cromwell, had failed. He was too upset to give her the sables. She should have no such gift from his hands! He was mad with rage. His wise marriage had brought him a woman who delighted him not. Because her name was Anne, he had thought of another Anne, and his vision of his bride had been a blurred Anne Boleyn, as meek as Jane Seymour. And here he was, confronted by a creature whose accents jarred on him, whose face and figure repelled him. He had been misled. Holbein had misled him! Cromwell had misled him. Cromwell! He gnashed his teeth over that name. Yes, Cromwell had brought about this unhappy state of affairs. Cromwell had brought him Anne of Cleves.

"Alas!" he cried. "Whom shall men trust! I see no such thing as hath been shown me of her pictures and report. I am ashamed that men have praised her as they have done, and I love her not!"

But he was polite enough to Anne in public, so that the crowds of his subjects, to whom pageantry was the flavouring in their dull dish of life, did not guess that the King was anything but satisfied. Anne in her cloth of gold and rich jewellery seemed beautiful enough to them; they did not know that in private the King was berating Cromwell, likening his new bride to a great Flanders mare, that his conscience was asking him if the lady's contract with the Duke of Lorraine did not make a marriage between herself and the King illegal.

Poor Anne was deliberately delayed at Dartford whilst Henry tried to find some excuse for not continuing with the marriage. She was melancholy. The King had shown his dislike quite clearly; she had seen the great red face grow redder; she had seen the small eyes almost disappear into the puffy flesh; she had seen the quick distaste. She herself was disappointed, such accounts had she had of the once-handsomest prince in Christendom; and in reality he was a puffed out, unwieldy, fleshy man with great white hands overloaded with jewels, into whose dazzling garments two men could be wrapped with room to spare; on his face was the mark of internal disease; and bandages bulged about his leg; he had the wickedest mouth and cruellest eyes she had ever seen. She could but, waiting at Dartford, remember stories she had heard of this man. How had Katharine met her death? What had she suffered before she died? All the world knew the fate of tragic Anne Boleyn. And poor Jane Seymour? Was it true that after having given the King a son she had been so neglected that she had died?

She thought of the long and tiring journey from Dusseldorf

to Calais, and the Channel crossing to her new home; she thought of the journey to Rochester; until then she had been reasonably happy. Then she had seen him, and seeing him it was not difficult to believe there was a good deal of truth in the stories she had heard concerning his treatment of his wives. And now she was to be one of them, or perhaps she would not, for, having seen the distaste in his face, she could guess at the meaning of this delay. She did not know whether she hoped he would marry her or whether she would prefer to suffer the humiliation of being sent home because her person was displeasing to him.

Meanwhile Henry was flying into such rages that all who must come into contact with him went in fear for their lives. Was there a previous contract? He was sure there was! Should he endanger the safety of England by producing another bastard? His conscience, his most scrupulous conscience, would not allow him to put his head into a halter until he was sure.

It was Cromwell who must make him act reasonably, Cromwell who would get a cuff for his pains.

"Your Most Gracious Majesty, the Emperor is being feted in Paris. An you marry not this woman you throw the Duke of Cleves into an alliance with Charles and Francis. We should stand alone."

Cromwell was eloquent and convincing; after all he was pleading for Cromwell. If this marriage failed, Cromwell failed, and he knew his head to be resting very lightly on his shoulders, and that the King would be delighted to find a reason for striking it off. But Henry knew that in this matter, Cromwell spoke wisely. If Henry feared civil war more than anything, then next he feared friendship between Charles and Francis, and this was what had been accomplished. He dared not refuse to marry Anne of Cleves.

"If I had known so much before, she should not have come hither!" he said, looking menacingly at Cromwell, as though the meetings between Charles and Francis had been arranged by him. Henry's voice broke on a tearful note. "But what remedy now! What remedy but to put my head in the yoke and marry this . . ." His cheeks puffed with anger and his eyes were murderous. "What remedy but to marry this great Flanders mare!"

There followed the ceremony of marriage with its gorgeously apparelled men and women, its gilded barges and banners and streamers. Henry in a gown of cloth of gold raised with great silver flowers, with his coat of crimson satin decorated with great flashing diamonds, was a sullen bridegroom. Cromwell was terrified, for he knew not how this would end, and he had in his mind such examples of men who had displeased the King as would make a braver man than he was tremble. The Henry of ten years ago would never have entered into this marriage; but this Henry was more careful of his throne. He spoke truthfully when he had said a few hours before the ceremony that if it were not for the sake of his realm he would never have done this thing.

Cromwell did not give up hope. He knew the King well; it

might be that any wife was better than no wife at all; and there were less pleasant-looking females than Anne of Cleves. She was docile enough and the King liked docility in women; the last Queen had been married for that very quality.

The morning after the wedding day he sought audience with the King; he looked in vain for that expression of satiety in the King's coarse red face.

"Well?" roared Henry, and Cromwell noticed with fresh terror that his master liked him no better this day than he had done on the previous one.

"Your Most Gracious Majesty," murmured the trembling Cromwell, "I would know if you are any more pleased with your Queen."

"Nay, my lord!" said the King viciously, and glared at Cromwell, laying the blame for this catastrophe entirely upon him. "Much worse! For by her breasts and belly she should be no maid; which, when I felt them, strake me so to the heart that I had neither will nor courage to prove the rest."

Cromwell left his master, trembling for his future.

✳

Catherine Howard could not sleep for excitement. At last she had come to court. Her grandmother had provided her with garments she would need, and Catherine had never felt so affluent in the whole of her eighteen years. How exciting it was to peep through the windows at personages who had been mere names to her! She saw Thomas Cromwell walking through the courtyards, cap in hand, with the King himself. Catherine shuddered at the sight of that man. "Beware of the blacksmith's son!" her grandmother had said. "He is no friend of the Howards." Always before Catherine had seen the King from a great distance; closer he seemed larger, more sparkling than ever, and very terrifying, so that she felt a greater urge to run from him than she did even from Thomas Cromwell. The King was loud in conversation, laughter and wrath, and his red face in anger was an alarming sight. Sometimes he would hobble across the courtyards with a stick, and she had seen his face go dark with the pain he suffered in his leg, and he would shout and cuff anyone who annoyed him. His cheeks were so puffed out and swollen that his eyes seemed lost between them and his forehead, and were more like the flash of bright stones than eyes. This King made Catherine shiver. Cranmer she saw too—quiet and calm in his archbishop's robes. She saw her uncle and would have hidden herself, but his sharp eyes would pick her out and he would nod curtly.

Catherine was enjoying life, for Derham could not pester her at court as he had done at the Duchess's house, and when she did not see him she could almost forget the sorrow that had come to her through him. She loved the Queen, and wept for her because she was so unhappy. The King did not love her; he was with her only in public. The ladies whispered together that when they went to the royal bedchamber at night the

King said good night to the Queen and that nothing passed between them until the morning when he said good morning. They giggled over the extraordinary relationship of the King and Queen; and Catherine was too inexperienced and too much in awe of them not to giggle with them, but she was really sorry for the sad-eyed Queen. But Catherine did refrain from laughing with them over the overcrowded and tasteless wardrobe of the Queen.

"Ah!" whispered the ladies. "You should have seen the other Queen Anne. What clothes she had, and how she knew the way to wear them! But this one! No wonder the King has no fancy for her. Ja, ja, ja! That is all she can say!"

Catherine said: "But she is very kind."

"She is without spirit to be otherwise!"

But that was not true. Catherine, who had been often beaten by the hard-handed Duchess, was susceptible to kindness; she sat with the Queen and learned the Flemish style of embroidery, and was very happy to serve Anne of Cleves.

There was something else that made Catherine happy. Thomas Culpepper was at court. She had not yet seen him, but each day she hoped for their reunion. He was, she heard, a great favourite with the King himself and it was his duty to sleep in the royal apartment and superintend those who dressed the King's leg. She wondered if he knew she was here, and if he were waiting for the reunion as eagerly as she was.

Gardiner, the Bishop of Winchester, gave a banquet one evening. Catherine was very excited about this, for she was going to sing, and it would be the first time she had ever sung alone before the King.

"You are a little beauty!" said one of the ladies. "What a charming gown!"

"My grandmother gave it to me," said Catherine, smoothing the rich cloth with the pleasure of one who has always longed for beautiful clothes and has never before possessed them.

"If you sing as prettily as you look," she was told, "you will be a successful young woman."

Catherine danced all the way down to the barge; she sang as they went along the river; she danced into the Bishop's house. Over her small head smiles were exchanged; she was infectiously gay and very young.

"Mind you do not forget your words."

"Oh, what if I do! I feel sure I shall!"

"Committed to the Tower!" they teased her, and she laughed with them, her cheeks aglow, her auburn curls flying.

She sat at the great table with the humblest of the ladies. The King, at the head of the table, was in a noisy mood. He was eating and drinking with great heartiness as was his custom, congratulating the Bishop on his cook's efforts, swilling great quantities of wine, belching happily.

Would His Most Gracious Majesty care for a little music? the Bishop would know.

The King was ever ready to be entertained, and there was nothing he liked better, when he was full of good food and wine, than to hear a little music. He felt pleasantly sleepy; he smiled with benevolent eyes on Gardiner. A good servant, a good servant. He was in a mellow mood; he would have smiled on Cromwell.

He looked along the table. A little girl was singing. She had a pretty voice; her flushed cheeks reminded him of June roses, her hair gleamed gold; she was tiny and plump and very pretty. There was something in her which startled him out of his drowsiness. It was not that she was the least bit like Anne. Anne's hair had been black as had her eyes; Anne had been tall and slender. How could this little girl be like Anne? He did not know what could have suggested such a thought to him, and yet there it was . . . but elusive, so that he could not catch it, could not even define it. All he could say was that she reminded him. It was the tilt of her head, the gesture of the hands, that graceful back bent forward, and now the pretty head tossed back. He was excited, as for a long time he had wanted to be excited. He had not been so excited since the early days of marriage with Anne.

"Who is the girl now singing?" he asked Gardiner.

"That, Your Majesty, is Norfolk's niece Catherine Howard."

The King tapped his knee reflectively. Now he had it. Anne had been Norfolk's niece too. The elusive quality was explained by a family resemblance.

"Norfolk's niece!" he said, and growled without anger, so that the growl came through his pouched lips like a purr. He watched the girl. He thought, By God, the more I see of her the more I like her!

He was comparing her with his pockmarked Queen. Give him English beauties, sweet-faced and sweet-voiced. He liked sonorous English on the tongue, not harsh German. Like a rose she was, flushed, laughing and happy.

"She seems little more than a child," he said to Gardiner.

Norfolk was beside the King. Norfolk was cunning as a monkey, artful as a fox. He knew well how to interpret that soft look in the royal eyes; he knew the meaning of the slurring tones. Norfolk had been furious when the King had chosen Anne Boleyn instead of his own daughter the Lady Mary Howard. Every family wanted boys, but girls, when they were as pleasant to the eye as Anne Boleyn and Catherine Howard, had their uses.

"We liked well your little niece's playing," said the King.

Norfolk was beside the King. Norfolk murmured that His Majesty was gracious, and that it gave him the utmost delight that a member of his family should give some small pleasure to her sovereign.

"She gives us much pleasure," said the King. "We like her manners and we like her singing. Who is her father?"

"My brother Edmund, sir. Your Majesty doubtless remembers him. He did well at Flodden Field."

The King nodded. "I remember well," he said kindly. "A good servant!" He was ready to see through a haze of benevolence, every member of a family which could produce such a charming child as Catherine Howard.

"Doubtless Your Most Gracious Majesty would do my little niece the great honour of speaking to her. A royal compliment on her little talents would naturally mean more to the child than the costliest gems."

"Right gladly I will speak to her. Let her be brought to me."

"Your Majesty, I would humbly beg that you would be patient with her simplicity. She has led but a sheltered life until recently she came to court. I fear she may seem very shy and displease you with her gaucherie. She is perhaps too modest."

"Too modest!" the King all but shouted. "How is it possible, my lord, for maidens to be too modest!" He was all impatience to have her close to him, to study the fresh young skin, to pat her shoulders and let her know she had pleased her king. "Bring her to me without delay."

Norfolk himself went to Catherine. She stopped playing and looked at him in fear. He always terrified her, but now his eyes glittered speculatively and in the friendliest manner.

Catherine stood up. "Have I done aught wrong?"

"Nay, nay!" said his Grace. "Your singing has pleased His Majesty and he would tell you how much. Speak up when he talks to you. Do not mumble, for he finds that most irritating. Be modest but not shy."

The King was waiting impatiently. Catherine curtseyed low and a fat, white, jewelled hand patted her shoulder.

"Enough!" he said, not at all unkindly, and she rose and stood trembling before him.

He said: "We liked your singing. You have a pretty voice."

"Your Majesty is most gracious. . . ." she stammered and blushed sweetly. He watched the blood stain her delicate cheeks. By God, he thought, there never has been such a one since Anne. And his eyes filled with sudden self-pity to think how ill life had used him. He had loved Anne who had deceived him. He had loved Jane who had died. And now he was married to a great Flanders mare, when in his kingdom, standing before him so close that he had but to stretch out his hands and take her, was the fairest rose that ever grew in England.

"We are glad to be gracious to those who please us," he said. "You are lately come to court? Come! You may sit here . . . close to us."

"Yes, please Your Majesty. I . . . I have lately come . . ."

She was a bud just unfolding, he thought; she was the most perfect creature he had ever seen, for while Anne had been irresistible, she had also been haughty, vindictive and demanding, whereas this little Catherine Howard with her doe's eyes and gentle frightened manner, had the beauty of Anne and the docility of Jane. Ah, he thought, how happy I should have been, if instead of that Flemish creature I had found this lovely girl at Rochester. How I should have enjoyed presenting her with costly sables; jewels too; there is naught I would not give to such a lovely child.

He leaned towards her; his breath, not too sweet, warmed her cheek, and she withdrew involuntarily; he thought this but natural modesty and was enchanted with her.

"Your uncle has been talking to me of you."

Her uncle! She blushed again, feeling that the Duke would have said nothing good of her.

"He told me of your father. A good man, Lord Edmund. And your grandmother the Dowager Duchess is a friend of ours."

She was silent; she had not dreamed of such success; she had known her voice was moderately good, nothing more, certainly not good enough to attract the King.

"And how do you like the court?" he asked.

"I like it very much, please Your Majesty."

"Then I am right glad that our court pleases you!" He laughed and she laughed too. He saw her pretty teeth, her little white throat, and he felt a desire to make her laugh some more.

"Now we have discovered you," he said, "we shall make you sing to us often. How will you like that, eh?"

"I shall find it a great honour."

She looked as if she meant this; he liked her air of candid youth.

He said, "Your name is Catherine, I know. Tell me, how old are you?"

"I am eighteen, sir."

Eighteen! He repeated it, and felt sad. Eighteen, and he close to fifty. Getting old; short of breath; quick of temper; often dizzy; often after meals suffering from diverse disorders of the body; his leg getting worse instead of better; he could not sit his horse as once he had done. Fifty . . . and eighteen!

He watched her closely. "You shall play and sing to us again," he said.

He wanted to watch her without talking; his thoughts were busy. She was a precious jewel. She had everything he would look for in a wife; she had beauty, modesty, virtue and charm. It hurt him to look at her and see behind her the shadow of his Queen. He wanted Catherine Howard as urgently as once he had wanted Anne Boleyn. His hunger for Catherine was more pathetic than that he had known for Anne, for when he had loved Anne he had been a comparatively young man. Catherine was precious because she was a beacon to light the dark days of his middle age with her youthful glow.

Sweetly she sang. He wanted to stretch out his hands and pet her and keep her by him. This was cold age's need of warm youth. He thought, I would be a parent and a lover to her, for she is younger than my daughter Mary, and she is lovely enough to make any but the blind love her, and those she would enchant with her voice.

He watched her and she played again; then he would have her sit with him; nor did she stir from his side the evening through.

✦

A ripple of excitement went through the court.

"Didst see the King with Mistress Catherine Howard last night?"

"I declare I never saw His Majesty so taken with a girl since Anne Boleyn."

"Much good will it do her. His mistress? What else since he has a queen?"

"The King has a way with queens, has he not?"

"Hush! Dost want to go to the Tower on a charge of treason?"

"Poor Queen Anne, she is so dull, so German! And Catherine Howard is the prettiest thing we have had at court for many years!"

"Poor Catherine Howard!"

"Poor, forsooth!"

"Would you change places with her? Remember . . ."

"Hush! They were unfortunate!"

Cromwell very quickly grasped the new complications brought about by the King's infatuation for Catherine Howard, and it seemed to him that his end was in sight. Norfolk could be trusted to exploit this situation to the full. Catherine was a Catholic, a member of the most devout Catholic family in England. Continental events loomed up darkly for Cromwell. When the Emperor had passed through France there were signs that his friendship with Francis was not quite as cordial as it had been. Charles was no longer thinking of attacking England, and it was only when such plans interested him that he would be eager to take Francis as an ally. Trouble was springing up over Charles's domains and he would have his hands tied very satisfactorily from Henry's point of view if not from Cromwell's. When the Duke of Cleves asked for help in securing the Duchy of Guelders, Henry showed that he was in no mood to give it.

Cromwell saw the position clearly. He had made no mistakes. He had merely gambled and lost. When the marriage with Anne of Cleves had been made it was necessary to the safety of England; now England had passed out of that particular danger and the marriage was no longer necessary, and the King would assuredly seize an excuse to rid himself of his most hated minister. Cromwell had known this all the time. He could not play a good game if he had not the cards. With Charles and Francis friendly, he had stood a chance of winning; when relations between these two were strained, Cromwell was unlucky. On Cromwell's advice Henry had put a very irritating yoke about his neck. Now events had shown that it was no longer necessary that the yoke should remain. And there was Norfolk, making the most of Cromwell's ill luck, cultivating his niece, arranging meetings between her and the King, offering up the young girl as a sacrifice from the house of Howard on that already bloodstained altar of the King's lusts.

Henry's mind was working rapidly. He must have Catherine Howard. He was happy; he was in love. Catherine was the sweetest creature in the world, and there was none but Catherine who could keep him happy. She was delightful; she was sweetly modest; and the more he knew her, the more she delighted him. Just to see her skipping about the Hampton Court gardens which he had planned with her cousin Anne, made him feel younger. She would be the perfect wife; he did not want her to be his mistress—she was too sweet and pure for that—he wanted her beside him on the throne, that he might live out his life with none other but her.

She was less shy with him now; she was full of laughter, but ready to weep for other people's sorrows. Sweet Catherine! The sweetest of women! The rose without a thorn! Anne had perhaps been the most gorgeous rose that ever bloomed, but oh, the thorns! In his old age this sweet creature should be beside him. And he was not so old! He could laugh throatily, holding her hand in his, pressing the cool, plump fingers against his thigh. He was not so old. He had years of pleasant living in front of him. He did not want riotous living, he told himself. All he had ever wanted was married happiness with one woman, and he had not found her until now. He must marry Catherine; he must make her his queen.

His conscience began to worry him. He realized that Anne's contract with the Duke of Lorraine had ever been on his mind, and it was for this reason that he had never consummated the marriage. So cursed had he been in his matrimonial undertakings, that he went cautiously. He had never been Anne's true husband because of his dread of presenting another bastard to the nation. Moreover the lady was distasteful to him and he suspected her virtue. Oh, he had said naught about it at the time, being over-merciful perhaps, being anxious not to accuse before he was sure. He had not been free when he entered into the marriage; only because he had felt England to be defenceless against the union of Charles and Francis had he allowed it to take place. England owed him a divorce, for had he not entered into this most unwelcome engagement for England's sake? And he owed England children. He had one boy and two girls—both of these last illegitimate; and the boy did not enjoy the best of health. He had failed to make the throne secure for Tudors; he must have an opportunity of doing so. Something must be done.

✦

The Dowager Duchess of Norfolk could scarcely believe her ears when she heard the news. The King and her granddaughter! What a wonderful day this was to bring her such news!

She would bring out her most costly jewels. "If Catherine could attract him in those simple things," she babbled, "how much more so will she when I have dressed her!"

For once she and the Duke were in agreement. He visited her, and the visit was the most amiable they had ever shared. The Dowager Duchess had never thought she and the Duke would one day put their heads together over the hatching of a plot. But when the Duke had gone, the Duchess was overcome with fears, for it seemed to her that another granddaughter looked at her from out of the dark shadows of her room and would remind her of her own tragic fate. How beautiful and proud that Queen Anne had been on the day of her coronation! Never would the Duchess be able to forget the sight of her entering the Tower to be received by her royal lover. And then, only three years later. . . .

The Duchess called for lights. "I declare the gloom of this

656

house displeases me. Light up! Light up! What are you wenches thinking of to leave me in the dark!"

She felt easier when the room was lighted. It was stupid to imagine for a moment that the dead could return. "She cannot die for what was done before," she muttered to herself; and she set about sorting out her most valuable jewels—some for Catherine in which to enchant the King; and some for herself when she should go to another coronation of yet another granddaughter.

*

The Earl of Essex, who had been such a short time before plain Thomas Cromwell, was awaiting death. He knew it was inevitable. He had been calculating and unscrupulous; he had been devilishly cruel; he had tortured men's bodies and sacrificed their flesh to the flames; he had dissolved the monasteries, inflicting great hardship on their inmates, and he had invented crimes for these people to have committed, to justify his actions; with Sampson, Bishop of Chichester, he had worked out a case against Anne Boleyn, and had brought about her death through the only man who would talk against her, a poor, delicate musician who had had to be violently tortured first; all these crimes—and many others—had he committed, but they had all been done at the command of his master. They were not Cromwell's crimes; they were Henry's crimes.

657

And now he awaited the fate which he had so many times prepared for others. It was ten years since the death of Wolsey, and they had been ten years of mounting power for Cromwell; and now here was the inevitable end. The King had rid himself of Wolsey—for whom he had had some affection—because of Anne Boleyn; now he would rid himself of Cromwell—whom, though he did not love him, he knew to be a faithful servant— for Catherine Howard. For though this young girl, whom the King would make his queen, bore no malice to any, and would never ask to see even an enemy punished but rather beg that he should be forgiven, yet was it through her that Cromwell was falling; for cruel Norfolk and Gardiner had risen to fresh power since the King had shown his preference for Norfolk's niece, and these two men, who represented Catholicism in all its old forms, would naturally wish to destroy one who, with staunch supporters like Thomas Wyatt, stood more strongly for the new religion than he would dare admit. Whilst he was despoiling the monasteries, he had been safe, and knowing this he had left one very wealthy institution untouched, so that in an emergency he might dangle its treasure before the King's eyes and so earn a little respite. This he had done, and in throwing in this last prize he had earned the title of Earl of Essex.

It was a brief triumph, for Cromwell's position was distressingly similar to that in which Wolsey had found himself. Had not Wolsey flung his own treasure to the King in a futile effort to save himself? Hampton Court and York House; his houses and plate and art treasures. Cromwell, as Wolsey before him, if it would please the King, must rid his master of a wife whom he, Cromwell, supported; but if he succeeded in doing this, he would put on the throne a member of the Howard family who had sworn to effect his destruction.

When the King realized that Cromwell was hesitating to choose between two evils, since he could not be certain as to which was the lesser, he lost patience, and declared that Cromwell had been working against his aims for a settlement of the religious problem, and this was, without a doubt, treason.

Now, awaiting his end, he recalled that gusty day when, as he travelled with the members of the privy council to the palace, a wind had blown his bonnet from his head. How significant had it been when they, discourteously, did not remove their bonnets, but had kept them on whilst he stood bare-headed! And their glances had been both eager and furtive. And then later he had come upon them sitting round the council chamber, talking together, insolently showing him that they would not wait for his coming; and as he would have sat down with them, Norfolk's voice had rung out, triumphant, the voice of a man who at last knows an old enemy is defeated. "Cromwell! Traitors do not sit with gentlemen!"

He had been arrested then and taken to the Tower. He smiled bitterly, imagining the King's agents making inventories of his treasures. How often had he been sent to do a similar errand in the King's name! He had gambled and lost; there was a small grain of comfort in the knowledge that it was not due to lack of skill, but ill luck which had brought about his end.

A messenger was announced; he came from the King. Cromwell's hopes soared. He had served the King well; surely His Majesty could not desert him now. Perhaps he could still be useful to the King. Yes! It seemed he could. The King needed Cromwell to effect his release from the marriage into which he had led him. Cromwell must do as he was bid. The reward? The King was ever generous, ever merciful, and Cromwell should be rewarded when he had freed the King. Cromwell was a traitor and there were two deaths accorded to traitors. One was the honourable and easy death by the axe. The other? Cromwell knew better than most. How many poor wretches had he condemned to die that way? The victim was hanged but not killed; he was disembowelled and his entrails were burned while the utmost care was taken to keep him alive; only then was he beheaded. This should be Cromwell's reward for his last service to his master: In his gracious mercy, the most Christian king would let him choose which way he would die.

Cromwell made his choice. He would never fail to serve the King.

Anne had been sent to Richmond. It was significant that the King did not accompany her. She was terrified. This had happened before, with another poor lady in the role she now must play. What next? she wondered. She was alone in a strange land, among people whose language she could not speak, and she felt that death was very close to her. Her brother the Duke of Cleves was far away and he was but insignificant compared with this great personage who was her husband, and who thought little of murder and practiced it as lightly as some people eat, drink and sleep.

She had endured such mental anguish since her marriage that she felt limp and unequal to the struggle she would doubtless have to put up for her life. Her nights were sleepless; her days were so full of terror that a tap on a door would set her shivering as though she suffered from some ague.

She had been Queen of England for but a few months and she felt as though she had lived through years of torment. Her husband made no attempt to hide his distaste for her. She was surrounded by attendants who mimicked her because they were encouraged in this unkindness by the King, who was ready to do any cruel act to discredit her, and who found great satisfaction in hurting her—and inspiring others to hurt her—as he declared her unpleasant appearance hurt him. The Lady Rochford, one of her ladies, who had been the wife of another queen's late brother, was an unpleasant creature, who listened at doors and spied upon her, and reported all that she said to the other ladies and tittered unkindly about her; they laughed at her clothes, which she was ready to admit were not as graceful as those worn in England. The King was hinting that she had led an immoral life before she came to England; this was so unjust and untrue that it distressed her more than anything else she had been called upon to endure, because she really believed Henry did doubt her virtue. She did not know him well enough to realize that this was characteristic of him, and that he accused others of his own failings because he drew moral strength from this attitude and deceived himself into thinking that he could not be guilty of that which he condemned fiercely in others. So poor Queen Anne was a most unhappy woman.

There was one little girl recently come to court, whom she could have loved; and how ironical it was that this child's beauty and charm should have increased the King's animosity towards herself. The King would rid himself of me, she thought, to put poor little Catherine Howard on the throne. This he may well do, and how I pity that poor child, for when I am removed, she will stand in my most unhappy shoes!

As she sat in the window seat a message was brought to her that the lords Suffolk and Southampton with Sir Thomas Wriothesley were without, and would speak with her.

The room began to swing round her. She clutched at the scarlet hangings to steady herself. She felt the blood drain away from her head. It had come. Her doom was upon her!

When Suffolk with Southampton and Wriothesley entered the room they found the Queen lying on the floor in a faint. They roused her and helped her to a chair. She opened her eyes and saw Suffolk's florid face close to her own, and all but fainted again; but that nobleman began to talk to her in soothing tones and his words were reassuring.

What he said seemed to Anne the happiest news she had ever heard in her life. The King, out of his regard for her—which meant his regard for the house of Cleves, but what did that matter!—wished to adopt her as his sister, providing she would resign her title of Queen. The King wished her no ill, but she well knew that she had never been truly married to His Majesty because of that previous contract with the Duke of Lorraine. This was why His Most Cautious Majesty had never consummated the marriage. All she need do was to behave in a reasonable manner, and she should have precedence at court over every lady, excepting only the King's daughters and her who would become his queen. The English taxpayers would provide her with an income of three thousand pounds a year.

The King's sister! Three thousand pounds a year! This was miraculous! This was happiness! That corpulent, perspiring, sullen, angry, spiteful, wicked monster of a man was no longer her husband! She need not live close to him! She could have her own establishment! She need not return to her own dull country, but she could live in this beautiful land which she had already begun to love in spite of its King! She was free.

She almost swooned again, for the reaction of complete joy after absolute misery was overwhelming.

Suffolk and Southampton exchanged glances with Wriothesley. The King need not have been so generous with his three thousand pounds. It had not occurred to him that Anne would be so eager to be rid of him. They would keep that from the

King; better to let His August Majesty believe that their tact had persuaded the woman it would be well to accept.

Anne bade her visitors a gay farewell. Never had Henry succeeded in making one of his wives so happy.

Catherine was bewildered. Quite suddenly her position had changed. Instead of being the humblest newcomer, she was the most important person at court. Everyone paid deference to her; even her grim old uncle had a pleasant word for her, so that Catherine felt she had misjudged him. The Dowager Duchess, her grandmother, would deck her out in the most costly jewels, but these were poor indeed compared with those which came from the King. He called her "The Rose without a Thorn"; and this he had had inscribed on some of the jewels he had given her. He had chosen her device, which was "No other Will but His."

Catherine was sorry for the poor Queen, and could not bear to think that she was displacing her; but when she heard that Anne appeared to be happier at Richmond than she had ever been at court, she began to enjoy her new power.

Gifts were sent to her, not only from the King, but from the courtiers. Her grandmother petted, scolded and warned at the same time. "Be careful! No word of what has happened with Derham must ever reach the King's ears."

"I would prefer to tell him all," said Catherine uneasily.

"I never heard such folly!" Her Grace's black eyes glinted. "Do you know where Derham is?" she asked. And Catherine assured her that she did not know.

"That is well," said the Duchess. "I and Lord William have spoken to the King of your virtues and how you will make a most gracious and gentle queen."

"But shall I?" asked Catherine.

"Indeed you shall. Now, no folly. Come let me try this ruby ring on your finger. I would have you know that the King, while liking well our talk, would have been most displeased with us had we done aught but sing your praises. Oh, what it is to be loved by a king! Catherine Howard, I declare you give yourself graces already!"

Catherine had thought that she would be terrified of the King, but this was not so. There was nothing for her to fear in this great soft man. His voice changed when he addressed her, and his hard mouth could express nothing but kindness for her. He would hold her hand and stroke her cheek and twine her hair about his fingers; and sometimes press his lips against the flesh on her plump shoulders. He told her that she would mean a good deal to him, that he wished above all things to make her his queen, that he had been a most unhappy man until he had set eyes on her. Catherine looked in wonder at the little tear-filled eyes. Was this the man who had sent her beautiful cousin to her death? How could simple Catherine believe ill of him when she stood before him and saw real tears in his eyes?

He talked of Anne, for he saw that Anne was in Catherine's

thoughts; she was, after all, her own cousin, and the two had known and been fond of one another.

"Come and sit upon my knee, Catherine," he said, and she sat there while he pressed her body against his and talked of Anne Boleyn. "Wert deceived as I was by all that charm and beauty, eh? Ah! But thou wert but a child and I am man. Didst know that she sought to take my life and poison my daughter Mary? Dost know that my son died through a spell she cast upon him?"

"It is hard to believe that. She was so kind to me. I have a jewelled tablet she gave me when I was but a baby."

"Sweet Catherine, I too had gifts from her. I too could not believe . . ."

It was easier for Catherine to believe the King who was close to her, when Anne was but a memory.

It was at this time that she met Thomas Culpepper. He was one of the gentlemen of the privy chamber, and had great charm of manner and personal beauty which had pleased the King ever since he had set eyes upon him. Thomas's intimate duties of superintending the carrying out of the doctor's orders regarding the King's leg kept him close to Henry, who had favoured him considerably, and had given him several posts which, while they brought little work, brought good remuneration; he had even given him an abbey. He liked Culpepper; he was amused by Culpepper. In his native Kent, the boy had involved himself in a certain amount of scandal, for it seemed he was wild and not over-scrupulous, but the King was as ready to forgive the faults of those he wished to keep around him, as he was to find fault with those he wished removed.

The knowledge that his cousin was at court soon reached Thomas Culpepper, for since her elevation, everyone was discussing Catherine Howard. Seeing her in the pond garden one afternoon, he went out to her. She was standing by a rose tree, the sun shining on her auburn hair. Thomas immediately understood the King's infatuation.

"You would not remember me," he said. "I am your cousin Thomas Culpepper."

Her eyes opened very wide and she gave a little trill of pleasure; she held out both her hands.

"Thomas! I had hoped to see you."

They stood holding hands; studying each other's faces.

How handsome he is! thought Catherine. Even more handsome than he was as a boy!

How charming she is! thought Thomas. How lovable—and in view of what has happened to her during the last weeks, how dangerously lovable! But to Thomas nothing was ever very interesting unless it held an element of danger.

He said, greatly daring: "How beautiful you have grown, Catherine!"

She laughed delightedly. "That is what everyone says to me now! Do you remember the stick you gave me with which to tap on the wall?"

They were laughing over their memories.

"And the adventures you used to have . . . and how we used to ride in the paddock . . . and how you . . ."

"Said I would marry you!"

"You did, you know, Thomas, and then you never did anything about it!"

"I never forgot!" he lied. "But now . . ." He looked across the garden and over the hedge to the windows of the palace. Even now, he thought, little hot, jealous eyes might have caught sight of him. Living close to the King he knew something of his rages. Dangerously sweet was this contact with Catherine.

"It is too late now," she said soberly, and she looked very sad. She saw Thomas as the lover to whom she had been betrothed for many years; she forgot Manox and Derham and believed that she had loved Thomas always.

"Suppose that we had married when it was suggested a year or so ago," said Thomas.

"How different our lives would have been then!"

"And now," he said, "I risk my life to speak to you."

Her eyes widened with terror. "Then we must not stay here." She laughed suddenly. They did not know the King, these people who were afraid of him. His Majesty was all kindness, all eagerness to make people happy really. As if he would hurt her cousin if she asked him not to!

"Catherine," said Thomas, "I shall risk my life again and again. It will be worth it."

He took her hand and kissed it, and left her in the pond garden.

They could not resist meeting secretly. They met in dark corridors; they feared that if it reached the ears of the King that they were meeting thus, there would be no more such meetings. Sometimes he touched her fingers with his, but nothing more; and after the first few meetings they were in love with each other.

There was a similarity in their natures; both were passionate, reckless people; they were first cousins and they knew now that they wished to enjoy a closer relationship; and because, when they had been children, they had plighted their troth in the paddock of Hollingbourne, they felt life had been cruel to them to keep them apart and bring them together only when it was too late for them to be lovers.

Catherine had little fear for herself, but she feared for him. He, a reckless adventurer who had been involved in more than one dangerous escape, was afraid not for himself but for her.

They would touch hands and cry out to each other: "Oh, why, oh, why did it have to happen thus!"

She would say to him, "I shall be passing along the corridor that leads to the music room at three of the clock this afternoon."

He would answer: "I will be there as if by accident."

All their meetings were like that. They would long for them all day, and then when they reached the appointed spot, it might be that someone was there, and it was impossible for them to exchange more than a glance. But to them both this danger was very stimulating.

There was one occasion when he, grown more reckless by the passing of several days which did not bring even a glimpse of her, drew her from the corridor into an antechamber and shut the door on them.

"Catherine," he said, "I can endure this no longer. Dost not realize that thou and I were meant one for the other from the first night I climbed into thy chamber? We were but children then, and the years have been cruel to us, but I have a plan. Thou and I will leave the palace together. We will hide ourselves and we will marry."

She was pale with longing, ever ready to abandon herself to the passion of the moment, but it seemed to her that she heard her cousin's voice warning her. Catherine would never know the true story of Anne Boleyn, but she had loved her and she knew her end had been terrible. Anne had been loved by the same huge man; those eyes had burned hotly for Anne; those warm, moist hands had caressed her. Anne had had no sad story of a cousin to warn her.

Culpepper was kissing her hands and her lips, Catherine's healthy young body was suggesting surrender. Perhaps with Manox or Derham she would have surrendered; but not with Culpepper. She was no longer a lighthearted girl. Dark shadows came pursuing her out of the past. Doll Tappit's high voice. "The cries of the torture chambers are terrible. . . ."

Catherine knew how the monks of the Charterhouse had died; she could not bear to think of others suffering pain, but to contemplate one she loved being vilely hurt was sufficient to stem her desire. She remembered how Derham had run for his life; but then she had been plain Catherine Howard. What of him who dared to love her whom the King had chosen for his queen!

"Nay, nay!" she cried, tears falling from her eyes. "It cannot be! Oh, that it could! I would give all my life for one year of happiness with you. But I dare not. I fear the King. I must stay here because I love you."

She tore herself away; there must be no more such meetings.

"Tomorrow . . ." she agreed weakly. "Tomorrow."

She ran to her apartment, where, since Anne had left for Richmond, she enjoyed the state of a queen. She was greeted by one of her attendants, Jane Rochford, widow of her late cousin George Boleyn. Lady Rochford looked excited. There was a letter for Catherine, she said.

"A letter?" cried Catherine. "From whom?"

Catherine did not receive many letters; she took this one and opened it; she frowned for she had never been able to read very easily.

Jane Rochford was at her side.

"Mayhap I could assist?"

Jane had been very eager to ingratiate herself with Catherine; she had not liked the last queen; Jane had decided to adhere to the Catholic cause and support Catherine Howard against Anne of Cleves.

Catherine handed her the letter.

"It is from a Jane Bulmer," said Jane, "and it comes from York."

"I remember. It is from Jane Acworth who went to York to marry Mr. Bulmer. Tell me what she says."

Jane Bulmer's letter was carefully worded. She wished Catherine all honour, wealth and good fortune. Her motive in writing was to ask a favour of Catherine, and this was that she should be found a place at court. Jane was unhappy in the country; she was desolate. A command from the future queen to Jane's husband to bring his wife to court would make Jane Bulmer very happy, and she begged for Catherine's help.

The threat was in the last sentence.

"I know the Queen of Britain will not forget her secretary. . . ."

Her secretary! Jane Bulmer it was who had written those revealing, those intimate and passionate letters to Derham; Jane Bulmer knew everything that had happened.

Catherine sat very still as Jane Rochford read to her; her face was rosy with shame.

Jane Rochford was not one to let such signs pass unnoticed. She, as well as Catherine, read into those words a hint of blackmail.

On a hot July day Cromwell made the journey from the Tower to Tyburn. Tyburn it was because it was not forgotten that he was a man of lowly origins; he could smile at this, though a short while ago it would have angered him; but what does a man care when his head is to be cut off, whether it be done at Tower Hill or Tyburn?

He had obeyed his master to the last; he had been more than the King's servant; he had been the King's slave. But to his cry for mercy, had his most gracious prince been deaf. He had done with Cromwell. He had not allowed Cromwell to speak in his own defence. Cromwell's fall would help to bring back Henry's popularity, for the people of England hated Cromwell.

His friends? Where were they? Cranmer? He could laugh at the thought of Cranmer's being his friend. Only a fool would expect loyalty in the face of danger from weak-kneed Cranmer. He knew that the Archbishop had declared himself smitten with grief; he had told the King that he had loved Cromwell, and the more for the love he had believed him to bear His Grace the King; he had added that although he was glad Cromwell's treason was discovered, he was very sorrowful, for whom should the King trust in future?

He had said almost the same words when Anne Boleyn had been taken to the Tower. Poor Cranmer! How fearful he was. He must have faced death a thousand times in his imagination. There was never a man quicker to dissociate himself from a fallen friend!

Crowds had gathered to see Cromwell's last moments. He recognized many enemies. He thought of Wolsey, who would have faced this, had he lived long enough. He had walked in the shadow of Wolsey, had profited by his example, by his brilliance and his mistakes; he had followed the road to power and had found it led to Tyburn.

There was one in the crowd who shed a tear for him. It was Thomas Wyatt, who had been as eager as Cromwell himself that the Lutheran doctrines should be more widely understood. Their eyes met. Cromwell knew that Wyatt was trying to reassure him, to tell him that cruelties he had inflicted on so many had been done at Henry's command and that Cromwell was not entirely responsible for them. This young man did not know of the part Cromwell had played in the destruction of Anne Boleyn. Cromwell hoped then that he never would. His heart warmed to Wyatt.

"Weep not, Wyatt," he said, "for if I were not more guilty than thou wert when they took thee, I should not be in this pass."

It was time for him to make his last speech, to lay his head upon the block. He thought of all the blood he had caused to be shed, and tried to pray, but he could think of nothing but blood, and the scream of men in agony and the creaking of the rack.

Onto his thick neck, the axe descended; his head rolled away from his body as four years before had Anne Boleyn's.

The King was enchanted with his bride. In the great hall at Hampton Court, he proclaimed her Queen. None had known the King in such humour for years; he was rejuvenated.

A few days after the proclamation, he took her from Hampton Court to Windsor, and astonished everyone by cutting himself off from the court that he might enjoy the company of his bride in private. Catherine seemed doubly pleasing in the King's eyes, coming after Anne of Cleves; she was gentle yet ever ready to laugh; she had no disconcerting wit to confound him; her conversation held not a trace of cleverness, only kindness. She was a passionate creature, a little afraid of him, but not too much so; she was responsive and womanly; and never had the King felt such drowsy and delicious peace. If she had a fault it was her generosity, her kindness to others. She would give away her clothes and jewels, explaining, her head a little on one side, her dewy lips parted, "But it becomes her so, and she had so little. . . ." Or, "She is poor, if we could but do something for her, how happy I should be!" She was irresistible and he could not bring himself to reprimand her for this over-lavishness; he liked it; for he too came in for his share of her generosity. He would kiss her and stroke her and tickle her; and have her shrieking with laughter. Never had he dreamed of such blessedness.

Anne of Cleves was ordered to come to court to pay homage to the new Queen. There was a good deal of speculation in the court as to how the displaced queen would feel when kneeling to one who had but a short time ago been her maid of honour. It was expected that Catherine would demand great homage from Anne of Cleves to prove to herself and to the court that she was safely seated on the throne and had command of the

675

King's affection. But when Anne came and knelt before the new Queen, Catherine impulsively declared that there should be no ceremony.

"You must not kneel to me!" she cried, and the two queens embraced each other with tears of affection in their eyes, and it was Anne of Cleves who was moved to pity, not Catherine Howard.

Catherine would do honour to her cousin's daughter, Elizabeth, partly because she was her cousin's daughter, and partly because, of all her stepchildren, she loved Elizabeth best.

Mary was disposed to be friendly, but only because Catherine came from a family which adhered to the old Catholic faith, and Mary's friendship for people depended entirely on whether or not they were what she called true Catholics. Mary was six years older than her father's wife, and she thought the girl over-frivolous. Catherine accepted Mary's disapproval of her at first because she knew the Princess had suffered so much, but eventually she was goaded into complaining that Mary showed her little respect; she added that if only Mary would remember that although she was young she was the Queen, she would be ready to be friendly. This resulted in a sharp reprimand to Mary from the King; but friendship was not made that way, and how could poor, plain, frustrated Mary help feeling certain twinges of jealousy for sparkling Catherine whose influence over the King appeared to be unlimited. Mary was more Spanish than English; she would often sink into deepest melancholy; she would spend hours on her knees in devotion, brooding on her mother's dreary tragedy and the break with Rome; preferring to do this rather than sing and dance and be gay. On her knees she would pray that the King might come back to the true faith in all its old forms, that he might follow the example of her mother's country and earn the approval of heaven by setting up an Inquisition in this careless island and torturing and burning all those who deserved such a fate, since they were heretics. How could soft-hearted, frivolous Catherine ever bring the King to take this duty upon himself! No, there could be no real friendship between Catherine and Mary.

Little Edward was not quite two years old; pale of face; solemn-eyed, he was watched over by his devoted nurse, Mrs. Sibell Penn, who was terrified that some cold breath of air might touch him and end his frail life.

Of course it was Elizabeth whom Catherine must love most, for the child already had a look of Anne, for all that she had inherited her father's colouring. She would have Elizabeth at the table with them, occupying the place of honour next to Mary. She begged privileges for Elizabeth.

"Ah!" said Henry indulgently. "It would seem that England has a new ruler, and that Queen Catherine!"

"Nay!" she replied. "For how could I, who am young and foolish, rule this great country? That is for one who is strong and clever to do."

He could not show his love sufficiently. "Do what thou wilt, sweetheart," he said, "for well thou knowest, I have heart to refuse thee naught."

He liked to watch them together—his favourite child and his beloved queen. Seeing them thus, he would feel a deep contentment creep into his mind. Anne's child is happy with my new queen, he would tell himself; and because it would seem to him that there might be a plea for forgiveness in that thought, he would hastily assure himself that there was nothing for Anne to forgive.

He and Catherine rode together in the park at Windsor. He had never wandered about so unattended before; and he enjoyed to the full each day he shared with this lovely laughing girl. It was pleasant to throw off the cares of kingship and be a lover. He wished he were not so weighty, though he never could abide lean men; still, to puff and pant when you were the lover of a sprightly young girl was in itself a sad state of affairs. But Catherine feigned not to notice the puffing and looked to it that he need not exert himself too much in his pursuit of her. She was perfect; his rose without a single thorn.

He was almost glad that the low state of the treasury would not allow for ceremony just at this time, for this enabled him to enjoy peace with his young bride.

They made a happy little journey from Windsor to Grafton where they stayed until September, and it was while they were at Grafton that an alarming incident took place.

Cranmer noted and decided to make the utmost use of it, although, knowing the amorous nature of the King, he could hope for little from it yet. Cranmer was uneasy, and had been since the arrest of Cromwell, for they had walked too long side by side for the liquidation of one not to frighten the other seriously. Norfolk was in the ascendant, and he and Cranmer were bitterly engaged in the silent, subtle warring of two opposing religious sects. Such as Catherine Howard were but counters to be moved this way and that by either side; and the fight was fierce and deadly. Cranmer, though a man of considerable intellectual power, was at heart a coward. His great aim was to keep his head from the block and his feet from the stake. He could not forget that he had lost his ally Cromwell and had to play this wily Norfolk single-handed. Cranmer was as determined to get Catherine Howard off the throne as the Catholics had been to destroy Anne Boleyn. At this time, he bowed before the new Queen; he flattered her; he talked of her in delight to the King, murmuring that he trusted His Majesty had now the wife his great goodness deserved. And now, with this incident coming to light and the marriage not a month old, Cranmer prayed that he might be able to make the utmost use of it and bring Catherine Howard to ruin and so serve God in the way He most assuredly preferred to be served.

It had begun with a few words spoken by a priest at Windsor. He had talked slightingly of the Queen, saying that he had been told once, when she was quite a child, she had led a most immoral life. This priest was immediately taken prisoner and put into the keep of Windsor Castle, while Wriothesley, at the bidding of the council, was sent to lay these matters before the King.

Catherine was in a little antechamber when this man arrived; she heard the King greet him loudly.

"What news?" cried Henry. "By God! You look glum enough!"

"Bad news, Your Majesty, and news it grieves me greatly to bring to Your Grace."

"Speak up! Speak up!" said the King testily.

"I would ask Your Majesty to be patient with me, for this concerns Her Majesty the Queen."

"The Queen!" Henry's voice was a roar of fear. The sly manner and the feigned sorrow in the eyes of the visitor were familiar to him. He could not bear that anything should happen to disturb this love idyll he shared with Catherine.

"The dribblings of a dotard doubtless," said Wriothesley. "But the council felt it their duty to warn Your Majesty. A certain priest at Windsor has said that which was unbefitting concerning the Queen."

Catherine clutched the hangings, and felt as though she were about to faint. She thought, I ought to have told him. Then he would not have married me. Then I might have married Thomas. What will become of me? What will become of me now?

"What's this? What's this?" growled the King.

"The foolish priest—doubtless a maniac—referred to the laxity of Her Majesty's behaviour when she was in the Dowager Duchess's care at Lambeth."

The King looked at Wriothesley in such a manner as to make that ambitious young man shudder. The King was thinking that if Catherine had been a saucy wench before he had set eyes on her, he was ready to forget it. He wanted no disturbance of this paradise. She was charming and good-tempered, a constant delight, a lovely companion, a most agreeable bed-fellow; she was his fifth wife, and his fourth had robbed him of any desire to make a hasty change. He wanted Catherine as he had made her appear to himself. Woe betide any who tried to destroy that illusion!

"Look ye here!" he said sternly. "I should have thought you would have known better than to trouble me with any fool-ish tale of a drunken priest. You say this priest but repeated what he had heard. You did right to imprison him. Release him now, and warn him. Tell him what becomes of men who speak against the King . . . and by God, those who speak against the Queen speak against the King! Tongues have been ripped out for less. Tell him that, Wriothesley, tell him that. As for him who spoke these evil lies to the priest, let him be confined until I order his release."

Wriothesley was glad to escape.

Catherine, trembling violently, thought: I must speak to my grandmother. I must explain to the King.

She half expected the King to order her immediate arrest, and that she would be taken to the Tower and have to lay her head on the block as her cousin had done. She was hysteri-cal when she ran out to the King; she was flushed with fear; impulsively she threw her arms about his neck and kissed him.

He pressed her close to him. He might still be doubtful, but he was not going to lose this. By God, he thought, if anyone says a word against my queen, he shall pay for it!

"Why, sweetheart?" he said, and turned her face to his, determined to read there what he wished to read. Such innocence! By God, those who talked against her deserved to have their heads on London Bridge—and should too! She was pure and innocent, just as Lord William and her grandmother had assured him. He was lucky—even though he were a king—to have such a jewel of womanhood.

The happy honeymoon continued.

The Dowager Duchess was closeted with the Queen.

"I declare," said Catherine, "I was greatly affrighted. I heard every word, and I trembled so that I scarce dared go out to the King when the man had gone!"

"And the King, said he naught to you?"

"He said naught."

"He has decided to ignore this, depend upon it."

"I feel so miserable. I would prefer to tell him. You understand, with Derham, it was as though we were married . . ."

"Hush! Do not say such things. I am an old woman and an experienced one; you are young and unwise. Take my advice."

"I will," said Catherine. "Of course I will. It was yours I took when I did not tell the King before my marriage."

"Pish!" said the Duchess, and then dropping her voice to a whisper: "I have heard from Derham."

"From Derham!"

"I said from Derham. He is back in my house. He is such a charming boy and I could not find it in my heart to keep up my anger against him. He still speaks of you with indiscreet devotion, and he has asked for something which I cannot advise you to refuse him. He says that he must see you now and then, that you have nothing to fear from him. He loves you too well to harm you."

"What does he ask?"

"A place at court!"

"Oh, no!"

"Indeed yes; and I feel that you would be very unwise to refuse it. Do not look so frightened. Remember you are the Queen."

Catherine said slowly: "I have Jane Bulmer here and Katharine Tylney as well as Margaret Morton. I would that I had refused them."

"Refuse them! You speak without thought. Have you forgotten that these people were at Lambeth and actually witnessed what took place between you and Derham!"

"I had rather they were not here. They are inclined to insolence as though they know I dare not dismiss them."

She did not tell the Duchess that Manox approached her too, that he had demanded a place at court. There was no need to disturb the Duchess further, and tell her that Manox, now one of the court musicians, had once been Catherine's lover.

"Now," said the Duchess, "you must listen to me. Derham must come to court. You cannot refuse him."

"I see that you are right," said Catherine wearily.

So came Derham.

⋅✦⋅

The King's delight in his Queen did not diminish with the passing of the months. They left Ampthill for More Park where they could enjoy an even more secluded life; Henry was impatient with any minister who dared disturb him, and gave special instructions that no one was to approach him; any matter which was urgent was to be set out in writing. He was happy, desperately warming himself by the fire of Catherine's youth; he doted on her; he caressed her even in public, declaring that at last he had found conjugal happiness. He felt this to be a reward for a life of piety. There was one further blessing he asked, and that was children. So far, there was little success, but what matter? Catherine in herself was as much as any man could reasonably ask.

She was such a soft-hearted little thing and could bear to hurt no one. She hated to hear of the executions which were taking place every day; she would put her plump little fingers into her ears, and he would pet her and murmur, "There, there, sweetheart, wouldst have me fete these traitors?"

"I know traitors must be severely dealt with," she said. "They must die, but let them die by the axe or the rope, not these lingering, cruel deaths."

And he, forgetting how he had spurned Jane Seymour and

684

threatened her when she would meddle, could deny his new Queen little.

Those Catholics who still hoped for reunion with Rome thought the moment ripe to strike at the men who had supported Cromwell, and Wyatt, among others, was sent to the Tower. He, bold as ever, had dared defend himself, and Catherine angered her uncle Norfolk by pleading for leniency towards Wyatt. She took warm clothes and food to the old Countess of Salisbury, who was still in the Tower.

The King remonstrated with her.

"It will not do, sweetheart, it will not do."

"Would you have me leave such a poor old lady to starve?"

He took her onto his knee, and touched her cheek in a manner meant to reprove her, but she, with a characteristic gesture, seized his finger and bit it softly, which amused him, so that he found himself laughing instead of scolding.

He could not help it. She was irresistible. If she would take clothes and food to the old Countess, then she must. He would try pleading with her again concerning the greater indiscretion of asking pardon for Wyatt.

"Now listen to me," he said. "Wyatt is a traitor."

"He is no traitor. He is a brave man. He does not cringe nor show fear, and is not afraid to state his opinions."

"Aye!" said the King slyly. "And he is the handsomest man in court, you are about to add!"

"He is assuredly, and I am certain he is a true friend to Your Majesty."

"So you find him handsomer than your King, eh?"

"The handsomest man, you said. We did not speak of kings!" She took his great face in her hands and surveyed him saucily. "Nay," she said, "I will say that Thomas Wyatt is the handsomest man in the court, but I would not include the King in that!" Which made him laugh and feel so gratified that he must kiss her and say to himself, A plague on Norfolk! Does he think to rule this realm! Wyatt is indeed a bold spirit and I was ever one to look for boldness in a man. If he is too anti-Catholic, he is at least honest. How does a king know when men will plot against him? Wyatt is too pleasant a man to die; his head is too handsome to be struck off his shoulders. Doubtless we can pardon Wyatt on some condition.

Norfolk was furious over the affair of Wyatt. He quarrelled with his stepmother.

"What means the Queen? Wyatt is our enemy. Has she not sense enough to know that!"

"Speak not thus of the Queen in my presence!" said the Dowager Duchess. "Or 'twill go ill with thee, Thomas Howard."

"You are an old fool. Who put the wench on the throne, I would ask you?"

"You may ask all you care to. I am willing to answer. The King put Catherine Howard on the throne because he loves her sweet face."

"Bah! You will go to the block one day, old woman, and that wench with you."

"This is treason!" cried Her Grace.

"Tut, tut," said the Duke and left her.

The Duchess was so furious that she went straight to the Queen.

"He was but feigning friendship for us," said Catherine. "I believe I ever knew it. . . ."

"I fear him," said the Duchess. "There is that in him to terrify a woman, particularly when . . ."

They looked at each other; then glanced over their shoulders. The past was something they must keep shut away.

"Tread warily with the Duke!" warned the Duchess.

But it was not in Catherine's nature to tread warily. She showed her displeasure in her coolness to the Duke. The King noticed it and was amused. He liked to see proud Norfolk slighted by this vivacious queen of his whose power flowed from himself.

Norfolk was filled with cold fury. This Catherine was every bit as unruly as his niece Anne Boleyn. If there was anything in that rumour which had risen up within a few weeks of her marriage, by God, he would not be the one to hold out a helping hand to Catherine Howard.

Sly Cranmer watched the trouble between Norfolk and his niece, and was pleased by it, for Norfolk was a worthy ally, and that they, enemies to one another, should be joined in common cause against Catherine Howard, was not an unsatisfactory state of affairs. But even if he had a case against Catherine, he would have to wait awhile, since it would be folly to present it to the King in his present amorous state. How much longer was the fat monarch going on cooing like a mating pigeon?

There was no sign of a change in the King's attitude towards Catherine. All through spring and summer as they journeyed from place to place, he was her devoted husband. He preferred comparative retirement in the country to state balls and functions.

Henry was, however, jolted out of his complacency by news of a papist revolt in the north. This was headed by Sir John Neville and there was no doubt that it had been strongly influenced from the Continent by Cardinal Pole. Up rose Henry, roaring like a lion who has slumbered too long. He would restrain his wrath no longer. He had, in his newly found happiness, allowed himself to be over-lenient. How could he go on enjoying bliss with Catherine if his throne was imperilled and snatched from him by traitors!

The old Countess of Salisbury could no longer be allowed to live. Her execution had been delayed too long. Catherine had pleaded for her, had conjured up pitiful pictures of her freezing and starving in the Tower. Let her freeze! Let her starve! So perish all traitors! She was the mother of a traitor—one of the greatest and most feared Henry had ever known. Cardinal Pole might be safe on the Continent, but his mother should suffer in his stead.

"To the block with her!" shouted Henry, and all Catherine's pleas could not deter him this time. He was gentle with her, soothing her. "Now, now, sweetheart, let such matters rest. She is not the poor old lady you might think her to be. She is a traitor and she has bred traitors. Come, come, wouldst thou have thy king and husband tottering from his throne? Thrones have to be defended now and then with blood, sweetheart."

So the old Countess was done to death in cruel fashion, for she, the last of the Plantagenets, kept her courage to the violent end. She refused to lay her head on the block, saying the sentence was unjust and she no traitor.

"So should traitors do," she said, "but I am none, and if you will have my head, you must win it if you can."

Of all murders men had committed at the King's command this was the most horrible, for the Countess was dragged by her hair to the block, and since she would not then submit her head peaceably, the executioner hacked at her with his axe until she, bleeding from many wounds, sank in her death agony to the ground, where she was decapitated.

Such deaths aroused Henry's wrath. The people loved to gloat over bloody details; they whispered together, ever fond of martyrs.

It had always been Henry's plan, since the break with Rome, to play the Catholics off against the Lutherans, just as he played Charles against Francis. The last insurrection had put the Catholics out of favour, and his conscience now gave him several twinges about Cromwell. He replied to his conscience by mourning that, acting on false accusations which those about him had made, he had put to death the best servant he had ever had. Thus could he blame the Catholics for Cromwell's death and exonerate himself. Norfolk was out of favour; Cranmer in the ascendant. Henry left the administration of his affairs in the hands of a few chosen anti-papists headed by Cranmer and Chancellor Audley, and proceeded north on a punitive expedition, accompanied by the Queen.

✦

Henry was wholehearted in most things he undertook. When he set out to stamp the impression of his power on his subjects, he did so with vigour; and as his method was cruelty, Catherine could not help being revolted by that tour to the north.

Loving most romantically the handsome Culpepper, she must compare him with Henry; and while she had been prepared to do her best and please the indulgent man she had so far known, she was discovering that this was not the real man, and she was filled with horror. There was no kindness in him. She was forced to witness the grovelling of those who had rebelled because they wished to follow what they believed to be true. As they went through county after county and she saw the cruelty inflicted, and worse still was forced to look on his delight in it, it seemed to her, that when he came to her, his hands dripped blood. She wished the King to be a loving monarch; she wished the people to do homage to him; but she wanted them to respect him without fearing him, as she herself was trying so desperately to do.

There had been many compensations which had come to her when she forsook Culpepper to marry Henry. Mary, Joyce and Isabel, her young sisters, had been lifted from their poverty; indeed, there was not one impecunious member of her family who had not felt her generosity. This did not only apply to her family but to her friends also. She wanted to feel happiness about her; she wanted to make the King happy; she wanted no one worried by poverty, inconvenienced by hardship, smitten with sorrow. She wanted a pleasant world for herself and everyone in it.

When they came to Hull and saw what was left of Constable, a prey to the flies, hanging on the highest gate where Norfolk had gleefully placed him full four years ago, she turned away sickened, for the King had laughingly pointed out this grim sight to her.

"There hangs a traitor . . . or what is left of him!"

She turned from the King, knowing that however she tried she would never love him.

"Thou art too gentle, sweetheart!" The King leaned towards her and patted her arm, showing that he liked her gentleness, even though it might make her shed a tear for his enemies.

Often she thought of Thomas Culpepper, who was in the retinue accompanying them. Often their eyes would meet, exchanging smiles. Jane Rochford noted this, and that peculiar twist of her character which had ever made her court danger though through doing so she could bring no gain to herself, made her say, "Your cousin Culpepper is a handsome young man. He loves you truly. I see it there in his eyes. And methinks Your Majesty is not indifferent to him, for who could be to such a handsome boy! You never meet him. You are over-cautious. It could be arranged. . . ."

This was reminiscent of the old days of intrigue, and

Catherine could not resist it. She felt that only could she endure Henry's caresses if she saw Thomas now and then. She carried in her mind every detail of Thomas's face so that when the King was with her, she could, in her imagination, put Thomas in his place, and so not show the repugnance to his caresses which she could not help but feel.

Derham came to her once or twice to write letters for her. He watched her with smoldering, passionate eyes, but she was not afraid of harm coming from Derham. He was devoted as ever, and though his jealousy was great, he would never do anything, if he could help it, to harm the Queen. Derham knew nothing of her love for Culpepper, and Catherine, not wishing to cause him pain, saw to it that he should not know, and now and then would throw him soft glances to show that she remembered all they had been to each other. In view of this Derham could not forbear to whisper to his friend Damport that he loved the Queen, and he was sure that if the King were dead he might marry her.

During that journey there were many meetings with Culpepper. Lady Rochford was in her element; she carried messages between the lovers; she listened at doors. "The King will be in council for two hours more. It is safe for Culpepper to come to the apartment. . . ." Catherine did not know that her relations with Culpepper were becoming a sly joke throughout the court and were discussed behind hands with many a suppressed giggle.

When they were at Lincoln she all but surrendered to

Culpepper. He would beg; she would hesitate; and then be firm in her refusals.

"I dare not!" wept Catherine.

"Ah! Why did you not fly with me when I asked it!"

"If only I had done so!"

"Shall we go on spoiling our lives, Catherine?"

"I cannot bear this sorrow, but never, never could I bear that harm should come to you through me."

Thus it went on, but Catherine was firm. When she felt weak she would seem to feel the presence of Anne Boleyn begging her to take care, warning her to reflect on her poor cousin's fate.

Because no one showed that the love between them was known, they did not believe it was known, and they grew more and more reckless. There was a time at Lincoln when they were alone until two in the morning, feeling themselves safe because Lady Rochford was keeping guard. They revelled in their secret meetings with ostrich-like folly. As long as they denied themselves the satisfaction their love demanded, they felt safe. No matter that people all around them were aware of their intrigue. No matter that Cranmer was but waiting an opportunity.

On this occasion at Lincoln, Katharine Tylney and Margaret Morton had been loitering on the stairs outside the Queen's apartment in a fever of excitement lest the King should come unexpectedly, and they be involved.

"Jesus!" whispered Katharine Tylney as Margaret came gliding into the corridor, "is not the Queen abed yet?"

Margaret, who a moment before had seen Culpepper emerge, answered: "Yes, even now." And the two exchanged glances of relief, shrugging their shoulders smiling over the Queen's recklessness and frivolity, reminding each other of her behaviour at Lambeth.

Many such dangerous meetings took place, with Lady Rochford always at hand, the Queen's attendant, always ready with suggestions and hints. Catherine had been indiscreet enough to write to Culpepper before this journey began. This was an indication of the great anxiety she felt for him, because Catherine never did feel happy with a pen, and to write even a few lines was a great effort to her. She had written this letter before the beginning of the tour when she and the King were moving about close to London and Culpepper was not with them. It was folly to write; and greater folly on Culpepper's part to keep the letter; but being in love and inspired by danger rather than deterred by it, they had done many foolish things and this was but one of them.

"I heartily recommend me unto you, praying you to send me word how that you do," wrote Catherine. *"I did fear you were sick and I never longed for anything so much as to see you. It makes my heart to die when I think that I cannot always be in your company. Come to me when Lady Rochford be here for then I shall be best at leisure to be at your commandment. . . ."*

And such like sentences all written out laboriously in Catherine's untrained hand.

She lived through the days, waiting for a glimpse of Culpepper, recklessly, dangerously, while the foolish Lady Rochford sympathized and arranged meetings.

The King noticed nothing. He felt pleased; once more he was showing rebels what happened to those who went against their king. He could turn from the flattery of those who sought his good graces to the sweet, youthful charm of Catherine Howard.

"Never was man so happy in his wife!" he said; and he thought that when he returned he would have the nation sing a Te Deum, for at last the Almighty had seen fit to reward his servant with a perfect jewel of womanhood.

✦

Cranmer was so excited he could scarcely make his plans. At last his chance had come. This was too much even for the King to ignore.

There was a man at court who was of little importance, but towards whom Cranmer had always had a kindly feeling. This man was a Protestant, stern and cold, a man who never laughed because he considered laughter sinful, a man who had the makings of a martyr, one who could find more joy in a hair shirt than in a flagon of good wine. This man's name was John Lassells, a protege of Cromwell's who had remained faithful to him; he preached eternal damnation for all those who did not accept the teachings of Martin Luther.

This John Lassells came to Cranmer with a story which set Cranmer's hopes soaring, that made him feel he could embrace the man.

"My lord," said Lassells most humbly, "there is on my conscience that which troubles me sorely."

Cranmer listened half-heartedly, feeling this was doubtless some religious point the man wished explained.

"I tremble for what this may mean," said Lassells, "for it concerns Her Grace the Queen."

Gone was Cranmer's lethargy; there was a flicker of fire in his eyes.

"My lord Archbishop, I have a sister, Mary, and Mary being nurse to Lord William Howard's first wife, was after her death taken into the service of the Dowager Duchess of Norfolk."

"Where the Queen was brought up," said Cranmer eagerly.

"I asked my sister Mary why she did not sue for service with the Queen, for I saw that many who had been in the Dowager Duchess's household now held places at court. My sister's answer was most disturbing. 'I will not,' she said: 'But I am very sorry for the Queen.' I asked why, and she answered, 'Marry, for she is both light in living and behaviour.' I asked how so, and she did tell me a most alarming story."

"Yes, yes?"

"There was one Francis Derham who had slept in bed with her for many nights, and another, Manox, had known her."

"Derham!" cried Cranmer. "Manox! They are both in the Queen's household."

He questioned Lassells further, and when he had learned all the man had to tell, he dismissed him after telling him he had indeed done the King a great service.

Cranmer was busy, glad of the absence of the King to give him a free hand. He sent Southampton to question Mary Lassells. Manox was arrested and brought before him and Wriothesley. Derham went to the Tower. Cranmer was going to garner each grain he gleaned, and when they were laid side by side he doubted not he would have good harvest. He waited impatiently for the return of the royal pair.

Henry was filled with satisfaction when he returned to Hampton Court. He was full of plans which he would lay before his confessor. A public thanksgiving should be prepared that the whole country might know, and thank God, that he had been blessed with a loving, dutiful and virtuous wife.

But Henry's satisfaction was short-lived. He was in the chapel at Hampton Court when Cranmer came to him; Cranmer's eyes were averted and in his hand he carried a paper.

"Most Gracious King," said Cranmer, "I fear to place this grave matter set out herein in your hands, and yet the matter being so grave I dare do naught else. I pray that Your Grace will read it when you are alone."

Henry read the report on Catherine; his anger was terrible, but it was not directed against Catherine but those who had given evidence against her. He sent for Cranmer.

"This is forged!" he cried. "This is not truthful! I have conceived such a constant opinion of her honesty that I know this!"

He paced up and down so that Cranmer's chicken heart was filled with fear. It was too soon. The King would not give up the Queen; rather he would destroy those who sought to destroy her.

"I do not believe this!" cried the King, but Cranmer had heard the quiver of doubt in his master's voice and rejoiced. "But," went on the King, "I shall not be satisfied until the certainty is known to me." He glowered at Cranmer. "There must be an examination. And . . . no breath of scandal against the Queen."

The King left Hampton Court, and Catherine was told to stay in her rooms. Her musicians were sent away and told that this was no time for music.

Over Hampton Court there fell a hush of horror like a dark curtain that shut away gaiety and laughter; thus it had been at Greenwich less than six years ago when Anne Boleyn had looked in vain for Brereton, Weston, Norris and Smeaton.

Catherine was chilled with horror; and when Cranmer with Norfolk, Audley, Sussex and Gardiner came to her, she knew that the awful doom she had feared ever since she had become the King's wife was about to fall upon her.

✦

Wriothesley questioned Francis Derham in his cell.

"You may as well tell the truth," said Wriothesley, "for others have already confessed it for you. You have spent a hundred nights naked in the bed of the Queen."

"Before she was Queen," said Derham.

"Ah! Before she was Queen. We will come to that later. You admit that there were immoral relations between you and the Queen?"

"No," said Derham.

"Come, come, we have ways of extracting the truth. There were immoral relations between you and the Queen."

"They were not immoral. Catherine Howard and I regarded each other as husband and wife."

Wriothesley nodded slowly.

"You called her 'wife' before others?"

"Yes."

"And you exchanged love tokens?"

"We did."

"And some of the household regarded you as husband and wife?"

"That is so."

"The Dowager Duchess and Lord William Howard regarded you as husband and wife?"

"No; they were ignorant of it."

"And yet it was no secret."

"No, but . . ."

"The entire household knew, with the exception of the Dowager Duchess and Lord William?"

"It was known among those with whom it was our custom to mix."

"You went to Ireland recently, did you not?"

"I did."

"And there were engaged in piracy?"

"Yes."

"For which you deserve to hang, but no matter now. Did you not leave rather abruptly for Ireland?"

"I did."

"Why?"

"Because Her Grace had discovered the relationship between Catherine and me."

"Was there not another occasion when she discovered you with her granddaughter?"

"Yes."

"It was in the maids' room and she entered and found you romping together, in arms kissing?"

He nodded.

"And what were Her Grace's reactions to that?"

"Catherine was beaten; I was warned."

"That seems light punishment."

"Her Grace believed it to be but a romp."

"And you joined the Queen's household soon after her marriage with the King? Mr. Derham, I suggest that you and the Queen continued to live immorally, in fact in adultery, after the Queen's marriage with His Majesty."

"That is not true."

"Is it not strange that you should join the Queen's household, and receive special favours, and remain in the role of Queen's attendant only?"

"It does not seem strange."

"You swear that no immoral act ever took place between you and the Queen after her marriage with the King?"

"I swear it."

"Come, Mr. Derham. Be reasonable. Does it seem logical to you in view of what you once were to the Queen?"

"I care not what it may seem. I only know that no act of immorality ever took place between us since her marriage."

Wriothesley sighed. "You try my patience sorely," he said, and left him.

He returned in half an hour accompanied by two burly men.

"Mr. Derham," said the King's secretary softly, "I would ask you once more to confess to adultery with the Queen."

"I cannot confess what is not so."

"Then I must ask you to accompany us."

Derham was no coward; he knew the meaning of that summons; they were going to torture him. He pressed his lips together, and silently prayed for the courage he would have need of. He had led an adventurous life of late; he had faced death more than once when he had fought on the rough sea for booty. He had taken his chances recklessly as the inevitable milestones on the road of adventure; but the cold-blooded horror of the torture chamber was different.

In the corridors of the Tower was the sickening smell of

death; there was dried blood on the floor of the torture rooms. If he admitted adultery, what would they do to Catherine? They could not hurt her for what was done before. They could not call that treason, even though she had deceived the King into thinking her a virgin. They could not hurt Catherine if he refused to say what they wished. He would not swerve. He would face all the torture in the world rather than harm her with the lies they wished him to tell. She had not loved him since his return from Ireland; but he had continued to love her. He would not lie.

They were stripping him of his clothes. They were putting him on the rack. Wriothesley, one of the cruellest men in all England, was standing over him implacably.

"You are a fool, Derham. Why not confess and have done!"

"You would have me lie?" asked Derham.

"I would have you save yourself this torture."

The ropes were about his wrists; the windlasses were turned. He tried to suppress his cries, for it was more cruel than his wildest imaginings. He had not known there could be such pain. He shrieked and they stopped.

"Come, Derham. You committed adultery with the Queen."

"No, no."

Wriothesley's cruel lips were pressed together; he nodded to the tormentors. It began again. Derham fainted and they thrust the vinegar brush under his nose.

"Derham, you fool. Men cannot endure much of this."

That was true; but there were men who would not lie to

save themselves from death, even if it must be death on the rack; and Derham, the pirate, was one of them.

When it would have been death to continue with the torture they carried him away; he was fainting, maimed and broken; but he had told them nothing.

✦

When the Dowager Duchess heard what had happened at Hampton Court she shut herself into her chamber and was sick with fear. The Queen under lock and key! Derham in the Tower! She remembered her sorrow when Anne was sent to the Tower; but now side by side with sorrow went fear, and out of these two was born panic.

She must not stay idle. She must act. Had she not assured His Majesty of Catherine's purity and goodness! And yet had she not beaten Catherine for her lewdness! Had she not warned Derham first, and had he not, later, run away to escape her anger when it had been discovered that he and Catherine had been living as husband and wife in her house!

She paced up and down her room. What if they questioned her! Her teeth chattered. She pictured the terrible end of the Countess of Salisbury, and saw herself running from the headsman's axe. She was rich; her house was chock full of treasure. Was not the King always ready to dispatch those who were rich, that their goods might fall into his hands! She pictured the Duke's sly eyes smiling at her. "That wench will go to the block!" he had said; and she had berated him, telling him he had better take care how he spoke of the Queen. Her stepson was her most deadly enemy and now he would have a chance of working openly against her.

She must waste no time. She must act. She went down to the great hall and called a confidential servant to her. She told him to go to Hampton Court, glean the latest news, and come back to her as fast as he could. She waited in mental anguish for his return, but when he came he could only tell her what she knew already. The Queen and Derham were accused of misconduct, and some of the Queen's attendants were accused of being in on the guilty secret.

She thought of Derham's friend Damport, who doubtless knew as much of Derham's secrets as any. She had some hazy plan of bribing him to silence on all he knew.

"I hear Derham is taken," she said plaintively, "and also the Queen; what is the matter?"

Damport said he thought Derham had spoken with indiscretion to a gentleman usher.

Her Grace's lips quivered; she said that she greatly feared that in consequence of evil reports some harm should fall the Queen. She looked fearfully at Damport and said she would like to give him a little gift. Thereupon she presented him with ten pounds. It was stupid and clumsy, but she was too frightened to know what she did. She murmured something about his saying nothing of Catherine Howard's friendship with Derham.

Her fear becoming hysterical, the Dowager Duchess paced from room to room. What if Catherine and Derham had exchanged letters when he had gone away to Ireland!

There were here in her house some trunks and coffers of Derham's, for before he had gone to court she had taken him back into her house; several of the trunks were those which he had left behind when he fled. He had not removed them when he went to court, for his lodging there was not large enough to accommodate them. What if in Derham's trunks and coffers there was some incriminating evidence?

Her legs shaking, her voice high with hysteria, she called to some of her most trusted servants. She told them that she feared a visit from the King's ambassadors at any moment; the Queen was in danger; all Derham's belongings must be searched for fear there might be something in them to incriminate the Queen; she implored her attendants to show their loyalty and help her.

There was a great bustling throughout the house; trunks were forced open; coffers were rifled. There were found some of those letters written by Jane Bulmer on Catherine's behalf, and which had been preserved by Derham; of these there was made a bonfire; the Duchess even destroyed articles which she suspected had been gifts from Catherine to Derham.

When this work was done she retired to her chamber, feeling old and very weary. But there was no rest for her. A knocking on her door heralded the advent of fresh trouble, the worst possible trouble.

"His Grace the Duke is below," said her frightened maid, "and he demands to see you immediately."

.✳.

Catherine, facing those five dreaded men, was numb with terror. Her limbs trembled so much, and her countenance was so wild, that they thought she would lose her reason. She had had a wild fit of laughing which had ended in weeping; she was more hysterical than had been her cousin, for Anne had not had a terrible example in her mind all the time.

There was one thing which terrified her beyond all others, and gave her great agony of mind. She could think of no way of warning Culpepper. She was almost mad with anxiety on his behalf.

Norfolk's cold eyes mocked her, seeming to say: So you thought yourself so clever, did you! You are another such as your cousin Anne Boleyn. Oh, did ever a man have such a pair of nieces!

Her uncle was more terrifying than the other four.

"Compose yourself! Compose yourself!" said Norfolk. "Think not to drown your guilt in tears!"

Cranmer seemed much kinder; he was ever cautious, knowing well the King's great tenderness for her; he was determined to go cautiously for fear he had to retrace his steps. It was to Cranmer whom she would talk if she talked at all.

In his soft voice he told her how grieved he was that this

should have befallen her. Francis Derham had confessed to having lived with her as her husband. Manox had also known her. It would be better for her to tell the truth, for the King, heartbroken at her deception, was inclined towards leniency.

Her answers were scarcely audible. She caught her breath every time one of them spoke, terrified that she would hear Culpepper's name. But when they did not speak of him, she came to the conclusion that they knew nothing of her love for him and his for her; and this so lightened her spirits that she seemed suddenly happy. She confessed readily to what she had done before her marriage to the King. Yes, Derham had called her wife; she had called him husband. Yes . . . yes. . . .

Norfolk, with never a thought of his own adultery with Bess Holland, tut-tutted in horror at such wickedness; but in comparison with him, the others seemed almost kind, and her hysteria was passing. They knew nothing against Thomas. They could send her to the block as they had her cousin, but Thomas Culpepper should not suffer through his love for her.

The council of five left her, and Cranmer prepared a report of the examination that he might show it to the King.

Henry was awaiting the report in feverish impatience. He could not hide his agitation. He had changed since he had read the paper containing the news which Cranmer had declared he was too moved to give his master by word of mouth. His usually purple face had gone a shade of grey the colour of parchment, and the veins, usually so full of rich red blood, now looked like brown lines drawn upon it.

Cranmer's voice took on those pained tones he could always assume on certain occasions. He talked of the abominable, base, and carnal life of the Queen; voluptuous and vicious were the words he used to describe her; and this woman had led the King to love her, had arrogantly coupled herself in marriage with him.

Norfolk watched the King and Cranmer uneasily. After all the wanton wench was his niece, and it was he who had helped to recommend her to the King. Norfolk was worried. He was possessed of great worldly riches. When a queen was found guilty of treason, members of her family often found themselves in like trouble. He had spoken with disgust of his niece whenever he could; he had whispered slander about her; his great wish was to dissociate himself from her. He was grieved, he told all; his house was plunged into deepest mourning because it had produced two such wanton and abandoned women as Anne Boleyn and Catherine Howard. He said he thought the only just fate that should be meted out to Catherine Howard was death by burning. He would be there to savour every one of her screams as she had a foretaste of the torment that would be eternally hers. His pity, he had announced, went to the King whom he loved and whom he hoped would not hold him in any way responsible for the vile creatures his house had produced to deceive his most loved monarch. He had quarrelled with his stepmother, whom all knew had had the confidence of the Queen; all were aware that he had never been a friend of that old woman nor of her vile granddaughter.

The King could do nothing but sit leaden-eyed. His dream was over; reality faced him. He had been deceived in her. She was not his jewel of womanhood; she was not entirely his. Others had enjoyed her; he was tortured by thoughts of them. He had loved her; she was to have been his last wife; she was to have made all his miserable matrimonial engagements worthwhile. He could not bear it. He put his hands to his face and tears gushed from his eyes.

Chapuys summed up the King's feelings when writing to his master. "This king," he wrote, "has wonderfully felt the case of the Queen, his wife, and has certainly shown greater sorrow at her loss than at the faults, loss or divorce of his preceding wives. It is like the case of the woman who cried more bitterly at the loss of her tenth husband than at the deaths of all the others together, though they had all been good men, but it was because she had never buried one of them before, without being sure of the next; and as yet this king has formed no plan or preference."

That was true. At the height of his jealousy of Anne, Jane had been waiting to comfort him; but in between Jane and Catherine he had had the disappointing experience of Anne of Cleves. He had lost Catherine and he felt cheated, since there was no beautiful and much-desired young woman waiting to console him. And indeed he wanted consolation from no one but Catherine herself. He was no longer a bull; he was a staid domesticated animal who wished only to spend his last days in peace with the mate he loved.

So he wept bitterly and unashamedly before his council, and Cranmer quaked to see those tears, for it seemed to him that there was a possibility of the King's trying to hush up this matter and take back the Queen. "The faults have been committed," those tears seemed to be telling Cranmer. "Let be!"

But what of Cranmer if Catherine Howard regained her influence with the King? Cranmer knew of two ways to stop this. He could have the scandal bruited abroad. How would Henry feel if those foreign princes knew that Henry had kept a wife who had deceived him? Spread the news abroad then; make it hard for him to take her back. There was another and even more satisfactory alternative: discover that she had had a lover even as she had loved with and been loved by the King.

Damport was arrested. He had been the greatest friend of Derham's; he had been in the Dowager Duchess's household; he had recently received a sum of money from Her Grace.

Damport was sweating with fear.

"My lords, I know nothing . . . nothing. . . ."

It is a terrible predicament for a man who knows nothing and yet must tell something. What could he tell them? Nothing! Nothing, but that which they knew already.

"Why did the Dowager Duchess of Norfolk give you money?"

"I know not! I know not!"

There was nothing they could extract from this young man but what they already knew, and Cranmer himself had given orders that they must get confessions.

"Come, Damport, you were the special friend of this man Derham."

"Yes, yes, yes. . . ."

"It will be much better for you if you talk."

"But I swear I know nothing . . . nothing. . . ."

They led him down to the torture chamber where Derham had gone before him, where Mark Smeaton had moaned in agony.

"Come, Damport. What is it to you? You have naught to lose. We do but ask for truth."

Damport's hair was wet on his forehead; sweat ran down his nose; he could but stare open-mouthed at those vile instruments; he could but retch from the stench of death.

"Why, Damport, that is a very fine set of teeth you have, and doubtless you are very proud of them!"

Damport looked about him as though seeking escape from such a situation, but the dark and slimy walls had no suggestion to offer; there was nothing to learn from them except that within them men had descended for many, many years to the level of the lowest animals. It seemed to Damport that the evil shadows that hung about the dim chamber were the ghosts of those who, having died in agony, had returned to watch the anguish of those doomed to follow them. These cruel tormentors, these examiners, felt not the presence of those sad ghosts; cruelty was commonplace to them; they had learned indifference to the groans of tortured men; one had but to look into their brute faces to know this.

Damport whimpered, "An I knew aught, I would tell it."

"We were saying those teeth were fine, Damport. Let us see whether they will look as fine when the brakes have done with them!"

It seemed that his head was being torn from his body; he felt a sickening crunch; his jerkin was wet and he felt its damp warmness on his chest; he smelled his own blood, and swooned. Words were like the beating of the blunt end of an axe on his head.

"Come, Damport, you know Derham committed adultery with the Queen."

They had torn out most of his teeth and all he could remember was that Derham had said that if the King were dead he would marry Catherine Howard. He told them this, fearing further torture. They were disappointed, but the man was bleeding badly and he could not stand for the pain; and his mouth was so swollen that if he would, he could not speak.

They led him from the torture chamber. They would have to tell Cranmer that they could get nothing from Damport and believed he had nothing to tell. Cranmer would be filled with that cold fury that was more terrifying than the hot rage of some men.

From Manox they could get nothing of interest. There was not sufficient evidence against him; he had been one of the humblest musicians, and there was really nothing against him;

he had not been in the Queen's presence, even while her ladies were with her. As for his relations with her at Horsham and Lambeth he was ready enough to talk of these. He was such an obvious rogue that torture would be wasted on him.

But Cranmer was not angry. He was in fact delighted. The King of France had sent condolences to Henry, telling him how grieved he was to hear news of the faults of her, so recently his Queen. That was good; but there was better still.

Why, thought Cranmer, should the Queen wish to surround herself with those who had helped her in her wantonness before her marriage, if it was not to help her in the same capacity after marriage? He would examine thoroughly all those women at the court of the Queen who had been in the service of the Dowager Duchess of Norfolk. There were several of them—Katharine Tylney, Margaret Morton, Jane Bulmer, and two named Wilkes and Baskerville being the chief among them. It was from Katharine Tylney and Margaret Morton that Cranmer learned of a certain night at Lincoln; Thomas Culpepper's name was mentioned. Lady Rochford had arranged interviews. There had been several meetings before the tour to the north and during it.

"Bring in Culpepper!" ordered Cranmer, and they brought in Culpepper.

He was a bold youth, fearless and courageous, such as Francis Derham.

A plague on courageous, gallant men! thought Cranmer, the coward. What trouble they give us!

Head held high, Culpepper admitted his love for the Queen, admitted that he would have married her if he could. No wrong, he said, had passed between them.

Cranmer laughed at that. He must admit that wrong had passed between them! How else could Cranmer be sure of enraging his lovesick king.

"Rack him until he confesses!" he ordered.

Derham had been a pirate; he had faced death more than once, and it held less horror for him than for a man like Cranmer who had never seen it come close to himself; it was with Culpepper as with Derham. Culpepper was a wild boy and had ever been a plague to his father; he was a rebellious, unruly boy with a taste for adventure and getting into trouble. There was one quality he had in common with Derham and that was bravery.

They put him on the rack. He endured that excruciating pain, that most exquisite of tortures, pressing his lips firmly together, and only now and then, and most shamefacedly, let out a groan of pain. He even smiled on the rack and tried to remember her face, anxious for him. "Oh, take care, Thomas. Take care lest thou shouldst suffer for love of me."

He thought she was with him, talking to him now. In his thoughts he answered her. "Sweet Catherine, dost think I would do aught that might hurt thee? Thou shalt never suffer through me, Catherine. Let them do what they will."

"Culpepper! Culpepper, you young fool! Will you speak?"

He gasped, for the pain was such as to make speech difficult.

"I have spoken."

"Again! Again! Work faster, you fools! He has to confess!"

But he did not confess, and they carried his poor suffering body away most roughly, for they had worked themselves weary over him in vain.

✦

The King's rage was terrible, when he heard that Culpepper was involved. Rage, misery, jealousy, self-pity, humiliation maddened him. He wept; he shut himself up; he would see no one. This . . . to happen to the King of England.

His face was clothed in grief; his sick leg throbbed with pain; his youth was gone, taking with it his hope of happiness. He was an old, sick man and Culpepper was a young and beautiful boy. He himself had loved to watch the grace of Culpepper; he had favoured the lad; he had winked at his wickedness and had said that what happened in Kent need not be remembered at court. He had loved that boy—loved him for his wit and his beauty; and this same boy, fair of face and clean of limb, had looked frequently on the unsightly weeping sore on the royal leg, and doubtless had laughed that all the power and riches in England could not buy youth and health such as he enjoyed.

Mayhap, thought the King angrily, he is less beautiful now his graceful limbs have been tortured; the King laughed deep sobbing laughter. Culpepper should die the death of a traitor; he should die ignobly; indignities should be piled upon his traitor's body; and when his head was on London Bridge, would she feel the same desire to kiss his lips? The King tormented himself with such thoughts of them together that could only come to a very sensual man, and the boiling blood in his head seemed as if it would burst it.

"She never had such delight in her lovers," he said, "as she shall have torture in death!"

Catherine, in those apartments which had been planned for Anne Boleyn and used so briefly by Jane, and briefer still by Anne of Cleves, was in such a state of terror that those who guarded her feared for her reason. She would fling herself onto her bed, sobbing wildly; then she would arise and walk about her room, asking questions about her death; she would have those who had witnessed the death of her cousin come to her and tell her how Anne had died; she would weep with sorrow, and then her laughter would begin again for it seemed ironical that Anne's fate should be hers. She was crazy with grief when she heard Culpepper was taken. She prayed incoherently. "Let them not harm him. Let me die, but let him be spared."

If I could but see the King, she thought, surely I could make him listen to me. Surely he would spare Thomas, if I asked him.

"Could I have speech with His Majesty? Just one moment!" she begged.

"Speech with His Majesty!" They shook their heads. How could that be! His Majesty was incensed by her conduct; he would not see her. And what would Cranmer say, Cranmer who would not know real peace until Catherine Howard's head was severed from her body!

She remembered the King as he had always been to her, indulgent and loving; even when he had reprimanded her for too much generosity, even when he, angered by the acts of traitors, had listened to her pleas for leniency, he had never shown a flicker of anger. Surely he would listen to her.

She made plans. If she could but get to the King, if she could but elude her jailers, she would know how to make herself irresistible.

She was calm now, watching for an opportunity. One quick movement of the hand to open the door, and then she would dash down the back stairs; she would watch and wait and pray for help.

The opportunity came when she knew him to be at mass in the chapel. She would run to him there, fling herself onto her knees, implore his compassion, promise him lifelong devotion if he would but spare Culpepper and Derham.

Those who were guarding her, pleased with her calmness, were sitting in a window seat, conversing among themselves of the strange happenings at court. She moved swiftly towards the door; she paused, threw a glance over her shoulder, saw that their suspicions had not been aroused, turned the handle, and was on the dark staircase before she heard the exclamation of dismay behind her.

Fleet with fear she ran. She came to the gallery; she could hear the singing in the chapel. The King was there. She would succeed because she must. Culpepper was innocent. He must not die.

Her attendants were close behind her, full of determination that her plan should not succeed, fully aware that no light punishment would be meted out to them should they let her reach the King. They caught her gown; they captured her just as she reached the chapel door. They dragged her back to the apartment. Through the gallery her screams rang out like those of a mad creature, mingling uncannily with the singing in the chapel.

A few days later she was taken from Hampton Court; she sailed down the river to a less grand prison at Sion House.

The Dowager Duchess lay in bed. She said to her attendants: "I cannot get up. I am too ill. I feel death approaching fast."

She was sick and her disease was fear. She had heard that Culpepper and Derham had been found guilty of treason. She knew that they had had no true trial, for how could men be sentenced to death for what could not be proved, and for that which they would not admit under the vilest torture! But these two brave men had not convinced their torturers that they would not eventually respond to the persuasions of the rack, and even after their sentence, daily they were taken to the torture chambers to suffer fresh agonies. But not once did either of them swerve from their protestations of the Queen's innocence since her marriage.

Never in the Dowager Duchess's memory had men been tried like this before. For those accused with Anne Boleyn there had been a trial, farcical as it was. Culpepper and Derham had been taken to Guildhall before the Lord Mayor but on either side of the Lord Mayor had sat Suffolk and Audley. Sentence had been quickly pronounced, and the two were judged guilty and condemned to die the horrible lingering death assigned to traitors.

The Dowager Duchess thought of these matters as she lay abed, staring up in terror when she heard the least sound from below. She knew inventories had been made of her goods, and she knew they could not fail to arouse the covetousness of the King, for they were great in value.

What hope had she of escaping death? Even the Duke, old soldier that he was, had shown that he thought the only safe thing for a Howard to do was retreat. He had gone into voluntary retirement, hoping that the King would forget him awhile, until the fortunes of the Howard family were in a happier state.

And as she lay there, that which she dreaded came to pass. Wriothesley, accompanied by the Earl of Southampton, had come to see her.

Her face was yellow when they entered; they thought she was not malingering but really suffering from some terrible disease. They dared not approach too near the bed, the fear of plague being ever in their minds.

"We but called to see how Your Grace does," said Wriothesley artfully, never taking his eyes from her face. "Do not distress yourself, this is but a visit; we would condole with you on the sad happenings which have befallen your family."

The colour returned slightly to her face. The men could see hope springing up. They exchanged glances. Their little ruse had succeeded, for she had always been a foolish woman ready to believe what she wished rather than what she should have known to be the truth; and she could not hide the wonderful feeling that after all she might be safe. The Dowager Duchess, these two men knew, suffered from no plague, but only from the qualms of a guilty conscience.

They questioned her. She wept and talked incoherently.

She knew nothing . . . nothing! She assured them. She had thought the attraction between Derham and her granddaughter but an affection between two who were united by the bonds of kinship. She had not thought to look for wickedness in that. But had she not found them together, in arms kissing? Had she thought that meet and proper in her whom the King had chosen to honour? Oh, but Catherine had been such a child, and there had been no harm . . . no harm that she had known of. But had she not been told of these things? Had she not beaten the girl, and had not Derham fled for his life?

"I knew it not! I knew it not!" she sobbed.

Wriothesley's cunning eyes took in each rich detail of the room.

"Methinks," he said, "Your Grace is well enough to be transported to the Tower."

At Tyburn a crowd had gathered to see the death of the Queen's lovers. Culpepper was first. How could the Queen have loved such a man? His face was emaciated; his lips drawn down; his skin like bad cheese; his eyes had sunk into black hollows. The people shuddered, knowing that they saw not the Queen's lover, but what the tormentors had made of him. Lucky Culpepper, because he was of noble birth, and was to be but beheaded!

Derham could say Lucky Culpepper! He was of not-such-noble birth, and although he begged the King for mercy, which meant that he asked to die by the axe or the rope, the King was in no mood for mercy. He saw no reason why sentence should not be carried out as ordained by the judges.

Derham's eyes were dazed with pain; he had suffered much since his arrest; he had not known there could be such cruelty in men; truly, he had known of those grim chambers below the fortress of the Tower of London, but to know by hearsay and to know by experience were two very different matters. He did not wish to live, for if he did he would never forget the gloomy dampness of grey stone walls, the terrible shrieks of agony, pain and the smell of blood and vinegar, and those awful great instruments, like monsters without thought, grimly obedient to the evil will of men.

This he had suffered and he had to suffer yet; he had been submerged in pain, but mayhap he had not yet tested its depth.

Nature was more merciful than men, providing for those who suffered great pain such blessedness as fainting; but men were cruel and brought their victims out of faints that the pain might start again.

He clung to the glorious memory of unconsciousness which must inevitably follow an excess of pain. There was another joy he knew, and it was this: He had not betrayed Catherine. They might kill Catherine, but not a drop of her blood should stain his hands. He had loved her; his intentions towards her had been ever honest. In the depth of his passion he had been unable to resist her; but that was natural; that was no sin. He had called her wife and she had called him husband, and it had been the dearest wish of his life that he should marry her. Now, here at Tyburn with the most miserable ordeal yet before him, he could feel lightness of spirit, for his end could not be far off, however they would revive him that he might suffer more. These men, whose cruel eyes were indifferent to his suffering, these monsters who were but hirelings of that spiteful murderer who stood astride all England and subdued her with torture and death, were to be pitied, as was Henry himself. For one day they must die, and they would not die as Derham died; they would not know his agony of body, but neither would they know his peace of mind.

The noose was about his neck; he swung in mid-air. There was a brief jolting pain, and the next he knew was that he was lying on hard wood and he could not breathe; he was choking; but they were tending him solicitously, that he might return to life and suffer more pain.

Now he was sufficiently recovered to smell the Tyburn crowd, to hear a faint hum of voices, to feel a man's hands on his body, to see a flash of steel, to be aware of agony. He felt the knife cold against his flesh. A searing hot pain ran through him. He writhed and screamed, but he seemed to hear a voice close to his ear murmur: "Soon now, Derham. Not long now, Derham. It cannot last. Remember they are helping you out of this wicked world."

He could smell the smoke. "Oh, God!" he moaned, and twisted and groaned afresh in his agony. He could smell his burning entrails. A thousand white hot knives were surely being plunged into him. He tried to raise himself. He tried to sob out to them to have pity. He could not speak. He could do nothing but endure, but give his tortured body up to a million gnawing devils. He had touched pain's depth, for there was never agony such as that endured by men who were hanged by the neck, and then revived that they might feel the knife that ripped their bodies, that they might feel the agony of their burning entrails.

Blessed blackness closed in on him, and the stroke of the axe which severed his head was like a gentle caress.

Jane Rochford was back in the Tower. She had been calm enough when they took her there, but now her eyes were wild, her hair hung loose about her face; she did not know why she was there; she talked to those who were not there.

"George! You here, George!" She went into shrieks of crazy

laughter. "So we meet here, George. It is so just that we should . . . so just."

She paused as though listening to the conversation of another; then she went into wild laughter that was followed by deep sobbing. Lady Rochford had gone mad.

She looked from her window and saw the Thames.

She said, "Why should you come in your pomp and I be here a prisoner? You have everything; I have nothing. The King loves you. George loves you. Oh, George, do not stand there in the shadows. Where is your head, George? Oh, yes, I remember. They took it off."

There was none who dared stay with her. It was uncanny to hear her talking to those who were not there. It was eerie to watch her eyes as she looked into space.

"Is it the ghost of George Boleyn she talks to?" it was whispered. "Is he really there and we see him not? Is he haunting her because she sent him to his death?"

Her shrieks terrified all those who heard them, but after a while a calmness settled on her, though the madness was still in her eyes.

She said quietly, "He has come to mock me now. He says that all my wickedness has but led me to the block. He puts his hands to his head and lifts it off to show me that he is not really George but George's ghost. He says the axe that killed him was wielded by me and it was called vindictiveness. And he says that the axe that will kill me will be wielded by me also and it is called folly. He says I am twice a murderess because I killed him and now I kill myself."

She flung herself against the window seat, her hands held up in supplication to an empty space.

Her attendants watched her fearfully; they were frightened by the uncanny ways of the mad.

Out of Sion House and down the river to the Tower passed the Queen's barge. She was composed now and looked very beautiful in her gown of black velvet. She thanked God that darkness had fallen and that she might not see the decomposing, fly-pestered heads of the men who had loved her. The suspense was over. Thomas was dead; Francis was dead; there but remained that Catherine should die. She thought with deep compassion of her poor old grandmother who was suffering imprisonment in the Tower. She thought of Manox and Damport and Lord William, who, with members of her family and her grandmother's household, had come under suspicion through her. She had heard that Mary Lassells had been commended for her honesty in bringing the case against the Queen to light; she had heard that the King, whose grief and rage had been great, was now recovering, and that he was allowing himself to be amused with entertainments devised by the most beautiful ladies of the court.

Catherine felt calm now, resenting none except perhaps her uncle Norfolk, who now, to save himself, was boasting that it was due to him that the old Dowager Duchess had been brought to her present state. For him, Catherine could feel little but contempt; she remembered her grandmother's telling her how cruel he had been to Anne Boleyn.

Lady Rochford was with Catherine; her madness had left her for a while though it would keep returning, and it was never known when she would think she saw visions. But there was some comfort for Catherine in having Jane Rochford with her, for she had been a witness of, and participator in, Anne's tragedy. She would talk of that sad time which was but six years ago, and Catherine gained courage in hearing how Anne had nobly conducted herself even to the block.

Sir John Gage, who had taken the place of Sir William Kingston as Constable of the Tower, came to her on the second day in the fortress.

"I come to ask that you prepare yourself for death," he told her solemnly.

She tried to be brave but she could not. She was not quite twenty years old, so young, so beautiful and in love with life; she was overtaken with hysteria, and wept continually and with such violence as was verging on madness.

In the streets people were murmuring against the King.

"What means this? Another Queen—and this time little more than a child to go to the block!"

"It is whispered that she has never done aught against even her enemies."

"Is it not strange that a man should be so cursed in his wives?"

Gage returned to her and told her she would die the next day.

She said: "I am ready!" And she asked that they should bring the block to her that she might practice laying her head upon it. "My cousin died most bravely I hear. I would follow her example. But she was a great lady and I fear I am not, nor ever were. What she could do naturally, I must practice."

It was a strange request but he could not deny it, and the block was brought to her room, where she had them place it in the centre thereof, and graciously she walked to it, looking so young and innocent that it was as though she played some child's game of executions. She laid her head upon it, and kept it there a long time so that the wood was wet with her tears.

She said she was tired and would sleep awhile, and she fell into a deep, peaceful sleep almost as soon as she lay down. In sleep, her auburn hair fell into disorder, her brow was smooth and untroubled; her mouth smiling.

She dreamed she saw her cousin Anne who caressed her as she had done when she was a baby, and bid her be of good cheer for the death was easy. A sharp, subtle pain and then peace. But Catherine could not be reassured, for it seemed to her that though she was innocent of adultery, she was in some measure to blame because of what had happened before her marriage. But her cousin continued to soothe her, saying: "Nay, I was more guilty than you, for I was ambitious and proud, and hurt many, while you never hurt any but yourself."

She was comforted, and clung to her dream. She knew now that she, like Anne, was innocent of any crime deserving of death. Anne had been murdered; she was about to be. But the death was quick and there was nothing to fear.

In the early morning, when they aroused her, she said almost calmly: "I had forgotten what the day was. Now I know. Today I am to die."

She walked with that slow dignity, which she had rehearsed last evening in her room, to the spot before the church where, six years before, Anne had died. She was dressed in black velvet, and was very pale. Her eyes were wide, and she tried to believe she saw her cousin, smiling at her from beyond the haze through which she herself must step. She thought as she walked, I must die like a queen, as Anne died.

She was accompanied by Jane Rochford, who was to die with her. Jane's dignity was as complete as that of the Queen. Her eyes were calm, and all the madness had passed from her now; she could face death gladly, for it seemed to her that only by dying could she expiate the sin she had committed against her husband.

The early February air was cold and river damp; the scene was ghostly. Catherine looked for her uncle's face among those of the people who gathered there to see her die, and felt a rush of gratitude to know she would be spared seeing him there.

She muttered a little prayer for her grandmother. She would not pray for Thomas and Francis for they were now at peace.

Had Anne felt this strange lightening of the heart when her death had been but a moment away; had she felt this queer feeling which had a touch of exultation in it?

She said she would speak a few words. Tears were in the eyes of many who beheld her, for she had none of that haughtiness which had characterized her tragic cousin. In her black velvet gown she looked what she was, a very young girl, innocent of any crime, whose tragedy was that she had had the misfortune to be desired by a ruthless man whose power was absolute. Some remembered that though Anne had been found guilty by a picked jury, she had had an opportunity of defending herself, and this she had done with a clarity, dignity and obvious truthfulness so that all unprejudiced posterity must believe in her innocence; but little Catherine Howard had had no such opportunity; contrary to English law she would be executed without an open trial, and there was but one word for such an execution, and that the ugly one of murder. Some must ask themselves what manner of man was this king of theirs, who twice in six years had sent a young wife to the block! They remembered that this Henry was the first King of England to shed women's blood on the block and burn them at the stake. Was the King's life so moral, they must ask themselves, that he dared express such horror at the frailty of this child?

But she was speaking, and her voice was so low that it was difficult to hear her, and as she spoke tears started from her eyes and ran down her smooth cheeks, for she was speaking of her lover Culpepper, the grisly spectacle of whose head all might see when crossing London Bridge.

She was trying to make these people understand her love for that young man, but she could not tell them how she had met and loved him when at Hollingbourne he had first come into her lonely life.

"I loved Culpepper," she said, and she tried to tell them how he had urged her not to marry the King. "I would rather have him for husband than be mistress of the world. . . . And since the fault is mine, mine also is the suffering, and my great sorrow is that Culpepper should have to die through me."

Her voice faltered; now her words grew fainter and the headsman looked about him, stricken with sorrow at what he must do, for she was so young, but a child, and hardened as he was, it moved him deeply that his should be the hand to strike off her head.

She turned her brimming eyes to him and begged he would not delay. She cried, "I die a queen, but I would rather die the wife of Culpepper. God have mercy on my soul. Good people . . . I beg you pray for me. . . ."

She fell to her knees and laid her head on the block not so neatly as she had done it in her room, but in such a way as to make many turn away and wipe their eyes.

She was praying when the headsman, with a swift stroke, let fall the axe.

Her attendants, their eyes blinded with tears, rushed forward to cover the mutilated little body with a black cloth, and to carry it away where it might be buried in the chapel, close to that spot where lay Anne Boleyn.

There was none to feel much pity for Lady Rochford. This gaunt woman was a striking contrast to the lovely young Queen. Jane mounted the scaffold like a pilgrim who has, after much tribulation, reached the end of a journey.

She spoke to the watching crowd and said that she was guiltless of the crime for which she was paying this doleful penalty; but she deserved to die, and she believed she was dying as a punishment for having contributed to the death of her husband by her false accusation of Queen Anne Boleyn. Almost with exultation she laid her head on the block.

"She is mad," said the watchers. "None but the insane could die so joyfully."

Jane was smiling after the axe had fallen and her blood gushed forth to mingle with that of the murdered Queen.

In his palace at Greenwich, the King stood looking over the river. He felt himself to be alone and unloved. He had lost Catherine. Her mutilated body was now buried beside that of another woman whom he had loved and whom he had killed as he had now killed Catherine.

He was afraid. He would always be afraid. Ghosts would haunt his life . . . myriads of ghosts, all the men and women whose blood he had caused to be shed. There were so many that he could not remember them all, although among their number there were a few he would never forget. Buckingham. Wolsey. More. Fisher. Montague. Exeter and the old Countess of Salisbury. Cromwell. These, he could tell his conscience he had destroyed for England's sake. But there were others he had tried harder to forget. Weston. Brereton. Norris. Smeaton. Derham. Culpepper. George Boleyn. Catherine . . . and Anne.

He thought of Anne, whom he had once loved so passionately; never had he loved one as he had her; nor ever would he; for his love for Catherine had been an old man's selfish love, the love of a man who is done with roving; but his love for Anne had had all the excitement of the chase, all the urgency of passionate desire; all the tenderness, romance and dreams of an idyll.

A movement beside him startled him and the hair was damp on his forehead, for it seemed to him that Anne was standing beside him. A second glance told him that it was but an image conjured up by the guilty mind of a murderer, for it was not Anne who stood beside him, but Anne's daughter. There were often times when she reminded him of her mother. Of all his children he loved her best because she was the most like him; she was also like her mother. There were times when she angered him; but then, her mother had angered him, and he had loved her. He loved Elizabeth, Elizabeth of the fiery hair and the spirited nature and the quick temper. She would never be the dark-browed beauty that her mother had been; she was tawny red like her father. He felt sudden anger sweep over him. Why, oh, why had she not been born a boy!

She did not speak to him, but stood quite still beside him, her attention caught and held, for a great ship—his greatest ship—was sailing towards the mouth of the river, and she was watching it, her eyes round with appreciation. He glowed with pride and warmed further towards her because she so admired the ships he had caused to be built.

To contemplate that ship lifted his spirits. He needed to lift his spirits, for he had been troubled, and to think one sees a ghost is unnerving to a man of deep-rooted superstitions. He found himself wondering about this man who was Henry of England, who to him had always seemed such a mighty figure, so right in all that he did.

He was a great king; he had done much for England, for he was England. He was a murderer; he knew this now and then; he knew it as he stood looking over the river, Anne's daughter beside him. He had murdered Anne whom he had loved best, and he had murdered Catherine whom he had also loved; but England he had begun to lift to greatness, because he and England were one.

He thought of this land which he loved, of April sunshine and soft, scented rain; of green fields and banks of wild flowers; and the river winding past his palaces to the sea. It was no longer just an island off the coast of Europe; it was a country becoming mighty, promising to be mightier yet; and through him had this begun to happen, for he would let nothing stand in the way of his aggrandizement, and he was England.

He thought backwards over bloodstained years. Wales subdued; but a few weeks ago he had assumed the title of King of Ireland; he planned to marry his son, Edward, to a Scottish princess. As he reached out for treasure so should England. He would unite these islands under England and then . . .

He wanted greatness for England. He wanted people, in years to come, when they looked back on his reign, not to think of the blood of martyrs but of England's glory.

There were dreams in his eyes. He saw his fine ships. He had made that great navy into the finest ever known. He had thought of conquering France, but he had never done so. France was powerful, and too much of England's best blood had been shed in France already. But there were new lands as yet undiscovered on the globe. Men sailed the seas from Spain and Portugal and found new lands. The Pope had drawn a line down the globe from pole to pole and declared that all lands discoverable on the east side of that line belonged to Portugal and west of it to Spain. But England had the finest ships in the world. Why not to England? War? He cared not for the shedding of England's blood, for that would weaken her and weaken Henry, for never since Wolsey had left him to govern England did he forget that England was Henry.

No bloodshed for England, for that was not the way to greatness. What if in generations to come England took the place of Spain! He had ever hated Spain as heartily as he loved England. What if English ships carried trade to the new lands, instead of war and pillage, instead of fanaticism and the Inquisition!

He had the ships. . . . If Spain were weak. . . . What a future for England!

He thought of his pale, puny son, Jane's son. No! It should have been Anne's son who carried England through these hazy dreams of his to their reality. He looked at Anne's girl—eager, vital, with so much of himself and so much of Anne in her.

Oh, Anne, why did you not give me a son! he thought. Oh, had this girl but been a boy!

What should scholarly Edward do for England? Would he be able to do what this girl might have done, had she been a boy? He looked at her flushed face, at her eyes sparkling as she watched the last of the ship, at her strong profile. A useless girl!

He was trembling with the magnitude of his thoughts, but his moment of clarity was gone. He was an old and peevish man; his leg pained him sorely, and he was very lonely, for he had just killed his wife whose youth and beauty were to have been the warm and glowing fire at which he would have warmed his old body.

He reminded his conscience—better preserved than his body—that Anne had been an adulteress, a traitress, that her death was not murder, only justice.

He scowled at Elizabeth; she was too haughty, too like her mother. He wished he could shut from his mind the sound of screaming, mingling with the chanting voices in the chapel. Catherine was a wanton, a traitress and adulteress, no less than Anne.

The ship was passing out of sight, and he was no longer thinking of ships, but of women. He pictured one, beautiful and desirable as Anne, demure and obedient as Jane, young and vivacious as Catherine. His hot tongue licked his lips, and he was smiling.

He thought, I must look for a new wife . . . for the sake of England.

More passion, politics, and drama—
don't miss these other great Tudor-era
novels by Jean Plaidy